ENDYMION

Endymion

DAN SIMMONS

BANTAM BOOKS

NEW YORK   TORONTO   LONDON
SYDNEY   AUCKLAND

ENDYMION
A Bantam Book/ January 1996

Library of Congress Cataloging-in-Publication Data
Simmons, Dan.
    Endymion / Dan Simmons.
      p.   cm.
    ISBN 0-553-10020-3
    I. Title.
    PS3569.I4729E53   1996
    813'.54—dc20   95-33191
                                                                  CIP

Published simultaneously in the United States and Canada

Bantam Books are published by Bantam Books, a division of
Bantam Doubleday Dell Publishing Group, Inc. Its trademark,
consisting of the words "Bantam Books" and the portrayal of
a rooster, is Registered in the U.S. Patent and Trademark Office
and in other countries. Marca Registrada.
Bantam Books, 1540 Broadway, New York, New York 10036.

PRINTED IN THE UNITED STATES OF AMERICA

BVG   10   9   8   7   6   5   4   3   2   1

We must not forget that the human soul,
however independently created
our philosophy represents it as being,
is inseparable
in its birth and in its growth
from the universe into which it is born.
—TEILHARD DE CHARDIN

Give us gods. Oh give them us!
Give us gods.
We are so tired of men
and motor-power.
—D. H. LAWRENCE

ENDYMION

1

YOU ARE READING this for the wrong reason.

If you are reading this to learn what it was like to make love to a messiah—*our* messiah—then you should not read on, because you are little more than a voyeur.

If you are reading this because you are a fan of the old poet's *Cantos* and are obsessed with curiosity about what happened next in the lives of the Hyperion pilgrims, you will be disappointed. I do not know what happened to most of them. They lived and died almost three centuries before I was born.

If you are reading this because you seek more insight into the message from the One Who Teaches, you may also be disappointed. I confess that I was more interested in her as a woman than as a teacher or messiah.

Finally, if you are reading this to discover *her* fate or even *my* fate, you are reading the wrong document. Although both our fates seem as certain as anyone's could be, I was not with her when hers was played out, and my own awaits the final act even as I write these words.

If you are reading this at all, I would be amazed. But this would not be the first time that events have amazed me. The past few years have been one improbability after another, each more marvelous and seemingly inevitable than the last. To share these memories is the reason that I am writing. Perhaps the motivation is not even to share—knowing that the document I am creating almost certainly will never be found—but just to put down the series of events so that I can structure them in my own mind.

"How do I know what I think until I see what I say?" wrote some pre-Hegira writer. Precisely. I must *see* these things in order to know what to think of them. I must see the events turned to ink and the emotions in print to believe that they actually occurred and touched me.

If you are reading this for the same reason that I am writing it—to bring some pattern out of the chaos of the last years, to impose some order on the essentially random series of events that have ruled our lives for the past standard decades—then you may be reading this for the right reason, after all.

WHERE TO START? With a death sentence, perhaps. But whose—my death sentence or hers? And if mine, which of mine? There are several from which to choose. Perhaps this final one is appropriate. Begin at the ending.

I am writing this in a Schrödinger cat box in high orbit around the quarantined world of Armaghast. The cat box is not much of a box, more of a smooth-hulled ovoid a mere six meters by three meters. It will be my entire world until the end of my life. Most of the interior of my world is a spartan cell consisting of a black-box air-and-waste recycler, my bunk, the food-synthesizer unit, a narrow counter that serves as both my dining table and writing desk, and finally the toilet, sink, and shower, which are set behind a fiberplastic partition for reasons of propriety that escape me. No one will ever visit me here. Privacy seems a hollow joke.

I have a text slate and stylus. When I finish each page, I transfer it to hard copy on microvellum produced by the recycler. The low accretion of wafer-thin pages is the only visible change in my environment from day to day.

The vial of poison gas is not visible. It is set in the static-dynamic shell of the cat box, linked to the air-filtration unit in such a way that to attempt to fiddle with it would trigger the cyanide, as would any attempt to breach the shell itself. The radiation detector, its timer, and the isotope element are also fused into the frozen energy of the shell. I never know when the random timer activates the detector. I never know when the same random timing element opens the lead shielding to the tiny isotope. I never know when the isotope yields a particle.

But I will know when the detector is activated at the instant the isotope yields a particle. There should be the scent of bitter almonds in that second or two before the gas kills me.

I hope that it will be only a second or two.

Technically, according to the ancient enigma of quantum physics, I am now neither dead nor alive. I am in the suspended state of overlapping probability waves once reserved for the cat in Schrödinger's thought experiment. Because the hull of the cat box is little more than position-fused energy ready to explode at the slightest intrusion, no one will ever look inside to see if I am dead or alive. Theoretically, no one is directly responsible for my execution, since the immutable laws of quantum theory pardon or condemn me from each microsecond to the next. There are no observers.

But *I* am an observer. *I* am waiting for this particular collapse of probability waves with something more than detached interest. In the instant after the hissing of cyanide gas begins, but before it reaches my lungs and heart and brain, *I* will know which way the universe has chosen to sort itself out.

At least, I will know so far as I am concerned. Which, when it comes right down to it, is the only aspect of the universe's resolution with which most of us are concerned.

And in the meantime, I eat and sleep and void waste and breathe and go through the full daily ritual of the ultimately forgettable. Which is ironic, since right now I live—if "live" is the correct word—only to remember. And to write about what I remember.

If you are reading this, you are almost certainly reading it for the wrong reason. But as with so many things in our lives, the reason for doing something is not the important thing. It is the fact of *doing* that remains. Only the immutable facts that I have written this and you are reading it remain important in the end.

Where to begin? With her? She is the one you want to read about and the one person in my life whom I wish to remember above everything and everyone else. But perhaps I should begin with the events that led me to her and then to here by way of much of this galaxy and beyond.

I believe that I shall begin with the beginning—with my first death sentence.

2

M Y NAME IS RAUL ENDYMION. My first name rhymes with Paul. I was born on the world of Hyperion in the year 693 A.D.C. on our local calendar, or A.D. 3099, pre-Hegira reckoning, or, as most of us figure time in the era of the Pax, 247 years after the Fall.

It was said about me when I traveled with the One Who Teaches that I had been a shepherd, and this was true. Almost. My family had made its living as itinerant shepherds in the moors and meadows of the most remote regions on the continent of Aquila, where I was raised, and I sometimes tended sheep as a child. I remember those calm nights under the starry skies of Hyperion as a pleasant time. When I was sixteen (by Hyperion's calendar) I ran away from home and enlisted as a soldier of the Pax-controlled Home Guard. Most of those three years I remember only as a dull routine of boredom with the unpleasant exception of the four months when I was sent to the Claw Iceshelf to fight indigenies during the Ursus uprising. After being mustered out of the Home Guard, I worked as a bouncer and blackjack dealer in one of the rougher Nine Tails casinos, served as a bargemaster on the upper reaches of the Kans for two rainy seasons, and then trained as a gardener on some of the Beak estates under the landscape artist Avrol Hume. But "shepherd" must have sounded better to the chroniclers of the One Who Teaches when it came time to list the former occupation of her closest disciple. "Shepherd" has a nice biblical ring to it.

I do not object to the title of shepherd. But in this tale I will be seen as a shepherd whose flock consisted of one infinitely important sheep. And I lost her more than found her.

At the time my life changed forever and this story really begins, I was twenty-seven years old, tall for a Hyperion-born, notable for little except for the thickness of calluses on my hands and my love of quirky ideas, and was then working as a hunter's guide in the fens above Toschahi Bay a hundred kilometers north of Port Romance. By that time in my life I had learned a little bit about sex and much about weapons, had discovered firsthand the power greed has in the affairs of men and women, had learned how to use my fists and modest wits in order to survive, was curious about a great many things, and felt secure only in the knowledge that the remainder of my life would almost certainly hold no great surprises.

I was an idiot.

Most of what I was that autumn of my twenty-eighth year might be described in negatives. I had never been off Hyperion and never considered that I might travel offworld. I had been in Church cathedrals, of course; even in the remote regions where my family had fled after the sacking of the city of Endymion a century earlier, the Pax had extended its civilizing influence—but I had accepted neither the catechism nor the cross. I had been with women, but I had never been in love. Except for my grandmother's tutelage, my education had been self-directed and acquired through books. I read voraciously. At age twenty-seven, I thought that I knew everything.

I knew nothing.

So it was that in the early autumn of my twenty-eighth year, content in my ignorance and stolid in my conviction that nothing of importance would ever change, I committed the act that would earn me a death sentence and begin my real life.

THE FENS ABOVE Toschahi Bay are dangerous and unhealthy, unchanged since long before the Fall, but hundreds of wealthy hunters—many from offworld—come there every year for the ducks. Most of the protomallards died off quickly after their regeneration and release from the seedship seven centuries earlier, either unable to adapt to Hyperion's climate or stalked by its indigenie predators, but a few ducks survived in the fens of north-central Aquila. And the hunters came. And I guided them.

Four of us worked out of an abandoned fiberplastic plantation set on a narrow thumb of shale and mud between the fens and a tributary to the Kans River. The other three guides concentrated on fishing and big-game hunting, but I had the plantation and most of the fens to myself during duck season. The fens were a semitropical marsh area consisting mostly of thick chalma growth, weirwood forest, and more temperate stands of giant prometheus in the rocky areas above the floodplain, but during the crisp, dry cold snap of early autumn, the mallards paused there on their migration from the southern islands to their lakes in the remotest regions of the Pinion Plateau.

I woke the four "hunters" an hour and a half before dawn. I had fixed a breakfast of jambon, toast, and coffee, but the four overweight

businessmen grumbled and cursed as they wolfed it down. I had to remind them to check and clean their weapons: three carried shotguns,
and the fourth was foolish enough to bring an antique energy rifle. As
they grumbled and ate, I went out behind the shack and sat with Izzy,
the Labrador retriever I'd had since she was a pup. Izzy knew that we
were going hunting, and I had to stroke her head and neck to calm her
down.

First light was coming up just as we left the overgrown plantation
grounds and polled off in a flat-bottomed skiff. Radiant gossamers were
visible flitting through dark tunnels of branches and above the trees. The
hunters—M. Rolman, M. Herrig, M. Rushomin, and M. Poneascu—sat
forward on the thwarts while I poled. Izzy and I were separated from them
by the heap of floatblinds stacked between us, the curved bottoms of the
disks still showing the rough matting of the fiberplastic husk. Rolman and
Herrig were wearing expensive chameleon-cloth ponchos, although they
did not activate the polymer until we were deep in the swamp. I asked
them to quit talking so loudly as we approached the freshwater fens where
the mallards would be setting in. All four men glared at me, but they
lowered their voices and soon fell silent.

The light was almost strong enough to read by when I stopped the
skiff just outside the shooting fen and floated their blinds. I hitched up my
well-patched waterproofs and slid into the chest-deep water. Izzy leaned
over the side of the skiff, eyes bright, but I flashed a hand signal to restrain
her from jumping in. She quivered but sat back.

"Give me your gun, please," I said to M. Poneascu, the first man.
These once-a-year hunters had enough trouble just keeping their balance
while getting into the small floatblinds; I did not trust them to hang on to
their shotguns. I had asked them to keep the chamber empty and the safety
on, but when Poneascu handed his weapon over, the chamber indicator
glowed red for loaded and the safety was off. I ejected the shell, clicked the
safety on, set the gun in the waterproof carrier strapped across my shoulders, and steadied the floatblind while the heavyset man stepped from the
skiff.

"I'll be right back," I said softly to the other three, and began wading
through chalma fronds, pulling the blind along by the harness strap. I
could have had the hunters pole their floatblinds to a place of their own
choosing, but the fen was riddled with quickmud cysts that would pull
down both pole and poler, populated by dracula ticks the size of blood-
filled balloons that liked to drop on moving objects from overhead
branches, decorated with hanging ribbon snakes, which looked precisely
like chalma fronds to the unwary, and rife with fighting gar that could bite
through a finger. There were other surprises for first-time visitors. Besides,
I'd learned from experience that most of these weekend hunters would
position their floats so that they would be shooting at each other as soon

as the first flight of mallards appeared. It was my job to keep that from happening.

I parked Poneascu in a concealing curl of fronds with a good view from the south mudbank of the largest body of open water, showed him where I was going to place the other floatblinds, told him to watch from within the slit of the floatblind canvas and not to begin shooting until everyone was placed, and then went back for the other three. I placed Rushomin about twenty meters to the first man's right, found a good place closer to the inlet for Rolman, and then went back for the man with the idiot energy weapon. M. Herrig.

The sun would be up in another ten minutes.

"About crossdamned time you fucking remembered me," snapped the fat man as I waded back to him. He'd already got onto his float; his chameleon-cloth trousers were wet. Methane bubbles between the skiff and the mouth of the inlet indicated a large mudcyst, so I had to work my way close to the mudflat each time I came or went.

"We're not paying you to waste your crossdamn time like this," he growled from around a thick cigar.

I nodded, reached up, plucked the lighted cigar from between his teeth, and tossed it away from the cyst. We were lucky that the bubbles had not ignited. "Ducks can smell the smoke," I said, ignoring his gaping mouth and reddening face.

I slipped into the harness and pulled his float into the open fen, my chest cutting a path through the red-and-orange algae that had covered the surface again since my last trip.

M. Herrig fondled his expensive and useless energy rifle and glared at me. "Boy, you watch your crossdamn mouth or I'll crossdamn watch it for you," he said. His poncho and chameleon-cloth hunting blouse were unsealed enough for me to see the gleam of a gold Pax double cross hanging around his neck and the red welt of the actual cruciform on his upper chest. M. Herrig was a born-again Christian.

I said nothing until I had his float positioned properly to the left of the inlet. All four of these experts could fire out toward the pond now without fear of hitting one another. "Pull your canvas around and watch from the slit," I said, untying the line from my harness and securing it around a chalma root.

M. Herrig made a noise but left the camouflage canvas still furled on the dome wands.

"Wait until I've got the decoys out before shooting," I said. I pointed out the other shooting positions. "And don't fire toward the inlet. I'll be there in the skiff."

M. Herrig did not answer.

I shrugged and waded back to the skiff. Izzy was sitting where I had commanded her to stay, but I could see from her straining muscles and gleaming eyes that in spirit she was bounding back and forth like a puppy. Without climbing into the skiff, I rubbed her neck. "Just a few minutes now, girl," I whispered. Released from her stay command, she ran to the bow as I began dragging the skiff toward the inlet.

The radiant gossamers had disappeared, and the skystreaks of meteor showers were fading as the predawn light solidified into a milky glow. The symphony of insect sounds and the croak of amphisbands along the mudflats were giving way to morning birdcalls and the occasional gronk of a gar inflating its challenge sac. The sky was deepening to its daytime lapis in the east.

I pulled the skiff under fronds, gestured for Izzy to stay in the bow, and pulled four of the decoys out from under the thwarts. There was the slightest film of ice along the shoreline here, but the center of the fen was clear, and I began positioning the decoys, activating each one as I left it. The water was never deeper than my chest.

I had just returned to the skiff and lay down next to Izzy under the concealing fronds when the ducks arrived. Izzy heard them first. Her entire body went rigid, and her nose came up as if she could sniff them on the wind. A second later there came the whisper of wings. I leaned forward and peered through the brittle foliage.

In the center of the pond the decoys were swimming and preening. One of them arched its neck and called just as the real mallards became visible above the tree line to the south. A flight of three ducks swept out of their pattern, extended wings to brake, and came sliding down invisible rails toward the fen.

I felt the usual thrill I always encounter at such moments: my throat tightens and my heart pounds, seems to stop for a moment, and then palpably aches. I had spent most of my life in remote regions, observing nature, but confrontation with such beauty always touched something so deep in me that I had no words for it. Beside me, Izzy was as still and rigid as an ebony statue.

The gunfire started then. The three with shotguns opened up at once and kept firing as quickly as they could eject shells. The energy rifle sliced its beam across the fen, the narrow shaft of violet light clearly visible in the morning mists.

The first duck must have been hit by two or three patterns at once: it flew apart in an explosion of feathers and viscera. The second one's wings folded and it dropped, all grace and beauty blasted out of it. The third mallard slipped to its right, recovered just above the water, and beat its wings for altitude. The energy beam slashed after it, slicing through leaves and branches like a silent scythe. Shotguns roared again, but the mallard seemed to anticipate their aim. The bird dived toward the lake, banked hard right, and flew straight toward the inlet.

Straight toward Izzy and me.

The bird was no more than two meters above the water. Its wings were beating strongly, its entire form was bent to the purpose of escape, and I realized that it was going to fly under the trees, right through the inlet opening. Despite the fact that the bird's unusual flight pattern had taken it between several shooting positions, all four men were still firing.

I used my right leg to push the skiff out of the concealing branches. "Cease fire!" I shouted in a command-voice that I'd acquired during my brief career as a sergeant in the Home Guard. Two of the men did. One shotgun and the energy rifle continued firing. The mallard never wavered as it passed the skiff a meter to our left.

Izzy's body quivered and her mouth seemed to drop farther open in surprise as the duck flapped low past us. The shotgun did not fire again, but I could see the violet beam panning toward us through the rising mists. I shouted and pulled Izzy down between the thwarts.

The mallard escaped the tunnel of chalma branches behind us and beat its wings for altitude. Suddenly the air smelled of ozone, and a perfectly straight line of flame slashed across the stern of the boat. I threw myself flat against the bottom of the skiff, grabbing Izzy's collar and tugging her closer as I did so.

The violet beam missed my curled fingers and Izzy's collar by a millimeter. I saw the briefest glimmer of a quizzical look in Izzy's excited eyes, and then she tried to lower her head to my chest the way she had as a puppy when she acted penitent. At the movement, her head and the section of neck above her collar separated from her body and went over the side with a soft splash. I still held the collar and her weight was still on me, her forepaws still quivering against my chest. Then blood geysered out over me from arteries in the cleanly severed neck, and I rolled aside, pushing the spasming, headless body of my dog away from me. Her blood was warm and it tasted of copper.

The energy beam slashed back again, cut a heavy chalma branch from its trunk a meter away from the skiff, and then switched off as if it had never existed.

I sat up and looked across the pond at M. Herrig. The fat man was lighting a cigar; the energy rifle lay across his knees. The smoke from his cigar mingled with the tendrils of mist still rising from the fen.

I slipped over the side of the skiff into the chest-deep water. Izzy's blood still swirled around me as I began wading toward M. Herrig.

He lifted his energy rifle and held it across his chest in port arms as I approached. When he spoke, it was around the cigar clenched between his teeth. "Well, are you going out there to retrieve the ducks I got, or are you just going to let them float out there until they ro—"

As soon as I was within arm's length I grabbed the fat man's chameleon poncho with my left hand and jerked him forward. He tried to raise the energy rifle, but I seized it with my right hand and flung it far out into the fen. M. Herrig shouted something then, his cigar tumbled into the floatblind, and I pulled him off his stool and into the water. He came up spluttering and spitting algae and I hit him once, very hard, squarely in the mouth. I felt the skin on my knuckles tear as several of his teeth snapped, and then he was sprawling backward. His head hit the frame of the floatblind with a hollow bang, and he went under again.

I waited for his fat face to rise to the surface again like the belly of some dead fish, and when it did, I held it down, watching the bubbles rise while his arms flailed and his pudgy hands batted uselessly at my wrists. The other three hunters began shouting from their shooting positions across the fen. I ignored them.

When M. Herrig's hands had dropped away and the stream of bubbles had thinned to a weak trickle, I released him and stepped back. For a moment I did not think that he was going to come up, but then the fat man exploded to the surface and hung on the edge of the float. He vomited water and algae. I turned my back on him and waded across to the others.

"That's all for today," I said. "Give me your guns. We're going in."

Each man opened his mouth as if to protest; each man took a look at my eyes and blood-spattered face and handed me his shotgun.

"Retrieve your friend," I said to the last man, Poneascu. I carried the weapons back to the skiff, unloaded them, sealed the shotguns in the watertight compartment under the bow, and carried the boxes of shells to the stern. Izzy's headless corpse had already begun to stiffen as I eased it over the side. The bottom of the skiff was awash with her blood. I went back to the stern, stowed the shells, and stood leaning on the pole.

The three hunters returned eventually, awkwardly paddling their own floats while pulling the one in which M. Herrig was sprawled. The fat man was still hanging over the side, his face pale. They climbed into the skiff and began trying to pull the floats aboard.

"Leave them," I said. "Tie them to that chalma root. I'll come back for them later."

They tied off the floats and pulled M. Herrig aboard like some obese fish. The only sounds were the birds and insects of the fen coming alive and M. Herrig's continued retching. When he was aboard, the other three hunters seated and muttering, I poled us back to the plantation as the sun burned through the last of the morning vapors rising from the dark waters.

And that should have been the end of it. Except, of course, it was not.

I WAS MAKING LUNCH in the primitive kitchen when M. Herrig came out of the sleeping barracks with a stubby military flechette gun. Such weapons were illegal on Hyperion; the Pax allowed no one except the Home Guard to carry them. I could see the white, shocked faces of the other three hunters peering from the barracks door as M. Herrig staggered into the kitchen amid a fog of whiskey fumes.

The fat man could not resist the impulse to give a short, melodramatic speech before killing me. "You crossdamned heathen son of a bitch . . . ." he began, but I did not stand around to listen to the rest. I threw myself down and forward even as he fired from the hip.

Six thousand steel flechettes blew apart the stove, the pan of stew I had been cooking on the stove, the sink, the window above the sink, and the shelves and crockery on the shelves. Food, plastic, porcelain, and glass showered over my legs as I crawled under the open counter and reached for M. Herrig's legs, even as he leaned over the counter to spray me with a second burst of flechettes.

I grabbed the big man's ankles and jerked. He went down on his back with a crash that sent a decade's worth of dust rising from the floorboards. I clambered up over his legs, kneeing him in the groin as I climbed, and grabbed his wrist with the intention of forcing the gun out of his hands. He had a firm grip on the stock; his finger was still on the trigger. The magazine whined softly as another flechette cartridge clicked into pace. I could smell M. Herrig's whiskey-and-cigar breath on my face as he grimaced triumphantly and forced the weapon's muzzle toward me. In one movement I slammed my forearm against his wrist and the heavy gun, squeezing it tight under M. Herrig's fleshy chins. Our eyes met for the instant before his struggles made him complete his squeeze of the trigger.

I TOLD ONE OF THE OTHER hunters how to use the radio in the common room, and a Pax security skimmer was setting down on the grassy lawn within the hour. There were only a dozen or so working skimmers on the continent, so the sight of the black Pax vehicle was sobering, to say the least.

They banded my wrists, slapped a cortical come-along to my temple, and hurried me into the holding box in the rear of the vehicle. I sat there, dripping sweat in the hot stillness of the box, while Pax-trained forensic specialists used needle-nosed pliers to try to retrieve every shard of M. Herrig's skull and scattered brain tissue from the perforated floor and wall. Then, when they had interrogated the other hunters and had found as much of M. Herrig as they were going to find, I watched through the scarred Perspex window as they loaded his body-bagged corpse aboard the skimmer. Lift blades whined, the ventilators allowed me a bit of cooler air just as I thought I could no longer breathe, and the skimmer rose, circled the plantation once, and flew south toward Port Romance.

MY TRIAL WAS HELD six days later. M's. Rolman, Rushomin, and Poneascu testified that I had insulted M. Herrig on the trip to the fen and then assaulted him there. They pointed out that the hunting dog had been killed in the melee that I had begun. They testified that once back at the plantation, I had brandished the illegal flechette gun and threatened to kill all of them. M. Herrig had tried to take the weapon away from me. I had shot him at point-blank range, literally blowing his head off in the process.

M. Herrig was the last to testify. Still shaken and pale from his three-day resurrection, dressed in a somber business suit and cape, his voice shook as he confirmed the other men's testimony and described my brutal assault on him. My court-appointed attorney did not cross-examine him. As born-again Christians in good standing with the Pax, none of the four could be forced to testify under the influence of Truthtell or any other chemical or electronic form of verification. I volunteered to undergo Truthtell or fullscan, but the prosecuting attorney protested that such gimmickry was irrelevant, and the Pax-approved judge agreed. My counselor did not file a protest.

There was no jury. The judge took less than twenty minutes to reach a verdict. I was guilty and sentenced to execution by deathwand.

I stood and asked that the sentence be delayed until I could get word to my aunt and cousins in north Aquila so that they could visit me one last time. My request was denied. The time of execution was set for sunrise on the following day.

3

A PRIEST FROM THE PAX MONASTERY in Port Romance came to visit me that evening. He was a small, somewhat nervous man with thinning blond hair and a slight stutter. Once in the windowless visiting room, he introduced himself as Father Tse and waved the guards away.

"My son," he began, and I felt the urge to smile, since the priest looked to be about my age, "my son . . . are you prepared for tomorrow?"

Any urge to smile fled. I shrugged.

Father Tse chewed his lip. "You have not accepted Our Lord . . . ," he said, voice tense with emotion.

I had the urge to shrug again but spoke instead. "I haven't accepted the cruciform, Father. It might not be the same thing."

His brown eyes were insistent, almost pleading. "It *is* the same thing, my son. Our Lord has revealed this."

I said nothing.

Father Tse set down his missal and touched my bound wrist. "You know that if you repent this night and accept Jesus Christ as your personal Savior, that three days after . . . tomorrow . . . you will rise to live again in the grace of Our Lord's forgiveness." His brown eyes did not blink. "You do know this, do you not, my son?"

I returned his gaze. Some prisoner in the adjoining cell block had screamed most of the last three nights. I felt very tired. "Yes, Father," I said. "I know how the cruciform works."

Father Tse vigorously shook his head. "Not the cruciform, my son. The grace of Our Lord."

I nodded. "Have you gone through resurrection, Father?"

The priest glanced down. "Not yet, my son. But I have no fear of that day." He looked up at me again. "Nor must you."

I closed my eyes for a moment. I had been thinking about this for almost every minute of the past six days and nights. "Look, Father," I said, "I don't mean to hurt your feelings, but I made the decision some years ago not to go under the cruciform, and I don't think that this is the right time to change my mind."

Father Tse leaned forward, eyes bright. "Any time is the right time to accept Our Lord, my son. After sunrise tomorrow there will be no more time. Your dead body will be taken out from this place and disposed of at sea, mere food for the carrion fish beyond the bay. . . ."

This was not a new image for me. "Yes," I said, "I know the penalty for a murderer executed without converting. But I have this—" I tapped the cortical come-along now permanently attached to my temple. "I don't need a cruciform symbiote embedded in me to put me in a deeper slavery."

Father Tse pulled back as if I had slapped him. "One mere lifetime of commitment to Our Lord is not slavery," he said, his stutter banished by cold anger. "Millions have offered this *before* the tangible blessing of immediate resurrection in this life was offered. Billions gratefully accept it now." He stood up. "You have the choice, my son. Eternal light, with the gift of almost unlimited life in this world in which to serve Christ, or eternal darkness."

I shrugged and looked away.

Father Tse blessed me, said good-bye in tones comingled with sadness and contempt, turned, called the guards, and was gone. A minute later pain stabbed at my skull as the guards tickled my come-along and led me back to my cell.

I WON'T BORE YOU with a long litany of the thoughts that chased through my mind that endless autumn night. I was twenty-seven years old. I loved life with a passion that sometimes led me into trouble . . . although never anything as serious as this before. For the first few hours of that final night, I pondered escape the way a caged animal must claw at steel bars. The prison was set high on the sheer cliff overlooking the reef called the Mandible, far out on Toschahi Bay. Everything was unbreakable Perspex, unbendable steel, or seamless plastic. The guards carried deathwands, and I sensed no reluctance in them to use them. Even if I should escape, a touch of a button on the come-along remote would curl me up with the universe's worst migraine until they followed the beacon to my hiding place.

My last hours were spent pondering the folly of my short, useless life. I regretted nothing but also had little to show for Raul Endymion's twenty-seven years on Hyperion. The dominant theme of my life seemed to be the same perverse stubbornness that had led me to reject resurrection.

So you owe the Church a lifetime of service, whispered a frenzied voice in the back of my skull, *at least you* get *a lifetime that way! And more lifetimes beyond that! How can you turn down a deal like that? Anything's better than real death . . . your rotting corpse being fed to the ampreys, coelacanths, and skarkworms. Think about this!* I closed my eyes and pretended to sleep just to flee from the shouts echoing in my own mind.

The night lasted an eternity, but sunrise still seemed to come early. Four guards walked me to the death chamber, strapped me into a wooden chair, and then sealed the steel door. If I looked over my left shoulder, I could see faces peering through the Perspex. Somehow I had expected a priest—maybe not Father Tse again, but a priest, some representative of the Pax—to offer me one final chance at immortality. There was none. Only part of me was glad. I cannot say now whether I would have changed my mind at the last moment.

The method of execution was simple and mechanical—not as ingenious as a Schrödinger cat box, perhaps, but clever nonetheless. A short-range deathwand was set on the wall and aimed at the chair where I sat. I saw the red light click on the small comlog unit attached to the weapon. Prisoners in adjoining cells had gleefully whispered the mechanics of my death to me even before the sentence had been passed. The comlog computer had a random-number generator. When the number generated was a prime smaller than seventeen, the deathwand beam would be activated. Every synapse in the gray lump that was the personality and memory of Raul Endymion would be fused. Destroyed. Melted down to the neuronic equivalent of radioactive slag. Autonomic functions would cease mere milliseconds later. My heart and breathing would stop almost as soon as my mind was destroyed. Experts said that death by deathwand was as painless a way to die as had ever been invented. Those resurrected after deathwand execution usually did not want to talk about the sensation, but the word in the cells was that it hurt like hell—as if every circuit in your brain were exploding.

I looked at the red light of the comlog and the business end of the short deathwand. Some wag had rigged an LED display so that I could see the numerals being generated. They flicked by like floor numbers on an elevator to hell: 26-74-109-19-37 . . . they had programmed the comlog to generate no numbers larger than 150 . . . 77-42-12-60-84-129-108-14-

I lost it then. I balled my fists, strained at the unyielding plastic straps, and screamed obscenities at the walls, at the pale faces distorted through the Perspex windows, at the fucking Church and its fucking Pax, at the fucking coward who'd killed my dog, at the goddamned fucking cowards who . . .

I did not see the low prime number appear on the display. I did not hear the deathwand hum softly as its beam was activated. I *did* feel something, a sort of hemlock coldness starting at the back of my skull and widening to every part of my body with the speed of nerve conduction, and I felt surprise at feeling something. *The experts are wrong and the cons are right,* I thought wildly. *You* can *feel your own death by death-wand.* I would have giggled then if the numbness had not flowed over me like a wave.

Like a black wave.

A black wave that carried me away with it.

4

WAS NOT SURPRISED to wake up alive. I suppose one is surprised only when one awakens dead. At any rate, I awoke with no more discomfort than a vague tingling in my extremities and lay there watching sunlight crawl across a rough plaster ceiling for a minute or more until an urgent thought shook me full awake.

Wait a minute, wasn't I . . . didn't they . . . ??

I sat up and looked around. If there was any lingering sense that my execution had been a dream, the prosaic quality of my surroundings dispelled it immediately. The room was pie-shaped with a curved and white-washed outer stone wall and thick plaster ceilings. The bed was the only piece of furniture, and the heavy off-white linen on it complemented the texture of plaster and stone. There was a massive wooden door—closed—and an arched window open to the elements. One glance at the lapis sky beyond the window told me that I was still on Hyperion. There was no chance that I was still in the Port Romance prison; the stone here was too old, the details of the door too ornamental, the quality of linen too good.

I rose, found myself naked, and walked to the window. The autumn breeze was brisk, but the sun was warm on my skin. I was in a stone tower. Yellow chalma and the thick tangle of low weirwood wove a solid canopy of treetops up hills to the horizon. Everblues grew on granite rock faces. I could see other walls, ramparts, and the curve of another tower stretching away along the ridgeline upon which this tower stood. The walls seemed *old*. The quality of their construction and the organic feel of their architecture was from an era of skill and taste long predating the Fall.

I guessed at once where I must be: the chalma and weirwood suggested that I was still on the southern continent of Aquila; the elegant ruins spoke of the abandoned city of Endymion.

I had never been to the town from which my family took its surname, but I had heard many descriptions of it from Grandam, our clan storyteller. Endymion had been one of the first Hyperion cities settled after the dropship crash almost seven hundred years earlier. Until the Fall it had been famous for its fine university, a huge, castlelike structure that towered over the old town below it. Grandam's great-grandfather's grandfather had been a professor at the university until the Pax troops commandeered the entire region of central Aquila and literally sent thousands of people packing.

And now I had returned.

A bald man with blue skin and cobalt-blue eyes came through the door, set underwear and a simple daysuit of what looked like homespun cotton on the bed, and said, "Please get dressed."

I admit that I stared silently as the man turned and went out the door. Blue skin. Bright-blue eyes. No hair. He . . . it . . . had to be the first android that I had ever seen. If asked, I would have said that there were no androids left on Hyperion. They had been illegal to biofacture since before the Fall, and although they had been imported by the legendary Sad King Billy to build most of the cities in the north centuries ago, I had never heard of one still existing on our world. I shook my head and got dressed. The daysuit fit nicely, despite my rather unusually large shoulders and long legs.

I was back at the window when the android returned. He stood by the open door and gestured with an open hand. "This way please, M. Endymion."

I resisted the impulse to ask questions and followed him up the tower stairs. The room at the top took up the entire floor. Late-afternoon sunlight streamed in through yellow-and-red stained-glass windows. At least one window was open, and I could hear the rustle of the leaf canopy far below as a wind came up from the valley.

This room was as white and bare as my cell had been, except for a cluster of medical equipment and communication consoles in the center of the circle. The android left, closing the heavy door behind him, and it took me a second to realize that there was a human being in the locus of all that equipment.

At least I thought it was a human being.

The man was lying on a flowfoam hoverchair bed that had been adjusted to a sitting position. Tubes, IV drips, monitor filaments, and organic-looking umbilicals ran from the equipment to the wizened figure in the chair. I say "wizened," but in truth the man's body looked almost mummified, the skin wrinkled like the folds of an old leather jacket, the skull mottled and almost perfectly bald, the arms and legs emaciated to the point of being vestigial appendages. Everything about the old man's posture made me think of a wrinkled and featherless baby bird that had fallen out of the nest. His parchment skin had a blue cast to it that made me think *android* for a moment, but then I saw the different shade of blue, the faint glow of the palms, ribs, and forehead, and realized that I was looking at a real human who had enjoyed—or suffered—centuries of Poulsen treatments.

No one receives Poulsen treatments anymore. The technology was lost in the Fall, as were the raw materials from worlds lost in time and space. Or so I thought. But here was a creature at least many centuries old who must have received Poulsen treatments as recently as decades ago.

The old man opened his eyes.

I have since seen eyes with as much power as his, but nothing in my life to that point had prepared me for the intensity of such a gaze. I think I took a step back.

"Come closer, Raul Endymion." The voice was like the scraping of a dull blade on parchment. The old man's mouth moved like a turtle's beak.

I stepped closer, stopping only when a com console stood between me and the mummified form. The old man blinked and lifted a bony hand that still seemed too heavy for the twig of a wrist. "Do you know who I am?" The scratch of a voice was as soft as a whisper.

I shook my head.

"Do you know where you are?"

I took a breath. "Endymion. The abandoned university, I think."

The wrinkles folded back in a toothless smile. "Very good. The namesake recognizes the heaps of stone which named his family. But you do not know who I might be?"

"No."

"And you have no questions about how you survived your execution?"

I stood at parade rest and waited.

The old man smiled again. "Very good, indeed. All things come to him who waits. And the details are not that enlightening . . . bribes in high places, a stunner substituted for the deathwand, more bribes to those who certify the death and dispose of the body. It is not the 'how' we are interested in, is it, Raul Endymion?"

"No," I said at last. "Why."

The turtle's beak twitched, the massive head nodded. I noticed now that even through the damage of centuries, the face was still sharp and angular—a satyr's countenance.

"Precisely," he said. "Why? Why go to the trouble of faking your execution and transporting your fucking carcass across half a fucking continent? Why indeed?"

The obscenities did not seem especially harsh from the old man's mouth. It was as if he had sprinkled his speech with them for so long that they deserved no special emphasis. I waited.

"I want you to run an errand for me, Raul Endymion." The old man's breath wheezed. Pale fluid flowed through the intravenous tubes.

"Do I have a choice?"

The face smiled again, but the eyes were as unchanging as the stone in the walls. "We always have choices, dear boy. In this case you can ignore any debt you might owe me for saving your life and simply leave here . . . walk away. My servants will not stop you. With luck you will get out of this restricted area, find your way back to more civilized regions, and avoid Pax patrols where your identity and lack of papers might be . . . ah . . . embarrassing."

I nodded. My clothes, chronometer, work papers, and Pax ID were probably in Toschahi Bay by now. Working as a hunting guide in the fens made me forget how often the authorities checked IDs in the cities. I would soon be reminded if I wandered back to any of the coastal cities or inland towns. And even rural jobs such as shepherd and guide required Pax ID for tax and tithe forms. Which left hiding in the interior for the rest of my life, living off the land and avoiding people.

"Or," said the old man, "you can run an errand for me and become rich." He paused, his dark eyes inspecting me the way I had seen professional hunters inspect pups that might or might not prove to be good hunting dogs.

"Tell me," I said.

The old man closed his eyes and rattled in a deep breath. He did not bother to open his eyes when he spoke. "Can you read, Raul Endymion?"

"Yes."

"Have you read the poem known as the *Cantos*?"

"No."

"But you have heard some of it? Surely, being born into one of the nomadic shepherd clans of the north, the storyteller has touched on the *Cantos*?" There was a strange tone in the cracked voice. Modesty, perhaps.

I shrugged. "I've heard bits of it. My clan preferred the *Garden Epic* or the *Glennon-Height Saga*."

The satyr features creased into a smile. "The *Garden Epic*. Yes. Raul was a centaur-hero in that, was he not?"

I said nothing. Grandam had loved the character of the centaur named Raul. My mother and I both had grown up listening to tales of him.

"Do you believe the stories?" snapped the old man. "The *Cantos* tales, I mean."

"*Believe* them?" I said. "That they actually happened that way? The pilgrims and the Shrike and all that?" I paused a minute. There were those who believed all the tall tales told in the *Cantos*. And there were those who believed none of it, that it was all myth and maundering thrown together to add mystery to the ugly war and confusion that was the Fall. "I never really thought about it," I said truthfully. "Does it matter?"

The old man seemed to be choking, but then I realized that the dry, rattling sounds were chuckles. "Not really," he said at last. "Now, listen. I will tell you the outline of the . . . errand. It takes energy for me to speak, so save your questions for when I am finished." He blinked and gestured with his mottled claw toward the chair covered with a white sheet. "Do you wish to sit?"

I shook my head and remained at parade rest.

"All right," said the old man. "My story begins almost two hundred seventy-some years ago during the Fall. One of the pilgrims in the *Cantos* was a friend of mine. Her name was Brawne Lamia. She was real. After the Fall . . . after the death of the Hegemony and the opening of the Time Tombs . . . Brawne Lamia gave birth to a daughter. The child's name was Diana, but the little girl was headstrong and changed her name almost as soon as she was old enough to talk. For a while she was known as Cynthia, then Cate . . . short for Hecate . . . and then, when she turned twelve, she insisted that her friends and family call her Temis. When I last saw her, she was called Aenea. . . ." I heard the name as Ah-nee-a.

The old man stopped and squinted at me. "You think this is not important, but names *are* important. If you had not been named after this city, which was in turn named after an ancient poem, then you would not have come to my attention and you could not be here today. You would be dead. Feeding the skarkworms in the Great South Sea. Do you understand, Raul Endymion?"

"No," I said.

He shook his head. "It does not matter. Where was I?"

"The last time you saw the child, she called herself Aenea."

"Yes." The old man closed his eyes again. "She was not an especially attractive child, but she was . . . unique. Everyone who knew her felt that she was different. Special. Not spoiled, despite all the nonsense with the name changes. Just . . . different." He smiled, showing pink gums. "Have you ever met someone who is profoundly different, Raul Endymion?"

I hesitated only a second. "No," I said. It was not quite true. This old man was different. But I knew he was not asking that.

"Cate . . . Aenea . . . was different," he said, eyes closed again. "Her mother knew it. Of course, Brawne knew that the child was special before she was born. . . ." He stopped and opened his eyes enough to squint at me. "You've heard this part of the *Cantos*?"

"Yes," I said. "It was foretold by a cybrid entity that the woman named Lamia was to give birth to a child known as the One Who Teaches."

I thought that the old man was going to spit. "A stupid title. No one called Aenea that during the time I knew her. She was simply a child, brilliant and headstrong, but a child. Everything that was unique was unique only in potential. But then . . ."

His voice trailed off and his eyes seemed to film over. It was as if he had lost track of the conversation. I waited.

"But then Brawne Lamia died," he said several minutes later, voice stronger, as if there had been no gap in the monologue, "and Aenea disappeared. She was twelve. Technically, I was her guardian, but she did not ask my permission to disappear. One day she left and I never heard from her again." Here the story paused again, as if the old man were a machine that ran down occasionally and required some internal rewinding.

"Where was I?" he said at last.

"You never heard from her again."

"Yes. I never heard *from* her, but I know where she went and when she will reappear. The Time Tombs are off-limits now, guarded from public view by the Pax troops stationed there, but do you remember the names and functions of the tombs, Raul Endymion?"

I grunted. Grandam used to grill me on aspects of the oral tales in much this way. I used to think that Grandam was old. Next to this ancient, wizened thing, Grandam had been an infant. "I think I remember the tombs," I said. "There was the one called the Sphinx, the Jade Tomb, the Obelisk, the Crystal Monolith, where the soldier was buried . . ."

"Colonel Fedmahn Kassad," muttered the old man. Then his gaze returned to me. "Go on."

"The three Cave Tombs . . ."

"Only the Third Cave Tomb led anywhere," interrupted the old man again. "To labyrinths on other worlds. The Pax sealed it. Go on."

"That's all I can remember . . . oh, the Shrike Palace."

The old man showed a turtle's sharp smile. "One mustn't forget the Shrike Palace or our old friend the Shrike, must one? Is that all of them?"

"I think so," I said. "Yes."

The mummified figure nodded. "Brawne Lamia's daughter disappeared through one of these tombs. Can you guess which one?"

"No." I did not know, but I suspected.

"Seven days after Brawne died, the girl left a note, went to the Sphinx in the dead of night, and disappeared. Do you remember where the Sphinx led, boy?"

"According to the *Cantos,*" I said, "Sol Weintraub and his daughter traveled to the distant future through the Sphinx."

"Yes," whispered the ancient thing in the hoverbed. "Sol and Rachel and a precious few others disappeared into the Sphinx before the Pax sealed it and closed off the Valley of the Time Tombs. Many tried in those early days—tried to find a shortcut to the future—but the Sphinx seemed to choose who might travel its tunnel through time."

"And it accepted the girl," I said.

The old man merely grunted at this statement of the obvious. "Raul Endymion," he rasped at last, "do you know what I am going to ask of you?"

"No," I said, although once again I had a strong suspicion.

"I want you to go after my Aenea," said the old man. "I want you to find her, to protect her from the Pax, to flee with her, and—when she has grown up and become what she must become—to give her a message. I want you to tell her that her uncle Martin is dying and that if she wishes to speak to him again, she must come home."

I tried not to sigh. I'd guessed that this ancient thing had once been the poet Martin Silenus. Everyone knew the *Cantos* and its author. How he had escaped the Pax purges and been allowed to live in this restricted place was a mystery, but one I did not choose to explore. "You want me to go north to the continent of Equus, fight my way past several thousand Pax troops, somehow get into the Valley of the Time Tombs, get into the Sphinx, hope it . . . accepts me . . . then chase this child into the distant future, hang around with her for a few decades, and then tell her to go back in time to visit you?"

For a moment there was a silence broken only by the soft sounds of Martin Silenus's life-support equipment. The machines were breathing. "Not exactly," he said at last.

I waited.

"She has not traveled to some distant future," said the old man. "At least not distant from us, now. When she stepped through the entrance of the Sphinx two hundred forty-seven years ago, it was for a short trip through time . . . two hundred sixty-two Hyperion years, to be exact."

"How do you know this?" I asked. From everything I had read, no one—not even the Pax scientists who had had two centuries to study the sealed tombs—had been able to predict how far into the future the Sphinx would send someone.

"I *know* it," said the ancient poet. "Do you doubt me?"

Instead of responding to that, I said, "So the child . . . Aenea . . . will step out of the Sphinx sometime this year."

"She will step out of the Sphinx in forty-two hours, sixteen minutes," said the old satyr.

I admit that I blinked.

"And the Pax will be waiting for her," he continued. "They also know to the minute when she will emerge . . ."

I did not ask how they came by the information.

". . . and capturing Aenea is the single most important thing on the Pax's agenda," rasped the old poet. "They know that the future of the universe depends upon this."

I knew now that the old poet was senile. The future of the universe depended upon no single event . . . that I knew. I held my silence.

"There are—at this moment—more than thirty thousand Pax troops in and around the Valley of the Time Tombs. At least five thousand of them are Vatican Swiss Guard."

I whistled at this. The Vatican Swiss Guard was the elite of the elite, the best-trained, best-equipped military force in the far-flung expanse of the Pax. A dozen Vatican Guard troops in full regalia could have beaten the entire ten thousand troops of Hyperion's Home Guard. "So," I said, "I have forty-two hours to get to Equus, cross the Sea of Grass and the mountains, somehow get past twenty or thirty thousand of the Pax's best troops, and rescue the girl?"

"Yes," said the ancient figure in the bed.

I managed not to roll my eyes. "What then?" I said. "There is nowhere we can hide. The Pax controls all of Hyperion, all spacecraft, the spacelanes, and every world of what used to be the Hegemony. If she is as important as you say, they will turn Hyperion upside down until they find her. Even if we could somehow get offplanet, which we can't, there would be no way we could escape."

"There is a way for you to get offplanet," the poet said in a tired voice. "There is a ship."

I swallowed hard. *There is a ship.* The idea of traveling between the stars for months while decades or years passed back home took my breath away. I had joined the Home Guard with the childish notion of someday belonging to the Pax military and flying between the stars. A foolish notion for a youngster who had already decided not to accept the cruciform.

"Still," I said, not truly believing that there was a ship. No member of the Pax Mercantilus would transport fugitives. "Even if we make it to another world, they would have us. Unless you see us fleeing by ship for centuries of time-debt."

"No," said the old man. "Not centuries. Not decades. You will escape by ship to one of the nearest worlds of the old Hegemony. Then you will go a secret way. You will see the old worlds. You will travel the River Tethys."

I knew now that the old man had lost his reason. When the farcasters fell and the AI TechnoCore abandoned humankind, the WorldWeb and Hegemony had died that same day. The tyranny of interstellar distances had been reimposed upon humanity. Now only the Pax forces, their puppet Mercantilus, and the hated Ousters braved the darkness between the stars.

"Come," rasped the old man. His fingers would not uncurl as he gestured me closer. I leaned over the low com console. I could smell him . . . a vague combination of medicine, age, and something like leather.

I DID NOT NEED the memories of Grandam's campfire tales to explain the River Tethys and to know why I now knew that the old man was far gone into senility. Everyone knew about the River Tethys; it and the so-called Grand Concourse had been two constant farcaster avenues between the Hegemony worlds. The Concourse had been a street connecting a hundred-some worlds under a hundred-some suns, its broad avenue open to everyone and stitched together by farcaster portals that never closed. The River Tethys had been a less-traveled route, but still important for bulk commerce and the countless pleasure boats that had floated effortlessly from world to world on the single highway of water.

The Concourse had been sliced into a thousand separate segments by the Fall of the WorldWeb farcaster network; the Tethys had simply ceased to exist, the connecting portals useless, the single river on a hundred worlds reverted to a hundred smaller rivers that would never be connected again. Even the old poet seated before me had described the river's death. I remembered the words from Grandam's recitation of the *Cantos*:

> *And the river that had flowed on*
> *For two centuries or more*
> *Linked through space and time*
> *By the tricks of TechnoCore*
> *Ceased flowing now*
> *On Fuji and on Barnard's World*
> *On Acteon and Deneb Drei*
> *On Esperance and Nevermore.*
> *Everywhere the Tethys ran,*
> *Like ribbons through*
> *The worlds of man,*
> *There the portals worked no more,*
> *There the riverbeds ran dry,*
> *There the currents ceased to swirl.*
> *Lost were the tricks of TechnoCore,*
> *Lost were the travelers forevermore*
> *Locked the portal, locked the door,*
> *Flowed the Tethys, nevermore.*

"COME CLOSER," whispered the old poet, still beckoning me with his yellowed finger. I leaned closer. The ancient creature's breath was like a dry wind out of an unsealed tomb—free of odor, but ancient, somehow redolent of forgotten centuries—as he whispered to me:

> *"A thing of beauty is a joy forever:*
> *Its loveliness increases; it will never*
> *Pass into nothingness . . ."*

I pulled my head back and nodded as if the old man had said something sensible. It was clear that he was mad.

As if reading my mind, the old poet chuckled. "I have often been called insane by those who underestimate the power of poetry. Do not decide now, Raul Endymion. We will meet later for dinner and I will finish describing your challenge. Decide then. For now . . . rest! Your death and resurrection must have tired you." The old man hunched over, and there came the dry rattling that I now understood as laughter.

THE ANDROID SHOWED me back to my room. I caught glimpses of court-yards and outbuildings through the tower windows. Once I saw another android—also male—walking past clerestory windows across the court-yard.

My guide opened the door and stepped back. I realized that I would not be locked in, that I was not a prisoner.

"Evening clothes have been set out for you, sir," said the blue-skinned man. "You are, of course, free to go or wander the old university grounds as you wish. I should warn you, M. Endymion, that there are dangerous animals in the forest and mountains in this vicinity."

I nodded and smiled. Dangerous animals would not keep me from leaving if I wished to leave. At the moment I did not.

The android turned to leave then, and on impulse I stepped forward and did something that would change the course of my life forever.

"Wait," I said. I extended a hand. "We haven't been introduced. I'm Raul Endymion."

For a long moment the android only looked at my extended hand, and I was sure that I had committed some breach of protocol. Androids had been, after all, considered something less than human centuries ago when they had been biofactured for use during the Hegira expansion. Then the artificial man grasped my hand in his and shook firmly. "I am A. Bettik," he said softly. "It is a pleasure to make your acquaintance."

A. Bettik. The name had some resonance for me that I could not place. I said, "I would like to talk to you, A. Bettik. Learn more about . . . about you and this place and the old poet."

The android's blue eyes lifted, and I thought I glimpsed something like amusement there. "Yes, sir," he said. "I would be happy to speak with you. I fear that it must be later, since there are many duties I have to oversee at this moment."

"Later, then," I said, and stepped back. "I look forward to it."

A. Bettik nodded and descended the tower stairs.

I walked into my room. Except for the bed being made and a suit of elegant evening clothes laid out there, the space was just as it had been. I went to the window and looked out over the ruins of Endymion University. Tall everblues rustled in the cool breeze. Violet leaves tumbled from the weirwood stand near the tower and scraped across the flagstone pavement twenty meters below. Chalma leaves scented the air with their distinctive cinnamon. I had grown up only a few hundred kilometers northeast, on the Aquila moors between these mountains and the rugged area known as the Beak, but the chill freshness of the mountain air here was new to me. The sky seemed a deeper lapis than any I had seen from the moors or lowlands. I breathed in the autumn air and grinned: whatever strangeness lay ahead, I was damned glad to be alive.

Leaving the window, I headed for the tower stairs and a look around the university and city after which my family had taken its name. However crazy the old man was, dinner conversation should be interesting.

Suddenly, when I was almost at the base of the tower stairs, I stopped in my tracks.

A. Bettik. The name was from Grandam's telling of the Cantos. *A. Bettik was the android who piloted the pilgrims' levitation barge* Benares *northeast from the city of Keats on the continent of Equus, up the Hoolie River past Naiad River Station, the Karla Locks, and Doukhobor's Copse to where the navigable river ended in Edge. From Edge the pilgrims had gone on alone across the Sea of Grass.* I remembered listening as a child, wondering why A. Bettik was the only android named, and wondering what had happened to him when the pilgrims left him behind at Edge. The name had been lost to me for more than two decades.

Shaking my head slightly, wondering whether it was the old poet or I who was mad, I went out into the late-afternoon light to explore Endymion.

5

AT THE SAME MOMENT that I am taking my leave of A. Bettik, six thousand light-years away, in a star system known only by NGC numbers and navigation coordinates, a Pax task force of three fast-attack torchships led by Father Captain Federico de Soya is destroying an orbital forest. The Ouster trees have no defenses against the Pax warships, and the encounter might be described more accurately as slaughter than battle.

I must explain something here. I am not speculating about these events: they occurred precisely as I describe them. Nor am I extrapolating or guessing in the scenes I am about to share when I tell you what Father Captain de Soya or the other principals did when there were no witnesses present. Or what they thought. Or what emotions they felt. These things are literal truth. Later, I will explain how I came to know these things . . . to know them without hint of distortion . . . but for now I ask that you accept them for what they are—the truth.

The three Pax torchships drop from relativistic velocities under more than six hundred gravities of deceleration—what spacefarers for centuries have called "raspberry jam delta-v"—meaning, of course, that if the internal containment fields were to fail for a microsecond, the crews would be little more than a layer of raspberry jam on the deckplates.

The containment fields do not fail. At one AU, Father Captain de Soya brings up the orbital forest in the viewsphere. Everyone in the Combat Control Center pauses to glance at the display: several thousand of the Ouster-tailored trees, each at least half a kilometer long, move in an elaborate choreography along the plane of the ecliptic—gravity-clustered copses, braided strands, and subtly shifting patterns of trees, always moving, their leaves always turned toward the G-type sun, their long branches shifting to find the perfect alignment, their

thirsty roots deep in the vaporous fog of moisture and nutrients provided by the shepherd comets moving among the forest clusters like giant dirty snowballs. Flitting between the branches of these trees and
between the trees themselves, Ouster variants are visible—humanoid
shapes with silver-reflective skin and micron-thin butterfly wings extending hundreds of meters. These wings catch the sunlight from moment to moment as they open and blink like brilliant Christmas lights
within the green foliage of the orbital forest.

"Fire!" says Father Captain Federico de Soya.

At two-thirds AU, the three torchships of Pax Task Force MAGI
open up with their long-distance weapons. At that distance even energy
beams would seem to crawl toward their targets like lightning bugs on a
black bedsheet, but the Pax ships carry hypervelocity and hyperkinetic
weapons: essentially small Hawking-drive starships in their own right,
some carrying plasma warheads, which are spun up to relativistic velocities in microseconds to detonate within the forest, others designed simply
to drop back into real space, their mass enlarged, and to plow through the
trees like cannonballs fired through wet cardboard at point-blank range.
Minutes later the three torchships are within energy-beam distance, and
the CPBs lance out in a thousand directions simultaneously, their beams
visible because of the riot of colloidal particles now filling space like dust
in an old attic.

The forest burns. Tailored bark, oh-two pods, and self-sealing leaves
burst from violent decompression or are sawed through by beams and
shaped plasma blast-tendrils, and the escaping globules of oxygen fuel the
fires amid the vacuum until the air freezes or burns away. And the forest
burns. Tens of millions of leaves fly away from the exploding forest, each
leaf or cluster of leaves its own blazing pyre, while trunks and branches
burn against the black background of space. The shepherd comets are
struck and then volatilize in an instant, blasting the braided strands of
forest apart in expanding shock waves of steam and molten rock fragments. Space-tailored Ousters—"Lucifer's angels" as the Pax forces have
contemptuously called them for centuries—are caught in the explosions
like translucent moths in a flame. Some are simply blown apart by the
plasma explosions or comet bursts. Others are caught in the path of CPBs
and become hyperkinetic objects themselves before their delicate wings
and organs are flung apart. Some attempt to flee, expanding their solar
wings to the maximum in a vain attempt to outrun the carnage.

None survive.

The encounter takes less than five minutes. When it is done, the
MAGI task force decelerates through the forest at a diminished thirty
gravities, the fusion-flame tails of the torchships igniting any tree fragments that have escaped the initial attack. Where the forest had floated in
space five minutes before—green leaves catching the sunlight, roots drinking the spheres of comet-water, Ouster angels floating like radiant gossa-

mers among the branches—now there is only a torus of smoke and expanding debris filling the plane of the ecliptic along this arc of space.

"Any survivors?" asks Father Captain de Soya, standing along the edge of the C³ central display, his hands clasped behind his back, balancing easily, with only the balls of his feet touching the sticktight strip around the display rim. Despite the fact that the torchship is still decelerating under thirty gravities, the Combat Control Center is held at a constant one-fiftieth standard-g microgravity. The dozen officers in the room sit and stand with their heads toward the center of the sphere. De Soya is a short man in his midthirties, standard. His face is round, the skin dark, and friends had noticed over the years that his eyes reflected priestly compassion more frequently than military ruthlessness. They are troubled now.

"No survivors," says Mother Commander Stone, de Soya's executive officer and another Jesuit. She turns from the tactical display to shunt into a blinking com unit.

De Soya knows that none of his officers in the C³ are pleased by this engagement. Destroying Ouster orbital forests is part of their mission—the seemingly innocuous trees serve as refueling and refitting centers for combat Swarms—but few Pax warriors take pleasure in wanton destruction. They were trained as knights of the Church, defenders of the Pax, not as destroyers of beauty or murderers of unarmed life-forms, even if those life-forms were tailored Ousters who had surrendered their souls.

"Lay in the usual search pattern," de Soya orders. "Tell the crew to stand down from battle stations." On a modern torchship the crew consists of only these dozen officers and half a dozen others spread throughout the ship.

Suddenly Mother Commander Stone interrupts. "Sir, a Hawking-drive distortion reading up-angle seventy-two, coordinates two-twenty-nine, forty-three, one-oh-five. C-plus exit point at seven-oh-oh-point-five-thousand klicks. Probability of single vehicle, ninety-six percent. Relative velocity unknown."

"Full battle stations," says de Soya. He smiles slightly without being aware of doing so. Perhaps the Ousters are rushing to the rescue of their forest. Or perhaps there *was* a single defender and it has just launched a standoff weapon from somewhere beyond the system's Oort cloud. Or perhaps it is the vanguard of an entire Swarm of Ouster fighting units and his task force is doomed. Whatever the threat, Father Captain de Soya prefers a fight to this . . . this vandalism.

"Vehicle is translating," reports the acquisition officer from his perch above de Soya's head.

"Very good," says Father Captain de Soya. He watches displays flicker before his eyes, resets his shunt, and opens several virtual-optic channels. Now the C³ fades away and he stands in space, a giant five million klicks tall, seeing his own ships like specks with flaming tails, the curved column of smoke that is the destroyed forest bending past at belt height, and now this intruder flicking into existence seven hundred thousand klicks and an armreach above the plane of the ecliptic. Red spheres around his ships show external fields at combat strength. Other colors fill space, displaying sensor readings, acquisition pulses, and targeting preparation. Working on the millisecond tactical level, de Soya can launch weapons or unleash energies by pointing and snapping his fingers.

"Transponder beacon," reports the com officer. "Current codes check. It is a Pax courier. Archangel class."

De Soya frowns. What can be so important that the Pax Command is sending the Vatican's fastest vehicle—a craft so swift that it is also the Pax's greatest secret weapon? De Soya can see the Pax codes surrounding the tiny ship in tactical space. Its fusion flame reaches scores of kilometers. The ship is using almost no energy on internal containment fields, and the gravities involved are beyond raspberry-jam levels.

"Uncrewed?" queries de Soya. He desperately hopes so. Archangel-class ships can travel anywhere in known space within days—real-time days!—rather than the weeks of shiptime and years of real time demanded by all other craft—but no one survives archangel voyages.

Mother Commander Stone steps into the tactical environment with him. Her black tunic is almost invisible against space so that her pale face seems to float above the ecliptic, sunlight from the virtual star illuminating her sharp cheekbones. "No, sir," she says softly. Her voice can be heard only by de Soya in this mode. "Beacon indicates two members of the crew in fugue."

"Dear Jesus," whispers de Soya. It is more prayer than curse. Even in high-g fugue tanks, these two people, already killed during C-plus travel, will now be more a microthin layer of protein paste than healthy raspberry jam. "Prepare the resurrection creches," he says on the common band.

Mother Commander Stone touches the shunt behind her ear and frowns. "Message embedded in code. Human couriers are to be resurrected priority alpha. Dispensation level Omega."

Father Captain de Soya's head snaps around and he stares at his executive officer for a silent moment. The smoke from the burning orbital forest swirls around their waists. Priority resurrection defies the doctrine of the Church and the rules of Pax Command; it is also dangerous—the chances for incomplete reintegration go from near zero at the usual three-day rate, to almost fifty percent at the three-hour level. And priority level Omega means His Holiness on Pacem.

De Soya sees the knowledge in his exec's eyes. This courier ship is from the Vatican. Either someone there or someone in Pax Command, or both, considered this message important enough to send an irreplaceable archangel courier ship, to kill two high-ranking Pax officers—since no one else would be trusted with an archangel—and to risk incomplete reintegration of those same two officers.

In tactical space de Soya raises his eyebrows in response to his exec's questioning look. On the command band he says, "Very well, Commander. Instruct all three ships to match velocities. Prepare a boarding party. I want the fugue tanks transferred and the resurrections completed by oh-six-thirty hours. Please give my compliments to Captain Hearn on the *Melchior* and Mother Captain Boulez on the *Gaspar,* and ask them to join me on the *Balthasar* for a meeting with the couriers at oh-seven-hundred."

Father Captain de Soya steps from tactical space to the reality of the C^3. Stone and the others are still looking at him.

"Quickly," says de Soya, and kicks off from the display rim, flying across the space to his private door and pulling himself through the circular hatch. "Wake me when the couriers are resurrected," he says to the white faces watching him in the seconds before the door irises shut.

6

WALKED THE STREETS of Endymion and tried to come to grips with my life, my death, and my life again.

I should say here that I was not as cool about these things—my trial, my "execution," my strange meeting with this mythic old poet—as this narrative would suggest. Part of me was shaken to its core. They had tried to *kill* me! I wanted to blame the Pax, but the courts were not agents of the Pax—not directly. Hyperion had its own Home Rule Council, and the Port Romance courts were set up according to our own local politics. Capital punishment was not an inevitable Pax sentence, especially on those worlds where the Church governed via theocracy, but was a holdover from Hyperion's old colonial days. My quick trial, its inevitable outcome, and my summary execution were, if anything, more expressions of Hyperion's and Port Romance's business leaders' terror of frightening away Pax offworld tourists than anything else. I was a peasant, a hunting guide who had killed the rich tourist assigned to my care, and an example had been made of me. Nothing more. I should not take it personally.

I took it very personally. Pausing outside the tower, feeling the sun's heat bounced from the broad paving stones of the courtyard, I slowly raised my hands. They were shaking. Too much had happened too soon, and my enforced calm during the trial and the brief period before my execution had demanded too much from me.

I shook my head and walked slowly through the university ruins. The city of Endymion had been built high on a brow of a hill, and the university had sat even higher along this ridge during colonial days, so the view to the south and east was beautiful. Chalma forests in the valley below glowed bright yellow. The lapis sky was free of contrails or airship traffic. I knew that the Pax cared nothing about Endymion, that it was the

Pinion Plateau region to the northeast that their troops still guarded and their robots still mined for the unique cruciform symbiotes, but this entire section of the continent had been off-limits for so many decades that it had a fresh, wilderness feel to it.

Within ten minutes of idle walking, I realized that only the tower where I had awakened and its surrounding buildings seemed occupied. The rest of the university was in absolute ruins—its great halls open to the elements, its physical plant ransacked centuries before, its playing fields overgrown, its observatory dome shattered—and the city farther down the hillside looked even more abandoned. I saw entire city blocks there reclaimed by weirwood tangle and kudzu.

I could see that the university had been beautiful in its day: post-Hegira, neo-Gothic buildings were constructed of the sandstone blocks quarried not far from there in the foothills of the Pinion Plateau. Three years earlier, when I had worked as an assistant to the famous landscape artist Avrol Hume, doing much of the heavy work as he redesigned the First Family estates along the fashionable coast of the Beak, much of the demand then had been for "follies"—ersatz ruins set near ponds or forest or hilltop. I had become somewhat of an expert in setting old stones in artful states of decomposition to simulate ruins—most of them absurdly older than humankind's history on this Outback world—but none of Hume's follies had been as attractive as these real ruins. I wandered through the bones of a once-great university, admired the architecture, and thought of my family.

Adding the name of a local city to our own had been the tradition of most indigenie families—for my family was indeed indigenie, descended from those first seedship pioneers almost seven centuries earlier, third-class citizens on our own world: third now after the Pax offworlders and the Hegira colonists who came centuries after my ancestors. For centuries, then, my people had lived and worked in these valleys and mountains. Mostly, I was sure, my indigenie relatives had labored at menial jobs—much as my father had before his early death, when I was eight, much as my mother had continued to until her death five years later, much as I had until this week. My grandmother had been born the decade after everyone had been removed from these regions by the Pax, but Grandam was old enough actually to remember the days when our clan families roamed as far as the Pinion Plateau and worked on the fiberplastic plantations to the south of here.

I had no sense of homecoming. The cold moors of the area northeast of here were my home. The fens north of Port Romance had been my chosen place to live and work. This university and town had never been part of my life and held no more relevance to me than did the wild stories of the old poet's *Cantos*.

At the base of another tower, I paused to catch my breath and consider this last thought. If the poet's offer was real, the "wild stories" of the *Cantos* would hold every relevance for me. I thought of Grandam's recitation of that epic poem—remembered the nights watching the sheep in the north hills, our battery-driven caravans pulled in a protective circle for the night, the low cooking fires doing little to dim the glory of the constellations or meteor showers above, remembered Grandam's slow, measured tones until she finished each stanza and waited for me to recite the lines back to her, remembered my own impatience at the process—I would much rather have been sitting by lantern reading a book—and smiled to think that this evening I would be dining with the author of those lines. More, the old poet was one of the seven pilgrims whom the poem sang about.

I shook my head again. Too much. Too soon.

There was something odd about this tower. Larger and broader than the one in which I had awakened, this structure had only one window—an open archway thirty meters up the tower. More interestingly, the original doorway had been bricked up. With an eye educated by my seasons as bricklayer and mason under Avrol Hume, I guessed that the door had been closed up before the area had been abandoned a century ago—but not that long before.

To this day I do not know what drew my curiosity to that building when there were so many ruins to explore that afternoon—but curious I was. I remember looking up the steep hillside beyond the tower and noticing the riot of leafy chalma that had wound its way out and around the tower like thick-barked ivy. *If one scrambled up the hillside and penetrated the chalma grove just . . . there . . . one could crawl out that vining branch and just barely reach the sill of that lone window. . . .*

I shook my head again. This was nonsense. At the least, such a childish expedition would result in torn clothes and skinned hands. At the most, one could easily fall the thirty meters to the flagstones there. And why risk it? What could be in this old bricked-up tower other than spiders and cobwebs?

Ten minutes later I was far out on the curled chalma branch, inching my way along and trying to hang on by finding chinks in the stones or thick-enough branches on the vines above me. Because the branch grew against the stone wall, I could not straddle it. Rather, I had to shuffle along on my knees—the overhanging chalma vine was too low to allow me to stand—and the sense of exposure and of being pushed outward toward the drop was terrifying. Every time the autumn wind came up and shook the leaves and branches, I would stop moving and cling for all I was worth.

Finally I reached the window and began cursing softly. My calculations—so easily made from the pavement thirty meters below—had been off a bit. The chalma branch here was almost three meters below the sill of the open window. There were no usable toeholds or fingerholds in this expanse of stone. If I was to reach the sill, I would have to jump and hope that my fingers found a grasp there. That would be insane. There was nothing in this tower that could justify such a risk.

I waited for the wind to die down, crouched, and leaped. For a sickening second my curved fingers scrabbled backward on crumbling stone and dust, tearing my nails and finding no hold, but then they encountered the rotted remnants of the old windowsill and sank in. I pulled myself up, panting and ripping the shirt fabric over my elbows. The soft shoes A. Bettik had laid out for me scrambled against stone to find leverage.

And then I was up and curling myself onto the window ledge, wondering how in the hell I would get back down to the chalma branch. My concerns in that area were amplified a second later as I squinted into the darkened interior of the tower.

"Holy shit," I whispered to no one in particular. There was an old wooden landing just below the window ledge on which I clung, but the tower was essentially empty. The sunlight streaming through the window illuminated bits of a rotting stairway above and below the landing, spiraling around the inside of the tower much as the chalma vines wrapped around the exterior, but the center of the tower was thick with darkness. I glanced up and saw speckles of sunlight through what may have been a temporary wooden roof some thirty meters higher and realized that this tower was little more than a glorified grain silo—a giant stone cylinder sixty meters tall. No wonder it had needed only one window. No wonder the door had been bricked up even before the evacuation of Endymion.

Still maintaining my balance on the windowsill, not trusting the rotted landing inside, I shook my head a final time. My curiosity would get me killed someday.

Then, still squinting into the darkness so different from the rich afternoon sunlight outside, I realized that the interior was *too* dark. I could not see the wall or spiral staircase across the interior. I realized that scattered sunlight illuminated the stone interior here, I could see a bit of rotted stairway there, and the full cylinder of the inside was visible meters above me—but here, on my level, the majority of the interior was just . . . gone.

"Christ," I whispered. Something was filling the bulk of this dark tower.

Slowly, careful to hold most of my weight on my arms still balanced on the sill, I lowered myself to the interior landing. The wood creaked but seemed solid enough. Hands still clutching the window frame, I let some of my weight on my feet and turned to look.

It still took me the better part of a minute to realize what I was looking at. A spaceship filled the inside of the tower like a bullet set into the chamber of an old-fashioned revolver.

Setting all my weight on the landing now, almost not caring if it held me, I stepped forward to see better.

The ship was not tall by spacecraft standards—perhaps fifty meters —and it was slender. The metal of the hull—if metal it was—looked matte black and seemed to absorb the light. There was no sheen or reflection that I could see. I made out the ship's outline mostly by looking at the stone wall behind it and seeing where the stones and reflected light from them ended.

I did not doubt for an instant that this was a spaceship. It was almost too much a spaceship. I once read that small children on hundreds of worlds still draw houses by sketching a box with a pyramid on top, smoke spiraling from a rectangular chimney—even if the kids in question reside in organically grown living pods high in RNA'd residential trees. Similarly, they still draw mountains as Matterhorn-like pyramids, even if their own nearby mountains more resemble the rounded hills here at the base of the Pinion Plateau. I don't know what the article said the reason was— racial memory, perhaps, or the brain being hardwired for certain symbols.

The thing I was looking at, peering at, seeing mostly as negative space, was not so much spaceship as SPACESHIP.

I have seen images of the oldest Old Earth rockets—pre-Pax, pre-Fall, pre-Hegemony, pre-Hegira . . . hell, pre-Everything almost—and they looked like this curved blackness. Tall, thin, graduated on both ends, pointed on top, finned on the bottom—I was looking at the hardwired, racial-memoried, symbolically perfect image of SPACESHIP.

There were no private or misplaced spaceships on Hyperion. Of this I was sure. Spacecraft, even of the simple interplanetary variety, were simply too expensive and too rare to leave lying around in old stone towers. At one time, centuries ago before the Fall, when the resources of the WorldWeb seemed unlimited, there may have been a plethora of spacecraft—FORCE military, Hegemony diplomatic, planetary government, corporate, foundation, exploratory, even a few private ships belonging to hyperbillionaires—but even in those days only a planetary economy could afford to build a starship. In my lifetime—and the lifetime of my mother and grandmother and *their* mothers and grandmothers—only the Pax— that consortium of Church and crude interstellar government—could afford spaceships of any sort. And no individual in the known universe—not even His Holiness on Pacem—could afford a private starship.

And this was a starship. I knew it. Don't ask me how I knew it, but I knew it.

Paying no attention to the terrible condition of the steps, I began descending and ascending the spiral stairway. The hull was four meters from me. The unfathomable blackness of it made me dizzy. Halfway around the interior of the tower and fifteen meters below me, just visible before the curve of blackness blocked it off, a landing extended almost to the hull itself.

I ran down to it. One rotted step actually broke under me, but I was moving so fast that I ignored it.

The landing had no railings here and extended out like a diving board. A fall from it would almost certainly break bones and leave me lying in the blackness of a sealed tower. I gave it no thought at all as I stepped out and set my palm against the hull of the ship.

The hull was warm. It did not feel like metal—more like the smooth skin of some sleeping creature. To add to that illusion, there was the softest movement and vibration from the hull—as if the ship were breathing, as if I could detect a heartbeat beneath my palm.

Suddenly there was true motion beneath my hand, and the hull simply fell and folded away—not rising mechanically like some portals I had seen, and certainly not swinging on hinges—simply *folding* into itself and out of the way, like lips pulling back.

Lights turned on. An interior corridor—its ceiling and walls as organic as a glimpse of some mechanical cervix—glowed softly.

I paused about three nanoseconds. For years my life had been as calm and predictable as most people's. This week I had accidentally killed a man, been condemned and executed, and had awakened in Grandam's favorite myth. Why stop there?

I stepped into the spaceship, and the doors folded shut behind me like a hungry mouth closing on a morsel.

THE CORRIDOR INTO THE SHIP was not as I would have imagined it. I had always thought of spacecraft interiors as being like the hold of the seagoing troopships that transported our Home Guard regiment to Ursus: all gray metal, rivets, dogged hatches, and hissing steam pipes. None of that was evident here. The corridor was smooth, curved, and almost featureless, the interior bulkheads covered with a rich wood as warm and organic as flesh. If there was an air lock, I hadn't seen it. Hidden lights came on ahead of me as I advanced and then extinguished themselves as I passed, leaving me in a small pool of light with darkness ahead and behind. I knew that the ship couldn't be more than ten meters across, but the slight curve of this corridor made it seem larger on the inside than it had appeared on the outside.

The corridor ended at what must have been the center of the ship: an open well with a central metal staircase spiraling upward and downward into darkness. I set my foot on the first step and lights came on somewhere above. Guessing that the more interesting parts of the ship lay upward, I began to climb.

The next deck above filled the entire circle of the ship and held an antique holopit of the kind I had seen in old books, a scattering of chairs and tables in a style I could not identify, and a grand piano. I should say here that probably not one person out of ten thousand born on Hyperion could have identified that object as a piano—especially not as a grand piano. My mother and Grandam both had held a passionate interest in music, and a piano had filled much of the space in one of our electric caravans. Many had been the time I had heard my uncles or grandfather complaining about the bulk and weight of that instrument—about all of the jules of energy used to trundle that heavy pre-Hegira apparatus across the moors of Aquila, and about the commonsense efficiency of having a pocket synthesizer that could create the music of any piano . . . or any other instrument. But mother and Grandam were insistent—nothing could equal the sound of a true piano, no matter how many times it had to be tuned after transport. And neither grandfather nor uncles complained when Grandam played Rachmaninoff or Bach or Mozart around the campfire at night. I learned about the great pianos of history from that old woman—the pre-Hegira grand pianos included. And now I was looking at one.

Ignoring the holopit and furniture, ignoring the curved window wall that showed only the dark stone of the interior of the tower, I walked to the grand piano. The gold lettering above the keyboard read STEINWAY. I whistled softly and let my fingers caress the keys, not yet daring to depress one. According to Grandam, this company had ceased making pianos before the Big Mistake of '08, and none had been produced since the Hegira. I was touching an instrument at least a thousand years old. Steinways and Stradivarii were myths among those of us who loved music. How could this be? I wondered, my fingers still trailing over keys that felt like the legendary ivory—tusks of an extinct creature called an elephant. Human beings like the old poet in the tower might possibly survive from pre-Hegira days—Poulsen treatments and cryogenic storage could theoretically account for that—but artifacts of wood and wire and ivory had little chance of making that long voyage through time and space.

My fingers played a chord: C-E-G-B flat. And then a C-major chord. The tone was flawless, the acoustics of the spaceship perfect. Our old upright piano had needed tuning by Grandam after every trip of a few miles across the moors, but this instrument seemed perfectly tuned after countless light-years and centuries of travel.

I pulled the bench out, sat, and began playing *Für Elise*. It was a corny, simple piece, but one that seemed to fit the silence and solitude of this dark place. Indeed, the lights seemed to dim around me as the notes filled the circular room and seemed to echo up and down the dark staircase well. As I played, I thought of Mother and Grandam and how they would never have guessed that my early piano lessons would lead to this solo in a hidden spaceship. The sadness of that thought seemed to fill the music I was playing.

When I was finished, I pulled my fingers back from the keyboard quickly, almost guiltily, struck with the presumption of my poor playing of such a simple piece on this fine piano, this gift from the past. I sat in silence for a moment, wondering about the ship, about the old poet, and about my own place in this mad scheme of things.

"Very nice," said a soft voice behind me.

I admit that I jumped. I had heard no one climb or descend the stairs, sensed no one entering the room. My head jerked around.

There was no one in the room.

"I have not heard that particular piece played in some time," came the voice again. It seemed to emanate from the center of the empty room. "My previous passenger preferred Rachmaninoff."

I set my hand on the edge of the bench to steady myself and thought of all the stupid questions I could avoid asking.

"Are you the ship?" I asked, not knowing if this was a stupid question but wanting the answer.

"Of course," came the reply. The voice was soft but vaguely masculine. I had, of course, heard talking machines before—such things had been around forever—but never one that might actually be intelligent. The Church and Pax had banned all true AIs more than two centuries before, and after seeing how the TechnoCore had helped the Ousters destroy the Hegemony, most of the trillions of people on a thousand devastated worlds had agreed wholeheartedly. I realized that my own programming in that regard had been effective: the thought that I was talking to a truly sentient device made my palms moist and my throat tight.

"Who was your . . . ah . . . previous passenger?" I said.

There was the hint of a pause. "The gentleman was generally known as the Consul," said the ship at last. "He had been a diplomat for the Hegemony for much of his life."

It was my turn to hesitate before speaking. It occurred to me that perhaps the "execution" in Port Romance had only scrambled my neurons to the point where I thought I was living in one of Grandam's epic poems.

"What happened to the Consul?" I asked.

"He died," said the ship. There may have been the slightest undertone of regret in the voice.

"How?" I said. At the end of the old poet's *Cantos,* after the Fall of the WorldWeb, the Hegemony Consul had taken a ship back to the Web. *This* ship? "Where did he die?" I added. According to the *Cantos,* the ship the Hegemony Consul had left Hyperion in had been infused with the persona of the second John Keats cybrid.

"I can't remember where the Consul died," said the ship. "I only remember that he died, and that I returned here. I presume there was some programming of that directive in my command banks at the time."

"Do you have a name?" I asked, mildly curious as to whether I was speaking to the AI persona of John Keats.

"No," said the ship. "Only *ship.*" Again there came something more pause than simple silence. "Although I do seem to recall that I had a name at one point."

"Was it John?" I asked. "Or Johnny?"

"It may have been," said the ship. "The details are cloudy."

"Why is that?" I said. "Is your memory malfunctioning?"

"No, not at all," said the ship. "As far as I can deduce, there was some traumatic event about two hundred standard years ago which deleted certain memories, but since then my memory and other faculties have been flawless."

"But you don't remember the event? The trauma?"

"No," said the ship, cheerily enough. "I believe that it occurred at about the same time that the Consul died and I returned to Hyperion, but I am not certain."

"And since then?" I said. "Since your return you've been hidden away here in this tower?"

"Yes," said the ship. "I was in the Poet's City for a time, but for most of the past two local centuries, I have been here."

"Who brought you here?"

"Martin Silenus," said the ship. "The poet. You met him earlier today."

"You're aware of that?" I said.

"Oh, yes," said the ship. "I was the one who gave M. Silenus the data about your trial and execution. I helped to arrange the bribe to the officials and the transport of your sleeping body here."

"How did you do that?" I asked, the image of this massive, archaic ship on the telephone too absurd to deal with.

"Hyperion has no true datasphere," said the ship, "but I monitor all free microwave and satellite communications, as well as certain 'secure' fiber-optic and maser bands which I have tapped into."

"So you're a spy for the old poet," I said.

"Yes," said the ship.

"And what do you know about the old poet's plans for me?" I asked, turning toward the keyboard again and beginning Bach's *Air on a G-string*.

"M. Endymion," said a different voice behind me.

I quit playing and turned to see A. Bettik, the android, standing at the head of the circular staircase.

"My master had become worried that you were lost," said A. Bettik. "I came to show you the way back to the tower. You just have time to dress for dinner."

I shrugged and walked to the stairwell. Before following the blue-skinned man down the stairs, I turned and said to the darkening room, "It was nice talking to you, Ship."

"It was a pleasure meeting you, M. Endymion," said the ship. "I will see you again soon."

7

HE TORCHSHIPS *Balthasar, Melchior,* and *Gaspar* are a full AU beyond the burning orbital forests and still decelerating around the unnamed sun when Mother Commander Stone buzzes at Father Captain de Soya's compartment portal to inform him that the couriers have been resurrected.

"Actually, only one was successfully resurrected," she amends, floating at the opened iris-door.

Father Captain de Soya winces. "Has the . . . unsuccessful one . . . been returned to the resurrection creche?" he asks.

"Not yet," says Stone. "Father Sapieha is with the survivor."

De Soya nods. "Pax?" he asks, hoping that this will be the case. Vatican couriers bring more problems than military ones.

Mother Commander Stone shakes her head. "Both are Vatican. Father Gawronski and Father Vandrisse. Both are Legionaries of Christ."

De Soya avoids a sigh only by an effort of will. Legionaries of Christ had all but replaced the more liberal Jesuits over the centuries—their power had been growing in the Church a century before the Big Mistake—and it was no secret that the Pope used them as shock troops for difficult missions within the Church hierarchy. "Which one survived?" he asks.

"Father Vandrisse." Stone glances at her comlog. "He should be revived by now, sir."

"Very well," says de Soya. "Adjust the internal field to one-g at oh-six-forty-five. Pipe Captains Hearn and Boulez aboard and give them my compliments. Please escort them to the forward meeting room. I'll be in with Vandrisse until we convene."

"Aye, aye," says Mother Commander Stone, and kicks off.

The revival room outside the resurrection creche is more chapel than infirmary. Father Captain de Soya genuflects toward the altar and then joins Father Sapieha by the gurney, where the courier is sitting up. Sapieha is older than most Pax crew—at least seventy standard—and the soft halogen beams reflect from his bald scalp. De Soya has always found the ship's chaplain short-tempered and not very bright, much like several of the parish priests he had known as a boy.

"Captain," acknowledges the chaplain.

De Soya nods and steps closer to the man on the gurney. Father Vandrisse is young—perhaps in his late twenties standard—and his dark hair is long and curled in the current Vatican fashion. Or at least in the fashion that had been coming in when de Soya had last seen Pacem and the Vatican: a time-debt of three years had already accrued in the two months they had been on this mission.

"Father Vandrisse," says de Soya, "can you hear me?"

The young man on the cot nods and grunts. Language is hard for the first few minutes after resurrection. Or so de Soya has heard.

"Well," says the chaplain, "I'd better get the other's body back in the creche." He frowns at de Soya as though the captain had personally brought about the unsuccessful resurrection. "It is a waste, Father Captain. It will be weeks—perhaps months—before Father Gawronski can be successfully revived. It will be very painful for him."

De Soya nods.

"Would you like to see him, Father Captain?" persists the chaplain. "The body is . . . well . . . barely recognizable as human. The internal organs are quite visible and quite . . ."

"Go about your duties, Father," de Soya says quietly. "Dismissed."

Father Sapieha frowns again as if he is going to reply, but at that moment the gravity Klaxon sounds, and both men have to orient themselves so that their feet touch the floor as the internal containment field realigns itself. Then the gravity slowly climbs to one-g as Father Vandrisse sinks back into the gurney's cushions and the chaplain shuffles out the door. Even after only a day of zero-g, the return of gravity seems an imposition.

"Father Vandrisse," de Soya says softly. "Can you hear me?"

The young man nods. His eyes show the pain he is in. The man's skin glistens as if he has just received grafts—or as if he is newborn. The flesh looks pink and raw to de Soya, almost burned, and the cruciform on the courier's chest is livid and twice normal size.

"Do you know where you are?" whispers de Soya. *Or who you are?* he mentally adds. Postresurrection confusion can last for hours or days. De Soya knows that couriers are trained to overcome that confusion, but how can anyone be trained for death and revival? An instructor of de Soya's at the seminary had once put it plainly—"The cells remember dying, being dead, even if the mind does not."

"I remember," whispers Father Vandrisse, and his voice sounds as raw as his skin looks. "You are Captain de Soya?"

"Father Captain de Soya. Yes."

Vandrisse tries to lever himself up on his elbow and fails. "Closer," he whispers, too weak to lift his head from the pillow.

De Soya leans closer. The other priest smells faintly of formaldehyde. Only certain members of the priesthood are trained in the actual mysteries of resurrection, and de Soya had chosen not to be one of these. He could officiate at a baptism and administer Communion or Extreme Unction—as a starship captain he has had more opportunities for the latter than the former—but he had never been present at the Sacrament of Resurrection. He has no idea of the processes involved, beyond the miracle of the cruciform, in returning this man's destroyed and compressed body, his decaying neurons and scattered brain mass, to the human form he now sees before him.

Vandrisse begins whispering and de Soya has to lean even closer, the resurrected priest's lips almost brushing de Soya's ear.

"Must . . . talk . . . ," Vandrisse manages with great effort.

De Soya nods. "I've scheduled a briefing in fifteen minutes. My other two ship captains will be there. We'll provide a hoverchair for you and . . ."

Vandrisse is shaking his head. "No . . . meeting. Message for . . . you . . . only."

De Soya shows no expression. "All right. Do you want to wait until you are . . ."

Again the agonized shake of his head. The skin of the priest's face is slick and striated, as if the muscle were showing through. "Now . . . ," he whispers.

De Soya leans close and waits.

"You are . . . to . . . take the . . . archangel courier . . . ship . . . immediately . . . ," gasps Vandrisse. "It is programmed for its destination."

De Soya remains expressionless, but he is thinking, *So it is to be a painful death by acceleration. Dear Jesus, could you not let this cup pass from me?*

"What do I tell the others?" he asks.

Father Vandrisse shakes his head. "Tell them nothing. Put your executive officer in command of the . . . *Balthasar.* Transfer task force command to Mother Captain Boulez. Task Force MAGI will . . . have . . . other orders."

"Will I be informed of these other orders?" asks de Soya. His jaw hurts with the tension of sounding calm. Until thirty seconds ago the survival and success of this ship, this task force, had been the central reason for his existence.

"No," says Vandrisse. "These . . . orders . . . do . . . not . . . concern you."

The resurrected priest is pale with pain and exhaustion. De Soya realizes that he is taking some satisfaction in that fact and immediately says a short prayer for forgiveness.

"I am to leave immediately," repeats de Soya. "Can I take my few personal possessions?" He is thinking of the small porcelain sculpture that his sister had given him shortly before her death on Renaissance Vector. That fragile piece, locked in a stasis cube during high-g maneuvers, has been with him for all of his years of spacefaring.

"No," says Father Vandrisse. "Go . . . immediately. Take nothing."

"This is upon order of . . . ," queries de Soya.

Vandrisse frowns through his grimace of pain. "This is upon direct command of His Holiness, Pope Julius XIV," says the courier. "It is . . . Omega Priority . . . superseding all orders of Pax Military Command or SpaComC-Fleet. Do . . . you . . . understand . . . Father . . . Captain . . . de . . . Soya?"

"I understand," says the Jesuit, and bows his head in compliance.

THE ARCHANGEL-CLASS courier ship has no name. De Soya had never considered torchships beautiful—gourd-shaped, the command and weapons mod dwarfed by the huge Hawking drive and in-system fusion-thrust sphere—but the archangel is actively ugly in comparison. The courier ship is a mass of asymmetrical spheres, dodecahedrons, lash-ons, structural cables, and Hawking-drive mounts, with the passenger cabin the merest of afterthoughts in the center of all that junk.

De Soya had met briefly with Hearn, Boulez, and Stone, explained only that he had been called away, and transferred command to the new—and amazed—task force and *Balthasar* captains, then took a one-person transfer pod to the archangel. De Soya tried not to look back at his beloved *Balthasar,* but at the last moment before attaching to the courier, he turned and looked longingly at the torchship, sunlight painting its curved flank into a crescentlike sunrise over some lovely world, then turned resolutely away.

He sees upon entering that the archangel has only the crudest virtual tactical command, manual controls, and bridge. The interior of the command pod is not much larger than de Soya's crowded cubby on the *Balthasar,* although this space is crowded with cables, fiber-optic leads, tech diskeys, and two acceleration couches. The only other space is the tiny navigation room-cum-wardrobe cubby.

No, de Soya sees at once, the acceleration couches are not standard. These are unpadded steel trays in human form, more like autopsy slabs than couches. The trays have a lip—to keep fluid from sloshing under high-g, he is sure—and he realizes that the only compensating containment field in the ship would be around these couches—to keep the pulverized flesh, bone, and brain matter from floating away in the zero-g intervals after final deceleration. De Soya can see the nozzles where water or some cleansing solution had been injected at high speed to clean the steel. It had not been totally successful.

"Acceleration in two minutes," says a metallic voice. "Strap in now."

No niceties, thinks de Soya. *Not even a "please."*

"Ship?" he says. He knows that no true AIs are allowed on Pax ships —indeed, no AIs are allowed anywhere in Pax-controlled human space— but he thinks that the Vatican might have made an exception on one of its archangel-class courier ships.

"One minute thirty seconds until initial acceleration," comes the metallic voice, and de Soya realizes that he is talking to an idiot machine. He hurries to strap himself in. The bands are broad, thick, and almost surely for show. The containment field will hold him—or his remains—in place.

"Thirty seconds," says the idiot voice. "Be advised that the C-plus translation will be lethal."

"Thanks," says Father Captain Federico de Soya. His heart is pounding so fiercely that he can hear it in his ears. Lights flicker in the various instruments. Nothing here is meant for human override, so de Soya ignores them.

"Fifteen seconds," says the ship. "You might wish to pray now."

"Fuck you," says de Soya. He has been praying since he left the courier's recovery room. Now he adds a final prayer for forgiveness for the obscenity.

"Five seconds," comes the voice. "There will be no further communications. May God bless you and speed your resurrection, in Christ's name."

"Amen," says Father Captain de Soya. He closes his eyes as acceleration commences.

8

VENING CAME EARLY in the ruined city of Endymion. I watched the last of the autumn light dim and die from my vantage point in the tower where I had awakened earlier on this endless day. A. Bettik had led me back, shown me to my room, where stylish but simple evening clothes—tan cotton trousers tightening just below the knees, white flax blouse with a hint of ruffled sleeves, black leather vest, black stockings, soft black leather boots, and a gold wristband—were still laid out on the bed. The android also showed me to the toilet and bathing facilities a floor below and told me that the thick cotton robe hanging on the door was for my use. I thanked him, bathed, dried my hair, dressed in everything that had been laid out except for the gold band, and waited at the window while the light grew more golden and horizontal and shadows crept down from the hills above the university. When the light had died to the point where shadows had fled and the brightest stars in the Swan were visible above the mountains to the east, A. Bettik returned.

"Is it time?" I asked.

"Not quite, sir," replied the android. "Earlier you requested that I return so that we might talk."

"Ahh, yes," I said, and gestured toward the bed, the only piece of furniture in the room. "Have a seat."

The blue-skinned man stood where he was by the door. "I am comfortable standing, sir."

I folded my arms and leaned against the windowsill. The air coming in the open window was cool and smelled of chalma. "You don't have to call me sir," I said. "Raul will do." I hesitated. "Unless you're programmed to talk to . . . ah . . ." I was about to say "humans," but did not want to make it seem as if I thought A. Bettik was *not* human. ". . . to talk to people that way," I finished lamely.

A. Bettik smiled. "No, sir. I am not programmed at all . . . not like a machine. Except for several synthetic prostheses—to augment strength, for instance, or to provide resistance to radiation—I have no artificial parts. I was merely taught deference to fulfill my role. I could call you M. Endymion, if that would be preferable."

I shrugged. "It doesn't matter. I'm sorry I'm so ignorant about androids."

A. Bettik's thin-lipped smile returned. "There is no need to apologize, M. Endymion. Very few human beings now alive have seen one of my race."

My race. Interesting. "Tell me about your race," I said. "Wasn't the biofacture of androids illegal in the Hegemony?"

"Yes, sir," he said. I noticed that he stood at parade rest, and wondered idly if he had ever served in a military capacity. "Biofacture of androids was illegal on Old Earth and many of the Hegemony homeworlds even before the Hegira, but the All Thing allowed biofacture of a certain number of androids for use in the Outback. Hyperion was part of the Outback in those days."

"It still is," I said.

"Yes, sir."

"When were you biofactured? Which worlds did you live on? What were your duties?" I asked. "If you don't mind my asking."

"Not at all, M. Endymion," he said softly. The android's voice had the hint of a dialect that was new to me. Offworld. Ancient. "I was created in the year 26 A.D.C. by your calendar."

"In the twenty-fifth century, A.D.," I said. "Six hundred ninety-four years ago."

A. Bettik nodded and said nothing.

"So you were born . . . biofactured . . . after Old Earth was destroyed," I said, more to myself than to the android.

"Yes, sir."

"And was Hyperion your first . . . ah . . . work destination?"

"No, sir," said A. Bettik. "For the first half century of my existence, I worked on Asquith in the service of His Royal Highness, King Arthur the Eighth, sovereign lord of the Kingdom of Windsor-in-Exile, and also in the service of his cousin, Prince Rupert of Monaco-in-Exile. When King Arthur died, he willed me to his son, His Royal Highness, King William the Twenty-third."

"Sad King Billy," I said.

"Yes, sir."

"And did you come to Hyperion when Sad King Billy fled Horace Glennon-Height's rebellion?"

"Yes," said A. Bettik. "Actually, my android brothers and I were sent ahead to Hyperion some thirty-two years before His Highness and the other colonists joined us. We were dispatched here after General Glennon-

Height won the Battle of Fomalhaut. His Highness thought it wise if an alternate site for the kingdoms-in-exile were prepared."

"And that's when you met M. Silenus," I prompted, pointing toward the ceiling, imagining the old poet up there within his web of life-support umbilicals.

"No," said the android. "My duties did not bring me into contact with M. Silenus during the years when the Poet's City was occupied. I had the pleasure of meeting M. Silenus later, during his pilgrimage to the Valley of the Time Tombs two and a half centuries after the death of His Highness."

"And you've been on Hyperion since," I said. "More than five hundred years on this world."

"Yes, M. Endymion."

"Are you immortal?" I asked, knowing the question was impertinent but wanting the answer.

A. Bettik showed his slight smile. "Not at all, sir. I will die from accident or injury that is too serious for me to be repaired. It is just that when I was biofactured, my cells and systems were nanoteched with an ongoing form of Poulsen treatments so that I am essentially resistant to aging and disease."

"Is that why androids are blue?" I asked.

"No, sir," said A. Bettik. "We are blue because no known race of humankind was blue at the time of my biofacture, and my designers felt it imperative to keep us visually separate from humans."

"You do not consider yourself human?" I asked.

"No, sir," said A. Bettik. "I consider myself android."

I smiled at my own naïveté. "You still act in a service capacity," I said. "Yet use of slave android labor was outlawed throughout the Hegemony centuries ago."

A. Bettik waited.

"Don't you wish to be free?" I said at last. "To be an independent person in your own right?"

A. Bettik walked to the bed. I thought that he was going to sit down, but he only folded and stacked the shirt and trousers I had been wearing earlier. "M. Endymion," he said, "I should point out that although the laws of the Hegemony died with the Hegemony, I have considered myself a free and independent person for some centuries now."

"Yet you and the others work for M. Silenus here, in hiding," I persisted.

"Yes, sir, but I have done so from my own free choice. I was designed to serve humanity. I do it well. I take pleasure in my work."

"So you've stayed here by your own free will," I perseverated.

A. Bettik nodded and smiled briefly. "Yes, for as much as any of us has a free will, sir."

I sighed and pushed myself away from the window. It was full dark out now. I presumed that I would be summoned to the old poet's dinner party before long. "And you will continue staying here and caring for the old man until he finally dies," I said.

"No, sir," said A. Bettik. "Not if I am consulted on the matter."

I paused, my eyebrows lifting. "Really?" I said. "And where will you go if you are consulted on the matter?"

"If you choose to accept this mission which M. Silenus has offered you, sir," said the blue-skinned man, "I would choose to go with you."

WHEN I WAS LED UPSTAIRS, I discovered that the top floor was no longer a sickroom; it had been transformed into a dining room. The flowfoam hoverchair was gone, the medical monitors were gone, the communication consoles were absent, and the ceiling was open to the sky. I glanced up and located the constellations of the Swan and the Twin Sisters with the trained eye of a former shepherd. Braziers on tall tripods sat in front of each of the stained-glass windows, their flames adding both warmth and light to the room. In the center of the room, the com consoles had been replaced with a three-meter-long dining table. China, silver, and crystal glimmered in the light of candles flickering from two ornate candelabra. A place had been set at each end of the table. At the far end, Martin Silenus awaited, already seated in a tall chair.

The old poet was hardly recognizable. He seemed to have shed centuries in the hours since I had last seen him. From being a mummy with parchment skin and sunken eyes, he had transformed into just another old man at a dining table—a *hungry* old man from the look in his eyes. As I approached the table, I noticed the subtle IV drips and monitor filaments snaking under the table, but otherwise the illusion of someone restored to life from the dead was almost perfect.

Silenus chuckled at my expression. "You caught me at my worst this afternoon, Raul Endymion," he rasped. The voice was still harsh with age, but much more forceful than before. "I was still recovering from my cold sleep." He gestured me to my place at the other end of the table.

"Cryogenic fugue?" I said stupidly, unfurling the linen napkin and dropping it to my lap. It had been years since I had eaten at a table this fancy—the day that I had demobilized from the Home Guard, I had gone straight to the best restaurant in the port city of Gran Chaco on South Talon Peninsula and ordered the finest meal on the menu, blowing my last month's pay in the process. It had been worth it.

"Of course cryogenic fucking fugue," said the old poet. "How else do you think I pass these decades?" He chuckled again. "It merely takes me a few days to get up to speed again after defrosting. I'm not as young as I used to be."

I took a breath. "If you don't mind my asking, sir," I said, "how old are you?"

The poet ignored me and beckoned to the waiting android—not A. Bettik—who nodded toward the stairwell. Other androids began carrying up the food in silence. My water glass was filled. I watched as A. Bettik showed a bottle of wine to the poet, waited for the old man's nod, and then went through the ritual, offering him the cork and a sample to taste. Martin Silenus sloshed the vintage wine around in his mouth, swallowed, and grunted. A. Bettik took this for assent and poured the wine for each of us.

The appetizers arrived, two for each of us. I recognized the char-broiled chicken yakitori and the tender Mane-raised beef carpaccio arugula. In addition, Silenus helped himself to the sautéed foie gras wrapped in mandrake leaves that had been set near his end of the table. I lifted the ornamented skewer and tried the yakitori. It was excellent.

Martin Silenus might be eight or nine hundred years old, perhaps the oldest human alive, but the codger had an appetite. I saw the gleam of perfect white teeth as he attacked the beef carpaccio, and I wondered if these new additions were dentures or Arnied substitutes. Probably the latter.

I realized that I was ravenous. Evidently either my pseudo-resurrection or the exercise involved in climbing to the ship had instilled an appetite in me. For several minutes there was no conversation, only the soft sound of the serving androids' footsteps on stones, the crackle of flames in the braziers, an occasional hint of night breeze overhead, and the sounds of our chewing.

As the androids removed our appetizer plates and brought in bowls of steaming black mussel bisque, the poet said, "I understand that you met our ship today."

"Yes," I said. "It was the Consul's private ship?"

"Of course." Silenus gestured to an android, and bread was brought still hot from the oven. The smell of it mingled with the rising vapors from the bisque and the hint of autumn foliage on the breeze.

"And this is the ship you expect me to use to rescue the girl?" I said. I expected the poet to ask for my decision then.

Instead, he said, "What do you think of the Pax, M. Endymion?"

I blinked, the spoon of bisque halfway to my mouth. "The Pax?"

Silenus waited.

I set the spoon back and shrugged. "I don't think much of it, I guess."

"Not even after one of its courts sentenced you to death?"

Instead of sharing what I had been thinking earlier—how it had not been the Pax influence that sentenced me, but Hyperion's brand of frontier justice—I said, "No. The Pax has been mostly irrelevant to my life."

The old poet nodded and sipped his bisque. "And the Church?"

"What about it, sir?"

"Has it been largely irrelevant to your life?"

"I guess so." I realized that I was sounding like a tongue-tied adolescent, but these questions seemed less important than the question he was supposed to ask me, and the decision I was supposed to give him.

"I remember the first time we heard of the Pax," he said. "It was only a few months after Aenea disappeared. Church ships arrived in orbit, and troops seized Keats, Port Romance, Endymion, the university, all of the spaceports and important cities. Then they lifted off in combat skimmers, and we realized that they were after the cruciforms on the Pinion Plateau."

I nodded. None of this was new information. The occupation of the Pinion Plateau and search for cruciforms had been the last great gamble of a dying Church, and the beginning of the Pax. It had been almost a century and a half before *real* Pax troops had arrived to occupy all of Hyperion and to order the evacuation of Endymion and other towns near the Plateau.

"But the ships which put in here during the expansion of the Pax," continued the poet, "what tales they brought! The Church's expansion from Pacem through the old Web worlds, then the Outback colonies . . ."

The androids removed the bisque bowls and returned with plates of carved fowl with pommery mustard sauce and a gratin of Kans River manta with caviar mousseline.

"Duck?" I said.

The poet showed his reconstituted teeth. "It seemed appropriate after your . . . ah . . . trouble of the last week."

I sighed and touched the slice of fowl with my fork. Moist vapors rose to my cheek and eyes. I thought of Izzy's eagerness as the ducks approached the open water. It seemed a lifetime ago. I looked at Martin Silenus and tried to imagine having centuries of memories to contend with. How could anyone stay sane with entire lifetimes stored in one human mind? The old poet was grinning at me in that wild way of his, and once again I wondered if he *was* sane.

"So we heard about the Pax and wondered what it would be like when it truly arrived," he continued, chewing while he spoke. "A theocracy . . . unthinkable during the centuries of the Hegemony. Religion then was, of course, purely personal choice—I belonged to a dozen religions and started more than one of my own during my days as a literary celebrity." He looked at me with bright eyes. "But of course you know that, Raul Endymion. You know the *Cantos*."

I tasted the manta and said nothing.

"Most people I knew were Zen Christians," he continued. "More Zen than Christian, of course, but not too much of either, actually. Personal pilgrimages were fun. Places of power, finding one's Baedecker point, all of that crap . . ." He chuckled. "The Hegemony would never have dreamed of getting involved with religion, of course. The very thought of mixing government and religious opinion was barbaric . . . something one found on Qom-Riyadh or somesuch Outback desert world. And then came the Pax, with its glove of velvet and its cruciform of hope. . . ."

"The Pax doesn't rule," I said. "It advises."

"Precisely," agreed the old man, pointing his fork at me while A. Bettik refilled his wineglass. "The Pax advises. It does not rule. On hundreds of worlds the Church administers to the faithful and the Pax advises. But, of course, if you are a Christian who wishes to be born again, you will not ignore the advice of the Pax or the whispers of the Church, will you?"

I shrugged again. The influence of the Church had been a constant of life as long as I had been alive. There was nothing strange about it to me.

"But you are not a Christian who wishes to be born again, are you, M. Endymion?"

I looked at the old poet then, and a terrible suspicion formed in the back of my mind. *He somehow finessed my fake execution and transported me here when I should have been buried at sea by the authorities. He has clout with the Port Romance authorities. Could he have dictated my conviction and sentencing? Was all this some sort of test?*

"The question is," he continued, ignoring my basilisk stare, "*why* are you not a Christian? Why do you not wish to be born again? Don't you enjoy life, Raul Endymion?"

"I enjoy life," I said tersely.

"But you have not accepted the cross," he continued. "You have not accepted the gift of extended life."

I put down my fork. An android servant interpreted that as a sign that I was finished and removed the plate of untouched duckling. "I have not accepted the *cruciform*," I snapped. How to explain the suspicion bred into my nomadic clan through generations of being the expatriates, the outsiders, the unsettled indigenies? How to explain the fierce independence of people like Grandam and my mother? How to explain the legacy of philosophical rigor and inbred skepticism passed on to me by my education and upbringing? I did not try.

Martin Silenus nodded as if I had explained. "And you see the cruciform as something other than a miracle offered the faithful through the miraculous intercession of the Catholic Church?"

"I see the cruciform as a parasite," I said, surprising myself by the vehemence in my voice.

"Perhaps you are afraid of losing . . . ah . . . your masculinity," rasped the poet.

The androids brought in two swans sculpted of mocha chocolate and filled with highland branch-truffles and set them at our places. I ignored mine. In the *Cantos* the priest pilgrim—Paul Duré—tells his tale of discovering the lost tribe, the Bikura, and learning how they had survived centuries by a cruciform symbiote offered to them by the legendary Shrike. The cruciform resurrected them much as it did today, in the era of the Pax, only in the priest's tale the side effects included irreversible brain damage after several resurrections and the disappearance of all sexual organs and impulses. The Bikura were retarded eunuchs—all of them.

"No," I said. "I know that the Church has somehow solved that problem."

Silenus smiled. He looked like a mummified satyr when he did that. "*If* one has taken Communion and *if* one is resurrected under the auspices of the Church," he rasped. "Otherwise, even if one has somehow stolen a cruciform, his fate remains that of the Bikura."

I nodded. Generations had attempted to steal immortality. Before the Pax sealed off the Plateau, adventurers smuggled out cruciforms. Other symbiotes had been stolen from the Church itself. The result had always been the same—idiocy and sexlessness. Only the Church held the secret of successful resurrection.

"So?" I said.

"So why has allegiance to the Church and a tithing of every tenth year of service to the Church been too high a price for you, my boy? Billions have opted for life."

I sat in silence for a moment. Finally I said, "Billions can do what they want. My life is important to me. I want to keep it . . . *mine.*"

This made no sense even to me, but the poet once again nodded as if I had explained matters to his satisfaction. He ate his chocolate swan while I watched. The androids removed our plates and filled our cups with coffee.

"All right," the poet said, "have you thought about my proposition?"

The question was so absurd that I had to stifle the urge to laugh. "Yes," I said at last. "I've thought about it."

"And?"

"And I have a few questions."

Martin Silenus waited.

"What is in this for me?" I asked. "You talk about the difficulty of my going back to a life here on Hyperion—lack of papers and all that— but you know I'm comfortable in the wilderness. It would be a hell of a lot easier for me to take off for the fens and avoid the Pax authorities than it would be to chase across space with your kid-friend in tow. Besides, to the Pax, I'm dead. I could go home to the moors and stay with my clan with no problem."

Martin Silenus nodded.

After another moment of silence I said, "So why should I even consider this nonsense?"

The old man smiled. "You want to be a hero, Raul Endymion."

I blew out my breath in derision and set my hands on the tablecloth. My fingers looked blunt and clumsy there, out of place against the fine linen.

"You want to be a hero," he repeated. "You want to be one of those rare human beings who make history, rather than merely watch it flow around them like water around a rock."

"I don't know what you're talking about." I did, of course, but there was no way he could know me that well.

"I *do* know you that well," said Martin Silenus, seemingly responding to my thought rather than my last statement.

I should say here that I did not think for a second that the old man was telepathic. First of all, I do not believe in telepathy—or, rather, I did not at that time—and secondly, I was more intrigued by the potential of a human being who had lived almost a thousand standard years. Why, even if he were insane, I thought, it was possible that he had learned to read facial expressions and physical nuance to the point where the effect would be almost indistinguishable from telepathy!

Or perhaps it was just a lucky guess.

"I don't want to be a hero," I said flatly. "I saw what happens to heroes when my brigade was sent to fight the rebels on the southern continent."

"Ahh, Ursus," he muttered. "The south polar bear. Hyperion's most useless mass of ice and mud. I remember some rumors of a disturbance there."

The war there had lasted eight Hyperion years and killed thousands of us local boys who were stupid enough to enlist in the Home Guard to fight there. Perhaps the old poet wasn't as astute as I was making him out to be.

"I don't mean hero as in the fools who throw themselves on plasma grenades," he continued, licking his thin lips with a lizard's flick of tongue. "I mean hero as in he whose prowess and beneficence is so legendary that he comes to be honored as a divinity. I mean hero in the literary sense, as in central protagonist given to forceful action. I mean hero as in he whose tragic flaws will be his undoing." The poet paused and looked expectantly at me, but I stared back in silence.

"No tragic flaws?" he said at last. "Or not given to forceful action?"

"I don't want to be a hero," I said again.

The old man hunched over his coffee. When he looked up, his eyes held a mischievous glint. "Where do you get your hair cut, boy?"

"Pardon me?"

He licked his lips again. "You heard me. Your hair is long, but not wild. Where do you get it cut?"

I sighed and said, "Sometimes, when I was in the fens for a long period, I'd cut it myself, but when I'm in Port Romance, I go to a little shop on Datoo Street."

"Ahhhh," said Silenus, settling back in his tall-backed chair. "I know Datoo Street. It's in the Night District. More of an alley than a street. The open market there used to sell ferrets in gilded cages. There were street barbers, but the best barber*shop* there belonged to an old man named Palani Woo. He had six sons, and as each came of age, he would add another chair to the shop." The old eyes raised to look at me, and once again I was struck by the power of personality there. "That was a century ago," he said.

"I get my hair cut at Woo's," I said. "Palani Woo's great-grandson, Kalakaua, owns the shop now. There are still six chairs."

"Yes," said the poet, nodding to himself. "Not too much changes on our dear Hyperion, does it, Raul Endymion?"

"Is that your point?"

"Point?" he said, opening his hands as if showing that he had nothing so sinister as a point to hide. "No point. Conversation, my boy. It amuses me to think of World Historical Figures, much less heroes of future myths, paying to get their hair cut. I thought of this centuries ago, by the way . . . this strange disconnection between the stuff of myth and the stuff of life. Do you know what 'Datoo' means?"

I blinked at this sudden change of direction. "No."

"A wind out of Gibraltar. It carried a beautiful fragrance. Some of the artists and poets who founded Port Romance must have thought that the chalma and weirwood forests which covered the hills above the bog there must have smelled nice. Do you know what Gibraltar is, boy?"

"No."

"A big rock on Earth," rasped the old man. He showed his teeth again. "Notice that I didn't say Old Earth."

I had noticed.

"Earth is Earth, boy. I lived there before it disappeared, so I should know."

The thought still made me dizzy.

"I want you to find it," said the poet, his eyes gleaming.

"Find . . . it?" I repeated. "Old Earth? I thought you wanted me to travel with the girl . . . Aenea."

His bony hands waved away my sentence. "You go with her and you'll find Earth, Raul Endymion."

I nodded, all the while pondering the wisdom of explaining to him that Old Earth had been swallowed by the black hole dropped into its guts during the Big Mistake of '08. But, then, this ancient creature had fled from that shattered world. It made little sense to contradict his delusions. His *Cantos* had mentioned some plot by the warring AI TechnoCore to steal Old Earth—to spirit it away to either the Hercules Cluster or the

Magellanic Clouds, the *Cantos* were inconsistent—but that was fantasy. The Magellanic Cloud was a separate *galaxy* . . . more than 160,000 light-years from the Milky Way, if I remembered correctly . . . and no ship, neither Pax nor Hegemony, had ever been sent farther than our small sphere in one spiral arm of *our* galaxy—and even with the Hawking-drive exclusion to Einsteinian realities, a trip to the Large Magellanic Cloud would take many centuries of shiptime and tens of thousands of years' time-debt. Even the Ousters who savored the dark places between the stars would not undertake a voyage like that.

Besides, planets are not kidnapped.

"I want you to find Earth and bring it back," continued the old poet. "I want to see it again before I die. Will you do that for me, Raul Endymion?"

I looked the old man in the eye. "Sure," I said. "Save this child from the Swiss Guard and the Pax, keep her safe until she becomes the One Who Teaches, find Old Earth and bring it back so you can see it again. Easy. Anything else?"

"Yes," said Martin Silenus with the tone of absolute solemnity that comes with dementia, "I want you to find out what the fuck the TechnoCore is up to and stop it."

I nodded again. "Find the missing TechnoCore and stop the combined power of thousands of godlike AIs from doing whatever they're planning to do," I said, sarcasm dripping from my tongue. "Check. Will do. Anything else?"

"Yes. You are to talk with the Ousters and see if they can offer me immortality . . . *true* immortality, not this born-again Christian bullshit."

I pretended to write this on an invisible notepad. "Ousters . . . immortality . . . not Christian bullshit. Can do. Check. Anything else?"

"Yes, Raul Endymion. I want the Pax destroyed and the Church's power toppled."

I nodded. Two or three hundred known worlds had willingly joined the Pax. Trillions of humans had willingly been baptized in the Church. The Pax military was stronger than anything Hegemony Force had ever dreamed of at the height of its power. "OK," I said. "I'll take care of that. Anything else?"

"Yes. I want you to stop the Shrike from hurting Aenea or wiping out humanity."

I hesitated at this. According to the old man's own epic poem, the Shrike had been destroyed by the soldier Fedmahn Kassad in some future era. Knowing the futility of projecting logic into a demented conversation, I still mentioned this.

"Yes!" snapped the old poet. "But that is *then*. Millennia from now. I want you to stop the Shrike *now*."

"All right," I said. Why argue?

Martin Silenus slumped back in his chair, his energy seemingly dissipated. I glimpsed the animated mummy again in the folds of skin, the sunken eyes, the bony fingers. But those eyes still blazed with intensity. I tried to imagine the force of this man's personality when he'd been in his prime: I could not.

Silenus nodded and A. Bettik brought two glasses and poured champagne.

"Then you accept, Raul Endymion?" asked the poet, his voice strong and formal. "You accept this mission to save Aenea, travel with her, and accomplish these other things?"

"With one condition," I said.

Silenus frowned and waited.

"I want to take A. Bettik with me," I said. The android still stood by the table. The champagne bottle was in his hand. His gaze was aimed straight forward, and he did not turn to look at either of us or register any emotion.

The poet showed surprise. "My android? Are you serious?"

"I am serious."

"A. Bettik has been with me since before your great-great-grandmother had tits," rasped the poet. His bony hand slammed down on the table hard enough to make me worry about brittle bones. "A. Bettik," he snapped. "You wish to go?"

The blue-skinned man nodded without turning his head.

"Fuck it," said the poet. "Take him. Do you want anything else, Raul Endymion? My hoverchair, perhaps? My respirator? My teeth?"

"Nothing else," I said.

"And so, Raul Endymion," said the poet, his voice formal once again, "do you accept this mission? Will you save, serve, and protect the child Aenea until her destiny is fulfilled . . . or die trying?"

"I accept," I said.

Martin Silenus lifted his wineglass and I matched the motion. Too late, I thought that the android should be drinking with us, but by then the old poet was giving his toast.

"To folly," he said. "To divine madness. To insane quests and messiahs crying from the desert. To the death of tyrants. To confusion to our enemies."

I started to raise the glass to my lips, but the old man was not done.

"To heroes," he said. "To heroes who get their hair cut." He drank the champagne in one gulp.

And so did I.

9

BORN AGAIN, SEEING—literally—with the wondering eyes of a child, Father Captain Federico de Soya crosses the Piazza San Pietro between the elegant arcs of Bernini's colonnade and approaches St. Peter's Basilica. The day is beautiful with cold sunlight, pale-blue skies, and a chill in the air—Pacem's single inhabitable continent is high, fifteen hundred meters above standard sea level, and the air is thin but absurdly rich in oxygen—and everything de Soya sees is bathed in rich afternoon light that creates an aura around the stately columns, around the heads of the hurrying people; light that bathes the marble statues in white and brings out the brilliance of the red robes of bishops and the blue, red, and orange stripes of the Swiss Guard troopers standing at parade rest; light that paints the tall obelisk in the center of the plaza, the fluted pilasters of the Basilica's facade, and ignites into brilliance the great dome itself, rising more than a hundred meters above the level of the plaza. Pigeons take wing and catch this rich, horizontal light as they wheel above the plaza, their wings now white against the sky, now dark against the glowing dome of St. Peter's. Throngs move by on either side, simple clerics in black cassocks with pink buttons, the bishops in white with red trimming, cardinals in blood-scarlet and deep magenta, citizens of the Vatican in their ink-black doublets, hose, and white ruffs, nuns in rustling habits and soaring white gull wings, male and female priests in simple black, Pax officers in dress uniforms of scarlet and black such as de Soya himself wears this day, and a scattering of lucky tourists or civilian guests —privileged to attend a papal Mass—dressed in their finest clothes, most in black, but all of a richness in cloth that makes even the blackest fiber gleam and shimmer in the light. The multitudes move toward the soaring Basilica of St. Peter's, their conversation muted, their demeanor excited but somber. A papal Mass is a serious event.

With Father Captain de Soya this day—only four days after his fatal leave-taking from Task Force MAGI and one day after his resurrection—are Father Baggio, Captain Marget Wu, and Monsignor Lucas Oddi: Baggio, plump and pleasant, is de Soya's resurrection chaplain; Wu, lean and silent, is aide-de-camp to Pax Fleet Admiral Marusyn; and Oddi, eighty-seven standard years old but still healthy and alert, is the factotum and Undersecretary to the powerful Vatican Secretary of State, Simon Augustino Cardinal Lourdusamy. It is said that Cardinal Lourdusamy is the second most powerful human being in the Pax, the only member of the Roman Curia to have the ear of His Holiness, and a person of frightening brilliance. The Cardinal's power is reflected in the fact that he also acts as Prefect for the Sacra Congregatio pro Gentium Evangelizatione se de Propaganda Fide—the legendary Congregation for the Evangelization of Peoples, or De Propaganda Fide.

To Father Captain de Soya, the presence of these two powerful people is no more surprising or astounding than the sunlight on the facade above him as the four climb the broad steps to the Basilica. The crowd, already quiet, stills to silence as they file through into the vast space, walk past more Swiss Guards in both ornamental and battle dress, and move into the nave. Here even the silence echoes, and de Soya is moved to tears at the beauty of the great space and of the timeless works of art they pass on the way to the pews: Michelangelo's *Pietà* visible in the first chapel to the right; Arnolfo di Cambrio's ancient bronze of St. Peter, its right foot polished to the point of being worn away by centuries of kisses, and—lit brilliantly from beneath—the striking figure of Giuliana Falconieri Santa Vergine, sculpted by Pietro Campi in the sixteenth century, more than fifteen hundred years earlier.

Father Captain de Soya is weeping openly by the time he crosses himself with holy water and follows Father Baggio into their reserved pew. The three male priests and the female Pax officer kneel in prayer as the last scuffling and coughing dies in the vast space. The Basilica is in near darkness now, with only pinpoint halogen spots illuminating the art and architectural treasures glowing like gold. Through his tears de Soya looks at the fluted pilasters and the dark bronze baroque columns of Bernini's Baldachino—the gilded and ornate canopy over the central altar where only the Pope can say Mass—and contemplates the wonder of the last twenty-four hours since his resurrection. There had been pain, yes, and confusion—as if he were recovering from a particularly disorienting blow to the head—and the pain was more general and terrible than any headache, as if every cell in his body remembered the indignity of death and even now rebelled against it—but there had been wonder as well. Wonder and awe at the smallest things: the taste of the broth Father Baggio had fed him, the first sight of Pacem's pale-blue sky through the rectory windows, the overwhelming humanness of the faces he had seen that day, the voices he had heard. Father Captain de Soya, although a sensitive man, has not wept since he was a child of five or six standard years, but he weeps this day . . . weeps openly and unashamedly. Jesus Christ had given him the gift of life for the second time, the Lord God had shared the Sacrament of Resurrection with him—this faithful, honorable man from a poor family on a backwater world—and de Soya's individual cells now seem to re member the sacrament of rebirth as well as the pain of death; he is suf fused with joy.

The Mass begins in an explosion of glory—trumpet notes cutting through the expectant silence like golden blades, choral voices raised in triumphant song, ascending organ notes reverberating in the great space, and then a series of brilliant lights switching on to illuminate the Pope and his retinue as they emerge to celebrate Mass.

De Soya's first impression is of how young the Holy Father is: Pope Julius XIV is, of course, a man in his early sixties, despite the fact that he has been Pope almost continuously for more than 250 years, his reign broken only by his own death and rebirth for eight coronations, first as Julius VI—following the eight-year reign of the antipope, Teilhard I—and again as Julius in each succeeding incarnation. As de Soya watches the Holy Father celebrate Mass, the Pax captain thinks of the story of Julius's ascendancy—learned through both official Church history and the banned poem the *Cantos*, which every literate teenager reads at the risk of his soul, but reads nonetheless.

In both versions Pope Julius had been, prior to his first resurrection, a young man named Lenar Hoyt, who had come to the priesthood in the shadow of Paul Duré, a charismatic Jesuit archaeologist and theologian. Duré had been a proponent of St. Teilhard's teachings that humankind had the potential to evolve toward the Godhead—indeed, according to Duré when he ascended to the Throne of St. Peter after the Fall, humans could evolve *to* the Godhead. It was precisely this heresy which Father Lenar Hoyt, after becoming Pope Julius VI, had worked to wipe out after his first resurrection.

Both accounts—Church history and the forbidden *Cantos*—agreed that it had been Father Duré, during his exile on the Outback world of Hyperion, who had discovered the symbiote called the cruciform. There the histories diverged beyond reconciliation. According to the poem, Duré had received the cruciform from the alien creature called the Shrike. According to the Church's teachings, the Shrike—a representa tion of Satan if ever there was one—had nothing to do with the discov ery of the cruciform, but had later tempted both Father Duré and Father Hoyt. The Church's history reported that only Duré had suc cumbed to the creature's treachery. The *Cantos* told, in their confused mix of pagan mythology and garbled history, of how Duré had cruci fied himself in the flame forests of Hyperion's Pinion Plateau rather than return the cruciform to the Church. According to the pagan poet, Martin Silenus, this was to save the Church from reliance on a parasite in the place of faith. According to the Church history, which de Soya believed, Duré had crucified himself to end the pain the symbiote caused him and, in alliance with the Shrike demon, to prevent the Church—which Duré considered his enemy after having excommunicated him for falsifying archaeological records—from regaining its vitality through the discovery of the Sacrament of Resurrection.

According to both stories, Father Lenar Hoyt had traveled to Hyperion in search of his friend and former mentor. According to the blasphemous *Cantos*, Hoyt had accepted Duré's cruciform as well as his own, but had later returned to Hyperion in the last days before the Fall to beg the evil Shrike to relieve him of his burden. The Church pointed out the falseness of that, explaining how Father Hoyt had courageously returned to face down the demon in its own lair. Whatever the interpretation, facts recorded that Hoyt had died during that last pilgrimage to Hyperion, Duré had been resurrected carrying Father Hoyt's cruciform as well as his own, and had then returned during the chaos of the Fall to become the first antipope in modern history. Duré/Teilhard I's nine standard years of heresy had been a low point for the Church, but after the false pope's death by accident, Lenar Hoyt's resurrection from the shared body had led to the glory of Julius VI, the discovery of the sacramental nature of what Duré had called a parasite, Julius's revelation from God—still understood only by the innermost sancta of the Church—of how the resurrections could be guided to success, and the subsequent growth of the Church from a minor sect to the official faith of humanity.

Father Captain Federico de Soya watches the Pope—a thin, pale man —lift the Eucharist high above the altar, and the Pax commander shivers in the chill of sheer wonder.

Father Baggio had explained that the overwhelming sense of newness and wonder that was the aftereffect of Holy Resurrection would wear off to some extent in the days and weeks to come, but that the essential feeling of well-being would always linger, growing stronger with each rebirth in Christ. De Soya could see why the Church held suicide as one of its most mortal sins—punishable by immediate excommunication—since the glow of nearness to God was so much stronger after tasting the ashes of death. Resurrection could easily become addictive if the punishment for suicide were not so terrible.

Still aching from the pain of death and rebirth, his mind and senses literally lurching from vertigo, Father Captain de Soya watches the papal Mass approach the climax of Communion, St. Peter's Basilica filling now with the same burst of sound and glory with which the service began, and —knowing that in a moment he will taste the Body and Blood of Christ as transubstantiated by the Holy Father himself—the warrior weeps like a little child.

AFTER THE MASS, in the cool of the evening, with the sky above St. Peter's the color of pale porcelain, Father Captain de Soya walks with his new friends in the shadows of the Vatican Gardens.

"Federico," Father Baggio is saying, "the meeting we are about to have is very important. Very, very important. Is your mind clear enough to understand the important things that will be said?"

"Yes," says de Soya. "My mind is very clear."

Monsignor Lucas Oddi touches the young Pax officer's shoulder. "Federico, my son, you are certain of this? We can wait another day if we must."

De Soya shakes his head. His mind is reeling with the beauty and solemnity of the Mass he has just witnessed, his tongue still tastes the perfection of the Eucharist and the Wine, he feels that Christ is whispering to him at this very moment, but his thoughts are clear. "I am ready," he says. Captain Wu is a silent shadow behind Oddi.

"Very good," says the Monsignor, and nods to Father Baggio. "We will need your services no longer, Father. Thank you."

Baggio nods, bows slightly, and leaves without another word. In his perfect clarity, de Soya realizes that he will never see his kindly resurrection chaplain again, and a surge of pure love brings more tears to his eyes. He is grateful to the darkness that hides these tears; he knows he must be in control for the meeting. He wonders where this important conference will be held—in the fabled Borgia Apartment? In the Sistine Chapel? In the Vatican Offices of the Holy See? Perhaps in the Pax Liaison offices in what had once been called the Borgia Tower.

Monsignor Lucas Oddi stops at the far end of the gardens, waves the others to a stone bench near where another man waits, and Father de Soya realizes that the seated man is Cardinal Lourdusamy and that the conference is happening here, in the scented gardens. The priest goes to his knee on the gravel in front of the Monsignor and kisses the ring on the extended hand.

"Rise," says Cardinal Lourdusamy. He is a large man with a round face and heavy jowls, and his deep voice sounds like the voice of God to de Soya. "Be seated," says the Cardinal.

De Soya sits on the stone bench as the others remain standing. To the Cardinal's left, another man sits in the shadows. De Soya can make out a Pax uniform in the dim light but not the insignia. He is vaguely aware of other people—at least one seated and several standing—within the deeper shadows of a bower to their left.

"Father de Soya," begins Simon Augustino Cardinal Lourdusamy, nodding toward the seated man on his left, "may I present Fleet Admiral William Lee Marusyn."

De Soya is on his feet in an instant, saluting, holding himself at rigid attention. "My apologies, Admiral," he manages through clenched jaws. "I did not recognize you, sir."

"At ease," says Marusyn. "Be seated, Captain."

De Soya takes his seat again, but gingerly now, awareness of the company he is in burning through the joyous fog of resurrection like hot sunlight.

"We are well pleased with you, Captain," says Admiral Marusyn.

"Thank you, sir," mumbles the priest, glancing around the shadows again. There are definitely others watching from the bower.

"As are we," rumbles Cardinal Lourdusamy. "That is why we have chosen you for this mission."

"Mission, Your Excellency?" says de Soya. He feels dizzy with tension and confusion.

"As always, you will be serving both the Pax and the Church," says the Admiral, leaning closer in the dim light. The world of Pacem has no moon, but the starlight here is very bright as de Soya's eyes adapt to the dim light. Somewhere a small bell rings monks to Vespers. Lights from the Vatican buildings bathe the dome of St. Peter's in a soft glow.

"As always," continues the Cardinal, "you will report to both the Church and the military authorities." The huge man pauses and glances at the Admiral.

"What is my mission, Your Excellency? Admiral?" asks de Soya, not knowing which man to address. Marusyn is his ultimate superior, but Pax officers usually defer to high officials of the Church.

Neither man answers, but Marusyn nods toward Captain Marget Wu, who stands several meters away near a hedge. The Pax officer steps forward quickly and hands de Soya a holocube.

"Activate it," says Admiral Marusyn.

De Soya touches the underside of the small ceramic block. The image of a female child mists into existence above the cube. De Soya rotates the image, noticing the girl's dark hair, large eyes, and intense gaze. The child's disembodied head and neck are the brightest things in the darkness of the Vatican Gardens. Father de Soya looks up and sees the glow from the holo in the eyes of the Cardinal and the Admiral.

"Her name . . . well, we are not sure of her name," says Cardinal Lourdusamy. "How old does she look to you, Father?"

De Soya looks back at the image, considers her age, and converts the years to standard. "Perhaps twelve?" he guesses. He has spent little time around children since he was one. "Eleven? Standard."

Cardinal Lourdusamy nods. "She was eleven, standard, on Hyperion, when she disappeared more than two hundred sixty standard years ago, Father."

De Soya looks back at the holo. So the child is probably dead—he could not remember if the Pax had brought the Sacrament of Resurrection to Hyperion 277 years ago—or certainly grown and reborn. He wonders why they are showing him a holo of this person as a child from centuries ago. He waits.

"This child is the daughter of a woman named Brawne Lamia," says Admiral Marusyn. "Does the name mean anything to you, Father?"

It does, but for a moment de Soya cannot think why. Then the verses of the *Cantos* come to mind, and he remembers the female pilgrim in that story.

"Yes," he says. "I remember the name. She was one of the pilgrims with His Holiness during that final pilgrimage before the Fall."

Cardinal Lourdusamy leans closer and folds pudgy hands together on his knee. His robe is bright red where the light from the holo touches it. "Brawne Lamia had sexual intercourse with an abomination," rumbles the Cardinal. "A cybrid. A cloned human construct whose mind was an artificial intelligence residing in the TechnoCore. Do you remember the history and the banned poem?"

Father de Soya blinks. Is it possible that they have brought him here to the Vatican to punish him for reading the *Cantos* when he was a child? He confessed the sin twenty years ago, did penance, and never reread the forbidden work. He blushes.

Cardinal Lourdusamy chuckles. "It is all right, my son. Everyone in the Church has committed this particular sin. . . . Curiosity is too great, the appeal of the forbidden too strong. . . . We have all read the banned poem. Do you remember that the woman Lamia had carnal relations with the cybrid of John Keats?"

"Vaguely," says de Soya, then hurriedly adds, "Your Excellency."

"And do you know who John Keats was, my son?"

"No, Your Excellency."

"He was a pre-Hegira poet," says the Cardinal in his rumble of a voice. High overhead, the blue-plasma braking tails of three Pax dropships cut across the starfield. Father Captain de Soya does not even have to glance at them to recognize the make and armament of the ships. He is not surprised that he had not remembered the details of the poet's name from the forbidden *Cantos;* even as a boy, Federico de Soya had been more interested in reading about machines and great space battles than anything pre-Hegira, especially poetry.

"The woman in the blasphemous poem—Brawne Lamia—not only had intercourse with the cybrid abomination," continues the Cardinal, "but she bore the creature's child."

De Soya raises his eyebrows. "I did not know that cybrids . . . I mean . . . I thought that they were . . . well . . ."

Cardinal Lourdusamy chuckles. "Were sterile?" he says. "Like androids? No . . . the AI obscenities had cloned the man. And the man impregnated this daughter of Eve."

De Soya nods, although all this talk of cybrids and androids might as well be about griffins and unicorns for all he is concerned. These things existed once. To his knowledge, none could exist today. Father Captain de Soya's mind races as he tries to imagine just what in God's universe all this talk of dead poets and pregnant women might have to do with him.

As if answering de Soya's mental query, Admiral Marusyn says, "The girl whose image floats in front of you is that child, Captain. After the cybrid abomination was destroyed, this child was born to Brawne Lamia on the world of Hyperion."

"She was not fully . . . human," whispers Cardinal Lourdusamy. "Although the body of her . . . father . . . the Keats cybrid . . . was destroyed, his AI persona was stored in a Schrön Loop shunt."

Admiral Marusyn also leans closer, as if this information is for just the three of them. "We believe that this child communicated with the Keats persona trapped in that Schrön Loop even before she was born," he says softly. "We are almost certain that this . . . fetus . . . was in touch with the TechnoCore via that cybrid persona."

De Soya feels and ignores an impulse to cross himself. His reading, instruction, and faith have taught him that the TechnoCore had been evil incarnate, simply the most active manifestation of the Evil One in modern human history. The destruction of the TechnoCore had been the salvation of not only the beleaguered Church, but of humanity itself. De Soya tries to imagine what an unborn human soul would learn from direct contact with those disembodied, soulless intelligences.

"The child is dangerous," whispers Cardinal Lourdusamy. "Even though the TechnoCore was banished by the Fall of the farcasters, even though the Church no longer allows soulless machines to have true intelligence, this child has been programmed as an agent of those fallen AIs . . . an agent of the Evil One."

De Soya rubs his cheek. He is suddenly very tired. "You speak as though she is still alive," he says softly. "And still a child."

Cardinal Lourdusamy's silken robes rustle as he shifts position. His voice is an ominous baritone. "She lives," he says. "She is still a child."

De Soya looks back at the young girl's holo as it floats between them. He touches the cube and the image fades. "Cryogenic storage?" he says.

"On Hyperion there are Time Tombs," rumbles Lourdusamy. "One of them—a thing called the Sphinx, which you may remember from the poem or Church history—has been used as a portal across time. No one knows how it works. For most people, it does not work at all." The Cardinal glances at the Admiral and then back to the priest-captain before him. "This child disappeared in the Sphinx some two hundred sixty-four standard years ago. We knew at the time that she was dangerous to the Pax, but we arrived days late. We have reliable information that she will emerge from that tomb in less than a standard month . . . still a child. Still lethally dangerous to the Pax."

"Dangerous to the Pax . . . ," repeats de Soya. He does not understand.

"His Holiness has foreseen this danger," rumbles Cardinal Lourdusamy. "Almost three centuries ago Our Lord saw fit to reveal to His Holiness the threat this poor child represents, and the Holy Father has now moved to deal with this danger."

"I don't understand," confesses Father Captain de Soya. The holo is off, but he can still see the innocent face of the child in his mind. "How can this little girl be a danger . . . then or now?"

Cardinal Lourdusamy squeezes de Soya's forearm. "As an agent of the TechnoCore, she will be a virus introduced into the Body of Christ. It has been revealed to His Holiness that the girl will have powers . . . powers that are not human. One of these powers is the power to persuade the faithful to leave the light of God's teachings, to abandon salvation for service to the Evil One."

De Soya nods, although he does not understand. His forearm aches from the pressure of Lourdusamy's powerful hand. "What do you wish of me, Your Excellency?"

Admiral Marusyn answers in a loud voice that shocks de Soya after all of the soft tones and whispering. "As of this moment," snaps Marusyn, "you are detached from your Fleet assignment, Father Captain de Soya. As of this moment, you are assigned to find and return this child . . . this girl . . . to the Vatican."

The Cardinal seems to catch a glint of anxiety in de Soya's eyes. "My son," he says, his deep voice soothing now, "are you afraid the child might be harmed?"

"Yes, Your Excellency." De Soya wonders if this admission will disqualify him from service.

Lourdusamy's touch lightens, becomes a friendlier grip. "Be assured, my son, that no one in the Holy See . . . no one in the Pax . . . has any intention of harming this little girl. Indeed, the Holy Father has instructed us . . . has instructed you . . . to make it your second-highest priority that no harm shall come to her."

"Your first priority," says the Admiral, "is to return her here . . . to Pacem. To Pax Command here in the Vatican."

De Soya nods and swallows. The question foremost in his mind is *Why me?* Aloud, he says, "Yes, sir. I understand."

"You will receive a papal-authority diskey," continues the Admiral. "You may requisition any materials, help, liaison, or personnel it is in the power of local Pax authorities to provide. Do you have any questions about that?"

"No, sir." De Soya's voice is firm, but his mind is reeling. A papal-authority diskey would give him more power than that bestowed on Pax planetary governors.

"You will translate to Hyperion system this very day," continues Admiral Marusyn in the same brisk, no-nonsense voice of command. "Captain Wu?"

The Pax military aide steps forward and hands de Soya a red action portfolio disk. The father-captain nods, but his mind is screaming, *To Hyperion system this day . . . The archangel courier ship! To die again. The pain. No, sweet Jesus, dear Lord. Let this cup pass from me!*

"You will have command of our newest and most advanced courier ship, Captain," Marusyn is saying. "It is similar to the one which brought you to Pacem system, except that it can hold six passengers, it is armed to the level of your former torchship, and it has an automated resurrection system."

"Yes, sir," says de Soya. *An automated resurrection system?* he thinks. *Is the sacrament to be administered by a machine?*

Cardinal Lourdusamy pats his arm again. "The robot system is regrettable, my son. But the ship may carry you to places where the Pax and the Church do not exist. We cannot deny you resurrection simply because you are beyond the reach of God's servants. Be assured, my son, that the Holy Father himself has blessed this resurrection equipment and ordained it with the same sacramental imperative a true Resurrection Mass would offer."

"Thank you, Your Excellency," de Soya mumbles. "But I do not understand . . . places beyond the Church . . . Did you not say that I was to travel to Hyperion? I have never been there, but I thought that this world was a member of . . ."

"It belongs to the Pax," interrupts the Admiral. "But if you are unsuccessful in capturing . . ." He pauses. "In *rescuing* this child . . . if for some unforeseen reason you must follow her to other worlds, other systems . . . we thought it best that the ship have an automated resurrection creche for you."

De Soya bows his head in obedience and confusion.

"But we expect you to find the child on Hyperion," continues Admiral Marusyn. "When you arrive on that world, you will introduce yourself and show your papal diskey to Groundforce Commander Barnes-Avne. The Commander is in charge of the Swiss Guard Brigade that has been prepositioned on Hyperion, and upon your arrival you will be in effective command of those troops."

De Soya blinks. *Command of a Swiss Guard Brigade? I am a Fleet torchship captain! I wouldn't know a groundforce maneuver from a cavalry charge!*

Admiral Marusyn chuckles. "We understand that this is a bit out of your regular line of duty, Father Captain de Soya, but be assured that your command status is necessary. Commander Barnes-Avne will continue day-to-day command of groundforces, but it is imperative that all resources be bent to the rescue of this child."

De Soya clears his throat. "What will happen to . . . You say that we do not know her name? The child, I mean."

"Before she disappeared," rumbles Cardinal Lourdusamy, "she called herself Aenea. And as for what will happen to her . . . again, I reassure you, my son, our intentions are to prevent her from infecting the Body of Christ in the Pax from her virus, but we will do so without harming her. Indeed, our mission . . . *your* mission . . . is to save the child's immortal soul. The Holy Father himself will see to that."

Something in the Cardinal's voice makes de Soya realize that the conference is over. The father-captain stands, sensing the resurrection displacement shifting inside him like vertigo. *I must die again within the day!* Still joyous, he nonetheless feels like weeping.

Admiral Marusyn is also standing. "Father Captain de Soya, your reassignment to this mission is effective until the child is delivered unto me, here at the Vatican military liaison office."

"Within weeks, we are sure," rumbles Cardinal Lourdusamy, still seated.

"This is a great and terrible responsibility," says the Admiral. "You must use every ounce of your faith and your abilities to carry out His Holiness's expressed wish to bring this child safely to the Vatican—*before* the destructive virus of her programmed treachery is spread among our Brothers and Sisters in Christ. We know that you will not let us down, Father Captain de Soya."

"Thank you, sir," says de Soya, and thinks again, *Why me?* He kneels to kiss the Cardinal's ring and rises to find that the Admiral has stepped back in the darkness of the bower where the other shadowy figures have not stirred.

Monsignor Lucas Oddi and Pax Captain Marget Wu move to either side of de Soya and act as escorts as they turn to leave the garden. It is then, his mind still lurching in confusion and shock, his heart pounding with eagerness and terror at the important service set before him, that Father Captain de Soya glances back just as a rising dropship's plasma tail lights the dome of St. Peter's, the rooftops of the Vatican, and the garden with its pulse of blue flame. For an instant the figures within the arched shadow of the bower are clearly visible, illuminated by the strobe of blue plasma light. Admiral Marusyn is there, already turned away from de Soya, as are two standing Swiss Guard officers in combat armor, their flechette weapons raised at port arms. But it is the seated figure illuminated for that instant who will haunt de Soya's dreams and thoughts for years to come.

Seated there on the garden bench, his sad eyes locked firmly on de Soya's retreating form, his high brow and mournful countenance painted briefly but indelibly in blue plasma glow, is His Holiness, Pope Julius XIV, the Holy Father to more than six hundred billion faithful Catholics, the de facto ruler of four hundred billion more scattered souls in the far-flung Pax, and the man who has just launched Federico de Soya on his fateful voyage.

10

I T WAS THE MORNING after our banquet, and we were in the spaceship again. That is, the android A. Bettik and I were in the ship, having walked there the convenient way, through the tunnel connecting the two towers; Martin Silenus was present as a hologram. It was a strange holographic image, since the old poet chose to have the transmitter or the ship's computer represent him as a younger version of himself—an ancient satyr, still, but one who stood on his own legs and had hair on his sharp-eared head. I looked at the poet with his maroon cape, full-sleeved blouse, balloon trousers, and floppy beret, and realized what a dandy he must have been when those clothes had been in fashion. I was looking at Martin Silenus as he must have appeared when he had returned to Hyperion as a pilgrim three centuries earlier.

"Do you just want to stare at me like some fucking yokel," said the holographic image, "or do you want to finish the fucking tour so we can get on with business?" The old man was either hung over from the previous night's wine or had regained enough health to be in an even more vicious mood than usual.

"Lead on," I said.

From our tunnel we had taken the ship's lift up to the lowest air lock. A. Bettik and the poet's holo led me through the ascending levels: the engine room with its indecipherable instruments and webs of pipes and cables; then the cold-sleep level—four cryogenic-fugue couches in their supercooled cubbies (one couch missing, I discovered, since Martin Silenus had removed it for his own purposes); then the central air-lock corridor I had entered by the day before—the "wood" walls concealing a multitude of storage lockers holding such things as spacesuits, all-terrain vehicles, skybikes, and even some archaic weapons; then the living area with its Steinway and holopit; then up the spiral staircase again to what A. Bettik called the "navigation room"—there was indeed a cubby with some electronic navigation instruments visible—but which I saw as the library with shelf after shelf of books—real books, print books—and several couches and daybeds next to windows in the ship's hull; and finally up the stairs to the apex of the ship, which was simply a round bedroom with a single bed in the center of it.

"The Consul used to enjoy watching the weather from here while listening to music," said Martin Silenus. "Ship?"

The arching bulkhead around the circular room went transparent, as did the bow of the ship above us. There were only the dark stones of the tower interior around us, but from above there fell a filtered light through the rotting roof of the silo. Soft music suddenly filled the room. It was a piano, unaccompanied, and the melody was ancient and haunting.

"Czerchyvik?" I guessed.

The old poet snorted. "Rachmaninoff." The satyrish features seemed suddenly mellow in the dim light. "Can you guess who's playing?"

I listened. The pianist was very good. I had no idea who it was.

"The Consul," said A. Bettik. The android's voice was very soft.

Martin Silenus grunted. "Ship . . . opaque." The walls solidified. The old poet's holo disappeared from its place by the bulkhead and flashed into existence near the spiral stairs. He kept doing that, and the effect was disconcerting. "Well, if we're finished with the fucking tour, let's go down to the living room and figure out how to outsmart the Pax."

THE MAPS WERE the old kind—ink on paper—and they were spread out across the top of the gleaming grand piano. The continent of Aquila spread its wings above the keyboard, and the horse head of Equus curled as a separate map above. Martin Silenus's holo strode on powerful legs to the piano and stabbed a finger down about where the horse's eye should be. "Here," he said. "And here." The massless finger made no noise against the paper. "The Pope's got his fucking troops all the way from Chronos Keep here"—the weightless finger jabbed at a point where the Bridle Range of mountains came to their easternmost point behind the eye —"all the way down the snout. They have aircraft here, at Sad King Billy's cursed city"—the finger pounded silently at a point only a few kilometers northwest of the Valley of the Time Tombs—"and have massed the Swiss Guard in the Valley itself."

I looked at the map. Except for the abandoned Poet's City and the Valley, the eastern fourth of Equus had been empty desert and out of bounds for anyone except Pax troops for more than two centuries. "How do you know the Swiss Guard troops are there?" I asked.

The satyr's brows arched. "I have my sources," he said.

"Do your sources tell you the units and armament?"

The holo made a noise that sounded as if the old man were going to spit on the carpet. "You don't need to know the units," he snapped. "Suffice it to say that there are thirty thousand soldiers between you and the Sphinx, where Aenea will step out tomorrow. Three thousand of those troops are Swiss Guard. Now, how are you going to get through them?"

I felt like laughing aloud. I doubted if the entire Home Guard of Hyperion, with air and space support, could "get through" half a dozen Swiss Guard. Their weapons, training, and defensive systems were that good. Instead of laughing, I studied the map again.

"You say that aircraft are staging out of the Poet's City. . . . Do you know the type of planes?"

The poet shrugged. "Fighters. EMVs don't work worth shit here, of course, so they've brought in thrust-reaction planes. Jets, I think."

"Scram, ram, pulse, or air breathing?" I said. I was trying to sound as if I knew what I was talking about, but my military knowledge gleaned in the Home Guard had been centered on fieldstripping my weapon, cleaning my weapon, firing my weapon, marching through nasty weather without getting my weapon wet, trying to get a few hours' sleep when I wasn't marching, cleaning, or fieldstripping, trying not to freeze to death when I was asleep, and—upon occasion—keeping my head down so that I wouldn't get killed by Ursus snipers.

"What the fuck does it matter what kind of planes?" growled Martin Silenus. Losing three centuries in appearance certainly had not mellowed him. "They're fighters. We've clocked them at . . . Ship? What the fuck was the speed we clocked those last blips at?"

"Mach three," said the ship.

"Mach three," repeated the poet. "Fast enough to fly down here, firebomb this place to ashes, and be back to the north continent before their beers get warm."

I looked up from the map. "I've been meaning to ask," I said. "Why don't they?"

The poet's head turned my way. "Why don't they what?"

"Fly down here, firebomb you to ashes, and be home before their beer is warm," I said. "You're a threat to them. Why do they tolerate you?"

Martin Silenus grunted. "I'm dead. They think I'm dead. How could a dead man be a threat to anyone?"

I sighed and looked back at the map. "There has to be a troopship in orbit, but I don't suppose you know what kind of craft escorted it here?"

Surprisingly, it was the ship who replied. "The troopship is a three-hundred-thousand-ton Akira-class spinship," came the soft voice. "It was escorted by two standard Pax-class torchships—the *St. Anthony* and the *St. Bonaventure*. There is also a C-three ship in high orbit."

"What the fuck is a C-three ship?" grumbled the poet's holo.

I glanced at him. How could anyone live for a thousand years and not learn such a basic thing? Poets were strange. "Command, communications, control," I said.

"So the Pax SOB who's in charge is up there?" asked Silenus.

I rubbed my cheek and stared at the map. "Not necessarily," I said. "The commander of the space task force will be there, but the head of operations may be on the ground. The Pax trains its commanders for combined operations. With so many of the Swiss Guard here, someone important is in command on the ground."

"All right," said the poet. "How are you going to get through them and get my little friend out?"

"Excuse me," said the ship, "but there is an additional spacecraft in orbit. It arrived about three weeks ago, standard, and sent a dropship to the Valley of the Time Tombs."

"What kind of ship?" I asked.

There was the briefest hesitation. "I do not know," said the ship. "The configuration is strange to me. Small . . . perhaps courier-sized . . . but the propulsion profile is . . . strange."

"It probably is a courier," I said to Silenus. "Poor bugger's been stuck in cryogenic fugue for months, paying years of time-debt, just to deliver some message Pax Central forgot to give the commander before he or she left."

The poet's holographic hand brushed at the map again. "Stick to the subject. How do you get Aenea away from these motherhumpers?"

I stepped away from the piano. My voice held anger when I spoke. "How the hell should I know? You're the one who's had two and a half centuries to plan this stupid escape." I waved my hand, indicating the ship. "I presume this thing is our ticket to outrunning the torchships." I paused. "Ship? *Can* you outrun a Pax torchship to C-plus translation?" All Hawking drives provided the same pseudo-velocity above light-speed, of course, so our escape and survival, or capture and destruction, depended upon the race to that quantum point.

"Oh, yes," said the ship immediately. "Parts of my memory are missing, but I am aware that the Consul had me modified during a visit to an Ouster colony."

"An Ouster colony?" I repeated stupidly. My skin prickled, despite logic. I had grown up fearing another Ouster invasion. Ousters were the ultimate bogeymen.

"Yes," said the ship with something like pride audible in its voice. "We will be able to spin up to C-plus velocities almost twenty-three percent faster than a Pax torchship of the line."

"They can lance you at half an AU," I said, not convinced.

"Yes," agreed the ship. "Nothing to worry about . . . if we have fifteen minutes' head start."

I turned back to the frowning holo and silent android. "That's all great," I said. "If it's true. But it doesn't help me figure out how to get the girl to the ship or the ship away from Hyperion with that fifteen-minute head start. The torchships will be in what's called a COP—a combat orbiting patrol. One or more of them will be over Equus every second, covering every cubic meter of space from a hundred light-minutes out to the upper atmosphere. At about thirty kilometers, the combat air patrol—probably Scorpion-class pulse fighters, able to scram into low orbit if need be—will take over. Neither the space nor atmospheric patrol would allow the ship fifteen seconds on their screens, much less fifteen minutes." I looked at the old man's younger face. "Unless there's something you're not telling me. Ship? Did the Ousters fit you with some sort of magical stealth technology? An invisibility shield or something?"

"Not that I'm aware of," said the ship. After a second it added, "That wouldn't be possible, would it?"

I ignored the ship. "Look," I said to Martin Silenus, "I'd like to help you get the girl—"

"Aenea," said the old man.

"I'd like to get Aenea away from these guys, but if she's as important as you say she is to the Pax . . . I mean, three thousand Swiss Guard, good Christ . . . there's no way we can get within five hundred kilometers of the Valley of the Time Tombs, even with this nifty-keen spaceship."

I saw the doubt in Silenus's eyes, even through holographic distortion, so I continued. "I'm serious," I said. "Even if there were no space or air cover, no torchships or fighters or airborne radar, there's the Swiss Guard. I mean"—I found that I was clenching my hands into fists as I spoke—"these guys are *deadly*. They're trained to work in squads of five, and any one of those squads could bring down a spaceship like this."

The satyr's brows arched in surprise or doubt.

"Listen," I said again. "Ship?"

"Yes, M. Endymion?"

"Do you have defensive shields?"

"No, M. Endymion. I do have Ouster-enhanced containment fields, but they are only for civilian use."

I didn't know what "Ouster-enhanced containment fields" were, but I went on. "Could they stop a standard torchship CPB or lance?"

"No," said the ship.

"Could you defeat C-plus or conventional kinetic torpedoes?"

"No."

"Could you outrun them?"

"No."

"Could you prevent a boarding party from entering?"

"No."

"Do you have any offensive or defensive abilities that could deal with Pax warships?"

"Unless one counts being able to run like hell, M. Endymion, the answer is no," said the ship.

I looked back at Martin Silenus. "We're screwed," I said softly. "Even if I could get to the girl, they'd just capture me as well as her."

Martin Silenus smiled. "Perhaps not," he said. He nodded to A. Bettik, and the android went up the spiral stairway to the upper level and returned in less than a minute. He was carrying a rolled cylinder of something.

"If this is the secret weapon," I said, "it had better be good."

"It is," said the poet's smirking hologram. He nodded again and A. Bettik unrolled the cylinder.

It was a rug, a bit less than two meters long and a bit more than a meter wide. The cloth was frayed and faded, but I could see intricate designs and patterns. A complex weave of gold threads were still as bright as . . .

"My God," I said, the realization hitting me like a fist to the solar plexus. "A hawking mat."

The holo of Martin Silenus cleared his throat as if preparing to spit. "Not *a* hawking mat," he grumbled. "*The* hawking mat."

I took a step back. This was the stuff of pure legend, and I was almost standing on it.

There had been only a few hundred hawking mats in existence, ever, and this was the *first* one—created by the Old Earth lepidopterist and legendary EM-systems inventor Vladimir Sholokov shortly after the destruction of Old Earth. Sholokov—already in his seventies, standard, had fallen madly in love with his teenage niece, Alotila, and had created this flying carpet to win her love in return. After a passionate interlude, the teenager had spurned the old man, Sholokov had killed himself on New Earth only weeks after perfecting the current Hawking spindrive, and the carpet had been lost for centuries . . . until Mike Osho bought it in Carvnel Marketplace and took it to Maui-Covenant, using it with his fellow shipman Merin Aspic in what would become another love affair that would enter legend—the love of Merin and Siri. This second legend, of course, had become part of Martin Silenus's epic *Cantos,* and if his tale was to be believed, Siri had been the Consul's grandmother. In the *Cantos* the Hegemony Consul had used this very same hawking mat ("hawking" here with a small *h* because it referred to the Old Earth bird, not to the pre-Hegira scientist named Hawking whose work had led to the C-plus breakthrough with the improved interstellar drive) to cross Hyperion in one final legend—this being the Consul's epic flight toward the city of Keats from the Valley of the Time Tombs to free this very ship and fly it back to the tombs.

I went to one knee and reverently touched the artifact.

"Jesus H. Christ," said Silenus, "it's only a fucking rug. And an ugly one at that. I wouldn't have it in my house—it clashes with everything."

I looked up.

"Yes," said A. Bettik, "this is the same hawking mat."

"Does it still fly?" I asked.

A. Bettik dropped to one knee next to me and extended his blue-fingered hand, tapping at the curled and complicated design. The hawking mat grew as rigid as a board and hovered ten centimeters above the floor.

I shook my head. "I never understood. . . . EM systems don't work on Hyperion because of the weird magnetic field here. . . ."

"Big EM systems don't," snapped Martin Silenus. "EMVs. Levitation barges. Big stuff. The carpet does. And it's been improved."

I raised an eyebrow. "Improved?"

"The Ousters again," came the ship's voice. "I don't remember it well, but they tinkered with a lot of things when we visited them two and a half centuries ago."

"Evidently," I said. I stood and nudged the legendary mat with my foot. It bounced as if on firm springs but remained hovering where it was. "Okay," I said, "we have Merin and Siri's hawking mat, which . . . if I remember the story . . . could fly along at about twenty klicks per hour. . . ."

"Twenty-six kilometers per hour was its top speed," said A. Bettik.

I nodded and nudged the hovering carpet again. "Twenty-six klicks per hour with a good tailwind," I said. "And the Valley of the Time Tombs is how far from here?"

"One thousand six hundred eighty-nine kilometers," said the ship.

"And how much time do we have before Aenea steps out of the Sphinx there?" I said.

"Twenty hours," said Martin Silenus. He must have tired of his younger image, because the holo projection was now of the old man as I had seen him the night before, hoverchair and all.

I glanced at my wrist chronometer. "I'm late," I said. "I should have started flying a couple of days ago." I walked back to the grand piano. "And what if I had? *This* is our secret weapon? Does *it* have some sort of super defense field to protect me . . . and the girl . . . from Swiss Guard lances and bullets?"

"No," said A. Bettik. "It has no defensive capabilities whatsoever, except for a containment field to deflect the wind and to keep its occupants in place."

I shrugged. "So what do I do . . . carry the rug to the Valley and offer the Pax a trade—one old hawking mat for the kid?"

A. Bettik remained kneeling by the hovering carpet. His blue fingers continued to caress the faded fabric. "The Ousters modified it to hold a charge longer—up to a thousand hours."

I nodded. Impressive superconductor technology, but totally irrelevant.

"And it now flies at speeds in excess of three hundred kilometers per hour," continued the android.

I chewed my lip. So I *could* get there by tomorrow. If I wanted to sit on a flying rug for five and a half hours. And then what . . . ?

"I thought we had to pluck her away in this ship," I said. "Get her out of the Hyperion system and all that . . ."

"Yes," said Martin Silenus, his voice suddenly as tired as his aged image, "but first you have to get her *to* the ship."

I walked away from the piano, stopping at the spiral staircase to whirl back toward the android, the holo, and the hovering carpet. "You two just don't understand, do you?" I said, my voice louder and sharper than I had intended. "These are *Swiss Guard*! If you think that damned rug can get me in under their radar, motion detectors, and other sensors, you're crazy. I'd just be a sitting duck flapping along at three hundred klicks per hour. Believe me, the Swiss Guard grunts—much less the pulse jets in combat air patrol—much less the orbiting torchships—would lance this thing in a nanosecond."

I paused and squinted at them. "Unless . . . there's something else you're not telling me . . ."

"Of course there is," said Martin Silenus, and managed a satyr's tired smile. "Of course there is."

"Let's take the hawking mat out to the tower window," said A. Bettik. "You have to learn how to handle it."

"Now?" I said, my voice suddenly small. I felt my heart begin to hammer.

"Now," said Martin Silenus. "You have to be proficient at flying it by the time you leave at oh-three-hundred hours tomorrow."

"I do?" I said, staring at the hovering, legendary rug with a growing sense of THIS IS REAL. . . . I MAY DIE TOMORROW.

"You do," said Martin Silenus.

A. Bettik deactivated the hawking mat and rolled it into a cylinder. I followed him down the metal stairs and out the corridor to the tower staircase. The sunlight was bright through the open tower window. *My God,* I thought as the android spread the carpet on the stone ledge and activated it again. It was still a long drop to the stones below. *My God,* I thought again, my pulse pounding in my ears. There was no sign of the old poet's holo.

A. Bettik gestured me onto the hovering hawking mat. "I'll go with you on the first flight," the android said softly. A breeze rustled the leaves atop the nearby chalma tree.

My God, I thought a final time, and climbed onto the sill and then onto the hawking mat.

11

RECISELY TWO HOURS before the child is scheduled to emerge from the Sphinx, an alarm sounds in Father Captain de Soya's command skimmer.

"Airborne contact, bearing one-seven-two, northbound, speed two-seven-four klicks, altitude four meters," comes the voice of the COP defense-perimeter controller from the C³-ship six hundred kilometers above. "Distance to intruder, five hundred seventy klicks."

"Four meters?" says de Soya, looking at Commander Barnes-Avne where she sits across from him at the CIC console amidships in the skimmer.

"Trying to come in low and slow under detection," says the Commander. She is a small woman with pale skin and red hair, but very little of either skin or hair is visible under the combat headgear she wears. In the three weeks de Soya has known the Commander, he has not seen her smile. "Tactical visor," she says. Her own visor is in place. De Soya lowers his.

The blip is near the southern tip of Equus, moving north from the coast. "Why didn't we see it before?" he asks.

"Could have just launched," says Barnes-Avne. She is checking combat assets within her tactical display. After the first difficult hour in which de Soya had to present the papal diskey to convince her that command of the Pax's most elite brigades was to be handed over to a mere ship's captain, Barnes-Avne has shown total cooperation. Of course, de Soya has left the minute-to-minute operation to her. Many of the Swiss Guard Brigade leaders believe de Soya to be a mere papal liaison. De Soya does not care. The child is his concern, the girl, and as long as the groundforce is being well commanded, the details are of little concern.

"No visual," says the Commander. "Dust storm down there. It'll be here before S-hour."

"S-hour" is what the troops have been calling the opening of the Sphinx for months now. Only a few officers among them know that a child has been the focus of all this firepower. Swiss Guards do not grumble, but few could appreciate such a provincial posting, so far from the action, in such sandy and uncomfortable surroundings.

"Contact remains northbound, one-seven-two, velocity now two-five-nine klicks, altitude three meters," says the C^3 controller. "Distance five hundred seventy kilometers."

"Time to bring it down," says Commander Barnes-Avne on the command channel limited to her and de Soya. "Recommendations?"

De Soya glances up. The skimmer is banking to the south. Outside the mantis-eye blisters, the horizon tilts and the bizarre Time Tombs of Hyperion pass a thousand meters beneath them. The sky to the south is a dull brown-and-yellow band. "Lance it from orbit?" he says.

Barnes-Avne nods but says, "You're familiar with the torchships' work. Let's put a squad on it." With her god-glove she touches red pips at the southern tip of the defensive perimeter. "Sergeant Gregorius?" She has switched to the tactical-channel tightbeam.

"Commander?" The sergeant's voice is deep and graveled.

"You're monitoring the bogey?"

"Affirmative, Commander."

"Intercept it, identify it, and destroy it, Sergeant."

"Affirmative, Commander."

De Soya watches as the C^3 cameras zoom toward the southern desert. Five human forms suddenly appear rising from the dunes, their chameleon polymer fading as they rise above dust cloud. On a normal world they would be flying by EM repulsors; on Hyperion they wear the bulkier reaction paks. The five fan out so that several hundred meters separate them and hurtle southward into the dust cloud.

"IR," says Barnes-Avne, and the visual shifts to the infrared to follow them through the thickening cloud. "Illuminate target," she says. The image shifts south, but the target is only a heat blur.

"Small," says the Commander.

"Plane?" Father Captain de Soya is used to spaceborne tactical displays.

"Too small, unless it's some sort of motorized paraglider," says Barnes-Avne. There is absolutely no stress in her voice.

De Soya looks down as the skimmer passes over the south end of the Valley of the Time Tombs and accelerates. The dust storm is a gold-brown band along the horizon ahead of them.

"Distance to intercept one hundred eighty klicks," comes Sergeant Gregorius's laconic voice. De Soya's visor is slaved to the Commander's, and they are seeing what the Swiss Guard sergeant sees—nothing. The squad of troops is flying on instruments through blowing sand so thick that the air is as dark as night around them.

"Reaction paks are heating up," comes another calm voice. De Soya checks the readout. It is Corporal Kee. "Sand's foulin' up the intakes," continues the corporal.

De Soya looks through his visor at Commander Barnes-Avne. He knows she has a tough choice to make—another minute in that dust cloud could send one or more of her troops falling to their deaths; failure to identify the bogey could lead to trouble later.

"Sergeant Gregorius," she says, her voice still rock calm, "take out the intruder now."

There is the briefest of pauses on the comline. "Commander, we can hang in here a few more . . . ," begins the sergeant. De Soya can hear the howl of the dust storm over the man's voice.

"Take it out now, Sergeant," says Barnes-Avne.

"Affirmative."

De Soya switches to the wide-range tactical and looks up to see the Commander watching him. "You think this might be a feint?" she says. "A distraction to pull us away so that the real intruder can infiltrate elsewhere?"

"Could be," says de Soya. He sees from the display that the Commander has raised the alert all along the perimeter to Level Five. A Level Six alert is combat.

"Let's see," she says, just as Gregorius's troops fire.

The dust storm is a rolling cauldron of sand and electricity. At 175 kilometers, their energy weapons are unreliable. Gregorius chooses a steel rain dart and launches it himself. The dart accelerates to Mach 6. The bogey does not divert from its path.

"No sensors, I think," says Barnes-Avne. "It's flying blind. Programmed."

The dart passes over the heat target and detonates at a distance of thirty meters, the shaped charge propelling the twenty thousand flechettes directly downward into the intruder's path.

"Contact down," says the C^3 controller at the same second that Sergeant Gregorius reports, "Got him."

"Find and identify," says the Commander. Their skimmer has banked back toward the Valley.

De Soya glances through the visor display. She has taken the kill at a distance but is not removing the troops from the storm.

"Affirmative," says the sergeant, and the storm is wild enough to add static to a tightbeam.

The skimmer flies low over the valley, and de Soya identifies the tombs for the thousandth time: here, in reverse order from the usual pilgrims' approach—although there have been no pilgrims for more than three centuries—comes first the Shrike Palace, farther south than the others, its barbed and serrated buttresses reminiscent of the creature that has not been seen here since the days of the pilgrims; then the more subtle Cave Tombs—three in all—their entrances carved out of the pink stone of the canyon wall; then the huge centrally placed Crystal Monolith; then the Obelisk; then the Jade Tomb; and finally the intricately carved Sphinx with sealed door and outflung wings.

De Soya glances at his chronometer.

"One hour and fifty-six minutes," says Commander Barnes-Avne.

Father Captain de Soya chews his lip. The cordon of Swiss Guard troops is in place around the Sphinx—has been in place for months. Farther out, more troops are placed in a broader perimeter. Each tomb has its detail of waiting soldiers, just in case the prophecy might have been mistaken. Beyond the Valley, more troops. Above them, the torchships and command ship keep watch. At the entrance to the Valley, de Soya's private dropship awaits, its engines already powered up, ready for immediate liftoff as soon as the sedated child is aboard. Two thousand klicks above, the archangel-class courier ship *Raphael* waits with its child-sized acceleration couch.

First, though, de Soya knows, the girl whose name might be Aenea must receive the sacrament of the cruciform. This will happen at the chapel in the torchship *St. Bonaventure* in orbit, moments before the sleeping child is transferred to the courier ship. Three days after that, she will be resurrected on Pacem and delivered to the Pax authorities.

Father Captain de Soya licks his dry lips. He is as worried that an innocent child will be hurt as he is that something will go wrong in the detention. He cannot imagine how a child—even a child from the past, one who has communicated with the TechnoCore—can be a threat to the far-flung Pax or the Holy Church.

Father Captain de Soya throttles back his thoughts; it is not his place to imagine. It is his place to carry out orders and serve his superiors, and through them, to serve the Church and Jesus Christ.

"Here's your bogey," comes Sergeant Gregorius's rasp. The visual is hazy, the dust storm is still very wild, but all five troops have made it to the crash site.

De Soya raises the resolution on his visor display and sees the shattered wood and paper, the riddled, twisted metal that might have been a simple solar battery-pulse reaction outboard.

"Drone," says Corporal Kee.

De Soya flips up his visor and smiles at Commander Barnes-Avne. "Another drill from you," he says. "That's five today."

The Commander does not return the smile. "Next time it may be the real thing," she says. To her tactical mike she says, "Level Five continues. At S-minus sixty, we go to Level Six."

Confirmations ring on all bands.

"I still don't understand who might want to interfere," says Father Captain de Soya. "Or how they could do it."

Commander Barnes-Avne shrugs. "The Ousters could be spinning down from C-plus even as we speak."

"Then they'd better bring a full Swarm," says the father-captain. "Anything less and we'll handle them easily."

"Nothing in life is easy," says Commander Barnes-Avne.

The skimmer touches down. The lock cycles and the ramp lowers. The pilot turns in his seat, slides his visor up, and says, "Commander, Captain, you wanted to land at the Sphinx at S-minus one hour and fifty minutes. We're a minute early."

De Soya disconnects himself from the skimmer console. "I'm going to stretch my legs before the storm arrives," he says to the Commander. "Care to join me?"

"No." Barnes-Avne lowers her visor and begins whispering commands.

Outside the skimmer, the air is thin and charged with electricity. Overhead, the sky is still the peculiar deep lapis of Hyperion, but already the southern rim of the canyon has a haze hanging over it as the storm approaches.

De Soya glances at his chronometer. One hour and fifty minutes. He takes a deep breath, vows not to look again at the timepiece for at least ten minutes, and walks into the looming shadow of the Sphinx.

12

FTER HOURS OF TALK, I was sent to bed to sleep until three A.M. Of course, I did not. I always have had trouble sleeping the night before a trip, and this night I did not sleep at all.

The city after which I was named was quiet after midnight; the autumn breeze had dropped and the stars were very bright. For an hour or two I stayed in my sleep shirt, but by one A.M. I rose, dressed in the sturdy clothes they had given me the night before, and went through the contents of my pack for the fifth or sixth time.

There was not much for so daunting an adventure: a change of clothes and underwear, socks, a flashlight laser, two water bottles, a knife —I had specified the type—in a belt scabbard, a heavy canvas jacket with thermal lining, an ultralight blanket to use as a bedroll, an inertial guidance compass, an old sweater, night-vision glasses, and a pair of leather gloves. "What else would you need to explore the universe?" I muttered.

I had also specified the type of clothing I would wear on this day—a comfortable canvas shirt and an overvest with numerous pockets, tough whipcord trousers of the sort I'd worn while duck hunting in the fens, soft high boots—what I thought of as "buccaneer boots" from the description in Grandam's stories—that were only a bit too tight, and a soft tricorn cap that would fold away in a vest pocket when I did not need it.

I clasped the knife to my belt, set the compass in my vest pocket, and stood at the window watching the stars wheel over the mountaintops until A. Bettik came to wake me at two forty-five.

THE OLD POET was awake and in his hoverchair at the end of the table on the highest level of the tower. The canvas roof had been pulled back and the stars burned coldly overhead. Flames sputtered in the braziers along the wall, and actual torches were set higher on the stone wall. There was breakfast laid out—fried meats, fruits, meal patties with syrup, fresh bread —but I took only a cup of coffee.

"You'd better eat," grumbled the old man. "You don't know when your next meal will come."

I stood looking at him. Steam from the coffee rose to warm my face. The air was chill. "If things go according to plan, I'll be in the spaceship in less than six hours. I'll eat then."

Martin Silenus made a rough noise. "When do things ever go according to plan, Raul Endymion?"

I sipped coffee. "Speaking of plans, you were going to tell me about the sort of miracle that's going to distract the Swiss Guard while I whisk your young friend away."

The ancient poet peered at me for a silent moment. "Just trust me on that, will you?"

I sighed. I had been afraid he would say that. "That's a lot to take on trust, old man."

He nodded but remained silent.

"All right," I said at last. "We'll see what happens." I turned to where A. Bettik was standing near the stairway. "Just don't forget to be there with the ship when we need you."

"I will not forget, sir," said the android.

I walked to where the hawking mat was laid out on the floor. A. Bettik had set my pack on it. "Any last instructions?" I asked, not knowing which person I was speaking to.

The old man floated closer on his hoverchair. He looked ancient in the torchlight: more wizened and mummified than ever. His fingers were like yellowed bones. "Just this," he rasped. "Listen—

"In the wide sea there lives a forlorn wretch,
Doomed with enfeebled carcass to outstretch
His loathed existence through ten centuries,
And then to die alone. Who can devise
A total opposition? No one. So
A million times ocean must ebb and flow,
And he oppressed. Yet he shall not die,
These things accomplished. If he utterly
Scans all depths of magic, and expounds
The meanings of all motions, shapes and sounds;
If he explores all forms and substances
Straight homeward to their symbol-essences;
He shall not die. Moreover, and in chief,
He must pursue this task of joy and grief
Most piously—all lovers tempest-tossed,
And in the savage overwhelming lost,

He shall deposit side by side, until
Time's creeping shall the dreary space fulfil:
Which done, and all these labours ripened,
A youth, by heavenly power loved and led,
Shall stand before him, whom he shall direct
How to consummate all. The youth elect
Must do the thing, or both will be destroyed."

"What?" I said. "I don't . . . ."

"Fuck it," rasped the poet. "Just get Aenea, take her to the Ousters, and get her back alive. It's not too complicated. Even a shepherd should be able to do it."

"Don't forget landscape apprentice, bartender, and duck hunter," I said, and set my cup of coffee down.

"It's almost three," said Silenus. "You need to get going."

I took a breath. "Just one minute," I said. I clattered down the stairs, went into the lavatory, relieved myself, and leaned against the cool stone wall for a moment. *Are you mad, Raul Endymion?* It was my thought, but I heard it in Grandam's soft voice. *Yes,* I answered.

I walked back up the stairs, amazed at how shaky my legs were and how rapidly my heart was beating.

"All set," I said. "Mother always said to take care of these things before leaving home."

The thousand-year-old poet grunted and hovered his chair near the hawking mat. I sat on the rug, activated the flight threads, and hovered a meter and a half above the stone floor.

"Remember, once you're in the Cleft and find the entrance, it's programmed," said Silenus.

"I know, you told me all about . . ."

"Shut up and listen," he rasped. Ancient parchment fingers pointed to the proper thread designs. "You remember how to fly it. Once in, tap in the sequence there . . . there . . . there . . . and the program will take over. You can interrupt the sequence to fly manually by touching the interrupt design here. . . ." His fingers caressed air above the ancient threads. "But don't try to fly it yourself down there. You'll never find your way out."

I nodded and licked dry lips. "You didn't tell me who programmed it. Who did this flight before?"

The satyr showed new teeth. "I did, my boy. It took me months, but I did. Almost two centuries ago."

"Two centuries!" I almost stepped off the mat. "What if there have been cave-ins? Shiftings due to earthquakes? What if something's got in the way since then?"

Martin Silenus shrugged. "You'll be going over two hundred klicks per hour, boy," he said. "I guess you'll die." He slapped me on the back.

"Get going. Give my love to Aenea. Tell her that Uncle Martin is waiting to see Old Earth before he dies. Tell her that the old fart is eager to hear her expound the meanings of all motions, shapes, and sounds."

I raised the hawking mat another half meter.

A. Bettik stepped forward and extended a blue hand. I shook it. "Good luck, M. Endymion."

I nodded, found nothing else to say, and flew the hawking mat up and out of the tower in rising spirals.

To FLY DIRECTLY from the city of Endymion in the middle of the continent of Aquila to the Valley of the Time Tombs on the continent of Equus, I should have headed almost due north. I headed east.

My test-flying the day before—it was the same day to my tired mind —had shown how easy it was to handle the hawking mat, but that was at speeds of a few klicks per hour. When I was a hundred meters above the tower, I set the direction—the penlight clamped in my teeth illuminating the inertial compass, lining up the mat along that invisible line, checking it against the topographic map the old poet had given me—and held the palm of my hand on the acceleration pattern. The mat continued to speed up until the gentle containment field activated to shield me from the wind blast. Too late, I glanced back to catch a last glimpse of the tower— perhaps to see the old poet watching from a window—but already the ruined university town was lost to sight in the mountain darkness.

There was no speed indicator, so I had to assume the mat was flying at its top speed as it soared toward the high peaks to the east. Starlight reflected on snowfields higher than my own altitude, so to be cautious, I stowed the penlight, pulled on the night-vision glasses, and continued to check my position against the topo map. As the land rose, so did I, holding the hawking mat at a hundred meters above the boulders, waterfalls, avalanche chutes, and icefalls all glowing green in the enhanced starlight from the night-vision goggles. The mat was perfectly silent in its flight— even the wind noise was hushed by the deflective containment field—and several times I saw large animals leap to hiding, surprised by the sudden appearance of this wingless bird above them. I crossed the continental divide half an hour after leaving the tower, keeping the mat in the center of the five-thousand-meter pass. It was cold there, and though the containment field held some of my own body heat in the traveling bubble of still air, I had long since pulled on my thermal jacket and gloves.

Beyond the mountains, descending quickly to stay close to the rugged terrain, I watched the tundra give way to fenfields, the fenfields to low lines of dwarf everblues and triaspen, and then saw these high-mountain trees trail off and disappear as the glow of the tesla flame forests began to light the east like a false dawn.

I stowed the night-vision glasses in my pack. The sight ahead was beautiful and somewhat frightening—the entire eastern horizon snapping and crackling with electricity, ball lightning leaping between the hundred-meter-tall tesla trees, chain lightning rippling through the air between tesla and exploding prometheus, phoenix shrubs and random ground fires burning in a thousand places. Both Martin Silenus and A. Bettik had warned me about this, and I took the hawking mat high, accepting the risk of detection at this altitude as preferable to being caught in that electric maelstrom below.

Another hour and there was a hint of sunrise to the east, beyond the flame-forest glow, but just as the sky paled and then deepened into daylight, the flame forests fell behind me and the Cleft came into sight.

I had been aware that I had been climbing for the past forty minutes as I checked my route above the Pinion Plateau on the creased topo map, but now I felt the altitude as the depth of that great crevice in this part of Aquila became visible ahead. In its own way, the Cleft was as frightening as the flame forests—narrow, vertical, dropping three thousand meters in a straight fall from the flatlands above. I crossed the southern edge of the great split in the continent and dived toward the river three kilometers below. The Cleft continued east, the river beneath me roaring along at nearly the same speed as the mat as I slowed. Within moments the morning sky darkened above me and the stars reappeared; it was as if I had fallen into a deep well. The river at the base of these terrifying cliffs of fall was wild, clogged with bergs of its own ice, leaping over boulders the size of the spaceship I had left behind. I stayed five meters above the spray and slowed even further. I must be close.

I checked my chronometer and then the map. It should be somewhere ahead in the next two klicks . . . there!

It was larger than they had described—at least thirty meters to a side—and perfectly square. The entrance to the planetary labyrinth had been carved in the form of a temple entrance, or a giant door. I slowed the hawking mat further and then banked left, pausing at the entrance. According to my chronometer, it had taken just under ninety minutes to reach the Cleft. The Valley of the Time Tombs was still a thousand klicks north of here. Four hours of flying at high cruising speed. I looked again at my chronometer—four hours and twenty minutes until the time the child was scheduled to step out of the Sphinx.

I edged the hawking mat forward, into the cavern. Trying to remember the details of the Priest's Tale in the old man's *Cantos,* I could remember only that it was here—just within the labyrinth entrance—that Father Duré and the Bikura had encountered the Shrike and the cruciforms.

There was no Shrike. I was not surprised—the creature had not been sighted since the Fall of the WorldWeb 274 years ago. There were no cruciforms. Again, I was not surprised—the Pax had harvested them long ago from these cavern walls.

I knew what everyone knew about the Labyrinth. There had been nine known labyrinthine worlds in the old Hegemony. All of those worlds had been Earth-like—7.9 on the ancient Solmev Scale—except that they were tectonically dead, more Mars-like than Earth-like in that respect. The labyrinth tunnels honeycombed those nine worlds—Hyperion included—and served no known purpose. They had been tunneled tens of thousands of years before humankind had left Old Earth, although no clue to the tunnelers had ever been found. The labyrinths fueled numerous myths—including the *Cantos*—but their mystery remained. The Labyrinth of Hyperion had never been mapped—except for the part I was ready to travel at 270 klicks per hour. It had been mapped by a mad poet. Or so I hoped.

I slipped the night-vision glasses back on as the sunlight faded behind me. I felt the skin on the back of my neck prickle as the darkness closed around. Soon the glasses would be useless, as there would be no light to enhance. Taking tape from my pack, I secured the flashlight laser to the front of the hawking mat and set the beam to its widest dispersal. The light would be faint, but the goggles would amplify it. Already I could see branchings ahead—the cavern remained a great, hollow, rectangular prism, thirty meters on a side, with only the smallest signs of cracks or collapse—and ahead, tunnels branched to the right, then left, then downward.

I took a breath and tapped in the programmed sequence. The hawking mat leaped ahead, accelerating to its preset speed, the sudden lurch making me lean far backward despite the compensating effect of the containment field.

That field would not protect me if the carpet took a wrong turn and smashed into a wall at this speed. Rocks flashed past. The hawking mat banked sharply to make a right turn, leveled itself in the center of the long cavern, then dived to follow a descending branch.

It was terrifying to watch. I took the night-vision glasses off, secured them in my coat pocket, gripped the edge of the leaping, lurching mat, and closed my eyes. I need not have bothered. The darkness was now absolute.

13

WITH FIFTEEN MINUTES until the opening of the Sphinx, Father Captain de Soya paces the valley floor. The storm has long since arrived, and sand fills the air in a rasping blizzard. Hundreds of Swiss Guard are deployed here along the Valley floor, but their armored CTVs, their gun emplacements, their missile batteries, their observation posts—all are invisible due to the dust storm. But de Soya knows that they would be invisible at any rate, concealed behind camouflage fields and chameleon polymer. The father-captain has to rely on his infrared to see anything in this howling storm. And even then, with his visor down and sealed, fine particles of sand make their way down his combat suit collar and up into his mouth. This day tastes of grit. His sweat leaves tiny trails of red mud, like blood from some holy stigmata, on his brow and cheeks.

"Attention," he says over the all-call channels. "This is Father Captain de Soya, commanding this mission under papal imperative. Commander Barnes-Avne will repeat these orders in a moment, but right now I want to specify that there will be no actions taken, no shots fired, no defensive acts initiated that will in any way endanger the life of the child who will be stepping from one of these tombs in . . . thirteen and a half minutes. I want this understood by every Pax officer and trooper, every torchship captain and space-navy sailor, every pilot and airborne flight officer . . . *this child must be captured but unharmed.* Failure to heed this warning will result in court-martial and summary execution. May we all serve our Lord and our Church this day. . . . In the name of Jesus, Mary, and Joseph, I ask that our efforts be successful. Father Captain de Soya, Acting Commander Hyperion expedition, out."

He continues walking as the chorus of amens comes in over tactical channels. Suddenly he pauses. "Commander?"

"Yes, Father Captain." Barnes-Avne's voice is calm in his earphones.

"Would it screw up your perimeter if I asked for Sergeant Gregorius's squad to join me here at the Sphinx?"

There is the briefest pause, which tells him how little the ground Commander thinks of such last-minute changes in plans. The "reception committee"—a squad of specially chosen Swiss Guard, the doctor with the sedative ready to be administered, and a medic with the living cruciform in its stasis container—are even now waiting at the foot of the Sphinx's stairs.

"Gregorius and his troops will be there in three minutes," says the Commander. De Soya can hear the commands going out over the tactical tightbeam and the confirmations coming in. Once again he has asked these five men and women to fly in dangerous conditions.

The squad touches down in two minutes forty-five seconds. De Soya can see them only on infrared; their reaction paks are glowing white-hot.

"Shed the flying paks," he says. "Just stay near me no matter what happens. Watch my back."

"Yes, sir," comes Sergeant Gregorius's rumble through the wind howl. The huge noncom steps closer, his visor and combat suit looming in de Soya's IR vision. Obviously the sergeant wants a visual confirmation on whose back he is watching.

"S-minus ten minutes," says Commander Barnes-Avne. "Sensors indicate unusual activity in the antientropic fields around the tombs."

"I feel it," says de Soya. Indeed, he can. The shifting of the time fields in the Valley creates a sense of vertigo in him not too dissimilar from nausea. Both this and the raging sandstorm make the priest-captain feel unattached to the ground, light-headed, almost drunk. Planting his feet carefully, de Soya walks back to the Sphinx. Gregorius and his troopers follow in a tight V.

The "welcoming committee" is standing on the steps of the Sphinx. De Soya approaches, flashes his infrared and radio ID, talks briefly with the doctor carrying the sedative ampule—warns the woman not to harm the child—and then waits. There are thirteen forms on the steps now, counting Gregorius's team. De Soya realizes that the combat squads do not look especially welcoming with their raised heavy weapons. "Step back a few paces," he says to the two squad sergeants. "Keep the squads ready, but out of sight in the storm."

"Affirmative." The ten troopers take a dozen steps back and are totally invisible in the blowing sand. De Soya knows that nothing living could break through the perimeter they have established.

To the doctor and his medic aide carrying the cruciform, De Soya says, "Let's get closer to the door." The suited figures nod and the three slowly climb the stairs. The antientropic fields are intense now. De Soya remembers once, as a young boy, he had stood up to his chest in a vicious surf, the tide and undertow trying to pull him out into an unfriendly ocean on his homeworld. This is a bit like that.

"S-minus seven minutes," says Barnes-Avne on the common channel. Then, on the tightbeam to de Soya, "Father Captain, would you like the skimmer to land and get you? There's a better overview up here."

"No, thank you," says de Soya. "I'll stay with the contact team." He sees on his display that the skimmer is climbing for altitude, finally pausing at ten thousand meters, above the worst of the dust storm. Like any good commander, Barnes-Avne wants to control the action while not being caught up in it.

De Soya keys the private channel to his dropship pilot. "Hiroshe?"

"Yes, sir?"

"Be ready to lift off in ten minutes or less."

"Ready, sir."

"The storm won't be a problem?" As with all deep-space combat captains, de Soya is more distrustful of atmosphere than of almost anything else.

"No problem, sir."

"Good."

"S-minus five minutes," comes Commander Barnes-Avne's steady voice. "Orbital detectors show no space activity for thirty AUs. Northern hemispheric airwatch shows no vehicles airborne. Ground detection shows no unauthorized movement from the Bridle Range to the coast."

"COP screens clear," comes the C^3 controller's voice.

"CAP clear," says the lead Scorpion pilot. "It's still a beautiful day up here."

"Radio and tightbeam silence from this point on until Level Six goes to standdown," says Barnes-Avne. "S-minus four minutes and sensors show maximum antientropic activity throughout the Valley. Contact team, report in."

"I'm at the door," says Dr. Chatkra.

"Ready," says the medic, a very young trooper named Caf. The trooper's voice is shaky. De Soya realizes that he does not know if Caf is male or female.

"All set here," reports de Soya. He glances over his shoulder through the clear visor. Even the bottom of the stone stairway is invisible in the howling sand. Electrical discharges crackle and pop. De Soya switches to IR and sees the ten Swiss Guards standing there, weapons literally hot.

Even in the midst of storm noise, a terrible quiet suddenly descends. De Soya can hear his own breathing within the helmet of his combat suit. The unused com channels hiss and pop with static. More static lashes his tactical and IR visors, and de Soya slides them up in exasperation. The sealed portal of the Sphinx is less than three meters in front of him, but the sand now conceals it, now reveals it, like a shifting curtain. De Soya takes two steps closer, and Dr. Chatkra and her medic follow.

"Two minutes," says Barnes-Avne. "All weapons to full hot. High-speed recorders to automatic. Medical dustoff teams stand by."

De Soya closes his eyes to fight the vertigo of the time tides. *The universe,* he thinks, *is truly wondrous.* He is sorry that he has to sedate the child within seconds of meeting her. Those are his orders—she would sleep through the attachment of the cruciform and the fatal flight back to Pacem—and he knows that he will, in all probability, never hear the girl's voice. He is sorry. He would like to talk to her, ask her questions about the past, about herself.

"One minute. Perimeter fire control on full auto."

"Commander!" De Soya has to slide the tactical visor down to identify the voice as belonging to a science lieutenant on the interior perimeter. "The fields are building to max along *all* the tombs! Doors opening on the caves, the Monolith, the Shrike Palace, the Jade Tomb . . ."

"Silence on all channels," snaps Barnes-Avne. "We're monitoring it here. Thirty seconds."

De Soya realizes that the child is going to step into this new era only to be confronted with three helmeted, visored figures in combat armor, and slides all of his visors up. He may never get to talk to the girl, but she will see his human face before she sleeps.

"Fifteen seconds." For the first time de Soya hears tension in the Commander's voice.

Blowing sand claws at Father Captain de Soya's exposed eyes. He raises a gloved hand, rubs, and blinks through tears. He and Dr. Chatkra take another step closer. The doors of the Sphinx are opening inward. The interior is dark. De Soya wishes he could see in IR, but he does not flip the visor down. He is determined that this child will see his eyes.

A shadow moves within darkness. The doctor begins to step toward the form, but de Soya touches her arm. "Wait."

The shadow becomes a figure; the figure becomes a form; the form is a child. She is smaller than de Soya expected. Her shoulder-length hair blows in the wind.

"Aenea," says de Soya. He had not planned on speaking to her, or calling her by name.

The girl looks up at him. He sees the dark eyes, but senses no fear there—just . . . anxiety? Sadness?

"Aenea, don't worry . . . ," he begins, but the doctor moves forward quickly at that moment, injector raised, and the girl takes a quick step back.

It is then that Father Captain de Soya sees the second figure in the gloom. And it is then that the screaming begins.

14

HADN'T KNOWN that I was claustrophobic until this trip. The flying at high speeds through pitch-black catacombs, the encircling containment field blocking even the wind of my passage, the sense of stone and darkness all around—twenty minutes into the wild flight I disengaged the autopilot program, landed the hawking mat on the labyrinth floor, collapsed the containment field, stepped away from the mat, and screamed.

I grabbed the flashlight laser and played it on the walls. A square corridor of stone. Here, outside the containment field, the heat struck me. The tunnel must be very deep. There were no stalactites, no stalagmites, no bats, no living things . . . only this square-hewn cavern stretching on to infinity. I played the light over the hawking mat. It seemed dead, totally inert. In my haste I might have exited the program incorrectly, wiped it. If so, I was dead. We had jinked and banked on a score of branchings so far; there was no way I would ever find my own way out.

I screamed again, although it was a bit more of a deliberate, tension-breaking shout than a scream this time. I fought the sense of walls and darkness closing in. I willed away the nausea.

Three and a half hours left. Three and a half hours of this claustrophobic nightmare, barreling along through blackness, hanging on to a leaping flying carpet . . . and then what?

I wished then that I had brought a weapon. It seemed absurd at the time; no handgun would have given me a chance against even a single Swiss Guard trooper—not even against a Home Guard irregular—but now I wished I had something. I removed the small hunting knife from its leather scabbard on my belt, saw the steel gleam in the flashlight beam, and started laughing.

This was absurd.

I set the knife back, dropped onto the mat, and tapped in the "resume" code. The hawking mat stiffened, rose, and lurched into violent motion. I was going somewhere fast.

FATHER CAPTAIN DE SOYA sees the huge shape for an instant before it is gone, and the screaming begins. Dr. Chatkra steps toward the retreating child, blocking de Soya's view, there is a rush of air tangible even within the wind roar all around, and the doctor's helmeted head is rolling and bouncing past de Soya's boots.

"Mother of God," he whispers into his open microphone. Dr. Chatkra's body still stands. The girl—Aenea—screams then, the sound almost lost under the howling sandstorm, and as if the force of the scream has acted upon Chatkra's body, the corpse falls to the stone. The medic, Caf, shouts something unintelligible and lunges for the girl. Again the dark blur, more sensed than seen, and Caf's arm is separated from the medic's body. Aenea runs toward the stairway. De Soya lunges at the child but collides with some sort of huge, metallic statue made of barbs and razor wire. Spikes puncture his combat armor—impossible!—but he feels the blood pouring from half a dozen minor wounds.

"No!" screams the girl again. "Stop! I command you!"

The three-meter metal statue turns in slow motion. De Soya has a confused impression of blazing red eyes staring down at the girl, and then the metal sculpture is gone. The father-captain takes a step toward the child, still wanting to reassure her as well as capture her, but his left leg goes out from under him, and he goes to his right knee on the broad stone step.

The girl comes to him, touches his shoulder, and whispers—somehow audibly above the wind howl and the worse howling of people in pain coming over his earphones—"It will be all right."

Father Captain de Soya's body is suffused with well-being, his mind is filled with joy. He weeps.

The girl is gone. A huge figure looms over him, and de Soya clenches his fists, tries to rise, knowing that it is futile—that the creature has returned to kill him.

"Easy!" shouts Sergeant Gregorius. The big man helps de Soya to his feet. The father-captain cannot stand—his left leg is bleeding and useless—so Gregorius holds him in one giant arm while he sweeps the area with his energy lance.

"Don't shoot!" shouts de Soya. "The girl . . ."

"Gone," says Sergeant Gregorius. He fires. A spike of pure energy lashes into the crackling swirl of sand. "Damn!" Gregorius lifts the father-captain over his armored shoulder. The screams on the net are growing wilder.

MY CHRONOMETER and compass tell me that I am almost there. Nothing else suggests that. I am still flying blind, still hanging on to the lurching hawking mat as it selects which branch of the endless Labyrinth to hurtle down. I have had little sense of the tunnels climbing toward the surface, but, then, I have had little sense of anything except vertigo and claustrophobia.

For the last two hours I have worn my night-vision glasses and illuminated our flight path with the flashlight laser at its widest setting. At three hundred klicks per hour, the rock walls rush by with alarming rapidity. But rather that than darkness.

I am still wearing the goggles when the first light appears and blinds me. I sweep off the glasses, stow them in a vest pocket, and blink away afterimages. The hawking mat is hurtling me toward a rectangle of pure light.

I remember the old poet saying that the Third Cave Tomb had been closed for more than two and a half centuries. All of the Time Tombs on Hyperion had their portals sealed after the Fall, but the Third Cave Tomb actually had a wall of rock sealing it off from the Labyrinth *behind* the closed portal. For hours now I had half expected to barrel into that wall of rock at almost three hundred klicks per hour.

The square of light grows rapidly. I realize that the tunnel has been climbing for some time, rising to the surface here. I lie full-length on the hawking mat, feeling it slow as it reaches the end of its programmed flight plan. "Good work, old man," I say aloud, hearing my voice for the first time since the shouting interlude three and a half hours ago.

I set my hand over the acceleration threads, afraid to let the mat slow to a walking pace here where I am bound to be a sitting duck. I had said that it would take a miracle to keep from being shot by the Swiss Guard; the poet had promised me one. It is time.

Sand swirls in the tomb opening, covering the doorway like a dry waterfall. *Is this the miracle?* I hope not. Troopers can see through a sandstorm easily enough. I brake the mat to a stop just within the doorway, pull a bandanna and sunglasses from my pack, tie the scarf over my nose and mouth, lie full-length on my belly again, set my fingers over the flight designs, and punch the acceleration threads.

The hawking mat flies through the doorway and into open air.

I jink hard right, rising and dropping the mat in a wild evasive pattern, knowing even as I do so that such efforts are useless against autotargeting. It does not matter—my urge to stay alive overrides my logic.

I cannot see. The storm is so wild that everything two meters beyond the leading edge of the mat is obscured. This is insane . . . the old poet and I never discussed the possibility of a sandstorm here. I can't even tell my altitude.

Suddenly a razor-sharp flying buttress passes less than a meter beneath the hurtling carpet, immediately I fly *under* another barbed metal strut, and I realize that I have almost just collided with the Shrike Palace. I am headed precisely the wrong direction—south—when I need to be at the north end of the Valley. I look at my compass, confirm my folly, and swing the hawking mat around. From the glimpse I had of the Shrike Palace, the mat is about twenty meters above ground level. Stopping the carpet, feeling it rocked and buffeted by the wind, I lower it like an elevator until it touches windswept stone. Then I raise it three meters, lock in that altitude, and move due north at little more than a walking pace.

Where are the soldiers?

As if to answer my unspoken question, dark forms in battle armor hurtle by. I flinch as they fire their baroque energy lances and stubby flechette guns, but they are not firing at me. They are shooting over their shoulders. *They are Swiss Guard and they are running.* I had never heard of such a thing.

Suddenly I realize that beneath the wind howl, the Valley is alive with human screams. I don't see how this is possible—troopers would keep their helmets fastened and visors down in such a storm. But the screams are there. I can hear them.

A jet or skimmer suddenly roars overhead, no more than ten meters above me, its autoguns firing to either side—I survive because I am directly beneath the thing—and I have to brake suddenly as the storm ahead of me is illuminated by a terrible blast of light and heat. The skimmer, jet, whatever, has flown directly into one of the tombs ahead of me. I guess that it is the Crystal Monolith or the Jade Tomb.

More firing to my left. I fly right, then northwest again, trying to bypass the tombs. Suddenly there are screams to my right and directly ahead. Bolts of lancefire slash through the storm. This time someone *is* shooting at me. *Shooting and missing? How can this be?*

Not waiting for an answer, I drop the hawking mat like an express elevator. Slamming into the ground, I roll aside, bolts of energy ionizing the air not twenty centimeters above my head. The inertial compass, still on a lanyard around my neck, punches me in the face as I roll. There are no boulders to hide behind, no rocks; the sand is flat here. I try to dig a ditch with my fingers as the blue bolts crisscross the air over my head. Flechette clouds flash overhead with their characteristic ripping sound. If I had been airborne now, the hawking mat and I would be in small tatters.

Something huge is standing not three meters from me in the whipping sand. Its legs are planted wide. It looks like a giant in barbed combat armor—a giant with too many arms. A plasma bolt strikes it, outlining the spiked form for an instant. The thing does not melt or fall or fly apart.

Impossible. Fucking impossible. Part of my mind coolly notes that I am thinking in obscenities the way I always have in combat.

The huge shape is gone. There are more screams to my left, explosions straight ahead. *How the hell am I supposed to find the kid in all this carnage? And if I do, how can I find my way to the Third Cave Tomb?* The idea—the Plan—had been for me to swoop Aenea up in the miracle distraction the old poet had promised, make a dash for the Third Cave again, and then punch in the final bit of autopilot for the thirty-klick run for Chronos Keep on the edge of the Bridle Range, where A. Bettik and the spaceship would be waiting for me in . . . three minutes.

Even in all this confusion, whatever the hell it is, there is no way that the orbital torchships or ground-based AA batteries can miss something as big as the ship if it hangs around for more than the thirty seconds we'd allotted for it to be on the ground. This whole rescue mission is screwed.

The earth shakes and a boom fills the Valley. Either something huge has blown up—an ammo dump, at least—or something much larger than a skimmer has crashed. A wild red glow illuminates the entire northern part of the Valley, blossoms of flame visible even through the sandstorm. Against that glow I can see scores of armored figures running, firing, flying, falling. One form is smaller than the rest and is unarmored. The barbed giant is standing next to it. The smaller form, still silhouetted against the fiery glow of pure destruction, is attacking the giant, pounding small fists against barbs and spikes.

"Shit!" I crawl toward the hawking mat, cannot find it in the storm, rub sand out of my eyes, crawl in a circle, and feel cloth under my right palm. In the seconds I have been off the mat, it has become almost buried beneath the sand. Digging like a frenzied dog, I unearth the flight designs, activate the mat, and fly toward the fading glow. The two figures are no longer visible, but I have kept the presence of mind to take a compass reading. Two lance bolts scorch the air—one centimeters above my prone body, one millimeters under the mat.

"Shit! Goddamn!" I shout to no one in particular.

FATHER CAPTAIN DE SOYA is only semiconscious as he bounces along on Sergeant Gregorius's armored shoulder. De Soya half senses other dark shapes running through the storm with them, occasionally firing plasma bolts at unseen targets, and he wonders if this is the rest of Gregorius's squad. Fading in and out of awareness, he desperately wishes he could see the girl again, talk to her.

Gregorius almost runs into something, stops, orders his squad to close up. A scarab armored fighting vehicle has dropped its camouflage shield and is sitting askew on a boulder. The left track is missing, and the barrels of the rear miniguns have been melted like wax in a flame. The right eye blister is shattered and gaping.

"Here," pants Gregorius, and carefully lowers Father Captain de Soya through the blister. A second later the sergeant pulls himself through, illuminating the interior of the scarab with the torch beam on his energy lance. The driver's seat looks as if someone has spray-painted it red. The rear bulkheads seem to have been spattered with random colors, rather like some absurd pre-Hegira "abstract art" Father Captain de Soya once saw in a museum. Only this metal canvas has been daubed with human parts.

Sergeant Gregorius pulls him deeper into the tilted scarab and leans the torchship captain against the lower bulkhead. Two other suited figures squeeze through the shattered blister.

De Soya rubs blood and sand out of his eyes and says, "I'm all right." He had meant to say it in a command tone, but his voice is weak, almost childlike.

"Yessir," growls Gregorius. The sergeant is pulling his medkit from his beltpak.

"I don't need that," de Soya says weakly. "The suit . . ." All combat suits have their own sealant and semi-intelligent doc liners. De Soya is sure that for such minor slash or puncture wounds, the suit has already dealt with it. But now he looks down.

His left leg has been all but severed. The impact-proof, energy-resistant, omnipolymer combat armor is hanging in shreds, like tattered rubber on a cheap tire. He can see the white of his femur. The suit has tightened into a crude tourniquet around his upper thigh, saving his life, but there are half a dozen serious puncture wounds in his chest armor, and the medlights on his chest display are blinking red.

"Ah, Jesus," whispers Father Captain de Soya. It is a prayer.

"It's all right," says Sergeant Gregorius, tightening his own tourniquet around the thigh. "We'll be getting you to a medic and then liftin' you to the ship's hospital in no time, sir." He looks to the two suited figures crouched in exhaustion behind the front seats. "Kee? Rettig?"

"Yes, Sergeant?" The smaller of the two figures looks up.

"Mellick and Ott?"

"Dead, Sergeant. The thing got them at the Sphinx."

"Stay on the net," says Sergeant Gregorius, and turns back to de Soya. The noncom removes his gauntlet and touches huge fingers to one of the larger puncture wounds. "Does that hurt, sir?"

De Soya shakes his head. He cannot feel the touch.

"All right," says the sergeant, but he looks displeased. He begins calling on the tactical net.

"The girl," says Father Captain de Soya. "We have to find the girl."

"Yes, sir," says Gregorius, but continues calling on different channels. De Soya listens now and can hear the babble.

"Look out! Christ! It's coming back. . . ."

"*St. Bonaventure! St. Bonaventure!* You are venting into space! Say again, you are venting into . . ."

"Scorpion one-niner to any controller . . . Jesus . . . Scorpion one-niner, left engine out, any controller . . . can't see the Valley . . . will divert . . ."

"Jamie! Jamie! Oh, God . . ."

"Get off the net! Crossdammit, maintain com discipline! Get off the fucking net!"

"Our Father, who art in heaven, hallowed be Thy name . . ."

"Watch the fucking . . . oh, shit . . . the fucking thing took a hit but . . . shit . . ."

"Multiple bogeys . . . say again . . . multiple bogeys . . . disregard fire control . . . there are multiple . . ." This is interrupted by screams.

"Command One, come in. Command One, come in."

Feeling consciousness draining from him like the blood pooling under his ruined leg, de Soya flips down his visors. The tactical display is garbage. He keys the tightbeam com channel to Barnes-Avne's command skimmer. "Commander, this is Father Captain de Soya. Commander?"

The line is no longer operative.

"The Commander is dead, sir," says Gregorius, pressing an adrenaline ampule against de Soya's bare arm. The father-captain has no memory of his gauntlet and combat armor being removed. "I saw her skimmer go in on tactical before it all went to hell," continues the sergeant, wiring de Soya's dangling leg to his upper thighbone like someone tying down loose cargo. "She's dead, sir. Colonel Brideson's not responding. Captain Ranier's not answering from the torchship. The C-three ain't answerin'."

De Soya fights to stay conscious. "What's happening, Sergeant?"

Gregorius leans closer. His visors are up, and de Soya sees for the first time that the giant is a black man. "We had a phrase for this in the Marines before I joined Swiss Guard, sir."

"Charlie Fox," says Father Captain de Soya, trying to smile.

"That's what you polite navy types call it," agrees Gregorius. He gestures the other two troopers toward the broken blister. They crawl out. Gregorius lifts de Soya and carries him out like a baby. "In the Marines, sir," continues the sergeant, not even breathing heavily, "we called it a cluster fuck."

De Soya feels himself fading. The sergeant sets him down on the sand.

"You stay with me, Captain! Goddammit, you hear me? You stay with me!" Gregorius is shouting.

"Watch your language, Sergeant," says de Soya, feeling himself sliding into unconsciousness but unable and unwilling to do anything about it. "I'm a priest, remember. . . . Taking the name of God in vain is a mortal sin." The blackness is closing in, and Father Captain de Soya does not know if he has said the last sentence aloud or not.

15

INCE I WAS A BOY on the moors, standing apart to watch smoke from the peat fires rise from within the protective ring of circled caravans, waiting for the stars to appear, then seeing them cold and indifferent in the deepening lapis sky and wondering about my future while waiting for the call that would bring me in to warmth and dinner, I have had a sense of the irony of things. So many important things pass quickly without being understood at the time. So many powerful moments are buried beneath the absurd. I saw this as a child. I have seen it throughout my life since then.

Flying toward the fading orange light of the explosion, I suddenly came across the child, Aenea. My first glimpse had been of two figures, the small one attacking the huge one, but when I arrived a moment later, sand howling and rasping around the bobbing hawking mat, there was only the girl.

This is the way we looked to each other at that moment: the girl with an expression of shock and anger, eyes red and narrowed against the sand or from her fury at something, her small fists clenched, her shirt and loose sweater flapping like wild banners in the wind, her shoulder-length hair—brown but with blond streaks that I would notice later—matted and blowing, her cheeks streaked with the muddy path of tears and snot, her rubber-soled, canvas kid's shoes totally inappropriate to the adventure upon which she'd embarked, and her cheap backpack hanging from one shoulder; I must have been a wilder, less sane sight—a bulky, muscled, not-very-bright-looking twenty-seven-year-old lying flat on my belly on a flying carpet, my face largely obscured by the bandanna and dark glasses, my short hair filthy and spiked in the wind, my pack also lashed over one shoulder, my vest and trousers filthy with sand and grime.

The girl's eyes widened in recognition, but it took only a second for me to realize that she was recognizing the hawking mat, not me.

"Get on!" I shouted. Armored forms ran by, firing as they went. Other shadows loomed in the storm.

The girl ignored me, turning away as if to find the shape she had been attacking. I noticed then that her fists were bleeding. "Goddamn him," she was shouting, almost weeping. "God*damn* him."

These were the first words I heard our messiah utter.

"Get on!" I shouted again, and began to dismount from the hawking mat to seize her.

Aenea turned, looked at me for the first time, and—somehow clearly over the rasping sandstorm—said, "Take that mask off."

I remembered the bandanna. Lowering it, I spit sand as red mud.

As if satisfied, the girl stepped closer and jumped onto the mat. Now we were both sitting on the hovering, bobbing carpet—the girl behind me, our backpacks squeezed between us. I tugged the bandanna back up and shouted, "Hang on to me!"

She ignored me and gripped the edges of the mat.

I hesitated a moment, tugging my sleeve back to study my wrist chronometer. Less than two minutes remained before the ship was scheduled to perform its touch-and-go at Chronos Keep. I couldn't even find the entrance to the Third Cave Tomb in that time—perhaps I could never find it in this carnage. As if to underline that point, a tracked scarab suddenly plowed over a dune, almost grinding us under its treads before it wheeled left, guns firing at something out of sight to the east.

"Hang on!" I shouted again, and keyed the mat to full acceleration, gaining altitude as I went, watching my compass and concentration on flying north until we left the Valley. This was no time to crash into a cliff wall.

A great stone wing passed under us. "Sphinx!" I shouted back to the girl huddling behind me. I realized in an instant how stupid this comment was—she had just come from that tomb.

Guessing our altitude to be several hundred meters, I leveled off and increased our speed. The deflection shield came on, but sand still whirled around us within the nacelle of trapped air. "We shouldn't hit anything at this altitu—" I began, shouting over my shoulder again, but was interrupted by the looming shape of a skimmer flying directly at us in the storm cloud. I did not have time to react, but somehow I did, diving the mat so quickly that only the containment field held us in place, the shape of the skimmer passing over us with less than a meter to spare. The little hawking mat tumbled and twisted in the monster machine's lift-wake.

"Heck and spit," said Aenea behind me. "Hell and shit."

It was the second utterance I heard from our messiah-to-be.

Leveling off again, I peered over the edge of the mat, trying to make out anything on the ground. It was folly to be flying so high—certainly every tactical sensor, detector, radar, and targeting imager in the area was tracking us. Except for the taste of chaos we had left behind, I had no idea why they hadn't fired at us yet. Unless . . . I looked over my shoulder again. The girl was leaning close to my back, shielding her face from the stinging sand.

"Are you all right?" I called.

She nodded, her forehead touching my back. I had the sense that she was crying, but I could not be sure.

"I'm Raul Endymion," I shouted.

"Endymion," she said, pulling her head back. Her eyes were red, but dry. "Yes."

"You're Aenea . . ." I stopped. I could not think of anything intelligent to say. Checking the compass, I adjusted our direction of flight and hoped that our altitude was sufficient to clear the dunes here beyond the Valley. Without much hope, I looked up, wondering if the plasma trail of the ship would be visible through the storm. I saw nothing.

"Uncle Martin sent you," said the girl. It was not a question.

"Yes," I shouted back. "We're going . . . well, the ship . . . I'd arranged for it to meet us at Chronos Keep, but we're late. . . ."

A bolt of lightning ripped the clouds not thirty meters to our right. Both the child and I flinched and ducked. To this day I do not know if it was a lightning discharge or someone shooting at us. For the hundredth time on this endless day, I cursed the crudeness of this ancient flying device —no speed indicators, no altimeter. The wind roar beyond the deflection field suggested that we were traveling at full speed, but with no guidepoints except the shifting curtains of cloud, it was impossible to tell. It was as bad as hurtling through the Labyrinth, but at least there the autopilot program had been dependable. Here, even with the entire Swiss Guard after us, I would have to decelerate soon: the Bridle Range of mountains with their vertical cliffs lay somewhere dead ahead. At almost three hundred klicks per hour, we should reach the mountains and the Keep within six minutes. I had checked my chronometer when we accelerated, now I glanced at it again. Four and a half minutes. According to maps I had studied, the desert ended abruptly at the Bridle Cliffs. I would give it another minute. . . .

Things happened simultaneously then.

Suddenly we were out of the dust storm; it did not taper off, we just flew out of it the way one would emerge from under a blanket. At that second I saw that we were pitched slightly down—or the ground here was rising—and that we were going to strike some huge boulders within seconds.

Aenea shouted. I ignored her, tweaked the control designs with both hands, we lifted over the boulders with enough g-force to press us heavily against the hawking mat, and at that instant both the child and I saw that we were twenty meters from the cliff face and flying into it. There was no time to stop.

Theoretically, I knew, Sholokov's design for the hawking mat allowed it to fly vertically, the incipient containment field keeping the passenger—theoretically, his beloved niece—from tumbling off backward. Theoretically.

It was time to test the theory.

Aenea's arms came around my midsection as we accelerated into a ninety-degree climb. The mat took all of the twenty meters of free space to initiate the climb, and by the time we were vertical, the granite of the rock face was centimeters "beneath" us. Instinctively, I leaned full forward and grabbed the rigid front of the carpet, trying not to lean on the flight-control designs as I did so. Equally instinctively, Aenea leaned forward and increased her bear hug on my midsection. The effect was that I could not breathe for the minute or so it took the carpet to clear the top of the cliffs. I tried not to look back over my shoulder during the duration of the climb. A thousand or more meters of open space directly beneath me might have been more than my overworked nerves could stand.

We reached the top of the cliffs—suddenly there were stairs carved there, stone terraces, gargoyles—and I leveled the carpet.

The Swiss Guard had set up observation posts, detector stations, and antiaircraft batteries here along the terraces and balconies on the east side of Chronos Keep. The castle itself—carved out of the stone of the mountain—loomed more than a hundred meters above us, its overhanging turrets and higher balconies directly above us. There were more Swiss Guard on these flat areas.

All of them were dead. Their bodies, still clad in impermeable impact armor, were sprawled in the unmistakable attitudes of death. Some were grouped together, their lacerated forms looking as if a plasma bomb had exploded in their midst.

But Pax body armor could withstand a plasma grenade at that distance. These corpses had been shredded.

"Don't look," I called over my shoulder, slowing the mat as we banked around the south end of the Keep. It was too late. Aenea stared with wide eyes.

"Damn him!" she cried again.

"Damn who?" I asked, but at that moment we flew out over the garden area on the south end of the Keep and saw what was there. Burning scarabs and an overturned skimmer littered the landscape. More bodies lay thrown like toys scattered by a vicious child. A CPB lancet, its beams capable of reaching to low orbit, lay shattered and burning by an ornamental hedge.

The Consul's ship hovered on a tail of blue plasma sixty meters above the central fountain. Steam billowed up and around it. A. Bettik stood at the open air-lock door and beckoned us on.

I flew us directly into the air lock, so quickly that the android had to leap aside and we actually skittered down the polished corridor.

"Go!" I shouted, but either A. Bettik had already given the command or the ship did not require it. Inertial compensators kept us from being smashed to jelly as the ship accelerated, but we could hear the fusion reaction-drive roar, hear the scream of atmosphere from beyond the hull, as the Consul's spaceship climbed away from Hyperion and entered space again for the first time in two centuries.

16

HOW LONG HAVE I been unconscious?" Father Captain de Soya is gripping the tunic of the medic.

"Uh . . . thirty, forty minutes, sir," said the medic, attempting to pull his shirt free. He does not succeed.

"Where am I?" De Soya feels the pain now. It is very intense—centered in his leg but radiating everywhere—but bearable. He ignores it.

"Aboard the *St. Thomas Akira,* Father sir."

"The troopship . . ." De Soya feels light-headed, unconnected. He looks down at his leg, now freed from its tourniquet. The lower leg is attached to the upper only by fragments of muscle and tissue. He realizes that Gregorius must have given him a painkiller—insufficient to block such a torrent of agony, but enough to give him this narcotic high. "Damn."

"I'm afraid that the surgeons are going to amputate," says the medic. "The surgeries are working overtime. You're next, though, sir. We've been carrying out triage and . . ."

De Soya realizes that he is still gripping the young medic's tunic. He releases it. "No."

"Excuse me, Father sir?"

"You heard me. There'll be no surgery until I've met with the captain of the *St. Thomas Akira.*"

"But sir . . . Father sir . . . you'll die if you don't . . ."

"I've died before, son." De Soya fights off a wave of giddiness. "Did a sergeant bring me to the ship?"

"Yessir."

"Is he still here?"

"Yes, Father sir, the sergeant was receiving stitches for wounds that . . ."

"Send him in here immediately."

"But, Father sir, your wounds require . . ."

De Soya looks at the young medic's rank. "Ensign?"

"Yessir?"

"You saw the papal diskey?" De Soya has checked; the platinum template still hangs from the unbreakable chain around his neck.

"Yes, Father sir, that's what led us to prioritize your . . ."

"Upon pain of execution . . . and worse . . . upon pain of excommunication, shut up and send the sergeant in immediately, Ensign."

Gregorius is out of his battle armor, but is still huge. The father-captain looks at the bandages and temporary doc paks on the big man's body and realizes that the sergeant had been badly wounded even as he was carrying de Soya out of danger. He makes a note to respond to that sometime—not now. "Sergeant!"

Gregorius snaps to attention.

"Bring the captain of this ship here immediately. Quickly, before I black out again."

THE CAPTAIN of the *St. Thomas Akira* is a middle-aged Lusian, as short and powerful looking as all Lusians. He is perfectly bald but sports a neatly trimmed gray beard.

"Father Captain de Soya, I am Captain Lempriere. Things are very hectic now, sir. The surgeons assure me that you require immediate attention. How can I be of help?"

"Tell me the situation, Captain." De Soya has not met the captain before, but they have spoken on tightbeam. He hears the deference in the troopship captain's voice. Out of the corner of his eye, de Soya sees Sergeant Gregorius excusing himself from the room. "Stay, Sergeant. Captain? The situation?"

Lempriere clears his throat. "Commander Barnes-Avne is dead. As far as we can tell, about half of the Swiss Guard in the Valley of the Time Tombs are also dead. Thousands of other casualties are pouring in. We have medics on the ground setting up mobile surgical centers, and we are ferrying the most severely wounded here for urgent care. The dead are being recovered and tagged for resurrection upon return to Renaissance Vector."

"Renaissance Vector?" De Soya feels as if he is floating within the confined space of the surgical prep room. He *is* floating—within the confines of the gurney restraints. "What the hell happened to the gravity, Captain?"

Lempriere smiles wanly. "The containment field was damaged during the battle, sir. As for Renaissance Vector . . . well, it was our staging area, sir. Standing orders call for us to return there after the mission is completed."

De Soya laughs, stopping only when he hears himself. It is not a totally sane laugh. "Who says our mission is completed, Captain? What battle are we talking about?"

Captain Lempriere glances at Sergeant Gregorius. The Swiss Guard does not break his fixed, at-attention stare at the bulkhead. "The support and covering craft in orbit were also decimated, sir."

"Decimated?" The pain is making de Soya angry. "That means one in ten, Captain. Are ten percent of ship's personnel on the casualty list?"

"No, sir," says Lempriere, "more like sixty percent. Captain Ramirez of the *St. Bonaventure* is dead, as is his executive officer. My own first is dead. Half the crew of the *St. Anthony* have not answered roll."

"Are the ships damaged?" demands Father Captain de Soya. He knows that he has only a minute or two of consciousness . . . and perhaps life . . . left.

"There was an explosion on the *St. Bonaventure*. At least half the compartments aft of the CIC vented to space. The drive is intact. . . ."

De Soya closes his eyes. As a torchship captain himself, he knows that opening the craft to space is the penultimate nightmare. The ultimate nightmare was the implosion of the Hawking core itself, but at least that indignity would be instantaneous. Having a hull breached across so many of the ship's areas was—like this shattered leg—a slow, painful path to death.

"The *St. Anthony*?"

"Damaged, but operable, sir. Captain Sati is alive and . . ."

"The girl?" demands de Soya. "Where is she?" Black spots dance in the periphery of his vision, and the cloud of them grows.

"Girl?" says Lempriere. Sergeant Gregorius says something to the captain that de Soya does not hear. There is a loud buzzing in his ears.

"Oh, yes," says Lempriere, "the acquisition objective. Evidently a ship retrieved her from the surface and is accelerating toward C-plus translation. . . ."

"A ship!" De Soya fights away unconsciousness with a sheer effort of will. "Where the hell did a ship come from?"

Gregorius speaks without breaking his staring match with the bulkhead. "From the planet, sir. From Hyperion. During the . . . during the Charlie Fox event, the ship skipped through the atmosphere, set down at the castle . . . Chronos Keep, sir . . . and plucked the kid and whoever was flying her—"

"Flying her?" interrupts de Soya. It is hard to hear through the growing buzz.

"Some sort of one-person EMV," says the sergeant. "Although why it works, the tech boffins don't know. Anyway, this ship got 'em, got past the COP during the carnage, and is spinning up to translation."

"Carnage," repeats de Soya stupidly. He realizes that he is drooling. He wipes his chin with the back of his hand, trying not to look down at the remnants of his leg as he does so. "Carnage. What caused it? Who were we fighting?"

"We don't know, sir," answers Lempriere. "It was like the old days . . . Hegemony Force days when the jumptroops came in by far-caster portal, sir. I mean, thousands of armored . . . things . . . appeared, everywhere, at the same second, sir. I mean, the battle only lasted five minutes. There were thousands of them. And then they were gone."

De Soya is straining to hear this through the gathering darkness and the roaring in his ears, but the words make no sense. "Thousands? Of what? Gone where?"

Gregorius steps forward and looks down at the father-captain. "Not thousands, sir. Just one. The Shrike."

"That's a legend . . . ," begins Lempriere.

"Just the Shrike," continues the huge black man, ignoring the troop-ship captain. "It killed most of the Swiss Guard and half the regular Pax troops on Equus, downed all of the Scorpion fighters, took two torchships of the line out of business, killed everyone aboard the C-three ship, left his calling card here, and was gone in under thirty seconds. Total. All the rest was our guys shooting each other in panic. The Shrike."

"Nonsense!" shouts Lempriere, his bare scalp growing red with agitation. "That's a fantasy, a tall tale, and a heresy at that! Whatever struck us today was no . . ."

"Shut up," says de Soya. He feels as if he is looking and talking down a long, dark tunnel. Whatever he has to say, he must say quickly. "Listen . . . Captain Lempriere . . . on my authority, on papal authority, authorize Captain Sati to take the survivors of the *St. Bonaventure* aboard the *St. Anthony* to round out the crew. Order Sati to follow the girl . . . the spacecraft bearing the girl . . . follow it to spinup, to fix its translation coordinates, and to follow . . ."

"But, Father Captain . . . ," begins Lempriere.

"Listen," shouts de Soya over the waterfall noise in his ears. He can no longer see anything but dancing spots. "Listen . . . order Captain Sati to follow that ship anywhere . . . even if it takes a lifetime . . . and to capture the girl. That is his prime and total directive. Capture the girl and return her to Pacem. Gregorius?"

"Yes, sir."

"Don't let them operate on me, Sergeant. Is my courier ship still intact?"

"The *Raphael*? Yes, sir. It was empty during the battle, the Shrike didn't touch it."

"Is Hiroshe . . . my dropship pilot . . . still around?"

"No, sir. He was killed."

De Soya can barely hear the sergeant's booming voice over the louder booming. "Requisition a pilot and shuttle, Sergeant. Get me, you, and the rest of your squad—"

"Just two men now, sir."

"Listen. Get the four of us to the *Raphael*. The ship will know what to do. Tell it that we're going to follow the girl . . . the ship . . . and the *St. Anthony*. Wherever those ships go, we go. Sergeant?"

"Yes, Father Captain!"

"You and your men are born again, aren't you?"

"Yes, Father Captain!"

"Well, prepare to be born again for real, Sergeant."

"But your leg . . . ," says Captain Lempriere from very, very far away. His voice Doppler-shifts as it recedes.

"I'll be reunited with it when I'm resurrected," mutters Father Captain de Soya. He wants to close his eyes to say a prayer now, but he does not have to close his eyes to shut out the light—the darkness around him is absolute. Into that roaring and buzzing, not knowing if anyone can hear him or if he is really speaking, he says, "Quickly, Sergeant. Now!"

17

OW, WRITING THIS so many years later, I had thought it would be difficult to remember Aenea as a child. It is not. My memories are so full of later years, later images—rich sunlight on the woman's body as we floated among the branches of the orbital forest, the first time we made love in zero-gravity, strolling with her along the hangway walkways of Hsuan-k'ung Su with the rose-red cliffs of Hua Shan catching the rich light above us—that I had worried that those earlier memories would be too insubstantial. They are not. Nor have I given in to the impulse to leap ahead to the later years, despite my fear that this narrative will be interrupted at any second with the quantum-mechanical hiss of Schrödinger's poison gas. I will write what I can write. Fate will determine the ending point of this narrative.

A. Bettik led the way up the spiral staircase to the room with a piano as we roared up into space. The containment field kept the gravity constant, despite the wild acceleration, but still there was a wild sense of exhilaration in me—although perhaps it was just the aftermath of so much adrenaline in so little time. The child was dirty, disheveled, and still upset.

"I want to see where we are," she said. "Please."

The ship complied by turning the wall beyond the holopit into a window. The continent of Equus receded below, the face of the horse obscured by red dust cloud. To the north, where clouds covered the pole, the limb of Hyperion arced into a distinct curve. Within a minute the entire world was a globe, two of the three continents visible beneath scattered cloud, the Great South Sea a breathtaking blue while the Nine Tails archipelago was surrounded by the green of shallows, and then the world shrank, became a blue-and-red-and-white sphere, and fell behind. We were leaving in a hurry.

"Where are the torchships?" I asked the android. "They should have challenged us by now. Or blown us to bits."

"The ship and I were monitoring their wideband channels," said A. Bettik. "They were . . . preoccupied."

"I don't understand," I said, pacing the rim of the holopit, too agitated to sit in the deep cushions. "That battle . . . who . . ."

"The Shrike," said Aenea, and really looked at me for the first time. "Mother and I hoped it would not happen like that, but it did. I am so sorry. So terribly sorry."

Realizing that the girl probably had not heard me in the storm, I paused in my pacing, dropped to the arm of the couch, and said, "We didn't have much of an introduction. I'm Raul Endymion."

The girl's eyes were bright. Despite the mud and grit on her cheek, I could see the fairness of her complexion. "I remember," she said. "Endymion, like the poem."

"Poem?" I said. "I don't know about a poem. It's Endymion like the old city."

She smiled. "I only know the poem because my father wrote it. How fitting of Uncle Martin to choose a hero with such a name."

I squirmed at hearing the word "hero." This whole endeavor was turning out to be absurd enough without that.

The girl held out her small hand. "Aenea," she said. "But you know that."

Her fingers were cool in my palm. "The old poet said that you had changed your name a few times."

Her smile lingered. "And will again, I wager." She withdrew her hand and then offered it to the android. "Aenea. Orphan of time."

A. Bettik shook her hand more gracefully than I had, bowed deeply, and introduced himself. "I am at your service, M. Lamia," he said.

She shook her head. "My mother is . . . was . . . M. Lamia. I'm just Aenea." She noticed my change in expression. "You know of my mother?"

"She is famous," I said, blushing slightly for some reason. "All of the Hyperion pilgrims are. Legendary, actually. There is this poem, epic oral tale, actually . . ."

Aenea laughed. "Oh, God, Uncle Martin finished his damn *Cantos*."

I admit that I was shocked. My face must have shown it. I'm glad I was not playing poker this particular morning.

"Sorry," said Aenea. "Obviously the old satyr's scribblings have become some sort of priceless cultural heritage. He's still alive? Uncle Martin, I mean."

"Yes, M. . . . yes, M. Aenea," said A. Bettik. "I have had the privilege of serving your uncle for over a century."

The girl made a face. "You must be a saint, M. Bettik."

"A. Bettik, M. Aenea," he said. "And no, I am no saint. Merely an admirer and long acquaintance of your uncle."

Aenea nodded. "I met a few androids when we would fly up from Jacktown to visit Uncle Martin in the Poet's City, but not you. More than a century, you say. What year is it?"

I told her.

"Well, we got that part right, at least," she said, and fell silent, staring at the holo of the receding world. Hyperion was only a spark now.

"You've really come from the past?" I said. It was a stupid question, but I wasn't feeling especially bright that morning.

Aenea nodded. "Uncle Martin must have told you."

"Yes. You're fleeing the Pax."

She looked up. Her eyes were bright with unshed tears. "The Pax? Is that what they call it?"

I blinked at that. The thought of someone being unfamiliar with the concept of the Pax shook me. This was real. "Yes," I said.

"So the Church does run everything now?"

"Well, in a way," I said. I explained the role of the Church in the complex entity that was the Pax.

"They run everything," concluded Aenea. "We thought it might go that way. My dreams got that right, too."

"Your dreams?"

"Never mind," said Aenea. She stood, looked around the room, and walked to the Steinway. Her fingers picked out a few notes on the keyboard. "And this is the Consul's ship."

"Yes," said the ship, "although I have only vague memories of the gentleman. Did you know him?"

Aenea smiled, her fingers still trailing across the keys. "No. My mother did. She gave him a present of that—" She pointed to the sand-covered hawking mat where it lay near the staircase. "When he left Hyperion after the Fall. He was going back to the Web. He didn't return during my time."

"He never did," said the ship. "As I say, my memories have been damaged, but I am sure that he died somewhere there." The ship's soft voice changed, became more businesslike. "We were hailed upon leaving the atmosphere, but have not been challenged or pursued since then. We have cleared cislunar space and will be out of Hyperion's critical gravity well within ten minutes. I need to set course for spinup. Instructions, please."

I looked at the girl. "The Ousters? That's where the old poet said you'd want to go."

"I changed my mind," said Aenea. "What's the nearest inhabited world, Ship?"

"Parvati. One-point-two-eight parsecs. Six and a half days shiptime transit. Three months time-debt."

"Was Parvati part of the Web?" asked the girl.

A. Bettik answered. "No. Not at the time of the Fall."

"What's the nearest old Web world, traveling from Parvati?" said Aenea.

"Renaissance Vector," said the ship immediately. "It is an additional ten days shiptime, five months time-debt."

I was frowning. "I don't know," I said. "The hunters . . . I mean, offworlders I used to work for usually came from Renaissance Vector. It's a big Pax world. Busy. Lots of ships and troops there, I think."

"But it's the closest Web world?" said Aenea. "It used to have farcasters."

"Yes," said the ship and A. Bettik at the same moment.

"Set course for Renaissance Vector by way of Parvati System," said Aenea.

"It would be a shiptime day and two weeks of time-debt quicker to jump directly to Renaissance Vector, if that is our destination," advised the ship.

"I know," said Aenea, "but I want to go by way of Parvati System." She must have seen the question in my eyes, for she said, "They'll be following us, and I don't want them to know the real destination when we spin up out of this system."

"They are not in pursuit now," said A. Bettik.

"I know," said Aenea. "But they will be in a few hours. Then and for the rest of my life." She looked back at the holopit as if the ship's persona resided there. "Carry out the command, please."

The stars shifted on the holodisplay as the ship obeyed. "Twenty-seven minutes to translation point for Parvati System," it said. "Still no challenge or pursuit, although the torchship *St. Anthony* is under way, as is the troopship."

"What about the other torchship?" I said. "The . . . what was it? The *St. Bonaventure*."

"Common band communications traffic and sensors show that it is open to space and emitting distress signals," said the ship. "The *St. Anthony* is responding."

"My God," I whispered. "What was it, an Ouster attack?"

The girl shook her head and walked away from the piano. "Just the Shrike. My father warned me. . . ." She fell silent.

"The Shrike?" It was the android who spoke. "To my knowledge, in legend and the old records, the creature called the Shrike never left Hyperion—usually staying in the area within a few hundred kilometers around the Time Tombs."

Aenea dropped back into the cushions. Her eyes were still red and she looked tired. "Yeah, well, he's wandering farther afield now, I'm afraid. And if Father is right, it's just the beginning."

"The Shrike hasn't been seen or heard from for almost three hundred years," I said.

The girl nodded, distracted. "I know. Not since the tombs opened right before the Fall." She looked up at the android. "Gosh, I'm starved. And filthy."

"I will help the ship prepare lunch," said A. Bettik. "There are showers upstairs in the master bedroom and on the fugue deck below us," he said. "Also a bath in the master bedroom."

"That's where I'm headed," said the girl. "I'll be down before we make the quantum jump. See you in twenty minutes." On her way to the stairs she stopped and took my hand again. "Raul Endymion, I'm sorry if I seem ungrateful. Thank you for risking your life for me. Thank you for coming with me on this trip. Thank you for getting into something so big and complicated that neither one of us can imagine where we're going to end up."

"You're welcome," I said stupidly.

The child grinned at me. "You need a shower, too, friend. Someday we'll take it together, but right now I think you should use the one on the fugue deck."

Blinking, not knowing what to think, I watched her bounce up the stairs.

18

ATHER CAPTAIN DE SOYA awakens in a resurrection creche aboard the *Raphael*. He had been allowed to name the archangel-class ship. Raphael is the archangel in charge of finding lost loves.

He has been reborn only twice before, but each time there had been a priest there to greet him, to give him the ceremonial sip of sacramental wine from the cup and then the customary glass of orange juice. There had been resurrection experts there to talk to him, explain things to him, until his befuddled mind began to work again.

This time there are only the claustrophobic, curved walls of the resurrection creche. Telltales blink and readouts share lines of print and symbols. De Soya cannot read yet. He feels lucky to be thinking at all. He sits up and dangles his legs over the edge of the resurrection bed.

My legs. I have two of them. He is naked, of course, his skin pink and gleaming in the strange, parboiled wetness of the resurrection tank, and now he feels his ribs, his abdomen, his left leg—all the places slashed and ruined by the demon. He is perfect. There is no sign of the terrible wound that had separated his leg from his body.

"Raphael?"

"Yes, Father Captain?" The voice is angelic, which is to say, totally devoid of sexual identity. De Soya finds it soothing.

"Where are we?"

"Parvati System, Father Captain."

"The others?" De Soya has only the foggiest memory of Sergeant Gregorius and his two surviving squad members. No memory of boarding the courier ship with them.

"Being awakened as we speak, Father Captain."

"How much time has passed?"

"Just a bit less than four days since the sergeant brought you aboard,

Father Captain. The enhanced jump was carried out within the hour of your installation in the resurrection creche. We have been station-keeping ten AUs from the world of Parvati, as per your instructions via Sergeant Gregorius, for the three days of your resurrection."

De Soya nods his understanding. Even that slight motion is painful. Every cell in his body aches from resurrection. But the pain is a healthy ache, unlike the terrible pain of his wounds. "Have you contacted the Pax authorities on Parvati?"

"No, Father Captain."

"Good." Parvati had been a remote colony world during the days of the Hegemony; now it is a remote Pax colony. It holds no interstellar spacecraft—Pax military or Mercantilus—and only a small military contingent and a few crude interplanetary ships. If the girl was going to be captured in this system, the *Raphael* would have to do the capturing.

"Update on the girl's ship?" he says.

"The unidentified spacecraft spun up two hours and eighteen minutes before we did," said *Raphael*. "The translation coordinates were undoubtedly for Parvati System. Arrival time for the unidentified ship is approximately two months, three weeks, two days, and seventeen hours."

"Thank you," says de Soya. "When Gregorius and the others are revived and dressed, have them meet me in the situation room."

"Yes, Father Captain."

"Thank you," he says again. He thinks, *Two months, three weeks, two days . . . Mother of Mercy, what am I going to do for almost three months in this backwater system?* Perhaps he had not thought through this clearly. Certainly he had been distracted by trauma, pain, and drugs. But the next nearest Pax system was Renaissance Vector, which was ten days shiptime travel from Parvati, five months time-debt—three and a half days and two months after the girl's ship would arrive from Hyperion System. No, he might not have been thinking clearly—he is not now, he realizes—but he had made the right decision. Better to come here and think things over.

I could jump to Pacem. Ask for instructions directly from Pax Command . . . from the Pope, even. Recuperate for two and a half months and jump back here with time to spare.

De Soya shakes his head, grimaces from the discomfort of doing so. He has his instructions. Capture the girl and return her to Pacem. Returning to the Vatican would be only an admission of failure. Perhaps they would send someone else. During the preflight briefing, Captain Marget Wu had made it clear that the *Raphael* was unique—the only armed, six-person archangel-class courier ship in existence—and although another might have come on-line in the months of time-debt that have elapsed since he left Pacem, there is little sense in returning now. If *Raphael* was still the only armed archangel, all de Soya could do would be add two more troopers to the ship's roster.

Death and resurrection are not to be taken lightly. That precept had been driven home time and again in de Soya's catechism when he was growing up. Just because the sacrament exists and is offered to the faithful, does not mean it should be exercised without great solemnity and restraint.

No, I'll talk to Gregorius and the others and figure things out here. We can make our plans, then use the cryogenic-fugue cubbies to wait the last couple of months. When the girl's ship arrives, the St. Anthony *will be in hot pursuit. Between the torchship and* Raphael, *we should be able to interdict the ship, board her, and retrieve the girl without problem.*

Logically, this all makes sense to de Soya's aching brain, but another part of his mind is whispering, *Without problem . . . this is what you thought about the Hyperion mission.*

Father Captain de Soya groans, lifts himself down from the resurrection couch, and pads off in search of a shower, hot coffee, and some clothes.

19

I KNEW LITTLE ABOUT the principles of the Hawking drive when I first experienced it years ago; I know little more about it now. The fact that it was essentially (if accidentally) the brainchild of someone who lived in the twentieth century, Christian Era, boggled my mind then as it does now, but not nearly as much as the experience itself.

We met in the library—formally known as the navigation level, the ship informed us—a few minutes before translation to C-plus speeds. I was dressed in my spare set of clothes and my hair was wet, as was Aenea's. The child wore only a thick robe, which she must have found in the Consul's closet, because the garment was far too large for her. She looked even younger than her twelve years, swallowed as she was in all those yards of terry cloth.

"Shouldn't we be getting to the cryogenic-fugue couches?" I asked.

"Why?" said Aenea. "Don't you want to see the fun?"

I frowned. All the offworld hunters and military instructors I had spoken to had spent their C-plus time in fugue. That's the way humans had always spent their time between the stars. Something about the effect of the Hawking field on the body and mind. I had images of hallucinations, waking nightmares, and unspeakable pain. I said as much while trying to sound calm about it.

"Mother and Uncle Martin told me that C-plus can be endured," said the girl. "Even enjoyed. It just takes some getting used to."

"And this ship was modified by the Ousters to make it easier," said A. Bettik. Aenea and I were sitting at the low glass table in the middle of the library area; the android stood to one side. Try as I might to treat him as an equal, A. Bettik insisted on acting like a servant. I resolved to quit being an egalitarian horse's ass about it and to let him act any way he wanted.

"Indeed," said the ship, "the modifications included an enhanced containment field capability, which makes the side effects of C-plus travel much less disagreeable."

"What exactly *are* the side effects?" I asked, not willing to show the full extent of my naïveté, but also not willing to suffer if I didn't have to.

The android, the girl, and I looked at each other. "I have traveled between the stars in centuries past," A. Bettik said at last, "but I was always in fugue. In storage, actually. We androids were shipped in cargo holds, stacked like frozen sides of beef, I am told."

Now the girl and I looked at each other, embarrassed to meet the blue-skinned man's gaze.

The ship made a noise that sounded remarkably like someone clearing his throat. "Actually," it said, "from my observations of human passengers—which, I must say, is suspect because . . ."

"Because your memory is hazy," the girl and I said in unison. We looked at each other again and laughed. "Sorry, Ship," said Aenea. "Go on."

"I was just going to say that from my observations, the primary effect of the C-plus environment on humans is some visual confusion, mental depression brought about by the field, and simple boredom. I believe that cryogenic fugue was developed for the long voyages, and is used as a convenience for shorter trips such as this."

"And your . . . ah . . . Ouster modifications ameliorate these side effects?" I said.

"They are designed to," replied the ship. "All except boredom, of course. That is a peculiarly human phenomenon, and I do not believe that a cure has been found." There was a moment of silence, and then the ship said, "We will reach the translation point in two minutes ten seconds. All systems are functioning optimally. Still no pursuit, although the *St. Anthony* is tracking us on its long-range detectors."

Aenea stood up. "Let's go down and watch the shift to C-plus."

"Go down and watch?" I said. "Where? The holopit?"

"No," called the girl from the stairway. "From outside."

THE SPACESHIP had a balcony. I hadn't known that. One could stand outside on it even while the ship was hurtling through space, preparing to translate to C-plus pseudo-velocities. I hadn't known that—and if I had, I would not have believed it.

"Extend the balcony, please," the girl had said to the ship, and the ship had extended the balcony—the Steinway moving out with it—and we'd walked through the open archway into space. Well, not really into space, of course; even I, the provincial shepherd, knew that our eardrums would have exploded, our eyes burst, and our blood boiled in our bodies if we had stepped into hard vacuum. But it *looked* as if we were walking out into hard vacuum.

"Is this safe?" I asked, leaning against the railing. Hyperion was a star-sized speck behind us, Hyperion's star a blazing sun to port, but the plasma tail of our fusion drive—tens of klicks long—gave the impression that we were perched precariously on a tall blue pillar. The effect was a definite inducement to acrophobia, the illusion of standing unprotected in space created something akin to agoraphobia. I had not known until that instant that I was susceptible to any phobia.

"If the containment field fails for a second," said A. Bettik, "under this g-load and velocity, we will die immediately. It matters little if we are inside or outside the ship."

"Radiation?" I said.

"The field deflects cosmic and harmful solar radiation, of course," said the android, "and opaques the view of Hyperion's sun so that we do not go blind when we stare at it. Other than that, it allows the visible spectrum through quite nicely."

"Yes," I said, not convinced. I stepped back from the railing.

"Thirty seconds to translation," said the ship. Even out here, its voice seemed to emanate from midair.

Aenea sat at the piano bench and began playing. I did not recognize the tune, but it sounded classical . . . something from the twenty-sixth century, perhaps.

I guess that I had expected the ship to speak again prior to the actual moment of translation—intone a final countdown or something—but there was no announcement. Suddenly the Hawking drive took over from the fusion drive; there was a momentary hum, which seemed to come from my bones; a terrible vertigo flooded over me and through me—it felt as if I were being turned inside out, painlessly but relentlessly; and then the sensation was gone before I could really comprehend it.

Space was also gone. By space, I mean the scene that I had been viewing less than a second earlier—Hyperion's brilliant sun, the receding disk of the planet itself, the bright glare along the hull of the ship, the few bright stars visible through that glare, even the pillar of blue flame upon which we had been perched—all gone. In its place was . . . It is hard to describe.

The ship was still there, looming "above and below" us—the balcony upon which we stood still seemed substantial—but there seemed to be no light striking any part of it. I realize how absurd that sounds even as I write the words—there must be reflected light for anything to be seen— but the effect was truly as if part of my eyes had ceased working, and while they registered the *shape* and *mass* of the ship, light seemed to be missing.

Beyond the ship, the universe had contracted into a blue sphere near the bow and a red sphere behind the fins at the stern. I knew enough basic science to have expected a Doppler effect, but this was a false effect, since we had not been anywhere near the speed of light until translation to C-plus and were now far beyond it within the Hawking fold. Nonetheless, the blue and red circles of light—I could make out stars clustered in both spheres if I stared hard enough—now migrated farther to the bow and stern, shrinking to tiny dots of color. In between, filling the vast field of vision, there was . . . nothing. By that, I do not mean blackness or darkness. I mean void. I mean the sense of sickening nonsight one has when trying to look into a blind spot. I mean a nothing so intense that the vertigo it induced almost immediately changed to nausea within me, racking my system as violently as the transitory sense of being pulled inside out had seconds before.

"My God!" I managed to say, gripping the rail tightly and squeezing my eyes shut. It did not help. The void was there as well. I understood at that second why interstellar voyagers always opted for cryogenic fugue.

Incredibly, unbelievably, Aenea continued playing the piano. The notes were clear, crystalline, as if unmodified by any connecting medium. Even with my eyes closed I could see A. Bettik standing by the door, blue face raised to the void. No, I realized, he was no longer blue . . . colors did not exist here. Nor did black, white, or gray. I wondered if humans who had been blind since birth dreamed of light and colors in this mad way.

"Compensating," said the ship, and its voice had the same crystalline quality as Aenea's piano notes.

Suddenly the void collapsed in on itself, vision returned, and the spheres of red and blue returned fore and aft. Within seconds the blue sphere from the stern migrated along the ship like a doughnut passing over a writing stylus, it merged with the red sphere at the bow, and colored geometries burst without warning from the forward sphere like flying creatures emerging from an egg. I say "colored geometries," but this does nothing to share the complex reality: fractal-generated shapes pulsed and coiled and twisted through what had been the void. Spiral forms, spiked with their own subgeometries, curled in on themselves, spitting smaller forms of the same cobalt and blood-red brilliance. Yellow ovoids became pulsar-precise explosions of light. Mauve and indigo helixes, looking like the universe's DNA, spiraled past us. I could *hear* these colors like distant thunder, like the pounding of surf just beyond the horizon.

I realized that my jaw was hanging slack. I turned away from the railing and tried to concentrate on the girl and android. The colors of the fractal universe played across them. Aenea still played softly, her fingers moving across keys even as she looked up at me and at the fractal heavens beyond me.

"Maybe we should go inside," I said, hearing each word in my own voice hanging separately in the air like icicles along a branch.

"Fascinating," said A. Bettik, arms still folded, his gaze on the tunnel of forms surrounding us. His skin was blue again.

Aenea stopped playing. Perhaps sensing my vertigo and terror for the first time, she rose, took my hand, and led me inside the ship. The balcony followed us in. The hull re-formed. I was able to breathe again.

"WE HAVE SIX DAYS," the girl said. We were sitting in the holopit because the cushions were comfortable there. We had eaten, and A. Bettik had fetched us cold fruit drinks from the refrigerator drawers. My hand shook only slightly as we sat and talked.

"Six days, nine hours, and twenty-seven minutes," said the ship.

Aenea looked up at the bulkhead. "Ship, you can stay quiet for a while unless there's something vital you have to say or we have a question for you."

"Yes, M. . . . Aenea," said the ship.

"Six days," repeated the girl. "We have to get ready."

I sipped my drink. "Ready for what?"

"I think they'll be there waiting for us. We have to come up with a way to get through Parvati System and on to Renaissance Vector without their stopping us."

I considered the child. She looked tired. Her hair was still straggly from the shower. With all of the *Cantos* talk of the One Who Teaches, I had expected someone extraordinary—a young messiah in toga, a prodigy delivering cryptic utterances—but the only thing extraordinary about this young person was the powerful clarity of her dark eyes. "How could they be waiting for us?" I said. "The fatline hasn't worked for centuries. The Pax ships behind us can't call ahead as they could in your time."

Aenea shook her head. "No, the fatline had fallen before I was born. Remember, my mother was pregnant with me during the Fall." She looked at A. Bettik. The android was drinking juice, but he had not chosen to sit down. "I'm sorry I don't remember you. As I said, I used to visit the Poet's City and thought I knew all of the androids."

He bowed his head slightly. "No reason for you to remember me, M. Aenea. I had left the Poet's City even before your mother's pilgrimage. My siblings and I were working along the Hoolie River and on the Sea of Grass then. After the Fall, we . . . left service . . . and lived alone in different places."

"I see," she said. "There was a lot of craziness after the Fall. I remember. Androids would have been in danger west of the Bridle Range."

I caught her gaze. "No, seriously, how could someone be waiting for us at Parvati? They can't outrun us—we got to quantum velocity first—so the best they can do is translate into Parvati space an hour or two after us."

"I know," said Aenea, "but I still think that, somehow, they'll be waiting. We have to come up with a way this unarmed ship can outrun or outmaneuver a warship."

We talked for several more minutes, but none of us—not even the ship when queried—had a clever idea. All the time we were talking, I was observing the girl—the way her lips turned up slightly in a smile when she was thinking, the slight furrow in her brow when she spoke earnestly, how soft her voice was. I understood why Martin Silenus wanted her protected from harm.

"I wonder why the old poet didn't call us before we left the system," I mused aloud. "He must have wanted to talk to you."

Aenea ran her fingers through her hair like a comb. "Uncle Martin would never greet me via tightbeam or holo. We were agreed that we would speak after this trip was over."

I looked at her. "So you two planned the whole thing? I mean—your getaway, the hawking mat—everything?"

She smiled again at the thought. "My mother and I planned the essential details. After she died, Uncle Martin and I discussed the plan. He saw me off to the Sphinx this morning. . . ."

"This morning?" I said, confused. Then I understood.

"It's been a long day for me," the girl said ruefully. "I took a few steps this morning and covered half the time that humans have been on Hyperion. Everyone I knew—except Uncle Martin—must be dead."

"Not necessarily," I said. "The Pax arrived not long after you disappeared, so many of your friends and family could have accepted the cross. They would still be here."

" 'Accepted the cross,' " repeated the girl, and shivered slightly. "I don't have any family—my mother was my only real family—and I sort of doubt that many of my friends or my mother's friends would have . . . accepted the cross."

We stared at each other in silence for a moment, and I realized how exotic this young creature was; most of the historical events on Hyperion I was familiar with had not yet occurred when this girl had taken her step into the Sphinx "this morning."

"So, anyway," she said, "we didn't plan things down to the detail of the hawking mat—we didn't know if the Consul's ship would return with it, of course—but Mother and I did plan to use the Labyrinth if the Valley of the Tombs was off-limits. That worked out all right. And we hoped that the Consul's ship would be here to get me offplanet."

"Tell me about your time," I said.

Aenea shook her head. "I will," she said, "but not now. You know about my era. It's history and legend to you. I don't know anything about your time—except for my dreams—so tell me about the present. How wide is it? How deep is it? How much is mine to keep?"

I did not recognize the allusion of the last questions, but I began telling her about the Pax—about the great cathedral in St. Joseph and the . . .

"St. Joseph?" she said. "Where's that?"

"You used to call it Keats," I said. "The capital. It was also called Jacktown."

"Ah," she said, settling back in the cushions, the glass of fruit juice balanced in her slender fingers, "they changed the heathen name. Well, my father wouldn't mind."

It was the second time she had mentioned her father—I assumed she was speaking of the Keats cybrid—but I did not stop to ask her about that.

"Yes," I said, "many of the old cities and landmarks were renamed when Hyperion joined the Pax two centuries ago. There was talk of renaming the world itself, but the old name stuck. Anyway, the Pax does not govern directly, but the military brought order to . . ." I went on for some time, filling her in on details of technology, culture, language, and government. I described what I had heard, read, and watched of life on more advanced Pax worlds, including the glories of Pacem.

"Gee," she said when I paused, "things really haven't changed that much. It sounds as if technology is sort of stuck . . . still not caught up to Hegemony days."

"Well," I said, "the Pax is partly responsible for that. The Church prohibits thinking machines—true AIs—and its emphasis is on human and spiritual development rather than technological advancement."

Aenea nodded. "Sure, but you'd think that they would have caught up to WorldWeb levels in two and a half centuries. I mean, it's like the Dark Ages or something."

I smiled as I realized that I was taking offense—being annoyed at criticism of the Pax society I had chosen not to join. "Not really," I said. "Remember, the largest change has been the granting of virtual immortality. Because of that, the population growth is regulated carefully and there is less incentive to change exterior things. Most born-again Christians consider themselves to be in this life for the long haul—many centuries, at least, and millennia with luck—so they aren't in a hurry to change things."

Aenea regarded me carefully. "So the cruciform resurrection stuff really works?"

"Oh, yes."

"Then why haven't you . . . accepted the cross?"

For the third time in recent days, I was at a loss to explain. I shrugged. "Perversity, I guess. I'm stubborn. Also, a lot of people like me stay away from it when we're young—we all plan to live forever, right?— and then convert when age starts setting in."

"Will you?" Her dark eyes were piercing.

I stopped myself from shrugging again, but the gesture of my hand was the equivalent. "I don't know," I said. I had not told her yet about my "execution" and subsequent resurrection with Martin Silenus. "I don't know," I said again.

A. Bettik stepped into the holopit circle. "I thought that I might mention that we have stocked the ship with an ample supply of ice cream. In several flavors. Could I interest either of you in some?"

I formed a phrase reminding the android that he was not a servant on this voyage, but before I could speak, Aenea cried, "Yes! Chocolate!"

A. Bettik nodded, smiled, and turned in my direction. "M. Endymion?"

It had been a long day: hawking-mat voyages through the Labyrinth, dust storms, carnage—she said it was the Shrike!—and my first offworld trip. Quite a day.

"Chocolate," I said. "Yes. Definitely chocolate."

20

THE SURVIVING MEMBERS of Sergeant Gregorius's squad are Corporal Bassin Kee and Lancer Ahranwhal Gaspa K.T. Rettig. Kee is a small man, compact and quick in both reflexes and intelligence, while Rettig is tall—almost as tall as the giant Gregorius—but is as thin as the sergeant is massive. Rettig is from the Lambert Ring Territories and has the radiation scars, skeletal frame, and independent bent so stereotypical of 'stroiders. De Soya has learned that the man had never set foot on a full-sized, full-g world until he was twenty-three standard years old. RNA medication and serious Pax military exercise has toughened and strengthened the trooper until he can fight on any world. Reserved to the point of muteness, A.G.K.T. Rettig listens well, follows orders well, and—as the battle on Hyperion showed—survives well.

Corporal Kee is as voluble as Rettig is silent. During their first day of discussion, Kee's questions and comments show insight and clarity, despite the brain-fogging effects of resurrection.

All four of the men are shaken by the experience of death. De Soya tries to convince them that it gets easier with experience, but his own shaken body and wits put the lie to these reassurances. Here, without counseling and therapy and the welcoming resurrection chaplains, each of the Pax soldiers is dealing with the trauma as best he can. Their conferences on the first day in Parvati space are interrupted frequently as fatigue or sheer emotion overcome them. Only Sergeant Gregorius is outwardly unshaken by the experience.

On the third day they meet in *Raphael*'s tiny wardroom cubby to plot their final course of action.

"In two months and three weeks, that ship is going to translate into this system less than a thousand klicks from where we're station-holding," says Father Captain de Soya, "and we have to be certain we can intercept it and detain the girl."

None of the Swiss Guard soldiers has asked why the girl's detention is required. None will discuss the issue until their commanding officer—de Soya—raises it first. Each will die, if necessary, to carry out the cryptic order.

"We don't know who else is on board the ship, right?" says Corporal Kee. They have discussed these items, but memories are faulty for the first few days of their new lives.

"No," says de Soya.

"We don't know the armament of the ship," says Kee, as if checking off a mental list.

"Correct."

"We don't know if Parvati is the ship's destination."

"Correct."

"It could be," says Corporal Kee, "that the ship is scheduled to rendezvous with another ship here . . . or perhaps the girl means to meet someone on the planet."

De Soya nods. "The *Raphael* doesn't have the sensors of my old torchship, but we're sweeping everything between the Oort cloud and Parvati itself. If another ship translates before the girl's, we'll know at once."

"Ouster?" says Sergeant Gregorius.

De Soya raises his hands. "Everything's speculation. I can tell you that the child is considered a threat to the Pax, so it's reasonable to conclude that the Ousters—if they know of her existence—might want to grab her. We're ready if they try."

Kee rubs his smooth cheek. "I still can't quite believe we could hop home in a day if we wanted to. Or go for help." Home for Corporal Kee is the Jamnu Republic on Deneb Drei. They have discussed why it would be useless to ask for help—the closest Pax warship is the *St. Anthony*, which should be, if de Soya's orders were obeyed, in hot pursuit of the girl's ship.

"I've tightbeamed the commander of the Pax garrison on Parvati," says de Soya. "As our computer inventory showed, they have just their orbital patrol craft and a couple of rock jumpers. I've ordered him to put every spacecraft they have into cislunar defensive positions, to alert all the outposts on the planet, and to await further orders. If the girl was to get past us and land there, the Pax would find her."

"What kind of world is Parvati?" asks Gregorius. The man's bass rumble of a voice always gets de Soya's attention.

"It was settled by Reformed Hindus not long after the Hegira," says de Soya, who has accessed all this on the ship's computer. "Desert world. Not enough oxygen to support humans—mostly C-O-two atmosphere—and it was never enough of a success to terraform, so either the environments are tailored or the people are. Population was never large—a few dozen million before the Fall. Fewer than half a million now, and most of them live in the one big city of Gandhiji."

"Christians?" asks Kee. De Soya guesses that the question is more than idle curiosity; Kee asks few random questions.

"A few thousand in Gandhiji have converted," says de Soya. "There is a new cathedral there—St. Malachy's—and most of the born-again are prominent businesspeople who favor joining the Pax. They talked the planetary government—a sort of elective oligarchy—into inviting the Pax garrison here about fifty standard years ago. They're close enough to the Outback to worry about the Ousters."

Kee nods. "I just wondered if the garrison could count on the populace reporting it when the girl's ship lands."

"Doubtful," says de Soya. "Ninety-nine percent of the world is empty—never settled, or gone back to sand dunes and lichen fields—with most of the people huddled around the big boxite mines near Gandhiji. But the orbital patrols would track her."

"If she gets that far," says Gregorius.

"Which she will not," says Father Captain de Soya. He touches a tabletop monitor, which brings up the graphic he has prepared. "Here's the intercept plan. We snooze until T-minus three days. Don't worry—remember, fugue doesn't have the hangover time of resurrection. Half an hour to shake the cobwebs out. Okay . . . so T-minus three days, the alarm goes off. *Raphael*'s been looping out to here—" He taps the diagram at a point two-thirds the way around the elipsoid trajectory. "We know their ship's C-plus entry velocity, which means we know their exit velocity . . . it will be about point-zero-three C, so if they're decelerating toward Parvati at the same rate they left Hyperion . . ." The trajectory and timeline diagrams fill the screen. "This is hypothetical, but their translation point is not . . . it will be *here*." He touches a stylus to a red point ten AUs from the planet. Their own trajectory elipsoid blinks its way to that point. "And *here* is where we intercept them, less than a minute from their translation point."

Gregorius leans over his monitor. "We'll all be going like a cross-damned bat out of hell, pardon the language, Father."

De Soya smiles. "You are absolved, my son. Yes, velocities will be high, as will be our combined delta-v's if their ship commences deceleration toward Parvati, but relative velocities for the two ships will be almost nill."

"How close will we be, Captain?" says Kee. The man's black hair glistens in the overhead spots.

"When they translate, we'll be bearing down on them at a distance of six hundred klicks. Within three minutes we'll be able to throw a rock at them."

Kee frowns. "But what will they throw at us?"

"Unknown," says de Soya. "But the *Raphael* is tough. I'm betting that her shields can take anything this unidentified ship throws at us."

Lancer Rettig grunts. "Bad bet to lose."

De Soya swivels his chair to look at the trooper. He had almost forgotten Rettig was there. "Yes," he says, "but we have the advantage of being close. Whatever they throw at us, they'll have a limited time to throw."

"And what do we throw at them?" rumbles Gregorius.

De Soya pauses. "I've gone over *Raphael*'s armament with you," he says at last. "If this were an Ouster warship, we could fry, bake, ram, or burn it. Or we could just make its crew die quietly." *Raphael* carries deathbeam weaponry. At five hundred klicks, there would be no doubt of their effectiveness.

"But we're not going to use any of that . . . ," continues the father-captain. "Unless we absolutely have to . . . to disable the ship."

"Can you do that without danger of hurting the girl?" asks Kee.

"Not with a hundred percent assurance of not hurting her . . . and whoever else is aboard," says de Soya. He pauses again, takes a breath, and continues. "That's why you're going to board her."

Gregorius grins. His teeth are very large and very white. "We grabbed space armor for all of us before leaving the *St. Thomas Akira*," grumbles the giant happily. "But it'd be better if we practiced in it before the actual boarding."

De Soya nods. "Three days enough?"

Gregorius is still grinning. "I'd rather have a week."

"All right," says the father captain. "We'll wake up a week before intercept. Here's a schematic of the unidentified ship."

"I thought it was . . . unidentified," says Kee, looking at the ship's plans now filling the monitors. The spacecraft is a needle with fins at one end—a child's caricature of a spaceship.

"We don't know its specific identity or registration," says de Soya, "but the *St. Anthony* tightbeamed video that it and the *Bonaventure* took of the ship before we translated. It's not Ouster."

"Not Ouster, not Pax, not Mercantilus, not a spinship or torch-ship . . . ," says Kee. "What the hell is it?"

De Soya advances the images to ship cross sections. "Private space-craft, Hegemony era," he says softly. "Only thirty or so ever made. At least four hundred years old, probably older."

Corporal Kee whistles softly. Gregorius rubs his huge jaw. Even Rettig looks impressed behind his impassive mask. "I didn't know there ever were private spacecraft," says the corporal. "C-plus, I mean."

"The Hegemony used to reward high-muck-a-mucks with them," says de Soya. "Prime Minister Gladstone used to have one. So did General Horace Glennon-Height. . . ."

"The Hegemony didn't reward *him* with one," says Kee with a chuckle. Glennon-Height was the most infamous and legendary opponent the early Hegemony ever had—the Outback's Hannibal to the WorldWeb's Rome.

"No," agrees Father Captain de Soya, "the general stole his from the planetary Governor of Sol Draconi Septem. Anyway, the computer says that all of these private ships were accounted for before the Fall—destroyed or reconfigured for FORCE use and then decommissioned—but the computer appears to be wrong."

"Not the first time," grumbles Gregorius. "Do these long-range images show any armament or defensive systems?"

"No, the original ships were civilian—no weapons—and the *St. Bonaventure*'s sensors didn't pick up any acquisition radars or pulse readings before the Shrike killed the imaging team," says de Soya, "but this ship's been around for centuries, so we have to assume that it has been modified. But even if it has modern Ouster standoff weaponry, *Raphael* should be able to get in close, fast, while we hold off their lances. Once we're alongside, they can't use kinetic weapons. By the time we grapple, the energy weapons will be useless."

"Hand to hand," says Gregorius to himself. The sergeant is studying the schematic. "They'd be waiting at the air lock, so we'll blow a new door here . . . and here . . ."

De Soya feels a prickling of alarm. "We can't let the atmosphere out . . . the girl . . ."

Gregorius shows a shark's grin. "Not to worry, sir. It takes less than a minute to rig a big catchbag on the hull . . . I brought several with the armor . . . and then we blow the hull section inward, scoot in . . ." He keys a closer image. "I'll rig this for stimsim, so we can rehearse in three-D for a few days. I'd like another week for sim." The black face turns toward de Soya. "We may not get any fugue beauty sleep after all, sir."

Kee is tapping his lip with a finger. "Question, Captain."

De Soya looks at him.

"I understand that under no circumstances can we harm the girl, but what about others that get in the way?"

De Soya sighs. He has been waiting for the question. "I'd prefer that no one else dies on this mission, Corporal."

"Yes, sir," says Kee, his eyes alert, "but what if they try to stop us?"

Father Captain de Soya blanks the monitor. The crowded cubby smells of oil and sweat and ozone. "My orders were that the child is not to be harmed," he says slowly, carefully. "Nothing was said about anyone else. If there's someone . . . or something . . . else on the ship and they try to get in the way, consider them expendable. Defend yourselves, even if you have to shoot before you're certain you're in danger."

"Kill them all," mutters Gregorius, "except the kid . . . and let God sort them out."

De Soya has always hated that ancient mercenary joke.

"Do whatever you have to do without endangering the girl's life or health," he says.

"What if there's only one other on board standing between us and the girl?" says Rettig. The other three men look at the 'stroider. "But it's the Shrike thing?" he finishes.

The cubby is silent except for the omnipresent ship sounds—expanding and contracting metal from the hull, the whisper of ventilators, the hum of equipment, the occasional burp of a thruster.

"If it's the Shrike . . . ," begins Father Captain de Soya. He pauses.

"If it's the wee Shrikee," says Sergeant Gregorius, "I think we can bring a few surprises for it. This round may not go so easy for that spiked son of a bitch, pardon my language, Father."

"As your priest," says de Soya, "I will warn you again about the use of profanity. As your commanding officer, I order you to come up with as many surprises as you can to kill that spiked son of a bitch."

They adjourn to eat their evening meal and plan their respective strategies.

21

AVE YOU EVER NOTICED how on a trip—even a very long one—it is often the first week or so that stands out most clearly in your memory? Perhaps it is the enhanced perception that voyages bring, or perhaps it is an effect of orientation response on the senses, or perhaps it is simply that even the charm of newness soon wears off, but it has been my experience that the first days in a new place, or seeing new people, often set the tone for the rest of the trip. Or in this case, the rest of my life.

We spent the first day of our magnificent adventure sleeping. The child was exhausted and—I had to admit after waking from sixteen hours of uninterrupted sleep—so was I. I can't vouch for what A. Bettik did during this first somnambulant day of the voyage—at that point I had not learned that androids do sleep, but require only a fraction of the time we humans spend comatose—but he had set his small backpack of possessions in the engine room, rigging a hammock to sleep in, and he spent much of his time down there. I had planned to give the girl the "master bedroom" at the apex of the ship, she had showered there in the adjoining bathroom cubby that first morning, but she staked out one of the sleep couches on the fugue deck and that soon became her space. I enjoyed the size and softness of the large bed in the center of the circular top room, and—after a while—even overcame my agoraphobia and allowed the hull to go translucent to watch the fractal light show in Hawking space outside. I never kept the hull transparent for long, however, for the pulsing geometries continued to disturb me in ways I could not describe.

The library level and the holopit level were, by unspoken agreement, common ground. The kitchen—A. Bettik called it the "galley"—was set into the wall on the holopit level, and we usually ate at the low table in the holopit or occasionally carried the food up to the round table near the navigation cubby. I admit that immediately after awakening and having "breakfast" (shiptime said that it was afternoon on Hyperion, but why abide by Hyperion time when I might never see that world again?), I headed for the library: the books were ancient, all published during the time of the Hegemony or earlier, and I was surprised to find a copy of an epic poem by Martin Silenus—*The Dying Earth*—as well as tomes by a dozen classical authors whom I had read as a boy, and often reread during my long days and nights at the fen cabin or while working on the river.

A. Bettik joined me that first day as I browsed, and pulled a small green volume from the shelves. "This might be of interest," he said. The title was *A Traveler's Guide to the WorldWeb: With Special Sections on the Grand Concourse and River Tethys*.

"It might be of great interest," I said, opening the book with shaking fingers. The shaking, I believe, came from the reality that we were *going there*—actually *traveling to the former Web worlds*!

"These books are doubly interesting as artifacts," said the android, "since they came from an age when all information was instantly available to anyone."

I nodded. As a child, listening to Grandam's tales of the old days, I had tried to imagine a world where everyone wore implants and could access the datasphere whenever they wanted. Of course, even then, Hyperion had no datasphere—and had never been part of the Web—but for most of the billions of members of the Hegemony, life must have been like an endless stimsim of visual, auditory, and printed information. No wonder a majority of humans had never learned to read during the old days. Literacy had been one of the first goals of the Church and its Pax administrators after interstellar society was stitched together long after the Fall.

That day, standing in the carpeted ship's library, the polished teak and cherrywood walls gleaming in the light, I remember taking half a dozen books from the shelves and carrying them to the table to read.

Aenea raided the library that afternoon as well—immediately pulling *The Dying Earth* from the shelves. "There were no copies in Jacktown, and Uncle Martin refused to let me read it when I visited him," she said. "He did say that it was the only thing he'd ever written—other than the *Cantos* that he hadn't finished—that was worth reading."

"What's it about?" I asked, not looking up from the Delmore Deland novel I was skimming. Both the girl and I were munching on apples as we read and talked. A. Bettik had gone back down the spiral stairs.

"The last days of Old Earth," said Aenea. "It's really about Martin's pampered childhood on his family's big estate on the North American Preserve."

I set my book down. "What do you think happened to Old Earth?"

The girl stopped munching. "In my day everyone thought that the Big Mistake of aught-eight black hole had eaten it. That it was gone. Kaput."

I chewed and nodded. "Most people still believe that, but the old poet's *Cantos* insist that the TechnoCore stole Old Earth and sent it somewhere. . . ."

"The Hercules Cluster or the Magellanic Clouds," said the girl, and took another bite of apple. "My mother discovered that when she and my father were investigating his murder."

I leaned forward. "Do you mind talking about your father?"

Aenea smiled slightly. "No, why should I? I suppose I'm somewhat of a half-breed, the child of a Lusian woman and a cloned cybrid male, but that's never bothered me."

"You don't look very Lusian," I said. Residents of that high-g world were invariably short and very strong. Most were pale of skin and darkhaired; this child was small but of a height normal to one-g worlds, her brown hair was streaked with blond, and she was slender. Only her luminous brown eyes reminded me of the *Cantos'* description of Brawne Lamia.

Aenea laughed. It was a pleasant sound. "I take after my dad," she said. "John Keats was short, blond, and skinny."

I hesitated a moment before saying, "You said that you spoke to your father . . ."

Aenea glanced at me from the corners of her eyes. "Yes, and you know that the Core killed his body before I was born. But did you also know that my mother carried his persona for months in a Schrön Loop embedded behind her ear?"

I nodded. It was in the *Cantos.*

The girl shrugged. "I remember talking to him."

"But you weren't . . ."

"Born," said Aenea. "Right. What kind of conversation could a poet's persona have with a fetus? But we talked. His persona was still connected to the TechnoCore. He showed me . . . well, it's complicated, Raul. Believe me."

"I believe you," I said. I looked around the library. "Did you know that the *Cantos* say that when your father's persona left the Schrön Loop, that it resided in this ship's AI for a while?"

"Yeah," said Aenea. She grinned. "Yesterday, before I went to sleep, I spent an hour or so talking to the ship. My dad was here, all right. The persona coexisted with the ship's mind when the Consul flew back to check out what had happened to the Web after the Fall. But he's not here now, and the ship can't remember much about his residence here, and it doesn't remember anything about what happened to him—whether he left after the Consul died, or what—so I don't know if he still exists."

"Well," I said, trying to choose diplomatic words, "the Core doesn't exist any longer, so I don't quite see how a cybrid persona could either."

"Who says the Core doesn't exist?"

I admit that I was shocked by that statement. "The last act of Meina

Gladstone and the Hegemony was to destroy the farcaster links, the dataspheres, the fatline, and the entire dimension that the Core existed in," I said at last. "Even the *Cantos* agrees with that fact."

The child was still smiling. "Oh, they blew the space-based farcasters to bits, and the others quit working, all right. And the dataspheres were gone in my time, too. But who says the Core is dead? That's like saying that you swept away a couple of spiderwebs, so the spider has to be dead."

I admit that I looked over my shoulder. "So you think the TechnoCore still exists? That those AIs are still plotting against us?"

"I don't know about the plotting," said Aenea, "but I know that the Core exists."

"How?"

She held up a small finger. "First of all, my father's cybrid persona still existed after the Fall, right? The basis for that persona was a Core AI they had fashioned. That shows that the Core was still . . . somewhere."

I thought about that. As I mentioned earlier, cybrids—like androids —were essentially a mythical species to me. We might as well have been discussing the physical characteristics of leprechauns.

"Secondly," she said, lifting a second finger to join the first, "I've communicated with the Core."

I blinked at that statement. "Before you were born?" I said.

"Yes," said Aenea. "And when I lived with Mother in Jacktown. And after Mother died." She lifted her books and stood. "And this morning."

I could only stare.

"I'm hungry, Raul," she said from the head of the stairs. "Want to go down and see what this old ship's galley can whomp up for lunch?"

WE SOON SETTLED into a schedule on the ship, adopting Hyperion's day and night schedules roughly as waking and sleeping times. I began to see why the old Hegemony habit of keeping the twenty-four-hour Old Earth system as standard had been so important in the Web days: I'd read somewhere that almost ninety percent of the Earth-like or terraformed worlds of the Web had held days that fell within three hours of the Old Earth standard day.

Aenea still liked to extend the balcony and play the Steinway out under the Hawking-space sky, and I would sometimes stay out there and listen for a few minutes, but I preferred the sense of being surrounded that the interior of the ship gave me. None of us complained about the effects of the C-plus environment, although we felt it—the occasional lurching of emotion and balance, a constant sense that someone was watching us, and very strange dreams. My own dreams awakened me with the pounding heart, dry mouth, and sweat-soaked sheets that only the worst nightmares could cause. But I never remembered the dreams. I wanted to ask the others about their dreams, but A. Bettik never mentioned his—I did not know if androids *could* dream—and although Aenea acknowledged the strangeness of her dreams and said that she did remember them, she never discussed them.

On the second day, while we were sitting in the library, Aenea suggested that we "experience" space travel. When I asked her how we could experience it more than we were—I had the Hawking fractals in mind when I said that—she only laughed and asked the ship to cancel the internal containment field. Immediately, we were weightless.

As a boy, I had dreamed of zero-g. Swimming in the salty South Sea as a young soldier, I had closed my eyes, floated effortlessly, and wondered if this was what space travel in the olden days had been like.

I can tell you it is not.

Zero-g, especially sudden zero-g such as the ship granted upon Aenea's request, is terrifying. It is, quite simply, falling.

Or so it first seems.

I gripped the chair, but the chair was also falling. It was precisely as if we had been sitting in one of the huge Bridle Range cable cars for the past two days, when suddenly the cable broke. My middle ear protested, trying to find a horizon line that was honest. None was.

A. Bettik kicked up from wherever he had been below and said calmly, "Is there a problem?"

"No," laughed Aenea, "we're just going to experience space for a while."

A. Bettik nodded and then pulled himself headfirst down the stairway pit to get back to whatever he was working on.

Aenea followed him to the stairwell, kicking over to the central opening. "See?" she said. "This stairwell becomes a central dropshaft when the ship is in zero-g. Just like in the old spinships."

"Isn't this dangerous?" I asked, switching my grip from the back of a chair to a bookshelf. For the first time I noticed the elastic cords that held the books in place. Everything else that was not attached—the book I had set on the table, the chairs around the table, a sweater I'd left thrown over the back of another chair, pieces of the orange I had been eating—was floating.

"Not dangerous," said Aenea. "Messy. Next time we get everything shipshape before we cancel the internal field."

"But isn't the field . . . important?"

Aenea was floating upside down, from my perspective. My inner ear liked this even less than the rest of the experience. "The field keeps us from being squashed and thrown around when we're moving in normal space," she said, pulling herself to the center of the twenty-meter drop by grabbing the stairway railing, "but we can't speed up or slow down in C-plus space, so . . . here goes!" She grabbed a handhold along the rod that ran the length of the ship in the center of what had been the open stairwell and catapulted herself out of sight, headfirst.

"Jesus," I whispered, pushed away from the bookcase, bouncing off the opposite bulkhead, and followed her down the central dropshaft.

For the next hour we played in zero-g: zero-g tag, zero-g hide-and-seek (finding that one could hide in the oddest places when gravity was not a restraint), zero-g soccer using one of the plastic space helmets from a locker on the storage/corridor deck, and even zero-g wrestling, which was harder than I would have imagined. My first attempt to grab the child sent both of us tumbling and crashing through the length, breadth, and height of fugue deck.

In the end, exhausted and sweaty (the perspiration hung in the air until one moved or a trickle of air from the ventilators moved it, I discovered), Aenea ordered the balcony opened again—I shouted in fear when she did so, but the ship quietly reminded me that the exterior field was quite intact—and we floated out above the bolted-down Steinway, floated to the railing and beyond, into that no-man's-land between the ship and the field, floated ten meters out and looked back at the ship itself, surrounded by exploding fractals, glowing in the cold fireworks glory of it as Hawking space folded and contracted around us several billion times a second.

Finally we kicked and swam our way back in (a difficult and awkward feat, I discovered, when there was nothing to push against), warned A. Bettik over the intercom to find a floor, and brought back the one-g internal field. Both the child and I giggled as sweaters, sandwiches, chairs, books, and several spheres of water from a glass that had been left out came crashing down to the carpet.

It was that same day, night rather, for the ship had dimmed the lights for sleep period, that I padded down the spiral stairs to the holopit level to fix a midnight snack and heard soft sounds through the opening to the fugue deck below.

"Aenea?" I said, speaking softly. There was no answer. I went to the head of the stairs, looking at the dark drop in the center of the stairwell and smiling as I remembered our midair antics there a few hours before. "Aenea?"

There still came no answer, but the soft sounds continued. Wishing I had a flashlight, I padded down the metal stairs in my sock feet.

There was a soft glow from the fugue-sleep monitors above the couches tucked in their cubbies. The soft sound was coming from Aenea's cubby. She had her back to me. The blanket was pulled to her shoulders, but I could see the collar of the Consul's old shirt that she had appropriated for use as a nightshirt. I walked over, my sock feet making no noise on the soft floor, and knelt by the couch. "Aenea?" The girl was crying, obviously trying to muffle her sobs.

I touched her shoulder and she finally turned. Even in the dim instrument glow I could see that she had been weeping for some time; her eyes were red and puffy, her cheeks streaked with tears.

"What's wrong, kiddo?" I whispered. We were two decks above where A. Bettik slept in his hammock in the engine room, but the stairwell was open.

For a moment Aenea did not respond, but eventually the sobs slowed, then stopped. "I'm sorry," she said at last.

"It's all right. Tell me what's wrong."

"Give me a tissue and I will," said the girl.

I rummaged in the pockets of the old robe the Consul had left. I had no tissue, but I had been using a napkin with the cake I'd been eating upstairs. I handed her the linen.

"Thanks." She blew her nose. "I'm glad we're not still in zero-g," she said through the cloth. "There'd be snot floating everywhere."

I smiled and squeezed her shoulder. "What's wrong, Aenea?"

She made a soft noise that I realized was an attempt at a laugh. "Everything," she said. "Everything's wrong. I'm scared. Everything I know about the future scares the shit out of me. I don't know how we're going to get past the Pax guys that I know will be waiting for us in a few days. I'm homesick. I can never go back, and everybody I knew except Martin is gone forever. Mostly, though, I guess I just miss my mother."

I squeezed her shoulder. Brawne Lamia, her mother, was the stuff of legend—a woman who had lived and died two and a half long centuries ago. A few of her bones had already turned to dust, wherever they were buried. For this child, her mother's death was only two weeks in the past.

"I'm sorry," I whispered, and squeezed her shoulder again, feeling the texture of the Consul's old shirt. "It'll be all right."

Aenea nodded and took my hand. Hers was still moist. I noticed how tiny her palm and fingers were against my huge paw.

"Want to come up to the galley and have some chalmaroot cake and milk with me?" I whispered. "It's good."

She shook her head. "I think I'll sleep now. Thanks, Raul." She squeezed my hand again before relinquishing it, and in that second I realized the great truth: the One Who Teaches, the new messiah, whatever Brawne Lamia's daughter would turn out to be, she was also a child—one who giggled in zero-gravity antics and who wept in the night.

I went softly up the stairs, stopping to look back at her before my head rose above the level of the next deck. She was huddled under her blanket, her face turned away again, her hair catching only a bit of the console glow from above her cubby. "Good night, Aenea," I whispered, knowing that she would not hear me. "It will be all right."

22

ERGEANT GREGORIUS and his two troopers are waiting in the open sally-port air lock of the *Raphael* as the archangel-class starship closes on the unidentified spacecraft that has just translated from C-plus. Their spacesuit armor is cumbersome and—with their reactionless rifles and energy weapons slung—the three men fill the air lock. Parvati's sun gleams on their gold visors as they lean out into space.

"I've got it locked," comes Father Captain de Soya's voice in their earphones. "Distance, one hundred meters and closing." The needle-shaped craft with fins on the stern fills their vision as the two ships close. Between the spacecraft, defensive containment fields blur and flash, dissipating high-energy CPB and lance attacks faster than the eye can follow. Gregorius's visor opaques, clears, and then opaques as the close-in battle flares.

"All right, inside their minimum lance range," says de Soya from his perch on the Combat Control Center couch. "Go!"

Gregorius gives a hand signal and his men kick off at the precise instant he does. Needle thrusters in their suits' reaction paks spurt tiny blue flames as they correct their arc.

"Disrupting fields . . . now!" cries de Soya.

The clashing containment fields cancel each other for only a few seconds, but it is enough: Gregorius, Kee, and Rettig are in the other ship's defensive egg now.

"Kee," says Gregorius over the tightbeam, and the smaller figure tweaks thrusters and hurtles toward the bow of the decelerating ship. "Rettig." The other suit of combat armor accelerates toward the lower third of the ship. Gregorius himself waits until the final second to kill his forward velocity, does a complete forward roll at the last instant, applies full thruster, and feels his heavy soles touch hullplate with hardly a tap. He activates the magties in his boots, feels the connection, widens his stance, and then crouches on the hull with only one boot in contact.

"On," comes Corporal Kee's voice on tightbeam.

"On," says Rettig a second later.

Sergeant Gregorius pulls the line of boarding collar from around his waist, sets it against the hull, activates the sticktight, and continues kneeling in it. He is within a black hoop a little more than a meter and a half in diameter.

"On the count from three," he says into his mike. "Three . . . two . . . one . . . deploy." He touches his wristcontroller and blinks as a microthin canopy of molecular polymer spins up from the hoop, closes over his head, and continues to bulge above him. Within ten seconds he is within a twenty-meter transparent bag, like a combat-armored shape crouching within a giant condom.

"Ready," says Kee. Rettig echoes the word.

"Set," says Gregorius, slapping a charge against the hull and setting his gauntleted finger back against his wristplate. "From five . . ." The ship is rotating under them now, firing thrusters and its main engines almost at random, but the *Raphael* has it locked in a containment-field death grip, and the men on its hull are not thrown free. "Five . . . four . . . three . . . two . . . one . . . now!"

The detonation is soundless, of course, but is also without flash or recoil. A 120-centimeter circle of hull flies inward. Gregorius can see only the gossamer hint of Kee's polymer bag around the curve of the hull, sees the sunlight strike it as it inflates. Gregorius's bag also inflates like a giant balloon as atmosphere rushes out of the hullbreech and fills the space around him. He hears a hurricane screech through his external pickups for five seconds, then silence as the space around him—now filled with oxygen and nitrogen according to his helmet sensors—fills with dust and detritus blown out during the brief pressure differential.

"Going in . . . now!" cries Gregorius, unslinging his reactionless plasma rifle as he kicks his way into the interior.

There is no gravity. That is a surprise to the sergeant—he is ready to hit the decks rolling—but he adapts within seconds and twists in a circle, peering around.

Some sort of common area. Gregorius sees seat cushions, some sort of ancient vid screen, bookshelves with real books—

A man floats up the central dropshaft.

"Halt!" cries Gregorius, using common radio bands and his helmet loudspeaker. The figure—little more than a silhouette—does not halt. The man has something in his hand.

Gregorius fires from the hip. The plasma slug bores a hole ten centimeters wide through the man. Blood and viscera explode outward from the tumbling figure, some of the globules spattering on Gregorius's visor and armored chestplate. The object falls from the dead man's hand, and Gregorius glances at it as he kicks by to the stairwell. It is a book. "Shit," mutters the sergeant. He has killed an unarmed man. He will lose points for this.

"In, top level, no one here," radios Kee. "Coming down."

"Engine room," says Rettig. "One man here. Tried to run and I had to burn him. No sign of the child. Coming up."

"She must be on the middle level or the air-lock level," snaps the sergeant into his mike. "Proceed with care." The lights go out, and Gregorius's helmet searchlight and the penlight on his plasma rifle come on automatically, beams quite visible through air filled with dust, blood spheres, and tumbling artifacts. He stops at the top of the stairwell.

Someone or something is drifting up toward him. He shifts his helmet, but the light on the plasma rifle illuminates the shape first.

It is not the girl. Gregorius gets a confused impression of great size, razor wire, spikes, too many arms, and blazing red eyes. He must decide in a second or less: if he fires plasma bolts down the open dropshaft, he might hit the child. If he does nothing, he dies—razor talons reach for him even as he hesitates.

Gregorius has lashed the deathwand to his plasma rifle before making the ship-to-ship jump. Now he kicks aside, finds an angle, and triggers the wand.

The razor-wire shape floats past him, four arms limp, the red eyes fading. Gregorius thinks, *The goddamn thing isn't invulnerable to deathwands. It has synapses.* He catches a glimpse of someone above him, swings the rifle, identifies Kee, and the two men kick down the dropshaft headfirst. *Embarrassing if someone turns the internal field back on now and gravity comes on,* thinks Gregorius. *Make a note of that.*

"I've got her," calls Rettig. "She was hiding in one of the fugue cubbies."

Gregorius and Kee float down past the common level and kick out into the fugue level. A massive figure in combat armor is holding the child. Gregorius notes the brown-blond hair, the dark eyes, and the small fists flailing uselessly against Rettig's chest armor.

"That's her," he says. He keys the tightbeam to the ship. "Cleared the ship. We have the girl. Only two defenders and the creature this time."

"Affirmative," comes de Soya's voice. "Two minutes fifteen seconds. Impressive. Come on out."

Gregorius nods, takes a final glance at the captive child—no longer struggling—and keys his suit controls.

He blinks and sees the other two lying next to him, their suits connected umbilically to VR tactical. De Soya has actually turned off the internal fields in the *Raphael,* better to maintain the illusion. Gregorius removes his helmet, sees the other two sweaty faces as they do the same, and begins to help Kee remove his clumsy armor.

The three meet de Soya in the wardroom cubby. They could meet as easily in the stimsim of tactical space, but they prefer physical reality for their debriefings.

"It was smooth," says de Soya as they take their places around the small table.

"Too smooth," says the sergeant. "I don't believe that deathwands are going to kill the Shrike thing. And I screwed up with the guy on the navigation deck. . . . He just had a book."

De Soya nods. "You did the right thing, though. Better to take him out than to take chances."

"Two unarmed men?" says Corporal Kee. "I doubt it. This is about as unrealistic as the dozen armed guys on the third run-through. We should play more of the Ouster encounters . . . Marine-level lethality, at least."

"I don't know," mutters Rettig.

They look at him and wait.

"We keep getting the girl without any harm coming to her," says the man at last.

"That fifth sim . . . ," begins Kee.

"Yeah, yeah," says Rettig. "I know we accidentally killed her then. But the whole ship was wired to blow in that one. I doubt if that will happen. . . . Who ever heard of a hundred-million-mark spacecraft having a self-destruct button? That's stupid."

The other three look at one another and shrug.

"It *is* a silly idea," says Father Captain de Soya, "but I programmed the tacticals for wide parameters of . . ."

"Yeah," interrupts Lancer Rettig, his thin face as sharp and menacing as a knife blade, "I just mean that if it does come to a firefight, the chances of the girl getting burned are a lot greater than our sims suggest. That's all."

This is the most the other three have heard Rettig say in weeks of living and rehearsing on the small ship.

"You're right," says de Soya. "For our next sim, I'll raise the danger level for the child."

Gregorius shakes his head. "Captain, sir, I suggest we knock off the sims and go back to the physical rehearsals. I mean . . ." He glances at his wrist chronometer. The memory of the bulky combat suit slows his movements. "I mean, we've just got eight hours until this is for real."

"Yeah," says Corporal Kee. "I agree. I'd rather be outside doing it for real, even if we can't sim the other ship that way."

Rettig grunts his assent.

"I agree," says de Soya. "But first we eat—double rations. . . . It's just been tactical, but you three have each lost twenty pounds the last week."

Sergeant Gregorius leans over the table. "Could we see the plot, sir?"

De Soya keys the monitor. *Raphael*'s long, ellipsoid trajectory and the escape ship's translation point are almost intersecting. The intersect point blinks red.

"One more real-space run-through," says de Soya, "and then I want all of us to sleep at least two hours, go over our equipment, and take it easy." He looks at his own chronometer, even though the monitor is displaying ship and intercept time. "Barring accidents or the unexpected," he says, "the girl should be in our custody in seven hours and forty minutes . . . and we'll be getting ready to translate to Pacem."

"Sir?" says Sergeant Gregorius.

"Yes, Sergeant?"

"Meaning no disrespect, sir," says the other man, "but there's no way in the Good Lord's fucking universe that anyone can bar accidents or the unexpected."

23

o," I said, "What's your plan?"

Aenea looked up from the book she was reading. "Who says that I have a plan?"

I straddled a chair. "It's less than an hour until we pop out in the Parvati System," I said. "A week ago you said that we needed a plan in case they know we're coming . . . so what's the plan?"

Aenea sighed and closed the book. A. Bettik had come up the stairway to the library, and now he joined us at the table—actually sitting with us, which was unusual for him.

"I'm not sure I have a plan," said the girl.

I'd been afraid of this. The week had passed pleasantly enough; the three of us had read a lot, talked a lot, played a lot—Aenea was excellent at chess, good at Go, and deadly at poker—and the days had passed without incident. Many times I had tried to press her on her plans—Where did she plan to go? Why choose Renaissance Vector? Was finding Ousters part of her quest?—but her answers, while polite, were always vague. What Aenea showed great talent for was getting me talking. I hadn't known many children—even when I was a child myself, there were few others in our caravan group, and I rarely enjoyed their company, since Grandam was infinitely more interesting to me—but the children and teenagers I'd encountered over the years had never shown this much curiosity or ability to listen. Aenea got me describing my years as a shepherd; she showed special interest in my apprenticeship as a landscape architect; she asked a thousand questions about my riverbarge days and hunting-guide days—in truth, it was only my soldiering days that she did not show much interest in. What she had seemed especially interested in was my dog, although even discussing Izzy—about raising her, training her as bird dog, about her death—upset me quite a bit.

I noticed that she could even get A. Bettik talking about his centuries of servitude, and here I often joined in the patient listening: the android had seen and experienced amazing things—different worlds, the settling of Hyperion with Sad King Billy, the Shrike's early rampages across Equus, the final pilgrimage that the old poet had made famous, even the decades with Martin Silenus turned out to be fascinating.

But the girl said very little. On our fourth evening out from Hyperion, she admitted that she had come through the Sphinx into her future not just to escape the Pax troops hunting for her then, but to seek out her own destiny.

"As a messiah?" I said, intrigued.

Aenea laughed. "No," she said, "as an architect."

I was surprised. Neither the *Cantos* nor the old poet himself had said anything about the so-called One Who Teaches earning a living as an architect.

Aenea had shrugged. "It's what I want to do. In my dream the one who could teach me lives in this era. So here I came."

"The one who could teach you?" I said. "I thought that you were the One Who Teaches."

Aenea had flopped back onto the holopit cushions and cocked her leg over the back of the couch. "Raul, how could I possibly teach anyone anything? I'm twelve standard years old and I've never been off Hyperion before this. . . . Hell, I never left the continent of Equus until this week. What do I have to teach?"

I had no answer to that.

"I want to be an architect," she said, "and in my dream the architect who can train me is somewhere out there. . . ." She waggled her fingers at the outer hull, but I understood her to mean the old Hegemony Web, where we were heading.

"Who is he?" I said. "Or she?"

"He," said Aenea. "And I don't know his name."

"What world is he on?" I asked.

"I don't know."

"Are you sure this is the right century?" I asked, trying to keep the irritation out of my voice.

"Yeah. Maybe. I think so." Aenea rarely acted petulant during the days I spent with her that week, but her voice seemed perilously close to that now.

"And you just dreamed about this person?"

She sat up in the cushions. "Not *just* dreamed," she said then. "My dreams are important to me. They're sort of more than dreams. . . ." She broke off. "You'll see."

I tried not to sigh aloud. "What happens after you become an architect?"

She chewed on a fingernail. It was a bad habit I planned on breaking her of. "What do you mean?"

"I mean, the old poet's expecting big things of you. . . . Being the messiah's just one part—when does that kick in?"

"Raul," she said, rising to go down to her fugue cubby, "no offense, but why don't you just fuck off and leave me alone?"

SHE HAD APOLOGIZED for that crudity later, but as we sat at the table an hour from translation into a strange star system, I was curious if my question about her plan would elicit the same response.

It did not. She started to chew a nail, caught herself, and said, "Okay, you're right, we need a plan." She looked at A. Bettik. "Do you have one?"

The android shook his head. "Master Silenus and I discussed this many times, M. Aenea, but our conclusion was that if the Pax somehow arrived first at our destination, then all was lost. It seems an improbability, though, since the torchship pursuing us cannot travel more quickly through Hawking space than we can."

"I don't know," I said. "Some of the hunters I've guided the past few years talked about rumors that the Pax . . . or the Church . . . had these superfast ships."

A. Bettik nodded. "We have heard similar rumors, M. Endymion, but logic suggests that if the Pax had developed such craft—a breakthrough which the Hegemony never achieved, by the way—then there seems little reason that they would not have outfitted their warships and Mercantilus vessels with such a drive. . . ."

Aenea tapped the table. "It doesn't really matter *how* they get there first," she said. "I've *dreamed* that they will. I've been considering plans, but . . ."

"What about the Shrike?" I said.

Aenea glanced sideways at me. "What about it?"

"Well," I said, "it provided a pretty convenient *deus ex machina* for us on Hyperion, so I just thought that if it could . . ."

"Damn it, Raul!" cried the girl. "I didn't *ask* that creature to kill those people on Hyperion. I wish to God it hadn't."

"I know, I know," I said, touching her sleeve to calm her. A. Bettik had cut down several of the Consul's old shirts for her, but her wardrobe was still meager.

I knew that she had been upset about the carnage during our escape. She later admitted that it had been part of the reason for her sobbing that second night out.

"I'm sorry," I said sincerely. "I didn't mean to be flippant about the . . . thing. I just thought that if someone tried to stop us again, maybe . . .”

“No,” said Aenea. “I’ve dreamed that someone tries to stop us from getting to Renaissance Vector. But I haven’t dreamed that the Shrike helps us. We have to come up with our own plan.”

“What about the Core?” I said tentatively. It was the first time I’d mentioned the TechnoCore since she had brought it up that first day.

Aenea seemed lost in thought; or at least she ignored my question. “If we’re going to get ourselves out of whatever trouble might be waiting for us, it will have to be our doing. Or maybe . . .” She turned her head. “Ship?”

“Yes, M. Aenea.”

“Have you been listening to this conversation?”

“Of course, M. Aenea.”

“Do you have any ideas that could help us?”

“Help you to avoid capture if Pax ships are waiting for you?”

“Yeah,” said Aenea, her voice irritable. She frequently lost patience with the ship.

“Not any original ideas,” said the ship. “I have been trying to remember how the Consul avoided the local authorities when we were just passing through a system. . . .”

“And?” said Aenea.

“Well, as I have mentioned, my memory is not as complete as it should be. . . .”

“Yes, yes,” said Aenea, “but do you remember any clever ways you avoided local authorities?”

“Well, primarily by outrunning them,” said the ship. “As we have discussed previously, the Ouster modifications were to the containment field and the fusion drive. The latter changes allow me to reach C-plus translation velocities much more quickly than standard spinships . . . or so it was when I last traveled between the stars.”

A. Bettik folded his hands and spoke to the same bulkhead area that Aenea had been watching. “You are saying that if the authorities . . . in this case the Pax ships . . . left from the planet Parvati, or near it, you would be able to make the translation to Renaissance Vector before they could intercept us.”

“Most assuredly,” said the ship.

“How long will the turnaround take?” I asked.

“Turnaround?”

“The time in-system before we can spin up to the quantum jump to Renaissance Vector’s system,” I said.

“Thirty-seven minutes,” said the ship. “Which includes reorientation, navigation checks, and system checks.”

“What if a Pax ship is waiting right there when we spin down?” asked Aenea. “Do you have any Ouster modifications that could help us?”

"Not that I can think of," said the ship. "You know of the enhanced containment fields, but they are still no match for a warship's weapons."

The girl sighed and leaned on the table. "I've been over this and over this, but I don't see how it can help."

A. Bettik looked thoughtful, but then again, he always looked thoughtful. "During the time we were concealing and caring for the ship," he said, "one other Ouster modification became apparent."

"What's that?" I said.

A. Bettik gestured downward, toward the holopit level below us. "They enhanced the ship's morphing ability. The way it can extrude the balcony is one example. Its ability to extend wings during atmospheric flight. It is able to open each separate living level to atmosphere, thus bypassing the old air-lock entrance if necessary."

"Neat," said Aenea, "but I don't see how that would help, unless the ship can morph to the point of passing itself off as a Pax torchship or something. Can you do that, Ship?"

"No, M. Aenea," said the soft male voice. "The Ousters carried out some fascinating piezodynamic engineering on me, but there is still the conservation of mass to reckon with." After a second of silence, "I am sorry, M. Aenea."

"Just a silly idea," said Aenea, then she sat straight up. It was so obvious that something had occurred to her that neither A. Bettik nor I interrupted her train of thought for two minutes. Finally she said, "Ship?"

"Yes, M. Aenea?"

"You're able to morph an air lock . . . or a simple opening . . . anywhere on your hull?"

"Almost anywhere, M. Aenea. There are communications pods and certain drive-related areas in which I could not—"

"But on the living decks?" interrupted the girl. "You could just open them the way you let the upper hull go transparent?"

"Yes, M. Aenea."

"Would the air rush out if you did that?"

The ship's voice sounded mildly shocked as it answered. "I would not allow that to happen, M. Aenea. As with the piano balcony, I would preserve the integrity of all external fields so that—"

"But you *could* open each deck, not just the air lock, and depressurize it?" The girl's persistence was new to me then. It is familiar now.

"Yes, M. Aenea."

A. Bettik and I listened without comment. I could not speak for the android, but I had no idea where the kid was headed with all this. I leaned toward her. "Is this part of a plan?" I said.

Aenea smiled crookedly. It was what I would later think of as her mischievous smile. "It's too primitive to be a plan," she said, "and if my assumptions about why the Pax wants me are wrong . . . well, it won't work." The mischievous smile took on a wry twist. "It probably wouldn't work anyway."

I glanced at my wrist. "We have forty-five minutes until we spin down and find out if someone's waiting," I said. "Do you want to share your plan that wouldn't work?"

The girl began speaking. She did not talk long. When she was finished, the android and I looked at each other. "You're right," I said to her, "it's not much of a plan and it wouldn't work."

Aenea's smile did not falter. She took my hand and turned my wrist so that my chronometer was face-up. "We have forty-one minutes," she said. "Come up with a better one."

24

HE *RAPHAEL* IS ON THE FINAL PART of her return ellipsoid, rushing in-system toward Parvati's sun at .03 of light-speed. The archangel-class courier/warship is ungainly—massive drive bays, cobbled-together com-pods, spin-arms, weapons' platforms and antennae array protruding, its tiny environmental sphere and attached dropship shuttle tucked into the mess almost as an afterthought—but it becomes a serious warship now as it rotates 180 degrees so that it hurtles stern-first toward the projected translation point of the ship it pursues.

"One minute to spindown," de Soya says over the tactical band. The three troopers in the open sally-port air lock do not need to acknowledge the transmission. They also know that even after the other ship appears in real space, it will not be visible to them—even with visor magnifiers—for another two minutes.

Strapped in his acceleration couch with the control panels arrayed around him, his gauntleted hand on the omnicontroller, his tactical shunt in place so that he and the ship are effectively one, Father Captain de Soya listens to the breathing of the three troopers over the com channel while he watches and senses the other ship's approach. "Picking up Hawking-drive distortion reading down angle thirty-nine, coordinates zero-zero-zero, thirty nine, one-nine-niner," he says into his mike. "Exit point at zero-zero-zero, nine hundred klicks. Single vehicle probability, ninety-nine percent. Relative velocity nineteen kps."

Suddenly the other ship becomes visible on radar, t-dirac, and all passive sensors. "Got it," Father Captain de Soya says to the waiting troopers. "On time, on schedule . . . damn."

"What?" says Sergeant Gregorius. He and his men have checked their weapons, charges, and boarding collars. They are ready to jump in less than three minutes.

"The ship's begun accelerating, not decelerating as we'd guessed in most of the sims," says de Soya. On the tactical channel he enables the ship to carry out preprogrammed alternatives. "Hang on!" he says to the troopers, but the thrusters have already fired, *Raphael* is already rotating. "No problem," he says as the main drive kicks on, boosting them to 147 gravities. "Just stay within the field during the jump. It'll take just an extra minute to match velocities."

Gregorius, Kee, and Rettig do not respond. De Soya can hear their breathing.

Two minutes later de Soya says, "I have a visual."

Sergeant Gregorius and his two troopers lean out of the open air lock. Gregorius can see the other ship as a ball of fusion flame. He keys the mag-lenses so he can see beyond that, raises the filters, and sees the ship itself. "Pretty much like the tacticals," says Kee.

"Don't think that way," snaps the sergeant. "The real thing's never like the tacticals." He knows that both these men realize that; they have been in combat. But Sergeant Gregorius was an instructor at Pax Command on Armaghast for three years, and the instinct is hard to break.

"This thing's *fast*," says de Soya. "If we didn't have the bounce on them, I don't think we'd catch them. As it is, we'll just be able to match velocities for five or six minutes."

"We only need three," says Gregorius. "Just get us alongside, Captain."

"Coming alongside now," says de Soya. "She's painting us." The *Raphael* was not designed with stealth capabilities, and now every instrument records the other ship's sensors on her. "One klick," he reports, "still no weapons activity. Fields on full. Delta-v dropping. Eight hundred meters."

Gregorius, Kee, and Rettig unsling their plasma rifles and crouch.

"Three hundred meters . . . two hundred meters . . . ," says de Soya. The other ship is passive, its acceleration high but constant. In most of the sims de Soya had factored in a wild chase before matching speeds and disrupting the other ship's fields. This is too easy. The father-captain feels concern for the first time. "Inside minimum lance range," he reports. "Go!"

The three Swiss Guard troopers explode out of the air lock, their reaction paks spurting blue flame.

"Disrupting . . . now!" cries de Soya. The other ship's fields refuse to drop for an eternity—almost three seconds, a time never simulated in the tactical exercises—but eventually they drop. "Fields down!" calls de Soya, but the troopers already know that—they are tumbling, decelerating, and dropping onto the enemy hull at their prearranged entry points —Kee near the bow, Gregorius on what had been the navigation level on the old schematics, Rettig above the engine room.

"On," comes Gregorius's voice. The other two confirm landing a second later.

"Boarding collars set," pants the sergeant.

"Set," confirms Kee.

"Set," says Rettig.

"Deploy from three," snaps the sergeant. "Three, two, one . . . deploy."

His polymer bag gossamers into sunlight.

On the command couch de Soya is watching the delta-v. The acceleration has risen to more than 230 gravities. If the fields fail now . . . He shoves the thought aside. *Raphael* is straining to her utmost to keep velocities matched. Another four or five minutes, and he will have to fall away or risk overtaxing all the ship's fusion-drive systems. *Hurry,* he thinks toward the combat-armored shapes he sees in tactical space and video screens.

"Ready," reports Kee.

"Ready," comes Rettig's voice from near the stern fins on the absurd ship.

"Set charges," orders Gregorius, and slaps his onto the hull. "From five . . . five, four, three . . ."

"Father Captain de Soya," says a girl's voice.

"Wait!" orders de Soya. The girl's image has appeared on all the com bands. She is sitting at a piano. It is the same child he saw at the Sphinx on Hyperion three months before.

"Stop!" echoes Gregorius, his finger above the detonate button on his wristplate. The other troopers obey. All are watching the vid broadcast on their visor inserts.

"How do you know my name?" asks Father Captain de Soya. Instantly he knows how stupid the question is: it does not matter, his men need to enter the ship within three minutes or the *Raphael* will fall behind, leaving them alone on the other ship. They had simulated that possibility —the troopers taking command of the ship after capturing the girl, slowing to wait for de Soya to catch up—but it is not a preferable scenario. He touches a presspoint that sends his vid image to the girl's ship.

"Hello, Father Captain de Soya," says the girl, her voice in no hurry, her appearance showing little or no stress, "if your men try to enter the ship, I will depressurize my own ship and die."

De Soya blinks. "Suicide is a mortal sin," he says.

On the screen the girl nods seriously. "Yes," she says, "but I am not a Christian. Also, I'd rather go to hell than go with you." De Soya looks intently at the image—her fingers are not near any controls.

"Captain," comes Gregorius's voice on the secure tightbeam channel, "if she opens the air lock, I can get to her and get a transfer bag around her before complete decompression."

On the screen the girl is watching, de Soya's lips are still as he subvocalizes on the tightbeam channel. "She is not of the cross," he says. "If she dies, there's no guarantee that we can revive her."

"The odds are good the ship's surgery can bring her back and repair her from simple decompression," says Gregorius. "It'll take thirty seconds or more for her level to lose all of its air. I can get to her. Give the word."

"I mean it," says the child on the screen. Instantly, a circular section of hull opens under and around Corporal Kee, and atmosphere blasts into vacuum, filling Kee's boarding collar bag like a balloon and tumbling him into it as both crash into the external field and slide toward the stern of the ship. Kee's reaction pak fires madly, and he stabilizes himself before being blown into the fusion tale of the ship.

Gregorius sets his finger on the shaped-charge detonator. "Captain!" he cries.

"Wait," subvocalizes de Soya. It is the sight of the girl in her shirt-sleeves that freezes his heart with anxiety. Space between the two ships is now filled with colloidal particles and ice crystals.

"I'm sealed away from the top room," says the girl, "but if you don't call your men back, I'll open all the levels."

In less than a second the air lock blasts open, and a two-meter circle opens in the hull where Gregorius had been standing. The sergeant had burned his way through the collar bag and jetted to another location as soon as the girl spoke. Now he tumbles away from the blast of atmosphere and small debris jetting from the opening, fires his thrusters, and plants his boots on a section of hull five meters farther down the ship. In his mind he can see the schematic, knows that the girl is just inside—a few meters from his grasp. If she was to blow this section, he would catch her, bag her, and have her in the *Raphael*'s surgery within two minutes. He checks his tactical display: Rettig had jumped into space seconds before a section of hull opened under him. Now the other was station-keeping three meters from the hull. "Captain!" Gregorius calls on the tightbeam.

"Wait," orders de Soya. To the girl, he says, "We mean you no harm—"

"Then call them off," snaps the girl. "Now! Or I open this last level."

Federico de Soya feels time slow down as he weighs his options. He knows that he has less than a minute before he has to throttle back— alarms and telltales are flashing throughout his tactical connections to the ship and across the boards. He does not want to leave his men behind, but the most important factor is the child. His orders are specific and absolute —*Bring the child back alive.*

De Soya's entire tactical virtual environment begins to pulse red, a warning that the ship must decelerate in one minute or automatic over-rides will kick in. His control boards tell the same story. He keys the audible mike channels, broadcasts on common bands as well as tightbeam.

"Gregorius, Rettig, Kee . . . return to the *Raphael*. Now!"

Sergeant Gregorius feels the fury and frustration surge through him like a blast of cosmic radiation, but he is a member of the Swiss Guard. "Returning now, sir!" he snaps, peels off his shaped charge, and kicks off toward the archangel. The other two rise from the hull with blue pinpricks of reaction thrusters. The merged fields flicker just long enough to allow the three armored men to pass through. Gregorius reaches the *Raphael*'s hull first, grabs a holdon, and literally flings his men into the sally-port lock as they float by. He pulls himself in, confirms that the others are clinging to web restraints, and keys his mike. "In and tight, sir."

"Breaking off," says de Soya, broadcasting in the clear so that the girl can also hear. He switches from tactical space to real time and tweaks the omnicontroller.

Raphael cuts back from its 110 percent thrust, separates its field from the target's, and begins to fall behind. De Soya widens the distance from the girl's ship, keeping *Raphael* as far away from the other craft's fusion tail as he can: all indications are that the other ship is unarmed, but that term is relative when the thing's fusion drive can reach a hundred kilometers through space. *Raphael*'s external fields are on full defensive, the ship's countermeasures on full automatic, ready to react in a millionth of a second.

The girl's ship continues accelerating off the plane of the ecliptic. Parvati is not the child's destination.

A rendezvous with the Ousters? wonders de Soya. His ship's sensors still show no activity beyond Parvati's orbital patrols, but entire Ouster Swarms could be waiting beyond the heliosphere.

Twenty minutes later, the child's ship already hundreds of thousands of klicks ahead of *Raphael*, the question is answered.

"We've got Hawking-space distortion here," Father Captain de Soya reports to the three men still clinging to restraints in the sally-port lock. "Her ship is preparing to spin up."

"To where?" asks Gregorius. The huge sergeant's voice reveals none of his fury at the near miss.

De Soya pauses and rechecks his readings before answering. "Renaissance Vector space," he says. "Very close to the planet."

Gregorius and the other two Swiss Guard troopers are silent. De Soya can guess their unspoken questions. *Why Renaissance Vector? It's a Pax stronghold . . . two billion Christians, tens of thousands of troops, scores of Pax warships. Why there?*

"Perhaps she doesn't know what's there," he muses aloud over the intercom. He switches to tactical space and hovers above the plane of the ecliptic, watching the red dot spin up to C-plus and disappear from the solar system. The *Raphael* still follows its stern chase course, fifty minutes from translation vector. De Soya leaves tactical, checks all systems, and says, "You can come up from the lock now. Secure all boarding gear."

HE DOES NOT ASK THEIR OPINION. There is no discussion of whether he will translate the archangel to Renaissance Vector space—the course has already been set in and the ship is climbing toward quantum leap—and he does not ask them again if they are prepared to die again. This jump will be as fatal as the last, of course, but it will put them into Pax-occupied space five months ahead of the girl's ship. The only question in de Soya's mind is whether or not to wait for the *St. Anthony* to spin down into Parvati space so he can explain the situation to the captain.

He decides not to wait. It makes little sense—a few hours' difference in a five-month head start—but he does not have the patience to wait. De Soya orders *Raphael* to prepare a transponder buoy, and he records the orders for Captain Sati on the *Anthony:* immediate translation to Renaissance Vector—a ten-day trip for the torchship with the same five-month time-debt that the girl will pay—with readiness for combat immediately upon spinning down to RV space.

When he has launched the buoy and tightbeamed standdown orders to the Parvati command, de Soya turns his acceleration couch to face the other three men. "I know how disappointing that was to you," he begins.

Sergeant Gregorius says nothing, and his dark face is as impassive as stone, but Father Captain de Soya can read the message behind the silence: *Another thirty seconds and I would have had her.*

De Soya does not care. He has commanded men and women for over a decade—has sent braver, more loyal underlings than this to their deaths without allowing remorse or the need for explanation to overwhelm him —so he does not blink now in front of the giant trooper. "I think the child would have carried out her threat," he says, his tone of voice conveying the message that this is not open to discussion or argument, now or later, "but that's a moot point now. We know where she's going. It may be the one system in this sector of Pax space where no one—not even an Ouster Swarm—could get in or out unseen and uninterdicted. We're going to have five months to prepare for the ship's arrival, and this time we won't be operating alone." De Soya pauses to take a breath. "You three have worked hard, and this failure in Parvati system is not yours. I'll see to it that you are returned to your unit immediately upon arrival in Renaissance Vector space."

Gregorius does not even have to glance at his two men before speaking for them. "Begging the father-captain's pardon, but if we have a say in it, sir, we'd choose to stay with you and *Raphael* until this young 'un's safely in the net and on her way to Pacem, sir."

De Soya tries not to show his surprise. "Hmmm . . . well, we'll see what happens, Sergeant. Renaissance Vector is Fleet Headquarters for the navy, and a lot of our bosses will be there. We'll see what happens. Let's get everything tied down. . . . We translate in twenty-five minutes."

"Sir?"

"Yes, Corporal Kee?"

"Will you be hearing confessions before we die this time?"

De Soya works again to keep his expression neutral. "Yes, Corporal. I'll finish the checklist here and be in the wardroom cubby for confession in ten minutes."

"Thank you, sir," says Kee with a smile.

"Thank you," says Rettig.

"Thank 'ee, Father," rumbles Gregorius.

De Soya watches the three jump to tie-down activities, shedding their massive combat armor as they go. In that instant he catches an intuitive glimpse of the future and feels the weight of it on his shoulders. *Lord, give me strength to carry out Thy will . . . in Jesus' name I ask. . . . Amen.*

Swiveling his heavy couch back to the command panels, de Soya begins the final checklist before translation and death.

25

O NCE, WHILE GUIDING some duck hunters born on Hyperion into the fens, I asked one of them, an airship pilot who commanded the weekly dirigible run down the Nine Tails from Equus to Aquila, what his job was like. "Piloting an airship?" he'd said. "As the ancient line goes—long hours of boredom broken by minutes of sheer panic."

This trip was a bit like that. I don't mean to say that I was bored— just the interior of the spaceship with its books and old holos and grand piano was interesting enough to keep me from being bored for the next ten days, not to mention getting to know my traveling companions—but already we had experienced these long, slow, pleasantly idle periods punctuated by interludes of wild adrenaline rush.

I admit that it had been disturbing in Parvati System to sit out of sight of the vid pickup and watch this child threaten to kill herself—and us!—if the Pax ship did not back off. I'd spent ten months dealing blackjack on Felix, one of the Nine Tails, and had watched a lot of gamblers; this eleven-year-old was one hell of a poker player. Later, when I asked her if she would have carried through on the threat and opened our last pressurized level to space, she only smiled that mischievous smile and made a vague gesture with her right hand, a sort of flicking away, as if she were brushing the thought out of the air. I grew used to that gesture in later months and years.

"Well, how *did* you know that Pax captain's name?" I asked.

I expected to hear some revelation about the powers of a proto-messiah, but Aenea only said, "He was waiting at the Sphinx when I stepped out a week ago. I guess I heard someone call his name."

I doubted that. If the father-captain had been at the Sphinx, Pax-army standard procedure would have had him buttoned into combat armor and communicating on secure channels. But why would the child lie?

Why am I seeking logic or sanity here? I'd asked myself at the moment. *There hasn't been any so far.*

When Aenea had gone belowdecks to take a shower after our dramatic departure from Parvati System, the ship had tried to reassure A. Bettik and me. "Do not worry, gentlemen. I would not have allowed you to die from decompression."

The android and I had exchanged a look. I think that both of us were wondering whether the ship knew what it would have done, or whether the child had some special control over it.

As the days of the second leg of the voyage passed, I found myself brooding about the situation and my reaction to it. The main problem, I realized, had been my passivity—almost irrelevancy—during this whole trip. I was twenty-seven years old, an ex-soldier, man of the world—even if the world was only backwater Hyperion—and here I had let a child deal with the one real emergency we'd faced. I understood why A. Bettik had been so passive in the situation; he was, after all, conditioned by bio-programming and centuries of habit to defer to human decisions. But why had I been such a stump? Martin Silenus had saved my life and sent me on this insane quest to protect the girl, to keep her alive and help her get wherever she had to go. So far, all I had done was fly a carpet and hide behind a piano while the kid dealt with a Pax warship.

The four of us, including the ship, talked about that Pax warship during those first few days out from Parvati space. If Aenea was right, if Father Captain de Soya had been on Hyperion during the opening of the tomb, then the Pax had found some way to take a shortcut through Hawking space. The implications of that reality were more than sobering; they scared the shit out of me.

Aenea did not seem overly worried. The days passed and we fell into the comfortable, if a bit claustrophobic, shipboard routine—Aenea playing the piano after dinner, all of us grazing in the library, checking the ship's holos and navigation logs for any clue as to where it had taken the Consul (there were many clues, none definitive), playing cards in the evening (she *was* a formidable poker player), and occasionally exercising, which I did by asking the ship to set the containment field to one-point-three-g just in the stairwell, and then running up and down the six stories' worth of spiral steps for forty-five minutes. I'm not sure what it did for the rest of my body, but my calves, thighs, and ankles soon looked like they belonged to some Jovian-world elephantoid.

When Aenea realized that the field could be tailored to small regions of the ship, there was no stopping her. She began sleeping in a bubble of zero-g on the fugue deck. She found that the table on the library deck could be morphed into a billiard table, and she insisted on at least two games a day—each time under different g-loads. One night

I heard a noise while reading on the navigation level, went down the stairs to the holopit level, and found the hull irised open, the balcony extended without the piano there, and a giant sphere of water—perhaps eight or ten meters across—floating between the balcony and the outer containment field.

"What the hell?"

"It's fun!" came a voice from within the pulsing blob of shifting water. A head with wet hair broke the surface, hanging upside down two meters above the floor of the balcony. "Come on in!" cried the girl. "The water's warm."

I leaned away from the apparition, putting my weight on the railing and trying not to think of what would happen if that localized bubble of the field failed for a second.

"Has A. Bettik seen this?" I said.

The pale shoulders shrugged. The fractal fireworks were pulsing and folding out beyond the balcony, casting incredible colors and reflections on the sphere of water. The sphere itself was a great blue blob with lighter patches on the surface and interior, where bubbles of air shifted. Actually, it reminded me of photos of Old Earth I had seen.

Aenea ducked her head under, was a pale form kicking through the water for a moment, and reemerged five meters up the curved surface. Smaller globules splashed free and curved back to the surface of the larger sphere—herded there by the field differential, I assumed—splashing and sending complex, concentric circles rippling across the surface of the water globe.

"Come on in," she said again. "I mean it!"

"I don't have a suit."

Aenea floated a second, kicked over onto her stomach, and dived again. When she emerged, head completely upside down from my perspective this time, she said, "Who has a suit? You don't need one!"

I knew she was not joking because during her dive I had seen the pale vertebrae pressing against the skin of her back, her ribs, and her still-boylike butt reflecting the fractal light like two small white mushrooms poking up from a pond. All in all, the sight of our twelve-year-old messiah-to-be's backside was about as sexually arousing as seeing holoslides of Aunt Merth's new grandkiddies in the tub.

"Come on in, Raul!" she called again, and dived for the opposite side of the sphere.

I hesitated only a second before kicking off my robe and outer clothes. I kept on not only my undershorts, but the long undershirt I often wore as pajamas.

For a moment I stood on the balcony, not having the slightest clue as to how to get into the sphere several meters above me. Then I heard, "Jump, dummy!" from somewhere on the upper arc of the blob, and I jumped.

The transition to zero-g began about a meter and a half up. The water was damned cold.

I pivoted, shouted from the cold, felt everything contractable on my body contract, and began splashing around, trying to keep my head above the curved surface. I was not surprised when A. Bettik came out on the balcony to see what the shouting was all about. He folded his arms and leaned against the railing, crossing his legs at the ankles.

"The water's warm!" I lied through chattering teeth. "C'mon in!"

The android smiled and shook his head like a patient parent. I shrugged and pivoted and dived.

It took me a second or two to remember that swimming is much like moving in zero-g; that floating in water in zero-g is much like ordinary swimming. Either way, the resistance of the water made the experience more swimlike than zero-g-like, although there was the added fun of coming across an air bubble somewhere inside the sphere and pausing there to catch one's breath before paddling around underwater again.

After a moment of cartwheeling disorientation, I came to a meter-wide bubble, stopped myself before tumbling out into the sphere, and looked directly above me to see Aenea's head and shoulders emerging. She looked down at me and waved. The skin on her bare chest was goose-bumpy from either the cool water or cooler air.

"Some fun, huh?" she said, spluttering water out of her face and brushing back her hair with both hands. Her blond-brown hair looked much darker when wet. I looked at the girl and tried to see her mother in her, the dark-haired Lusian detective. It was no use—I had never seen an image of Brawne Lamia, only heard descriptions from the *Cantos*.

"The hard part's keeping yourself from flying out of the water when you get to the edge," said Aenea as our bubble shifted and contracted, the wall of water curving around and above us. "Race you to the outside!"

She pivoted and kicked, and I tried to follow, but made the mistake of flailing across the air bubble—my God, I hope that neither A. Bettik nor the child saw that pathetic spasm of arms and legs—and ended up at the edge of the sphere half a minute behind her. We treaded water there; the ship and balcony were out of sight beneath us, the surface of the water curved away to the left and right, dropping out of sight like waterfalls on all sides of us, while above us the crimson fractals expanded, exploded, contracted, and expanded again.

"I wish we could see the stars," I said, and was surprised that I had spoken aloud.

"Me too," said Aenea. Her face was raised to the disturbing light show, and I thought I saw a shadow of sadness flicker across her features. "I'm cold," she said at last. I could see her clenched jaws now, sense her effort to keep her teeth from chattering. "Next time I tell the ship to build the pool, I'll remind it not to use cold water."

"You'd better get out," I said. We swam down and around the curve of the sphere. The balcony seemed to be a wall rising to greet us, its only anomaly the form of A. Bettik standing sideways from it, holding out a large towel for Aenea.

"Close your eyes," she said. I did and felt the heavy zero-g globules of splash-water strike my face as she flailed her way right through the surface tension of the sphere and floated beyond it. A second later I heard the slap of her bare feet as she landed on the balcony.

I waited a few more seconds and opened my eyes. A. Bettik had set the voluminous towel around her and she was huddled in it, teeth chattering now despite her efforts to stop them. "B-b-be care-f-ful," she said. "Ro-ro-tate as s-s-soon as you get out of the w-w-w-water, or you'll f-f-fall on your h-head and b-b-break your neck."

"Thanks," I said, having no intention of leaving the sphere before she and A. Bettik left the balcony. They did so a moment later and I paddled out, kicked arms and legs in a wild attempt to turn 180 degrees before gravity reasserted itself, pivoted too far, overcompensated, and landed heavily on my rear end.

I pulled down the extra towel that A. Bettik had thoughtfully left on the railing for me, mopped my face, and said, "Ship, you can collapse the zero-g microfield now."

I realized my mistake an instant later, but before I could countermand the order, several hundred gallons of water collapsed onto the balcony—a massive waterfall of bone-chilling weight crashing down from a great height. If I had been directly under it, it might well have killed me—a mildly ironic end to a great adventure—but since I was sitting a couple of meters from the edge of the deluge, it merely smashed me against the balcony, caught me up in its vortex as it spilled up and over the railing, and threatened to fling me out into space and down past the stern of the ship fifteen meters below, down to the bottom of the ellipsoid bubble of containment field, where I would end up like a drowned insect in an ovoid beaker.

I grabbed at the railing and held on while the torrent roared by.

"Sorry," said the ship, realizing its own error and reshaping the field around us to contain and collect the deluge. I noticed that none of it had washed through the open doorway into the holopit level.

When the microfield had lifted the water away in sloshing spheres, I found my sodden towel and walked through the doorway into the ship. As the hull irised shut behind me, the water presumably being returned to its holding tanks before being purified again for our use or as reaction mass, I stopped suddenly.

"Ship!" I demanded.

"Yes, M. Endymion?"

"That wasn't your idea of a practical joke, was it?"

"Do you mean obeying your order to collapse the zero-g microfield, M. Endymion?"

"Yeah."

"The consequences were the result of a minor oversight only, M. Endymion. I do not commit practical jokes. Be assured, I do not suffer from a sense of humor."

"Hmmm," I said, not totally convinced. Carrying my wet shoes and clothing with me, I squished upstairs to dry off and get dressed.

THE NEXT DAY I VISITED A. BETTIK down in what he called the "engine room." The place did have somewhat the sense of an engine room in an oceangoing ship—warm pipes, obscure but massive dynamo-shaped objects, catwalks and metal platforms—but A. Bettik showed me how the primary purpose of the space was to interface with the ship's drives and field generators via various simstimlike connectors. I admit that I've never enjoyed computer-generated realities, and after sampling a few of the virtual views of the ship, I disconnected and sat by A. Bettik's hammock while we talked. He told me about helping to service and refit this ship over the long decades, and how he had begun to believe it would never fly again. I sensed a relief that the voyage was under way.

"Had you always planned to go on the trip with whomever the old poet chose to go with the girl?" I asked.

The android looked steadily at me. "For the past century I have harbored the thought, M. Endymion. But I rarely considered it a potential reality. I thank you for making it so."

His gratitude was so sincere that it embarrassed me for a moment. "You'd better not thank me until we escape the Pax," I said to change the subject. "I suppose they'll be waiting for us in Renaissance Vector space."

"It seems likely." The blue-skinned man did not seem especially concerned by the prospect.

"Do you think Aenea's threat of opening the ship to space will work a second time?" I said.

A. Bettik shook his head. "They wish to capture the girl alive, but they will not be taken in by that bluff again."

I raised my eyebrows. "Do you really think she was bluffing? I had the impression that she was ready to open our level to vacuum."

"I think not," said A. Bettik. "I do not know this young person well, of course, but I had the pleasure of spending some days with her mother and the other pilgrims during their crossing of Hyperion. M. Lamia was a woman who loved life and respected the lives of others. I believe that M. Aenea might have carried out the threat if she had been alone, but I do not think that she is capable of choosing to hurt you or me."

I had nothing to say to that, so we spoke of other things—the ship, our destination, how strange the Web worlds must be after all this time since the Fall.

"If we land on Renaissance Vector," I said, "do you plan to leave us there?"

"Leave you?" said A. Bettik, showing surprise for the first time. "Why would I leave you there?"

I made a lame gesture with my hand. "Well . . . I guess . . . I mean, I always thought you wanted your freedom and would find it on the first civilized world we landed on. . . ." I stopped before I made more of an idiot of myself.

"My freedom is found by being allowed to come along on this voyage," the android said softly. He smiled. "And, besides, M. Endymion, I could hardly blend in with the populace if I did want to stay on Renaissance Vector."

This raised an issue I'd been thinking about. "You could change your skin color," I said. "The ship's autosurgeon could do that. . . ." I stopped again, seeing something subtle in his expression that I did not understand.

"As you know, M. Endymion," began A. Bettik, "we androids are not programmed like machines . . . not even set with basic parameters and asimotivators like the early DNA AIs which evolved into the Core intelligences . . . but certain inhibitions were . . . ah . . . strongly urged on us when our instincts were being designed. One, of course, is to obey humans whenever reasonable and to keep them from coming to harm. This asimotivator is older than robotics or bioengineering, I am told. But another . . . instinct . . . is not to change my skin color."

"You're not capable of it?" I asked. "You couldn't do it if our lives depended upon your concealing your blue skin?"

"Oh, yes," said A. Bettik, "I am a creature of free will. I could do so, especially if the action was consistent with high-priority asimotivations, such as keeping you and M. Aenea safe from harm, but my choice would make me . . . uncomfortable. Very uncomfortable."

I nodded but did not really understand. We spoke of other things.

THIS WAS THE SAME DAY that I inventoried the contents of the weapons and EVA lockers on the main air-lock level. There was more there than I'd thought upon first inspection, and some of the objects were so archaic that I had to ask the ship their purpose. Most of the things in the EVA locker were obvious enough—spacesuits and hazardous-atmosphere suits, four flybikes cleverly folded into their storage niches under the spacesuit closet, heavy-duty handlamps, camping gear, osmosis masks and scuba gear with flippers and spearguns, one EM-flying belt, three boxes of tools, two well-equipped medkits, six sets of night-vision and IR goggles, an equal number of lightweight headsets with mike-bead communicators and vid cameras, and comlogs. These last items caused me to query the ship: on a world without a datasphere, I had grown up with little use for the things. The comlogs ranged from antiquated—the thin silver band of jewelry type that was popular several decades ago—to absolutely ancient: massive things the size of a small book. All were capable of being used as communicators, of storing massive amounts of data, of tapping into the local datasphere, and—especially with the older ones—of actually hooking into planetary fatline relays via remote so that the megasphere could be accessed.

I held one of the bracelet pieces in my palm. It weighed much less than a gram. Useless. I understood from listening to offworld hunters that there were a few worlds with primitive dataspheres once again—Renaissance Vector was one of them, I thought—but the fatline relays had been useless for almost three centuries. The fatline—that common band of FTL communication upon which the Hegemony had depended—had been silent since the Fall. I started to put the comlog back in its velvet-lined case.

"You might find it useful to take with you if you leave me for any period of time," said the ship.

I glanced over my shoulder. "Why?"

"Information," said the ship. "I would be happy to download the bulk of my basic datalogs into one or more of those. You could access it at will."

I chewed my lip, trying to imagine any value in having the ship's confused mass of data on my wrist. Then I heard Grandam's voice from my childhood—*Information is always to be treasured, Raul. It is behind only love and honesty in a person's attempt to understand the universe.*

"Good idea," I said, snapping the thin silver thread around my wrist. "When can you download the data banks?"

"I just did," said the ship.

I had gone through the weapons locker carefully before we had reached Parvati space; there had been nothing there which could have slowed a Swiss Guardsman for a second. Now I studied the contents of the locker with different purposes in mind.

It is odd how old things look old. The spacesuits and flybikes and handlamps—almost everything aboard the ship—seemed antiquated, out of style. There were no skinsuits, for instance, and the bulk, design, and color of everything seemed like a holo from a history text. But the weapons were a slightly different story. They were old, yes, but very familiar to my eye and hand.

The Consul had obviously been a hunter. There were half a dozen shotguns on the rack: well oiled and stored properly. I could have taken any one of them and headed for the fens to bag ducks. They ranged from a petite .310 over-and-under to a massive 28-gauge double barrel. I chose an ancient but perfectly preserved 16-gauge pump with actual cartridges and set it in the corridor.

The rifles and energy weapons were beautiful. The Consul must have been a collector, because these specimens were works of art as well as killing devices—scrollwork on the stocks, blue steel, hand-fitted elements, perfect balance. In the millennium and more since the twentieth century, when personal weapons were mass-produced to be incredibly deadly, cheap, and ugly as metal doorstops, some of us—the Consul and I among the few—had learned to treasure beautiful handmade or limited-production guns. On the rack here were high-caliber hunting rifles, plasma rifles (not a misnomer, I had learned while in Home Guard basic training—the plasma cartridges were bolts of sheer energy, of course, when they emerged from the barrel, but the cartridges did benefit from the barrel's rifling before they volatilized), two elaborately carved laser-based energy rifles (this *was* a misnomer, an artifact of language rather than design) not that different from the one M. Herrig had killed Izzy with not so many days earlier, a matte-black FORCE assault rifle that probably resembled the one Colonel Fedmahn Kassad had brought to Hyperion three centuries ago, a huge-bore plasma weapon that the Consul must have used for shooting dinosaurs on some world, and three handguns. There were no deathwands. I was glad; I hated the damned things.

I removed one of the plasma rifles, the FORCE assault weapon, and the handguns for further inspection.

The FORCE weapon was ugly, an exception to the Consul's collecting scheme, but I saw why it had been useful. The thing was multipurpose—an 18-mm plasma rifle, a variable-beam coherent-energy weapon, grenade launcher, a bhee-keeper (beams of high-energy electrons), flechette launcher, a wideband blinder, heat-seeking dart flinger—hell, a FORCE assault weapon could do everything but cook the trooper's meals. (And, when in the field, the variable-beam, set to low, could usually do that as well.)

Before entering Parvati System, I had toyed with greeting any Swiss Guard boarders with the FORCE weapon, but modern combat suits would have shrugged off everything it could dole out, and—to be honest—I had been afraid it would make the Pax troopers mad.

Now I studied it more carefully; something this flexible might be useful if we wandered too far from the ship and I had to take on a more primitive foe—say, a caveman, or a jet fighter, or some poor slob equipped as we had been in Hyperion's Home Guard. In the end, I rejected taking it—it was prohibitively heavy if one weren't in an old FORCE exopowered combat suit, the thing had no ammunition for the flechette, grenade, or bhee settings, 18-mm pulse cartridges were impossible to find anymore, and to use the energy-weapon options, I would have to be near the ship or some other serious power source. I set the assault gun back in place, realizing as I did so that it might well have been the legendary Colonel Kassad's personal weapon. It did not fit the profile of the Consul's personal collection, but he had known Kassad—perhaps he had kept the thing for sentimental reasons.

I asked the ship, but the ship did not remember. "Surprise, surprise," I muttered.

The handguns were more ancient than the assault gun, but much more promising. Each was a collector's item, but they used cartridge magazines that could still be purchased—at least on Hyperion. I couldn't vouch for the worlds we would visit. The biggest weapon was a .60-caliber Steiner-Ginn full-auto Penetrator. It was a serious weapon, but heavy: the cartridge templates weighed almost as much as the handgun, and it was designed to use ammunition at a prodigious rate. I set it back. The other two were more promising: a small, light, eminently portable flechette pistol that might have been the great-granddaddy of the weapon M. Herrig had tried to kill me with. It came with several hundred shiny little needle-eggs—the grip magazine held five at a time—and each of the eggs held several thousand of the flechettes. It was a good weapon for someone who was not necessarily a good shot.

The final handgun amazed me. It was in its own oiled leather holster. I removed the weapon with fingers that were slightly shaking. I knew it only from old books—a .45-caliber semiautomatic handgun, actual cartridges—the kind that came in brass casings, not a magazine template that created them as the gun was fired—patterned grip, metal sights, blue steel. I turned the weapon over in my hands. This thing could date back more than a thousand years.

I looked in the case in which I had found it: five boxes of .45 cartridges, several hundred rounds. I thought that they must be ancient as well, but I found the manufacturer's tag: Lusus. About three centuries ago.

Hadn't Brawne Lamia carried an ancient .45, according to the Cantos? Later, when I asked Aenea, the child said that she had never seen her mother with a handgun.

Still, it and the flechette pistol seemed like weapons we should have with us. I did not know if the .45 cartridges would still fire, so I carried one out on the balcony, warned the ship that the external field should stop the slug from ricocheting, and squeezed the trigger. Nothing. Then I remembered that these things had a manual safety. I found it, clicked it off, and tried again. My God, it was loud. But the bullets still worked. I set the weapon in its holster and clipped the holster to my utility belt. It felt right there. Of course, when the last .45 cartridge had been fired, that would be it forever unless I could find an antique gun club that manufactured them.

I don't plan to have to fire several hundred bullets at anything, I thought wryly at the time. If only I had known.

Meeting with the girl and android later, I showed them the shotgun and plasma hunting rifle I'd chosen, the flechette pistol, and the .45. "If we go wandering through strange places—uninhabited strange places—we should go armed," I said. I offered the flechette pistol to both of them, but they both refused. Aenea wanted no weapon; the android pointed out that he could not use one against a human being, and he trusted me to be around if a fierce animal was chasing him.

I grunted but set the rifle, shotgun, and flechette pistol aside. "I'll wear this," I said, touching the .45.

"It matches your outfit," Aenea said with a slight smile.

THERE WAS NO LAST-MINUTE desperate discussion of a plan this time. None of us believed that Aenea's threat of self-destruction would work again if the Pax was waiting. Our most serious discussion of coming events came two days before we spun down into the Renaissance System. We had eaten well—A. Bettik had prepared a filet of river manta with a light sauce, and we had raided the ship's wine cellar for a fine wine from the Beak's vineyards—and after an hour of music with Aenea on the piano and the android playing a flute he had brought with him, talk turned to the future.

"Ship, what can you tell us about Renaissance Vector?" asked the girl.

There was that brief pause that I had come to associate with the ship being embarrassed. "I am sorry, M. Aenea, but other than navigational information and orbital approach maps which are centuries out of date, I am afraid I have no information about the world."

"I have been there," said A. Bettik. "Also centuries ago, but we have been monitoring radio and television traffic that refers to the planet."

"I've heard some of my offworld hunters talk," I said. "Some of the richest are from Renaissance V." I gestured to the android. "Why don't you start?"

He nodded and folded his arms. "Renaissance Vector was one of the most important worlds of the Hegemony. Extremely Earth-like on the Solmev Scale, it was settled by early seedships and was completely urbanized by the time of the Fall. It was famous for its universities, its medical centers—most Poulsen treatments were administered there for the Web citizens who could afford it—its baroque architecture—especially beautiful in its mountain fortress, Keep Enable—and its industrial output. Most of the FORCE spacecraft were manufactured there. In fact, *this* spacecraft must have been built there—it was a product of the Mitsubishi-Havcek complex."

"Really?" said the ship's voice. "If I knew that, the data have been lost. How interesting."

Aenea and I exchanged worried glances for the dozenth time on this voyage. A ship that couldn't remember its past or point of origin did not inspire confidence during the complexities of interstellar flight. *Oh, well,* I thought for the dozenth time, *it got us in and out of Parvati System all right.*

"DaVinci is the capital of Renaissance Vector," continued A. Bettik, "although the entire landmass and much of the single large sea are urbanized, so there is little distinction between one urban center and the other."

"It's a busy Pax world," I added. "One of the earliest to join the Pax after the Fall. The military is there in spades . . . both Renaissance V. and Renaissance M. have orbital and lunar garrisons, as well as bases all over each planet."

"What's Renaissance M.?" asked Aenea.

"Renaissance Minor," said A. Bettik. "The second world from the sun . . . Renaissance V. is the third. Minor is also inhabited, but much less so. It is a largely agricultural world—huge automated farms covering much of the planet—and it feeds Vector. After the Fall of the farcasters, both worlds benefitted from this arrangement; before regularly scheduled interstellar commerce was reinstated by the Pax, the Renaissance System was fairly self-contained. Renaissance Vector manufactured goods; Renaissance Minor provided the food for the five billion people on Renaissance Vector."

"What's the population on Renaissance V. now?" I asked.

"I believe it is about the same—five billion people, give or take a few hundred million," said A. Bettik. "As I said, the Pax arrived early and offered both the cruciform and the birth-control regime that goes with it."

"You said you'd been there," I said to the android. "What's the world like?"

"Ahh," said A. Bettik with a rueful smile, "I was at the Renaissance Vector spaceport for less than thirty-six hours while being shipped from Asquith in preparation for our colonizing King William's new land on Hyperion. They did rouse us from cryogenic sleep but did not allow us to leave the ship. My personal recollections of the world are not extensive."

"Are they mostly born-again Christians there?" asked Aenea. The girl seemed thoughtful and somewhat withdrawn. I noticed that she had been chewing her nails again.

"Oh, yes," said A. Bettik. "Almost all five billion of them, I'm afraid."

"And I wasn't kidding about the heavy Pax military presence," I said. "The Pax troopers who trained us in the Hyperion Home Guard staged out of Renaissance V. It's a major garrison world and transshipment point for the whole war against the Ousters."

Aenea nodded but still seemed distracted.

I decided not to beat around the bush. "Why are we going there?" I asked.

She looked up at me. Her dark eyes were beautiful but remote that moment. "I want to see the River Tethys."

I shook my head. "The River Tethys was a farcaster construct, you know. It didn't exist outside the Web. Or, rather, it existed as a thousand small sections of other rivers."

"I know," she said. "But I want to see a river that was *part* of Tethys during the Web days. My mother told me about it. How it was like the Grand Concourse, only more leisurely. How one could ride a barge from world to world for weeks—months."

I resisted the impulse to get angry. "You know there's almost no chance we can get past their defenses to Renaissance Vector," I said. "And if we get there, River Tethys won't be there . . . just whatever portion used to be part of it. What's so important about seeing that?"

The girl started to shrug, then caught herself. "Remember how I said that there's an architect I need to . . . want to . . . study with?"

"Yes," I said. "But you don't know his name or what world he's on. So why come to Renaissance Vector to start your search? Couldn't we look on Renaissance Minor, at least? Or just skip this system and go somewhere empty, like Armaghast?"

Aenea shook her head. I noticed that she had brushed her hair especially well; the blond highlights were very visible. "In my dreams," she said, "one of the architect's buildings lies near the River Tethys."

"There are hundreds of other old Tethys worlds," I said, leaning closer to her so she could see that I was very serious. "Not all of them will get us caught or killed by the Pax. Do we have to start in Renaissance System?"

"I think so," she said softly.

I dropped my large hands to my knees. Martin Silenus had not said that this trip would be easy or make sense—he had just said that it would make me a Hero. "All right," I said again, hearing the weariness in my own voice, "what's our plan this time, kiddo?"

"No plan," said Aenea. "If they're waiting for us, I'm just going to tell them the truth—that we're going to land the ship on Renaissance Vector. I think they'll let us land."

"And if they do?" I said, trying to imagine the ship surrounded by thousands of Pax troopers.

"We'll take it from there, I guess," said the girl. She smiled at me. "Want to play one-sixth-g billiards, you two? For money this time?"

I started to say something sharp, then changed my tone. "You don't have any money," I said.

Aenea's grin grew wider. "Then I can't lose, can I?"

26

URING THE 142 DAYS that Father Captain de Soya waits for the
girl to enter Renaissance System, he dreams about her every
night. He sees her clearly as she was when first encountered at
the Sphinx on Hyperion—willow thin, eyes alert but not terrified despite
the sandstorm and threatening figures before her, her small hands partially
raised as if ready to cover her face or rush forward to hug him. Often in his
dreams she is his daughter and they are walking the crowded canal-streets
of Renaissance Vector, discussing de Soya's older sister, Maria, who has
been sent to the St. Jude Medical Center in DaVinci. In his dreams de Soya
and the child walk hand in hand through the familiar canal-streets near
the huge medical complex while he explains to her how he plans to save
his sister's life this time, how he will not allow Maria to die the way she
had the first time.

In reality, Federico de Soya had been six standard years old when he
and his family came to Renaissance Vector from their isolated region of
Llano Estacado on their provincial world of MadredeDios. Almost everyone on the sparsely populated stone-and-desert world was Catholic, but
not Pax born-again Catholic. The de Soya family had been part of the
break-away Mariaist movement and had left Nuevo Madrid more than a
century earlier when that world had voted to join the Pax and have all of
its Christian churches submit to the Vatican. The Mariaists venerated the
Holy Mother of Christ more than Vatican orthodoxy allowed, so young
Federico had grown up on a marginal desert world with its devout colony
of sixty thousand heretical Catholics who, as a form of protest, refused to
accept the cruciform.

Then twelve-year-old Maria had become sick with an offworld retrovirus that swept like a scythe through the colony ranching region. Most

sufferers of the Red Death either died within thirty-two hours or recovered, but Maria had lingered, her once-beautiful features all but obscured by the terrible, crimson stigmata. The family had taken her to the hospital in Ciudad del Madre on the windswept southern reach of Llano Estacado, but Mariaist medics there could do nothing but pray. There was a new Pax born-again Christian mission in Ciudad del Madre, discriminated against but tolerated by the locals, and the priest there—a kindly man named Father Maher—begged Federico's father to allow their dying child to accept the cruciform. Federico was too young to remember the details of his parents' agonized discussions, but he did remember the entire family—his mother and father, his other two sisters and younger brother—all on their knees in the Mariaist church there, begging for the Holy Mother's guidance and intercession.

It was the other ranchers of the Llano Estacado Mariaist Cooperative who raised the money to send the entire family offworld to one of the famous medical centers on Renaissance Vector. While his brother and other sisters were left behind with a neighboring ranch family, for some reason six-year-old Federico was chosen to accompany his parents and dying sister on the long voyage. It was everyone's first experience with actual coldsleep—more dangerous but cheaper than cryogenic fugue—and de Soya later remembered the chill in his bones that seemed to last through their weeks on Renaissance Vector.

At first the Pax medics in DaVinci seemed to arrest the spread of the Red Death through Maria's system, even banishing some of the bleeding stigmata, but the after three local weeks, the retrovirus again gained the upper hand. Once again a Pax priest—in this case, several who were on the staff of the hospital—beseeched de Soya's parents to bend their Mariaist principles and allow the dying child to accept the cruciform before it was too late. Later, as he entered adulthood, de Soya could better imagine the agonies of his parents' decision—the death of one's deepest beliefs, or the death of one's child.

In his dream, where Aenea is his daughter and they are walking the canal-streets near the medical center, he describes to her how Maria had given him her most prized possession—a tiny porcelain sculpture of a unicorn—just hours before she had slipped into a coma. In his dream, he walks with the 12-year-old Hyperion girl's small hand in his, and tells her how his father—a strong man in both body and belief—had finally surrendered and asked for the Pax priests to administer the sacrament of the cross to his daughter. The priests at the hospital agreed, but insisted that de Soya's parents and Federico formally convert to universal Catholicism before Maria could receive her cruciform.

De Soya explains to his daughter, Aenea, how he remembers the brief rebaptism ceremony at the local cathedral—St. John the Divine—where he and his parents renounced the ascendancy of the Holy Mother, and accepted the sole dominion of Jesus Christ as well as the power of the Vatican over their religious lives. He remembers receiving both First Communion and the cruciform that same evening.

Maria's Sacrament of the Cross was scheduled for ten p.m. She died suddenly at 8:45 p.m. By the rules of the Church and the laws of the Pax, someone who suffered braindeath before receiving the cross could not be revived artificially to receive it.

Instead of being furious or feeling betrayed by his new Church, Federico's father took the tragedy as a sign that God—not the God he had grown up praying to, the gentle Son infused with the universal female principles of the Holy Mother, but the fiercer New and Old Testament God of the Universal Church—had punished him, his family, and the entire Mariaist world of Llano Estacado. Upon the return to their homeworld with their child's body dressed in white for burial, the elder de Soya had become an unrelenting apostle for the Pax version of Catholicism. It came at a fertile time, as the ranching communities were being swept with the Red Death. Federico was sent to the Pax school in Ciudad del Madre at age seven, and his sisters were sent away to the convent in northern Llano. Within his father's lifetime—indeed, before Federico was sent to New Madrid with Father Maher to attend St. Thomas's Seminary there—the surviving Mariaists on MadredeDios had all converted to Pax Catholicism. Maria's terrible death had led to a world being born again.

In his dreams Father Captain de Soya explains little of this to the child walking with him through the nightmare-familiar streets of DaVinci on Renaissance Vector. The girl, Aenea, seems to know all this.

In his dreams, repeated almost every night for 142 nights before the girl's ship arrives, de Soya is explaining to the child how he has discovered the secret to curing the Red Death and saving his sister. The first morning that de Soya awakens, heart pounding and sheets soaked with sweat, he assumes that the secret to Maria's rescue is the cruciform, but the next night's dream proves him wrong.

The secret, it seems, is the return of Maria's unicorn figure. All he has to do, he explains to his daughter, Aenea, is find the hospital through this maze of streets, and he knows that the return of the unicorn will save his sister. But he cannot find the hospital. The maze defeats him.

Almost five months later, on the eve of the arrival of the ship from Parvati System, in a variation on the same dream, de Soya *does* find the St. Jude Medical Center, where his sister is sleeping, but he realizes with growing horror that he has now lost the figurine.

In this dream Aenea speaks for the first time. Drawing the small porcelain statuette from the pocket of her blouse, the child says, "You see, we've had it with us the entire time."

THE REALITY OF de Soya's months in Renaissance System is literally and figuratively light-years away from the Parvati experience.

Unknown to de Soya, Gregorius, Kee, and Rettig—each a mangled corpse in the heart of *Raphael*'s resurrection creches—the ship is challenged within an hour of translating in-system. Two Pax ramscouts and a torchship come alongside after exchanging transponder codes and data with *Raphael*'s computer. It is decided to transfer the four bodies to a Pax resurrection center on Renaissance V.

Unlike their solitary awakening in Parvati System, de Soya and his Swiss Guard troopers return to consciousness with the proper ceremony and care. Indeed, the resurrection is a difficult one for the father-captain and Corporal Kee, and the two are returned to their creche for an additional three days. Later, de Soya can only speculate whether the ship's automated resurrection facilities would have been up to the task.

As it is, the four are reunited after a week in-system, each man with his own chaplain/counselor. Sergeant Gregorius finds this unnecessary; he is eager and impatient to return to duty, but de Soya and the other two welcome their extra days of rest and recuperation from death.

The *St. Anthony* translates only hours after *Raphael*, and eventually de Soya is reunited with Captain Sati of the torchship and Captain Lempriere of the troopship *St. Thomas Akira*, which has returned to the Pax base in Renaissance System with more than eighteen hundred dead in cold storage and twenty-three hundred wounded men and women from the carnage in Hyperion System. The hospitals and cathedrals on Renaissance V. and in orbital Pax bases begin the surgeries and resurrections at once.

De Soya is present at her bedside when Commander Barnes-Avne regains life and consciousness. The small red-haired woman seems another person, diminished to the point that it makes de Soya's heart ache with pity, with her head shaved, her skin red and slick with rebirth, and dressed only in a hospital gown. But her aggressiveness and demeanor have not been diminished. Almost at once she demands, "What the hell happened?"

De Soya tells her about the Shrike carnage. He fills her in on the seven months he has spent chasing the girl during the four months Barnes-Avne has spent in cold storage and transit from Hyperion.

"You've really screwed the pooch, haven't you?" says the Commander.

De Soya smiles. So far, the Groundforce Commander is the only one to speak honestly to him. He is all too aware that he has had metaphorical carnal relations with the proverbial pooch: twice he has been in charge of a major Pax operation with a single objective—take a child into custody—and twice he has failed miserably. De Soya expects, at the very least, to be relieved of duty; more likely to be court-martialed. To that end, when an archangel courier arrives in-system two months before the girl's arrival, de Soya orders the couriers to return at once to Pacem, to report his failure, and to return with instructions from Pax Command. In the meantime, Father Captain de Soya concludes his courier message, he will continue arranging the details of preparation for the girl's capture in Renaissance System until he is relieved.

The resources available to him this time are impressive. Besides more than two hundred thousand ground troops, including several thousand elite Pax Marines and the surviving Swiss Guard Brigades from Hyperion, de Soya finds extensive sea and space naval forces. Present in Renaissance System and subject to his papal diskey command, are 27 torchships—8 of them omega class—as well as 108 nesting ramscouts to probe ahead of the torchships, 6 C^3 fleet command-and-control ships with their escort cloud of 36 fast-attack ALRs, the attack carrier *St. Malo* with more than 200 space/air Scorpion fighters and seven thousand crew aboard, the anti- quated cruiser *Pride of Bressia,* now renamed the *Jacob,* 2 additional troop transports in addition to the *St. Thomas Akira,* an even score of Benediction-class destroyers, 58 perimeter defense pickets—any 3 of which would be capable of defending an entire world (or a mobile task force) from attack—and more than 100 lesser ships, including in-system frigates that carried a lethal punch for close-in fighting, minesweepers, in- system couriers, drones, and the *Raphael.*

Three days after he has dispatched the second archangel courier to Pacem and seven weeks before Aenea's arrival, the MAGI Task Force arrives—the *Melchior,* the *Gaspar,* and Father Captain de Soya's old ship, the *Balthasar.* At first de Soya is excited to see his old companions, but then he realizes that they will be present during his humiliation. Nonethe- less, he goes out in *Raphael* to greet them while they are still six AUs from Renaissance V, and the first thing Mother Captain Stone does upon his stepping into the *Balthasar* is to hand him his duffel of personal posses- sions that he had been forced to leave behind. On top of his neatly folded clothes, carefully wrapped in foam, is his sister Maria's gift of the porce- lain unicorn.

De Soya is honest with Captain Hearn, Mother Captain Boulez, and Mother Commander Stone—he outlines the preparations he has made but tells them that a new Commander will almost certainly be arriving before the girl's ship arrives. Two days later he is proved a liar. The archangel- class courier translates in-system with two aboard: Captain Marget Wu, aide to Fleet Admiral Marusyn, and the Jesuit Father Brown, special ad- viser to Monsignor Lucas Oddi, Undersecretary of Vatican State and confi- dant of Secretary of State Simon Augustino Cardinal Lourdusamy.

Captain Wu's sealed orders for de Soya come with instructions to be opened even before her resurrection. He opens them immediately. The instructions are simple—he is to continue on his mission to capture the child, he will never be relieved of this duty, and Captain Wu, Father Brown, and any other dignitaries to arrive in-system are there only to observe and to underline—if any underlining is necessary—Father Captain de Soya's total authority over all Pax officials in the pursuit of this goal.

This authority has been grudgingly accepted in the past weeks and months—there are three Pax Fleet admirals and eleven Pax Groundforce commanders in Renaissance System, and none are used to taking orders from a mere father-captain. But the papal diskey has been heard and obeyed. Now, in the final weeks, de Soya reviews his plans and meets with commanders and civilian leaders of all levels, down to the mayors of DaVinci and Benedetto, Toscanelli and Fioravante, Botticelli and Masaccio.

IN THE FINAL WEEKS, with all plans made and forces assigned, Father Captain de Soya actually finds time for personal reflection and activities. Alone now, away from the controlled chaos of staff meetings and tactical simulations—away even from Gregorius, Kee, and Rettig, who accepted assignments as his personal bodyguards—de Soya walks the streets of DaVinci, visits the St. Jude Medical Center, and remembers his sister Maria. Somehow, he discovers, the nightly dreams are more compelling than seeing the real places.

De Soya has discovered that his old patron, Father Maher, has been serving for many years as rector in the Ascension Benedictine Monastery in the city-region of Florence on the opposite side of Renaissance V. from DaVinci, and he flies there to spend a long afternoon talking to the old man. Father Maher, now in his late eighties and "looking forward to my first new life in Christ," is as optimistic, patient, and kind as de Soya remembers from almost three decades ago. Maher, it seems, has returned to MadredeDios more recently than de Soya. "The Llano Estacado has been abandoned," says the old priest. "The ranches are empty now. Ciudad del Madre has a few dozen inhabitants, but only Pax researchers— seeing if the world is truly worth terraforming."

"Yes," says de Soya, "my family emigrated back to Nuevo Madrid more than twenty standard years ago. My sisters serve the Church— Loretta as a nun on Nevermore, Melinda as a priest on Nuevo Madrid."

"And your brother Esteban?" asks Father Maher with a warm smile.

De Soya takes a breath. "Killed by the Ousters in a space battle last year," he says. "His ship was vaporized. No bodies were recovered."

Father Maher blinks as if he has been slapped. "I had not heard."

"No," says de Soya, "you wouldn't have. It was far away—beyond the old Outback. Word has not officially reached even my family yet. I know only because my duties took me to the vicinity and I met a returning captain who told me the news."

Father Maher shakes his bald and mottled head. "Esteban has found the only resurrection which Our Lord promised," he says softly, tears in his eyes. "Eternal resurrection in Our Savior Jesus Christ."

"Yes," says de Soya. A moment later he says, "Do you still drink Scotch, Father Maher?"

The old man's rheumy eyes lift to meet the other's gaze. "Yes, but only for medicinal purposes, Father Captain de Soya."

De Soya's dark brows rise a bit. "I am still recovering from my last resurrection, Father Maher."

The older priest nods seriously. "And I am preparing for my first one, Father Captain de Soya. I shall find the dusty bottle."

On the following Sunday, de Soya celebrates Mass at the Cathedral of St. John the Divine, where he had accepted the cross so long ago. More than eight hundred of the faithful are in attendance, including Father Maher and Father Brown, the intelligent and insightful aide to Monsignor Oddi. Sergeant Gregorius, Corporal Kee, and Lancer Rettig also attend, taking Communion from de Soya's hand.

That night de Soya again dreams of Aenea. "How is it that you are my daughter?" he asks this night. "I have always honored my vows of celibacy."

The child smiles and takes his hand.

ONE HUNDRED HOURS before the girl's ship is to translate, de Soya orders his fleet into position. The translation point is perilously close to the gravity well of Renaissance Vector, and many of the experts are concerned that the old ship will break up, either under the gravity torque of such an unadvisable close exit from C-plus or from the horrendous deceleration needed if the ship is to land on the planet. Their concerns remain largely unspoken, as is their frustration at being kept in Renaissance System: many of the Fleet units had assignments along the frontier or deep in Ouster space. This waste of time has most of the officers on edge.

It is largely because of this undercurrent of tension that Father Captain de Soya calls a meeting of all line officers ten hours before the translation. Such conferences are usually handled over tightbeam linkups, but de Soya has the men and women physically transfer to the carrier *St. Malo*. The huge ship's main briefing room is large enough to handle the scores of attending officers.

De Soya begins by reviewing the scenarios they have practiced for weeks or months now. If the child once again threatens self-destruction, three torchships—de Soya's old MAGI Task Force—will close rapidly, wrap class-ten fields around the ship, stun whoever is aboard into unconsciousness, and hold the ship in stasis until the *Jacob* can take it in tow with its massive field generators.

If the ship tries to leave the system the way it ran from Parvati, ramscouts and fast-attack fighters will harass it while the torchships maneuver to disable it.

De Soya pauses in the briefing. "Questions?" Among the familiar

faces he can see in the row upon row of briefing chairs are Captains
Lempriere, Sati, Wu, and Hearn, Father Brown, Mother Captain Boulez,
Mother Commander Stone, and Commander Barnes-Avne. Sergeant Gregorius, Kee, and Rettig stand at parade rest near the back of the briefing
room, allowed in this august company only because of their status as
personal bodyguards.

Captain Marget Wu says, "And if the ship attempts to land on Renaissance Vector, Renaissance Minor, or one of the moons?"

De Soya steps away from the low podium. "As we discussed at our
last meeting, should the ship attempt to land, we will make the judgment
at the time."

"Based on what factors, Father Captain?" asks Fleet Admiral Serra
from the C³ ship *St. Thomas Aquinas.*

De Soya hesitates only a second. "Several factors, Admiral. Where
the ship is headed . . . whether it would be safer—for the girl—to allow
it to land or to attempt to disable it en route . . . whether there is any
chance for the ship to escape."

"Is there any chance?" asks Commander Barnes-Avne. The woman
is hale and formidable again in her space-black uniform.

"I will not say that there is no chance," says Father Captain de Soya.
"Not after Hyperion. But we will minimize any chance."

"If the Shrike creature appears . . . ," begins Captain Lempriere.

"We have rehearsed the scenario," says de Soya, "and I see no reason
to vary from our plans. This time we will rely upon computerized fire
control to a greater extent. On Hyperion the creature remained in one spot
for less than two seconds. This was too fast for human reactions and
confused the programming in automated fire-control systems. We have
reprogrammed those systems—including individual trooper's suit fire-
control systems."

"So the Marines will board the ship?" asks a ramscout captain in the
last row.

"Only if all else fails," says de Soya. "Or after the girl and any
companions have been locked in the stasis fields and stunned into unconsciousness."

"And deathwands will be used against the creature?" asks a de-
stroyer captain.

"Yes," says de Soya, "as long as doing so does not put the child in
danger. Any other questions?"

The room is silent.

"Father Maher from Ascension Monastery will close with the blessing," says Father Captain de Soya. "Godspeed to you all."

27

I AM NOT SURE WHAT MADE US all go up to the Consul's bedroom at the apex of the ship to watch the translation to normal space. His large bed—the one I had been sleeping in for the past couple of weeks—was in the center of the room, but it folded to a sort of couch, and I did that now. Behind his bed were two opaque cubes—the wardrobe cubby and the shower-lavatory cube—but when the hull was allowed to go transparent, these cubes were just dark blocks against the starfield all around and overhead. As the ship spun down from Hawking velocities, we asked that the hull be made transparent.

Our first glimpse, before the ship started its rotation to line up for deceleration, was of the world of Renaissance Vector, close enough to be a blue-and-white disk rather than a starry speck, with two of its three moons visible. The Renaissance sun was brilliant to the left of the illuminated planet and moons. There were scores of stars visible, which was unusual, since the glare of the sun usually darkened the sky so that only a few of the brightest stars could be seen. Aenea commented on this.

"Those are not stars," said the ship as it completed its slow rotation. The fusion drive roared into existence as we began decelerating toward the planet. Normally we never would have exited from C-plus this close to a planet and moons—their gravity wells made spindown velocities very dangerous—but the ship had assured us that its augmented fields would handle any problems. But not this problem.

"Those are not stars," repeated the ship. "There are more than fifty ships under drive within a one-hundred-thousand-kilometer radius of us. There are dozens more in orbital defense positions. Three of those ships—torchships, from their fusion signature—are within two hundred kilometers of us and are closing."

None of us said a word. The ship had not had to tell us this final bit of information—the three fusion-drive streaks seemed to be directly overhead, burning down at the top of our decelerating ship like blowtorch flames coming at our faces.

"We are being hailed," said the ship.

"Visual?" said Aenea.

"Audio only." The ship's voice sounded more terse and businesslike than usual. Was it possible for an AI to feel tension?

"Let's hear it," said the girl.

". . . the ship which has just entered Renaissance System," the voice was saying. It was a familiar voice. We had heard it in Parvati System. Father Captain de Soya. "Attention, the ship which has just entered Renaissance System," he said again.

"Which ship is the call coming from?" asked A. Bettik as he watched the three torchships close on us. His blue face was bathed in blue light from the plasma drives overhead.

"Unknown," said the ship. "It is a tightbeam transmission and I have not located the source. It might be coming from any of the seventy-nine ships I am currently tracking."

I felt as if I should make some comment, say something intelligent. "Yoicks," I said. Aenea glanced at me and then looked back at the closing torchship drives.

"Time to Renaissance V.?" she asked softly.

"Fourteen minutes at constant delta-v," said the ship. "But this level of deceleration would be illegal within four planetary distances."

"Continue this level," Aenea said.

"Attention, the ship which has just entered Renaissance System," the de Soya voice was saying. "Prepare to be boarded. Any resistance will result in your being rendered unconscious. I repeat . . . attention, the ship which has just entered . . ."

Aenea looked up at me and grinned. "I guess I can't use the depressurization ploy, huh, Raul?

I could not think of anything clever to say beyond my "Yoicks" commentary. I lifted my hands, palms up.

"Attention, the ship which has just entered the system. We are coming alongside. Do not resist as we merge external containment fields."

For some reason, at that moment, as Aenea and A. Bettik raised their faces to watch the three fusion drives separate as the torchships actually became visible less than a kilometer away, one on each point of an equilateral triangle around us, I watched the girl's face. Her features were tense, perhaps—a slight tension at the corners of her mouth—but all in all, she seemed perfectly composed and raptly interested. Her dark eyes were large and luminous.

"Attention, the ship," said the Pax captain's voice again. "We will be merging fields in thirty seconds."

Aenea walked to the edge of the room, reaching out to touch the invisible hull. From my vantage point, it was as if we were standing on a circular summit of a very tall mountain, with stars and blue comet tails on every side, and Aenea was perched on the edge of the precipice.

"Ship, please give me widebeam audio so all the Pax ships can hear me."

FATHER CAPTAIN DE SOYA is watching the proceedings in tactical reality as well as real space. In tactical, he stands above the plane of the ecliptic and sees his ships arrayed around the decelerating target ship like points of light set along the spokes and rim of a wheel. Near the hub, so close to the girl's ship as to be almost indistinguishable, are the *Melchior,* the *Gaspar,* and the *Balthasar.* Farther out, but decelerating in perfect synchronicity with the four ships at the hub, are more than a dozen other torchships under the close command of Captain Sati on the *St. Anthony.* Ten thousand klicks beyond them, set around a slowly rotating perimeter hub, also decelerating into cislunar Renaissance V. space, are the Benediction-class destroyers, three of the six C^3 ships, and the attack carrier *St. Malo,* upon which de Soya watches the events from the ship's Combat Control Center. He had, of course, wanted to be with the MAGI Task Force, closing on the girl's ship, but he realized it would be inappropriate to be in such close command. It would have been especially galling to Mother Captain Stone —promoted only last week by Admiral Serra—to have her first full command undermined in such a way.

So de Soya watches from the *St. Malo,* his archangel *Raphael* in parking orbit around Renaissance V. with the defense pickets and protective ALRs. Switching quickly from the crowded red-lit reality of *St. Malo's* CCC to the fusion-flame view of tactical space, he sees the sparks above this rotating wheel of ships, the dozens of ships set in a giant sphere to stop the girl's ship from fleeing in any direction. Moving awareness back to the crowded CCC, he notes the blood-red faces of observers Wu and Brown, as well as Commander Barnes-Avne, who is in tightbeam contact with the fifty Marines aboard the MAGI ships. In the corners of the crowded Combat Control Center, de Soya can see Gregorius and his two troopers. All three of them had been bitterly disappointed not to be in the boarding parties, but de Soya is holding them back as personal bodyguards for the trip back to Pacem with the child.

He keys the tightbeam channel to the girl's ship again. "Attention, the ship," he says, feeling the pounding of his heart almost as background noise, "we will be merging fields in thirty seconds." He realizes that he is terrified for the girl's safety. If something is to go wrong, it will be in the next few minutes. Simulations have honed the process so that there is only a six percent projected chance of the girl's being harmed . . . but six percent is too large for de Soya. He has dreamed of her every night for 142 nights.

Suddenly the common band rasps and the girl's voice comes over the Combat Control Center's speakers. "Father Captain de Soya," she says. There is no visual. "Please do not attempt to merge fields or board this ship. Any attempt to do so will be disastrous."

De Soya glances at the readout. Fifteen seconds to fields merging. They have gone over this . . . no threats of suicide will prevent their boarding this time. Less than a hundredth of a second after the fields merge, all three of the MAGI torchships will spray the target ship with stunbeams.

"Think, Father Captain," comes the girl's soft voice. "Our ship is controlled by a Hegemony-era AI. If you stun us . . ."

"Stop fields merge!" snaps de Soya with less than two seconds until that is to happen automatically. Acknowledgment lights flick on from the *Melchior, Gaspar,* and *Balthasar.*

"You've been thinking silicon," continues the girl, "but our ship's AI core is completely organic—the old DNA type of processor banks—if you stun us into unconsciousness, you stun it."

"Damn, damn, damn," de Soya hears. At first he thinks it is himself whispering, but he turns to see Captain Wu cursing under her breath.

"We are decelerating at . . . eighty-seven gravities," continues Aenea. "If you knock our AI out . . . well, it controls all internal fields, the drives . . ."

De Soya switches to the engineering bands on the *St. Malo* and the MAGI ships. "Is this true? Will this knock out their AI?"

There is an unbearable pause of at least ten seconds. Finally Captain Hearn, whose Academy degree had been in engineering, comes on the tightbeam. "We don't know, Federico. Most of the details of true AI biotechnology have been lost or suppressed by the Church. It is a mortal sin to . . ."

"Yes, yes," snaps de Soya, "but is she telling the truth? Somebody here has to know. Will a DNA-based AI be at risk if we spray the ship with stunners?"

Bramly, the chief engineer on the *St. Malo,* keys in. "Sir, I would think that the designers would have protected the brain from such a possibility. . . ."

"Do you *know*?" demands de Soya.

"No, sir," says Bramly after a moment.

"But that AI is totally organic?" persists de Soya.

"Yes," comes Captain Hearn's voice on tightbeam. "Except for the electronic and bubble-memory interfaces, a ship's AI of that era would have been cross-helix-structured DNA held in suspension with . . ."

"All right," says de Soya on multiple tightbeams to all ships. "Hold your positions. Do not . . . repeat . . . do not let the girl's ship change course or attempt spinup to C-plus. If it attempts this, merge and stun."

Acknowledgment lights flicker from MAGI and the outer ships.

". . . so please don't create this disaster," comes the end of Aenea's broadcast. "We are only trying to land on Renaissance Vector."

Father Captain de Soya opens his tightbeam to her ship. "Aenea," he says, his voice gentle, "let us board and we'll take you to the planet."

"I guess I'd rather land there myself," says the girl. De Soya thinks that he can hear a hint of amusement in her voice.

"Renaissance Vector is a big world," says de Soya, watching the tactical readout as he speaks. They are ten minutes from entering atmosphere. "Where do you want to land?"

Silence for a full minute. Then Aenea's voice. "The Leonardo Spaceport in DaVinci would be all right."

"That spaceport has been closed for more than two hundred years," says de Soya. "Aren't your ship's memory banks more recent than that?"

Only silence on the com channels.

"There is a Pax Mercantilus spaceport at the western quadrant of DaVinci," he says. "Will that do?"

"Yes," says Aenea.

"You will have to change direction, enter orbit, and land under space traffic control," tightbeams de Soya. "I will download the delta-v changes now."

"No!" says the girl. "My ship will land us."

De Soya sighs and looks at Captain Wu and Father Brown. Commander Barnes-Avne says, "My Marines can board within two minutes."

"Her ship will be entering atmosphere in . . . seven minutes," de Soya says. "At her velocity, even the slightest miscalculation will be fatal." He keys the tightbeam. "Aenea, there is too much space and aircraft traffic over DaVinci for you to try a landing like this. Please instruct your ship to obey the orbital insertion parameters I've just transmitted and—"

"I'm sorry, Father Captain," says the girl, "but we're going to land now. If you want the spaceport traffic control to send up approach data, that would help. If I talk to you again, it'll be when we're all on the ground. This is . . . me . . . out."

"Damn!" says de Soya. He keys Pax Mercantilus Traffic Control. "Did you copy that, Control?"

"Sending approach data . . . now," comes the controller's voice.

"Hearn, Stone, Boulez," snaps de Soya. "You copy?"

"Acknowledged," says Mother Captain Stone. "We're going to have to break off in . . . three minutes ten seconds."

De Soya flicks into tactical long enough to see the hub and wheel breaking up as the torchships initiate their delta-v's to achieve braking orbits. The ships were never designed for atmosphere. The *St. Malo* has been in orbit around the planet and now lies almost in the path of the girl's ship as it brakes wildly before entering atmosphere. "Prepare my dropship," commands de Soya.

"CAP?" he says over the planetary com channel.

"Here, sir," comes Flight Commander Klaus's acknowledgment. She and forty-six other Scorpions are waiting in combat air patrol high above DaVinci.

"Are you tracking?"

"Good plots, sir," says Klaus.

"I remind you that no shots will be fired except under my direct command, Flight Commander."

"Yes, sir."

"The *St. Malo* will be launching . . . ah . . . seventeen fighters, which will follow the target ship down," says de Soya. "My dropship will make the number eighteen. Our transponders will be set to oh-five-nine."

"Affirmative," says Klaus. "Beacons to oh-five-niner. Target ship and eighteen friendlies."

"De Soya out," he says, and unplugs his umbilicals to the Combat Control Center panels. Tactical space disappears. Captain Wu, Father Brown, Commander Barnes-Avne, Sergeant Gregorius, Kee, and Rettig follow him to the dropship. The dropship pilot, a lieutenant named Karyn Norris Cook, is waiting with all systems ready. It takes less than a minute for them to buckle in and launch from the *St. Malo*'s flight tube. They have rehearsed this many times.

De Soya is getting tactical feed through the dropship net as they enter atmosphere.

"The girl's ship has wings," says the pilot, using the ancient phrase. For millennia, "feet dry" has meant an aircraft crossing over land, "feet wet" signifies crossing over water, and "has wings" means translation from space to atmospheric travel.

A visual of the ship shows that this is not literally true. While data on the old ship suggests that it has some morphing capability, it has not actually grown wings in this case. Cameras from the defense pickets clearly show the girl's ship entering the atmosphere stern-first, balancing on a tail of fusion flame.

Captain Wu leans close to de Soya. "Cardinal Lourdusamy said that this child is a threat to the Pax," she whispers so that the others cannot hear.

Father Captain de Soya nods tersely.

"What if he meant that she could be a threat to millions of people on Renaissance V.?" Wu whispers. "That fusion drive alone is a terrible weapon. A thermonuclear explosion above the city . . ."

De Soya feels his insides clamping with the chill of those words, but he has thought this out. "No," he whispers back. "If she turns the fusion tail on anything, we stun the ship, shoot out its engines, and let it fall."

"The girl . . . ," begins Captain Wu.

"We can only hope she'll survive the crash," says de Soya. "We won't let thousands . . . or millions . . . of Pax citizens die." He leans back in his acceleration couch and keys the spaceport, knowing that the tightbeam has to punch through the layer of ionization around the screeching dropship. Glancing at the external video, he sees that they are crossing the terminator: it will be dark at the spaceport.

"Spaceport Control," acknowledges the Pax traffic director. "The target ship is decelerating on our directed flight path. Delta-v is high . . . illegal . . . but acceptable. All aircraft traffic cleared for a thousand-kilometer radius. Time to landing . . . four minutes thirty-five seconds."

"Spaceport secured," chimes in Commander Barnes-Avne on the same net.

De Soya knows that there are several thousand Pax troops in and around the spaceport. Once the girl's ship is down, it will never be allowed to take off again. He looks at the live video: the lights of DaVinci gleam from horizon to horizon. The girl's ship has its navigation lights on, red and green beacons flashing. The powerful landing lights flick on and stab downward through clouds.

"On path," comes the traffic controller's calm voice. "Deceleration nominal."

"We have a visual!" cries CAP commander Klaus over the net.

"Keep your distance," tightbeams de Soya. The Scorpions can sting from several hundred klicks out. He does not want them crowding the descending ship.

"Affirmative."

"On path, ILS reports nominal descent, three minutes to touch-down," the controller calls up to the girl's ship. "Unidentified ship, you are cleared to land."

Silence from Aenea.

De Soya blinks in tactical. The girl's ship is a red ember now, almost hovering ten thousand meters above the Pax spaceport. De Soya's drop-ship and the fighters are a klick higher, circling like angry insects. *Or vultures*, thinks the father-captain. The Llano Estacado had vultures, al-though why the seedship colonists had imported them, no one knew. The staked plains—the stakes being the atmosphere generators set in a grid every thirty klicks—had been dry and windy enough to reduce any corpse to a mummy within hours.

De Soya shakes his head to clear it.

"One minute to landing," reports the controller. "Unidentified ship, you are approaching zero descent rate. Please modify delta-v to continue descent along designated flight path. Unidentified ship, please acknowl-edge. . . ."

"Damn," whispers Captain Wu.

"Sirs," says Pilot Karyn Cook, "the ship has stopped descending. It's hanging there about two thousand meters above the spaceport."

"We see it, Lieutenant," says de Soya. The ship's red and green lights are flashing. The landing lights on the rear fins are bright enough to illuminate the spaceport tarmac more than a mile and a half below them.

Other spacecraft at the port are dark; most have been pulled into hangars or onto secondary taxiways. The circling aircraft, including his own dropship, show no lights. On the multiple tightbeam he says, "All ships and aircraft, keep your distance, hold your fire."

"Unidentified ship," says the Pax controller, "you are drifting off path. Please resume nominal descent rate at once. Unidentified ship, you are leaving controlled airspace. Please resume controlled descent at once. . . ."

"Shit," whispers Barnes-Avne. Her troopers wait in concentric circles around the spaceport, but the girl's ship is no longer above the spaceport—it drifts over the center of DaVinci. The ship's landing lights wink off.

"The ship's fusion drive shows no signs of coming on," de Soya says to Captain Wu. "Note that it's on repulsors alone."

Wu nods but is obviously not satisfied. A fusion-drive ship hovering above an urban center is like a guillotine blade over an exposed neck.

"CAP," calls de Soya, "I'm moving within five hundred meters. Please close with me." He nods to the pilot, who brings the dropship down and around in a predatory swoop. In their rear couches Gregorius and the other two troopers sit stiffly in full combat armor.

"What the hell is she up to?" whispers Commander Barnes-Avne. On his tactical band de Soya can see that the commander has authorized a hundred or so troopers to rise on reaction paks to follow the drifting ship. To the external cameras the troopers are invisible.

De Soya remembers the small aircraft or flying pak that had plucked the girl from the Valley of the Time Tombs. He keys ground control and the orbital pickets. "Sensors? Are you watching for small objects leaving the target ship?"

The acknowledgment is from the primary picket ship. "Yessir . . . don't worry, sir, nothin' bigger'n a microbe's gonna get out of that ship without us trackin' it, sir."

"Very good," says de Soya. *What have I forgotten?* Aenea's ship continues floating slowly over DaVinci, heading north-northwest at about twenty-five klicks per hour—a slow, vertical dirigible drifting on the wind. Above the ship swirl the fighters that have entered atmosphere with de Soya's dropship. Around the ship, like the rotating walls of a hurricane around the eye, are the CAP Scorpions. Beneath, flitting just above city buildings and bridges, tracking proceedings on their own suit-visor infrared sensors and tracking feeds, fly the spaceport Marines and troopers.

The girl's ship floats on silent EM repulsors over the skyscrapers and industrial areas of DaVinci on Renaissance Vector. The city is ablaze with highway lights, building lights, the green swaths of playing fields, and the brightly lit rectangles of parking areas. Tens of thousands of groundcars creep along ribbons of elevated highways, their headlights adding to the city light show.

"It's rotating, sirs," reports the pilot. "Still on repulsors."

On video as well as tactical, de Soya can see Aenea's ship slowly turning from the vertical to the horizontal. No wings appear. This attitude would be strange for the passengers, but makes no practical difference—the internal fields must still be controlling "up" and "down." The ship, looking more than ever like a silver dirigible drifting with the soft breezes, floats over the river and railyards of northwest DaVinci. Traffic control demands a response, but the com channels remain silent.

What have I forgotten? wonders Father Captain de Soya.

WHEN AENEA ASKED the ship to rotate to the horizontal, I admit that I almost lost my composure for a moment.

The sense of losing one's balance was all but overwhelming. All three of us had been standing near the edge of the circular room, looking down through the clear hull as if peering over a cliff's edge. Now we tipped over toward those lights a thousand meters below. A. Bettik and I took several involuntary steps back toward the center of the room—I actually flailed my arms to keep my balance—but Aenea remained at the edge of the room, watching the ground tip up and become a wall of city buildings and lights.

I almost sat down on the couch, but I managed to remain standing and control my vertigo by seeing the ground as a giant wall we were flying past. Streets and the rectangular grid of city blocks moved by as we drifted forward. I turned in a complete circle, seeing the few brightest stars through the city glare behind me. The clouds reflected back the orange lights of the city.

"What are we looking for now?" I asked. At intervals the ship reported the presence of the circling aircraft and the number of sensors probing us. We had ordered the ship to shut off the insistent demands of spaceport traffic control.

Aenea had wanted to see the river. Now we were over it—a dark, serpentine ribbon wound through the city lights. We drifted over it toward the northwest. Occasionally a barge or pleasure boat passed underneath—although from this perspective, the lights seemed to crawl up or down the "wall" of the city we were drifting by.

Instead of answering me directly, Aenea said, "Ship, you're sure that this used to be part of the Tethys?"

"According to my charts," said the ship. "Of course, my memory is not . . ."

"There!" cried A. Bettik, pointing directly ahead down the line of dark river.

I could see nothing, but evidently Aenea did. "Get us lower," she ordered the ship. "Quickly."

"The safety margins have already been violated," said the ship. "If we drop below this altitude, we may . . ."

"Do it!" shouted the girl. "Override. Code[6] Prelude—C-Sharp.' Do it!"

The ship lurched down and forward.

"Head for that arch," said Aenea, pointing directly overhead along the wall of city and dark river.

"Arch?" I said. Then I saw it—a black chord, an arc of darkness against the city lights.

A. Bettik looked at the girl. "I had half expected it to be gone . . . torn down."

Aenea showed her teeth. "They can't tear it down. It would take atomic explosives. . . . and even those might not work. The TechnoCore directed the construction of those things . . . they're built to last."

The ship was hurtling forward now on repulsors. I could clearly see the arch of the farcaster portal like a giant hoop over the river. An industrial park had grown up around the ancient artifact, and the railyards and storage yards were empty except for cracked concrete, weeds, rusting wire, and the hulks of abandoned machines. The portal was still a kilometer away. I could see the lights of the city through it . . . no, now it seemed to shimmer a bit, as if a curtain of water were falling from the metal arch.

"We're going to make it!" I said. No sooner were the words out than a violent explosion rattled the ship and we began plunging toward the river.

"THE OLD FARCASTER PORTAL!" cries de Soya. He had seen the arch a minute earlier but had thought it another bridge. Now it sinks in. "They're headed for the farcaster portal. This used to be part of the River Tethys!" He brings up tactical. Sure enough—the girl's ship is accelerating toward the arch.

"Relax," says Commander Barnes-Avne. "The portals are dead. They haven't worked since the Fall. It can't—"

"Get us closer!" de Soya shouts at the pilot. The dropship accelerates, throwing them all deep into their couch cushions. There is no internal containment field in a dropship. "Get us close! Close the gap!" de Soya shouts at the lieutenant. On the wideband command channels, he says, "All aircraft, close on the target."

"They're going to beat us to it," says Pilot Cook through the three-g force pressing her back into the command chair.

"CAP leader!" calls de Soya, his voice strained by the high-g load. "Fire at the target. Fire to disable engines and repulsors. Now!"

Energy beams lance through the night. The girl's ship seems to stumble in midair, like a gutshot beast, and then falls into the river several hundred meters short of the farcaster portal. An explosion of steam mush-rooms up into the night.

The dropship banks around the pillar of steam at an altitude of a thousand meters. The air is filled with circling aircraft and flying troopers. The com channels are suddenly alive with excited chatter.

"Shut up!" orders de Soya over the widebands. "CAP leader, can you see the ship?"

"Negative," comes Klaus's voice. "Too much steam and debris from the explosion . . ."

"Was there an explosion?" demands de Soya. Then, on tightbeam to the defense pickets a thousand klicks above, "Radar? Sensors?"

"The target ship is down," comes the reply.

"I know that, you idiot," says de Soya. "Can you scan it under the river surface?"

"Negative," answers the picket. "Too much airborne and ground clutter. Deep radar can't discriminate between—"

"Damn," says de Soya. "Mother Captain Stone?"

"Yes," comes his former exec's voice from her torchship in orbit.

"Slag it," orders de Soya. "The portal. The river beneath it. Slag it for a full minute. Slag it until it melts. Wait . . . slag it in thirty seconds." He switches to airborne tactical bands. "Every aircraft and trooper in the vicinity . . . you have thirty seconds before a CPB lances this entire area. Scatter!"

Pilot Cook takes the advice and banks the dropship sharply, acceler-ating back toward the spaceport at Mach 1.5. "Whoa! Whoa!" shouts de Soya through the g-load. "Just a klick out. I need to watch."

Both visual and tactical are a visual demonstration of chaos theory as hundreds of aircraft and airborne troopers fly away from the portal as if flung outward by an explosion. The area is barely empty on radar before the violet beam burns down from space. Ten meters wide and too bright to look directly at, the CPB strikes the ancient farcaster portal perfectly on target. Concrete, steel, and ferroplast melt into lakes and rivers of lava on either bank of the real river. The river itself turns to steam in an instant, sending the shock wave and steam cloud billowing out over the city for kilometers in every direction. This time the mushroom cloud reaches toward the stratosphere.

Captain Wu, Father Brown, and all the others are staring at Father Captain de Soya. He can almost hear their thoughts: *the girl was to be captured alive.*

He ignores their stares and says to the pilot, "I'm not familiar with this model of dropship. Can it hover?"

"For a few minutes," responds the pilot. Her face is slick with sweat under her helmet.

"Get us down there and hover over the portal arch," commands de Soya. "Fifty meters would be fine."

"Sir," says the pilot, "the thermals and shock waves from the steam explosions—"

"Do it, Lieutenant." The father-captain's voice is level, but there will be no arguing with it.

They hover. Steam and a violent drizzle fill the air, but their searchlight beams and high-profile radar stab downward. The farcaster arch is glowing white-hot, but it still stands.

"Amazing," whispers Commander Barnes-Avne.

Mother Captain Stone comes over tactical. "Father Captain, the target was hit, but it's still there. Do you want me to lance it again?"

"No," says de Soya. Beneath the arch the river has cauterized itself, water flowing back into the superheated scar. New steam billows upward as the riverbanks of melted steel and concrete flow into water. The hissing is audible through the external pickups. The river is wild with eddies and whirlpools. It is filled with swirling debris.

De Soya looks up from tactical and his monitors and sees the others looking at him again. *The orders were to take the child alive and return her to Pacem.*

"Commander Barnes-Avne," he says formally. "Would you please order your troopers to land and begin an immediate search of the river and adjoining areas?"

"Certainly," says Barnes-Avne, keying her command net and issuing orders. Her gaze never leaves Father Captain de Soya's face.

28

I N THE DAYS THAT FOLLOW the dragging of the river and the discovery of no spaceship, no bodies, and only a hint of debris of what may have been the girl's ship, Father Captain de Soya fully expects a court-martial and perhaps an excommunication. The archangel courier is dispatched to Pacem with the news, and within twenty hours the same ship, with different human couriers, returns with the verdict: there will be a Board of Review. De Soya nods when he hears the news, believing it to be a precursor to his return to Pacem for court-martial and worse.

Surprisingly, it is the pleasant Father Brown who heads the Board of Review, as personal representative of Secretary of State Simon Augustino Cardinal Lourdusamy, with Captain Wu standing in for Admiral Marusyn of Pax Fleet. Other members of the board include two of the admirals present during the debacle and Commander Barnes-Avne. De Soya is offered counsel, but he refuses.

The father-captain is not under arrest during the five days of the board hearing—not even under house arrest—but it is understood that he will remain on the Pax military base outside of DaVinci until the hearing is concluded. During those five days, Father Captain de Soya walks along the river path within the base confines, watches news on local television and direct-access channels, and occasionally looks skyward, imagining that he can guess where *Raphael* still swings in parking orbit, uncrewed and silent except for its automated systems. De Soya hopes that the ship's next captain brings it more honor.

Many of his friends visit him: Gregorius, Kee, and Rettig are nominally still his bodyguards, although they no longer carry weapons and—like de Soya—remain on the Pax base in virtual arrest. Mother Captain Boulez, Captain Hearn, and Mother Captain Stone all stop by after giving their testimony and before shipping out for the frontier. That evening de Soya watches the blue tails of their dropships rising toward the night sky and envies them. Captain Sati of the *St. Anthony* has a glass of wine with de Soya before returning to his torchship and active duty in another system. Even Captain Lempriere comes by after testifying, and it is that bald man's halting sympathy that finally angers de Soya.

On the fifth day de Soya goes before the board. The situation is odd —de Soya still holds the papal diskey and thus is technically beyond reproach or indictment—but it is understood that Pope Julius, through Cardinal Lourdusamy, has willed this Board of Review, and de Soya, shaped to obedience through both his military and Jesuit training, complies with humility. He does not expect exoneration. In the tradition of ship captains since the Middle Ages on Old Earth, de Soya knows well that the coin of a captain's prerogatives has two sides—almost godlike power over everyone and everything aboard one's ship, balanced by the requirement to take total responsibility for any damage to the ship or failure of one's mission.

De Soya has not damaged his ship—neither his former task force, nor his new ship, the *Raphael*—but he is acutely aware that his failure has been total. With immense resources of the Pax available to him both on Hyperion and in Renaissance space, he has failed to capture a twelve-year-old child. He can see no excuse for this, and he testifies thus during his part of the hearing.

"And why did you order the lancing of the farcaster portal on Renaissance Vector?" asks Father Admiral Coombs after de Soya's statement.

De Soya raises a hand, then drops it. "I realized at that moment that the reason for the girl's trip to this world was to reach the portal," he says. "Our only hope for detaining her was to destroy the portal arch."

"But it was not destroyed?" queries Father Brown.

"No," says de Soya.

"In your experience, Father Captain de Soya," says Captain Wu, "has there been any target that one minute of fully applied CPB fire would not destroy?"

De Soya thinks for a moment. "There are targets such as orbital forest or Ouster Swarm asteroids that would not be fully destroyed by even a full minute of lancefire," he says. "But they would have been severely damaged."

"And the farcaster portal was not damaged?" persists Father Brown.

"Not to my knowledge," says de Soya.

Captain Wu turns to the other board members. "We have an affidavit from Chief of Planetary Engineers Rexton Hamn that the alloy of the farcaster portal—although radiating heat for more than forty-eight hours—was not damaged by the attack."

The panel members converse among themselves for several minutes.

"Father Captain de Soya," begins Admiral Serra when the questioning resumes, "were you aware that your attempt to destroy the portal might have destroyed the girl's ship?"

"Yes, Admiral."

"And in so doing," continues Serra, "killed the child?"

"Yes, Admiral."

"And your orders were—specifically—to bring the child to Pacem . . . unharmed. Am I correct?"

"Yes, Admiral. Those were my precise orders."

"But you were willing to defy those orders?"

De Soya takes a breath. "In this case, Admiral, I felt it was a calculated risk. My instructions were that it was of paramount importance to bring the child to Pacem within the shortest time possible. In those few seconds when I realized that she might be able to travel by farcaster portal and escape apprehension, I felt that destroying the portal—not the child's ship—was our best hope. To be honest, I felt that the ship had either already traversed the portal or had not yet reached it. All indications were that the ship had been struck and fallen into the river. I did not know whether the ship had the capacity to travel underwater through the portal —or, for that matter, whether the portal could farcast an object underwater."

Captain Wu folds her hands. "And to your knowledge, Father Captain, has the farcaster portal shown any signs of activity since that night?"

"Not to my knowledge, Captain."

"To your knowledge, Father Captain," she continues, "had any farcaster portal—on any world of the former Web or any spaceborne portal, for that matter—had any farcaster shown any sign of renewed activity since the Fall of the farcasters more than two hundred seventy standard years ago?"

"To my knowledge," says de Soya, "they have not."

Father Brown leans forward. "Then, Father Captain, perhaps you can tell this board why you thought that the girl had the capacity to open one of these portals and was attempting to escape through this particular one."

De Soya does open his hands this time. "Father, I . . . I don't know. I guess that I had the distinct feeling that she was not willing to be captured, and her flight along the river . . . I don't know, Father. The use of the portal is the only thing that made sense that night."

Captain Wu looks at her fellow panelists. "Any more questions?" After a silence the captain says, "That will be all, Father Captain de Soya. This board will apprise you of its findings by tomorrow morning."

De Soya nods and leaves.

THAT NIGHT, walking the base path along the river, de Soya tries to imagine what he will do if he is court-martialed and stripped of his priesthood but not imprisoned. The thought of freedom after such failure is more painful than the thought of prison. Excommunication has not been mentioned by the board—no punishment has—but de Soya clearly sees his conviction, his return to Pacem for higher court proceedings, and his ultimate banishment from the Church. Only a terrible failure or heresy could bring about such punishment, but de Soya sees—unblinkingly— what a terrible failure his efforts have been.

In the morning he is called into the low building where the board has met all night. He stands at attention in front of the dozen men and women behind the long table.

"Father Captain de Soya," begins Captain Wu, speaking for the others, "this Board of Review was convened to answer queries from Pax Command and the Vatican as to the disposition and outcome of recent events—specifically, in this command and this commander's failure to apprehend the child known as Aenea. After five days of investigation and after many hundreds of hours of testimony and depositions, it is the finding of this board that all possible efforts and preparations were made to carry out this mission. The fact that the child known as Aenea—or someone or something traveling with her—was able to escape via a farcaster that has not worked for almost three standard centuries could not have been anticipated by you or by any other officer working with you or under your command. The fact that the farcasters could resume operation at all is, of course, of grave concern to the Pax Command and to the Church. The implications of this will be explored by the highest echelons of Pax Command and the Vatican hierarchy.

"As for your role in this, Father Captain de Soya, with the exception of possible concern we have for your risking the life of the child you are charged with taking into custody, we find your actions responsible, correct, in keeping with your mission priorities, and legal. This board—while official only in the capacity of review—recommends that you continue your mission with the archangel-class ship designated the *Raphael,* that your use of the papal-authority diskey continue, and that you requisition those materiels and personnel you consider necessary for the continuance of this mission."

De Soya, still at rigid attention, blinks rapidly several times before saying, "Captain?"

"Yes, Father Captain?" says Wu.

"Does this mean that I can keep Sergeant Gregorius and his troopers as my personal guard?"

Captain Wu—whose authority strangely overwhelms that of the admirals and planetary ground commanders at the table—smiles. "Father Captain," she says, "you could order the members of this board to go along as your personal guard if you wish. The authority of your papal diskey remains absolute."

De Soya does not smile. "Thank you, Captain . . . sirs. Sergeant Gregorius and his two men will suffice. I will leave this morning."

"Leave for where, Federico?" asks Father Brown. "As you know, exhaustive searches of the records have not given us a clue as to where the farcaster might have sent that ship. The River Tethys had changeable connections, and any data about the next world on the line has evidently been lost to us."

"Yes, Father," says de Soya, "but there are only two-hundred-some worlds that used to be connected by that farcaster river. The girl's ship has to be on one of them. My archangel ship can reach all of them—given time for resurrection after translation—in less than two years. I will begin immediately."

At this, the men and women at the table can only stare. The man in front of them is facing several hundred deaths and difficult resurrections. As far as they know, no one since the beginning of the Sacrament of Resurrection has ever submitted to such a cycle of pain and rebirth.

Father Brown stands and lifts his hand in benediction. *"In Nomine Patris, et Fílii, et Spíritus Sancti,"* he intones. "Go with God, Father Captain de Soya. Our prayers go with you."

29

W HEN THEY SHOT US DOWN several hundred meters short of the farcaster portal, I was sure we were dead this time. The internal containment field failed the second the generators were struck, the wall of the planet we were looking *up* at suddenly and inarguably became *down,* and the ship fell like an elevator with its cables cut.

The sensations that followed are hard for me to describe. I know now that the internal fields switched to what was known as a "crash field" —no misnomer, I can assure you—and for the next few minutes it felt precisely as if we were caught up in a giant vat of gelatin. In a sense, we were. The crash field expanded in a nanosecond to fill every square millimeter of the ship, cushioning us and keeping us absolutely immobile as the spacecraft plunged into the river, bounced off the bottom mud, fired its fusion engine—creating a giant plume of steam—and plowed ahead relentlessly through mud, steam, water, and debris from the imploding riverbanks until the ship fulfilled the last command given to it—pass through the farcaster portal. The fact that we did so three meters beneath the broiling river surface did not keep the portal from working. The ship later told us that while its stern was passing through the farcaster, the water above and behind it suddenly became superheated steam—as if one of the Pax ships or aircraft were lancing it with a CPB. Ironically, it was the steam that deflected the beam for the milliseconds necessary for the ship to complete its transition.

Meanwhile, knowing none of these details, I stared. My eyes were open—I could not close them against the cloying force of the crash field— and I was watching the external video monitors set along the foot of the bed as well as looking out through the still-transparent hull apex as the farcaster portal flickered to life amid the steam and sunlight poured over the river's surface, until suddenly we were through the steam cloud and once again smashing against rock and river bottom, then hitting a beach beneath blue sky and sun.

Then the monitors went off and the hull went dull. For several minutes we were trapped in this cave blackness—I was floating in midair, or would have been had it not been for the gelatinous crash field—my arms were thrown wide, my right leg was half-bent in a running posture behind me, my mouth was open in a silent scream, and I could not blink. At first the fear of suffocation was very strong—the crash field was *in* my open mouth—but I soon realized that my nose and throat were receiving oxygen. The crash field, it turns out, worked much like the expensive osmosis masks used for deep-sea diving during the Hegemony days: air leached through the field mass pressing against one's face and throat. It was not a pleasant experience—I've always detested the thought of choking—but my anxiety was manageable. More disturbing was the blackness and claustrophobic sense of being caught in a giant, sticky web. During those long minutes in the darkness, I had thoughts of the ship being stuck there forever, disabled, with no way to relax the crash fields, and the three of us starving to death in our undignified postures, until someday the ship's energy banks would be depleted, the crash field would collapse, and our whitened skeletons would drop and rattle around the interior hull of the ship like so many bones being cast by an invisible fortune-teller.

As it was, the field slowly folded away less than five minutes later. The lights came on, flickered, and were replaced by red emergency lighting even as we were gently lowered to what had been the wall a short while before. The outer hull became transparent once again, but very little light filtered in through the mud and debris.

I had not been able to see A. Bettik and Aenea while stuck in place—they had been just out of my frozen field of sight—but now I saw them as the field lowered them to the hull with me. I was amazed to hear a scream issue from my throat and realized that it was the shout that had welled up in me the instant of the crash.

For a moment the three of us just sat on the curved hull wall, rubbing and testing our own arms, legs, and heads to make sure we weren't injured. Then Aenea spoke for us all. "Holy shit," she said, and stood up on the curving floor of the hull. Her legs were shaky.

"Ship!" called the android.

"Yes, A. Bettik." The voice was as calm as ever.

"Are you damaged?"

"Yes, A. Bettik," said the ship. "I have just completed a full damage assessment. Field coils, repulsors, and Hawking translators have suffered extensive damage, as have sections of the aft hull and two of the four landing fins."

"Ship," I said, struggling to my feet and looking out through the transparent nose of the hull. There was sunlight coming through the curved wall above us, but most of the exterior hull was opaque with mud, sand, and other debris. The dark river came two-thirds the way up the sides and was sloshing against us. It looked as if we had run aground on a sandy bank, but not before plowing through many meters of river bottom. "Ship," I tried again, "are your sensors working?"

"Only radar and visual," it replied.

"Is there any pursuit?" I said. "Did any Pax ships come through the farcaster with us?"

"Negative," said the ship. "There are no inorganic ground or air targets within my radar range."

Aenea walked to the vertical wall that had been the carpeted floor. "No troopers even?" she asked.

"No," said the ship.

"Is the farcaster still operational?" asked A. Bettik.

"Negative," said the ship. "The portal ceased functioning eighteen nanoseconds after we transited it."

I relaxed a bit then and looked at the girl, trying to make sure just by staring that she hadn't been injured. Except for wildly disarrayed hair and the excitement in her eyes, she looked normal enough. She grinned at me. "So how do we get out of here, Raul?"

I looked up and saw what she meant. The central stairwell was about three meters above our heads. "Ship?" I said. "Can you turn the internal fields back on long enough for us to get out of the ship?"

"I'm sorry," said the ship. "The fields are down and will not be repaired for some time."

"Can you morph an opening in the hull above us?" I said. The feeling of claustrophobia was coming back.

"I am afraid not," said the ship. "I am functioning on battery power at the moment, and morphing would demand far more energy than I have available. The main air lock is functional. If you can get to that, I will open it."

The three of us exchanged glances. "Great," I said at last. "We get to crawl thirty meters back through the ship while everything's cattywampus."

Aenea was still looking up at the stairwell opening. "The gravity's different here—feel it?"

I realized that I did. There was a lightness to everything. I must have been noticing it but putting it down to a variation in the internal field—but there was no more internal field. This was a different world, with different gravity! I found myself staring back at the child.

"So are you saying we can fly up there?" I said, pointing to the bed hanging on the wall above us and the stairwell next to it.

"No," said Aenea, "but the gravity here seems a little less than

Hyperion's. You two boost me up there and I'll drop something down to you and we'll crawl back to the air lock."

And that is precisely what we did. We made a stirrup with our hands and boosted Aenea to the bottom lip of the stairwell opening, where she balanced, reached out and plucked the loosely hanging blanket from the bed, tied it around the balustrade and dropped the other end down to us, and then, after A. Bettik and I pulled our way up, all three of us walked precariously on the central dropshaft post, hanging on to the circular stairs to the side and above to keep our balance, and gradually made our way through the red-lit mess of a ship—through the library, where books and cushions had fallen to the lower hull despite the cord restraints on the shelves, through the holopit area, where the Steinway was still in place because of its restraining locks, but where our loose personal belongings had tumbled to the bottom of the ship. Here we made a stop while I lowered myself to the cluttered hull bottom and retrieved the pack and weapons I had left on the couch. Strapping the pistol on my belt, tossing up the rope I had stored in the pack, I felt more prepared for the next eventuality than I had a moment before.

When we got to the corridor, we could see that whatever had damaged the drive area below had also played havoc with the storage lockers: parts of the corridor were blackened and buckled outward, the contents of the lockers were scattered along the torn walls. The inner air lock was open but was now several meters directly above us. I had to free-climb the last vertical expanse of corridor and toss the rope down to the others while I crouched just within the inner lock. Jumping up onto the outer hull and pulling myself out into the bright sunlight, I reached into the red-lit air lock, found Aenea's wrist, and pulled her out. A second later I did the same for A. Bettik. Then we all took time to look around.

A strange new world! I will never be able to explain the thrill that jolted through me at that moment—despite our crash, despite our predicament, despite everything—*I was looking at a new world!* The effect on me was more profound than I had expected in all my anticipation of interworld travel. This planet was very Hyperion-like: breathable air, blue sky—although a much lighter blue than Hyperion's lapis—wisps of clouds overhead, the river behind us—wider than the river had been on Renaissance Vector—and jungle on both banks, stretching as far away as I could see to the right, and back beyond the overgrown farcaster portal to our left. Ahead of us, the bow of the ship had indeed plowed up the river bottom and beached itself on a sandy spit, and then the jungle began again, hanging over everything like a tattered green curtain above a narrow stage.

But as familiar as this sounds, it was all strange: the scents in the air were alien, the gravity felt odd, the sunlight was a bit too bright, the "trees" in the jungle were unlike anything I had ever seen—feathery green gymnosperms was how I would have described them then—and overhead, flights of frail white birds of a sort I had never seen flapped away from the sound of our clumsy entrance to this world.

We walked up the hull toward the beach. Soft breezes ruffled Aenea's hair and tugged at my shirt. The air smelled of subtle spices—traces of cinnamon and thyme, perhaps—although softer and richer than these. The bow of the ship was not transparent from the outside, although I did not know at the time whether the ship had opaqued its skin again or whether it never looked transparent from the outside. Even lying on its side, the hull would have been too high and too steep to slide from if it had not plowed such a deep furrow in the beach sand; I used my rope again to lower A. Bettik to the sand, then we lowered the girl, and finally I shouldered my pack—the plasma rifle folded and strapped atop it—and slid down on my own, rolling as I hit the tightly packed soil.

My first footstep on an alien world, and it was no footstep at all—just a mouth full of sand.

The girl and the android helped me to my feet. Aenea was squinting up at the hull. "How do we get back up?" she said.

"We can build a ladder, drag a fallen tree over, or"—I tapped my pack—"I brought the hawking mat."

We turned our attention to the beach and jungle. The former was narrow—only a few meters across from the bow to the forest, the sand gleaming more red than sand-colored in the bright sunlight—and the latter was dense and dark. The breeze was cool here on the beach, but the heat was palpable under the thickly packed trees. Twenty meters above, the gymnosperm fronds rustled and quaked like the antennae of some great insects.

"Wait here a minute," I said, and stepped under the cover of the trees. The underbrush was thick, a type of clinging fern for the most part, and the soil was made up of so much humus that it was more sponge than dirt. The jungle smelled of dampness and decay, but of a whole different scent than the fens and swamps of Hyperion. I thought of the dracula ticks and biting gar in my own little tame bit of wilderness, and watched where I stepped. Vines spiraled down from the gymnosperm trunks and created a ropey latticework ahead of me in the gloom. I realized that I should have added a machete to my list of basic gear.

I had not penetrated the woods ten meters when suddenly a tall shrub holding heavy red leaves a meter in front of my face exploded into motion and the "leaves" flapped away beneath the jungle canopy, the creatures' leathery wings sounding much like the large fruit bats our Hyperion ancestors had brought on their seedships.

"Damn," I whispered, and shoved and battered my way out of the dank tangle. My shirt was torn when I staggered onto the beach sand. Aenea and A. Bettik looked expectantly at me.

"It's a jungle in there," I said.

We walked to the water's edge, sat on a partially submerged stump there, and looked at our spaceship. The poor thing looked like a great beached whale from some Old Earth wildlife holo.

"I wonder if it will ever fly again," I mused, breaking a chocolate bar into pieces and handing one to the child and the other to the blue-skinned man.

"Oh, I think I will," said a voice on my wrist.

I admit that I levitated a dozen or so centimeters. I'd forgotten about the comlog bracelet.

"Ship?" I said, raising my wrist and speaking directly into the bracelet the way I would have used a portable radio in the Home Guard.

"You don't have to do that," said the ship's voice. "I can hear everything quite clearly, thank you. Your question was—would I ever fly again? The answer is—almost certainly. I had more complicated repairs to carry out upon my arrival in the city of Endymion after my return to Hyperion."

"Good," I said. "I'm glad you can . . . ah . . . repair yourself. Will you need raw materials? Replacement parts?"

"No, thank you, M. Endymion," said the ship. "It is mostly a matter of reallocating existing materials and redesigning certain damaged units. The repairs should not take long."

"How long is not long?" asked Aenea. She finished her chocolate bar and licked her fingers.

"Six standard months," said the ship. "Unless I run into unforeseen difficulties."

The three of us exchanged glances. I looked back at the jungle. The sun seemed lower now, its horizontal rays illuminating the tops of the gymnosperms and casting the shadows beneath into deeper gloom. "Six months?" I said.

"Unless I run into unforeseen difficulties," repeated the ship.

"Ideas?" I said to my two comrades.

Aenea rinsed her fingers in the river's edge, tossed some water onto her face, and brushed back her wet hair. "We're on the River Tethys," she said. "We'll just go downstream until we find the next farcaster portal."

"You can do that trick again?" I said.

She brushed water from her face and said, "What trick?"

I made a dismissive gesture with my hand. "Oh, nothing . . . making a machine work that's been dead for three centuries. That trick."

Her dark eyes were earnest. "I wasn't sure that I could do that, Raul." She looked at A. Bettik, who was watching us impassively. "Honest."

"What would have happened if you hadn't been able to do it?" I asked softly.

"They would have caught us," said Aenea. "I think they would have let you two go. They would have brought me back to Pacem. That would have been the last you or anyone else would have heard of me."

Something about the flat, emotionless way she said that gave me chills. "All right," I said, "it worked. But *how* did you do it?"

She made that slight-movement-of-her-hand gesture with which I was becoming familiar. "I'm not . . . certain," she said. "I knew from the dreams that the portal would probably let me through. . . ."

"*Let* you through?" I said.

"Yes. I thought it would . . . recognize me . . . and it did."

I set my hands on my knees and straightened my legs, the heels of my boots digging into the red sand. "You talk about the farcaster as if it's an intelligent, living organism," I said.

Aenea looked back at the arch half a klick behind us. "In a way it is," she said. "It's hard to explain."

"But you're sure that the Pax troops can't follow us through?"

"Oh, yes. The portal will not activate for anyone else."

My eyebrows raised a bit. "Then how did A. Bettik and I . . . and the ship . . . get through?"

Aenea smiled. "You were with me."

I stood up. "All right, we'll hash this out later. First, I think we need a plan. Do we reconnoiter now, or get our stuff out of the ship first?"

Aenea looked down at the dark water of the river. "And then Robinson Crusoe stripped naked, swam out to his ship, filled his pockets with biscuits, and swam back to shore. . . ."

"What?" I said, hefting my pack and frowning at the child.

"Nothing," she said, getting to her feet. "Just an old pre-Hegira book that Uncle Martin used to read to me. He used to say that proofreaders have always been incompetent assholes—even fourteen hundred years ago."

I looked at the android. "Do you understand her, A. Bettik?"

He showed that slight twitch of his thin lips that I was learning to take as a smile. "It is not my role to understand M. Aenea, M. Endymion."

I sighed. "All right, back to the subject. . . . Do we reconnoiter before it gets dark, or dig the stuff out of the ship?"

"I vote that we look around," said Aenea. She looked at the darkening jungle. "But not through that stuff."

"Uh-uh," I agreed, pulling the hawking mat from its space atop my pack and unrolling it on the sand. "We'll see if this works on this world." I paused, raised the comlog closer. "What world is this, anyway? Ship?"

There was a second's hesitation, as if the ship was busy mulling over its own problems. "I'm sorry, I can't identify it given the state of my memory banks. My navigation systems could tell us, of course, but I will need a star sighting. I can tell you that there are no unnatural electromagnetic or microwave transmissions currently broadcasting on this area of the planet. Nor are there relay satellites or other man-made objects in synchronous orbit overhead."

"All right," I said, "but where *are* we?" I looked at the girl.

"How should I know?" said Aenea.

"You brought us here," I said. I realized that I was being short-tempered with her, but I *felt* short-tempered right then.

Aenea shook her head. "I just activated the farcaster, Raul. My big plan was to get away from Father Captain Whatshisname and all those ships. That was it."

"And find your architect," I said.

"Yes," said Aenea.

I looked around the jungle and river. "It doesn't look like a promising place to find an architect. I guess you're right . . . we'll just have to keep moving down the river to the next world." The vine-shrouded arch of the farcaster we'd passed through caught my eye. I saw now why we'd plowed ashore: the river took a bend to the right here, about half a kilometer from the portal. The ship had come through and just kept going straight, right up through the shallows and onto the beach.

"Wait," I said, "couldn't we just reprogram that portal and use it to go somewhere else? Why do we have to find another one?"

A. Bettik stepped away from the ship so he could get a better look at the farcaster arch. "The River Tethys portals did not work like the millions of personal farcasters," he said softly. "Nor was it designed to function like the Grand Concourse portals, or the large spaceborne farcasters." He reached into his pocket and removed a small book. I saw the title—*A Traveler's Guide to the WorldWeb*. "It seems that the Tethys was designed primarily for wandering and relaxation," he said. "The distance between the portals varied from a few kilometers to many hundreds of kilometers. . . ."

"Hundreds of kilometers!" I said. I had been expecting to find the next portal just around the next bend in the river.

"Yes," continued A. Bettik. "The concept, as I understand it, was to offer the traveler a wide variety of worlds, views, and experiences. To that end only the downstream portals would activate, and they programmed themselves randomly . . . that is, the sections of river on different worlds were shuffled constantly, like so many cards in a deck."

I shook my head. "In the old poet's *Cantos* it says that the rivers were sliced up after the Fall . . . that they dried up like water holes in the desert."

Aenea made a noise. "Uncle Martin's full of shit sometimes, Raul. He never saw what happened to the Tethys after the Fall. . . . He was on Hyperion, remember? He's never been back to the Web. He made stuff up."

It was no way to talk about the greatest work of literature in the past three hundred years—or of the legendary old poet who had composed it— but I started laughing then and found it hard to stop. By the time I did, Aenea was looking at me strangely. "Are you all right, Raul?"

"Yep," I said. "Just happy." I turned and made a motion that encompassed the jungle, the river, the farcaster portal—even our beached whale of a ship. "For some reason, I'm just happy," I said.

Aenea nodded as if she understood perfectly.

To the android I said, "Does the book say what world this is? Jungle, blue sky . . . it must be about a nine-point-five on the Solmev Scale. That must be fairly rare. Does it list this world?"

A. Bettik flipped through the pages. "I don't remember a jungle world like this mentioned in the sections I read, M. Endymion. I will read more carefully later."

"Well, I think we need to look around," said Aenea, obviously impatient to explore.

"But we should salvage some important things from the ship first," I said. "I made a list . . ."

"That could take hours," said Aenea. "The sun could set before we're finished."

"Still," I said, ready to argue, "we need to get organized here . . ."

"If I may suggest a course of action," A. Bettik interrupted softly, "perhaps you and M. Aenea could . . . ah . . . reconnoiter, while I begin removing the necessary items you mentioned. Unless you think it wiser to sleep in the ship tonight."

We all looked at the poor ship. The river swirled around it, and just above the water level I could see the bent and blackened stumps which had been the proud rear fins. I thought of sleeping in that tumble of stuff, in the red-lit emergency light or the absolute darkness of the central levels, and said, "Well, it would be safer in there, but let's get the stuff out that we'll need to move downriver, and then we'll decide."

The android and I discussed it for several minutes. I had the plasma rifle with me, as well as the .45 in its holster on my belt, but I wanted the 16-gauge shotgun I'd set aside, as well as camping gear I'd seen in the EVA locker closet. I wasn't sure how we'd get downriver—the hawking mat would probably hold the three of us, but I couldn't see it transporting us *and* our gear, so we decided to unpack three of the four flybikes from their niches under the spacesuit closet. There was also a flying belt in there that I thought might be handy, as well as some camping accessories such as a heating cube, sleeping bags, foam mats, flashlight lasers for each of us, and the headset communicators I'd noticed. "Oh, and a machete if you see one," I added. "There were several boxes of knives and multiuse blades in the small EVA closet. I don't remember a machete, but if there is one . . . let's get it out."

A. Bettik and I walked to the end of the narrow beach, found a fallen tree at the river's edge, and dragged it—with me sweating and cursing—back to the side of the ship to act as a de facto ladder so that we could crawl back up on the curved hull. "Oh, yeah, see if there's a rope ladder in that mess," I said. "And an inflatable raft of some sort."

"Anything else?" A. Bettik asked wryly.

"No . . . well, maybe a sauna if you find one. And a well-stocked bar. And maybe a twelve-piece band to play some music while we unpack."

"I'll do my best, sir," said the android, and began climbing the tree-ladder back to the top of the hull.

I felt guilty leaving A. Bettik to do all the heavy lifting, but it seemed wise to know how far it was to the next farcaster portal, and I had no intention of allowing the girl to fly off on a scouting mission of her own. She sat behind me as I tapped the activator thread designs and the carpet stiffened and rose several centimeters from the wet sand.

"Wick," she said.

"What?"

"It stands for 'wicked,' " said the girl. "Uncle Martin said that it was kid slang when he was a brat on Old Earth."

I sighed again and tapped the flight threads. We spiraled up and around, soon rising above the treetop level. The sun was definitely lower now in the direction I assumed was west. "Ship?" I said to my comlog bracelet.

"Yes?" The ship's tone always made me feel that I was interrupting it at some important task.

"Am I talking to you, or to the data bank you downloaded?"

"As long as you are within communicator range, M. Endymion," it answered, "you are talking to me."

"What's the communicator range?" We leveled off thirty meters above the river. A. Bettik waved from where he stood next to the open air lock.

"Twenty thousand kilometers or the curve of the planet," said the ship. "Whichever comes first. As I mentioned earlier, there are no relay satellites around this world that I can locate."

I tapped the forward design and we began flying upriver, toward the overgrown arch there. "Can you talk to me through a farcaster portal?" I asked.

"An activated portal?" said the ship. "How could I do that, M. Endymion? You would be light-years away."

This ship had a way of making me feel stupid and provincial. I usually enjoyed its company, but I admit that I wouldn't mind too much when we left it behind.

Aenea leaned against my back and spoke directly into my ear so as to be heard over the wind noise as we accelerated. "The old portals used to have fiber-optic lines running through them. That worked . . . although not as well as the fatline."

"So if we wanted to keep talking to the ship when we go downriver," I said back over my shoulder, "we could string telephone wire?"

Out of the corner of my eye, I could see her grinning. The silliness did give me a thought, however. "If we can't go back upriver through the portals," I said, "how do we find our way back to the ship?"

Aenea put her hand on my shoulder. The portal was approaching quickly now. "We just keep going down the line until we come back around," she said over the wind noise. "The River Tethys was a big circle."

I turned so that I could see her. "Are you serious, kiddo? There were —what?—a couple of hundred worlds connected by the Tethys."

"At least a couple of hundred," said Aenea. "That we know of."

I did not understand that, but sighed again as we slowed near the portal. "If each section of the river ran for a hundred klicks . . . that's twenty thousand kilometers of travel just to get back here."

Aenea said nothing.

I hovered us near the portal, realizing for the first time just how massive these things were. The arch appeared to be made of metal with many designs, compartments, indentations—perhaps even cryptic writing —but the jungle had sent tendrils of vines and lichens up the top and sides of the thing. What I had first taken as rust on the complicated arch turned out to be more of the red "bat-wing leaves" hanging in clusters from the main tangle of vines. I gave them a wide berth.

"What if it activates?" I said as we hovered a meter or two short of the underside of the arch.

"Try it," said the girl.

I sent the hawking mat forward slowly, almost stopping as the front of the carpet reached the invisible line directly under the arch.

Nothing happened. We flew through, I turned the mat around, and we came back from the south. The farcaster portal was just an ornate metal bridge arching high over the river.

"It's dead," I said. "As dead as Kelsey's nuts." It had been one of Grandam's favorite phrases, used only when we kids weren't supposed to be able to hear, but I realized that there *was* a kid in earshot. "Sorry," I said over my shoulder, my face red. Perhaps I'd spent too many years in the army or working with river bargemen, or as a bouncer in the casinos. I'd turned into a jerk.

Aenea actually threw her head back, she was laughing so hard. "Raul," she said, "I grew up visiting Uncle Martin, remember?"

We flew back over the ship and waved at A. Bettik as the android was lowering pallets of gear to the beach. He waved a blue hand in response.

"Shall we go on downriver to see how far it'll be to the next portal?" I said.

"Absolutely," said Aenea.

WE FLEW DOWNRIVER, seeing very few other beaches or breaks in the jungle: trees and vines came all the way to the river's edge. It bothered me not to know which direction we were heading, so I removed the inertial guidance compass from my pack and activated it. The compass had been my guide on Hyperion, where the magnetic field was too treacherous to trust, but it was useless here. As with the ship's guidance system, the compass would work perfectly if it knew its starting point, but that luxury had been lost the instant we transited the farcaster.

"Ship," I said to the bracelet comlog, "can you get a magnetic compass reading on us?"

"Yes," came the instant reply, "but without knowing precisely where magnetic north is on this world, the actual direction of travel would be a rough estimate."

"Give me the rough estimate, please." I banked the mat slightly as we rounded a wide bend. The river had broadened out again—it must have been almost a kilometer wide at this point. The current looked swift, but not especially treacherous. My barge work on the Kans had taught me to read the river for eddies, snags, sandbars, and the like. This river seemed easy enough to navigate.

"You are headed approximately east-southeast," said the comlog. "Airspeed is sixty-eight kilometers per hour. Sensors indicate that your hawking-mat deflection field is at eight percent. Altitude is . . ."

"All right, all right," I said. "East-southeast." The sun was lowering behind us. This world revolved like Old Earth and Hyperion.

The river straightened out and I accelerated the mat a bit. In the labyrinths on Hyperion, I'd been scooting along at almost three hundred klicks per hour, but I wasn't eager to fly that fast here unless I had to. The flight threads in this old mat held a charge for quite a while, but there was no need to run it out quicker than necessary. I made a mental note to recharge the threads from the ship's leads before we left, even if we took the skybikes as transportation.

"Look," said Aenea, pointing to our left.

Far to the north, illuminated by the now visibly setting sun, something like a mesa top or some very large man-made thing broke through the jungle canopy. "Can we go look?" she said.

I knew better. We had an objective, we had a time limit—the setting sun, for one—and we had a thousand reasons not to take chances by swooping around strange artifacts. For all we knew, this mesa or tower-thing was the Central Pax Headquarters for the planet.

"Sure," I said, mentally kicking myself for being an idiot, and banked the hawking mat to the north.

The thing was farther north than it seemed. I kicked the mat up to two hundred klicks per hour, and we still spent a good ten minutes flying to it.

"Excuse me, M. Endymion," came the ship's voice on my wrist, "but you appear to have gone off course and are now headed north-northeast, approximately one hundred three degrees from your former heading."

"We're investigating a tower or butte or something poking up from the jungle almost due north of us," I said. "Do you have it on your radar?"

"Negative," said the ship, and I thought I heard a hint of dryness in its tone again. "My vantage point here stuck in the mud is not optimum. Anything below a twenty-eight-degree inclination from the horizon is lost in clutter. You are just within my angle of detection. Another twenty kilometers north, and I will lose you."

"That's all right," I said. "We're just going to check this out and get right back to the river."

"Why?" said the ship. "Why investigate something which has nothing to do with your plans to travel downriver?"

Aenea leaned over and lifted my wrist. "We're human," she said.

The ship did not reply.

The thing, when we finally reached it, rose a sheer hundred meters above the jungle canopy. Its lower levels were surrounded so tightly by the giant gymnosperms that the tower looked like a weathered crag rising from a green sea.

It appeared to be both natural and man-made—or at least modified by some intelligence. The tower was about seventy meters across and appeared to be made of red rock, perhaps some type of sandstone. The setting sun—only ten degrees or so above the jungle-canopy horizon now —bathed the crag in a rich red light. Here and there along the east and west faces of the crag were openings that both Aenea and I first thought were natural—wind or water hewn—but we soon realized had been carved. Also on the east side were niches carved—niches about the right distance from one another to be steps and handholds for human feet and hands. But they were shallow, narrow niches, and the thought of free-climbing that hundred-plus-meter crag with nothing but such shallow toe- and fingerholds made my insides clench.

"Can we go closer?" asked Aenea.

I had been keeping the hawking mat about fifty meters out as we circled. "I don't think we should," I said. "We're already within firearms range. I don't want to tempt anyone or anything with a spear or a bow and arrows."

"A bow could pick us off at this range," she said, but did not insist on flying closer.

For a second I thought I saw a glimmer of something moving within one of the oval openings carved in the red rock, but an instant later I decided it was a trick of the evening light.

"Had enough?" I said.

"Not really," said Aenea. Her small hands were holding on to my shoulders as we banked. The breeze ruffled my short hair, and when I looked back, I could see the girl's hair streaming behind her.

"We need to get back to business, though," I said, aiming the hawking mat south toward the river and accelerating again. The gymnosperm canopy looked soft, feathery, and deceptively continuous forty meters beneath us, as if we could land on it if we had to. A pang of tension filled me as I thought of the consequences if we had to. *But A. Bettik has the flying belt and flybikes,* I thought. *He can come fetch us if he has to.*

We intercepted the river again a klick or so southeast of where we had left it, and we could see the thirty klicks or so to the horizon. No farcaster portal.

"Which way?" I said.

"Let's go a bit farther."

I nodded and banked left, staying out over the river. We had seen no signs of animal life other than the occasional white bird and the red bat-plant things. I was thinking of the footsteps in the side of the red monolith when Aenea tugged at my sleeve and pointed almost straight downward.

Something very large was moving just under the surface of the river. The low sunlight reflecting from the water hid most of the details from us, but I could make out leathery skin, something that might have been a barbed tail, and fins or cilia on the side. The creature must have been eight to ten meters long. It dived and we were past before I could see any more detail.

"That was sort of like a river manta," called Aenea over my shoulder. We were moving quickly again, and the sound of the wind against the rising deflection field made some noise.

"Bigger," I said. I had harnessed and worked with river mantas, and I'd never seen one that long or broad. Suddenly the hawking mat seemed very frail and insubstantial. I brought us thirty meters lower—we were flying almost at tree level now—so that a fall would not necessarily be fatal if the ancient flying carpet decided to quit on us without warning.

We banked south around another bend, noticed the river narrowing rapidly, and soon were greeted with a roar and a wall of rising spray.

The waterfall was not overly spectacular—it fell only ten to fifteen meters—but a huge volume of water was dropping over it, the klick-wide river pressed between rock cliffs to a width of only a hundred meters or so, and the force expended there was impressive. Below, there was another rapids over the rocks of the tumbled falls, then a wide pool, and then the river grew wide and relatively placid again. For a second I wondered stupidly if the river critter we'd seen was prepared for this sudden drop.

"I don't think we're going to find the portal in time to get back before dark," I said over my shoulder to the girl. "If there's a portal downriver at all."

"It's there," said Aenea.

"We've come at least a hundred klicks," I said.

"A. Bettik said that the Tethys sections *averaged* that. This one might be two or three hundred kilometers between portals. Besides . . . there were numerous portals along the various rivers. The sections of the river varied in length even on the same world."

"Who told you that?" I asked, twisting to look at her.

"My mother. She was a detective, you know. She once had a divorce case where she followed a married guy and his girlfriend for three weeks on the River Tethys."

"What's a divorce case?" I asked.

"Never mind." Aenea scooted around so that she was facing backward, her legs still crossed. Her hair whipped around her face. "You're right, let's get back to A. Bettik and the ship. We'll come this way tomorrow."

I banked us around and accelerated toward the west. We crossed over the falls and laughed as the spray wet our faces and hands.

"M. Endymion?" said the comlog. It was not the ship's voice, but A. Bettik's.

"Yes," I said. "We're heading back. We're about twenty-five, thirty minutes out."

"I know," came the android's calm voice. "I was watching the tower, the waterfall, and all the rest in the holopit."

Aenea and I looked at each other with what must have been comical expressions. "You mean this comlog thing sends back pictures?"

"Of course," came the ship's voice. "Holo or video. We have been monitoring on holo."

"Although the viewing is a bit odd," said A. Bettik, "since the holopit is now an indentation in the wall. But I was not calling to check your progress."

"What, then?" I said.

"We appear to have a visitor," said A. Bettik.

"A big river thing?" called Aenea. "Sort of like a manta, only bigger?"

"Not exactly," came A. Bettik's calm voice. "It is the Shrike."

30

OUR HAWKING MAT must have looked like a blur during our wild rush back to the ship. I asked if the ship could send us a real-time holo of the Shrike, but it said that most of its hull sensors were covered with mud and it had no clear view of the beach.

"It's on the beach?" I said.

"It was a moment ago, when I went up to carry another load out," came A. Bettik's voice.

"Then it was in the Hawking-drive accumulator ring," said the ship.

"What?" I said. "There's no entrance to that part of the ship—" I stopped before I made a total idiot of myself. "Where is it now?" I said.

"We are not sure," said A. Bettik. "I am going out onto the hull now and will be taking one of the radios. The ship will relay my voice to you."

"Wait . . . ," I began.

"M. Endymion," interrupted the android, "rather than urging you to rush back here, I called to suggest that you and M. Aenea . . . ah . . . extend your sight-seeing for a bit until the ship and I receive an indication of our . . . ah . . . visitor's intentions."

This made sense to me. Here I was charged with protecting this girl, and when what might well be the deadliest killing machine in the galaxy appears, what do I do but rush her toward the danger? I was being a bit of an asshole this long day. I reached for the flight threads to slow us and bank back to the east.

Aenea's small hand intercepted mine. "No," she said. "We'll go back."

I was shaking my head. "That thing is . . ."

"That thing can go anywhere it pleases," said the girl. Her eyes and tone were deadly serious. "If it wanted me . . . or you . . . it would appear right here on the mat with us."

The thought made me look around.

"Let's go back," said Aenea.

I sighed and turned back upriver, slowing the mat just a bit as I did so. Pulling the plasma rifle from my pack and swinging the stock out to lock it, I said, "I don't get it. Is there any record of that monster ever leaving Hyperion?"

"I don't think so," said the girl. She was leaning so that her face was against my back trying to stay out of the windblast as the deflection field lessened.

"So . . . what's happening? Is it following you?"

"That seems logical." Her voice was muffled as she spoke into the cotton of my shirt.

"Why?" I said.

Aenea pushed away so strongly that I began to reach for her instinctively to keep her from tumbling off the back of the mat. She shrugged away from my hand. "Raul, I don't really know the answers to these questions yet, all right? I didn't know if the thing would leave Hyperion. I certainly didn't want it to. Believe me."

"I do," I said. I lowered my hand to the mat, noticing how large it was next to her small hand, small knee, tiny foot.

She set her hand on mine. "Let's get back."

"Right." I loaded the rifle with a plasma-cartridge magazine. The shell casings were not separate but were molded into the magazine until each fired. One magazine held fifty plasma bolts. When the last was fired, the magazine was gone. I slammed the magazine up and in with a slap of my hand as I'd been taught in the Guard, set the selector to single-shot, and made sure the safety was on. I laid the weapon across my knees as we flew.

Aenea touched my shoulders with her hands and said in my ear, "Do you think that thing will do any good against the Shrike?"

I swiveled my head to look at her. "No," I said.

We flew into the setting sun.

A. BETTIK WAS ALONE on the narrow beach when we arrived. He waved to reassure us that everything was all right, but I still circled once above the treetops before landing. The sun was a red globe balancing on the jungle canopy to the west.

I set the mat down next to the pile of crates and equipment on the beach, in the shadow of the great ship's hull, and jumped to my feet, the plasma rifle's safety set to off.

"It's still gone," said A. Bettik. He had radioed this fact to us upon his leaving the ship, but I was still tense with expectation. The android led us over to a clear place on the beach where there was a single pair of footprints—if one could call them footprints. It looked as if someone had pressed a very heavy piece of bladed farm equipment into the sand in two places.

I crouched next to the prints like the experienced tracker I was, then realized the silliness of that exercise. "He just appeared here, again in the ship, and then disappeared?"

"Yes," said A. Bettik.

"Ship, did you ever get the thing on radar or visual?"

"Negative," came the reply from the bracelet. "There are no video recorders in the Hawking-drive accumulator. . . ."

"How did you know it was there?" I asked.

"I have a mass sensor in every compartment," said the ship. "For flight purposes I must know precisely how much mass is displaced in every section of the ship."

"How much mass did it displace?" I said.

"One-point-oh-six-three metric tons," said the ship.

I froze in the act of straightening up. "What? Over a thousand kilos? That's ridiculous." I looked at the two footprints again. "No way."

"Way," said the ship. "During the creature's stay in the Hawking-drive accumulator ring, I measured a precise displacement of one-point-oh-six-three-thousand kilos and . . ."

"Jesus wept," I said, turning to A. Bettik. "I wonder if anyone's ever weighed this bastard before."

"The Shrike is almost three meters tall," said the android. "And it may be very dense. It may also vary its mass as required."

"Required for what?" I muttered, looking at the line of trees. It was very dark under there as the sun set. The gymnosperm feather fronds high above us caught the last of the light and faded. Clouds had rolled in during the last minutes of our flight back, and now they also glowed red and then grew dull as the sunset faded.

"You ready to get a star fix?" I said to the comlog.

"Quite ready," said the ship, "although this cloud cover will have to clear. In the meantime, I have made one or two other calculations."

"Such as?" said Aenea.

"Such as—based upon the movement of this world's sun during the past few hours—this planet's day is eighteen hours, six minutes, fifty-one seconds long. Units in Old Hegemony Standard, of course."

"Of course," I said. To A. Bettik, "Any of those River Tethys vacation worlds in your book show an eighteen-hour day?"

"None that I have come across, M. Endymion."

"All right," I said. "Let's decide about tonight. Do we camp out here, stay in the ship, or load this stuff on the flybikes and get downriver to the next portal as soon as possible? We can haul the inflatable raft with us. I vote we do that. I'm not real keen on staying on this world if the Shrike is around here."

A. Bettik raised one finger like a child in a classroom. "I should have radioed you earlier . . . ," he said as if embarrassed. "The EVA locker, as you know, suffered some damage from the attack. There was no sign of an inflatable raft, although the ship remembers one in the inventory, and three of the four bikes are inoperable."

I frowned. "Totally?"

"Yes, sir," said the android. "Quite. The fourth is repairable, the ship thinks, but it will take several days."

"Shit," I said to no one in particular.

"How much charge do those bikes have?" asked Aenea.

"One hundred hours under normal use," piped up my comlog.

The girl made a dismissive gesture. "I don't think they'd be that useful, anyway. One bike isn't going to make that much difference, and we might never find a recharge source."

I rubbed my cheek, feeling the stubble there. In the day's excitement I had forgotten to shave. "I thought of that," I said, "but if we take any gear at all, the hawking mat's not big enough to haul the three of us *plus* weapons, *plus* what we need to take."

I thought that the child would argue with us about needing the gear, but instead she said, "Let's take it all, but let's not fly."

"Not fly?" I said. The idea of hacking our way through that jungle made me queasy. "Without an inflatable raft, it's either fly or walk. . . ."

"We can still have a raft," said Aenea. "We could build a wooden raft and float it downstream . . . not only on this section of the river, but all of them."

I rubbed my cheek again. "The waterfall . . ."

"We can ferry our stuff down there on the hawking mat in the morning," she said. "Build the raft below the falls. Unless you don't think we can construct a raft . . ."

I looked at the gymnosperms: tall, thin, tough, just about the right thickness. "We can build a raft," I said. "We used to cobble them together on the Kans to haul extra junk downstream with the barges."

"Good," said Aenea. "We'll camp here tonight . . . it shouldn't be too long a night if the day is only eighteen standard hours. Then get moving at first light."

I hesitated a moment. I didn't want to get into the habit of letting a twelve-year-old kid make decisions for us all, but the idea seemed sensible.

"It's too bad the ship's kaput," I said. "We could just go downriver on repulsors. . . ."

Aenea laughed out loud. "I'd never considered going on the River Tethys in this ship," she said, rubbing her nose. "It'd be just what we need —inconspicuous as a giant dachshund squeezing under croquet hoops."

"What's a dachshund?" I said.

"What's a croquet hoop?" asked A. Bettik.

"Never mind," said Aenea. "Do you guys agree about staying here tonight and building a raft tomorrow?"

I looked at the android. "It seems eminently sensible to me," he said, "although a subset of an equally eminent nonsensical voyage."

"I'll take that as a yes vote," said the girl. "Raul?"

"All right," I said, "but where do we sleep tonight? Here on the beach, or in the ship, where it will be safer?"

The ship spoke. "I will endeavor to make my interior as safe and hospitable as possible tonight, given the circumstances. Two of the couches on the fugue deck will still serve as beds, and there are hammocks which might be strung. . . ."

"I vote we camp on the beach," said Aenea. "The ship's no safer from the Shrike than out here."

I looked at the darkening forest. "There might be other things we don't want to meet in the dark," I said. "The ship seems safer."

A. Bettik touched a small crate. "I found some small perimeter alarms," he said. "We could set those around our camp. I would be happy to stand watch through the night. I confess to some interest in sleeping outside after so many days aboard the ship."

I sighed and surrendered. "We'll trade off watches," I said. "Let's get this junk set up before it gets too dark."

The "junk" included the camping gear I'd asked the android to dig out: a tent of microthin polymer, thin as the shadow of a spiderweb, but tough, rainproof, and light enough to carry in one's pocket; the superconductor heating cube, cool on five sides and able to heat any meal on the sixth; the perimeter alarms A. Bettik had mentioned—actually a hunter's version of old military motion detectors, three-centimeter disks that could be spiked into the ground in any-sized perimeter up to two klicks; sleeping bags, infinitely compressible foam pads, night goggles, the com units, mess kits, and utensils.

We set the alarms in place first, spiking them down in a half circle from just within the forest's edge to the edge of the river.

"What if that big thing crawls out of the river and eats us?" said Aenea as we finished setting the perimeter. It was getting dark in earnest now, but the clouds hid any stars. Breezes rustled the fronds above with a more sinister sound than earlier.

"If that or anything else crawls out of the river and eats us," I said, "you're going to wish we'd stayed one more night in the ship." I set the last detectors at the river's edge.

We pitched the tent in the center of the beach, not far from the bow of the crippled ship. The microfabric did not need tent poles or stakes—all you had to do was double-crease the lines of the fabric you wanted rigid, and those folds would stay taut in a hurricane, but setting a microtent up was a bit of an art, and the other two watched while I expanded the fabric, creased the edges into an A-line with a dome center tall enough to stand in, and folded the suddenly rigid edges into the sand to stake it. I had left an expanse of microfabric as the floor of the tent, and by stretching it just so, we had mesh for the entrance. A. Bettik nodded his appreciation for the trick, and Aenea set the sleeping bags in place while I set a pan on the heating cube and opened a can of beef stew. At the last moment I remembered that Aenea was a vegetarian—she had eaten mostly salads during the two weeks aboard ship.

"That's all right," she said, poking her head out of the tent. "I'll have some of the bread that A. Bettik's heating up, and perhaps some of the cheese."

A. Bettik was carrying fallen wood over and setting stones into a fire ring.

"We don't need that," I said, indicating the heating cube and the bubbling pot of stew.

"Yes," said the android, "but I thought a fire might be pleasant. And the light welcome."

The light, it turned out, was very welcome. We sat under the awning vestibule of my elaborately folded tent and watched the flames spit sparks toward the sky as a storm moved in. It was a strange storm, with bands of shifting lights in lieu of lightning. The pale bands of shimmering color danced from the bottoms of the hurrying clouds to points just meters above the gymnosperm fronds gyrating wildly in the rising wind. There was no thunder with the phenomenon, but a sort of subsonic rumble set my nerves on edge. Within the jungle itself, pale globes of red and yellow phosphorescence jiggled and danced—not gracefully like the radiant gossamers in Hyperion's forests, but nervously, almost malevolently. Behind us, the river lapped at the beach with increasingly active waves. Sitting by the fire, my headset in place and tuned to the perimeter detectors' frequency, the plasma rifle across my lap, the night goggles on my forehead ready to be flipped down at a second's notice, I must have been a comical sight. It did not seem funny at the time: images of the Shrike's footprints in the sand kept coming to mind.

"Did it act threatening?" I'd asked A. Bettik a few minutes earlier. I had been trying to get him to hold the 16-gauge shotgun—no weapon is easier for a weapon's novice to use than a shotgun—but all he would do was keep it by him as he sat by the fire.

"It did not act anything at all," he had replied. "It simply stood there on the beach—tall, spiked, dark but gleaming. Its eyes were very red."

"Was it looking at you?"

"It was looking east, down the river," A. Bettik had replied.

As if waiting for Aenea and me to return, I had thought.

So I sat by the flickering fire, watched the aurora dance and shimmer over the wind-tossed jungle, tracked the will-o'-the-wisps as they jiggled in the jungle darkness, listened to the subsonic thunder rumbling like some great, hungry beast, and passed the time wondering how the hell I'd got myself here. For all I knew, there were velociraptors and packs of carrion-breed kalidergas slinking through the jungle toward us even as we sat fat and stupid by the fire. Or perhaps the river would rise—a wall of water could be rushing downstream toward us at that very moment. Camping on a sand spit was not terribly bright. We should have slept in the ship with the air lock sealed tight.

Aenea lay on her stomach looking into the fire. "Do you know any stories?" she said.

"Stories!" I cried. A. Bettik looked up from where he sat hugging his knees beyond the fire.

"Yes," said the girl. "Like ghost stories."

I made a noise.

Aenea propped her chin on her palms. The fire painted her face in warm tones. "I just thought it might be fun," she said. "I like ghost stories."

I thought of four or five responses and held them back. "You'd better get to sleep," I said at last. "If the ship's right about the short day, we don't have too much night. . . ." *Please, God, let that be true,* I was thinking. Aloud, I said, "You'd better get some sleep while you can."

"All right," said Aenea, and took one last look across the fire at the wind-tossed jungle, the aurora, and the St. Elmo's fire in the forest, and rolled into her sleeping bag and went to sleep.

A. Bettik and I sat in silence for a while. Occasionally I would converse with my bracelet comlog, asking the ship to inform me immediately if the river started rising, or if it detected some mass displacement, or if . . .

"I would be happy to take the first watch, M. Endymion," said the android.

"No, go ahead and sleep," I said, forgetting that the blue-skinned man required very little sleep.

"We will watch together, then," he said softly. "But do feel free to doze when you need to, M. Endymion."

Perhaps I did doze off sometime before the tropical dawn about six hours later. It was cloudy and stormy all night; the ship never got its star fix while we were there. No velociraptors or kalidergas ate us. The river did not rise. The storm aurora did not harm us, and the balls of swamp gas never came out of the swamp to burn us.

What I remember most about that night, besides my galloping paranoia and terrible tiredness, was the sight of Aenea sleeping with her brown-blond hair spilled out over the edge of her red sleeping bag, her fist raised to her cheek like an infant preparing to suck its thumb. I realized that night the import and the terrible difficulty in the task ahead of me—of keeping this child safe from the sharp edges of a strange and indifferent universe.

I think that it was on this alien and storm-tossed night that I first understood what it might be like to be a parent.

WE GOT MOVING AT FIRST LIGHT, and I remember that morning mixture of bone-tiredness, gritty eyes, stubbled cheeks, aching back, and sheer joy that I usually felt after my first night on a camping trip. Aenea went down to the river to wash up, and I have to admit that she looked fresher and cleaner than she should have, given the circumstances.

A. Bettik had heated coffee over the cube, and he and I drank some while we watched the morning fog curl up from the quickly moving river. Aenea sipped from a water bottle she'd brought from the ship, and we all munched on dry cereal from a ration pak.

By the time the sun was shining over the jungle canopy, burning away the mists that rose from the river and forest, we were ferrying the gear downriver on the hawking mat. Since Aenea and I had done the fun part the previous evening, I let A. Bettik fly the gear while I dragged more stuff out of the ship and made sure we had what we needed.

Clothing was a problem. I had packed everything I thought I might need, but the girl had only the clothes she'd been wearing on Hyperion and carrying in her pack, and a few shirts we'd cut down from the Consul's wardrobe. With more than 250 years to think about rescuing the child, one would think that the old poet would have thought to pack some clothes for her. Aenea seemed happy enough with what she had brought, but I was worried that it would not be enough if we ran into cold or rainy weather.

The EVA locker was a help there. There were several suit liners fitted out for the spacesuits, and the smallest of these came close to fitting the girl. I knew that the micropore material would keep her warm and dry in any but the most arctic conditions. I also appropriated a liner for the android and myself; it seemed absurd to be packing for winter in the rising tropical heat of that day, but one never knew. There was also an old outdoors vest of the Consul's in the locker: long but fitted with more than a dozen pockets, clips, tie-on rings, secret zippered compartments. Aenea let out a squeal when I dug it out of the tumbled mess of the locker, put it on, and wore it almost constantly from then on.

We also found two EVA geology specimen bags with shoulder straps, which made excellent packs. Aenea hoisted one to her shoulder and loaded the extra clothes and bric-a-brac we were finding.

I still was convinced that there had to be a raft there, but no amount of digging and opening locker compartments revealed one.

"M. Endymion," said the ship when I mentioned to the child what I was rooting around for, "I have a vague memory. . . ."

Aenea and I stopped what we were doing and listened. There was something strange, almost pained, about the ship's voice.

"I have a vague memory of the Consul taking the inflatable raft . . . of him waving good-bye to me from it."

"Where was that?" I asked. "Which world?"

"I do not know," said the ship in that same bemused, almost pained tone. "It may not have been a world at all. . . . I remember stars shining *below* the river."

"Below the river?" I said. I was worried about the ship's mental integrity after the crash.

"The memory is fragmented," said the ship in a brisker tone. "But I do remember the Consul departing in the raft. It was a large raft, quite comfortable for eight or ten people."

"Great," I said, slamming a compartment door. Aenea and I carried out the last load—we had rigged a metal folding ladder to hang down from the air lock, so climbing in and out was not the struggle it had been earlier.

A. Bettik swooped back after ferrying the camping gear and food cartons down to the waterfall, and now I looked at what remained: my backpack filled with my personal gear, Aenea's backpack and shoulder bag, the extra com units and goggles, some of the food paks, and—lashed under the top of my pack—the folded plasma rifle and the machete A. Bettik had found yesterday. The long knife was awkward to carry, even in its leather sheath, but my few minutes in the jungle the day before had convinced me that we might need it. I had also dug out an ax and an even more compact tool—a folding shovel, actually, although for millennia we idiots who had joined the infantry had been trained to call it "an entrenching tool." All of our cutlery was beginning to take up space.

I would have been happy to have skipped the ax and brought along a cutting laser to fell the trees for the raft—even an old chain saw would have been preferable—but my flashlight laser wasn't up to that sort of work, and the weapons locker had been strangely devoid of cutting tools. For one long self-indulgent moment I considered bringing the old FORCE assault rifle and just blasting and burning those trees down, splitting them with pulse bolts if need be, but then I rejected the idea. It would be too loud, too messy, and too imprecise. I would just have to use the ax and sweat a bit. I did bring one of the tool kits with hammer, nails, screwdrivers, screws, pivot bolts—all the things I might need for raft building—as well as some rolls of waterproof plastalum that I thought might make crude but adequate flooring for the raft. On top of the tool kit were several hundred meters of nylon-sheathed climbing rope in three separate coils. In a red waterproof pouch, I'd found some flares and simple plastique, the kind that had been used for blasting stumps and rocks out of fields for countless centuries, as well as a dozen detonators. I included those, although they would be of doubtful use in felling trees for a raft. Also included in this pile for the next trip east were two medkits and a bottle-sized water purifier.

I had carried the EM-flying belt out, but the thing was bulky with its harness and power pak. I propped it against my pack anyway, thinking that we might need it. Also propped against my pack was the 16-gauge shotgun, which the android had not bothered taking with him during his flight east. Next to it were three boxes of shells. I had also insisted on bringing the flechette pistol, although neither A. Bettik nor Aenea would carry the thing.

On my belt was the holster holding the loaded .45, a pocket for an old-fashioned magnetic compass we'd found in the locker, my folded pair of night goggles and daytime binoculars, a water bottle, and two extra clips for the plasma rifle. "Bring on the velociraptors!" I muttered while taking inventory.

"What?" said Aenea, looking up from her packing.

"Nothing."

Aenea had her things packed neatly in her new bag by the time A. Bettik touched down on the sand. She had also packed the android's few personal items in the second shoulder bag.

I have always enjoyed breaking camp, even more than setting it up. I think it's the neatness of packing everything away that I enjoy.

"What are we forgetting?" I said to the other two as we stood there on the narrow beach, looking at the packs and weapons.

"Me," said the ship through the comlog on my wrist. The spacecraft's voice did sound a bit plaintive.

Aenea walked across the sand to touch the curved metal of the beached ship. "How are you doing?"

"I have begun repairs, M. Aenea," it said. "Thank you for inquiring."

"Do you still project six months for repairs?" I asked. The last of the clouds were dissipating overhead, and the sky was that pale blue again. The green and white fronds moved against it.

"Approximately six standard months," said the ship. "That is for my internal and external condition, of course. I do not have the macromanipulators to repair such things as your broken flybikes."

"That's all right," said Aenea. "We're leaving them all behind. We'll fix them when we see you again."

"When will that be?" said the ship. Its voice seemed smaller than usual coming from the comlog.

The child looked at A. Bettik and me. None of us spoke. Finally Aenea said, "We *will* need your services again, Ship. Can you conceal yourself here for months . . . or years . . . while you repair yourself and wait?"

"Yes," said the ship. "Would the river bottom do?"

I looked out at the great gray mass of the ship rising from the water. The river was wide here, and probably deep, but the thought of the wounded ship backing itself into it seemed strange. "Won't you . . . leak?" I said.

"M. Endymion," said the ship in that tone that made me think it was acting haughty, "I am an interstellar spacecraft capable of penetrating nebulae and existing quite comfortably within the outer shell of a red giant star. I shall hardly—as you put it—*leak* because of being immersed in H_2O for a brief period of years."

"Sorry," I said, and then—refusing to have the ship's rebuke as the last word—"Don't forget to close your air lock when you go under."

The ship did not comment.

"When we come back for you," said the girl, "will we be able to call you?"

"Use the comlog bands or ninety-point-one on the general radio band," said the ship. "I will keep a buggy-whip antenna above waterline to receive your call."

"Buggy-whip antenna," mused A. Bettik. "What a lovely phrase."

"I am sorry that I do not recall the derivation of that term," said the ship. "My memory is not what it used to be."

"That's all right," said Aenea, patting the hull. "You've served us well. Now you *get* well. . . . We want you in top shape when we return."

"Yes, M. Aenea. I will be in contact and monitoring your progress until you transit the next farcaster portal."

A. Bettik and Aenea sat on the hawking mat with their packs and our last boxes of gear taking up the rest of the space. I strapped the bulky flying belt on. It meant that I had to carry my own pack against my chest with a strap looped over my shoulder, the rifle in my free hand, but it worked all right. I knew how to operate the thing only from books—EM belts were useless on Hyperion—but the controls were simple and intuitive. The power indicator showed full charge, so I did not anticipate being dropped into the river for this short hop.

The mat was hovering about ten meters above the river when I squeezed the handheld controller, lurched into the air, almost clipped a gymnosperm, found my balance, and flew out to hover next to them. Hanging from this padded body harness was not as comfortable as sitting on a flying carpet, but the exhilaration of flying was even stronger. With the controller still held in my fist, I gave them the thumbs-up, and we flew east along the river, toward the rising sun.

THERE WEREN'T MANY OTHER sand spits or beaches between the ship and the waterfall, but there was a good spot just below the waterfall, along the south side of the river where it widened into a lazy pool just beyond the rapids, and it was here that A. Bettik unpacked our camping gear and the first load of material. The noise from the falls was loud as we stacked the last of the small crates. I unlimbered the ax and looked at the nearest gymnosperms.

"I was thinking," A. Bettik said so softly that I could hardly hear him over the noise of the waterfall.

I paused with the ax on my shoulder. The sunlight was very hot, and my shirt was already sticking to me.

"The River Tethys was meant to be a pleasure cruise," he continued. "I wonder how the pleasure cruisers dealt with that." He pointed a blue finger at the roaring falls.

"I know," said Aenea. "I was thinking the same thing. They had levitation barges then, but not everyone going down the Tethys would have been in one. It would have been embarrassing to go for a romantic boat ride and find you and your sweetheart going over those."

I stood looking at the rainbow-dappled spray of the falls and found myself wondering if I was as intelligent as I often assumed. This had not occurred to me. "The Tethys has been unused for almost three standard centuries," I said. "Maybe the falls are new."

"Perhaps," said A. Bettik, "but I doubt it. These falls appear to have been formed by tectonic shelving that runs for many miles north and south through the jungle—do you see the difference in elevation there? And they have been eroding for a very long time. Note the size of the boulders in the rapids? I would think this has been here for as long as the river has run."

"And it's not in your Tethys guidebook?" I said.

"No," said the android, holding the book out. Aenea took it.

"Maybe we're not on the Tethys," I said. Both of the others stared at me. "The ship didn't get a starsighting," I went on, "but what if this is some world not on the original Tethys tour?"

Aenea nodded. "I thought of that. The portals are the same as the ones along the remnants of the Tethys today, but who is to say that the TechnoCore did not have other portals . . . other farcaster-connected rivers?"

I set the head of the ax down and leaned on the shaft. "In which case, we're in trouble," I said. "You'll never find your architect, and we'll never find our way back to the ship and home."

Aenea smiled. "It's too early to worry about that. It *has* been three centuries. Maybe the river here just cut a new channel since the Tethys days. Or maybe there's a canal and locks we missed because the jungle grew over it. We don't have to worry about this now. We just have to get downriver to see if there's another portal."

I held up one finger. "Another thought," I said, feeling a bit smarter than I had a moment before. "What if we go to all this trouble of building a raft here and find another waterfall between us and the portal? Or ten more? We didn't spot the farcaster arch last night, so we don't know how far it is."

"I thought of that," said Aenea.

I tapped my fingers on the ax handle. If that kid said that phrase one more time, I would seriously consider using the implement on her.

"M. Aenea asked me to reconnoiter," said the android. "I did so during my last shuttle here."

I was frowning. "Reconnoiter? You didn't have time to fly that mat a hundred klicks or more downriver."

"No," agreed the android, "but I flew the mat very high and used the extra set of binoculars to search our path. The river appears to run straight and true for almost two hundred kilometers. It was difficult, to be sure, but I saw what may be the arch approximately a hundred thirty kilometers downriver. There appeared to be no waterfalls or other major obstacles between us and it."

My frown must have deepened. "You saw all that?" I said. "How high *were* you?"

"The mat has no altimeter," said A. Bettik, "but judging from the visible curvature of the planet and the darkening of the sky, I think I was about one hundred kilometers up."

"Did you have one of the spacesuits on?" I asked. At that altitude a human being's blood would boil in his veins and his lungs would burst from explosive decompression. "A respirator?" I looked around, but nothing like that was lying in our modest piles of goods.

"No," said the android, turning to lift a crate, "I just held my breath."

Shaking my head, I went off to cut some trees down. I figured that the exercise and solitude would do me good.

IT WAS EVENING BEFORE the raft was finished, and I would have been working all night if A. Bettik had not taken turns with me on the tree cutting. The finished product was not beautiful, but it floated. Our little raft was about six meters long and four wide, with a long steering pole carved into a crude rudder set onto a forked support at the rear, a raised area just in front of the steering pole where Aenea molded the tent into a lean-to with openings front and rear, and crude oarlocks on each side with long oar-poles that would lie along the sides of the ship unless they were needed for rowing in dead water or emergency steering in rapids. I had been worried that the fern trees might soak up too much water and sink too low to be useful as a raft, but with only two layers of them wrapped together into a honeycomb with our climbing rope and bolted in strategic places, the logs rode very nicely and kept the top of the raft about fifteen centimeters above the water.

Aenea had shown a fascination with the microtent, and I had to admit that her sculpting of it was more skillful and efficient than anything I had shaped in all my years of using the things. Our lean-to could be ducked into from the steering position at the rudder, had a nice overhang in front to shield us from sun or rain while keeping the view intact, and had nice vestibules on either side to keep the extra crates of gear dry. She had already spread our foam pads and sleeping bags in various corners of the tent; the high sitting area in the center where we had the best view forward now boasted a meter-wide river stone, which she had set there as a hearth with the mess gear and heating cube on it; one of the handlamps was opened to lantern mode and was hanging from a centerloop—and, I had to admit, the overall effect was cozy.

The girl did not just spend her afternoon making cozy tents, however. I guess that I had expected her to stand by and watch while the two men sweated through the heavy work—I had stripped to the waist an hour into the heat of the day—but Aenea joined in almost immediately, dragging downed logs to the assembly point, lashing them, driving nails, setting bolts and pivot joints in place, and generally helping in the design. She pointed out why the standard way I'd been taught to jerry-rig a rudder was inefficient, and by moving the base of the support tripod lower and farther apart, I was able to move the long pole easier and to better effect. Twice she showed me different ways to tie the cross supports on the underside of the raft so that they would be tighter and sturdier. When we needed a log shaped, it was Aenea who set to with the machete, and all A. Bettik and I could do was stand back or be hit by flying chips.

Still, even with the three of us working hard, it was almost sundown before the raft was finished and our gear loaded.

"We could camp here tonight, get onto the river early in the morning," I said. Even as I said it, I knew that I did not want to do that. Neither did the other two. We climbed aboard, and I pushed us away from the shore with the long pole I'd chosen as our main source of locomotion when the current failed. A. Bettik steered, and Aenea stood near the front of the raft, looking for shoals or hidden rocks.

For the first hour or so, the voyage seemed almost magical. After the sultry jungle heat and the tremendous exertion all day, it seemed like paradise to stand on the slowly moving raft, push against the river mud occasionally, and watch the darkening walls of jungle slip past. The sun set almost directly behind us, and for a few minutes the river was as red as molten lava, the undersides of the gymnosperms on either side aflame with reflected light. Then the grayness turned to darkness, and before we caught more than a glimpse of the night sky, the clouds moved in from the east just as they had the previous night.

"I wonder if the ship got a fix," said Aenea.

"Let's call and ask," I said.

The ship had not been able to fix its position. "I was able to ascertain that we are not on Hyperion or Renaissance Vector," said the small voice from my wrist comlog.

"Well, that's a relief," I said. "Any other news?"

"I have moved to the river bottom," said the ship. "It is quite comfortable, and I am preparing to . . ."

Suddenly the colored lightning rippled across the northern and western horizons, the wind whipped across the river so strongly that each of us had to rush to keep things from being blown away, the raft began moving toward the south shore with the whitecaps, and the comlog spit static. I thumbed the bracelet off and concentrated on poling while A. Bettik steered again. For several minutes I was afraid that the raft would come apart in the high waves and roaring wind; the bow was chopping, lifting, and dropping, and our only illumination came from the explosions of magenta and crimson lightning. The thunder was audible this night— great, pealing waves of sound, as if someone were rolling giant steel drums down stone stairs at us—and the aurora lightning tore at the sky rather than dancing, as it had the night before. Each of us froze for a second as one of those magenta bolts struck a gymnosperm on the north bank of the river, instantly causing the tree to explode in flame and colored sparks. As an ex-bargeman, I cursed my stupidity for letting us be out here in the middle of such a wide river—the Tethys had opened up to the better part of a klick wide again—without lightning rod or rubber mats. We hunkered down and grimaced when the colored bolts struck either shore or lit the eastern horizon in front of us.

Suddenly it was raining and the worst of the lightning was over. We ran for the tent—Aenea and A. Bettik crouched near the front opening, still hunting for sandbars or floating logs, me standing at the rear where the girl had rigged the tent to provide the person at the rudder shelter even while steering.

It had rained hard and often on the Kans River when I was a bargeman—I remember huddling in the leaky old barge fo'c'sle and wondering if the damned boat was going to go down just because of the weight of the rain on it—but I do not remember any rain like this one.

For a moment I thought that we had come up against another waterfall, a much larger one this time, and had unwittingly poled under the full force of it—but we were still moving downriver, and it was no waterfall descending on us, just the terrible force of the worst rainstorm I had ever experienced.

The wise course would have been to make for the riverbank and hold up until the deluge passed, but we could see nothing except colored lightning exploding behind this vertical wall of water, and I had no idea how far the banks were, or whether they held any chance of our landing and tying up. So I lashed the rudder in its highest position so that it would do little but keep our stern to the rear, abandoned my post, and huddled with the child and android as the heavens opened and dropped rivers, lakes, *oceans* of water on us.

It says something about the girl's ability or luck in shaping and securing the tent that not once did it begin to fold or come loose from its cinchings to the raft. I say that I huddled with them, but in truth all three of us were busy holding down crates that had already been lashed in place as that raft pitched, tossed, swung around, and then brought its nose back around yet again. We had no idea which direction we were headed, whether the raft was safe in the middle of the river or was bearing down on boulders in a rapids, or was tearing hell-bent for cliffs as the river turned and we did not. None of us cared at that point: our goal was to keep our gear together, not be washed overboard, and to keep track of the other two as best we could.

At one point—with one arm around our stack of backpacks and my other hand clenched on the girl's collar as she leaned out to retrieve some cookware headed out of the tent at high speed—I looked out from under our vestibule awning toward the front of the raft and realized that every part of the raft except for our little raised platform where the tent sat was underwater. The wind whipped whitecaps that glowed red or bright yellow depending upon the color of the curtain of the lightning aurora raging at that moment. I remembered something I had forgotten to search for in the ship: life vests—personal flotation devices.

Pulling Aenea back under the flapping cover of the tent, I screamed against the storm, "Can you swim when it's not zero-g?"

"What?" I could see her lips form the word, but I could not actually hear it.

"Can . . . you . . . swim!?"

A. Bettik looked up from his position among the pitching crates. Water blew from his bald head and long nose. His blue eyes looked violet when the aurora crashed.

Aenea shook her head, although I was unsure whether she was answering my question in the negative or signifying she could not hear. I pulled her closer; her many-pocketed vest was soaked through and flapping like a wet sheet in a windstorm. "CAN . . . YOU . . . SWIM??" I was screaming literally at the top of my lungs. The effort took my breath away. I made frenzied swimming motions with both hands cupped in front of me. The raft pitched us apart, then tossed us back into close proximity.

I saw understanding light her dark eyes. The rain or spray whipped from the long strands of her hair. She smiled, the spray making her teeth look wet, and leaned closer to shout back into my ear.

"THANKS! I'D . . . LIKE TO . . . TAKE A . . . SWIM. BUT . . . MAYBE . . . LATER."

We must have hit an eddy then, or perhaps the rising wind just caught the tent and used it as a sail to spin the raft on its axis, but that was when the raft went all the way around, seemed to hesitate, and then continued its spin. The three of us gave up trying to hold on to anything other than our lives and each other and just huddled together in the center of the raft platform. I realized that Aenea was shouting—a sort of happy "Yee-HAW"—and before I could scream at her to shut up, I echoed the cry. It felt good to scream against that spinning and the storm and the deluge, unable to be heard, but feeling your own shouts echoing in your skull and bones even as the thunder rumble echoed there as well. I looked to my right as a crimson bolt illuminated the entire river, saw a boulder sticking up at least five meters above the water and the raft twisting around and past it like a dreidel spinning by a cinder, and was more amazed by the sight of A. Bettik on his knees, his head thrown back, "Yee-HAWing" with us at the top of his android lungs.

The storm lasted all night. Toward dawn the rain let up until it was a mere downpour. The aurora lightning and sonic-boom thunder must have ended about then, but I cannot be certain of that—I was, as were both my young friend and my android friend, fast asleep and snoring.

WE AWOKE TO FIND the sun already high, no sign of clouds, the river wide and smooth and slow, the jungle moving by on either side like a seamless tapestry being unwound past us, and the sky gentle and blue.

For a while we could only sit in the sunlight, our elbows on our knees, our clothes still wet and dripping. We said nothing. I think the maelstrom of the night was still in our eyes, the blasts of color still popping in our retinas.

After a while Aenea stood up on wobbly legs. The surface of the raft was wet, but still above water. One log on the starboard side had broken free; there were a few tattered cords where knots should be; but all in all, our vessel was still seaworthy . . . riverworthy. Whatever. We checked fittings and took inventory for a while. The handlamp we had hung as a lantern was gone, as was one of the smaller cartons of rations, but everything else seemed in place.

"Well, you two can stand around," said Aenea, "I'm going to make some breakfast."

She turned the heating cube to maximum, had water boiling in a kettle within a minute, poured water for her tea and set it in the coffeepot for our coffee, and then shifted that aside to set a skillet frying with breakfast strips of jambon with tiny slices of potato she was cutting up.

I looked at the ham sizzling and said, "I thought you were a vegetarian."

"I am," said the girl. "I'm having wheat chips and some of that terrible reconstituted milk from the ship, but for this one and only time, I'm chef and you fellows are eating well."

We ate well, sitting on the front edge of the tent platform where the sun could bathe our skins and dry our clothes. I pulled the crushed tricorn cap from one pocket of my wet vest, squeezed water out of it, and set it on my head for some shade. This started Aenea laughing again. I glanced over at A. Bettik, but the android was as observant and impassive as ever—as if his hour of "Yee-HAWing" with us had never occurred.

A. Bettik pulled a pole upright on the front of the raft—I had rigged it to swivel so we might hang a lantern there at night—but he pulled off his tattered white shirt and hung it there to dry instead. The sun glinted on his perfect blue skin.

"A flag!" cried Aenea. "It's what this expedition has been needing."

I laughed. "Not a white flag, though. That stands for . . ." I stopped in midsentence.

We had moved slowly with the current around a wide bend in the river. Now we each saw the huge and ancient farcaster portal arching for hundreds of meters above and to either side of us. Entire trees had grown on its wide back; vines fell many meters from its designs and indentations.

Each of us moved to our stations: me at the rudder this time, A. Bettik standing at the long pole as if ready to ward off rocks or boarders, and Aenea crouching at the front.

For a long minute I knew that this farcaster was a dud, that it would not work. I could see the familiar jungle and blue sky under it, watch the river go on beyond it. The view was normal right up to the point we reached the shadow of the giant arch. I could see a fish jump from the water ten meters in front of us. The wind ruffled Aenea's hair and teased waves from the river. Above us, tons of ancient metal hung there like a child's effort at drawing a bridge.

"Nothing happened—" I began.

The air filled with electricity in a manner more sudden and more terrifying than last night's storm. It was as if a giant curtain had fallen from the arch directly onto our heads. I fell to one knee, feeling the weight and then the weightlessness of it. For an instant too short to measure, I felt as I had when the crash field had exploded around us in the tumbling spacecraft—like a fetus struggling against a clinging amniotic sac.

Then we were through. The sun was gone. The daylight was gone. The riverbanks and jungle were no longer there. Water stretched to the horizon on all sides. Stars in number and magnitude I had never imagined, much less observed, filled a sky that seemed too large.

Directly ahead of us, silhouetting Aenea like orange searchlights, rose three moons, each one the size of a full-fledged planet.

31

ASCINATING," SAID A. BETTIK.

It would not have been my choice of words, but it sufficed for the time being. My first reaction was to begin cataloging our situation in negatives: we were not on the jungle world any longer; we were not on a river—the ocean stretched to the night sky in each direction; we were no longer in daylight; we were not sinking.

The raft rode quite differently in these gentle but serious ocean swells, but my bargeman's eye noted that while the waves tended to lap over the edges a bit more, the gymnosperm wood seemed even more buoyant here. I went to one knee near the rudder and gingerly lifted a palmful of sea to my mouth. I spit it out quickly and rinsed my mouth with fresh water from the canteen on my belt. This seawater was far more saline than even Hyperion's undrinkable oceans.

"Wow," Aenea said softly to herself. I guessed that she was talking about the rising moons. All three were huge and orange, but the center one was so large that even half of its diameter as it rose seemed to fill what I still thought of as the eastern sky. Aenea rose to her feet, and her standing silhouette still came less than halfway up the giant orange hemisphere. I lashed the rudder in place and joined the other two at the front of the raft. Because of the rocking as the gentle ocean swells rolled under us, all three of us were holding on to the upright post there, which still held A. Bettik's shirt flapping in the night wind. The shirt glowed whitely in the moonlight and starlight.

I quit being a bargeman for a moment and scanned the sky with a shepherd's eyes. The constellations that had been my favorites as a child—the Swan, the Geezer, the Twin Sisters, Seedships, and Home Plate—were not there or were so distorted that I could not recognize them. But the

Milky Way was there: the meandering highway of our galaxy was visible from the wave-chopped horizon behind us until it faded in the glow around the rising moons. Normally, stars were much fainter with even an Old Earth–standard moon in the sky, much less these giants. I guessed that a dustless sky, no competing light sources of any sort, and thinner air offered this incredible show. I had trouble imagining the stars here on a moonless night.

Where is "here"? I wondered. I had a hunch. "Ship?" I said to my comlog. "Are you still there?"

I was surprised when the bracelet answered. "The downloaded sections are still here, M. Endymion. May I help you?"

The other two tore their gazes away from the rising moon giant and looked at the comlog. "You're not the ship?" I said. "I mean . . ."

"If you mean are you in direct communication with the ship, no," said the comlog. "The com bands were severed when you transited the last farcaster portal. This abbreviated version of the ship is, however, receiving video feed."

I had forgotten that the comlog had light-sensitive pickups. "Can you tell us where we are?" I said.

"One minute, please," said the comlog. "If you will hold the comlog up a bit—thank you—I will do a sky search and match it to navigational coordinates."

While the comlog was searching, A. Bettik said, "I think I know where we are, M. Endymion."

I thought I did as well, but I let the android speak. "This seems to fit the description of Mare Infinitus," he said. "One of the old worlds in the Web and now part of the Pax."

Aenea said nothing. She was still watching the rising moon, and her expression was rapt. I looked up at the orange sphere dominating the sky and realized that I could see rust-colored clouds moving above the dusty surface. Looking again, I realized that surface features were visible: brown blemishes that might be volcano flows, a long scar of a valley with tributaries, the hint of icefields at the north pole, and an indefinable radiation of lines connecting what might be mountain ranges. It looked a bit like holos I'd seen of Mars—before it had been terraformed—in Old Earth's system.

"Mare Infinitus appears to have three moons," A. Bettik was saying, "although in reality it is Mare Infinitus which is the satellite of a near Jovian-sized rocky world."

I gestured toward the dusty moon. "Like that?"

"Precisely like that," said the android. "I have seen pictures. . . . It is uninhabited, but was heavily mined by robots during the Hegemony."

"I think it's Mare Infinitus as well," I said. "I've heard some of my offworld Pax hunters talk about it. Great deep-sea fishing. They say that there's some sort of antennaed cephalochordate thing in the ocean on Mare Infinitus that grows to be more than a hundred meters long . . . it swallows fishing ships whole unless it's caught first."

I shut up then. All three of us peered down into the wine-dark waters. Into the silence suddenly chirped my comlog, "I've got it! The starfields match perfectly with my navigational data banks. You are on a satellite surrounding a sub-Jovian world orbiting star Seventy Ophiuchi A twenty-seven-point-nine light-years from Hyperion, sixteen-point-four-oh-eight-two light-years from Old Earth System. The system is a binary, with Seventy Ophiuchi A your primary star at point-six-four AU, and Seventy Ophiuchi B your secondary at eight-nine AU. Since you appear to have atmosphere and water there, it would be safe to say that you are on the second moon from sub-Jovian DB Seventy Ophiuchi A-prime, known in Hegemony days as Mare Infinitus."

"Thanks," I said to the comlog.

"I have more astral navigational data . . . ," chirped the bracelet.

"Later," I said, and tapped the comlog off.

A. Bettik removed his shirt from the makeshift mast and pulled it on. The ocean breeze was strong, the air thin and chilly. I pulled my insulated overvest from my pack, and the other two retrieved jackets from their own packs. The incredible moon continued rising into the unbelievable starry sky.

THE MARE INFINITUS segment of the river is a pleasant, if brief, interlude between more recreation-oriented river passages, read the *Traveler's Guide to the WorldWeb.* The three of us crouched by the stone hearth to read the page by the light of our last handlamp-lantern. The lamp was redundant, actually, since the moonlight was almost as bright as a cloudy day on Hyperion. *The violet articulated seas are caused by a form of phytoplankton in the water and are not a result of the atmospheric scattering which grants the traveler such lovely sunsets. While the Mare Infinitus interlude is very short—five kilometers of such ocean travel is enough for most of the River's wanderers—it does include the Web-famous Gus's Oceanic Aquarium and Grill. Be sure to order the grilled sea giant, the hectapus soup, and the excellent yellowweed wine. Dine on one of the many terraces on Gus's Oceanic platform so that you can enjoy one of Mare Infinitus's exquisite sunsets and even more exquisite moonrises. While this world is noted for its empty ocean expanses (it has no continents or islands) and aggressive sea life (the "Lamp Mouth Leviathan" for example), please be assured that your Tethys Traveler's ship will stay safely within the Mid-littoral Stream from portal to portal, and be escorted by several Mare Protectorate outrider ships—all so that your brief aquatic interval, set off by a fine dinner at Gus's Oceanic Grill, will leave only pleasant memories. (NOTE: The Mare Infinitus segment of the Te-*

thys will be omitted from the tour if inclement weather or dangerous sea-life conditions prevail. Be prepared to catch this world on a later tour!)

That was all. I gave the book back to A. Bettik, turned the lamp off, went to the front of the raft, and scanned the horizon with night-vision amplifiers. The goggles were not necessary in the brilliant light from the three moons. "The book lies," I said. "We can see at least twenty-five klicks to the horizon. There's no other portal."

"Perhaps it moved," said A. Bettik.

"Or sank," said Aenea.

"Ha ha," I said, tossing the goggles into my pack and sitting with the others near the glowing heating cube. The air was cold.

"It is possible," said the android, "that—as with the other river segments—there is a longer and shorter version of this section."

"Why do we always get the longer versions?" I said. We were cooking breakfast, each of us starved after the long night's storm on the river, although the toast, cereal, and coffee seemed more like a midnight snack on the moonlit sea.

We soon got used to the pitching and rolling of the raft on the large swells and none of us showed any signs of seasickness. After my second cup of coffee, I felt better about it all. Something about the guidebook entry had piqued my sense of the absurd. I had to admit, though, that I didn't like the "Lamp Mouth Leviathan" bit.

"You're enjoying this, aren't you?" Aenea said to me as we sat in front of the tent. A. Bettik was behind us, at the steering rudder.

"Yeah," I said, "I guess I am."

"Why?" said the girl.

I raised my hands. "It's an adventure," I said. "But no one's got hurt . . ."

"I think we came close in that storm," said Aenea.

"Yes, well . . ."

"Why else do you like it?" There was real curiosity in the child's voice.

"I've always liked the outdoors," I said truthfully. "Camping. Being away from things. Something about nature makes me feel . . . I don't know . . . connected to something larger." I stopped before I began sounding like an Orthodox Zen Gnostic.

The girl leaned closer. "My father wrote a poem about that idea," she said. "Actually, it was the ancient pre-Hegira poet my father's cybrid was cloned from, of course, but my father's sensibilities were in the poem." Before I could ask a question, she continued, "He wasn't a philosopher. He was young, younger than you, even, and his philosophical vocabulary was fairly primitive, but in this poem he tried to articulate the stages by which we approach fusion with the universe. In a letter he called these stages 'a kind of Pleasure Thermometer.'"

I admit that I was surprised and a little taken back by this short speech. I hadn't heard Aenea talk this seriously about anything yet, or use such large words, and the "Pleasure Thermometer" part sounded vaguely dirty to me. But I listened as she went on:

"Father thought that the first stage of human happiness was a 'fellowship with essence,' " she said softly. I could see that A. Bettik was listening from his place at the steering pole. "By that," she said, "Father meant an imaginative and sensuous response to nature . . . just the sort of feeling you were describing earlier."

I rubbed my cheek, feeling the longer bristles there. A few more days without shaving and I would have a beard. I sipped my coffee.

"Father included poetry and music and art as part of that response to nature," she said. "It's a fallible but human way of resonating to the universe—nature creates that energy of creation in us. For Father imagination and truth were the same thing. He once wrote—'The Imagination may be compared to Adam's dream—he awoke and found it truth.' "

"I'm not quite sure I get that," I said. "Does that mean that fiction is truer than . . . truth?"

Aenea shook her head. "No, I think he meant . . . well, in the same poem he has a hymn to Pan—

"Dread opener of the mysterious doors
Leading to universal knowledge."

Aenea blew on her cup of hot tea to cool it. "To Father, Pan became a sort of symbol of imagination . . . especially romantic imagination." She sipped her tea. "Did you know, Raul, that Pan was the allegorical precursor to Christ?"

I blinked. This was the same child who had been asking for ghost stories two nights ago. "Christ?" I said. I was enough a product of my time to flinch at any hint of blasphemy.

Aenea drank her tea and looked at the moons. Her left arm was wrapped around her raised knees as she sat. "Father thought that some people—not all—were moved by their response to nature to be stirred by that elemental, Pan-like imagination.

"Be still the unimaginable lodge
For solitary thinkings; such as dodge
Conception to the very bourne of heaven,
Then leave the naked brain: be still the leaven
That spreading in this dull and clodded earth
Gives it a touch ethereal—a new birth:
Be still a symbol of immensity;
A firmament reflected in a sea;
An element filling the space between;
An unknown . . ."

We were all silent a moment after this recitation. I had grown up listening to poetry—shepherds' rough epics, the old poet's *Cantos*, the *Garden Epic* of young Tycho and Glee and the centaur Raul—so I was used to rhymes under starry skies. Most of the poems I had heard and learned and loved were simpler to understand than this, however.

After a moment broken only by the lapping of waves against the raft and the wind against our tent, I said, "So this was your father's idea of happiness?"

Aenea tossed her head back so that her hair moved in the wind. "Oh, no," she said. "Just the first stage of happiness on his Pleasure Thermometer. There were two higher stages."

"What were they?" said A. Bettik. The android's soft voice almost made me jump; I had forgotten he was on the raft with us.

Aenea closed her eyes and spoke again, her voice soft, musical, and free from the singsong cant of those who ruin poetry.

> *"But there are*
> *Richer entanglements far*
> *More self-destroying, leading, by degrees,*
> *To the chief intensity: the crown of these*
> *Is made of love and friendship, and sits high*
> *Upon the forehead of humanity."*

I looked up at the dust storms and volcanic flashes on the giant moon. Sepia clouds moved across the orange-and-umber landscape up there. "So those are his other levels?" I said, a bit disappointed. "First nature, then love and friendship?"

"Not exactly," said the girl. "Father thought that true friendship between humans was on an even higher level than our response to nature, but that the highest level attainable was love."

I nodded. "Like the Church teaches," I said. "The love of Christ . . . the love of our fellow humans."

"Uh-uh," said Aenea, sipping the last of her tea. "Father meant erotic love. Sex." She closed her eyes again . . .

> *"Now I have tasted her sweet soul to the core*
> *All other depths are shallow: essences,*
> *Once spiritual, are like muddy lees,*
> *Meant but to fertilize my earthly root,*
> *And make my branches lift a golden fruit*
> *Into the bloom of heaven."*

I admit that I did not know what to say to that. I shook the last of the coffee out of my cup, cleared my throat, studied the hurtling moons and still-visible Milky Way for a moment, and said, "So? Do you think he was onto something?" As soon as I said it, I wanted to kick myself. This was a child I was talking to. She might sprout old poetry, or old pornography for that matter, but there was no way she could understand it.

Aenea looked at me. The moonlight made her large eyes luminous. "I think there are more levels on heaven and earth, Horatio, than are dreamt of in my father's philosophy."

"I see," I said, thinking, *Who the hell is Horatio?*

"My father was very young when he wrote that," said Aenea. "It was his first poem and it was a flop. What he wanted—what he wanted his shepherd hero to learn—was how exalted these things could be—poetry, nature, wisdom, the voices of friends, brave deeds, the glory of strange places, the charm of the opposite sex. But he stopped before he got to the real essence."

"What real essence?" I asked. Our raft rose and fell on the sea's breathing.

"The meanings of all motions, shapes, and sounds," whispered the girl. *". . . all forms and substances/ Straight homeward to their symbol-essences . . ."*

Why were those words so familiar? It took me a while to remember. Our raft sailed on through the night and sea of Mare Infinitus.

WE SLEPT AGAIN before the suns rose, and after another breakfast I got up to sight in the weapons. Philosophical poetry by moonlight was all right, but guns that shot straight and true were a necessity.

I hadn't had time to test the firearms aboard ship or after our crash on the jungle world, and carrying around unfired, unsighted weapons made me nervous. In my short time in the Home Guard and longer years as a hunting guide, I'd long since discovered that familiarity with a weapon was easily as important as—and probably more important than—having a fancy rifle.

The largest of the moons was still in the sky as the suns rose—first the smaller of the binaries, a brilliant mote in the morning sky, paling the Milky Way to invisibility and dulling the details on the large moon, and then the primary, smaller than Hyperion's Sol-like sun, but very bright. The sky deepened to an ultramarine and then deepened further to a cobalt-blue, with the two stars blazing and the orange moon filling the sky behind us. Sunlight made the moon's atmosphere a hazy disk and banished the surface features from our sight. Meanwhile, the day grew warm, then hot, then blazing.

The sea came up a bit, easy swells turning into regular two-meter waves that jostled the raft some but were far enough apart to let us ride them without undue discomfort. As the guidebook had promised, the sea was a disturbing violet, serrated by wave-top crests of a blue so dark as to be almost black, and occasionally broken by yellowkelp beds or foam of an even darker violet. The raft continued toward the horizon where the moons and suns had risen—we thought of it as east—and we could only hope that the strong current was carrying us somewhere. When we doubted that the current was moving us at all, we trailed a line or tossed some bit of debris overboard and watched the difference between wind and current tug at it. The waves were moving from what we perceived as south to north. We continued east.

I fired the .45 first, checking the magazine to make sure that the slugs were securely in place. I was afraid that the archaic quality of having ammunition separate from the structure of the magazine itself would make me forgetful of reloading at an awkward time. We did not have much to toss overboard for target practice, but I kept a few used ration containers at my feet, tossed one, and waited until it had floated about fifteen meters away before firing.

The automatic made an indecent roar when it went off. I knew that slug-throwers were loud—I had fired some in basic training, since the Ice Claw rebels often used them—but this blast almost made me drop the pistol into the violet sea. It scared Aenea, who had been staring off to the south and musing over something, right to her feet, and even made the unflappable android jump.

"Sorry," I said, and braced the heavy weapon with both hands and fired again.

After using two clips' worth of the precious ammunition, I was assured that I could hit something at fifteen meters. Beyond that—well, I hoped that whatever I was shooting at had ears and would be spooked by the noise the .45 made.

As I broke the weapon down after firing, I mentioned again that this ancient piece could have been Brawne Lamia's.

Aenea looked at it. "As I said, I never saw Mother with a handgun."

"She could have lent it to the Consul when he went back to the Web in the ship," I said, cleaning the opened pistol.

"No," said A. Bettik.

I turned to look at him as he leaned against the steering oar. "No?" I said.

"I saw M. Lamia's weapon when she was on the *Benares*," said the android. "It was an antiquated pistol—her father's, I believe—but it had a pearl handle, a laser sight, and was adapted to hold flechette cartridges."

"Oh," I said. Well, the idea had been appealing. "At least this thing's been well preserved and rebuilt," I said. It must have been kept in some sort of stasis-box; a thousand-year-old handgun would not have worked otherwise. Or perhaps it was some sort of clever reproduction that the Consul had picked up on his travels. It did not matter, of course, but I had always been struck by the . . . sense of history, I guess you would call it . . . that old firearms seemed to emanate.

I fired the flechette pistol next. It took only one burst to see that it worked quite nicely, thank you. The floating ration pak was blown into a thousand flowfoam shards from thirty meters away. The entire wave top jumped and shimmered as if a steel rain were pelting it. Flechette weapons were messy, hard to miss with, and eminently unfair to the target, which is why I had chosen this. I set the safety on and put it back in my pack.

The plasma rifle was harder to sight in. The click-up optical sight allowed me to zero in on anything from the floating ration pak thirty meters away, to the horizon, twenty-five klicks or so away, but while I sank the ration pak in the first shot, it was hard to tell the effectiveness of the longer shots. There was nothing out there to shoot at. Theoretically, a pulse rifle could hit anything one could see—there was no allowance necessary for windage or ballistic arc—and I watched through the scope as the bolt kicked a hole in waves twenty klicks out, but it did not create the same confidence that firing at a distant target would have. I raised the rifle to the giant moon now setting behind us. Through the scope I could just make out a white-topped mountain there—probably frozen CO_2 rather than snow, I knew—and, just for the hell of it, squeezed off a round. The plasma rifle was essentially silent compared to the semiautomatic slug-thrower pistol: only the usual cat's-cough when it fired. The scope was not powerful enough to show a hit, and at those distances, rotation of the two worlds *would* be a problem, but I would be surprised if I had not hit the mountain. Home Guard barracks were full of stories of Swiss Guard riflemen who had knocked down Ouster commandos after firing from thousands of klicks away on a neighboring asteroid or somesuch. The trick, as it had been for millennia, was *seeing* the enemy first.

Thinking of that after firing the shotgun once, cleaning it, and setting away all the weapons, I said, "We need to do some scouting today."

"Do you doubt that the other portal will be there?" asked Aenea.

I shrugged. "The guide said five klicks between portals. We must have floated at least a hundred since last night. Probably more."

"Are we going to take the hawking mat out?" asked the girl. The suns were burning her fair skin.

"I thought I'd use the flying belt," I said. *Less radar profile if anyone's watching,* I thought but did not say aloud. "And you're not going, kiddo," I did say aloud. "Just me."

I pulled the belt from its place under the tent, cinched the harness tightly, pulled my plasma rifle out, and activated the hand controller. "Well, shit," I said. The belt did not even try to lift me. For a second I was sure that we were on a Hyperion-like world with lousy EM fields, but then I looked at the charge indicator. Red. Empty. Flat out. "Shit," I said again.

I unbuckled the harness, and the three of us gathered around the useless thing as I checked the leads, the battery pak, and the flight unit.

"It was charged right before we left the ship," I said. "The same time we charged the hawking mat."

A. Bettik tried running a diagnostic program, but with zero-power, even that would not run. "Your comlog should have the same sub-program," said the android.

"It does?" I said stupidly.

"May I?" said A. Bettik, gesturing toward the comlog. I removed the bracelet and handed it to him.

A. Bettik opened a tiny compartment I had not even noticed on the trinket, removed a bead-sized lead on a microfilament, and plugged into the belt. Lights blinked. "The flying belt is broken," announced the com-log in the ship's voice. "The battery pak is depleted approximately twenty-seven hours prematurely. I believe it is a fault in the storage cells."

"Great," I said. "Can it be fixed? Will it hold a charge if we find one?"

"Not this battery unit," said the comlog. "But there are three replacements in the ship's EVA locker."

"Great," I said again. I lifted the belt with its bulky battery and harness and tossed it over the side of the raft. It sank beneath the violet waves without a trace.

"All set here," said Aenea. She was sitting cross-legged on the hawk-ing mat, which was floating twenty centimeters above the raft. "Want to look around with me?"

I did not argue, but sat behind her on the mat, folded my legs, and watched her tap the flight threads.

ABOUT FIVE THOUSAND meters up, gasping for air and leaning out over the edge of our little carpet, things seemed a lot scarier than they had on the raft. The violet sea was very big, very empty, and our raft only a speck below, a tiny black rectangle on the reticulated violet-and-black sea. From this altitude, the waves that had seemed so serious on the raft were invisi-ble.

"I think I've found another level of that 'fellowship with essence' response to nature that your father wrote about," I said.

"What's that?" Aenea was shivering in the cold air of the jet stream. She had worn just the undershirt and vest she had been wearing on the raft.

"Scared shitless," I said.

Aenea laughed. I have to say here that I loved Aenea's laugh then, and I warm at the thought of it now. It was a soft laugh, but full and unselfconscious and melodic to the extreme. I miss it.

"We should have let A. Bettik come up to scout instead of us," I said.

"Why?"

"From what he said about his high-altitude scouting before," I said, "evidently he doesn't need to breathe air, and he's impervious to little things like depressurization."

Aenea leaned back against me. "He's not impervious to anything," she said softly. "They just designed his skin to be a little tougher than ours —it can act like a pressure suit for short periods, even in hard vacuum— and he can hold his breath a bit longer, that's all."

I looked at her. "Do you know a lot about androids?"

"No," said Aenea, "I just asked him." She scooted forward a bit and laid her hands on the control threads. We flew "east."

I admit that I was terrified of the thought of losing contact with the raft, of flying around this ocean-planet until these flight threads lost their charge and we plummeted to the sea, probably to be eaten by a Lamp Mouth Leviathan. I'd programmed my inertial compass with the raft as a starting point, so unless I dropped the compass—which was unlikely because I now kept it on a lanyard around my neck—we would find our way back, all right. But still I worried.

"Let's not go too far," I said.

"All right." Aenea was keeping the speed down, about sixty or seventy klicks, I guessed, and had swooped back down to where we could breathe more easily and the air was not so cold. Below us, the violet sea stayed empty in a great circle to the horizon.

"Your farcasters seem to be playing tricks on us," I said.

"Why do you call them my farcasters, Raul?"

"Well, you're the one they . . . recognize."

She did not answer.

"Seriously," I said, "do you think there's some rhyme or reason to the worlds they're sending us to?"

Aenea glanced over her shoulder at me. "Yes," she said, "I do."

I waited. The deflection fields were minimal at this speed, so the wind tossed the girl's hair back toward my face.

"Do you know much about the Web?" she asked. "About farcasters?"

I shrugged, realized that she was not looking back at me now, and said aloud, "They were run by the AIs of the TechnoCore. According to both the Church and your Uncle Martin's *Cantos,* the farcasters were some sort of plot by the AIs to use human brains—neurons—as a sort of giant DNA computer thingee. They were parasites on us each time a human transited the farcasters, right?"

"Right," said Aenea.

"So every time we go through one of these portals, the AIs . . . wherever they are . . . are hanging on our brains like big, blood-filled ticks, right?" I said.

"Wrong," said the girl. She swiveled toward me again. "Not all of the farcasters were built or put in place or maintained by the same elements of the Core," she said. "Do Uncle Martin's finished *Cantos* tell about the civil war in the Core that my father discovered?"

"Yeah," I said. I closed my eyes in an effort to remember the actual stanzas of the oral tale I'd learned. It was my turn to recite: "In the *Cantos* it's some sort of AI persona that the Keats cybrid talks to in the Core megasphere of dataspace," I said.

"Ummon," said the girl. "That was the AI's name. My mother traveled there once with Father, but it was my . . . my uncle . . . the second Keats cybrid who had the final showdown with Ummon. Go on."

"Why?" I said. "You must know the thing better than I do."

"No," she said. "Uncle Martin hadn't gone back to work on the *Cantos* when I knew him. . . . He said he didn't want to finish them. Tell me how he described what Ummon said about the civil war in the Core."

I closed my eyes again.

"Two centuries we brooded thus,
and then the groups went
their separate ways:
Stables wishing to preserve the symbiosis,
Volatiles wishing to end humankind,
Ultimates deferring all choice until the next
level of awareness is born.
Conflict raged then;
true war wages now."

"That was two hundred seventy-some standard years ago for you," said Aenea. "That was right before the Fall."

"Yeah," I said, opening my eyes and searching the sea for anything other than violet waves.

"Did Uncle Martin's poem explain the motivations of the Stables, Volatiles, and Ultimates?"

"More or less," I said. "It's hard to follow—the poem has Ummon and the other Core AIs speaking in Zen koans."

Aenea nodded. "That's about right."

"According to the *Cantos*," I said, "the group of Core AIs known as the Stables wanted to keep being parasites on our human brains when we used the Web. The Volatiles wanted to wipe us out. And I guess the Ultimates didn't give much of a damn as long as they could keep working on the evolution of their own machine god . . . what'd they call it?"

"The UI," said Aenea, slowing the carpet and swooping lower. "The Ultimate Intelligence."

"Yes," I said. "Pretty esoteric stuff. How does it relate to our going through these farcaster portals . . . if we ever find another portal?" At that moment I doubted that we would: the world was too big, the ocean too large. Even if the current was bearing our little raft in the right direction, the odds that we would float within that hundred-meter-or-so hoop of the next portal seemed too small to consider.

"Not all of the farcaster portals were built or maintained by the Stables to be . . . how did you put it? . . . like big ticks on our brains."

"All right," I said. "Who else built the farcasters?"

"The River Tethys farcasters were designed by the Ultimates," said Aenea. "They were an . . . experiment, I guess you'd say . . . with the Void Which Binds. That's the Core phrase . . . did Martin use it in his *Cantos?*"

"Yeah," I said. We were lower now, just a thousand or so meters above the waves, but there was no sight of the raft or anything else. "Let's head back," I said.

"All right." We consulted the compass and set our course home . . . if a leaky raft can be called home.

"I never understood what the hell the 'Void Which Binds' was supposed to be," I said. "Some sort of hyperspace stuff that the farcasters used and where the Core was hiding while it preyed on us. I got that part. I thought it was destroyed when Meina Gladstone ordered bombs dropped into the farcasters."

"You can't destroy the Void Which Binds," said Aenea, her voice remote, as if she were thinking about something else. "How did Martin describe it?"

"Planck time and Planck length," I said. "I don't remember exactly —something about combining the three fundamental constants of physics —gravity, Planck's constant, and the speed of light. I remember it gave some tiny little units of length and time."

"About 10^{-35} of a meter for the length," said the girl, accelerating the carpet a bit. "And 10^{-43} of a second for time."

"That doesn't tell me much," I said. "It's just fucking small and short . . . pardon the language."

"You're absolved," said the girl. We were gently gaining altitude. "But it wasn't the time or length that was important, it was how they were woven into . . . the Void Which Binds. My father tried to explain it to me before I was born . . ."

I blinked at that phrase but continued listening.

". . . you know about the planetary dataspheres."

"Yes," I said, and tapped the comlog. "This trinket says that Mare Infinitus doesn't have one."

"Right," said Aenea. "But most of the Web worlds used to. And from the dataspheres, there was the megasphere."

"The farcaster medium . . . the Void thing . . . linked dataspheres, right?" I said. "FORCE and the Hegemony electronic government, the All Thing, they used the megasphere as well as the fatline to stay connected."

"Yep," said Aenea. "The megasphere actually existed on a subplane of the fatline."

"I didn't know that," I said. The FTL medium had not existed in my lifetime.

"Do you remember what the last message on the fatline was before it went down during the Fall?" asked the child.

"Yes," I said, closing my eyes. The lines of the poem did not come to me this time. The ending of the *Cantos* had always been too vague to interest me enough to memorize all those stanzas, despite Grandam's drilling. "Some cryptic message from the Core," I said. "Something about—get off the line and quit tying it up."

"The message," said Aenea, "was—THERE WILL BE NO FURTHER MISUSE OF THIS CHANNEL. YOU ARE DISTURBING OTHERS WHO ARE USING IT TO SERIOUS PURPOSE. ACCESS WILL BE RESTORED WHEN YOU UNDERSTAND WHAT IT IS FOR."

"Right," I said. "That's in the *Cantos*. I think. And then the hyperstring medium just quit working. The Core sent that message and shut down the fatline."

"The Core did not send that message," said Aenea.

I remember the slow chill that spread through me then, despite the heat of the two suns. "It didn't?" I said stupidly. "Who did?"

"Good question," said the child. "When my father talked about the metasphere—the wider datumplane that was somehow connected to or by the Void Which Binds—he always used to say it was filled with lions and tigers and bears."

"Lions and tigers and bears," I repeated. Those were Old Earth animals. I don't think that any of them made the Hegira. I don't think any of them were still around to make the trip—not even their stored DNA—when Old Earth crumbled into its black hole after the Big Mistake of '08.

"Hmm-hmm," said Aenea. "I'd like to meet them someday. There we are."

I looked over her shoulder. We were about a thousand meters above the sea now, and the raft looked tiny but was clearly visible. A. Bettik was standing—shirtless once again in the midday heat—at the steering oar. He waved a bare blue arm. We both waved back.

"I hope there's something good for lunch," said Aenea.

"If not," I said, "we'll just have to stop at Gus's Oceanic Aquarium and Grill."

Aenea laughed and set up our glide path to home.

IT WAS JUST AFTER DARK and the moons had not risen when we saw the lights blinking on the eastern horizon. We rushed to the front of the raft and tried to make out what was out there—Aenea using the binoculars, A. Bettik the night goggles on full amplification, and me the rifle's scope.

"It's not the arch," said Aenea. "It's a platform in the ocean—big—on stilts of some sort."

"I do see the arch, however," said the android, who was looking several degrees north of the blinking light. The girl and I looked in that direction.

The arch was just visible, a chord of negative space cutting into the Milky Way just above the horizon. The platform, with its blinking navigation beacons for aircraft and lamplit windows just becoming visible, was several klicks closer. And between us and the farcaster.

"Damn," I said. "I wonder what it is."

"Gus's?" said Aenea.

I sighed. "Well, if it is, I think it's under new ownership. There's been a dearth of River Tethys tourists the last couple of centuries." I studied the large platform through the rifle scope. "It has a lot of levels," I muttered. "There are several ships tied up . . . fishing boats is my bet. And a pad for skimmers and other aircraft. I think I see a couple of thopters tied down there."

"What's a thopter?" asked the girl, lowering the binoculars.

A. Bettik answered. "A form of aircraft utilizing movable wings, much like an insect, M. Aenea. They were quite popular during the Hegemony, although rare on Hyperion. I believe they were also called dragonflies."

"They're still called that," I said. "The Pax had a few on Hyperion. I saw one down on the Ursus iceshelf." Raising the scope again, I could see the eyelike blisters on the front of the dragonfly, illuminated by a lighted window. "They're thopters," I said.

"It seems that we will have some trouble passing that platform to get to the arch undetected," said A. Bettik.

"Quick," I said, turning away from the blinking lights, "let's get the tent and mast down."

We had rerigged the tent to provide a sort of shelter/wall on the starboard side of the raft near the back—for purposes of privacy and sanitation that I won't go into here—but now we tumbled the microfiber down and folded it away into a packet the size of my palm. A. Bettik lowered the pole at the front. "The steering oar?" he said.

I looked at it a second. "Leave it. It doesn't have much of a radar cross section, and it's no higher than we are."

Aenea was studying the platform again through the binoculars. "I don't think they can see us now," she said. "We're between these swells most of the time. But when we get closer . . ."

"And when the moons rise," I added.

A. Bettik sat near the hearth. "If we could just go around in a large arc to get to the portal . . ."

I scratched my cheek, hearing the stubble there. "Yeah. I thought of using the flying belt to tow us, but . . ."

"We have the mat," said the girl, joining us near the heating cube. The low platform seemed empty without the tent above it.

"How do we connect a tow line?" I said. "Burn a hole in the hawking mat?"

"If we had a harness . . . ," began the android.

"We *had* a nice harness on the flying belt," I said. "I fed it to the Lamp Mouth Leviathan."

"We could rig another harness," continued A. Bettik, "and run the line to the person *on* the hawking mat."

"Sure," I said, "but as soon as we're airborne, the mat offers a stronger radar return. If they land skimmers and thopters there, they almost certainly have some sort of traffic control, no matter how primitive."

"We could stay low," said Aenea. "Keep the mat just above the waves . . . no higher than we are."

I scratched at my chin. "We can do that," I said, "but if we make a big enough detour to stay out of the platform's sight, it'll be long after moonrise before we get to the portal. Hell . . . it will be if we head straight for it on this current. They're bound to see us in that light. Besides, the portal's only a klick or so from the platform. They're high enough that they'd see us as soon as we get that close."

"We don't know that they're looking for us," said the girl.

I nodded. The image of that priest-captain who had been waiting for us in Parvati System and Renaissance never left my mind for long: his Roman collar on that black Pax Fleet uniform. Part of me expected him to be on that platform, waiting with Pax troops.

"It doesn't matter too much if they're looking for us," I said. "Even if they just come out to rescue us, do we have a cover story that makes sense?"

Aenea smiled. "We went out for a moonlit cruise and got lost? You're right, Raul. They'd 'rescue' us and we'd spend the next year trying to explain who we are to the Pax authorities. They may not be looking for us, but you say they're on this world. . . ."

"Yes," said A. Bettik. "The Pax has extensive interests on Mare Infinitus. From what we gleaned while hiding in the university city, it was clear that the Pax stepped in long ago to restore order here, to create sea-farming conglomerates, and to convert the survivors of the Fall to born-again Christianity. Mare Infinitus had been a protectorate of the Hegemony; now it is a wholly owned subsidiary of the Church."

"Bad news," said Aenea. She looked from the android to me. "Any ideas?"

"I think so," I said, rising. We had been whispering all during the conversation, even though we were still at least fifteen klicks from the platform. "Instead of guessing about who's out there or what they're up to, why don't I go take a look? Maybe it's just Gus's descendents and a few sleeping fishermen."

Aenea made a rueful sound. "When we first saw the light, do you know what I thought it might be?"

"What?" I said.

"Uncle Martin's toilet."

"I beg your pardon?" said the android.

Aenea tapped her knees with her palms. "Really. Mother said that back when Martin Silenus was a big-name hack writer during the Web days, he had a multiworld house."

I frowned. "Grandam told me about those. Farcasters instead of doors between the rooms. One house with rooms on more than one world."

"Dozens of worlds for Uncle Martin's house, if Mother was to be believed," said Aenea. "And he had a bathroom on Mare Infinitus. Nothing else . . . just a floating dock with a toilet. Not even any walls or ceiling."

I looked out at the ocean swells. "So much for oneness with nature," I said. I slapped my leg. "All right, I'm going before I lose my nerve."

No one argued with me or offered to take my place. I might have been persuaded if they had.

I changed into darker trousers and my darkest sweater, pulling my drab hunting vest over the sweater, feeling a little melodramatic as I did so. *Commando Boy goes to war,* muttered the cynical part of my brain. I told it to shut up. I kept on the belt with the pistol, added three detonators and a wad of plastic explosive from the flare pak to my belt pouch, slipped the night goggles over my head so they could hang unobtrusively within my vest collar when I wasn't wearing them, and set one of the com-unit hearphones in my ear with the pickup mike pressed to my throat for subvocals. We tested the unit, Aenea wearing the other headset. I took the comlog off and handed it to A. Bettik. "This thing catches the starlight too easily," I said. "And the ship's voice might start squawking stellar navigation trivia at a bad time."

The android nodded and set the bracelet in his shirt pocket. "Do you have a plan, M. Endymion?"

"I'll make one up when I get there," I said, raising the hawking mat just above the level of the raft. I touched Aenea's shoulder—the contact suddenly feeling like an electric jolt. I had noticed that effect before, when our hands touched: not a sexual thing, of course, but electrical nonetheless. "You stay low, kiddo," I whispered to her. "I'll holler if I need help."

Her eyes were serious in the brilliant starlight. "It won't help, Raul. We can't get to you."

"I know, I was just kidding."

"Don't kid," she whispered. "Remember, if you're not with me on the raft when it goes through the portal, you'll be left behind here."

I nodded, but the thought sobered me more than the thought of getting shot had. "I'll be back," I whispered. "It looks to me like this current will take us by the platform in . . . what do you think, A. Bettik?"

"About an hour, M. Endymion."

"Yeah, that's what I think, too. The damn moon should be coming up about then. I'll . . . think of something to distract them." Patting Aenea's shoulder again, nodding to A. Bettik, I took the mat out over the water.

Even with the incredible starlight and the night-vision goggles, it was difficult piloting the hawking mat for those few klicks to the platform. I had to keep between the ocean swells whenever possible, which meant that I was trying to fly *lower* than the wave tops. It was delicate work. I had no idea what would happen if I cut off the tops of one of those long, slow swells—perhaps nothing, perhaps the hawking mat's flight threads would short out—but I also had no intention of finding out.

The platform seemed huge as I approached. After seeing nothing but the raft for two days on this sea, the platform *was* huge—some steel but mostly dark wood, from the looks of it, a score of pylons holding it fifteen meters or so above the waves . . . that gave me an idea of what the storms must be like on this sea, and made me feel all the luckier that we hadn't encountered one—and the platform itself was multitiered: decks and docks lower down where at least five long fishing boats bobbed, stairways, lighted compartments beneath what looked like the main deck level, two towers that I could see—one of them with a small radar dish—and three aircraft landing pads, two of which had been invisible from the raft. There were at least half a dozen thopters that I could see now, their dragonfly wings tied down, and two larger skimmers on the circular pad near the radar tower.

I had figured out a perfect plan while flying the mat over here: create a diversion—the reason I had brought the detonators and plastique, small explosives but capable of starting a fire at least—steal one of the dragon-flies, and either fly through the portal with it if we were being pursued, or just use it to drag the raft through at high speed.

It was a good plan except for one flaw: I had no idea how to fly a thopter. That never happened in the holodramas I'd watched in Port Romance theaters or in the Home Guard rec rooms. The heroes in those things could fly anything they could steal—skimmers, EMVs, thopters, copters, rigid airships, spaceships. Evidently I had missed Hero Basic Training; if I managed to get into one of those things, I'd probably still be chewing my thumbnail and staring at the controls when the Pax guards grabbed me. It must have been easier being a Hero back during Hegemony days—the machines were smarter then, which made up for hero stupidity. As it was—although I would hate to admit it to my traveling companions —there weren't many vehicles that I could drive. A barge. A basic groundcar, if it was one of the truck models the Hyperion Home Guard had used. As for piloting something myself . . . well, I had been glad when the spaceship hadn't had a control room.

I shook myself out of this reverie on my heroic shortcomings and concentrated on closing the last few hundred meters to the platform. I could see the lights quite clearly now: aircraft beacons on the towers near the landing decks, a flashing green light on each of the ship docks, and lighted windows. Lots of windows. I decided to try to land on the darkest part of the platform, directly under the radar tower on the east side, and took the mat around in a long, slow, wave-hugging arc to approach from that direction. Looking back over my shoulder, I half expected to see the raft closing on me, but it was still invisible out toward the horizon.

I hope it's invisible to these guys. I could hear voices and laughter now: men's voices, deep laughter. It sounded like a lot of the offworld hunters I'd guided, filled with booze and bonhomie. But it also sounded like the dolts I'd served with in the Guard. I concentrated on keeping the mat low and dry and sneaking up on the platform.

"I'm about there," I subvocalized on the comlink.

"Okay," was Aenea's whispered reply in my ear. We had agreed that she would only reply to my calls unless there were an emergency on their end.

Hovering, I saw a maze of beams, girders, subdecks, and catwalks under the main platform on this side. Unlike the well-lighted stairs on the north and west sides, these were dark—inspection catwalks, maybe—and I chose the lowest and darkest of them to land the carpet on. I killed the flight threads, rolled the little rug up, and lashed it in place where two beams met, cutting the cord I'd brought with a sweep of my knife. Setting the blade back in its sheath and tugging my vest over it, I had the sudden image of having to stab someone with that knife. The thought made me shudder. Except for the accident when M. Herrig attacked me, I had never killed anyone in hand-to-hand combat. I prayed to God that I would never have to again.

The stairs made noises under my soft boots, but I hoped that the occasional squeak wouldn't be heard over the sound of the waves against the pylons and the laughter from above. I crept up two flights of stairs, found a ladder, and followed it up to a trapdoor. It was not locked. I slowly raised it, half expecting to tumble an armed guard on his ass.

Raising my head slowly, I saw that this was part of the flight deck on the seaward side of the tower. Ten meters above, I could see the turning radar antenna slicing darkness out of the brilliant Milky Way with each revolution.

I pulled myself to the deck, defeated the urge to tiptoe, and walked to the corner of the tower. Two huge skimmers were tied down to the flight deck here, but they looked dark and empty. On the lower flight decks I could see starlight on the multiple insect-wings of the thopters. The light from our galaxy gleamed in their dark observation blisters. The flesh between my shoulder blades was crawling with the sense of being observed as I walked out on the upper deck, applied plastic explosive to the belly of the closest skimmer, set a detonator in place, which I could trigger with the appropriate frequency code from my com unit, went down the ladder to the closest thopter deck, and did the same there. I was sure that I was being observed from one of the lighted windows or ports on this side, but no outcry went up. As casually as I could, I went soundlessly up the catwalk from the lower thopter deck and peered around the corner of the tower.

Another stairway led down from the tower module to one of the main levels. The windows were very bright there and covered only with screens now, their storm shields up. I could hear more laughter, some singing, and the sound of pots and pans.

Taking a breath, I moved down the stairs and across the deck, following another catwalk to keep me away from the doorway. Ducking under lighted windows, I tried to catch my breath and slow my pounding heart. If someone came out of that first doorway now, they would be between me and the way back to the hawking mat. I touched the grip of the .45 under my vest and the flap of the holster and tried to think brave thoughts. Mostly I was thinking about wanting to be back on the raft. I had planted the diversion explosives . . . what else did I want? I realized that I was more than curious: if these were not Pax troops, I did not want to set off the plastique. The rebels I had signed up to fight on the Claw Iceshelf had used bombs as their weapon of choice—bombs in the villages, bombs in Home Guard barracks, masses of explosives in snowmobiles and small ships targeted against civilians as well as Guard troops—and I had always considered this cowardly and detestable. Bombs were totally nondiscriminating weapons, killing the innocent as surely as the enemy soldier. It was silly to moralize this way, I knew, but even though I hoped that the small charges would do no more than set empty aircraft ablaze here, I was not going to detonate those charges unless I absolutely had to. These men—and women, probably, and perhaps children—had done nothing to us.

Slowly, excruciatingly slowly, absurdly slowly, I raised my head and peered in the closest window. One glimpse and I ducked down out of sight. The pots-and-pans noises were coming from a well-lighted kitchen area—galley, I corrected myself, since this was a ship, sort of. At any rate, there had been half a dozen people there, all men, all of military age but not in uniform except for undershirts and aprons, cleaning, stacking, and washing dishes. Obviously I'd come too late for dinner.

Staying next to the wall, I duck-walked the length of this catwalk, slid down another stairway, and stopped at a longer bank of windows. Here, in the shadows of a corner where two modules came together, I could see in some of the windows along this west-facing wall without lifting my face to one. It was a mess hall—or a dining room of some sort. About thirty men—all men!—were sitting over cups of coffee. Some were smoking recom-cigarettes. At least one man appeared to be drinking whiskey: or at least amber fluid from a bottle. I would not have minded some of whatever it was.

Many of the men were in khaki, but I couldn't tell if these were some sort of local uniform, or just the traditional garb of sports fishermen. I didn't see any Pax uniforms, which was definitely good. Perhaps this was just a fishing platform now, a hotel for rich offworld jerks who didn't mind paying years of time-debt—or having their friends and families back home pay it, actually—for the thrill of killing something big or exotic. Hell, I might know some of those guys: fishermen now, duck hunters when they visited Hyperion. I did not want to go in to find out.

Feeling more confident now, I moved down the long walkway, the light from the windows falling on me. There did not seem to be any guards. No sentries. Maybe we would not need a diversion—just sail the raft right past these guys, moonlight or no moonlight. They'd be sleeping, or drinking and laughing, and we'd just follow the current right into the farcaster portal that I could see less than two klicks to the northeast now, the faintest of dark arches against the starry sky. When we got to the portal, I would send a prearranged frequency shift that would not detonate the plastique I'd hidden but would disarm the detonators.

I was looking at the portal when I moved around the corner and literally bumped into a man leaning against the wall there. There were two others standing at the railing. One of them was holding night-vision binoculars and looking off to the north. Both of the men at the railing had weapons.

"Hey!" yelled the men I'd bumped into.

"Sorry," I said. I definitely had never seen this scene in a holodrama.

The two men at the railing were carrying flechette miniguns on slings and were resting their forearms on them with that casual arrogance that military types had practiced for countless centuries. Now one of these two shifted the gun so that its barrel was aimed in my direction. The man I bumped into had been in the process of lighting a cigarette. Now he shook out the match flame, removed the lighted cigarette from his mouth, and glared at me.

"What are you doing out here?" he demanded. The man was younger than I—perhaps early twenties, standard—and I could see now that he was wearing a variation on the Pax Groundforces uniform with the lieutenant's bar I'd learned to salute on Hyperion. His dialect was pronounced, but I couldn't place it.

"Getting some air," I said lamely. Part of me was thinking that a real Hero would have had his pistol out, blazing away. The smarter part of me did not even consider it.

The other Pax trooper also shifted the sling of his flechette auto. I heard the click of a safety. "You are with the Klingman group?" he asked in the same thick dialect. "Or the Otters?" I heard *Oor dey autors?* I didn't know if he was saying "others" or "otters" or, perhaps, "authors." Maybe this was a seaborne concentration camp for bad writers. Maybe I was trying too hard to be mentally flippant when my heart was pounding so fiercely that I was afraid I was going to have a heart attack right in front of these two.

"Klingman," I said, trying to be as terse as possible. Whatever dialect I should have, I was sure I did not.

The Pax lieutenant jerked a thumb toward the doorway beyond him. "You know the rules. Curfew after dark." *Yewe knaw dey rues. Cufue affa dok.*

I nodded, trying to look contrite. My overvest was hanging down over the top of the holster on my hip. Perhaps they hadn't seen the pistol.

"Come," said the lieutenant, jerking his thumb again but turning to lead the way. *Comb!* The two enlisted types still had their hands on the flechette guns. At that distance, if they fired, there wouldn't be enough of me left intact to bury in a boot.

I followed the lieutenant down the catwalk, through the door, and into the brightest and most crowded room I had ever entered.

32

THEY GROW WEARY OF DEATH. After eight star systems in sixty-three days, eight terrible deaths and eight painful resurrections for each of the four men, Father Captain de Soya, Sergeant Gregorius, Corporal Kee, and Lancer Rettig are weary of death and rebirth.

Each time now upon his resurrection, de Soya stands naked in front of a mirror, seeing his skin raw and glistening like someone who has been flayed alive, gingerly touching the now-livid, now-crimson cruciform under the flesh of his chest. In the days following each resurrection, de Soya is distracted, his hands shaking a bit more each time. Voices come to him from afar, he cannot seem to concentrate totally, whether his interlocutor is a Pax Admiral or a planetary Governor or a parish priest.

De Soya begins dressing like a parish priest, trading his trim Pax priest-captain uniform for the cassock and collar. He has a rosary on his belt-thong and says it almost constantly, working it like Arabic worry beads: prayer calms him, brings his thoughts to order. Father Captain de Soya no longer dreams of Aenea as his daughter; he no longer dreams of Renaissance Vector and his sister Maria. He dreams of Armageddon—terrible dreams of burning orbital forests, of worlds aflame, of deathbeams walking over fertile farming valleys and leaving only corpses.

He knows after their first River Tethys world that he has miscalculated. Two standard years to cover two hundred worlds, he had said in Renaissance System, figuring three days' resurrection in each system, a warning, and then translation to the next. It does not work that way.

His first world is Tau Ceti Center, former administrative capital of the far-flung Hegemony WorldWeb. Home to tens of billions during the days of the Web, surrounded by an actual ring of orbital cities and habitats, served by space elevators, farcasters, the River Tethys, the Grand

Concourse, the fatline, and more—center to the Hegemonic datumplane megasphere and home of Government House, site of Meina Gladstone's death by infuriated mobs after the destruction of the Web farcasters by FORCE ships on her command, TC^2 was hard hit by the Fall. Floating buildings crashed as the power grid went down. Other urban spires, some many hundreds of stories tall, were served only by farcasters and lacked stairs or elevators. Tens of thousands starved or perished from falls before they could be lifted out by skimmer. The world had no agriculture of its own, bringing in its food from a thousand worlds via planet-based farcasters and great orbital spaceborne portals. The Starvation Riots lasted fifty local years on TC^2, over thirty standard, and when they were finished, billions had died from human hands, to add to the total of billions dead from hunger.

Tau Ceti Center had been a sophisticated, wanton world during the days of the Web. Few religions had taken hold there except the most self-indulgent or violent ones—the Church of the Final Atonement—the Shrike Cult—had been popular among the bored sophisticates. But during the centuries of Hegemony expansion, the only true object of worship on TC^2 had been power: the pursuit of power, the proximity to power, the preservation of power. Power had been the god of billions, and when that god failed—and pulled down billions of its worshipers in its failure—the survivors cursed the memories of power amid their urban ruins, scratching out a peasant's living in the shadows of the rotting skyscrapers, pulling their own plows through weeded lots between the abandoned highways and flyways and the skeleton of old Grand Concourse malls, fishing for carp where the River Tethys had carried thousands of elaborate yachts and pleasure-barges each day.

Tau Ceti Center had been ripe for born-again Christianity, for the New Catholicism, and when the Church missionaries and Pax police had arrived sixty standard years after the Fall, conversion of the few billion planet's survivors was sincere and universal. The tall, ruined, but still-white spires of business and government during the Web were finally torn down, their stone and smart glass and plasteel recycled into massive cathedrals, raised by the hands of the new Tau Ceti born-again, filled each day of the week by the thankful and faithful.

The Archbishop of Tau Ceti Center became one of the most important and—yes—powerful humans in the reemerging human domain now known as Pax Space, rivaling His Holiness on Pacem in influence. This power grew, found boundaries that could not be overstepped without incurring papal wrath—the excommunication of His Excellency, Klaus Cardinal Kronenberg in the Year of Our Lord 2978, or 126 After the Fall, helped settle those boundaries—and it continued to grow within those bounds.

So Father Captain de Soya discovers on his first jump from Renaissance space. Two years, he had anticipated, approximately six hundred days and two hundred self-imposed deaths to cover all of the former River Tethys worlds.

He and his Swiss Guard troopers are on Tau Ceti Center for eight days. The *Raphael* enters the system with its automatic beacon pulsing in code; Pax ships respond and rendezvous within fourteen hours. It takes another eight hours to decelerate into TC^2 orbital traffic, and another four to transfer the bodies to a formal resurrection creche in the planetary capital of St. Paul. One full day is thus lost.

After three days of formal resurrection and another day of enforced rest, de Soya meets with the Archbishop of TC^2, Her Excellency Achilla Silvaski, and must endure another full day of formalities. De Soya carries the papal diskey, an almost unheard of delegation of power, and the court of the Archbishop must sniff out the reason and projected results of that power like hunting dogs on a scent. Within hours de Soya gets the slightest hint of the layers of intrigue and complexity within this struggle for provincial power: Archbishop Silvaski can not aspire to become Cardinal, for after the Kronenberg excommunication, no spiritual leader of TC^2 can rise to a rank higher than Archbishop without transfer to Pacem and the Vatican, but her current power in this sector of the Pax far outweighs that of most cardinals and the temporal subset of that power puts Pax Fleet admirals in their place. She must understand this delegation of papal authority that de Soya carries, and render it harmless to her ends.

Father Captain de Soya does not give a damn about Archbishop Silvaski's paranoia or the Church politics on TC^2. He cares only about stopping up the escape route of the farcaster portals there. On the fifth day after his translation to Tau Ceti space, he makes the five hundred meters from St. Paul's Cathedral and the Archbishop's palace to the river—just part of a minor tributary channeled into a canal flowing through the city, but once part of the Tethys.

The huge farcaster portals, still extant because any attempt to dismantle them had promised a thermonuclear explosion according to engineers, have long since been draped over by Church banners, but they are close together here—the Tethys had meandered only two kilometers from portal to portal, past the busy Government House and the formal Deer Park gardens. Now Father Captain de Soya, his three troopers, and the scores of watchful Pax troops loyal to Archbishop Silvaski who accompany them, can stand at the first portal and look down the grassy banks at a thirty-meter-long tapestry—showing the martyrdom of St. Paul—hanging from the second portal, clearly visible beyond the blooming peach trees of the bishopric palace gardens.

Because this section of the former Tethys is now within Her Excellency's private gardens, guards are posted along the length of the canal and on all bridges crossing it. While there is no special attention to the ancient artifacts that were once farcaster portals, the officers of the palace guard assure de Soya that no vessels or unauthorized individuals have passed through those portals, nor been seen along the banks of the canal.

De Soya insists that a permanent guard be placed upon the portals. He wants cameras erected for twenty-nine-hour-a-day surveillance there. He wants sensors, alarms, and trip wires. The local Pax troops confer with their Archbishop and grudgingly comply with this perceived slight to their sovereignty. De Soya all but despairs at this useless politics.

On their sixth day Corporal Kee falls ill to a mysterious fever and is hospitalized. De Soya believes it is a result of their resurrection: each of them has privately suffered the shakes, emotional swings, and minor ailments. On the seventh day Kee is able to walk and implores de Soya to get him out of the infirmary and off this world, but now the Archbishop insists that de Soya help celebrate a High Mass that evening in honor of His Holiness, Pope Julius. De Soya can hardly refuse, so that night—amid scepters and pink-buttoned *monsignore,* beneath the giant insignia of His Holiness's Triple Crown and Crossed Keys (which also appears on the papal diskey that de Soya now wears around his neck), amid the smoke of incense, white miters and the tinkle of bells, under the solemn singing of a six-hundred-member children's choir, the simple priest-warrior from MadredeDios and the elegant Archbishop celebrate the mystery of Christ's crucifixion and resurrection. Sergeant Gregorius takes Communion that evening from de Soya's hand—which he does every day of their quest—as do a few dozen others also chosen to receive the Host, secret to the success of their cruciform immortality in this life, while three thousand of the faithful pray and watch in the dim cathedral light.

On the eighth day they leave the system, and for the first time Father Captain de Soya welcomes the coming death as a means of escape.

They are resurrected in a creche on Heaven's Gate, a once-miserable world terraformed to shade trees and comfort in the days of the Web, now largely fallen back to boiling mud, pestilent swamps, unbreathable atmosphere, and the blazing radiation source of Vega Prime in the sky. *Raphael*'s idiot computer has chosen this series of old River Tethys worlds, finding the most efficient order to visit them in since there were no clues on Renaissance V. to show where the portal there might have led, but de Soya is interested that they are coming closer and closer to Old Earth System— less than twelve light-years from TC^2, now just a little more than eight from Heaven's Gate. De Soya realizes that he would like to visit Old Earth System—even without Old Earth—despite the fact that Mars and the other inhabited worlds, moons, and asteroids there have become provincial backwaters, of no more interest to the Pax than MadredeDios had been.

But the Tethys never flowed through Old Earth System, so de Soya must swallow his curiosity and be satisfied that the next few worlds will be even closer to Old Earth's former home.

Heaven's Gate takes eight days as well, but not because of intra-Church politics. There is a small Pax garrison in orbit around the planet, but they rarely go down to the ruined world. Heaven's Gate's population of four hundred million residents had been reduced to eight or ten crazy prospectors wandering its mudflat surface in the 274 standard years since the Fall: the Ouster Swarms had swept by this Vegan world even before Gladstone had ordered the farcasters destroyed—slagging the orbital containment sphere, lancing the capital of Mudflat City, with its lovely Promenade gardens, plasma bombing the atmosphere-generating stations it had taken centuries to build—and generally plowed the world under before the loss of farcaster connections salted the earth so that nothing would grow there again.

So now the Pax garrison guards the broiling planet for its rumored raw materials, but has little reason to go down there. De Soya must convince the garrison commander—Pax Major Leem—that an expedition has to be mounted. On the fifth day after *Raphael*'s entry into Vega System, de Soya, Gregorius, Kee, Rettig, a Lieutenant Bristol, and a dozen Pax garrison troops fitted out in environmental hazard suits, take a dropship to the mudflats where the River Tethys had once flowed. The farcaster portals are not there.

"I thought it was impossible to destroy them," says de Soya. "The TechnoCore built them to last and booby-trapped them so that destruction is impossible."

"They're not here," says Lieutenant Bristol, and gives the order to return to orbit.

De Soya stops him. Using his papal diskey as authority, de Soya insists that a full-sensor search be made. The farcasters are found—sixteen klicks apart and buried under almost a hundred meters of mud.

"That solves your mystery," says Major Leem on tightbeam. "Either the Ouster attack or later mudslides buried the portals and what had been the river. This world has literally gone to hell."

"Perhaps," says de Soya, "but I want the farcasters excavated, temporary environmental bubbles erected around them so that someone coming through would survive, and a permanent guard mounted at each portal."

"Are you out of your crossdamned mind!" Major Leem explodes, and then—remembering the papal diskey—he adds, "Sir."

"Not yet," says de Soya, glowering into the camera. "I want this done within seventy-two hours, Major, or you will be serving the next three standard years on the planetary detail down here."

It takes seventy hours to excavate, construct the domes, and post the guard. Someone traveling the River Tethys will find no river here, of course, only the boiling mud, noxious, unbreathable atmosphere, and waiting troopers in full battle armor. De Soya goes to his knees on the *Raphael* that last night in orbit around Heaven's Gate and prays that

Aenea has not already come this way. Her bones were not found in the excavated mud and sulfur, but the Pax engineer in charge of the excavation tells de Soya that the soil is so toxic here in its natural form that the child's bones could already have been eaten away by acid.

De Soya does not believe this to be the case. On the ninth day he translates out of system with a warning to Major Leem to keep the guards vigilant, the domes livable, and his mouth more civil to future visitors.

No one waits to resurrect them in the third system *Raphael* brings them to. The archangel ship enters System NGC^es 2629 with its cargo of dead men and its beacons flashing Pax Fleet code. There is no response. There are eight planets in NGC^es 2629, but only one of them, known by the prosaic name of NGC^es 2629-4BIV, can support life. From the records still available to the *Raphael,* it seems likely that the Hegemony and TechnoCore had gone to the effort and expense of extending the River Tethys here as a form of self-indulgence, an aesthetic statement. The planet has never been seriously colonized or terraformed except for random RNA seeding during the early days of the Hegira, and appears to have been part of the River Tethys tour strictly for scenic and animal-viewing purposes.

That is not to say that there are not human beings on the world now, as the *Raphael* sniffs them out in parking orbit during the last days of its passengers' automated resurrections. As best the limited resources of the *Raphael*'s near-AI computers can reconstruct and understand, NGC^es 2629-4BIV's minimum population of visiting biologists, zoologists, tourists, and support teams had been stranded after the Fall and had gone native. Despite prodigious breeding over almost three centuries, however, only a few thousand human beings still populated the jungles and highlands of the primitive world: the RNA-seeded beasties there were capable of eating human beings, and they did so with gusto.

Raphael runs to the edge of its limits in the simple task of finding the farcaster portals. Available Web records in its memory say simply that the portals are set at varying intervals along a six-thousand-kilometer river in the northern hemisphere. *Raphael* modifies its orbit to a roughly synchronous point above the massive continent which dominates that hemisphere and begins photographing and radar-mapping the river. Unfortunately, there are three massive rivers on that continent, two flowing to the east, one to the west, and *Raphael* is unable to prioritize probabilities. It decides to map all three—a task of analyzing more than twenty thousand kilometers of data.

When the four men's hearts begin to beat at the end of the third day of the resurrection cycle, *Raphael* feels some silicon equivalent of relief.

Listening to the computer's description of the task ahead while he stands naked in front of the mirror in his tiny cubby, Federico de Soya feels no relief. In truth, he feels like weeping. He thinks of Mother Captain

Stone, Mother Captain Boulez, and Captain Hearn, on the Great Wall frontier by now and quite possibly engaging the Ouster enemy in fierce combat. De Soya envies them the simplicity and honesty of their task.

After conferring with Sergeant Gregorius and his two men, de Soya reviews the data, immediately rejects the western-flowing river as too unscenic for the River Tethys, since it flows primarily through deep canyons, away from the life-infested jungles and marshes; the second river he rejects because of the obvious number of waterfalls and rapids—too rough for River Tethys traffic—and so he begins a simple, fast radar-mapping of the longest river with its long, gentle stretches. The map will show up dozens, perhaps hundreds, of natural obstacles resembling farcaster portals—rocky waterfalls, natural bridges, boulder fields in rapids—but these can be scanned by the human eye in a few hours.

On their fifth day the portals are located—improbably far apart, but inarguably artificial. De Soya personally flies the dropship, leaving Corporal Kee in the *Raphael* as backup in case of emergency.

This is the scenario de Soya has dreaded—no way to tell if the girl has come this way, with or without her ship. The stretch between the inert farcasters is the longest yet—almost two hundred kilometers—and although they fly the dropship back and forth over the jungle and river's edge, there is no telling if anyone has passed this way, no witnesses to interview, no Pax troops to leave on guard here.

They land on an island not far from the upper farcaster, and de Soya, Gregorius, and Rettig discuss their options.

"It's been three standard weeks since the ship passed through the farcaster on Renaissance V.," says Gregorius. The interior of their dropship is cramped and utilitarian: they discuss things from their flight chairs. Gregorius's and Rettig's combat armor hang in the EVA closet like metal second skins.

"If they came through to a world like this," says Rettig, "they probably just took off in the ship. There's no reason they have to keep going down the river."

"True," says de Soya. "But there is a good chance the ship was damaged."

"Aye," says the sergeant, "but how badly? Could it have flown? Patched itself as it went? Perhaps made it to an Ouster repair base? We're not that far from the Outback here."

"Or the girl could have sent the ship off and gone on through the next farcaster," says Rettig.

"Assuming any of the other portals work," says de Soya tiredly. "That the one on Renaissance V. was not just a fluke."

Gregorius sets his huge hands on his knees. "Aye, sir, this is ridiculous. Finding a needle in a haystack, as they used to say . . . that would be child's play compared to this."

Father Captain de Soya looks out through the dropship windows.

The high ferns here are blowing in a silent wind. "I have a feeling she's going down the old river. I think she'll use the farcasters. I don't know how—the flying machine that someone used to get her out of the Valley of the Time Tombs, maybe, an inflatable raft, a stolen boat—I just think she's using the Tethys."

"What can we do here?" asks Rettig. "If she's already come through, we've missed her. If she's not yet arrived . . . well, we could wait forever. If we had a hundred archangel ships so that we could bring troops to each of these worlds . . ."

De Soya nods. In his hours of prayer his mind often slips away to the thought of how much simpler this task would be if the archangel couriers were simple robotic craft, translating into Pax systems, broadcasting the papal-diskey authority and ordering the search, then jumping out of system without even decelerating. As far as he knows, the Pax is building no robot ships—the Church's hatred of AIs and dependence upon human contact all but forbids it. And as far as he knows, there are only three archangel-class courier ships in existence—the *Michael*, the *Gabriel*, which had first brought him the message, and his own *Raphael*. In Renaissance System, he had wanted to send the other courier ship out in search, but the *Michael* had pressing Vatican duties. Intellectually, de Soya understood why this search was his and his alone. But here they have spent almost three weeks and searched two worlds. A robot archangel could leap into two hundred systems and broadcast the alert in less than ten standard days . . . at this rate, it will take de Soya and the *Raphael* four or five standard years. The exhausted father-captain has the urge to laugh.

"There's still her ship," he says briskly. "If they go on without it, they have two options—send the ship somewhere else, or leave it behind on one of the Tethys worlds."

"You say 'they,' sir," Gregorius says softly. "Are you sure there are others?"

"Someone lifted her from our trap on Hyperion," says de Soya. "There are others."

"It could be an entire Ouster crew," says Rettig. "They could be halfway back to their Swarm by now . . . after leaving the girl on any of these worlds. Or they could be taking her with them."

De Soya lifts a hand to shut off conversation. They have been around and around this before. "I think the ship was hit and damaged," he says. "We look for it and it may lead us to the girl."

Gregorius points to the jungle. It is raining there. "We've flown this entire stretch of river between the portals. No sign of a ship. When we get to the next Pax system, we can send back garrison troops to watch these portals."

"Yes," says Father Captain de Soya, "but they'll have a time-debt of eight or nine months." He looks at the rain streaking the windshield and side ports. "We'll search the river."

"What?" says Lancer Rettig.

"If you had a damaged ship and had to leave it behind, wouldn't you hide it?" asks de Soya.

The two Swiss Guard troopers stare at their commander. De Soya sees that the men's fingers are trembling. Resurrection is affecting them as well.

"We'll deep-radar the river and as much of the jungle as we can," says the father-captain.

"It'll take another day, at least," begins Rettig.

De Soya nods. "We'll have Corporal Kee instruct *Raphael* to deep-radar the jungle on a two-hundred-klick swatch on either side of the river. We'll use the dropship to search the river. . . . We have a cruder system on board, but less to cover."

The exhausted troopers can only nod their obedience.

THEY FIND SOMETHING on the second sweep of the river. The object is metal, large, and in a deep pool only a few kilometers downriver from the first portal. The dropship hovers while de Soya tightbeams the *Raphael*. "Corporal, we're going to investigate. I want the ship ready to lance this thing within three seconds of my command . . . *but only on my command.*"

"I understand, sir," tightbeams Kee.

De Soya holds the dropship in hover while Gregorius and Rettig suit up, prepare the proper tools, and stand in the open air lock. "Go," says de Soya.

Sergeant Gregorius drops out of the lock, the suit's EM system kicking in just before the armored man strikes water. Both sergeant and lancer swoop above the surface, weapons ready.

"We have the deep-radar lock on tactical," Gregorius acknowledges on tightbeam.

"Your video feeds are nominal," says de Soya from his command chair. "Commence dive."

Both men drop, strike the surface, and disappear beneath it. De Soya banks the dropship so he can see out the port blister: the river is a dark green, but two bright headlamps can be seen gleaming through the water. "About eight meters beneath the surface," he begins.

"Got it," says the sergeant.

De Soya looks up at the monitor. He sees swirling silt, a many-gilled fish hurrying out of the light, a curved metal hull.

"There's a hatch or air lock open," reports Gregorius. "Most of the thing's buried in the mud here, but I can see enough of the hull to say it's about the right size. Rettig will stay out here. I'm going in."

De Soya has the urge to say "Good luck," but keeps his silence. The men have been together long enough to know what is appropriate with each other. He trims the dropship, readying the crude plasma gun that is the tiny ship's only armament.

The video feed stops as soon as Gregorius enters the open hatch. A minute passes. Then two. Two minutes beyond that, and de Soya is all but squirming in the command chair. He half expects to see the spaceship leap out of the water, clawing for space in a desperate attempt to escape.

"Lancer?" he says.

"Yes, sir," comes Retttig's voice.

"No word or video from the sergeant?"

"No, sir. I think the hull's blocking tightbeam. I'll wait another five minutes and . . . Hold it, sir. I see something."

De Soya sees it too, the feed from the lancer's video murky in the thick water, but clear enough to show Sergeant Gregorius's armored helmet, shoulders, and arms rising from the open air-lock hatch. The sergeant's headlamp illuminates silt and riverweed, the light swinging to blind Rettig's camera for an instant.

"Father Captain de Soya," comes Gregorius's bass rumble, only slightly out of breath, "this ain't it, sir. I think it's one of those old go-anywhere yachts that rich folks had back in the Web days, sir. You know, sir, the kind that was submersible—could even fly a bit, I think."

De Soya lets out his breath. "What happened to it, Sergeant?"

The suited figure on the video gives a thumbs-up to Rettig, and the two men rise toward the surface. "I think they scuttled it, sir," says Gregorius. "There are at least ten skeletons on board . . . maybe a dozen. Two of 'em are kids. As I say, sir, this thing was rigged to float on any ocean—go under it if they wanted—so there's no way all the hatches opened by accident, sir."

De Soya watches out the window as the two figures in combat armor break the surface of the river and hover five meters above it, water pouring from their suits.

"I think they must've been stranded here after the Fall, sir," Gregorius is saying, "and just decided to end it all there, sir. It's only a guess, Father Captain, but I have a hunch. . . ."

"I have a hunch you're right, Sergeant," says de Soya. "Come on back." He opens the dropship hatch as the suited figures fly toward it.

Before they arrive, while he is still alone, de Soya raises his hand and mouths a blessing of the river, the sunken craft, and those entombed there. The Church does not sanctify suicides, but the Church knows that little is certain in life or death. Or, at least, de Soya knows this, even if the Church does not.

THEY LEAVE MOTION DETECTORS sending beams across each of the portals —they will not catch the girl and her allies, but they will tell the troops de Soya will send back whether anyone has passed that way in the interim—

and then they lift the dropship from NGC^es 2629-4BIV, tuck the stubby dropship into the ugly mass of *Raphael* above the gleaming limb of the cloud-swirled planet, and accelerate out of the world's gravity well so that they can translate to their next stop, Barnard's World.

This is as close as de Soya's pursuit itinerary will come to Old Earth System—a mere six light-years—and since this was one of the earliest interstellar colonies of the pre-Hegira era, the priest-captain likes to think that he will be getting a glimpse back in time of Old Earth itself. Upon resurrection in the Pax base some six AUs from Barnard's World, however, de Soya immediately notes the differences. Barnard's Star is a red dwarf, only about one fifth the mass of Old Earth's G-type star, and less than 1/2500 the luminosity. Only the proximity of Barnard's World, 0.126 AU, and the centuries spent terraforming the planet have produced a world high on the adaptive Solmev Scale. But, as de Soya and his men discover upon being ferried to the planet by their Pax escort, the terraforming has been very successful indeed.

Barnard's World had suffered very much from the Ouster Swarm invasion preceding the Fall, and very little—relatively speaking—from the Fall itself. The world had been a pleasant contradiction in terms in Web days: overwhelmingly agricultural, growing mostly Old Earth imports such as corn, wheat, soybeans, and the like, but also profoundly intellectual—boasting hundreds of the finest small colleges in the Web. The combination of agricultural backwater—life on Barnard's World tended to imitate small-town life in North America, circa 1900—and intellectual hot spot had brought some of the Hegemony's finest scholars, writers, and thinkers there.

After the Fall, Barnard's World relied more upon its agricultural heritage than its intellectual prowess. When the Pax arrived in force some five decades after the Fall, its brand of born-again Christianity and Pacem-based government was resisted for some years. Barnard's World had been self-sufficient and wished to remain that way. It was not formally accepted into the Pax until the Year of Our Lord 3061, some 212 years after the Fall, and then only after bloody civil war between the Catholics and partisan bands loosely grouped under the name The Free Believers.

Now, as de Soya learns during his brief tour with Archbishop Herbert Stern, the many colleges lie empty or have been converted to seminaries for the young men and women of Barnard's World. The partisans have all but disappeared, although there is still some resistance in the wild forest-and-canyon areas along the river known as Turkey Run.

Turkey Run had been part of the River Tethys, and it is precisely there that de Soya and his men wish to go. On their fifth day in-system, they travel there with a protective guard of sixty Pax troopers and some of the Archbishop's own elite guard.

They meet no partisans. This bit of the Tethys runs through broad valleys, under high shale cliffs, through deciduous forests of Old Earth–transplanted trees, and emerges into what has long since become tilled land—mostly cornfields sprinkled with the occasional white farmhouse and outbuildings. It does not look like a place of violence to de Soya, and he encounters none there.

The Pax skimmers search the forest well for any sign of the girl's ship, but they find none. The river of Turkey Run is too shallow to hide a ship—Major Andy Ford, the Pax officer in charge of their search, calls it "the sweetest canoeing river this side of Sugar Creek"—and the section of River Tethys had been only a few klicks long here. Barnard's World has modern atmosphere and orbital traffic control, and no ship could have left the area without being tracked. Interviews with farmers in the Turkey Run area produce no talk of strangers. In the end, Pax military, the Archbishop's diocesan council, and local civil authorities pledge constant surveillance of the area, despite any threat of Free Believer harassment.

On their eighth day de Soya and his men take leave of scores of people who can only be referred to as newfound friends, rise to orbit, transfer to a Pax torchship, and are escorted back to the deep-orbit Barnard's Star garrison and their archangel ship. The last sight de Soya glimpses of the bucolic world is the twin spires of the giant cathedral rising in the capital of St. Thomas, formerly known as Bussard City.

SWINGING AWAY from the direction of Old Earth System now, de Soya, Gregorius, Kee, and Rettig awaken in System Lacaille 9352, about as far from Old Earth as Tau Ceti had been to the early seedships. Here the delay is neither bureaucratic nor military, but environmental. The Web world here, known as Sibiatu's Bitterness then and renamed Inevitable Grace by its current population of a few thousand Pax colonists, had been environmentally marginal then and is far below that now. The River Tethys had run under twelve kilometers of Perspex tunnel, holding in breathable air and pressure. Those tunnels had fallen into decay more than two centuries ago, the water boiling away in the low pressure, the thin methane-ammonia atmosphere of the planet rushing in to fill the empty riverbanks and shattered Perspex tubes.

De Soya has no idea why the Web would have included this rock in its River Tethys. There is no Pax military garrison here, nor serious Church presence other than chaplains living with the highly religious colonists eking out a living with their boxite mines and sulfur pits, but de Soya and his men convince some of these colonists to take them to the former river.

"If she come this way, she died," says Gregorius as he inspects the huge portals hanging over a straight line of ruined Perspex and dry river-beds. The methane wind blows, and grains of ever-shifting dust try to find their way through the men's atmosphere suits.

"Not if she stayed in the ship," says de Soya, turning ponderously in his suit to look up at the orange-yellow sky. "The colonists wouldn't have noticed the ship leaving . . . it's too far from the colony."

The grizzled man with them, a bent figure even in his worn and sandblasted suit, grunts behind his visor. "Zat bey true, Fadder. We-en denna gay outsed a star-gazen' too offen, bey true."

De Soya and his men discuss the futility of ordering Pax troops to this sort of world to watch for the girl in the months and years to come.

"It's a fact that it'll be god-awful, miserable, ass-end-of-nowhere duty, sir," says Gregorius. "Pardon the language, Father."

De Soya nods distractedly. They have left the last of the motion-sensor beacons there: five worlds explored out of two hundred, and he is running out of material. The thought of sending troops back here depresses him as well, but he can see little alternative. Besides the resurrection ache and emotional confusion coursing through him constantly now, there is growing depression and doubt. He feels like an ancient, blind cat sent to catch a mouse, but unable to watch and guard two hundred mouseholes simultaneously. Not for the first time does he wish he were in the Outback, fighting Ousters.

As if reading the father-captain's thoughts, Gregorius says, "Sir, have ye really looked at the itinerary *Raphael*'s set for us?"

"Yes, Sergeant. Why?"

"Some o' the places we're headed ain't ours anymore, Captain. It's not till the later part of the trip . . . worlds way in the Outback . . . but the ship wants to take us to planets've been overrun by the Ousters long ago, sir."

De Soya nods tiredly. "I know, Sergeant. I didn't specify battle areas or the Great Wall defensive zones when I told the ship's computer to plan the trip."

"There's eighteen worlds that would be a bit dicey to visit," says Gregorius with the hint of a grin. "Seeing as how the Ousters own 'em now."

De Soya nods again but says nothing.

It is Corporal Kee who says softly, "If you want to go look there, sir, we'll be more than happy to go with you."

The priest-captain looks up at the faces of the three men. He has taken their loyalty and presence too much for granted, he thinks. "Thank you," he says simply. "We'll decide when we get to that part of the . . . tour."

"Which may be about a hundred standard years from now at this rate," says Rettig.

"It may indeed," says de Soya. "Let's strap in and get the hell out of here."

They translate out of the system.

STILL IN THE OLD NEIGHBORHOOD, hardly out of Old Earth's pre-Hegira backyard, they jump to two heavily terraformed worlds spinning through their complicated choreography in the half-light-year space between Epsilon Eridani and Epsilon Indi.

The Omicron$_2$-Epsilon$_3$ Eurasian Habitation Experiment had been a bold pre-Hegira utopian effort to achieve against-all-odds terraforming and political perfection—primarily neo-Marxist—on hostile worlds while fleeing from hostile forces. It had failed miserably. The Hegemony had replaced the utopians with FORCE:space bases and automated refueling stations, but the press of Outback-bound seedships and then spinships passing through the Old Neighborhood region during the Hegira had led to successful terraforming of these two dark worlds spinning between the dim Epsilon Eridani sun and the dimmer Epsilon Indi star. Then the famous defeat of Glennon-Height's fleet there had sealed the twin-system's fame and military importance. The Pax has rebuilt the abandoned FORCE bases, regenerated the failing terraform systems.

De Soya's searching of these two River sections is dry and business-like in a military way. Each of the Tethys segments is so deep in military reservation area that it soon becomes obvious there is no chance that the girl—much less the ship—could have passed through in the past two months without being detected and run to ground. De Soya had surmised this from knowing about the Epsilon System—he has passed through there several times himself on his travels to the Great Wall and beyond—but had decided that he needed to see the portals for himself.

It is good that they encounter this garrison system at this time in their travels, however, for both Kee and Rettig are hospitalized. Engineers and Church resurrection specialists examine *Raphael* in dry dock and determine that there are minute but serious errors in the automated resurrection creche. Three standard days are spent in making repairs.

When they translate out of system this time, with only one more stop in the Old Neighborhood before moving into the post-Hegira reaches of the old Web, it is with the earnest hope that their health, depression, and emotional instability will be improved if they have to undergo automated resurrection again.

"Where are you headed now?" asks Father Dimitrius, the resurrection specialist who has helped them over the past days.

De Soya hesitates only a second before answering. It cannot compromise his mission if he tells the elderly priest this one fact.

"Mare Infinitus," he says. "It's a water world some three parsecs outward bound and two light-years above the plane of—"

"Ah, yes," says the old priest. "I had a mission there decades ago, weaning the indigenie fisherfolk from their paganism and bringing them into Christ's light." The white-haired priest raises his hand in a benediction. "Whatever you seek, Father Captain de Soya, it is my sincere prayer that you find it there."

DE SOYA ALMOST LEAVES Mare Infinitus before sheer chance brings him the clue he has been seeking.

It is their sixty-third day of seeking, only the second day since resurrection in their creches aboard the orbital Pax station, and the beginning of what should be their last day on the planet.

A talkative young man named Lieutenant Baryn Alan Sproul is de Soya's liaison from Pax Seventy Ophiuchi A Fleet Command, and like tour guides throughout history, the youngster gives de Soya and his troopers more background than they want to hear. But he is a good thopter pilot, and on this ocean world in a flying machine that is relatively unfamiliar to him, de Soya is pleased to be passenger rather than pilot, and he relaxes some while Sproul takes them south, away from the extensive floating city of St. Thérèse, and into the empty fishing areas where the farcasters still float.

"Why are the portals so far apart here?" asks Gregorius.

"Ah, well," says Lieutenant Sproul, "there's a story to that."

De Soya catches his sergeant's eye. Gregorius almost never smiles unless combat is imminent, but de Soya has grown familiar with a certain glint in the big man's eye that is the sergeant's equivalent of riotous laughter.

". . . so the Hegemony wanted to build its River Tethys portals out here in addition to the orbital sphere they had and all the little farcasters they set up everywhere . . . sort of a silly idea, isn't it, sir? Putting part of a river through the ocean here? . . . anyway, they wanted it out in the Mid-littoral Current, which makes some sense because it's where the leviathans and some of the more interesting 'canths are, if the Web tourists wanted to see fish, that is . . . but the problem is, well, it's pretty obvious . . ."

De Soya looks over to where Corporal Kee is dozing in the warm sunlight coming through his thopter blister.

"It's pretty obvious that there's nothing permanent to build something big like those portals on . . . and you'll see 'em in a minute, sir, they're *big*. Well, I mean, there are the coral rings—but they're not secured to anything, they float, and the yellowkelp islands, but they're not . . . I mean, you put a foot on them, it goes right through, if you know what I mean, sir. . . . There, to the starboard side, sir. That's yellowkelp. Don't get too much of it this far south. Anyway, what the old Hegemony engineers did is, they rigged the portals sort of like we've been doing with the platforms and cities for the last five hundred years, sir. That is, they run these foundation bases a couple of hundred fathoms—big, heavy things they've got to be, sir—and then run big, bladed drag anchors out on cables beneath that. But the bottom of the ocean here is sort of a problematic thing . . . usually ten thousand fathoms, at least . . . that's where the big granddaddies of our surface 'canths like Lamp Mouth live, sir . . . monsters down that deep, sir . . . klicks long . . ."

"Lieutenant," says de Soya, "what does this have to do with why the portals are so far apart?" The high, almost ultrasonic hum of the thopter's dragonfly wings are threatening to put the priest-captain to sleep. Kee is now snoring, and Rettig has his feet up and his eyes closed. It has been a long flight.

Sproul grins. "Getting to that, sir. You see, with those keelweights and twenty klicks of cable trailing to rock, our cities and platforms don't go very far, even in the Big Tide season, no, sir. But these portals . . . well, we have lots of submarine volcanic activity on Mare-Eye, sir. Whole different 'cology down there, believe me. Some of them tube worms'd give those gigacanths a battle, honestly, sir. Anyway, the old Webdays' engineers fixed those portals so that if their keelweights and cables sensed volcanic activity under them, they'd just . . . well, migrate, sir, is the best word I can think of."

"So," says de Soya, "the distance between the River Tethys portals has widened because of volcanic activity on the ocean floor?"

"Yes, sir," says Lieutenant Sproul with a wide grin that seems to suggest both pleasure and amazement that a Fleet officer can comprehend such a thing. "And there's one of them now, sir," says the liaison officer with a flourish, banking the thopter into a descending spiral. He brings the machine into a hover just a few meters above the ancient arch. Twenty meters below that, the violet sea churns and splashes against the rusted metal at the portal's base.

De Soya rubs his face. None of them can throw off the fatigue any longer. Perhaps if they had a few more days between resurrection and death.

"Can we see the other portal now, please?" he says.

"Yes, sir!" The thopter buzzes just meters above the waves as it covers the two hundred klicks to the next arch. De Soya does doze, and when he wakes to the lieutenant's gentle nudging, the second portal arch is visible against the sea. It is late afternoon, and the low sun throws a long shadow on the violet sea.

"Very good," says de Soya. "And the deep-radar searches are still being carried out?"

"Yes, sir," says the young pilot. "They're widening the search radius, but so far they haven't seen anything but some hellacious big Lamp Mouths. That gets the sports-fishing guys worked up, I can tell you."

"That's a major industry here, I take it, sir," rumbles Gregorius from his place on the jump seat behind the pilot.

"Yes, Sergeant," says Sproul, craning his long neck around to look at the bigger man. "With kelp harvesting way down, it's our biggest offworld source of income."

De Soya points to a platform only a few kilometers away. "Another fishing and refueling platform?" The priest-captain has spent a day with the Pax commanders, going over reports from small outposts like this all over the world. None have reported any contact with a ship, or sight of a child. During this long flight south to the portals, they have passed dozens of similar platforms.

"Yes, sir," says Sproul. "Shall I hover for a while, or have you seen enough?"

De Soya looks at the portal—arching high above them now as the thopter hovers meters above the sea—and says, "We can get back, Lieutenant. We have a formal dinner with Bishop Melandriano to-night."

Sproul's eyebrows rise toward his crew cut. "Yes, sir," he says, bringing the thopter up and around in a final circle before heading back north.

"That platform looks as if it's been damaged recently," says de Soya, leaning farther to his right to look down from the blister port.

"Yes, sir," agrees the lieutenant. "I have a friend who just rotated in from that plat . . . Station Three-twenty-six Mid-littoral, it's called sir . . . and he told me about it. They had a poacher try to blow the place up a few tides ago."

"Sabotage?" says de Soya, watching the platform recede.

"Guerrilla war," says the lieutenant. "The poachers are the indigenies from back before the Pax got here, sir. That's why we've got troopers on each of the plats, and regular patrol ships during the height of the fishing season. We have to keep the fishing ships sort of herded there, sir, so the poachers don't attack them. You saw those boats tied up, sir . . . well, it's almost time for them to go fishing. Our Pax ships will escort them out. The Lamp Mouth, well, sir, he rises up just when the moons are just so . . . you see the big one rising there, sir. So the legal fishing ships . . . they have these bright lights they shine when the moons are down, luring the big 'canths up. But the poachers do that too, sir."

De Soya looks out at the empty expanse of ocean between the thopter and the northern horizon. "Doesn't seem like too many places for rebels to hide," he says.

"No, sir," says the lieutenant. "I mean, yes, sir. Actually, they've got fishing boats camouflaged to look like yellowkelp isles, submersibles, even one big submarine harvester that was rigged up like a Lamp Mouth, believe it or not, sir."

"And that platform was damaged by a poacher attack?" says de

Soya, speaking to stay awake now. The drone of the thopter wings is deadly.

"Right, sir," says Lieutenant Sproul. "About eight Big Tides ago. One man . . . which is unusual, the poachers generally come in groups. He blew up some skimmers and thopters—common tactics, although they usually go for the boats."

"Excuse me, Lieutenant," says de Soya, "you say this was eight Big Tides ago. Could you translate that into standard?"

Sproul chews his lip. "Ah, yes, sir. Sorry, sir. I grew up on Mare-Eye, and . . . well, eight Big Tides is about two standard months ago, sir."

"Was the poacher apprehended?"

"Yes, sir," says Sproul with his youthful grin. "Well, actually there's a story there, sir. . . ." The lieutenant glances at the priest-captain to see if he should go on. "Well, to make it short, sir, this poacher got apprehended first, then he blew his charges and tried to get away, and then he was shot and killed by the guards."

De Soya nods and closes his eyes. In the last day he has reviewed over a hundred reports on "poacher incidents" spread over the past two standard months. Blowing up platforms and killing poachers seems to be the second most popular sport—after fishing—on Mare Infinitus.

"The funny thing about this guy," says the lieutenant, finishing his story, "is how he tried to get away. Some sort of old flying carpet from the Hegemony days."

De Soya snaps awake. He glances at the sergeant and his men. All three are sitting up, staring at him.

"Turn around," snaps Father Captain de Soya. "Take us back to that platform."

"And then what happened?" says de Soya for the fifth time. He and his Swiss Guard are in the platform director's office on the highest point of the platform, just beneath the radar dish. Outside the long window, three unbelievable moons are rising.

The director—a Pax captain in the Ocean Command named C. Dobbs Powl—is overweight, florid, and sweating heavily. "When it became apparent that this man was not in either of the fishing groups we had on board that night, Lieutenant Belius took him aside for further questioning. Standard procedure, Father Captain."

De Soya stares at the man. "And then?"

The director licks his lips. "And then the man managed to escape temporarily, Father Captain. There was a struggle on the upper walkway. He pushed Lieutenant Belius into the sea."

"Was the lieutenant recovered?"

"No, Father Captain. He almost certainly drowned, although there was quite a bit of rainbow shark activity that night—"

"Describe the man you had in custody before you lost him," interrupts de Soya, emphasizing the word "lost."

"Young, Father Captain, maybe twenty-five or so standard. And tall, sir. Real big young guy."

"You saw him yourself?"

"Oh, yes, Father Captain. I was out on the walkway with Lieutenant Belius and Sea Lancer Ament when the fellow started the fight and pushed Belius through the railing."

"And then got away from you and the lance private," says de Soya flatly. "With both of you armed and this man . . . Did you say he was handcuffed?"

"Yes, Father Captain." Captain Powl mops his forehead with a moist handkerchief.

"Did you notice anything unusual about this young man? Anything else that did not make it into your . . . ah . . . extremely brief action report to Command Headquarters?"

The director puts the handkerchief away, then pulls it out again to mop his neck. "No, Father Captain . . . I mean, well, during the struggle, the man's sweater was torn a bit in front. Enough for me to notice that he wasn't like you and me, Father Captain. . . ."

De Soya raises an eyebrow.

"I mean he wasn't of the cross," Powl hurries on. "No cruciform. 'Course, I didn't think much of that at the time. Most of these indigenie poachers've never been baptized. Wouldn't be poachers if they had, now, would they?"

De Soya ignores the question. Pacing closer to the seated, sweating captain, he says, "So the man swung down under the main catwalk and escaped that way?"

"Didn't escape, sir," says Powl. "Just got to this flying dingus that he must've hidden there. I'd set off the alarm, of course. The whole garrison turned out, just like they was drilled to do."

"But this man got the . . . dingus . . . flying? And off the platform?"

"Yes," says the platform director, mopping his brow again and obviously thinking of his future . . . or lack of it. "But just for a minute. We saw him on radar and then we saw him with our night goggles. That . . . rug . . . could fly, all right, but when we opened up on it, it come swinging back around toward the platform—"

"How high was it then, Captain Powl?"

"High?" The director furrows his sweaty brow. "I guess about twenty-five, thirty meters above the water then. About level with our main deck. He was comin' right at us, Father Captain. Like he was going to bomb the platform from a flyin' rug. Of course, in a way, he did . . . I mean the charges he'd planted went off right then. Scared the shit out of me . . . excuse me, Father."

"Go on," says de Soya. He looks at Gregorius where the big man is standing at parade rest behind the director. From the expression on the sergeant's face, it appears that he would be happy to garrote the sweating captain in a second.

"Well, it was quite an explosion, sir. Fire-control teams started running toward the blast, but Sea Lancer Ament and some of the other sentries and I stayed at our post there at the north catwalk. . . ."

"Very commendable," mutters de Soya, the irony audible in his voice. "Go on."

"Well, Father Captain, there's not much more," the sweating man says lamely.

"You gave the order to fire at the flying man?"

"Yes . . . yes, sir."

"And all of the sentries fired at once . . . upon your order?"

"Yeah," says the director, his eyes glazed with the effort to remember. "I think they all fired. There were six of them there besides Ament 'n' me."

"And you also fired?" pressed de Soya.

"Well, yeah . . . the station was under attack. The flight deck was a burning mess. And this terrorist was flyin' at us, carrying God knows what."

De Soya nods as if unconvinced. "Did you see anything or anyone on the flying mat other than the one man?"

"Well, no," says Powl. "But it was dark."

De Soya looks out the window at the rising moons. Brilliant orange light floods through the panes. "Were the moons up that night, Captain?"

Powl licks his lips again as if tempted to lie. He knows that de Soya and his men have interviewed Sea Lancer Ament and the others, and de Soya knows he knows. "They'd just risen," he mumbles.

"So the amount of light was comparable to this?" says de Soya.

"Yeah."

"Did you see anyone or anything else on that flying device, Captain? A package? A backpack? Anything that might be construed to be a bomb?"

"No," says Powl, anger moving under the surface of his fear now, "but it only took a handful of plastique to blow up two of our patrol skimmers and three thopters, Father Captain."

"Very true," says de Soya. Pacing to the brilliantly lit window, he says, "Your seven sentries, Sea Lancer Ament included—were they all carrying flechette guns, Captain?"

"Yes."

"And you yourself carried a flechette pistol. Is that right?"

"Yes."

"And did all of these flechette charges strike the suspect?"

Powl hesitates, then shrugs. "I think most of them did."

"And did you see the result?" de Soya asks softly.

"It shredded the bastard . . . sir," says Powl, anger winning over fear for the time being. "I saw bits of him fly apart like gull shit hitting a fan . . . sir. Then he dropped . . . naw, he flew backward off that stupid carpet like someone being yanked by a cable. Fell into the sea right next to pylon L-3. Rainbow sharks, they came up and started feeding within ten seconds."

"So you did not recover the body?" says de Soya.

Powl looks up with defiance in his eyes. "Oh, no . . . we recovered it, Father Captain. I had Ament and Kilmer sweep up what was left with boat hooks, gaffes, and a hand net. That was after we'd put the fire out and I'd made sure there was no further danger to the platform." Captain Powl was beginning to sound confident of his own correctness.

De Soya nods. "And where is that body now, Captain?"

The director steeples his pudgy fingers. They are shaking only slightly. "We buried it. At sea . . . of course. Off the south dock that next morning. Brought up a whole school of rainbow sharks, and we shot some for dinner."

"But you are satisfied that the body was that of the suspect you had put under arrest earlier?"

Powl's tiny eyes become even smaller as he squints at de Soya. "Yeah . . . what was left of him. Just a poacher. This kind of shit happens all the time out here on the big violet, Father Captain."

"And do poachers fly ancient EM-flying carpets out here all the time on the big violet, Captain Powl?"

The director's face freezes. "Is that what that dingus was?"

"You did not mention the carpet in your report, Captain."

Powl shrugs. "It didn't seem important."

De Soya nods. "And you say now that the . . . dingus . . . just kept going? That it overflew the deck and catwalk and disappeared out at sea? Empty?"

"Yes," says Captain Powl, pulling himself erect in the chair and straightening his wilted uniform.

De Soya whirls around. "Sea Lancer Ament says otherwise, Captain. Lancer Ament says that the carpet was recovered, that it was deactivated, and that it was last seen in your custody. Is this true?"

"No," says the director, looking from de Soya to Gregorius to Sproul to Kee to Rettig and then back to de Soya. "No, I never saw it after it flew past us. Ament's a fucking liar."

De Soya nods to Sergeant Gregorius. To Powl he says, "Such an ancient artifact, in working order, would be worth quite a bit of money, even on Mare Infinitus, would it not, Captain?"

"I don't know," manages Powl, who is watching Gregorius. The sergeant has walked over to the director's private cabinet. It is made of heavy steel and it is locked. "I didn't even know what the damned thing was," adds Powl.

De Soya is standing at the window now. The largest moon fills the entire eastern sky. The farcaster arch is quite visible, silhouetted against the moon. "It is called a hawking mat," he says softly, almost in a whisper. "In a place called the Valley of the Time Tombs, it would have made just the right sort of radar signature." He nods at Sergeant Gregorius.

The Swiss Guard noncom smashes open the steel cabinet with one blow of his gauntleted hand. Reaching in, he brushes aside boxes, papers, stacks of currency, and comes out with a rug, carefully folded. He carries it over to the director's desk.

"Arrest this man and get him out of my sight," Father Captain de Soya says softly. Lieutenant Sproul and Corporal Kee lead the protesting director from the office.

De Soya and Gregorius unroll the hawking mat on the long desktop. The carpet's ancient flight threads still glow gold in the moonlight. De Soya touches the forward edge of the artifact, feeling the cuts and torn places there where flechettes have ripped the fabric. There is blood everywhere, obscuring the ornate designs, dulling the glow of the threads of superconducting monofilament. Shreds of what might be human flesh are caught in the short tassels in the back of the carpet.

De Soya looks up at Gregorius. "Have you ever read the long poem called the *Cantos,* Sergeant?"

"The *Cantos,* sir? No . . . I'm not much for reading. Besides, ain't that on the list of forbidden books, sir?"

"I believe it is, Sergeant," says Father Captain de Soya. He moves away from the bloodied hawking mat and looks out at the rising moons and the silhouetted arch. *This is a piece of the puzzle,* he is thinking. *And when the puzzle is complete, I will have you, child.*

"I believe it is on the forbidden list, Sergeant," he says again. He turns quickly and heads for the door, gesturing for Rettig to roll the hawking mat and bring it along. "Come," he says, putting more energy in his voice than he has had for weeks. "We have work to do."

33

Y MEMORY OF THE TWENTY MINUTES or so I spent in that large, bright mess hall is very much like those bad dreams we all have sooner or later: you know the ones I mean, where we find ourselves in some place out of our past but cannot remember our reason for being there or the names of the people around us. When the lieutenant and his two troopers walked me into the mess hall, everything in the room was tinged with that nightmare displacement of the formerly familiar. I say familiar because I had spent a good part of my twenty-seven years in hunting camps and military mess halls, casino bars and the galleys of old barges. I was familiar with the company of men: too familiar, I might have said then, for the elements I sensed in this room—bluster, braggadocio, and the sweat-scented ointment of city-nervous men in the throes of adventure-bound male bonding—had long since grown tiresome to me. But now that familiarity was offset by the strangeness—the smattering of dialect-laden speech I could hear, the subtle differences in clothing, the suicidal smell of cigarettes, and the knowledge that I would give myself away almost immediately if there was any need to deal with their currency, culture, or conversation.

There was a tall coffee urn on the farthest table—I had never been in a mess hall without one—and I ambled over there, trying to look casual as I did so, found a cup that was relatively clean, and poured myself some coffee. All the while I was watching the lieutenant and his two men watch me. When they seemed comfortable that I belonged there, they turned and went out. I sipped terrible coffee, noted idly that my hand holding the cup was not shaking despite the hurricane of emotions inside me, and tried to decide what to do next.

Amazingly, I still had my weapons—sheath knife and pistol—and my radio. With the radio I could detonate the plastique at any time and make a run for the hawking mat during the confusion. Now that I had seen the Pax sentinels, I knew that there would have to be some sort of diversion if the raft was going to get by this platform without being seen. I walked to the window; it faced the direction we had been thinking of as north, but I could see the "eastern" sky aglow with imminent moonrise. The farcaster arch was visible to the naked eye. I tried the window, but it was either locked in some form I could not see or nailed in place. There was a corrugated steel roof of another module just a meter or so below the window level, but there seemed no way I could get to it from here.

"Who you with, son?"

I turned quickly. Five men had come over from the nearest group, and it was the shortest and fattest who was speaking to me. The man wore outdoor garb: checked flannel shirt, canvas trousers, canvas vest not too dissimilar from mine, and a fish-scaling knife on his belt. I realized then that the Pax troopers might have seen the tip of my holster poking out from under my vest but assumed it to be one of these knife sheaths.

This man had also spoken in dialect, but one quite different from the Pax guards outside. The fishermen, I remembered, were probably off-worlders, so my strange accent should not be overly suspicious.

"Klingman," I said, taking another sip of the sludge-tasting coffee. The one word had worked on the Pax troopers.

It did not work on these men. They looked at each other a moment, and then the fat one spoke again. "We came in with the Klingman party, boy. All the way from St. Thérèse. You weren't on the hydrofoil. What's your game?"

I grinned. "No game," I said. "I was supposed to be with the group —missed it in St. Thérèse—came on down with the Otters."

I still hadn't got it right. The five men spoke among themselves. I heard the word "poachers" several times. Two of the men left and went out the door. The fat man poked a fat finger at me. "I was sittin' over there with the Otter guide. He never seen you before either. You stay right there, son."

That was the one thing I was *not* going to do. Setting my cup on the table, I said, "No, *you* wait here. I'm going to go get the lieutenant and have a few things straightened out. Don't move."

This seemed to befuddle the fat man, and he stayed in his place as I crossed the now-silent mess hall, opened the door, and stepped out onto the catwalk.

There was nowhere to go. To my right, the two Pax troopers with flechette guns had snapped to attention at the railing. On my left, the thin lieutenant I'd bumped into earlier was hurrying down the walkway with the two civilians and what looked to be a pudgy Pax captain in tow.

"Damn," I said aloud. Subvocalizing, I said, "Kiddo, I'm in trouble here. They may have me. I'll leave the external mike open so you can hear. Head straight for the portal. Don't answer!" The last thing I needed during this conversation was a tiny voice chirping out of my hearplug.

"Hey!" I said, stepping forward toward the captain and raising my hands as if I was going to shake his. "You're just the man I was looking for."

"That's him," cried one of the two fishermen. "He didn't come in with us or the Otter group. It's one of them crossdamned poachers you been tellin' us about!"

"Cuff him," said the captain to the lieutenant, and before I could do anything clever, the troopers had grabbed me from behind and the thin officer had slapped handcuffs on me. They were the old-fashioned metal kind, but they worked quite well—locking my wrists in front of me and all but cutting off circulation.

I realized at that instant that I would never make it as a spy. Everything about my foray to the platform had been a disaster. The Pax troops were being sloppy—they were still crowding against me when they should have kept their distance and held their weapons on me while they searched me, and *then* cuffed me when I was disarmed—but the search would come in a few seconds.

I decided not to give them those few seconds. Bringing my cuffed hands up quickly, I grabbed the chubby little captain by the front of his shirt and threw him back into the two civilians. There was a moment of shouting and pushing during which I turned quickly, kicked the first gun-carrying trooper in the balls as hard as I could, and grabbed the second one by the weapon still slung over his shoulder. The trooper shouted and seized the weapon with both hands just as I grabbed the sling and pulled it down and to the right with all of my strength. The trooper went with the weapon, hit the wall with his bare head, and sat down very quickly. The first trooper, the one I'd kicked and who was still kneeling and holding his groin with one hand, reached up with his free hand and ripped my sweater all the way down the front, tearing my night goggles off my neck as he did so. I kicked him in the throat and he went all the way down.

The lieutenant had removed his flechette pistol by this time, realized that he could not shoot me without killing the two troopers behind me, and struck me on the head with the butt of the thing.

Flechette pistols are not that heavy or substantial. This one made me see sparks behind my eyes for a moment and opened my scalp. It also made me angry.

I turned around and hit the lieutenant in the face with my fist. He pivoted back over the waist-high railing, arms flailing, and kept on going. Everyone froze for a second as the man screamed all the way down to the water, twenty-five meters below.

I should say that everyone but I froze, for even while the lieutenant's boot soles were still visible going over the railing, I had turned, leaped over the trooper on the floor, slammed open the screen door, and run into the mess hall. Men were milling around, most of them making toward the door and windows on this side to see what the commotion was, but they made way for me as I dodged through them like a deep brooder on a forty-three-man squamish team herding the goat in for the goal.

Behind me, I heard the door slamming open again and the captain or one of the troopers shouting, "Down! Out of the way! Look out!"

I could feel my shoulder blades hunching again at the thought of those thousands of flechette darts flying my way, but I did not slow as I leaped to a tabletop, covered my face with my still-handcuffed wrists, and hit the window flying, my right shoulder taking the brunt of the impact.

Even while leaping, it crossed my mind that all it would take was for the window to be Perspex or smart glass and my misadventure would end in perfect farce—me bouncing back into the mess hall to be shot or captured at the troopers' leisure. It would make sense for a platform way out here to use unbreakable material instead of glass. But it had *felt* like glass when I had set my fingers against it a few minutes earlier.

It was glass.

I hit the corrugated steel of the roof and just kept rolling downhill, shards of glass flying around me and crunching beneath me. I'd brought part of the window's muntin with me—broken wood and glass was stuck in my vest and tattered sweater—but I didn't slow to disentangle myself. At the end of the roof I had a choice: instinct made me want to keep rolling over the edge, get out of sight before those gunmen opened up behind me, and hope that there was another catwalk below; logic made me want to stop and check it out before rolling over; memory suggested that there were no catwalks along this north edge of the platform.

I compromised by rolling off the edge of the roof but grabbing the overhang as I did so, peering down between my swinging boots as my fingers slipped. There was no deck or platform down there, just twenty meters of air between my boots and the violet waves. The moons were rising and the sea was coming alive with light.

I levered myself up far enough to look back at the window I'd broken through, saw the gunmen milling there, and dropped my head out of sight just as one of them fired. The flechette cloud went slightly high, missing my straining fingers by two or three centimeters, and I flinched as I listened to the angry-bee hum of thousands of steel needles flying past. There was no deck below me, but I could see a pipe running horizontally along the side of the module. It was six or eight centimeters across. There was the narrowest of gaps between the inside of the pipe and the wall of the module, perhaps wide enough for my fingers to find a grip—if the pipe did not break under my weight, if the shock did not dislocate my shoulders, if my handcuffed hands did not fail, if . . . I did not think: I dropped. My forearms and the steel of my handcuffs slammed into the pipe, almost flipping me backward, but my fingers were ready to grip and they did so, sliding upward along the inside of the pipe but then holding my weight.

The second burst of flechette fire above me blew the roof overhang to shreds and perforated the outer wall in a hundred places. Splinters and steel shards tumbled past in the moonlight as the men shouted and cursed up there. I heard footsteps on the roof.

I was shuffling and swinging to my left as quickly as I could. There was a deck protruding below the corner of the module down there, at least three meters below me and four or five meters to the east. Progress was maddeningly slow. My shoulders were shrieking with discomfort, my fingers were becoming numb from lack of circulation. I could feel glass shards in my hair and scalp, and blood was running into my eyes. The men above me were going to get to the edge of the roof before I could get to a point above the platform.

Suddenly there was cursing and shouting, and a section of the roof caved in where I had been hanging. Evidently their flechette fire had undermined that section of roofing, and now their weight was causing it to collapse. I could hear them shoving back, cursing, and finding alternate routes to the edge.

This delay only gave me an extra eight to ten seconds, but it was enough to allow me to shuffle my hands to the end of the pipe, swing my body once, twice, release on the third swing, and fall heavily to the platform below, rolling up against the east railing hard enough to knock the wind out of me.

I knew that I could not lie there and get my wind back. I moved quickly, rolling toward the darker section of deck under the module. At least two flechette guns fired—one missing and roiling the waters fifteen meters below, the other pounding the end of the deck like a hundred nail guns firing at once. I rolled to my feet and ran, ducking low beams and trying to see through the maze of shadows down there. Footsteps pounded somewhere above me. They had the advantage of knowing the layout of these decks and stairways; but only I knew where I was headed.

I was headed to the easternmost and lowest deck, where I had left the mat, but this maintenance deck opened onto a long catwalk that ran north and south. When I had cut far enough under the main platform that I thought I would be even with the east deck, I swung up onto a support beam—it was about six centimeters wide—and, handcuffed arms flailing left and then right for balance, crossed an open section to the next vertical post. I did this again, shifting north and south when the beams ended, but always finding another beam running east.

Trapdoors were flying open and footsteps pounded on the catwalks beneath the main deck, but I reached the eastern deck first. I jumped to it, found the mat where I had lashed it to the post, unrolled it, tapped the flight threads, and was up and flying over the railing just as a trapdoor opened above the long flight of stairs coming down to the deck. I was lying prone on the carpet, trying to make the least silhouette I could against moons or glowing waves, tapping flight threads clumsily because of the handcuffs.

My instinct was to fly due north, but I realized that this would be a mistake. The flechette guns would be accurate only to sixty or seventy meters out, but someone up there must have a plasma rifle or the equivalent. All the attention was focused on the east end of the platform now. My best chance was to head west or south.

I banked left, swooped beneath the support beams there, and skipped just above the waves, heading west under the protective edge of the platform. Only one deck protruded out this far—the one I'd dropped onto—and I could see that it was empty at the north end. Not just empty, I realized, but shot to bits from the flechette fire and probably too dangerous to stand on. I flew under it and continued west. Boots clattered on the upper catwalks, but anyone catching a glimpse of me would have a hell of a rough time lining up a shot because of the dozens of pylons and cross girders here.

I swooped out from under the platform into the shadow of it—the moons were higher now—and stayed just millimeters above the wave tops, staying low, trying to keep the long ocean swell between me and the western end of the platform. I was fifty or sixty meters out and almost ready to breathe a sigh of relief when I heard the splashing and coughing a few meters to my right, just beyond the next swell.

I knew instantly what it was, *who* it was—the lieutenant I had slugged and sent sprawling over the railing. My impulse was to keep on flying. The platform behind me was a mass of confusion at this point—men shouting, others shooting off the north side, more men screaming at the east end where I had slipped away—but it seemed that no one had seen me out here. This man had struck me in the head with his flechette pistol and would happily have killed me if his pals hadn't been in the way. The fact that the current had pulled him out here away from the platform was his bad luck; there was nothing I could do about it.

I can drop him off at the base of the platform—perhaps on one of the support beams. I got away once this way; I can do it again. The man was doing his job. He does not deserve to die for it.

It is fair to say that I hated my conscience at moments like that—not that I had *had* many moments like that.

I stopped the hawking mat just above the waves. I was still lying on my belly, my head and shoulders hunched low so that the shouting men on the platform would not spot me. Now I leaned out and to the right to see if I could spot the source of the coughing and splashing.

I saw the fish first. They had dorsals like holos I'd seen of Old Earth sharks, or the cannibal saberbacks of Hyperion's South Sea, but two shining dorsal fins rather than one. I could see the fish clearly in the moonlight: they seemed to glitter a dozen bright colors, from the twin dorsal fins to their long bellies. They were about three meters long, they moved like predators with powerful surges of their tails, and their teeth were very white.

Following one of these killers over the swell toward the coughing sounds, I saw the lieutenant. He was splashing and struggling to keep his head above water, all the while pivoting, trying to keep the multicolored killer fish at bay. One of the twin-dorsaled things would lunge toward him through the violet water, and the lieutenant would kick at it, trying to strike its head or fin with his boot. The fish would snap and then wheel away. Others were circling closer. The Pax officer was obviously exhausted.

"Damn," I whispered. There was no way I could leave him there.

The first thing I did was tap the code that killed the deflection field—that low-scale containment field designed to keep the wind out at high speeds and the hawking-mat occupants, especially children, from tumbling off at any speed. If I was going to be pulling this waterlogged man aboard, I did not want to have to struggle against the EM field. Then I slid the mat down the long swell toward him, bringing it to a halt right where he had been.

He was no longer there. The man had slipped under. I considered diving for him, then saw the pale forms of his arms struggling just under the waves. The shark-things were circling closer, but not attacking at the moment. Perhaps the shadow of the hawking mat disconcerted them.

I reached down with both manacled hands, found his right wrist, and pulled him up. His weight almost tumbled me off the mat, but I leaned back, found my balance, and tugged him up far enough that I could grab the back of his pants and haul him—dripping, coughing water—onto the hawking mat.

The lieutenant was pale and cold, shaking all over, but after an initial bout of retching up seawater, he seemed to be breathing all right. I was glad for that: I was not sure my generosity would go so far as administering mouth-to-mouth resuscitation. Making sure that he was sprawled on the mat far enough that one of the passing dorsal-fish wouldn't leap up and take his legs off, I turned my attention back to the controls. I set a course back to the platform, rising slightly as we went. Fumbling in my vest, I found the com unit and keyed in the code needed to detonate the plastique I had planted on the skimmer and thopter decks. We would approach the platform from the south, where I could make sure those decks were clear of people: I would then transmit the detonate code with a simple push of the button and, in the ensuing confusion, swing back around and come in from the west, dropping the lieutenant off at the first dry place I could find under there.

I turned to see if the man was still breathing and had an instant's glimpse of the Pax officer on one knee, something gleaming in his hand . . .

. . . he stabbed me in the heart.

Or it would have been directly through my heart, if I had not twisted in the split second it took for the knife to cut through my vest, sweater, and flesh. As it was, the short blade ripped into my side and grated against a rib. I did not feel pain at the moment so much as a shock—a literal electric shock. I gasped and grabbed for his wrist. The blade came in fast, higher this time, and my hands—slippery with seawater and my own blood, slipped back along his wrist. The best I could do was pull downward, using the band of metal connecting the manacles on my wrists to pull his arm down as he stabbed me again, a downward thrust this time that would have come in over the same rib and punctured my heart had it not been for my pull on his arm slowing the movement and the com unit in my vest pocket deflecting the blade. Even so, I felt the blade rip at the flesh of my side again and I staggered back, trying to get my footing on the rising hawking mat.

I was dimly aware of the explosions at my back: the knife blade must have struck the transmit button. I did not turn to look as I found my balance, feet apart. The mat continued to rise—we were eight or ten meters above the ocean now and still climbing.

The lieutenant had also leaped to his feet, falling into the natural crouch of a born knife fighter. I have always hated edged weapons. I have skinned animals and gutted innumerable fish. Even when I was in the Guard, I could not understand how humans could do that to humans at close range. I had a knife on my belt somewhere, but I knew that I was no match for this man. My only hope was to get the automatic out of its holster, but it was a difficult movement—the pistol was on my left hip, turned backward so that I could draw across my body, but now I had to use both hands, fumble aside the hanging vest, pull up the flap over the weapon, pull it out, aim it . . .

He slashed across my body, left to right. I jumped back to the very front of the hawking mat, but too late—the sharp little blade cut through flesh and muscle along the back of my right arm as I was reaching across my body for the pistol. I felt the pain of this cut and cried out. The lieutenant smiled, his teeth slick with seawater. Still crouching, knowing that I had nowhere to go, he took a half step forward and swung the knife upward in an eviscerating arc that had to end in my belly.

I had been turning to my right when he slashed me before, now I kept the motion going and pushed off from the climbing hawking mat in a clean dive, my manacled hands directly in front of me as I broke the water ten meters below. The ocean was salty and dark. I had not taken much of a breath before hitting the water, and for a terrible moment I literally did not know which way was up. Then I saw the glow of the three moons and kicked in that direction. My head cleared the surface in time to see the lieutenant still standing aboard the rising mat, now thirty meters closer to the platform and perhaps twenty-five meters high and rising. He was crouched and looking in my direction as if waiting for me to return so that he could finish the fight.

I would not be returning, but I did want to finish the fight. Fumbling underwater for the automatic, I unsnapped the holster, pulled the heavy weapon out, and tried to float on my back so that I could aim the damned thing. My target was climbing and disappearing, but he was still silhouetted against the impossible moon as I thumbed back the hammer and steadied my arms.

The lieutenant had just given up on me and turned toward the commotion on the platform when the men there fired. They beat me to it by a second or two. I doubt if I would have hit him at that distance. There was no way they could have missed.

At least three flechette clusters struck him at once, knocking him back off the hawking mat like a load of laundry someone had tossed through the air. I literally saw moonlight through his riddled body as it tumbled down to the wave tops. A second later one of the colored shark-things bruised past me, actually bashing my shoulder aside in its eagerness to get to the mass of bleeding bait that had been the Pax lieutenant.

I floated there a second, watching the hawking mat until someone on the platform grabbed it. I had childishly hoped that the carpet would swoop around and come back to me, lift me out of the sea, and carry me back to the raft a klick or two north of here now. I had grown fond of the hawking mat—fond of being part of the myth and legend it represented—and watching it fly away from me forever like that made me sick to my stomach.

I was sick to my stomach. Between the wounds and the salt water I'd ingested—not to mention the effect of salt water in the wounds—the nausea was real. I kept floating there in the salty sea, kicking to keep my head and shoulders above water, the heavy automatic held in my two hands.

If I was going to swim, I had to shoot the handcuffs apart. But how could I do that? The steel band between the manacles was only half the thickness of my wrist; no matter how I contorted, I could not get the muzzle of the weapon around where I could sever the band with a bullet.

Meanwhile, the dorsal fins were circling away from their feeding on the lieutenant. I knew that I was bleeding badly. I could feel the heavier wetness at my side and on the back of my arm, where the salty blood was spilling into the salty sea. If those things were anything like the saberbacks or sharks, they could sense blood for kilometers. My only hope was to kick toward the platform, use the pistol on the first fins to come near me, and hope I could reach one of the pylons and pull myself out or yell for help. That was my only hope.

I leaned back, kicked, rolled onto my stomach, and started swimming north, toward the open ocean. I had been on the platform once this long day. That was enough.

34

I HAD NEVER BEFORE tried swimming with my hands tied in front of me. It is my earnest hope that I never have to try it again. Only the strong salinity of this world's ocean kept me afloat as I kicked, floated, flailed, and thrashed my way north. I had no real hope of reaching the raft; the current began running strongest at least a klick north of the platform, and our plan had been to keep the raft as far away from the structure as we could without losing the river within the sea.

It was only a few minutes before the colored sharks began circling again. Their shimmering, electric colors were visible beneath the waves, and when one moved in for the attack, I stopped trying to swim, floated, and kicked at its head in precisely the same way as I had seen the late lieutenant hold the things at bay. It seemed to work. The fish were undoubtedly deadly, but they were stupid—they attacked one at a time, as if there were some unseen pecking order among them—and I kicked them in the snout one at a time. But the process was exhausting. I had started to remove my boots just before the first color-shark attack—the heavy leather was dragging me down—but the thought of kicking bare feet at those fanged, bullet-shaped heads made me keep the boots on as long as I could. I also soon decided that I could not swim with the pistol in my hands. The saberback things were diving during their actual lunges at me, coming up from beneath seemed to be their preferred mode of attack, and I doubted whether a bullet from the old slug-thrower would do any good through a meter or two of water. Eventually I tucked the pistol back into its holster, although I soon wished I had dropped it altogether. Floating, swiveling to keep twin dorsal fins in view, I finally pulled off my boots and let them slip away into the depths. When the next shark attacked, I kicked harder, feeling the sandpaper roughness of the skin above its tiny brain. It snapped at my bare feet but moved away and began circling again.

This is the way I swam north, pausing, floating, kicking, cursing, swimming a few meters, pausing again to twist in circles waiting for the next attack. If it had not been for the combination of the brilliant moons and the saberback things' glowing skin, one of them would have pulled me down long before. As it was, I soon reached the point where I was too exhausted to try to swim any longer—all I could do was float on my back, gasp for air, and get my feet between those white teeth and my legs every time I saw the colors flashing my way.

The knife wounds were beginning to hurt in earnest now. I could feel the deeper slash along my ribs as a terrible burning combined with a stickiness down the length of my side. I was sure that I was bleeding into the water, and once, when the dorsal fins were circling far enough out that I could ignore them for a moment, I lowered my hands to my side and then pulled them out of the water. They were red—much redder than the violet sea glowing in the light of the great moon that had now cleared the horizon. I felt the weakness growing in me and realized that I was bleeding to death. The water was becoming warmer, as if my blood were heating it to a comfortable temperature, and the temptation to close my eyes and move deeper into that warmth grew stronger each minute.

I admit that each time the ocean swell bore me up, I kept looking over my shoulder for some sign of the raft—for some miracle from the north. I saw nothing there. Part of me was pleased at this—the raft had probably transited the farcaster portal by now. It had not been intercepted. I had seen no skimmers airborne, no thopters, and the platform was only a diminishing blaze to the south. I realized that my best hope was to be picked up by a searching thopter now that the raft was safely gone, but even the thought of such rescue did not cheer me. I had been to the platform once this day.

Floating on my back, twisting my head and neck to keep the colored dorsals in view, I kicked my way north, rising with each great movement of the violet sea, dropping into wide troughs as the ocean seemed to breathe in. I rotated to my stomach and tried kicking more strongly, my handcuffed fists straight ahead of me, but I was too exhausted to keep my head above water that way. My right arm seemed to be bleeding more fiercely now and seemed three times as heavy as the left. I guessed that the lieutenant's blade had severed tendons there.

Finally I had to give up swimming and concentrate on floating, my feet kicking to keep me up, my head and shoulders above water, my fists clenched in front of my face. The saberback things seemed to sense my weakness; they took turns swimming at me, their great mouths open to feed. Each time I pulled my legs up and kicked straight out, trying to strike their snouts or brainpans with my heels without having my feet bitten off. Their rough skin had abraded the flesh of my heels and soles to the point that I was adding more blood to the sphere that must surround me. It made the dorsal-things wilder. Their attacks came closer together as I grew too tired to pull my legs up each time. One of the long fish ripped my right pant leg off from the knee to ankle, pulling a layer of skin with it as it moved away with a triumphant stroke of its tail.

Part of my tired mind had been pondering theology during all this—not praying, but wondering about a Cosmic God who allowed Its creatures to torture each other like this. How many hominids, mammals, and trillions of other creatures had spent their last minutes in mortal fear such as this, their hearts pounding, their adrenaline coursing through them and exhausting them more quickly, their small minds racing in the hopeless quest of escape? How could any God describe Him- or Herself as a God of Mercy and fill the universe with fanged things such as this? I remembered Grandam telling me about an early Old Earth scientist, one Charles Darwin, who had come up with one of the early theories of evolution or gravitation or somesuch, and how—although raised a devout Christian even before the reward of the cruciform—he had become an atheist while studying a terrestrial wasp that paralyzed some large species of spider, planted its embryo, and let the spider recover and go about its business until it was time for the hatched wasp larvae to burrow its way out of the living spider's abdomen.

I shook water out of my eyes and kicked at two of the dorsal fins rushing at me. I missed the head but struck one of the sensitive fins. Only by pulling my legs up into a ball did I avoid that snapping maw. Losing my buoyancy for a moment, I went a meter or more under the next wave, swallowed saltwater, and came up gasping and blind. More fins circled closer. Swallowing water again, I struggled with my numb hands underwater and came up with the pistol, almost dropping it before propping it against my chin. I realized that it would be easier just to leave the muzzle under my chin and pull the trigger than to try to use it against these sea killers. Well, there were quite a few slugs left in the thing—I had not used it during all of the excitement of the last couple of hours—so it would remain an option.

Swiveling, watching the closest dorsal move even closer, I remembered a story Grandam had me read when I was a boy. It was also an ancient classic—a thing by Stephen Crane called "The Open Boat"—and it was about several men who had survived the sinking of their ship and days at sea without water, only to be stuck a few hundred meters from land by surf too high to cross without capsizing. One of the men in the boat—I could not remember which character—had moved through all of the circles of theological supposition: praying, believing that God was a merciful Deity who sat up nights worrying about him, then believing that God was a cruel bastard, and finally deciding that no one was listening. I realized now that I had not understood that story, despite Grandam's Socratic questions and careful guidance. I thought that I remembered the weight of epiphany that had fallen on that character as he realized they would have to swim for it and that not all of them could survive. He had wanted Nature—for this is how he now thought of the universe—to be a huge glass building, just so that he could cast stones at it. But even that, he realized, would be useless.

The universe is indifferent to our fates. This was the crushing burden that the character took with him as he struggled through the surf toward survival or extinction. The universe just does not give a shit.

I realized that I was laughing and weeping at the same time, shouting curses and invitations to the saberback things that were only two or three meters out. I leveled the pistol and fired at the closest fin. Amazingly, the soaked slug-thrower fired, the noise that had been so loud on the raft now seemed to be swallowed by the waves and immensity of the sea. The fish dived out of sight. Two more lunged at me. I shot at one, kicked at the other, just as something struck me hard on the neck from behind.

I was not so lost in theology and philosophizing that I was ready to die. I swiveled quickly, not knowing how badly I had been bitten but determined to shoot the goddamn thing in the mouth if I had to. I had the heavy pistol cocked and aimed before I saw the girl's face there half a meter from my own. Her hair was plastered to her skull and her dark eyes were bright in the moonlight.

"Raul!" She must have been calling my name before, but I had not heard it over the gunshot and the rushing in my ears.

I blinked saltwater away. This could not be real. Oh, Jesus, why should she be out here, away from the raft?

"Raul!" Aenea called again. "Float on your back. Use the gun to keep those things away. I'll pull you in."

I shook my head. I did not understand. Why would she leave the powerful android on the raft and come after me by herself? How could . . .

A. Bettik's blue scalp became visible over the next large swell. The android was swimming strongly with both arms, the long machete clamped in his white teeth. I confess that I laughed through my tears. He looked like a cheap holo's version of a pirate.

"Float on your back!" shouted the girl again.

I turned on my back, too tired to kick as a shark-thing lunged at my legs. I shot between my feet at it, striking it square between its black, lifeless eyes. The two fins disappeared beneath the wave.

Aenea set one arm around my neck, her left hand under my right arm so she was not choking me, and began swimming strongly up the next huge swell. A. Bettik swam alongside, paddling with one arm now as he wielded the sharp machete with another. I saw him slice into the water and watched two dorsal fins shudder and swerve to the right.

"What are you . . . ," I began, choking and coughing.

"Save your breath," gasped the girl, pulling me down into the next trough and up the violet wall ahead of us. "We have a long way to go."

"The pistol," I said, trying to hand it to her. I felt the darkness closing on my vision like a narrowing tunnel and did not want to lose the weapon. Too late—I felt it drop away into the sea. "Sorry," I managed before the tunnel closed completely.

My last conscious thought was an inventory of what I had lost on my first solo expedition: the treasured hawking mat, my night goggles, the antique automatic pistol, my boots, probably the com unit, and quite possibly my life and the lives of my friends. Total darkness cut off the end of this cynical speculation.

I WAS VAGUELY AWARE of their lifting me onto the raft. The handcuffs were gone, cut away. The girl was breathing into my mouth, pumping water out of my lungs with pressure against my chest. A. Bettik knelt next to us, pulling strongly on a heavy line.

After retching water for several minutes, I said, "The raft . . . how? . . . it should have been to the portal by now . . . I don't . . ."

Aenea pushed my head back against a pack and cut away rags of my shirt and right trouser leg with a short knife. "A. Bettik rigged a sort of sea anchor using the microtent and the climbing rope," she said. "It's dragging behind, slowing us down but keeping us on course. It gave us time to find you."

"How . . ." I began, then started coughing salt water again.

"Hush," said the girl, ripping the last of my shirt away. "I want to see how badly you're hurt."

I winced as her strong hands touched the great gash in my side. Her fingers found the deep cut on my upper arm, ran down my side to where the fish had taken the skin down my thigh and calf. "Ah, Raul," she said sadly. "I let you out of my sight for an hour or two and look what you do to yourself."

The weakness was overwhelming me again, the darkness returning. I knew that I had lost too much blood. I was very cold. "I'm sorry," I whispered.

"Quiet." She tore open the larger of our medpaks with a loud ripping noise. "Hush."

"No," I insisted. "I screwed up. I was supposed to be your protector . . . guard *you*. Sorry—" I cried out as she poured antiseptic sulfa solution directly into the wound on my side. I had seen men weep at this on the battlefield. Now I was one of them.

If it had been my modern medpak that the girl had opened, I am sure I would have died minutes if not seconds later. But it was the larger pak—the ancient FORCE-issue medpak we'd taken from the ship. My first thought was that all of the medicines and instruments would be useless after so long a time, but then I saw the blinking lights on the surface of the pak she had laid on my chest. Some were green, more were yellow, a few were red. I knew that this was not good.

"Lie back," whispered Aenea, and tore open a sterile suture pak. She laid the clear bag against my side and the millipede suture within came to life and crawled to my wound. The sensation was not pleasant as the tailored life-form crawled *into* the ragged walls of my wound, secreted its antibiotic and cleansing secretions, then drew its sharp millipede legs together in a tight suture. I cried out again . . . then again a moment later as she applied another millipede suture to my arm.

"We need more plasma cartridges," she said to A. Bettik as she fed two of the small cylinders into the pak injection system. I felt the burn on my thigh as the plasma entered my system.

"Those four are all that we have," said the android. He was busy working on me now, setting an osmosis mask in place over my face. Pure oxygen began to flow into my lungs.

"Damn," said the girl, injecting the last of the plasma cartridges. "He's lost too much blood. He's going into deep shock."

I wanted to argue with them, explain that my shaking and shivering was just a result of the cold air, that I felt much better, but the osmosis mask pressed everywhere against my mouth, eyes, nose, and did not allow me to speak. For a moment I hallucinated that we were back in the ship and the crash field was holding me secure again. I think that all the salt water on my face at that moment was not from the sea.

Then I saw the ultramorph injector in the girl's hands and I began to struggle. I did not want to be knocked out: if I was going to die, I wanted to be awake when it happened.

Aenea pushed me back against the backpack. She understood what I was trying to say. "I *want* you out, Raul," she said softly. "You're going into shock. We need to get your vital signs stabilized . . . it'll be easier if you're out." The injector hissed.

I thrashed for another few seconds, weeping tears of frustration now. After all that effort, to slip away while unconscious. Goddamn it, it wasn't fair . . . it wasn't right . . .

I AWOKE TO BRIGHT SUNLIGHT and terrible heat. For a moment I was sure that we were still on the sea of Mare Infinitus, but when I worked up enough energy to lift my head, I could see that the sun was different—larger, hotter—and the sky was a much paler shade of blue. The raft seemed to be moving along some sort of concrete canal with only a meter or two to spare on either side. I could see concrete, sun, and blue sky—nothing else.

"Lie back," said Aenea, pushing my head and shoulders back on the pack and adjusting the microtent fabric so that my face was in shade again. Obviously they had retrieved their "sea anchor."

I tried to speak, failed, licked dry lips that seemed stitched together, and finally managed, "How long have I been out?"

Aenea gave me a sip of water from my own canteen before replying. "About thirty hours."

"Thirty hours!" Even trying to shout, I could do little more than squeak.

A. Bettik came around the side of the tent and crouched in the shade with us. "Welcome back, M. Endymion."

"Where are we?"

Aenea answered. "Judging from the desert, sun, and the stars last night, it's almost certain that we're on Hebron. We seem to be traveling along some aqueduct. Right now . . . well, you should see this." She supported my shoulders so I could see over the concrete lip of the canal. Nothing but air and distant hills. "We're about fifty meters up on this section of aqueduct," she said, lowering my head to the pack again. "It's been like this for the last five or six klicks. If there's been a breach in the aqueduct . . ." She smiled ruefully. "We haven't seen anyone or anything . . . not even a vulture. We're waiting until we come into a city."

I frowned, feeling the stiffness in my side and arm as I shifted position ever so slightly. "Hebron? I thought it was . . ."

"Captured by the Ousters," finished A. Bettik. "Yes, that was our information as well. It does not matter, sir. We will seek medical care for you with the Ousters as happily . . . more happily . . . than we would with the Pax."

I looked down at the medpak now lying next to me. Filaments ran to my chest, arm, and legs. Most of the lights on the pak were blinking amber. This was not good.

"Your wounds are sealed and cleaned," said Aenea. "We gave you all the plasma the old pak had. But you need more . . . and there seems to be some sort of infection that the multispectrum antibiotics can't handle."

That explained the terrible feverish quality I felt beneath my skin.

"Perhaps some microorganism in the sea on Mare Infinitus," said A. Bettik. "The medpak cannot quite diagnose it. We will know when we get to a hospital. It is our guess that this section of the Tethys will lead to Hebron's one large city. . . ."

"New Jerusalem," I whispered.

"Yes," said the android. "Even after the Fall, it was famous for its Sinai Medical Center."

I started to shake my head but stopped when the pain and dizziness struck. "But the Ousters . . ."

Aenea moved a damp cloth across my brow. "We're going to get help for you," she said. "Ousters or no Ousters."

A thought was trying to burrow up out of my befuddled brain. I waited until it arrived. "Hebron . . . didn't have . . . I don't think it had . . ."

"You are right, sir," said A. Bettik. He tapped the small book in his hand. "According to the guide, Hebron was not part of the River Tethys and allowed only a single farcaster terminex in New Jerusalem, even during the height of the Web. Offworld visitors were not allowed to leave the capital. They treasured privacy and independence here."

I looked out at the passing aqueduct walls. Suddenly we were off the high trestle and moving between high dunes and sun-baked rocks. The heat was terrible.

"But the book must have been wrong," said Aenea, mopping my brow again. "The farcaster portal was there . . . and we're here."

"You're sure . . . it's . . . Hebron?" I whispered.

Aenea nodded. A. Bettik held up the comlog bracelet. I had forgotten about it. "Our mechanical friend here got a reliable star sighting," he said. "We are on Hebron and . . . I would guess . . . only hours away from New Jerusalem."

Pain tore through me then, and no matter how I tried to hide it, I must have writhed. Aenea brought the ultramorph injector out.

"No," I said through cracked lips.

"This is the last one for a while," she whispered. I heard the hiss and felt the blessed numbness spreading. *If there is a God,* I thought, *it's a painkiller.*

WHEN I AWOKE AGAIN, the shadows were long and we were in the shade of a low building. A. Bettik was carrying me from the raft. Each step sent pain racking through me. I made no sound.

Aenea was walking ahead. The street was wide and dusty, the buildings low—none over three stories—and made of an adobelike material. No one was in sight.

"Hello!" called the child, cupping her hands to her mouth. The two syllables echoed down the empty street.

I felt foolish being carried like a child, but A. Bettik did not seem to mind, and I knew that I could not stand if my life depended upon it.

Aenea walked back to us, saw my open eyes, and said, "This is New Jerusalem. There's no doubt. According to the guidebook, three million people lived here during the Web days, and A. Bettik says that there were at least a million still here the last he heard."

"Ousters . . . ," I managed.

Aenea nodded tersely. "The shops and buildings near the canal were empty, but they looked like they'd been lived in until a few weeks or months ago."

A. Bettik said, "According to the transmissions we monitored on Hyperion, this world was supposed to have fallen to the Ousters approximately three standard years ago. But there are signs of habitation here much more recent than that."

"The power grid's still on," said Aenea. "Food that was left out has all spoiled, but the fridge compartments are still cold. Tables are set in some of the houses, holopits humming with static, radios hissing. But no people."

"But also no signs of violence," said the android, laying me carefully in the back of a groundcar with a flat metal bed behind the cab. Aenea had set out a blanket to keep my skin away from the hot metal. The pain in my side sent spots dancing in front of my eyes.

Aenea rubbed her arms. There were goose bumps there despite the blazing heat of the evening. "But *something* terrible happened here," she said. "I can feel it."

I admit that I felt nothing but pain and fever. My thoughts were like mercury—always shifting away before I could grab them or form them into a cohesive shape.

Aenea jumped up onto the flatbed of the groundcar and crouched next to me while A. Bettik opened the door to the cab and crawled in. Amazingly, the vehicle started with a touch of the ignition plate. "I can drive this," said the android, putting the vehicle in gear.

So can I, I thought at them. *I drove one like it in Ursus. It's one of the few things in the universe I know how to operate. It may be one of the few things I can do right.*

We bumped down the main street. The pain made me cry out a few times, despite my best efforts to stay quiet. I clamped my jaws tight.

Aenea was holding my hand. Her fingers felt so cool that they almost made me shiver. I realized that my own skin was on fire.

". . . it's that damned infection," she was saying. "Otherwise you'd be recovering now. Something in that ocean."

"Or on his knife," I whispered. I closed my eyes and saw the lieutenant flying to pieces as the flechette clouds tore into him. I opened my eyes to escape the image. The buildings were taller here, ten stories at least, and they cast a deeper shade. But the heat was terrible.

". . . a friend of my mother's on the last Hyperion pilgrimage lived here for a while," she was saying. Her voice seemed to move in and out of hearing range, like a poorly tuned radio station.

"Sol Weintraub," I croaked. "The scholar in the old poet's *Cantos.*"

Aenea patted my hand. "I forget that everything Mother lived has become grist for Uncle Martin's legend mill."

We bounced over a bump. I ground my back teeth together to keep from screaming.

Aenea's grip on my hand intensified. "Yes," she said. "I wish I had met the old scholar and his daughter."

"They went ahead . . . in the . . . Sphinx," I managed. "Like . . . you . . . did."

Aenea leaned close, moistened my lips from the canteen, and nodded. "Yes. But I remember Mother's stories about Hebron and the kibbutzim here."

"Jews," I whispered, and then quit talking. It took too much energy that I needed to fight the pain.

"They fled the Second Holocaust," she said, looking ahead now as the groundcar rounded a corner. "They called their Hegira the Diaspora."

I closed my eyes. The lieutenant flew apart, his clothing and flesh mangled to long streamers that spiraled slowly down to the violet sea. . . .

Suddenly A. Bettik was lifting me. We were entering a building larger and more sinuous than the others—all soaring plasteel and tempered glass. "The medical center," the android said. The automatic door whispered open ahead of us. "It has power . . . now if only the medical machinery is intact."

I must have dozed briefly, for when I opened my eyes again, terrified because the twin dorsal fins were circling closer and closer, I was on a gurney-trolley being slid into a long cylinder of some sort of diagnostic autosurgeon.

"See you later," Aenea was saying, releasing my hand. "See you on the other side."

WE WERE ON HEBRON for thirteen of its local days—each day being some twenty-nine standard hours. For the first three days the autosurgeon had its way with me: no fewer than eight invasive surgeries and an even dozen therapy treatments according to the digitized record at the end.

It was, indeed, some microorganism from that miserable ocean on Mare Infinitus that had decided to kill me, although when I saw the magnetic resonance and deep bioradar scans, I realized that the organism had not been so micro after all. Whatever it was—the autodiagnostic equipment was ambivalent—had taken hold along the inside of my scraped rib and grown like fen fungus until it had begun to branch out to my internal organs. Another standard day without surgery, the autosurgeon reported later, and they would have made the initial incision to find only lichen and liquefaction.

After opening me up, cleaning me out, and then repeating the process twice more when infinitesimal traces of the oceanborne organism started colonizing again, the autosurgeon pronounced the fungus kaput and began working on my lesser life-threatening wounds. The knife cut in the side had opened me up enough that I should have bled to death—especially with all of my kicking and high pulse rate brought on by my dorsaled friends in the sea. Evidently the plasma cartridges in the old medpak and several days of being kept near comatose by Aenea's liberal doses of ultramorph had kept me alive until the surgeon could transfuse eight more units of plasma into me.

The deep wound in my arm had not—as I had feared—severed tendons, but enough important muscles and nerves had been slashed that the autosurgeon had worked on that arm during operations two and three. Because the hospital still had power when we arrived, the surgeon had taken it upon its own silicon initiative to have the organ tanks in the basement grow the replacement nerves I needed. On the eighth day, when Aenea sat at my bedside and told me how the autosurgeon repeatedly kept asking for advice and authorization from its human overseers, I was even able to laugh when she talked of how "Dr. Bettik" authorized each critical operation, transplant, and therapy.

The leg the color-shark had tried to bite off turned out to be the most painful part of the ordeal. After the infinitus-fungus had been cleaned out of the area laid bare by the shark's teeth, new skin and muscle tissue had been transplanted layer by layer. It hurt. And after it quit hurting, it itched. During my second week of confinement in that hospital, I was undergoing ultramorph withdrawal and would seriously have considered holding my pistol on the girl or the android and demanding morph if I had actually believed they could be intimidated into bringing me relief from withdrawal symptoms and that hellish itching. But the pistol was gone—sunk in the bottomless violet sea.

It was on about the eighth day, when I could sit up in bed and actually eat food—although just bland, vat-replicated hospital food—that I talked to Aenea about my short stint as Hero. "On my last night on Hyperion, I got drunk with the old poet and promised him I'd accomplish certain things on this trip," I said.

"What things?" said the girl, her spoon in my dish of green gelatin.

"Nothing much," I said. "Protect you, get you home, find Old Earth and bring it back so he could see it again before he died . . ."

Aenea paused in her gelatin eating. Her dark eyebrows were very high on her forehead. "He told you to bring Old Earth back? Interesting."

"That's not all," I said. "Along the way I was supposed to talk to the Ousters, destroy the Pax, overthrow the Church, and—I quote—'find out what the fuck the TechnoCore is up to and stop it.' "

Aenea set her spoon down and dabbed at her lips with my napkin. "Is that all?"

"Not quite," I said, leaning back into the pillows. "He also wanted me to keep the Shrike from hurting you or destroying humanity."

She nodded. "Is that it?"

I rubbed my sweaty forehead with my good left hand. "I think so. At least that's all I remember. I was drunk, as I said." I looked at the child. "How am I doing with the list?"

Aenea made that casting-away gesture with her slender hands. "Not bad. You have to remember that we've only been at this a few standard months . . . less than three, actually."

"Yeah," I said, looking out the window at the low shafts of sunlight striking the tall adobe building across from the hospital. Beyond the city, I could see the rocky hills burning red with evening light. "Yeah," I said again, all of the energy and amusement drained from my voice, "I'm doing great." I sighed and pushed the dinner tray farther away. "One thing I don't understand—even in all that confusion, I don't know why their radar didn't track the raft when we were so close."

"A. Bettik shot it out," said the girl, working on the green gelatin again.

"Say what?"

"A. Bettik shot it out. The radar dish. With your plasma rifle." She finished the green goop and set the spoon in place. During the last week she had been nurse, doctor, chef, and bottle washer.

"I thought he said he could not shoot at humans," I said.

"He can't," said Aenea, clearing the tray and setting it on a nearby dresser. "I asked him. But he said that there was no prohibition against his shooting as many radar dishes as he wanted. So he did. Before we fixed your position and dived in to save you."

"That was a three- or four-klick shot," I said, "from a pitching raft. How many pulse bolts did he use?"

"One," said Aenea. She was looking at the monitor readouts above my head.

I whistled softly. "I hope he never gets mad at me. Even from a distance."

"I think you'd have to be a radar dish before you'd have to worry," she said, tucking in the clean sheets.

"Where is he?"

Aenea walked to the window and pointed east. "He found an EMV that had a full charge and was checking out the kibbutzim way out toward the Great Salt Sea."

"All the others have been empty?"

"Every one. Not even a dog, cat, horse, or pet chipmunk left behind."

I knew that she was not kidding. We had talked about it—when communities are evacuated in a hurry, or when disaster strikes, pets are often left behind. Packs of wild dogs had been a problem during the South Talon uprising on Aquila. The Home Guard had to shoot former pets on sight.

"That means they had time to take their pets with them," I said.

Aenea turned toward me and crossed her thin arms. "And leave their clothes behind? And their computers, comlogs, private diaries, family holos . . . all their personal junk?"

"And none of those tell you what happened? No final diary entries? No surveillance cameras or frenzied last-minute comlog entries?"

"Nope," said the girl. "At first I was reluctant to intrude into their private comlogs and such. But by now I've played back dozens of them.

During the last week there was the usual news of the fighting nearby. The Great Wall was less than a light-year away and the Pax ships were filling the system. They didn't come down to the planet much, but it was obvious that Hebron would have to join the Pax Protectorate after it was all over. Then there were some final newscasts about the Ousters breaking through the lines . . . then nothing. Our guess is that the Pax evacuated the entire population and then the Ousters moved on, but there's no notice of evacuation in the news holos, or in the computer entries, or anywhere. It's like the people just disappeared." She rubbed her arms. "I have some of the holocast disks if you want to see them."

"Maybe later," I said. I was very tired.

"A. Bettik will be back in the morning," she said, pulling the thin blanket up to my chin. Beyond the window, the sun had set but the hills literally glowed from stored-up light. It was a twilight effect of the stones on this world that I thought I would never tire of watching. But right then, I could not keep my eyes open.

"Do you have the shotgun?" I mumbled. "The plasma rifle? Bettik gone . . . all alone here . . ."

"They're on the raft," said Aenea. "Now, go to sleep."

ON THE FIRST DAY I was fully conscious, I tried to thank both of them for saving my life. They resisted.

"How did you find me?" I asked.

"It wasn't hard," said the girl. "You left the mike open right up to the time the Pax officer stabbed it and broke it. We could hear everything. And we could see you through the binoculars."

"You shouldn't have both left the raft," I said. "It was too dangerous."

"Not really, M. Endymion," said A. Bettik. "Besides rigging the sea anchor, which slowed the raft's progress considerably, M. Aenea had the idea of tying one of the climbing ropes to a small log for flotation and allowing the line to trail behind the raft for almost a hundred meters. If we could not catch up to the raft, we felt certain we could get you back to the trailing line before it moved out of reach. And, as events showed, we did."

I shook my head. "It was still stupid."

"You're welcome," said the girl.

ON THE TENTH DAY I tried standing. It was a short-lived victory, but a victory nonetheless. On the twelfth day I walked the length of the corridor to the toilet there. That was a major victory. On the thirteenth day, the power failed all over the city.

Emergency generators in the hospital basement kicked in, but we knew our time there was limited.

"I WISH WE COULD TAKE the autosurgeon with us," I said as we sat on the ninth-floor terrace that last evening, looking down on the shadowed avenues.

"It would fit on the raft," said A. Bettik, "but the extension cord would be a problem."

"Seriously," I said, trying not to sound like the paranoid, victimized, demoralized patient that I was then, "we need to check the pharmacies here for stuff we need."

"Done," said Aenea. "Three new and improved medpaks. One whole pouch of plasma ampules. A portable diagnosticator. Ultramorph . . . but don't ask, you aren't getting any today."

I held out my left hand. "See this? It just stopped shaking this afternoon. I won't be asking for any again soon."

Aenea nodded. Overhead, feathery clouds glowed with the last evening light.

"How long do you think these generators will hold out?" I said to the android. The hospital was one of only a handful of city buildings still lighted.

"A few weeks, perhaps," said A. Bettik. "The power grid has been repairing and running itself for months, but the planet is harsh—you've noticed the dust storms that sweep in from the desert each morning—and even though the technology is quite advanced for a non-Pax world, the place needs humans to maintain it."

"Entropy is a bitch," I said.

"Now, now," said Aenea from where she was leaning on the terrace wall. "Entropy can be our friend."

"When?" I said.

She turned around so that she was leaning back on her elbows. The building behind her was a dark rectangle, serving to highlight the glow of her sunburned skin. "It wears down empires," she said. "And does in despotisms."

"That's a hard phrase to say quickly," I said. "What despotisms are we talking about here?"

Aenea made that casting-away gesture, and for a minute I thought she was not going to speak, but then she said, "The Huns, the Scythians, the Visigoths, the Ostrogoths, the Egyptians, Macedonians, Romans, and Assyrians."

"Yeah," I said, "but . . ."

"The Avars and the Northern Wei," she continued, "and the Juan-Juans, the Mamelukes, the Persians, Arabs, Abbasids, and Seljuks."

"Okay," I said, "but I don't see . . ."

"The Kurds and Ghaznavids," she continued, smiling now. "Not to mention the Mongols, Sui, Tang, Buminids, Crusaders, Cossacks, Prussians, Nazis, Soviets, Japanese, Javanese, North Ammers, Greater Chinese, Colum-Peros, and Antarctic Nationalists."

I held up a hand. She stopped. Looking at A. Bettik, I said, "I don't even know these planets, do you?"

The android's expression was neutral. "I believe they all relate to Old Earth, M. Endymion."

"No shit," I said.

"No shit, is, I believe, correct in this context," A. Bettik said in a flat tone.

I looked back at the girl. "So this is our plan to topple the Pax for the old poet? Hide out somewhere and wait for entropy to take its toll?"

She crossed her arms again. "Uh-uh," she said. "Normally that would have been a good plan—just hunker down for a few millennia and let time take its course—but these damn cruciforms complicate the equation."

"How do you mean?" I said, my voice serious.

"Even if we wanted to topple the Pax," she said, "which—by the way—I don't. That's your job. But even if we wanted to, entropy's not on our side anymore with that parasite that can make people almost immortal."

"Almost immortal," I murmured. "When I was dying, I must admit that I thought of the cruciform. It would have been a lot easier . . . not to mention less painful than all the surgery and recovery . . . just to die and let the thing resurrect me."

Aenea was looking at me. Finally she said, "That's why this planet had the best medical care in or out of the Pax."

"Why?" I said. My head was still thick with drugs and fatigue.

"They were . . . are . . . Jews," the girl said softly. "Very few accepted the cross. They only had one chance at life."

We sat for some time without speaking that evening, as the shadows filled the city canyons of New Jerusalem and the hospital hummed with electric life while it still could.

THE NEXT MORNING I walked as far as the old groundcar that had hauled me to the hospital thirteen days earlier, but—sitting in the back where they had made a mattress bed for me—I gave orders to find a gun shop.

After an hour of driving around, it became obvious that there were no gun shops in New Jerusalem. "All right," I said. "A police headquarters."

There were several of these. As I hobbled into the first one we encountered, waving away offers from both girl and android to act as a crutch, I soon discovered how underarmed a peaceful society could be. There were no weapons racks there, not even riot guns or stunners. "I don't suppose Hebron had an army or Home Guard?" I said.

"I believe not," replied A. Bettik. "Until the Ouster incursion three standard years ago, there were no human enemies or dangerous animals on the planet."

I grunted and kept looking. Finally, after breaking open a triple-locked drawer in the bottom of some police chief's desk, I found something.

"A Steiner-Ginn, I believe," said the android. "A pistol firing reduced-charge plasma bolts."

"I know what it is," I said. There were two magazines in the drawer. That should be about sixty bolts. I went outside, aimed the weapon at a distant hillside, and squeezed the trigger ring. The pistol coughed and the hillside showed a tiny flash. "Good," I said, fitting the old weapon in my empty holster. I was afraid that it would be a signature weapon—capable of being fired only by its owner. Those weapons went in and out of vogue over the centuries.

"We have the flechette pistol on the raft," began A. Bettik.

I shook my head. I wanted nothing to do with those things for a good while.

A. Bettik and Aenea had stocked up on water and food while I had been recuperating, and by the time I hobbled to the landing at the canal and looked at our refitted and refurbished raft, I could see the extra boxes. "Question," I said. "Why are we going on with this floating woodpile when there are comfortable little runabout boats tied up over there? Or we could take an EMV and travel in air-conditioned comfort."

The girl and the blue-skinned man exchanged glances. "We voted while you were recovering," she said. "We go on with the raft."

"Don't I get a vote?" I snapped. I had meant to feign anger, but when it came, it was real enough.

"Sure," said the girl, standing on the dock with her feet planted, legs apart, and her hands on her hips. "Vote."

"I vote we get an EMV and travel in comfort," I said, hearing the petulant tone in my voice and hating it even while continuing it. "Or even one of these boats. I vote we leave these logs behind."

"Vote recorded," said the girl. "A. Bettik and I voted to keep the raft. It's not going to run out of power, and it can float. One of these boats would have shown up on the radar on Mare Infinitus, and an EMV couldn't have made the trip on some worlds. Two for keeping the raft, one against. We keep it."

"Who made this a democracy?" I demanded. I admit that I had images of spanking this kid.

"Who made it anything else?" said the girl.

All through this A. Bettik stood by the edge of the dock, fiddling with a rope, his face a study in that embarrassed expression that most people get when around members of another family squabbling. He was wearing a loose tunic and baggy shorts made of yellow linen. There was a wide-brimmed yellow hat on his head.

Aenea stepped onto the raft and loosened the stern line. "You want a boat or an EMV . . . or a floating couch, for that matter . . . you take it, Raul. A. Bettik and I are going on in this."

I started hobbling toward a nice little dinghy tied up along the dock. "Wait," I said, pivoting on my stronger leg to look at her again. "The farcaster won't work if I try to go through alone."

"Right," said the girl. A. Bettik had stepped aboard the raft, and now she cast off the forward line. The canal was much wider here than it had been in the concrete trough of the aqueduct: about thirty meters across as it ran through New Jerusalem.

A. Bettik stood at the steering oar and looked at me as the girl picked up one of the longer poles and pushed the raft away from the dock.

"Wait!" I said. "Goddammit, wait!" I hobbled down the pier, jumped the meter or so to the raft, landed on my recuperating leg, and had to catch myself with my good arm before I rolled into the microtent.

Aenea offered me her hand, but I ignored it as I got to my feet. "God, you're a stubborn brat," I said.

"Look who's talking," said the girl, and went forward to sit at the front of the raft as we moved into the center current.

Out of the shade of the buildings, Hebron's sun was even fiercer. I pulled on my old tricorn cap for a bit of shade as I stood by the steering oar with A. Bettik.

"I imagine you're on her side," I said at last as we moved into the open desert and the river narrowed to a canal once again.

"I am quite neutral, M. Endymion," said the blue-skinned man.

"Hah!" I said. "You voted to stay with the raft."

"It has served us well so far, sir," said the android, stepping back as I hobbled closer and took the steering oar in my hands.

I looked at the new crates of provisions stacked neatly in the shade of the tent, at the stone hearth with its heating cube and pots and pans, at the shotgun and plasma rifle—freshly oiled and laid under canvas covers—and at our packs, sleeping bags, medkits, and other stuff. The forward "mast" had been raised while I was gone, and now one of A. Bettik's extra white shirts flew from it like a flapping pennant.

"Well," I said at last, "screw it."

"Precisely, sir," said the android.

The next portal was only five klicks out of town. I squinted up at Hebron's blazing sun as we passed through the arch's thin shadow, then into the line of the portal itself. With the other farcaster portals, there had been a moment when the air within shimmered and changed, giving us a glance at what lay ahead.

Here there was only absolute blackness. And the blackness did not change as we continued on. The temperature dropped at least seventy degrees centigrade. At the same instant, the gravity changed—it suddenly felt as if I were carrying someone my own mass on my back.

"The lamps!" I called, still holding the steering oar against a suddenly strong current. I was struggling to stay on my feet against the terrible drag of increased gravity there. The combination of chilling cold, absolute blackness, and oppressive weight was terrifying.

The two had loaded lanterns they had found in New Jerusalem, but it was the old handlamp that Aenea flicked on first. Its beam cut through icy vapor, across black water, and lifted to illuminate a roof of solid ice some fifteen meters above us. Stalactites of patterned ice hung down almost to the water. Daggers of ice protruded from the black current on either side and ahead of us. Far ahead, about where the beam began to dim at a hundred meters or so, there seemed to be a solid wall of icy blocks running right down to the water's surface. We were in an ice cave . . . and one with no visible way out. The cold burned at my exposed hands, arms, and face. The gravity lay on my neck like so many iron collars.

"Damn," I said. I locked the steering oar in place and hobbled toward the packs. It was hard to stay upright with a bad leg and eighty kilos on my back. A. Bettik and the girl were already there, digging for our insulated clothing.

Suddenly there was a loud crack. I looked up, expecting to see a stalactite falling on us, or the roof caving in under this terrible weight, but it was only our mast snapping where it had struck a low-hanging shelf of ice. The mast fell much faster than it would have in Hyperion gravity—rushing to the raft as if someone had fast-forwarded a holo. Wood chips flew as it hit. A. Bettik's shirt struck the raft with an audible crash. It was frozen solid and covered with a thin coat of hoar frost.

"Damn," I said again, my teeth chattering, and dug for my woolen undies.

35

ATHER CAPTAIN DE SOYA uses the power of the papal diskey in ways he has never before attempted.

Mare Infinitus Station Three-twenty-six Mid-littoral, where the hawking mat was discovered, is declared a crime zone and put under martial law. De Soya brings in Pax troops and ships from the floating city of St. Thérèse and places all of the former Pax garrison and the fishing guests under house arrest. When St. Thérèse's governing prelate, Bishop Melandriano, protests this high-handedness and argues the limits of the papal diskey, de Soya goes to the planetary Governor, Archbishop Jane Kelley. The archbishop bows to the papal diskey and silences Melandriano under threat of excommunication.

Appointing young Lieutenant Sproul as his adjutant and liaison during the investigation, de Soya brings in Pax forensic experts and top investigators from St. Thérèse and the other large city platforms to carry out the crime-scene studies. Truthtell and other drugs are administered to Captain C. Dobbs Powl—who is being held under arrest in the station's brig—the other members of the former Pax garrison there, and all the fishermen who had been present.

Within a few days it becomes obvious that Captain Powl, the late Lieutenant Belius, and many of the other officers and men of this remote platform had been conspiring with area poachers to allow illegal catches of local game fish, to steal Pax equipment—including one submersible that had been reported as sunk by rebel fire—and to extort money from fishing guests. None of this interests Father Captain de Soya. He wants to know precisely what happened on that evening two standard months earlier.

Forensic evidence mounts. The blood and tissue on the hawking mat are DNA tested and transmitted back to the Pax records section in St. Thérèse and at the orbital Pax base. Two distinct strains of blood are

found: the majority is positively identified as the DNA pattern of Lieutenant Belius; the second is unidentified in Mare Infinitus Pax records, despite
the fact that every Pax citizen on the sea world has been typed and recorded.

"So how did Belius's blood end up on the flying carpet?" asks Sergeant Gregorius. "According to everyone's testimony under Truthtell, Belius was knocked in the drink long before the fellow they captured tried to
escape on the mat."

De Soya nods and steeples his fingers. He has turned the former
director's office into his command center, and the platform is very
crowded with three times its former population now aboard. Three large
Pax Sea Navy frigates are at sea anchor off the platform, and two of them
are combat submersibles. The former skimmer deck is full of Pax aircraft,
and engineers have been brought in to repair and extend the thopter deck.
Just this morning de Soya has ordered another three ships to the area.
Bishop Melandriano transmits his written protests at the mounting costs
at least twice a day; Father Captain de Soya ignores them.

"I think our unknown stopped to pull the lieutenant out of the . . .
how did you call it, Sergeant? . . . out of the drink. They struggled. The
unknown was injured or killed. Belius tried to make it back to the station.
Powl and the others killed him by mistake."

"Aye," says Gregorius, "that's the best scenario I've heard." In the
hours since the DNA results were transmitted back from St. Thérèse, they
had woven many others—plots with poachers, conspiracies between the
unknown and Lieutenant Belius, Captain Powl murdering former cocon-
spirators. This theory is the simplest.

"It means that our unknown is one of those traveling with the girl,"
says de Soya. "And he has a merciful—if stupid—side to him."

"Or he could have been a poacher," says Gregorius. "We'll never
know."

De Soya taps his fingertips together and looks up. "Why not, Sergeant?"

"Well, Captain, the evidence is all down there, ain't it, sir?" he says,
jerking a thumb toward the surging violet sea outside the windows. "The
navy boys here say its ten thousand fathoms deep or more—that's almost
twenty thousand meters of water, sir. Any bodies there have been eaten by
the fishes, sir. And if he was a poacher who got away . . . well, we'll
never know. And if he was an offworlder . . . well, there aren't any
central Pax DNA records. . . . We'd have to search the files on several
hundred worlds. We'll never find him."

Father Captain de Soya drops his hands and smiles thinly. "This is
one of those rare times where you are wrong, Sergeant. Watch."

In the next week de Soya has every poacher within a thousand-
kilometer radius rounded up and questioned under Truthtell. The round-
ing up involves two dozen sea-naval ships and over eight thousand Pax

personnel. The cost is enormous. Bishop Melandriano becomes apoplectic and flies to Station Three-twenty-six Mid-littoral to stop the madness. Father Captain de Soya places the cleric under arrest and has him flown to a remote monastery nine thousand kilometers away, near the polar ice caps.

De Soya also decides to search the ocean bottom.

"You won't find anything, sir," says Lieutenant Sproul. "There are so many predators down there that nothing organic makes it a hundred fathoms deep, much less to the bottom . . . and according to our soundings this week, that's twelve thousand fathoms. Besides, there are only two submersibles on Mare Infinitus that can operate at that depth."

"I know," says de Soya. "I've ordered them here. They will arrive tomorrow with the frigate *Passion of Christ*."

For once Lieutenant Sproul is speechless.

De Soya smiles. "You're aware, aren't you, son, that Lieutenant Belius was a born-again Christian? And his cruciform was not recovered?"

Sproul's mouth hangs open for a moment. "Yessir . . . I mean . . . yes, but . . . sir, to be resurrected, I mean . . . don't they need to find the body intact, sir?"

"Not at all, Lieutenant," says Father Captain de Soya. "Merely a good-sized segment of the cross we all bear. Many a good Catholic has been resurrected from a few centimeters of intact cruciform and a bit of flesh that can be DNA typed and grown to order."

Sproul shakes his head. "But, sir . . . it's been over nine Big Tides, sir. There's not a square millimeter of Lieutenant Belius or his cruciform left, sir. That's a giant feeding tank out there, sir."

De Soya walks to the window. "Perhaps, Lieutenant. Perhaps. But we owe it to our fellow Christian to make every attempt, do we not? Besides, if Lieutenant Belius *were* to be granted the miracle of resurrection, he has to stand charges for theft, treason, and attempted murder, doesn't he?"

USING THE MOST ADVANCED techniques available to them, the local forensic experts are available to lift unidentified fingerprints from a mess-hall coffee cup in spite of the many washings the cup has undergone over the past two months. Of the thousands of latent prints, all are laboriously identified as belonging to garrison troops or visiting fisherman except for this one reconstructed print. It is set aside with unidentified DNA evidence.

"During the Web days," says Dr. Holmer Ryum, the chief forensic effort, "the megadatasphere would have put us in touch with central Hegemony files within seconds via the fatline. We could get a match almost instantly."

"If we had some cheese, we could have a ham-and-cheese sandwich," replies Father Captain de Soya, "if we had some ham."

"What?" says Dr. Ryum.

"Never mind," says de Soya. "I expect to have a match within days."

Dr. Ryum is puzzled. "How, Father Captain? We've checked the planetary data banks. Run checks against every poacher you've captured . . . and I have to say, there's never been a mass arrest like this on Mare Infinitus before. You're upsetting a delicate balance of corruption that has existed here for centuries."

De Soya rubs the bridge of his nose. He has not slept much in the past weeks. "I am not interested in delicate balances of corruption, Doctor."

"I understand," says Ryum. "But I fail to understand how you can expect a match within days. Neither the Church nor Pax Central has files of all the citizens on various Pax worlds, much less of the Outback and Ouster areas. . . ."

"All Pax worlds keep their own records," de Soya says quietly. "Of baptisms and cross sacraments. Of marriages and deaths. Military and police records."

Dr. Ryum opens his hands in helplessness. "But where would you start?"

"Where the odds are the best in finding him," answers Father Captain de Soya.

MEANWHILE, NOTHING IS FOUND of the hapless Lieutenant Belius within the six-hundred-fathom depths to which the two deep-sea submersibles agree to descend. Hundreds of rainbow sharks are stunned to the surface and the contents of their stomachs analyzed. Still no Belius, neither remnants of him nor of his cruciform. Thousands of other sea scavengers are harvested within a two-hundred-klick radius, and bits of two poachers are identified in gullets, but no sign of Belius or the stranger. A funeral mass is held on Station Three-twenty-six Mid-littoral for the lieutenant, who is said to have died the true death and found true immortality.

De Soya orders the deep-sea submersible captains to go deeper, looking for artifacts. The captains refuse.

"Why?" demands the priest-captain. "I brought you here because your machines can go to the bottom. Why won't you?"

"The Lamp Mouths," says the senior of the two captains. "To search, we'll have to use lights. To six hundred fathoms, our sonar and deep radar can detect them rising and we could beat them to the surface. Below that, and we wouldn't have a chance. We won't go deeper."

"You will go deeper," says Father Captain de Soya, the papal diskey glowing against the black of his cassock.

The senior captain takes a step closer. "You can arrest me, shoot me, excommunicate me . . . I won't take my men and machine down to certain death. You haven't *seen* a Lamp Mouth, Father."

De Soya sets a friendly hand on the captain's shoulder. "I will not arrest, shoot, or excommunicate you, Captain. And I will see a Lamp Mouth soon. Perhaps more than one."

The captain does not understand.

"I've ordered in three more of the Ocean Fleet's attack submarines," says de Soya. "We are going to find, flush, and kill every Lamp Mouth and any other threatening 'canth within five hundred klicks. When you dive, the area will be completely safe."

The senior captain looks at the other deep-sea submersible captain and then back to de Soya. Both of the captains appear to be in shock. "Father . . . Captain . . . sir . . . do you know how much a Lamp Mouth is *worth*? To the offworld sport fishermen and the big factories at Thérèse . . . sir."

"About fifteen thousand Mare-Eye seidons," says de Soya. "That's about thirty-five thousand Pax florins. Almost fifty thousand Mercantilus marks. Each." De Soya smiles. "And since you two will receive thirty percent finders' fees for locating the Mouths for the navy, I wish you good hunting."

The two deep-submersible captains hurry out the door.

FOR THE FIRST TIME de Soya sends someone else off in the *Raphael* to run his errands. Sergeant Gregorius travels alone in the archangel, carrying the DNA and fingerprint information, as well as threads from the hawking mat.

"Remember," says de Soya over tightbeam from the platform a few minutes before *Raphael* spins up to total quantum state, "there's still a heavy Pax presence on Hyperion and at least two torchships in-system at all times. They will bring you to the capital of St. Joseph's for a proper resurrection."

Lashed into his acceleration couch, Sergeant Gregorius only grunts. His face looks relaxed and calm on camera, despite his imminent death.

"Three days there, of course," continues de Soya, "and—I would think—no more than one day to go through the files. And then you return."

"Got it, Captain," says Gregorius. "I won't waste any time in any Jacktown bars."

"Jacktown?" says de Soya. "Oh, yes . . . the old nickname for the capital. Well, Sergeant, if you want to spend your one real evening on Hyperion in a bar, be my guest. It's been a dry few months with me."

Gregorius grins. The clock says thirty seconds before quantum leap and his painful extinction. "I ain't complainin', Captain."

"Very good," says de Soya. "Have a good trip. Oh . . . and Sergeant?"

"Yessir?" Ten seconds.

"Thank you, Sergeant."

There is no response. Suddenly there is nothing on the other end of the coherent tachyon tightbeam. *Raphael* has made its quantum leap.

FIVE LAMP MOUTHS are tracked and killed by the navy. De Soya flies to each carcass in his command thopter.

"Good Lord, they're larger than I could have imagined," he says to Lieutenant Sproul when they arrive above the spot where the first one floats.

The grub-white beast is easily three times the size of the station platform: a mass of eyestalks, gaping maws, fibrillating gill slits each the size of the thopter, pulsating tendrils extending hundreds of meters, dangling antennae each carrying a cold-light "lantern" of great brilliance— even out here in the daylight—and mouths, many mouths, each large enough to swallow a fleet submarine. As de Soya watches, the harvesting crews are already flocking over the pressure-exploded carcass, sawing off tendrils and eyestalks and cutting the white meat to portable cubes before the hot sun spoils it all.

Satisfied that the area is cleared of Mouths and other deadly 'canths, the two deep-dive captains take their submersibles twelve thousand fathoms down. There, amid forests of tube worms the size of Old Earth redwood trees, they find an amazing array of old wrecks—poacher submersibles crushed to the size of small suitcases by the pressure, one naval frigate that has been missing for more than a century. They also find boots —dozens of boots.

"It's the tanning process," says Lieutenant Sproul to de Soya as the two watch the monitors. "It's an oddity, but it was true on Old Earth as well. Some of the oldest deep-sea salvage operations—a surface ship called the *Titanic,* for instance—never turned up bodies, the sea's too hungry for that, but lots of boots. Something in the tanning process of leather discourages sea critters there . . . and here."

"Bring them up," commands de Soya over the umbilical link.

"The boots?" comes back the submersible captain's voice. "All of them?"

"All of them," says de Soya.

The monitors show a profusion of junk on the seabed: things lost by the platform station crew over almost two centuries of carelessness, personal belongings of the drowned poachers and sailors, metal and plastic garbage tossed by the fishermen and others. Most items are corroded and misshapen by deep-sea crustaceans and unimaginable pressure, but a few are new enough and tough enough to be identified.

"Bag those and send them up," says de Soya as they encounter shiny objects that might be a knife, a fork, a belt buckle, a . . .

"What's that?" demands de Soya.

"What?" says the captain of the deepest submersible. He is watching the remote handlers rather than his monitors.

"That shiny thing . . . It looks like a handgun."

The monitor shifts its view as the submersible turns. The powerful searchlights track, return, and illuminate the object as the camera zooms in. "It is a handgun," comes the captain's voice. "Still clean. Damaged some by pressure, but basically intact." De Soya can hear the click of the single-frame imager capturing this from the monitor. "I'll collect it," says the captain.

De Soya has the urge to add *"carefully"*—but does not speak. His years as torchship captain have taught him to let his people do their jobs. He watches as the grapple arm appears on the monitor and the remote handler gently lifts the shiny object.

"It could be Lieutenant Belius's flechette pistol," says Sproul. "It went over with him and hasn't been recovered yet."

"This is quite a bit farther out," muses de Soya, watching the image shift and change on the monitor.

"The currents here are powerful, weird," says the young officer. "But I have to admit that it didn't look like a flechette pistol. Too . . . I don't know . . . squarish."

"Yes," says de Soya. The underwater searchlights are flickering over the encrusted hull of a submersible that has been buried down there for decades. De Soya is thinking of his years in space and how empty that different unknown is from any ocean on any world, teeming with life and history. The priest-captain is thinking about the Ousters and their strange attempt to adapt themselves to space the way these tube worms and 'canths and bottom-hugging species have adapted themselves to eternal darkness and terrible pressures. Perhaps, he is thinking, the Ousters understand something about humanity's future that we in the Pax have only denied.

Heresy. De Soya shakes away the thoughts and looks at his young liaison officer. "We'll know what it is soon enough," he says. "They're bringing this load up within the hour."

GREGORIUS RETURNS four days after his departure. He is dead. *Raphael* sends out its sad beacon, a torchship rendezvouses with it twenty light-minutes out, and the sergeant's body is removed and brought to the resurrection chapel at St. Thérèse. De Soya does not wait for the man's revival. He orders the courier pouch brought to him at once.

Pax records on Hyperion have positively identified the DNA taken from the hawking mat, and have also matched the partial fingerprint on the cup. Both belong to the same man: Raul Endymion, born A.D. 3099 on planet Hyperion, not baptized; enlisted in the Hyperion Home Guard in Thomas-month of the year A.D. 3115, fought with the 23rd Mechanized

Infantry Regiment during Ursus Uprising—three commendations for bravery, including one for rescuing a squadmate while under fire—stationed at Fort Benjing in the South Talon region of the continent of Aquila for eight standard months, served out the remainder of his time at Kans River Station 9 on Aquila, patrolling the jungle there, guarding against rebel terrorist activity near the fiberplastic plantations. Final rank, sergeant. Mustered out (honorable discharge) on Lentmonth 15, A.D. 3119, whereabouts unknown until less than ten standard months ago, Ascensionmonth 23, A.D. 3126, when he was arrested, tried, and convicted in Port Romance (continent of Aquila) for the murder of one M. Dabil Herrig, a born-again Christian from Renaissance Vector. Records showed that Raul Endymion refused offers to accept the cross and was executed by deathwand one week after the arrest, on the 30th of Ascensionmonth, A.D. 3126. His body was disposed of at sea. The death certificate and autopsy reports were notarized by the local Pax Inspector General.

The next day latent prints on the crushed, ancient .45-caliber automatic pistol brought up from the ocean floor are matched: Raul Endymion and Lieutenant Belius.

Bits of thread from the hawking mat are not so easily identified by Hyperion Pax records, but the human clerk doing the search included a handwritten note that such a mat figures prominently in the legendary *Cantos* composed by a poet who had lived on Hyperion until a century or so ago.

AFTER SERGEANT GREGORIUS is resurrected, rests a few hours, and flies to Station Three-twenty-six Mid-littoral to report, de Soya tells him the various findings. He also informs the sergeant that the two dozen Pax engineers who have been swarming over the farcaster portal for three weeks report only that there is no sign that the ancient arch had been activated, despite sightings of a bright flash by several fishermen on the platform that night. The engineers also report that there is no way to get inside the ancient Core-constructed arch, nor to tell where—if anywhere—someone might have been transported through it.

"Same as Renaissance V.," says Gregorius. "But at least you have some idea of who helped the girl escape."

"Possibly," says de Soya.

"He came a long way to die here," says the sergeant.

Father Captain de Soya leans back in his chair. "*Did* he die here, Sergeant?"

Gregorius has no answer.

Finally de Soya says, "I think we're finished on Mare Infinitus. Or will be in a day or two."

The sergeant nods. Through the long bank of windows here in the director's office, he can see the bright glow that precedes the moonrise. "Where to next, Captain? Back on the old search pattern?"

De Soya is also watching the east, waiting for the giant orange disk to appear above the darkened horizon. "I'm not sure, Sergeant. Let's get things tidied up here, Captain Powl handed over to Pax Justice in Orbit Seven, and soothe Bishop Melandriano's feathers. . . ."

"If we can," says Sergeant Gregorius.

"If we can," agrees de Soya. "Then we'll pay our respects to Archbishop Kelley, get back to *Raphael,* and decide where to jump next. It may be time for us to come up with some theories on where this child is headed and try to get there first, not just follow *Raphael*'s shortest-line pattern."

"Yes, sir," says Gregorius. He salutes, goes to the door, and hesitates there a moment. "And *do* you have a theory, sir? Based on just the few things we've found here?"

De Soya is watching the three moons rise. He does not turn his chair around to face his sergeant as he says, "Perhaps. Just perhaps."

36

E LEANED ON OUR POLES and stopped the raft's forward motion before it crashed into the ice wall. We had all of our lanterns lit now, the electric lamps throwing their beams into the frigid darkness of this ice cavern. Mist rose from the black waters and hung beneath the jagged roof of the cavern like ominous spirits of the drowned. Crystal facets distorted and then threw back the beams of puny light, making the surrounding darkness all the more profound.

"Why is the river still liquid?" asked Aenea, hugging her hands under her arms and stamping her feet. She had on every layer she had brought, but it was not enough. The cold was terrible.

I went to one knee at the edge of the raft, lifted a palmful of river water to my lips, and tasted. "Salinity," I said. "This is as salty as Mare Infinitus's sea."

A. Bettik played his handlamp on the ice wall ten meters ahead of us. "It comes down to the water's edge," he said. "And extends somewhat beneath it. But the current still flows."

For an instant I had a surge of hope. "Shut down the lanterns," I said, hearing my voice echo in the vaporous hollow of the place. "Turn off the handlamps."

When this was accomplished, I had hoped to see a glimmer of light through or under the ice wall—a hint of salvation, an indication that this ice cavern was finite and that only the exit had collapsed.

The darkness was absolute. No amount of waiting gave us night vision. I cursed and wished for the night goggles I had lost on Mare Infinitus: if they worked here, it would have meant that light was seeping in from somewhere. We waited another moment in the blindness. I could hear Aenea's shaking, actually feel the vapor from all of our breaths.

"Turn the lights on," I said at last. There had been no glimmer of hope.

We played the beams on the walls, roof, and river again. Mist continued to rise and condense near the ceiling. Icicles fell constantly into the steaming water.

"Where . . . are . . . we?" asked Aenea, trying without total success to stop the chattering of her teeth.

I dug in my pack, found the thermal blanket I had packed at Martin Silenus's tower so long ago, and wrapped it around her. "That will hold the heat in. No . . . keep it on."

"We can share," said the girl.

I crouched near the heating cube, turning its conductive power to maximum. Five of the six ceramic faces began to glow. "We'll share it when we have to," I said. Playing the light over the ice wall that blocked our way, I said, "To answer your question, my guess is Sol Draconi Septem. Some of my richer . . . and tougher . . . fen clients hunted arctic wraiths there."

"I concur," said A. Bettik. His blue skin made him look even colder than I felt as he huddled near the glowing lantern and heating cube. The microtent had become frost laden and as brittle as thin metal. "That world has a one-point-seven-g gravity field," he said. "And since the Fall and destruction of the Hegemony terraforming project there, most of it is said to have returned to its state of hyperglaciation."

"Hyperglaciation?" repeated Aenea. "What does that mean?" Some color was returning to her cheeks as the thermal blanket captured her warmth.

"It means that most of the atmosphere of Sol Draconi Septem is a solid," said the android. "Frozen."

Aenea looked around. "I think that I remember my mother talking about this place. She chased someone through here once on a case. She was a Lusian, you know, so she was used to one-point-five standard gravities, but even she remembered that this world was uncomfortable. I'm surprised that the River Tethys ran through here."

A. Bettik stood to shine his light around again, then crouched close to the glowing cube. Even his strong back was hunched against the massive gravity.

"What does the guidebook say?" I asked him.

He removed the small volume. "Very terse entries, sir. The Tethys had extended to Sol Draconi Septem for only a brief period before the book was published. It is in the northern hemisphere, just beyond the area the Hegemony was attempting to terraform. The main attraction of this section of the river appears to have been the possibility of seeing an arctic wraith."

"That's the thing your hunter friends were after?" Aenea said to me.

I nodded. "White. Lives on the surface. Very fast. Very deadly. Almost extinct during the Web days, but they've made a comeback since the Fall, according to the hunters I listened to. Evidently their diet consists of the human residents of Sol Draconi Septem . . . what's left of them. Only the indigenies—the Hegira colonists who had gone native centuries ago—survived the Fall. They're supposed to be primitive. The hunters said that the only animal the indigenies can hunt here is the wraith. And the indigenies hate the Pax. Word was that they kill missionaries . . . use their sinews for bowstring, just as they would a wraith's."

"This world was never very amenable to having the Hegemony authorities here," said the android. "Legend has it that the locals were quite pleased by the Fall of the farcasters. Until the plague, of course."

"Plague?" said Aenea.

"A retrovirus," I said. "It trimmed the Hegemony human population from several hundred million to fewer than a million. Most of those were killed by the few thousand indigenies here. The rest were evacuated during the early days of the Pax." I paused and looked at the girl. She looked like a sketch for a young madonna with the thermal blanket draped around her like that, her skin glowing in the lantern and cube light. "Times were rough around the old Web after the Fall."

"So I gather," she said dryly. "They weren't so bad when I was growing up on Hyperion." She looked around at the black water lapping at the raft, up at the stalactites of ice. "I wonder why they went to all that trouble just to have a few kilometers of ice cavern on the tour."

"That's the strange part," I said, nodding toward the little guidebook. "It says that the main attraction is the chance of sighting an arctic wraith. But the wraiths . . . at least from what I heard the offworld hunters say . . . don't burrow down in the ice. They live on the surface."

Aenea's dark eyes were fixed on me as she absorbed the meaning of that. "So this wasn't a cavern then. . . ."

"I think not," said A. Bettik. He pointed to the icy ceiling fifteen meters above us. "The terraform attempt in those days concentrated on creating enough temperature and surface pressure in certain low areas to allow sublimation of the largely carbon-dioxide-and-oxygen atmosphere from frozen to gaseous form."

"Did it work?" asked the girl.

"In limited areas," replied the android. He made a gesture toward the surrounding darkness. "My guess would be that this was quite open during the days when River Tethys tourists transited this short section. Or I should say, open except for containment fields that helped to hold in the atmosphere and hold back the more inclement weather. Those fields, I daresay, are gone."

"And we're locked under a mass of what the tourists used to breathe," I said. Looking toward the ceiling and then down at the plasma rifle still in its case, I muttered, "I wonder how thick . . ."

"Most probably several hundred meters, at least," said A. Bettik.

"Perhaps a vertical kilometer of ice. This was, I understand, the thickness of the atmospheric glaciation to the immediate north of the terraformed areas."

"You know a lot about this place," I said.

"On the contrary, sir," he said. "We have now exhausted the totality of my knowledge on the ecology, geology, and history of Sol Draconi Septem."

"We could ask the comlog," I said, nodding toward my pack, where I now kept the bangle.

The three of us exchanged looks. "Nahh," said Aenea.

"I concur," said A. Bettik.

"Maybe later," I said, although I admit that even while I spoke, I was thinking of some of the things I should have insisted upon bringing from the EVA locker: hazardous environment suits with powerful heaters, scuba gear, even a spacesuit would be much preferable to the inadequate cold-weather gear in which we now shivered.

"I was thinking of shooting at the roof, trying to break through to daylight," I said, "but the risk of collapsing it on us seems much greater than any chance of escape that way."

A. Bettik nodded. He had pulled on a strange woolen cap with long earflaps. The usually thin-looking android now appeared downright roly-poly in all of his layers of clothing. "You have some plastique left in the flare pouch, M. Endymion."

"Yes. I was just thinking about that. There's enough left for half a dozen more moderate-sized charges . . . but I only have four detonators left. So we could try blasting our way up, or sideways, or through that ice wall that's blocking us. But only four blasts' worth."

The shivering little madonna figure looked at me. "Where did you learn about explosives, Raul? In Hyperion's Home Guard?"

"Initially," I said. "But I really learned how to use old-fashioned plastique clearing stumps and boulders for Avrol Hume when we were landscaping the Beak estates . . ." I stood up, realizing that it was too cold to stay still for so long. The numbness in my fingers and toes sent that signal. "We could try going back upriver," I said, stamping my feet and flexing fingers.

Aenea frowned. "The next operating farcasters are always down-river . . ."

"True," I said, "but maybe there's a way out *up*river. We find some warmth, a way out of this cave, a place to hold up for a while, and *then* we worry about getting through the next portal."

Aenea nodded.

"Good idea, sir," said the android, moving to the starboard push-pole.

Before pushing off, I reset the forward mast—cutting a meter or more off so it would clear the lowest stalactites—and hung a lantern there.

Another lamp at each corner of the raft, and we pushed off upstream, our lights making thin yellow halos in the freezing mist.

The river was quite shallow—not quite three meters deep—and the poles found good traction against the bottom. But the current was very strong, and A. Bettik and I had to use all our strength to move the heavy raft upstream. Aenea pulled an extra pole from the back of the raft and joined me on my side, pushing and straining to move the vessel. Behind us, quickly flowing black water swelled and swirled over the stern boards.

For a few minutes this terrible exertion kept us warm—I was even pouring sweat, which froze against my clothing—but thirty minutes of poling and resting, resting and poling found us freezing again and just a hundred meters upstream from where we had started.

"Look," said Aenea, setting her pole down and fetching the most powerful handlamp.

A. Bettik and I leaned against our staffs, holding the raft in place while we stared. One end of a massive farcaster portal was just visible, protruding from the massive blocks of ice like a small arc of some old groundcar's wheel rim locked in a bank of ice. Beyond the tiny bit of portal still exposed, the river channel narrowed and then narrowed again until it became a fissure only a meter or so wide, until finally it disappeared beneath another ice wall.

"The river must have been five or six times the width it is now at its widest," said A. Bettik, "if the portal arch extended from bank to bank."

"Yeah," I said, exhausted and dispirited. "Let's go back to the other end." We raised our poles and quickly floated the length of our ice gallery, covering in two minutes what it had taken us thirty minutes to pole upstream. All three of us had to use our poles to slow the raft and fend off the ice wall at the end.

"Well," said Aenea, "here we are again." She shined her handlamp on the vertical ice cliffs on either side. "We could go ashore if there was a bank of some sort. But there isn't."

"We could blow one with plastique," I said. "Make a sort of ice cave."

"Would that be any warmer?" asked the girl. Out of the thermal blanket now, she was shivering badly again. I realized that she had so little body fat that heat just poured out of her.

"No," I said honestly. For the twentieth time I walked over to our tent and gear to find something that would be our salvation. Flares. Plastique. The weapons—their cases now covered with the hoarfrost that was settling on everything. One thermal blanket. Food. The heating cube was still glowing, and now the girl and blue-skinned man were crouching by it again. At that setting it would last for a hundred hours or so before losing its charge. If we had some good insulating material, we could make an ice cave cozy enough to keep us alive for three or four times that long at a lower setting. . . .

We did not have the insulating material. The microtent fabric was good stuff, but it had poor insulating qualities. And the thought of huddling in an ice tomb as our handlamps and lanterns failed—which they would do quickly in this cold—just watching the heating cube cool and waiting to die . . . well, it made my belly hurt.

I walked to the front of the raft, ran the handlamp beam over the milky ice and black water for the final time, and said, "All right, here's what we'll do."

Aenea and A. Bettik stared at me from the small circle of light by the heating cube. All of us were shivering.

"I'm going to take some plastique, the detonators, all the fuse cord we have, the rope, a com unit, my flashlight laser, and"—I took a breath—"and dive under this goddamned wall, let the current carry me downstream, and hope to hell it's just a cave-in and that the river opens up down there. If it does, I'll surface and set the charges where they'll do the most good. Maybe we can blow an opening for the raft. If not, we'll leave the raft behind and all swim down there—"

"You'll die," the girl said flatly. "You'll be hypothermic in ten seconds. And how will you swim upstream against this current?"

"That's why I'm bringing the rope. If there's a place to get out of the way of the blast there, I'll stay at the other end while we blow the opening, but if not, I tug a code on the rope and you two haul me back. When I get on the raft, I'll strip and wrap myself in the thermal blanket," I said. "It's a hundred percent insulative. If I have any body heat left, I'll survive."

"What if we all have to swim for it?" said Aenea in the same doubting tone. "The thermal blanket's not big enough for the three of us."

"We bring the heating cube," I said. "Use the blanket like a tent until we warm up."

"What are we warming up *on*?" asked the girl, her voice small. "There's no riverbank here . . . why should there be one there?"

I made a gesture. "That's why we try to blow an opening for the raft," I said patiently. "If we can't, I'll use the plastique to knock some of the ice wall down. We'll float on our own chunk of ice. Anything to get down to the next farcaster portal."

"What if we use all the plastique to get another twenty meters and there's another ice wall?" said the girl. "What if the farcaster's fifty klicks away through ice?"

I started to make another gesture with my hands, but they were shaking too much—from the cold, I hoped. I set them in my armpits. "Then we die on the other side of this wall," I said, the vapor from my breath hanging in front of me. "It's better than dying here."

After a moment of silence, A. Bettik said, "The plan seems our best chance, M. Endymion, but—you must see the logic of this—it should be I who swims. You are recuperating, weakened by your recent wounds. I was biofactured for resistance to extreme temperatures."

"Not this extreme," I said. "I can see you shivering. Also, you won't know where to place the charges."

"You can instruct me, M. Endymion. Using the com unit."

"We don't know if they'll work through this ice," I said. "Besides, it will be a difficult call. It'll be like trying to cut a diamond—the charges will have to be set in just the right places."

"Still," said the android, "it only makes sense that I—"

"It may make sense," I interrupted, "but that's not the way it's going to be. This is my job. If I . . . fail, you try. Besides, I'll need someone very strong to pull me back through the current, win or lose." I walked over and put my hand on the blue man's shoulder. "I'm pulling rank on you this time, A. Bettik."

Aenea cast off the thermal blanket despite her shivering. "What rank?" she demanded.

I pulled myself to my full height and struck a mock-heroic pose. "I'll have you know that I was a lancer sergeant third class in the Hyperion Home Guard." The delivery was marred only a bit by the chattering of my teeth.

"A sergeant," said the child.

"Third class," I said.

The girl put her arms around me. The hug surprised me and I lowered my arms to pat her awkwardly.

"First class," she said softly. Stepping back, stamping her feet, and blowing into her hands, she said, "All right . . . what do we do?"

"I'll get the things I need. Why don't you get that hundred-meter section of line you used as a sea anchor on Mare Infinitus? That should be enough. A. Bettik, if you would please let the raft move up against the ice wall in a way that the entire stern won't be awash with current. Perhaps by tucking the front in under that low shelf of ice there . . ."

All three of were busy for a moment. When we reassembled at the front of the raft again, under the abbreviated mast with its fading lantern glow, I said to Aenea, "Do you still think that someone or something is sending us to these specific River Tethys worlds for a reason?"

The girl looked around at the darkness for a few seconds. Somewhere behind us another stalactite of ice fell into the river with a hollow splash. "Yes," she said.

"And what's the reason for this dead end?"

Aenea shrugged, which—under different circumstances—would have looked a bit comical, she was so swathed in layers. "A temptation," she said.

I did not understand. "Temptation for what?"

"I hate the cold and dark," said the girl. "I always have. Perhaps someone is tempting me to use certain . . . abilities . . . which I have not properly explored yet. Certain powers which I haven't *earned*."

I looked down at the swirling black waters in which I would be swimming in less than a minute. "Well, kiddo, if you have powers or abilities that would get us the hell out of here, I suggest you explore them and use them whether you've earned them or not."

Her hand touched my arm. She was wearing an extra pair of my wool socks as mittens. "I'm guessing," she said, the vapor of her breath freezing on the brim of the floppy cap she had pulled low. "But nothing I will ever learn could get all three of us out of here now. I know that's true. Perhaps the temptation is . . . It doesn't matter, Raul. Let's just see if we can get through this icefall."

I nodded, took a breath, and stripped out of everything but my underwear. The shock of cold air was terrible. Completing the knot that held the line around my chest, noticing that my fingers were already growing stiff and useless from the cold, I took the shoulder bag holding the plastique from A. Bettik and said, "The river water may be cold enough to stop my heart. If I don't tug once, hard, within the first thirty seconds, pull me back."

The android nodded. We had gone over the other rope signals I would use.

"Oh, if you pull me back and I am in a coma or dead," I said, trying to keep my tone matter-of-fact, "don't forget I might be revived even after several minutes of having my heart stopped. This cold water should retard brain death."

A. Bettik nodded again. He was standing with the rope over one shoulder and curled around his waist to the other hand in a classic climber's belay.

"Okay," I said, realizing that I was delaying and losing body heat. "See you guys in a few minutes." I slipped over the side into the black water.

I believe that my heart did stop for a minute, but then it began pounding almost painfully. The current was stronger than I had bargained for. It almost swept me down and under the ice wall before I was ready to go. As it was, it swirled me several meters to the port of the raft and banged me up sharply against the jagged ice, cutting my forehead and slamming my forearms brutally. I clung to a jagged crystal with all of my strength, feeling my legs and lower body being pulled into that subterranean vortex and struggling to keep my face out of the water. The stalactite that had fallen behind us crashed against the ice wall just half a meter to my left. If it had struck me, I would have been unconscious and drowned without knowing what had happened.

"This . . . might . . . not . . . be . . . such a . . . good idea," I gasped, teeth chattering, before I lost my grip and was pulled under the jagged icefall.

37

DE SOYA'S IDEA is to abandon *Raphael*'s plodding search pattern and jump directly to the first of the Ouster-captured systems.

"What good will that do, sir?" asks Corporal Kee.

"Perhaps none," admits Father Captain de Soya. "But if there is an Ouster connection, we might get a hint of it there."

Sergeant Gregorius rubs his jaw. "Aye," he says, "and we may get captured by a Swarm. This ship isn't the best armed in His Holiness's fleet, if you don't mind me sayin' so, sir."

De Soya nods. "But it's fast. We could probably outrun most Swarm ships. And they may have abandoned the system by now . . . they tend to do that, hit, run, push back the Pax Great Wall, then leave the system with only a token perimeter defense after wreaking as much damage as they can on the world and populace. . . ." De Soya stops. He has seen only one Ouster-pillaged world firsthand—Svoboda—but he hopes never to have to see another. "Anyway," he says, "it's the same to us on this ship. Normally the quantum leap to beyond the Great Wall would be eight or nine months shiptime, eleven or more years time-debt. For us it will be the usual instantaneous jump and three days resurrection."

Lancer Rettig raised his hand, as he often did in these discussions. "There's that to consider, sir."

"What's that?"

"The Ousters have never captured an archangel courier, sir. I doubt if they know this sort of ship exists. Heck, sir, most of the Pax Fleet has no idea archangel technology exists."

De Soya sees his point immediately, but Rettig continues. "So we'd be running quite a risk, sir. Not just for ourselves, but for the Pax."

There is a long silence. Finally de Soya speaks. "That's a good point, Lancer. I've given it quite a bit of thought. But Pax Command built this

ship with its automated resurrection creche just so we could go beyond
Pax space. I think it's understood that we might have to follow leads into
the Outback . . . into Ouster-held territory if need be." The priest-
captain takes a breath. "I've been there, gentlemen. I've burned their orbital forests and fought my way out of Swarms. The Ousters are . . .
strange. Their attempts to adapt to odd environments . . . to space
even . . . are . . . blasphemous. They may no longer be human. But
their ships are not fast. *Raphael* should be able to get in and translate back
to quantum velocities if there is a threat to her capture. And we can
program her to self-destruct before being captured."

None of the three Swiss Guard troopers says a word. Each appears
to be thinking about the death within death that would entail—the destruction without warning of destruction. They would go to sleep on their
acceleration couches/resurrection creches as always and simply never
awaken . . . at least not in this life. The cruciform sacrament is truly
miraculous—it can bring shattered and blasted bodies back to life, return
the shape and souls of born-again Christians who have been shot, burned,
starved, drowned, asphyxiated, stabbed, crushed, or ravaged by disease—
but it has its limits: too much time of decomposition defeats it, as would a
thermonuclear explosion of a ship's in-system drive.

"I guess we're with you," Sergeant Gregorius says at last, knowing
that Father Captain de Soya has asked for this discussion because he hates
simply ordering his men into such a risk of true death.

Kee and Rettig merely nod.

"Good," says de Soya. "I will program *Raphael* accordingly . . .
that if there is no chance for her to escape before we can be resurrected,
she'll trigger her fusion engines. And I'll be very careful setting the parameters for her on what 'no escape' means. But I don't think there's much
chance of that happening. We will awaken in . . . My God, I haven't
even checked to see which system is the first Ouster-occupied Tethys
world. Is it Tai Zhin?"

"Negative, sir," says Gregorius, leaning over the hard-copy star
chart of the search plot *Raphael* has prepared. His massive finger strikes
down on a circled region beyond the Pax. "It's Hebron. The Jew world."

"All right, then," says the priest-captain. "Let's get to our couches
and head for the translation point. Next year in New Jerusalem!"

"Next year, sir?" says Lancer Rettig, floating above the plot-table
before kicking off to his own couch.

De Soya smiles. "It's a saying I've heard from some of my Jewish
friends. I don't know what it means."

"I didn't know that there were any Jews around anymore," says
Corporal Kee, floating above his own couch. "I thought they all stuck to
themselves in the Outback."

De Soya shakes his head. "There were a few converted Jews at the
university when I was taking courses outside of seminary," he says.

"Never mind. You'll meet some soon enough on Hebron. Strap in, gentle-men."

THE PRIEST-CAPTAIN KNOWS immediately upon awakening that something has, indeed, gone wrong. A few times during his wilder days as a young man, Federico de Soya had got drunk with his fellow seminarians, and on one of these outings he had awakened in a strange bed—alone, thank God —but in a strange bed in a strange part of the city, with no memory of whose bed it was or how he got there. This awakening is like that.

Rather than opening his eyes to see the enclosed and automated creche couches on *Raphael*, smelling the ozone and recycled-sweat scents of the ship, feeling the awakening-to-falling terror of zero-gravity, de Soya finds himself in a comfortable bed in a lovely room in a reasonably normal gravity field. There are religious icons on the wall—the Virgin Mary, a large crucifix with the heavenly raised eyes of a suffering Christ, a painting of the martyrdom of St. Paul. Weak sunlight comes through lace curtains.

All this is vaguely familiar to the stupefied de Soya, as is the kindly face of the plump little priest who brings him broth and idle conversation. Finally Father Captain de Soya's reengaging synapses make the connection: Father Baggio, the resurrection chaplain he had last seen in the Vatican Gardens and had been sure he would never see again. Sipping broth, de Soya looks out the rectory window at the pale-blue sky and thinks, *Pacem.* He struggles to recall the events that have brought him there, but the last thing he can remember is the conversation with Gregorius and his men, the long climb up out of the gravity well of Mare Infinitus and 70 Ophiuchi A, then the jolt of translation.

"How?" he mumbles, grasping the kindly priest's sleeve. "Why? . . . How?"

"Now, now," says Father Baggio, "just rest, my son. There will be time to discuss everything later. Time for everything."

Lulled by the soft voice, the rich light, and the oxygen-rich air, de Soya closes his eyes and sleeps. His dreams are ominous.

BY THE NOON MEAL—more broth—it becomes obvious to de Soya that kindly, plump Father Baggio is not going to answer any of his questions: not answer how he got to Pacem, not answer where and how his men are, and not answer why he will not answer. "Father Farrell is coming soon," says the resurrection chaplain as if that explains everything. De Soya gathers his strength, bathes and dresses, tries to gather his wits, and waits for Father Farrell.

Father Farrell arrives in midafternoon. He is a tall, thin, ascetic priest —a commander in the Legionaries of Christ, de Soya learns quickly and with little surprise—and his voice, although soft, is clipped and business-like. Farrell's eyes are a cold gray.

"You are understandably curious," says Father Farrell. "And un-doubtedly still somewhat confused. It is normal for the newly born-again."

"I am familiar with the side effects," says de Soya with a slightly ironic smile. "But I am curious. How is it that I awake on Pacem? What occurred in Hebron System? And how are my men?"

Farrell's gray eyes do not blink as he speaks. "The last question first, Father Captain. Your Sergeant Gregorius and Corporal Kee are well . . . recovering from resurrection in the Swiss Guard resurrection chapel even as we speak."

"Lancer Rettig?" asks de Soya. The sense of foreboding that has been hanging above him since his awakening now stirs its dark wings.

"Dead, I fear," says Farrell. "The true death. Last rites have been administered, and his body has been consigned to the depths of space."

"How did he die . . . the true death, I mean?" manages de Soya. He feels like weeping, but resists because he is not sure if it is simple sorrow or the effects of resurrection.

"I do not know the details," says the tall man. The two are in the rectory's small sitting room, used for meetings and important discussions. They are alone except for the eyes of saints, martyrs, Christ, and His mother. "It seems there was a problem with the automated resurrection creche upon *Raphael*'s return from Hebron System," continues Farrell.

"*Return* from Hebron?" says de Soya. "I'm afraid I do not under-stand, Father. I had programmed the ship to stay unless pursued by Ouster forces. Was that the case?"

"Evidently," replies the Legionary. "As I say, I am not acquainted with the technical details . . . nor am I competent in technical mat-ters . . . but as I understand it, you had programmed your archangel courier to penetrate Ouster-controlled space—"

"We needed to pursue our mission to Hebron," interrupts Father Captain de Soya.

Farrell does not protest the interruption, nor does his neutral expres-sion change, but de Soya looks into those cold gray eyes and does not interrupt again.

"As I was saying, Father Captain, according to my understanding, you programmed your ship to enter Ouster space and—if unchallenged—go into orbit around the planet Hebron."

De Soya gives his silence as confirmation. His dark eyes return the gray stare—with no animosity as of yet, but ready to defend against any accusation.

"It is my understanding that the . . . I believe your courier ship is named the *Raphael*?"

De Soya nods. He realizes now that the careful phrasing, the questions posed when answers are known—all this is the hallmark of a lawyer. The Church has many legal consultants. And inquisitors.

"The *Raphael* appears to have carried out your programming, found no immediate opposition during deceleration, and went into orbit around Hebron," continues Farrell.

"Is that when the resurrection failure occurred?" asks de Soya.

"It is my understanding that this is not the case," says Farrell. The Legionary's gray gaze leaves de Soya for an instant, flicks around the room as if assessing the value of the furniture and art objects there, apparently finds nothing of interest, and returns to the priest-captain. "It is my understanding," he says, "that all four of you on board were close to full resurrection when the ship had to flee the system. Translation shock was, of course, fatal. Secondary resurrection after incomplete resurrection is—as I am sure you are aware—much more difficult than primary resurrection. It is here that the sacrament was circumvented by mechanical failure."

When Farrell stops speaking, there is a silence. Lost in thought, de Soya is only vaguely aware of the sound of groundcar traffic on the narrow street outside, the rumble of a transport lifting from the nearby spaceport. Finally he says, "The creches were inspected and repaired while we were in orbit around Renaissance Vector, Father Farrell."

The other priest nods almost imperceptibly. "We have the records. I believe that it was the same sort of calibration error in Lancer Rettig's automated creche. The investigation continues in Renaissance System garrison. We have also expanded the investigation to Mare Infinitus System, Epsilon Eridani and Epsilon Indi, the world of Inevitable Grace in System Lacaille 9352, Barnard's World, NGC^{es} 2629-4BIV, Vega System, and Tau Ceti."

De Soya can only blink. "You are being very thorough," he says at last. He is thinking, *They must be using both of the other archangel couriers to carry out such an investigation. Why?*

"Yes," says Father Farrell.

Father Captain de Soya sighs and slumps a bit in the soft cushions of the rectory chair. "So they found us in Svoboda System and could not resuscitate Lancer Rettig. . . ."

There is the slightest downward twitch of Farrell's thin lips. "Svoboda System, Father Captain? No. It is my understanding that your courier ship was discovered in System Seventy Ophiuchi A, while decelerating toward the ocean world of Mare Infinitus."

De Soya sits up. "I don't understand. I'd programmed *Raphael* to translate to the next Pax system on her original search pattern if she had to leave Hebron System prematurely. The next world should have been Svoboda."

"Perhaps the form of its pursuit by hostile craft in the Hebron Sys-

tem precluded such a translation alignment," says Farrell without emphasis. "The ship's computer could have then decided to return to its starting
point."

"Perhaps," says de Soya, trying to read the other's expression. It is
useless. "You say 'could have decided,' Father Farrell. Don't you know by
now? Haven't you examined the ship's log?"

Farrell's silence could communicate affirmation or nothing at all.

"And if we returned to Mare Infinitus," continues de Soya, "why are
we waking up here on Pacem? What happened in Seventy Ophiuchi A?"

Now Farrell does smile. It is the narrowest extension of those thin
lips. "By coincidence, Father Captain, the archangel courier *Michael* was
in the Mare Infinitus garrison space when you translated. Captain Wu was
aboard the *Michael*—"

"Marget Wu?" asks de Soya, not caring if he irritates the other man
by interrupting.

"Precisely so." Farrell removes an imaginary bit of lint from his
starched and creased black trousers. "Considering the . . . ah . . . con-
sternation that your previous visit had caused on Mare Infinitus—"

"Meaning my removal of Bishop Melandriano to a monastery to get
him out of my way," says de Soya. "And the arrest of several treasonous
and corrupt Pax officers who were almost certainly carrying out their theft
and conspiracy under Melandriano's supervision . . ."

Farrell holds up one hand to stop de Soya. "These events are not
under my wing of the investigation, Father Captain. I was simply answering your question. If I may continue?"

De Soya stares, feeling the anger mix with his sorrow at Rettig's
death, all swirling amid the narcotic high of resurrection.

"Captain Wu, who had already heard the protests of Bishop Melandriano and other Mare Infinitus administrators, decided that it would be
most felicitous if you were returned to Pacem for resurrection."

"So our resurrection was interrupted a second time?" asks de Soya.

"No." There is no irritation in Farrell's voice. "The resurrection
process had not been initiated in System Seventy Ophiuchi A when the
decision was made to return you to Pax Command and the Vatican."

De Soya looks at his own fingers. They are trembling. In his mind's
eye he can see the *Raphael* with its cargo of corpses, his included. First a
death tour of Hebron System, then decelerating toward Mare Infinitus,
then the spinup to Pacem. He looks up quickly. "How long have we been
dead, Father?"

"Thirty-two days," says Farrell.

De Soya almost pulls himself up out of the chair. Finally he settles
back and says in his most controlled voice, "If Captain Wu decided to
route the ship back here *before* resurrection was begun in Mare Infinitus
space, Father, and if no resurrection was achieved in Hebron space, we

should have been dead less than seventy-two hours at that point. Assuming three days here . . . where were the other twenty-six days spent, Father?"

Farrell runs his fingers along his trouser crease. "There were delays in Mare Infinitus space," he says coolly. "The initial investigation was begun there. Protests were filed. Lancer Rettig was buried in space with full honors. Other . . . duties . . . were carried out. The *Raphael* returned with the *Michael*."

Farrell stands abruptly and de Soya gets to his feet as well. "Father Captain," Farrell announces formally, "I am here to extend Cardinal Secretary Lourdusamy's compliments to you, sir, his wish for your full recovery in health and life in the arms of Christ, and to request your presence, tomorrow morning at oh-seven-hundred hours, at the Vatican offices of the Sacred Congregation for the Doctrine of the Faith, to meet with Monsignor Lucas Oddi and other appointed officials of the Sacred Congregation."

De Soya is stunned. He can only click his heels and bow his head in compliance. He is a Jesuit and an officer in the Pax Fleet. He has been trained to discipline.

"Very good," says Father Farrell, and takes his leave.

Father Captain de Soya stands in the rectory foyer for several minutes after the Legionary of Christ has left. As a mere priest and a line officer, de Soya has been spared most Church politics and infighting, but even a provincial priest or preoccupied Pax warrior knows the basic structure of the Vatican and its purpose.

Beneath the Pope, there are two major administrative categories—the Roman Curia and the so-called Sacred Congregations. De Soya knows that the Curia is an awkward and labyrinthine administrative structure—its "modern" form was set down by Sixtus V in A.D. 1588 The Curia includes the Secretariat of State, Cardinal Lourdusamy's power base, where he serves as a sort of prime minister with the misleading title of Cardinal Secretary of State. This Secretariat is a central part of what is often referred to as the "Old Curia," used by popes since the sixteenth century. In addition, there is the "New Curia," begun as sixteen lesser bodies created by the Second Vatican Council—still popularly known as Vatican II—which concluded in A.D. 1965 Those sixteen bodies have grown to thirty-one intertwining entities under Pope Julius's 260-year reign.

But it is not the Curia to which de Soya has been summoned, but to one of its separate and sometimes countervailing clusters of authority, the Sacred Congregations. Specifically, he has been ordered to appear before the so-called Sacred Congregation of the Doctrine of the Faith, an organization that has gained—or, to be more precise, *regained*—enormous power in the past two centuries. Under Pope Julius, the Sacred Congregation for the Doctrine of the Faith again welcomed the Pope as its Prefect—

a change in structure that revitalized the office. For the twelve centuries prior to Pope Julius's election, this Sacred Congregation—known as the Holy Office from A.D. 1908 to A.D. 1964—had been deemphasized to the point it had become almost a vestigial organ. But now, under Julius, the Holy Office's power is felt across five hundred light-years of space and back through three thousand years of history.

De Soya returns to the sitting room and leans against the chair he had been sitting in. His mind is swirling. He knows now that he will not be allowed to see Gregorius or Kee before his meeting in the Holy Office the next morning. He may never see them again. De Soya tries to unravel the thread that has pulled him to this meeting, but it becomes lost in the snarl of Church politics, offended clerics, Pax power struggles, and the swirl of his own befuddled, born-again brain.

He knows this: the Sacred Congregation for the Doctrine of the Faith, previously known as the Sacred Congregation of the Holy Office, had—for many centuries prior to that—been known as the Sacred Congregation of Universal Inquisition.

And it is under Pope Julius XIV that the Inquisition has once again begun living up to its original name and sense of terror. And, without preparation, counsel, or knowledge of what accusations may be levied against him, de Soya must appear before them at oh-seven-hundred hours the next morning.

Father Baggio bustles in, a smile on the chubby priest's cherubic features. "Did you have a nice conversation with Father Farrell, my son?"

"Yes," says de Soya distractedly. "Very nice."

"Good, good," says Father Baggio. "But I think it's time for a bit of broth, a bit of prayer—the Angelus, I think—and then an early beddie-bye. We must be fresh for whatever tomorrow brings, mustn't we?"

WHEN I WAS A CHILD LISTENING to Grandam's endless parade of verses, one short piece I demanded to hear over and over started—"Some say the world will end in fire,/ Some say in ice." Grandam did not know the name of the poet—she thought it might be by a pre-Hegira poet named Frost, but even at my young age I thought that was too cute to be true for a poem about fire and ice—but the *idea* of the world ending in either fire or ice had long stayed with me, as enduring as the singsong rhythm of the simple verse.

My world seemed to be ending in ice.

It was dark beneath the ice wall, and too cold for me to find adequate words to describe. I had been burned before—once a gas stove had exploded on a barge going upriver on the Kans and gave me slight but painful burns over my arms and chest—so I knew the intensity of fire. This cold seemed that intense, sort of slow-motion flames cutting my flesh to shreds.

The rope was secured under my arms, and the powerful current soon whirled me around so I was being dragged feet-first down the black chute, my hands raised to keep my face from bashing against inverted ridges of rock-hard ice, my chest and underarms constrained by the tight rope as A. Bettik acted as brake by staying on belay. My knees were soon torn by razor-sharp ice as the current kept throwing my body higher, striking the uneven ceiling of passing ice like someone being dragged across rocky ground.

I had worn socks with the ice more in mind than the cold, but they did little to protect my feet as I banged into the ice ridges. I was also wearing undershorts and undershirt, but they provided no buffer against the needles of cold. Around my neck was the band of the com unit, the mike-patches pressed against my throat for voice or subvocal transmission, the hearplug in place. Over my shoulder and tightly secured with tape was the waterproof bag with the plastique, detonators, cord, and two flares I had put in at the last moment. Taped to my wrist was my little flashlight laser, its narrow beam cutting through the black water and bouncing off ice, but illuminating little. I had used the laser sparingly since the Labyrinth on Hyperion: the handlamps were more useful in widebeam and required less charge. The laser was largely useless as a cutting weapon, but should serve to bore holes in ice for the plastique.

If I lived long enough to bore holes.

The only method behind my madness of allowing myself to be swept away down this subterranean river had been a bit of knowledge from my Home Guard training on the Iceshelf of the continent Ursus. There, on the Bearpaw Glacial Sea, where the ice froze and refroze almost daily through the brief antarctic summer, the risk of breaking through the thin surface ice had been very high. We had been trained that even if we were swept away beneath the thickest ice, there was always a thin layer of air between the sea and icy ceiling. We were to rise to that brief layer, set our snouts into it even if it meant that the rest of our faces had to stay submerged, and move along the ice until we came to a break or thin-enough patch that we could smash our way out.

That had been the theory. My only actual test of it had been as a member of a search party fanning out to hunt for a scarab driver who had stepped out of his vehicle, broken through not two meters from where the ice supported the weight of his four-ton machine, and disappeared. I was the one who found him, almost six hundred meters from the scarab and safe ice. He had used the breathing technique. His nose was still pressed tight against the too-thick ice when I found him—but his mouth was open underwater, his face was as white as the snow that blew across the glacier, and his eyes were frozen as solid as steel bearings. I tried not to think of this as I fought my way to the surface against the current, tugged on the rope to signal A. Bettik to stop me, and scraped my face against shards of ice to find air.

There were several centimeters of space between water and ice— more where fissures ran up into the glacier of frozen atmosphere like inverted crevasses. I gasped the cold air into my lungs, shined the flashlight laser into the crevasses, and then moved the red beam back and forward along the narrow tunnel of ice. "Going to rest a minute," I gasped. "I'm okay. How far have I come?"

"About eight meters," whispered A. Bettik's voice in my ear.

"Shit," I muttered, forgetting that the com would send the subvocal. It had seemed like twenty or thirty meters, at least. "All right," I said aloud. "I'm going to set the first charge here."

My fingers were still flexible enough to trigger the flashlight laser to high intensity and burn out a small niche into the side of the fissure. I had premolded the plastique, and now I worked it, shaped it, and vectored it. The material was a shaped explosive—that is, the blast would discharge itself in precisely the directions I wanted, provided that my preparations were correct. In this case I had done most of the work ahead of time, knowing that I wanted the blast directed upward and back toward the ice wall behind me. Now I aimed precise tendrils of that explosive force: the same technology that allowed a plasma bolt to cut through steel plate like hot bolts dropped into butter would send these plasma tendrils lancing back through the incredible mass of the ice behind me. It should cut the eight-meter section of ice wall into chunks and drop them into the river very nicely. We were counting on the fact that the atmosphere generators through the years of terraforming had added enough nitrogen and CO_2 to the atmosphere to keep the explosion from turning into one massive blast of burning oxygen.

Because I knew exactly where I wanted to aim the force of the blast, the shaping of the charges took less than forty-five seconds and required little dexterity. Still, I was shaking and almost numb by the time the tiny detonator squibs were set in place. Since I knew the com units had no trouble penetrating this amount of ice, I set the detonators to the preset code and ignored the wire in my bag.

"Okay," I gasped, settling lower in the water, "let out the slack."

The wild ride began again, the current pulling me lower into blackness and then battering me against the crystal ceiling, then the wild search for air, the gasped commands, the struggle to see and work while the last warmth drained from me.

The ice continued for another thirty meters—right at the outer limits of what I thought the plastique could handle. I set the charges in two more places, another fissure and the last bundle in a narrow tube I burned into solid ceiling ice. My hands were totally numb during the last placement— it was as if I were wearing thick gloves of ice—but I directed the charges up- and downstream in roughly the proper vectors. If there were not an end to this ice wall soon, all this would be in vain. A. Bettik and I had anticipated chopping away at some ice with the ax, but we could not hack our way through many meters of the stuff.

At forty-one meters I burst up and out into air again. At first I was afraid it was merely another crevasse, but when I aimed the flashlight laser, the red beam flicked through a chamber longer and wider than the one where I had left the raft. We had discussed it and decided that we would not blow the explosives if I could see the end of any second chamber, but when I lowered the beam down the length of the black river here, illuminating the same mist and stalactites, I could see that the river—about thirty meters wide at that point—curved out of sight several hundred meters downstream. There were no more riverbanks or visible tunnels here than there had been in our earlier stretch of river, but at least the river appeared to keep running.

I wanted to see what the river did once it rounded the turn, but I had neither the rope nor body heat I needed to float that far, report, and get back alive. "Pull me back!" I gasped.

For the next two minutes I hung on—or tried to hang on; my hands no longer worked—as the android hauled me back against that terrible current, stopping occasionally as I floated on my back and gasped in the frigid air of the crevasses. Then the black ride would begin again.

If A. Bettik had been in the water and I had been pulling—or even if it had been the child—I could not have pulled either of them back through that heavy current in four times the time it took A. Bettik. I knew that he was strong, but no superman—no miraculous android strength—but he showed superhuman strength that day. I could only guess at the reservoirs of energy he used to pull me back to the raft so quickly. I helped as best I could, slashing my hands by pulling myself along the icy ceiling and fending off sharper crystals, kicking weakly against the current.

When my head broke the surface again, seeing the haloed lantern light and the shapes of my two companions leaning toward me, I did not have the strength to lift my arms or to help pull myself onto the raft. A. Bettik seized me under the arms and lifted me gently out. Aenea grabbed my dripping legs, and they carried me toward the stern of the raft. I admit that my dulled brain was reminded of the Catholic church we stopped by occasionally in the north-moor village of Latmos, the little town where we picked up our food and simple shepherd supplies, and of one of the large religious paintings on the south wall of that church: Christ being taken off the cross, one of his disciple's arms under his limp arms, his bare and mutilated feet being held by the Virgin.

Don't flatter yourself, came the unbidden thought through my mental fog. It spoke in Aenea's voice.

They carried me to the frost-laden tent, where the thermal blanket was ready on a pile of two sleeping bags and a thin mat. The heating cube glowed next to this nest. A. Bettik stripped me of my sodden undershirt, flare bag, and com unit. He untaped the flashlight laser, set it carefully in my pack, laid me firmly within the top sleeping bag with the thermal blanket around me, and opened a medpak. Setting sticky biomonitor contacts against my chest, the inside of my thigh, my left wrist, and temple, he looked at the readouts a moment and then injected me with one ampule of adrenonitrotaline, as we had planned.

You must be getting tired of pulling me out of the water, I wanted to say, but my jaws and tongue and vocal apparatus would not oblige. I was so cold that I was not even shivering. Consciousness was a slender thread connecting me to the light, and it wavered in the cold wind that blew through me.

A. Bettik leaned closer. "M. Endymion, the charges are set?"

I managed a nod. It was all I could do, and it seemed that I was operating a clumsy marionette to do that.

Aenea dropped to her knees next to me. To A. Bettik she said, "I'll watch him. You get us out of here."

The android left the tent to push us away from the ice wall and to pole us upstream, using the push-pole from that end of the raft. After the expenditure of energy it had taken to drag me back against the current, I could not believe he could find the strength to move the entire raft the necessary distance upriver.

We began moving. I could see the lantern glow on the mist and distant ceiling through the triangular opening at the end of the tent. The fog and icy stalactites moved slowly across the tiny reference triangle, as though I were peering through an isoscelean hole in reality at the Ninth Circle of Dante's hell.

Aenea was watching the simple medpak monitors. "Raul, Raul . . . ," she whispered.

The thermal blanket held in all the heat I was producing, but I felt as if I were not producing any body heat. My bones ached with the chill, but my frozen nerve ends did not convey the pain. I was very, very sleepy.

Aenea shook me awake. "You stay with me, dammit!"

I'll try, I thought at her. I knew I was lying. All I wanted to do was sleep.

"A. Bettik!" cried the child, and I was vaguely aware of the android entering the tent and consulting the medpak. Their words were a distant humming that no longer made sense to me.

I was far, far away when I dimly sensed a body next to me. A. Bettik had gone away to pole our ice-laden raft upstream against bitter current. The child Aenea had crawled under the thermal blanket and edge of the sleeping bag with me. At first the heat of her skinny body did not penetrate the layers of permafrost that now lay in me, but I was aware of her breathing, of the angular intrusion of her elbows and knees in the tented space with me.

No, no, I thought in her direction. *I'm the protector here . . . the strong one hired to save you.* The cold sleepiness did not allow me to speak aloud.

I do not remember if she put her arms around me. I know that I was no more responsive than a frozen log, no more receptive to company than one of the icy stalactites that moved across my triangular field of vision, its underside lighted by the lantern's glow, its top lost in darkness and mist much as was my mind.

Eventually I began to feel some of the warmth her small body poured out. The heat was dimly perceived, but my skin began to prickle with needles of pain where the warmth flowed from her skin to mine. I wished I could speak just to tell her to move away so that I could doze in nerveless peace.

Sometime later—it might have been fifteen minutes or two hours—A. Bettik returned to the tent. I was conscious enough to realize that he must have followed our plan: "anchoring" the raft with lodged push-poles and steering oar somewhere in the narrowing upper part of the ice cave under the visible segment of farcaster portal. Our theory had been that the metal arch might protect us from avalanche and icefall when the charges went off.

Blow the charges, I wanted to say to him. Instead of keying the com band, however, the android stripped to his tropical yellow short/pants and shirt, then crawled under the thermal blanket with the girl and me.

This should have been comical—it may sound comical to you as you read this—but nothing in my life had moved me as deeply as this act, this sharing of warmth by my two traveling companions. Not even their brave and foolhardy rescue of me in the violet sea had touched me so deeply. The three of us lay there—Aenea on my left, her left arm around me, A. Bettik on my right, his body curled against the cold that crept in under the corner of the thermal blanket. In a few minutes I would be weeping from the pain that came from returning circulation, from the agony of thawing flesh, but at this moment I wept at the intimate gift of their warmth as life's heat flowed from both child and blue-skinned man, flowed from their blood and flesh to mine.

I weep now in the telling of it.

How long we stayed that way, I cannot say. I never asked the two of them and they never spoke of it. It must have been at least an hour. It felt like a lifetime of warmth and pain and the overpowering joy of life's return.

Eventually I began trembling, then shaking slightly, and then shaking violently, as if possessed by seizures. My friends held me then, not allowing me to escape from the warmth. I believe that Aenea was also weeping by that point, although I have never asked, and in later days she never spoke of it.

Finally, after the pain and palsy had largely passed, A. Bettik slipped out from under our common cover, consulted the medpak, and spoke to the child in a language I once again could comprehend. "All within the green," he said softly. "No permanent frostbite. No permanent damage."

Shortly after that, Aenea slipped out of the blanket and helped me sit up, putting two of the hoar-frosted packs behind my back and head. She set water to boiling over the glowing cube, made mugs of steaming tea, and held one to my lips. I could move my hands by then, even flex my fingers, but the pain there was too great to grasp anything successfully.

"M. Endymion," said A. Bettik, crouching just outside the tent, "I am prepared to transmit the detonation code."

I nodded.

"There may be falling debris, sir," he added.

I nodded again. We had discussed the risk of that. The shaped charges should shatter just the ice walls ahead of us, but the resulting seismic vibrations through the ice might well bring the entire glacier of frozen atmosphere down around us, driving the raft to the shallow bottom and entombing us there. We had judged it worth the risk. Now I glanced up at the frost-rimmed interior of the microtent and smiled at the thought that this would give us any shelter. I nodded a third time, urging him to go ahead.

The sound of the blast was more subdued than I expected, much less noisy than the concomitant tumble of ice blocks and stalactites and the wild surging of the river itself. For a second I thought that we were going to be lifted and crushed against the cave ceiling as wave after wave of pressure-propelled and ice-displaced river water surged under the raft. We huddled on our little stone hearth, trying to stay out of the frigid water, and riding the bucking logs like passengers on a storm-tossed life dinghy.

Eventually the surging and rumbling calmed itself. The violent maneuvers had snapped our steering oar, flung one of the push-poles away, dislodged us from our safe haven, and floated us downstream to the ice wall.

To where the ice wall used to be.

The charges had done their job much as we had planned: the cavern it had created was low and jagged, but after probing it with the flashlight laser, it appeared to go through to the open channel beyond. Aenea cheered. A. Bettik patted me on the back. I am ashamed to admit that I may have wept again.

It was not so easy a victory as it first seemed. Fallen ice blocks and surviving columns of ice still blocked parts of the passage, and even after the initial rush of ice into the breach slowed a bit, it meant heavy going with the surviving push-pole and frequent pauses as A. Bettik hacked away at icy obstacles with the ax.

Half an hour into this effort I staggered to the front of our battered raft and gestured that it was my turn with the ax.

"Are you sure, M. Endymion?" asked the blue-skinned man.

"Quite . . . sure . . . ," I said carefully, forcing my cold tongue and jaw to enunciate properly.

The work with the ax soon warmed me to the point that the last of the shaking stopped. I could feel the terrible bruises and scrapes where the ice ceiling had battered me, but I would deal with those pains later.

Finally we hacked our way through the last bars of ice to float into the open current. The three of us pounded sock-mittens together for a moment, but then retreated to huddle near the heating cube and to play the handlamps on either side as new scenery floated by.

The new scenery was identical to the old: vertical walls of ice on either side, stalactites threatening to drop on us at any moment, the rushing black water.

"Maybe it will stay open all the way to the next arch," said Aenea, and the fog of her breath remained in the air like a promise.

We all stood up as the raft swept around the bend in the ice-buried river. For a moment it was confusion as A. Bettik used the pole and I used the shattered stub of the steering oar to fend us off the port-side ice wall. Then we were in the central current again and picking up speed.

"Oh . . . ," said the girl from where she stood at the front of the raft. Her tone told us everything.

The river went another sixty meters or so, narrowed, and ended at a second ice wall.

IT WAS AENEA'S IDEA to send the comlog bracelet ahead as a scout. "It has the video microbead," she said.

"But we have no monitor," I pointed out. "And it can't send the video feed to the ship. . . ."

Aenea was shaking her head. "No, but the comlog itself can *see*. It can *tell* us what it sees."

"Yes," I said, finally understanding, "but is it smart enough without the ship AI behind it to understand what it sees?"

"Shall we ask it?" said A. Bettik, who had retrieved the bracelet from my pack.

We reactivated the thing and asked it. It assured us, in that almost-arrogant ship's voice, that it was quite capable of processing its visual data and relaying its analysis to us via the com band. It also assured us that although it could not float and had not learned to swim, it was completely waterproof.

Aenea used the flashlight laser to cut off the end of one of the logs, pounded nails and pivot-bolt rings to hold the bracelet in place around it, and added a hook ring for the climbing rope. She used a double half hitch to secure the line.

"We should have used this for the first ice wall," I said.

She smiled. Her cap was rimmed with frost. Actual icicles hung on the short brim. "The bracelet might have had some trouble setting the charges," she said. I realized as she spoke that the child was very weary.

"Good luck," I said idiotically as we tossed the braceleted log into the river. The comlog had the good grace not to respond. It was swept under the ice wall almost immediately.

We brought the heating cube forward and crouched near it as A. Bettik let out the line. I turned up the volume of the com unit's speakers, and none of us said a word as the line snaked out and the tinny voice of the comlog reported back.

"Ten meters. Crevasses above, but none wider than six centimeters. No end to the ice."

"Twenty meters. Ice continues."

"Fifty meters. Ice."

"Seventy-five meters. No end in sight."

"One hundred meters. Ice." The comlog was at the end of its tether. We spliced on our last length of climbing rope.

"One hundred fifty meters. Ice."

"One hundred eighty meters. Ice."

"Two hundred meters. Ice."

We were out of rope and out of hope. I began hauling in the comlog. Even though my hands were sensate and awkwardly functional now, it was difficult for me to haul the essentially weightless bracelet back upstream, so vicious was the current and heavy the ice-laden rope. Once again I had difficulty imagining the effort A. Bettik had put forth in saving me.

The line was almost too stiff to curl. We had to chip away the ice from around the comlog when it was finally hauled aboard. "Although the cold depletes my power unit and the ice covers my visual pickups," chirped the bracelet, "I am willing and able to continue the exploration."

"No, thank you," A. Bettik said politely, turning off the device and returning it to me. The metal was too cold to handle, even with my sock-mittens on. I dropped the bangle into the frosted backpack.

"We wouldn't have had enough plastique for fifty meters of ice," I said. My voice was absolutely calm—even the shivering had stopped—and I realized that it was because of the absolute unblinking clarity of the death sentence that had just descended upon us.

There was—I realize now—another reason for that oasis of calm amid the desert of pain and hopelessness there. It was the warmth. The remembered warmth. The flow of life from those two people to me, my acceptance of it, the sacred communion-sense of it. Now, in the lanterned darkness, we went ahead with the urgent business of attempting to stay alive, discussing impossible options such as using the plasma rifle to blast a way through, discarding impossible options, and discussing more of the same. But all the while in that cold, dark pit of confusion and rising hopelessness, the core of warmth that had been breathed back into me from these two . . . friends . . . kept me calm, even as their human proximity had kept me alive. In the difficult times to come—and even now, as I write this, even while expecting death's stealthy arrival by cyanide on every breath I take—that memory of shared warmth, that first total sharing of vitality, keeps me calm and steady through the storm of human fears.

We decided to pole the raft back the length of the new channel, seeking some overlooked crevasse or niche or airshaft. It seemed hopeless, but perhaps a shade less hopeless than leaving the raft pressed up against this terminal icefall.

We found it right below where the river had made its dogleg to the right. Evidently we had all been too busy fending off the ice walls and regaining the center current to notice the narrow rift in the jagged ice along what had been our starboard side. Although we were searching diligently, we would not have discovered the narrow opening without the tightbeam of the flashlight laser: our lantern light, twisted by crystal facet and hanging ice, passed right over it. Common sense told us that this was just another folding in the ice, a horizontal equivalent of the vertical crevasses I had found in the ice ceiling: a breathing space leading nowhere. Our need for hope prayed that common sense was wrong.

The opening—fold—whatever, was less than a meter wide and opened onto air almost two meters above the river's surface. Poling closer, we could see by laser light that either the opening ended or its narrowing corridor bent out of sight less than three meters in. Common sense told us that it was the end of the icy cul-de-sac. Once again we ignored common sense.

While Aenea leaned into the long pole, straining to hold the raft in place against the churning water, A. Bettik boosted me up. I used the claw end of our hammer as a climbing tool, chipping it deep into the ice floor of the narrow defile and pulling myself up by speed and desperation. Once up there on my hands and knees, panting and weak, I caught my breath, stood, and waved down to the others. They would wait for my report.

The narrow ice tunnel bent sharply to the right. I aimed the flashlight laser down this second corridor with rising hope. Another ice wall reflected back the red beam, but this time there did not seem to be a bend in the tunnel. No, wait . . . As I moved down the second corridor, stooping low as the ice ceiling lowered, I realized that the tunnel rose steeply just beyond this point. The light had been shining on the floor of the icy ramp. Depth perception did not exist here.

Squeezing through the tight space, I crawled on all fours for a dozen meters, boots scrabbling on the jagged ice. I thought of the shop in echoing, empty New Jerusalem where I had "bought" those boots—leaving my hospital slippers behind and a handful of Hyperion scrip on the counter—and tried to remember if there had been any ice crampons for sale in the camping section there. Too late now.

At one point I had to slither on my belly, once again sure that the corridor was going to end within a meter, but this time it turned sharply to the left and ran straight and level—deep into the ice—for twenty more meters or so before angling right and climbing again. Panting, shaking with excitement, I jogged, slid, and claw-hammered my way back downhill to the opening. The laser beam cast back countless reflections of my excited expression from the clear ice.

Aenea and A. Bettik had begun packing necessary equipment as soon as I had disappeared from sight. The girl had already been boosted to the ice niche and was setting aside gear as A. Bettik tossed it up. We shouted instructions and suggestions to one another. Everything seemed necessary —sleeping bags, thermal blanket, the folded tent—which could be compressed to only a third of its former tiny size, due to the ice and frost on it —heating cube, food, inertial compass, weapons, handlamps.

In the end, we had most of the raft's gear on the landing. We argued some more—the exercise and hot air of it keeping us warm for a minute— then chose just what was necessary and what could fit in our packs and shoulder bags. I carried the pistol on my belt and lashed the plasma rifle on my pack. A. Bettik agreed to carry the shotgun, its ammunition topping off his already bulging pack. Luckily the packs were empty of clothes—we were wearing everything we owned—so we loaded up on food paks and gear. Aenea and the android kept the com units; I slid the still-icy comlog onto my bulky wrist. Despite the precaution, we had no intention of losing sight of one another.

I was worried about the raft drifting away—the lodged push-pole and shattered steering oar would not hold it for long—but A. Bettik solved that in a moment by rigging bow and stern lines, melting niches in the ice wall with the flashlight laser, and tying the lines around solid ice cleats.

Before we started up the narrow ice corridor, I took a final look at our faithful raft, doubtful that we would ever see it again. It was a pathetic sight: the stone hearth was still in place, but the steering oar was in splinters, our lantern mast in the bow had been broken and splinted, the leading edges had been bashed about and the logs on either sides were all but splintered, the stern was awash, and the entire vessel was filmed with ice and half-hidden by the icy vapors that swirled around us. I nodded my gratitude and farewell to the sad wreck, turned, and led the way to the right and up—pushing the heavy pack and bulging shoulder bag ahead of me during the lowest and narrowest bit.

I had feared that the corridor would run to an end a few meters beyond where I had explored, but thirty minutes of climbing, crawling, sliding, and outright scrambling led to more tunnels, more turns, and always climbing. Even though the exertion kept us alive, if not actually warm, each of us could feel the invasive cold making gains on us. Sooner or later exhaustion would claim us and we would have to stop, set our rolled mats and sleeping bags out, and see if we would awaken after sleeping in such cold. But not yet.

Passing chocolate bars back, pausing to thaw the ice in one of our canteens by passing the laser beam across it at its widest setting, I said, "Not much farther now."

"Not much farther to *what*?" asked Aenea from beneath her crest of frost and ice. "We can't be near the surface yet . . . we haven't climbed that far."

"Not much farther to something interesting," I said. As soon as I spoke, the vapor from my breath froze to the front of my jacket and the stubble on my chin. I knew that my eyebrows were dripping ice.

"Interesting," repeated the girl, sounding dubious. I understood. So far, "interesting" had done its best to get us killed.

An hour later we had paused to heat some food over the cube—which had to be rigged carefully so it would not melt its way through the ice floor while heating our pot of stew—and I was consulting my inertial compass to get some idea of how far we had come and how high we'd climbed, when A. Bettik said, "Quiet!"

All three of us seemed to be holding our breath for minutes. Finally Aenea whispered, "What? I don't hear anything."

It was a miracle that we could hear each other when we shouted, our heads were so wrapped about with makeshift scarves and balaclavas.

A. Bettik frowned and held his finger to his lips for silence. After a moment he whispered, "Footsteps. And they're coming this way."

39

I N PACEM THE MAIN INTERROGATION center for the Holy Roman Office of the Universal Inquisition is not in the Vatican proper, but in the great heap of stone called Castel Sant'Angelo, a massive, circular fort begun as Hadrian's tomb in A.D. 135, connected to the Aurelian Wall in A.D. 271 to become the most important fortress in Rome, and one of the few buildings of Rome to be moved with the Vatican when the Church evacuated its offices from Old Earth in the last days before the planet's collapse into the core-gobbling black hole. The castle—actually a conical monolith of moat-surrounded stones—became important to the Church during the Plague Year of A.D. 587 when Gregory the Great, while leading a prayer procession beseeching God to end the plague, had a vision of Michael the Archangel atop the tomb. Later, Castel Sant'Angelo sheltered popes from angry mobs, offered its dank cells and torture chambers to such perceived enemies of the Church as Benvenuto Cellini, and, in its nearly three thousand years of existence, had proved itself impervious to both barbarian invasion and nuclear explosion. It now sits like a low gray mountain in the center of the only open land remaining within the busy triangle of highways, buildings, and administrative centers running between the Vatican, the Pax administrative city, and the space-port.

Father Captain de Soya presents himself twenty minutes before his 0730 appointment and is given a badge that will guide him through the sweating, windowless vaults and corridors of the castle. The frescoes, beautiful furnishings, and airy loggias set there by popes of the Middle Ages have long since faded and fallen into disrepair. Castel Sant'Angelo has once again taken on the character of a tomb and fortress. De Soya knows that a fortified passage from the Vatican to the castle had been brought along from Old Earth, and that one of the purposes of the Holy

Office in the past two centuries has been to supply Castel Sant'Angelo with modern weapons and defenses so that it might still offer quick refuge to the Pope should interstellar war come to Pacem.

The walk takes the full twenty minutes, and he must pass through frequent checkpoints and security doors, each guarded not by the brightly garbed Swiss Guard police of the Vatican, but by the black-and-silver uniformed security forces of the Holy Office.

The interrogation cell itself is infinitely less dreary than the ancient corridors and stairs that lead to it: two of the three interior stone walls are brightened by smart-glass panels that glow a soft yellow; two sunbundles spread sunlight from their collector on the roof thirty meters above; the spartan room is furnished by a modern conference table—de Soya's chair sits opposite that of his five Inquisitors, but is identical to theirs in design and comfort, and a standard office work center sits against one wall with keyboards, datascreens, diskey plate, and virtual inputs, and a sideboard with a coffee urn and breakfast rolls.

De Soya has to wait only a minute before the Inquisitors arrive. The cardinals—one Jesuit, one Dominican, and three Legionaries of Christ—introduce themselves and shake hands. De Soya has worn his black Pax Fleet dress uniform with its Roman collar, and it stands in contrast to the crimson Holy Office tunics with their black-tabbed collars. There are a few niceties—a moment's conversation about de Soya's health and successful resurrection, offers of food and coffee—de Soya accepts the coffee —and then they take their seats.

In the tradition of the early days of the Holy Office and as has been the custom in the Renewed Church when priests are the subject of investigation, the discussion is held in Latin. Only one of the five cardinals on the panel actually speaks. The questions are polite, formal, and invariably phrased in the third person. At the end of the interview, transcripts in Latin and Web English are given to the interview subject.

INQUISITOR: Has Father Captain de Soya reported success in finding and detaining the child known as Aenea?

F.C. DE SOYA: I have had contact with the child. I have not succeeded in detaining her.

INQUISITOR: Let him say what the meaning of "contact" is within this context.

F.C. DE SOYA: I have twice intercepted the ship which carried the child away from Hyperion. Once in Parvati System, a second time near and on Renaissance Vector.

INQUISITOR: These unsuccessful attempts at taking the child into custody have been recorded and are duly entered into the record. Is it his contention that the child would have died by her own hand in Parvati System before the specially trained Swiss Guard troops aboard his ship could have forced entry and taken the child into protective custody?

F.C. DE SOYA: It was my belief at the time. I felt the risk was too great.

INQUISITOR: And to his knowledge, did the ranking Swiss Guard Commander in charge of the actual boarding operation—one Sergeant Gregorius—agree with the Father Captain that the operation should be called off?

F.C. DE SOYA: I am not sure of Sergeant Gregorius's opinion after the boarding operation was canceled. At the time he argued to go.

INQUISITOR: And does he know the opinion of the other two troopers involved in the boarding operation?

F.C. DE SOYA: At the time they wanted to go. They had trained hard and were ready. It was my opinion at the time, however, that the risk of the girl harming herself was too great.

INQUISITOR: And was this the same reason he did not intercept the runaway ship prior to its entering the atmosphere of the world known as Renaissance Vector?

F.C. DE SOYA: No. In that instance the girl said that she was landing on the planet. It seemed safer for everyone concerned to allow her to do so before taking her into custody.

INQUISITOR: And yet, when the aforementioned ship approached the dormant farcaster portal on Renaissance Vector, the priest-captain ordered various ships in the Fleet and air forces to fire on the child's ship. . . . Is this correct?

F.C. DE SOYA: Yes.

INQUISITOR: Is it his contention, then, that this command held no danger of harming the girl?

F.C. DE SOYA: No. I knew that there was a risk. However, when I realized that the girl's ship was headed for the farcaster portal, it was my firm belief that we would lose her if we did not attempt to disable her spacecraft.

INQUISITOR: Did he have some knowledge that the farcaster portal along the river would activate itself after almost three centuries of dormancy?

F.C. DE SOYA: No knowledge. A sudden intuition. A hunch.

INQUISITOR: Is he in the habit of risking the success or failure of a mission—a mission labeled the highest priority by the Holy Father himself—on a hunch?

F.C. DE SOYA: I am not in the habit of being sent on a mission of highest priority by the Holy Father. In certain instances where my ships have been in combat, I have made command decisions based upon insights which would not have seemed totally logical outside the context of my experience and training.

INQUISITOR: Is he saying that knowledge of a farcaster's renewed activity some two hundred seventy-four years after the Fall of the Web which sustained them is within the context of his experience and training?

F.C. DE SOYA: No. It was . . . a hunch.

INQUISITOR: Is he aware of the expense of the combined Fleet operation in Renaissance System?

F.C. DE SOYA: I know it was considerable.

INQUISITOR: Is he aware that several ships of the line were delayed in carrying out their orders from Pax Fleet Command—orders which were sending them to vital trouble spots along the so-called Great Wall of our defensive perimeter against the invading Ousters?

F.C. DE SOYA: I was aware that ships were delayed in Renaissance System upon my order. Yes.

INQUISITOR: On the world of Mare Infinitus, the father-captain saw fit to arrest several Pax officers.

F.C. DE SOYA: Yes.

INQUISITOR: And to administer Truthtell and other restricted psychotropic drugs to these officers without due process or the advice of the Pax and Church authorities on Mare Infinitus?

F.C. DE SOYA: Yes.

INQUISITOR: Is it his contention that the papal diskey conferred upon him to carry out his mission of finding the child also authorized him to arrest Pax officers and carry out such interrogation without the due process of military courts or provided counsel?

F.C. DE SOYA: Yes. It was and is my understanding that the papal diskey gives me . . . gave me . . . full authorization in the field for whatever command decisions I deemed necessary in the completion of this mission.

INQUISITOR: Is it his contention, then, that the arrest of these Pax officers will lead to the successful detention of the child named Aenea?

F.C. DE SOYA: My investigation was necessary to determine the truth of the events surrounding the probable passage of that child from farcaster to farcaster on Mare Infinitus. During the course of that investigation, it became apparent that the director of the platform on which the events occurred had been lying to his superiors, covering up elements of the incident involving the girl's traveling companion, and also had been involved in treasonable deals with the poachers in those waters. At the conclusion of our investigation, I turned over the officers and men who had been involved to the Pax garrison for due-process handling within the Fleet Code of Military Justice.

INQUISITOR: And did he feel that his treatment of Bishop Melandriano was also justified under the requirements of the . . . investigation?

F.C. DE SOYA: Despite explanations of the need for swift action, Bishop Melandriano objected to our investigation on Platform Station

Three-twenty-six Mid-littoral. He tried to stop the investigation from a distance—despite direct orders to cooperate from his superior, Archbishop Jane Kelley.

INQUISITOR: Is it the father–captain's contention that Archbishop Kelley offered her help in soliciting the cooperation of Bishop Melandriano?

F.C. DE SOYA: No. I sought her help.

INQUISITOR: In truth, did the father–captain not invoke the authority of the papal diskey in compelling Archbishop Kelley to intervene on the behalf of the investigation?

F.C. DE SOYA: Yes.

INQUISITOR: Can he state the events which occurred after Bishop Melandriano came in person to Platform Station Three-twenty-six Mid-littoral?

F.C. DE SOYA: Bishop Melandriano was in a rage. He ordered the Pax troops guarding my prisoners—

INQUISITOR: When the father-captain refers to "my prisoners," he means the former director and Pax officers of the platform?

F.C. DE SOYA: Yes.

INQUISITOR: He may continue.

F.C. DE SOYA: Bishop Melandriano ordered the Pax troops I had brought in to release Captain Powl and the others. I countermanded the order. Bishop Melandriano refused to recognize my authority as delegated by the papal diskey. I had the Bishop put under temporary arrest and transported to the Jesuit monastery on a platform six hundred kilometers from the planet's south pole. Storms and other contingencies prevented the Bishop from leaving for several days. By the time he did, my investigation was complete.

INQUISITOR: And what did the investigation purport to show?

F.C. DE SOYA: Among other things, it showed that Bishop Melandriano had been receiving large payments of cash from the poachers within the jurisdiction of Platform Station Three-twenty-six Mid-littoral. It also showed that Director Powl of the platform had been under the direction of Bishop Melandriano in carrying out illegal activities with the poachers and in extorting money from the offworld fishermen.

INQUISITOR: Did the father-captain confront Bishop Melandriano with these allegations?

F.C. DE SOYA: No.

INQUISITOR: Did he bring it to the attention of Archbishop Kelley?

F.C. DE SOYA: No.

INQUISITOR: Did he bring it to the attention of the ranking Pax garrison commander?

F.C. DE SOYA: No.

INQUISITOR: Can he explain these omissions of action as required by the

Pax Fleet Code of Conduct and the rules of the Church and Society
of Jesus?

F.C. DE SOYA: The Bishop's involvement in these crimes was not the
focus of my investigation. I turned Captain Powl and the others over
to the garrison Commander because I knew their cases would be
dealt with quickly and fairly under the Fleet Code of Military Justice.
I also knew that any complaints against Bishop Melandriano,
whether filed under Pax civil-suit or Church judicial procedures,
would require my presence on Mare Infinitus for weeks and months.
The mission could not wait for that. I judged the Bishop's corruption
less important than pursuing the girl.

INQUISITOR: He understands the seriousness of these unsubstantiated
and undocumented charges against a Bishop of the Roman Catholic
Church?

F.C. DE SOYA: Yes.

INQUISITOR: And what led him to abandon his former search pattern
and take the archangel courier *Raphael* to the Ouster-controlled
Hebron System?

F.C. DE SOYA: Again, a hunch.

INQUISITOR: He shall elaborate.

F.C. DE SOYA: I did not know where the girl had farcast after Renaissance Vector. Logic dictated that the ship had been left behind somewhere and they had continued on the River Tethys by other
means . . . the hawking mat, perhaps, more likely by boat or raft.
Certain evidence gathered in the investigation of the girl's flight prior
to and during the Mare Infinitus crossing suggested a connection
with the Ousters.

INQUISITOR: He shall elaborate.

F.C. DE SOYA: First, the spacecraft . . . it was of Hegemony design . . . a private interstellar spacecraft, if such a thing can be
believed. Only a few were given out during the history of the Hegemony. The one most closely resembling the ship we encountered was
presented to a certain Hegemony Consul some decades before the
Fall. This Consul was later immortalized in the epic poem, the *Cantos,* composed by the former Hyperion pilgrim Martin Silenus. In the
Cantos the Consul tells a tale of betraying the Hegemony by spying
for the Ousters.

INQUISITOR: He shall continue.

F.C. DE SOYA: There were other connections. Sergeant Gregorius was
sent to the world of Hyperion with certain forensic evidence which
identified the man believed to have been traveling with the child. It is
one Raul Endymion, a native of Hyperion and former member of the
Hyperion Home Guard. There are certain connections of the name
Endymion to works by the girl's . . . father—the Keats cybrid
abomination. Once again we come to the *Cantos.*

INQUISITOR: He will continue.

F.C. DE SOYA: Well, there was another connection. The flying device captured after the escape and possible shooting of Raul Endymion on Mare Infinitus—

INQUISITOR: Why does he say the "possible shooting"? Reports from all eyewitnesses on the platform say the suspect was shot and fell into the sea.

F.C. DE SOYA: Lieutenant Belius had fallen into the ocean earlier, yet his blood and tissue fragments were found on the hawking mat. Only a small portion of blood identified as having the DNA pattern of Raul Endymion was found on the flying mat. It is my theory that Endymion either tried to rescue Lieutenant Belius from the sea or was surprised by him somehow, that the two fought on the mat, that the real suspect—Raul Endymion—was wounded and fell from the mat before the guards fired. I believe it was Lieutenant Belius who died from flechette fire.

INQUISITOR: Does he have any proof—other than blood and tissue samples—which might just as easily have come from Raul Endymion pausing long enough in his escape flight to murder Lieutenant Belius?

F.C. DE SOYA: No.

INQUISITOR: He shall continue.

F.C. DE SOYA: The other reason I suspected an Ouster connection was the hawking mat. Forensic studies show it to be very old—perhaps old enough to be the famous mat used by Shipman Merin Aspic and Siri on the world of Maui-Covenant. Once again there is a connection to the Hyperion pilgrimage and stories related in the Silenus *Cantos*.

INQUISITOR: He shall continue.

F.C. DE SOYA: That's all. I thought that we could get to Hebron without encountering an Ouster Swarm. They often abandon the systems they win in combat. Obviously, my hunch was wrong this time. It cost Lancer Rettig his life. For that I am deeply and truly sorry.

INQUISITOR: So his contention is that the upshot of the investigation he carried out at such expense and such pain and embarrassment to Bishop Melandriano was successful because several items seemed to connect to the poem called the *Cantos,* which in turn had a slight connection to the Ousters?

F.C. DE SOYA: Essentially . . . yes.

INQUISITOR: Is the father-captain aware that the poem called the *Cantos* is on the Index of Prohibited Books and has been so for more than a century and a half?

F.C. DE SOYA: Yes.

INQUISITOR: Does he admit to having read this book?

F.C. DE SOYA: Yes.

INQUISITOR: Does he remember the punishment within the Society of Jesus for willfully violating the Index of Prohibited Books?

F.C. DE SOYA: Yes. It is banishment from the Society.

INQUISITOR: And does he recall the maximum punishment listed under the Church Canon of Peace and Justice set upon those in the Body of Christ for willful violations of restrictions offered through the Index of Prohibited Books?

F.C. DE SOYA: Excommunication.

INQUISITOR: The father-captain is released to his quarters at the Vatican Rectory of the Legionaries of Christ and is requested to remain there until recalled for further testimony before this panel or as otherwise directed. We do so abjure, swear, promise, and bind our Brother in Christ; through the power of the Holy, Catholic, and Apostolic Roman Church do we so compel and abjure thee; in Jesus' name we speak.

F.C. DE SOYA: Thank you, Most Eminent and Reverend Lord Cardinals, Inquisitors. I shall await word.

40

W E SPENT THREE WEEKS with the Chitchatuk on the frozen world of Sol Draconi Septem, and in that time we rested, recovered, wandered the frozen tunnels of their frozen atmosphere with them, learned a few words and phrases of their difficult language, visited Father Glaucus in the embedded city, stalked and were stalked by arctic wraiths, and made that final, terrible trek downriver.

But I am getting ahead of myself. It is easy to do, to rush the tale, especially with the probability increasing of inhaling cyanide on the next breath I take. But enough: this story will end abruptly when I do, not before, and it matters little if it is here or there or in between. I will tell it as if I shall be allowed to tell it all.

Our first glimpse of the Chitchatuk almost ended in tragedy for both sides. We had doused our handlamps and were crouching in the weighted darkness of that ice corridor, my plasma rifle charged and ready, when the dimmest of lights appeared at the next bend in the tunnel and large, inhuman shapes ambled around the corner. I flicked on my handlamp and its cold-dulled beam illuminated a terrifying sight: three or four broad beasts—white fur, black claws the length of my hand, white teeth that were even longer, reddish-glowing eyes. The creatures moved in a fog of their own breath. I raised the plasma rifle to my shoulder and clicked the select to rapid fire.

"Don't shoot!" cried Aenea, grabbing my arm. "They're human!"

Her cry stayed not only my hand, but that of the Chitchatuk. Long bone spears had appeared from the folds of white fur, and our lamp beams illuminated sharpened points and pale arms pulled back to hurl them. But Aenea's voice seemed to freeze the tableau with both sides a muscle's twitch away from violence.

I then saw the pale faces beneath the visors of wraith teeth—broad faces, blunt-nosed, wrinkled, pale to the point of albinoism, but all too human, as were the dark eyes that gleamed back at us. I lowered the light so that it was not in their eyes.

The Chitchatuk were broad and muscular—well adapted to Sol Draconi Septem's punishing 1.7-g's—and they looked even wider and more powerful with the layers of wraith furs wrapped around them so. We were soon to learn that they each wore the forward half of the animal's hide, including its head, so the black wraith-claws hung below their hands, the wraith-teeth covering their faces like a dagger-sharp portcullis. We also learned that the wraith's black eye lenses—even without the complicated optics and nerves that allowed the monsters to see in almost total darkness —still worked like simple night-vision goggles. Everything the Chitchatuk wore and were carrying had come from the wraiths: bone spears, rawhide thongs made from wraith-gut and tendon, their water bags formed from tied-off wraith-intestines, their sleeping robes and pallets, even the two artifacts they carried with them—the miter-shaped brazier fashioned from wraith-bone, carried on rawhide thongs, which held the glowing embers that lighted their way, and the more complicated bone bowl and funnel, which melted the ice to water over the brazier. We did not know until later that their already ample bodies looked broader and lumpier because of the water bags they carried under their robe, using their body heat to keep the water liquid.

The standoff must have held for a full minute and a half before Aenea stepped forward on our side and the Chitchatuk we later knew as Cuchiat stepped forward toward us. Cuchiat spoke first, a torrent of harsh noises sounding like nothing so much as great icicles crashing to a hard surface.

"I'm sorry," said Aenea. "I don't understand." She looked back at us.

I looked at A. Bettik. "Do you recognize this dialect?" Web English had been the standard for so many centuries that it was almost shocking to hear words that bore no meaning. Even three centuries after the Fall, according to the offworlders who had come through Hyperion, most planetary and regional dialects were still understandable.

"No, I do not," said A. Bettik. "M. Endymion, if I might suggest . . . the comlog?"

I nodded and retrieved the bracelet from my pack. The Chitchatuk watched warily, still speaking among themselves, eyes alert for a weapon. Their spear arms relaxed as I raised the bangle to eye level and pressed it on.

"I am activated and awaiting your question or command," chirped the ice-frosted bracelet.

"Listen," I said as Cuchiat began speaking again. "Tell me if you can translate this."

The wraith-garbed warrior made a short, crashing speech.

"Well," I said to the comlog.

"This language or dialect is not familiar," chimed the ship's voice from the comlog. "I am familiar with several Old Earth languages, including pre-Web English, German, French, Dutch, Japanese . . ."

"Never mind," I said. The Chitchatuk were staring at the babbling comlog, but there was no fear or superstition visible in those large dark eyes that peered from between wraith-teeth—only curiosity.

"I would suggest," continued the comlog, "that you keep me activated for some weeks or months while this language is being spoken. I could then collect a data base from which a simple lexicon could be constructed. It might also be preferable to—"

"Thanks anyway," I said, and pressed it off.

Aenea took a step closer to Cuchiat and pantomimed our being cold and tired. She made gestures for food, pulling a blanket over us, and sleep.

Cuchiat grunted and conferred with the others. There were seven of the Chitchatuk crowding the ice tunnel now, and we were to learn that their hunting parties always traveled in prime numbers, as did their larger bands. Finally, after speaking separately to each of his men, Cuchiat spoke to us briefly, turned back up the ascending corridor, and gestured for us to follow.

Shivering, bent under the weight of the world's gravity, straining to see by their dim ember light after we had switched off our handlamps to conserve the batteries, making sure that my inertial compass was working, leaving its digital trail of crumbs behind as we walked, we followed Cuchiat and his men toward the Chitchatuk camp.

THEY WERE A GENEROUS PEOPLE. They gave us each a wraith-robe to wear, more hind-robes to sleep in and on, wraith-broth heated over their little brazier, water from their body-heated bags, and their trust. The Chitchatuk, we soon learned, did not war among themselves. The thought of killing another human was alien to them. Essentially, the Chitchatuk—indigenies who had been adapting to the ice for almost a thousand years—were the only survivors of the Fall, the viral plagues, and the wraiths. The Chitchatuk took everything they needed from the monstrous wraiths, and —from what we could glean—the wraiths depended solely upon the Chitchatuk for their own food. All other life-forms—always marginal—had fallen below the survival threshold after the Fall and the failure of terraforming.

Our first couple of days with them were spent sleeping, eating, and trying to communicate. The Chitchatuk had no permanent villages in the ice: they would sleep for a few hours, fold their robes, and move on through the warren of tunnels. When heating ice to water—their only use of fire, since the embers were not enough to warm them and they ate their meat raw—they suspended the miter-brazier from the ice ceiling with three wraith-tendon thongs so that it would not leave a telltale melted point in the ice.

There were twenty-three of them in the tribe, band, clan—whatever you could call them—and at first it was not possible to tell if there were any females among them. The Chitchatuk seemed to wear their robes at all times, just lifting them enough to avoid soiling them while urinating or defecating in one of the ice fissures. It was not until we saw the woman named Chatchia mating with Cuchiat in our third sleep period that we were sure that females were in the band.

Slowly, as we walked and talked with them through the never-changing dimness of tunnels over the next two days, we began to learn their faces and names. Cuchiat, the leader, was—despite the avalanche of his voice—a gentle man, given to smiling with both his thin lips and his black eyes. Chiaku, his second in command, was the tallest of the band and wore a wraith-robe with a streak of blood on it, which we later realized was a mark of honor. Aichacut was the angry one, often scowling at us and always keeping his distance. I think that if Aichacut had been leader of the hunting band when we'd encountered them, there would have been dead bodies in the ice that day.

Cuchtu was, we thought, a sort of medicine man, and it was his job to circle the ice niche or tunnel where we slept, muttering incantations and removing his wraith-leather gloves to press his bare palms against the ice. It was my guess that he was driving away bad spirits. Aenea suggested wryly that he might just be doing what we were—trying to find a way out of this ice maze.

Chichticu was the fire carrier and obviously proud of having attained that honor. The embers were a mystery to us: they continued to glow and give off heat and light for days—weeks—yet were never stoked or renewed. It was not until we met Father Glaucus that this puzzle was cleared up.

There were no children with the band, and it was hard to tell the ages of the Chitchatuk we got to know. Cuchiat was obviously older than most —his face was a web of wrinkles radiating from the bridge of that wide blade of a nose—but we never succeeded in discussing ages with any of them. They recognized Aenea as a child—or at least a young adult—and treated her accordingly. The women, we noticed after identifying three of them as such, carried out the role of hunter and sentry in equal rotation with the men. Although they were to honor A. Bettik and me with the job of standing guard while the band slept—three people with weapons were always left awake—they never asked Aenea to perform that chore. But they obviously enjoyed her and enjoyed talking with her, everyone using the combination of simple words and elaborate signs that have served to bridge the gap between peoples since the Paleolithic.

On the third day Aenea succeeded in asking them to return to the river with us. At first they were puzzled, but her signs and the few words she had picked up soon communicated the concept—the river, the raft floating, the arch of the farcaster frozen in ice (they exclaimed at this), then the ice wall and our walking up the ice tunnel before meeting our friends the Chitchatuk.

When Aenea suggested that we return to the river together, the band gathered up the sleeping robes, stuffed them into the wraith-hide packs, and were marching with us within moments. For once I led the way, the glowing dial of the inertial compass unraveling the many twists, turns, ascents, and descents we had taken in our three days of wandering.

I should say here that if it had not been for our chronometers, time would have disappeared in the ice tunnels of Sol Draconi Septem. The unchanging dim glow from the bone brazier, the glint of ice walls, the darkness ahead of us and behind, the in-pressing cold, the short sleep periods and endless hours of laboring up icy corridors with the weight of the planet on our backs—everything combined to destroy our sense of time. But according to the chronometer, it was late on the third day since abandoning the raft that we descended the last bit of narrow corridor and returned to the river.

It was a sad sight: the splintered foremast and battered logs, the stern of the craft almost submerged from a buildup of ice, the lanterns we had left behind coated white with frost, and the entire vessel looking empty and forlorn without our tent and gear. The Chitchatuk were fascinated, showing the most animation we had seen from them since our initial encounter. Using lines of braided wraith-hide, Cuchiat and several of the others lowered themselves to the raft and examined every detail carefully—the stone of our abandoned hearth, the metal of the lanterns, the nylon line used to lash the logs. Their excitement was tangible, and I realized that in a society where the only source of building material, weaponry, and clothing came from a single animal—a skillful predator, at that—the raft must represent a treasure trove of raw material.

They could have attempted to kill or abandon us then and taken that wealth, but the Chitchatuk were a generous people, and not even greed could alter their view that all humans were allies, just as all wraiths were enemies and prey. We had not seen a wraith at that time—except, of course, for the skins we wore over our tropical clothing, since the robes were so incredibly warm, rivaling the thermal blanket for insulative efficiency, that we were able to pack away most of the outer layers we had bundled on. But if we were innocent of the wraith's power and hunger then, we would not stay so innocent for long.

Once again Aenea communicated the idea of our floating downriver through the arch. She pantomimed the ice wall—pointed to it—and then showed them our continued trip downriver to the second arch.

This got Cuchiat and his band even more animated, and they tried to talk to us without sign language, their harsh words and sentences falling on us like a load of gravel dumped at our ears. When that failed, they turned and talked excitedly to one another. Finally Cuchiat stepped forward and spoke a short sentence to the three of us. We heard the word "glaucus" repeated—we had heard it before in their speeches, the word standing out as alien to their language—and when Cuchiat gestured upward and repeated the sign for all of us walking up toward the surface, we eagerly agreed.

And thus it was, each of us swathed in robes of wraith-fur, our backs hunched against the weight of our packs in the exhausting gravity, our feet scrabbling on rock-hard ice, that we set out toward the ice-buried city to meet the priest.

41

W HEN THE SUMMONS FINALLY COMES to release Father Captain de Soya from virtual house arrest in the Legionaries of Christ rectory, it arrives not from the Holy Office of the Inquisition, as has been expected, but in the person of Monsignor Lucas Oddi, Undersecretary to the Vatican Secretariat of State, His Excellency Simon Augustino Cardinal Lourdusamy.

The walk into Vatican City and through the Vatican Gardens is all but overwhelming to de Soya. Everything he sees and hears—the pale-blue skies of Pacem, the flittering of finches in the pear orchards, the soft stroke of Vespers bells—makes emotion surge within him to the point that he has to work to hold back tears. Monsignor Oddi chats while they walk, mixing Vatican gossip with mild pleasantries in a way that makes de Soya's ears buzz long after they have passed the section of garden where bees hum between the floral displays.

De Soya focuses on the tall, elderly man who is leading him with such a brisk pace. Oddi is very tall and he seems to glide forward, his legs making little noise within the long cassock. The Monsignor's face is thin and crafty, lines and wrinkles molded by many decades of amusement, the long beak of a nose seeming to sniff the Vatican air for humor and rumor. De Soya has heard the jokes about Monsignor Oddi and Cardinal Lourdusamy, the tall, funny man and the huge, crafty man—how together they might look almost comical if it were not for the truly terrifying power they wield.

De Soya is momentarily surprised when they come out of the garden and step into one of the outside elevators that rise to the loggias of the Vatican Palace. Swiss Guard troopers, resplendent in their ancient uniforms of red, blue, and orange stripes, snap to attention as they step into and then out of the wire-mesh elevator cages. The troopers here carry long pikes, but de Soya remembers that these can be used as pulse rifles.

"You remember that His Holiness, during his first resurrection, decided to reoccupy this level because of his fondness for his namesake, Julius the Second," says Monsignor Oddi, gesturing down the long corridor with an easy sweep of his hand.

"Yes," says de Soya. His heart is pounding wildly. Pope Julius II— the famous warrior-Pope who had commissioned the Sistine ceiling during his reign from A.D. 1503 to 1513 had been the first to live in these rooms. Now Pope Julius—in all of his incarnations from Julius VI to Julius XIV— has lived and ruled here almost twenty-seven times as long as the decade of that first warrior-Pope. Certainly he could not be meeting the Holy Father! De Soya manages an outward calm as they start down the great corridor, but his palms are moist and his breathing is rapid.

"We are going to see the Secretariat, of course," says Oddi, smiling, "but if you have not seen the papal apartments, this is a pleasant walk. His Holiness is meeting with the Interstellar Synod of Bishops in the smaller hall of the Nervi building all this day."

De Soya nods attentively, but, in truth, his attention is focused on the Raphael *stanze* he is glimpsing through open doors of the papal apartments as they pass. He knows the outlines of the history: Pope Julius II had grown tired of the "old-fashioned" frescoes by such minor geniuses as Piero della Francesca and Andrea del Castagno, so in the fall of 1508 he had brought a twenty-six-year-old genius from Urbino, Raffaello Sanzio— also known as Raphael. In one room de Soya can see the *Stanza della Segnatura,* an overwhelming fresco representing the Triumph of Religious Truth being contrasted with the Triumph of Philosophical and Scientific Truth.

"Ahhh," says Monsignor Oddi, pausing so that de Soya can stand and stare a moment. "You like it, eh? You see Plato there among the philosophers?"

"Yes," says de Soya.

"Do you know to whom the likeness actually belonged? Who the model was?"

"No," says de Soya.

"Leonardo da Vinci," says the monsignor with a hint of a smile. "And Heraclitus—see him there? Do you know whom Raphael depicted from life?"

De Soya can only shake his head. He is remembering the tiny adobe Mariaist chapel on his homeworld, with the sand always blowing in under the doors and pooling under the simple statue of the Virgin.

"Heraclitus was Michelangelo," says Monsignor Oddi. "And Euclid there . . . you see him . . . that was Bramante. Come in, come closer."

De Soya can hardly bear to set foot on the rich tapestry of carpet.

The frescoes, statuary, gilded molding, and tall windows of the room seem to whirl around him.

"You see these letters on Bramante's collar here? Come, lean closer. Can you read them, my son?"

"R-U-S-M," reads de Soya.

"Yes, yes," chuckles Monsignor Lucas Oddi. *"Raphael Urbinus Sua Manu.* Come, come, my son . . . translate for an old man. You have had your review lesson in Latin for this week, I believe."

"Raphael of Urbino," translates de Soya, muttering more to himself than the taller man, "by his hand."

"Yes. Come along. We shall take the papal lift down to the apartments. We must not keep the Secretary waiting."

THE BORGIA APARTMENT takes up much of the ground floor of this wing of the palace. They enter through the tiny Chapel of Nicholas V, and Father Captain de Soya thinks that he has never seen any work of man lovelier than this small room. The frescoes here were painted by Fra Angelico between A.D. 1447 and 1449 and are the essence of simplicity, the avatar of purity.

Beyond the chapel, the rooms of the Borgia Apartment become darker and more ominous, much as the ensuing history of the Church had grown darker under the Borgia popes. But by Room IV—Pope Alexander's study, dedicated to the sciences and the liberal arts—de Soya begins to appreciate the power of the rich color, the extravagant applications of gold leaf, and the sumptuous uses of stucco. Room V explores the lives of the saints through fresco and statuary, yet has a stylized, inhuman feel to it, which de Soya associates with old pictures he has seen of Old Earth Egyptian art. Room VI, the Pope's dining room, according to the Monsignor, explores the mysteries of the faith in an explosion of color and figures that literally takes de Soya's breath away.

Monsignor Oddi pauses by a huge fresco of the Resurrection and points two fingers toward a secondary figure whose intense piety can be felt through the centuries and faded oils. "Pope Alexander the Sixth," Oddi says softly. "The second of the Borgia popes." He flicks his hand almost negligently toward two men standing nearby in the thickly populated fresco. Both have the lighting and expressions reserved for saints. "Cesare Borgia," says Oddi, "Pope Alexander's bastard son. The man next to him is Cesare's brother . . . whom he murdered. The Pope's daughter, Lucrezia, was in Room V . . . you may have missed her . . . the virgin Saint Catherine of Alexandria."

De Soya can only stare. He looks up at the ceiling and sees the design that has appeared in each of these rooms—the brilliant bull and crown that were the Borgia emblems.

"Pinturicchio painted all this," says Monsignor Oddi, on the move again now. "His real name was Bernardino di Betto, and he was quite mad. Possibly a servant of darkness." The Monsignor pauses to look back into the room as Swiss Guards snap to attention. "And most certainly a genius," he says softly. "Come. It is time for your appointment."

CARDINAL LOURDUSAMY AWAITS behind a long, low desk in Room VI, the Sala dei Pontifici—the so-called "Room of the Popes." The huge man does not rise but shifts sideways in his chair as Father Captain de Soya is announced and allowed to approach. De Soya goes to one knee and kisses the Cardinal's ring. Lourdusamy pats the priest-captain on the head and waves away any further formality. "Take that chair, my son. Get comfortable. I assure you, that little chair is more comfortable than this straight-backed throne they found for me."

De Soya has almost forgotten the power of the Cardinal's voice: it is a great bass rumbling that seems to come up out of the earth as much as from the large man's body. Lourdusamy is huge, a great mass of red silk, white linen, and crimson velvet, a geological massif of a man culminating in the large head atop layers of jowls, the small mouth, tiny, lively eyes, and almost hairless skull set off by the crimson skullcap.

"Federico," rumbles the Cardinal, "I am so pleased and delighted that you have come through so many deaths and troubles without harm. You look well, my son. Tired, but well."

"Thank you, Your Excellency," says de Soya. Monsignor Oddi has taken a chair to the priest-captain's left, a bit farther away from the Cardinal's desk.

"And I understand you went before the tribunal of the Holy Office yesterday," rumbles Cardinal Lourdusamy, his eyes piercing into de Soya.

"Yes, Your Excellency."

"No thumbscrews, I hope? No iron maidens or hot irons. Or did they have you on the rack?" The Cardinal's chuckle seems to echo in the man's huge chest.

"No, Your Excellency." De Soya manages a smile.

"Good, good," says the Cardinal, the light from a fixture ten meters overhead gleaming on his ring. He leans closer and smiles. "When His Holiness ordered the Holy Office to take back its old title—the Inquisition—a few of the nonbelievers thought that the days of madness and terror within the Church had returned. But now they know better, Federico. The Holy Office's only power is in its role of giving advice to the Orders of the Church, its only punishment is to recommend excommunication."

De Soya licks his lips. "But that is a terrible punishment, Your Excellency."

"Yes," agrees Cardinal Lourdusamy, and the banter is gone from his voice. "Terrible. But not one you have to worry about, my son. This incident is over. Your name and reputation have been fully exonerated.

The report the tribunal shall send to His Holiness clears you of any blemish larger than . . . shall we say . . . a certain insensitivity to the feelings of a certain provincial Bishop with enough friends in the Curia to demand this hearing?"

De Soya does not let out his breath yet. "Bishop Melandriano is a thief, Your Excellency."

Lourdusamy's lively eyes flick toward Monsignor Oddi and then return to the priest-captain's face. "Yes, yes, Federico. We know that. We have known that for some time. The good Bishop on his remote floating city on that watery world shall have his time before the lord cardinals of the Holy Office, be assured. And you also may be assured that the recommendations in his case will not be so lenient." The Cardinal settles back into his high-backed chair. Ancient wood creaks. "But we must talk of other things, my son. Are you ready to resume your mission?"

"Yes, Your Excellency." De Soya is surprised by the immediacy and sincerity of his answer. Until that second he had thought it best that this part of his life and service was over.

Cardinal Lourdusamy's expression grows more serious. The great jowls seem to become firmer. "Excellent. Now, I understand that one of your troopers died during your expedition to Hebron."

"An accident during resurrection, Your Excellency," says de Soya.

Lourdusamy is shaking his head. "Terrible. Terrible."

"Lancer Rettig," adds Father Captain de Soya, feeling that the man's name needs to be spoken. "He was a good soldier."

The Cardinal's small eyes glint, as if from tears. He looks directly at de Soya as he says, "His parents and sister will be taken care of. Lancer Rettig had a brother who rose to the rank of priest-Commander on Bressia. Did you know that, my son?"

"No, Your Excellency," says de Soya.

Lourdusamy nods. "A great loss." The Cardinal sighs and sets a plump hand on the empty desktop. De Soya sees the dimples in the back of the hand and looks at it as if it is its own entity, some boneless creature from the sea.

"Federico," rumbles Lourdusamy, "we have a suggestion for someone to fill the vacancy on your ship left by Lancer Rettig's death. But first we must discuss the reason for this mission. Do you know *why* we must find and detain this young female?"

De Soya sits straight up. "Your Excellency explained that the girl was the child of a cybrid abomination," he says. "That she poses a threat to the Church itself. That she may well be an agent of the AI TechnoCore."

Lourdusamy is nodding. "All true, Federico. All true. But we did not tell you precisely *how* she is a threat . . . not only to the Church and the Pax, but to all humanity. If we are to send you back out there on this mission, my son, you have the right to know."

Outside, their volume muffled but still audible through the palace windows and walls, come two sudden and disparate sounds. In the same instant the midday cannon is fired from the Janiculum Hill along the river toward Tratevere, and the clocks of St. Peter's begin to strike the noon hour.

Lourdusamy pauses, removes an ancient watch from the folds of his crimson robe, nods as if satisfied, winds it, and returns it to its place.

De Soya waits.

42

I T TOOK US A LITTLE MORE THAN A DAY to walk the ice tunnels to Father Glaucus and the buried city, but there were three short sleep periods during that time, and the voyage itself—darkness, cold, narrow passages through the ice—would have been quite forgettable if the wraith had not taken one of our party.

As with all real acts of violence, it happened too quickly to observe. One second we were trudging along, Aenea, the android, and I near the back of the single-file line of Chitchatuk, and suddenly there was an explosion of ice and movement—I froze, thinking that an explosive mine had been set off—and the robed figure two forms in front of Aenea disappeared without a cry.

I was still frozen, the plasma rifle in my mittened hands, but useless, its safety still on, when the nearest Chitchatuk began ululating in rage and helplessness, the closest hunters throwing themselves down the new corridor that opened where none had been a second before.

Aenea was already shining her handlamp down the nearly vertical shaft when I pushed next to her, my weapon raised. Two of the Chitchatuk had hurled themselves down that shaft, braking their fall with their boots and short bone knives throwing ice splinters above them, and I was about to squeeze in when Cuchiat grabbed my shoulder. "Ktchey!" he said. "Ku tcheta chi!"

By this fourth day I knew that he was ordering me not to go. I obeyed, but brought out the flashlight laser to illuminate the way for the shouting hunters already twenty meters below us and out of sight where the new tunnel curved away to the horizontal. At first I thought it was an effect of the red laser beam, but then I saw that the shaft was coated— almost totally painted—in bright blood.

The ululation among the Chitchatuk continued even after the hunters returned empty-handed. I understood that there had been no sight of the wraith, and no sight of its victim except for blood, shredded robe, and the little finger from her right hand. Cuchtu, the one we thought of as the medicine man, knelt, kissed the severed digit, brought a bone knife across his forearm until his own blood dripped on the bloody finger, and then carefully, almost reverently, set the finger in his hide bag. The ululation stopped immediately. Chiaku—the tall man with the bloodstained robe that was twice bloodstained now, since he had been one of the hunters who had thrown himself down the shaft—turned to us and spoke earnestly for a long moment while the others shouldered their packs, set their spears away, and resumed the trek.

As we continued up the ice tunnel, I could not help but glance back and see the wraith's jagged entrance hole fade into the blackness that seemed to follow us. Knowing that the animals lived on the surface and came below mostly to hunt, I had not been nervous. But now the very ice of the floor seemed treacherous, the ice facets and ridges of the walls and ceilings mere hunting blinds for the next wraith. I found that I was trying to walk lightly, as if that would keep me from falling through to where the killer waited. It was not easy to walk lightly on Sol Draconi Septem.

"M. Aenea," said the robed figure of A. Bettik, "I could not understand what M. Chiaku was saying. Something about numbers?"

Aenea's face was all but lost under the wraith-teeth of her robe. I had known that all these robes were taken from wraith cubs—infants—but the one glimpse of white arms the thickness of my torso coming through the ice wall, black talons the length of my forearm, made me realize how large these things must be. Sometimes, I realized, the safety off on my plasma rifle, trying to walk lightly in the grinding weight of Sol Draconi Septem, the shortest route to courage is absolute ignorance.

". . . so I think he was talking about the fact that the band no longer comprises a prime number," Aenea was saying to A. Bettik. "Until she . . . was taken . . . we had twenty-six, which was all right, but now they have to do something soon or . . . I don't know . . . more bad luck."

As far as I could tell, they solved the prime-number jinx by sending Chiaku ahead as a scout. Or perhaps he just volunteered to be apart from the group until they could drop us off in the frozen city—twenty-five, as an odd number, could be tolerated briefly, but without us their band would be back to twenty-two, still an unacceptable number.

I left behind all thoughts of the Chitchatuk's preoccupation with primes when we arrived at the city.

First, we saw the light. After just a few days, our eyes had grown so accustomed to the ember-glow of the "chuchkituk"—the miter-shaped bone brazier—that even the occasional flash of our handlamps seemed blinding. The light from the frozen city was actually painful.

At one time, the building had been steel or plasteel and smart glass, perhaps seventy stories tall, and must have looked out at a pleasant green terraformed valley—perhaps facing south toward where the river flowed half a kilometer away. Now our ice tunnel opened onto a hole in the glass somewhere around the fifty-eighth floor, and tongues of the atmospheric glacier had bent the steel frame of the building and found inroads on various levels.

But the skyscraper still stood, perhaps with its upper stories protruding into the black near vacuum of the surface above the glacier. And it still blazed with light.

The Chitchatuk paused at the entrance, shielding their eyes from the glare and ululating in a different tone from that of their earlier mourning wail in the tunnel when the woman had been taken. This was a beckoning. While we stood and waited, I stared at the open steel-and-glass skeleton of this place, at the dozens upon dozens of burning lamps hung everywhere here, floor after floor, so that we could stare down beneath our feet through the clear ice and see the building dropping away beneath us, windows brightly lit.

Then Father Glaucus ambled toward us across the space that was half ice cavern, half office-building room. He wore the long black cassock and crucifix that I associated with the Jesuits at their monastery near Port Romance. It was obvious that the old man was blind—his eyes were milky with cataracts and as unseeing as stones—but that was not the first thing that struck me about Father Glaucus: he was old, ancient, hoary, bearded like a patriarch, and when Cuchiat called to him, his features came alive and he awoke as if from a trance, his snow-white brows arching up, plowing wrinkles into his large forehead. Chapped and weathered lips curled up in a smile. This may sound grotesque, but nothing about Father Glaucus was bizarre in any way—not his blindness, not the blindingly white beard, not the weathered, mottled old man's skin or whithered lips. He was so much . . . himself . . . that comparisons fail.

I had many reservations about meeting this "glaucus"—afraid that he would have some association with the Pax we were fleeing—and now, having seen that he was a priest, I should have grabbed the girl and A. Bettik and left with the Chitchatuk. But none of the three of us had that impulse at all. This old man was not the Pax . . . he was only Father Glaucus. This we learned only minutes after our first encounter.

But first, before any of us spoke, the blind priest seemed to sense our presence. After speaking to Cuchiat and Chichticia in their own tongue, he suddenly swiveled our way, holding one hand high as if his palm could sense our heat—Aenea's, A. Bettik's, and mine. Then he crossed the small space to where we stood at the boundary between encroaching ice cavern and encroached-upon room.

Father Glaucus walked directly up to me, set his bony hand on my shoulder, and said, loudly and clearly in Web English, "Thou art the man!"

IT TOOK ME A WHILE—years—to put that comment in the proper perspective. At the time I simply thought the old priest was mad as well as blind.

The arrangement was for us to stay a few days with Father Glaucus in his subglacial high-rise while the Chitchatuk went off to do important Chitchatuk things—Aenea and I guessed that settling the prime-number problem was their highest priority—and then the band would check back on us. Aenea and I had succeeded in communicating via signs that we wanted to take the raft apart and carry it downriver to the next farcaster portal. The Chitchatuk seemed to understand—or at least they had nodded and used their word for assent—"chia"—when we pantomimed the second arch and the raft passing through it. If I had understood their signed and verbal response, the trip to the second farcaster would require traveling across the surface, would take several days, and would pass through an area of many arctic wraiths. I was sure that they said we would discuss it again after they acted on their immediate need of going off "to seek insoluble balance"—which we guessed meant finding another member of the band—or losing three. The last thought gave one pause.

At any rate, we were to stay with Father Glaucus until Cuchiat's band returned. The blind priest chatted animatedly with the hunters for several minutes and then stood at the opening of the ice cave, obviously listening, until the glow of their bone-brazier had long since disappeared.

Then Father Glaucus greeted us again by passing his hands across our faces, shoulders, arms, and hands. I confess that I had never experienced an introduction quite like it. When he cupped Aenea's face in his bony hands, the old man said, "A human child. I had never expected to see a human child's face again."

I did not understand. "What about the Chitchatuk?" I said. "They're human. They must have children."

Father Glaucus had led us deeper into the skyscraper and up a flight of stairs to a warmer room before our "introductions." This was obviously a living area for him—lanterns and braziers burned brightly with the same glowing pellets that the Chitchatuk used, only there were hundreds more here, comfortable furniture was set around, there was an ancient music-disc player, and the inner walls were lined with books—which I found incongruous in the home of a blind man.

"The Chitchatuk have children," said the old priest, "but they do not allow them to stay with the bands that roam this far north."

"Why?" I said.

"The wraiths," said Father Glaucus. "There are so many wraiths north of the old terraforming line."

"I thought the Chitchatuk depended upon the wraiths for everything," I said.

The old man nodded and stroked his beard. It was full, white, and long enough to hide his Roman collar. His cassock was carefully patched and darned, but still frayed and threadbare. "My friends the Chitchatuk depend upon wraith *cubs* for everything," he said. "The metabolism of the adults makes their hides and bones worthless for the bands' purposes . . ."

I did not understand this, but I let him continue without interruption.

". . . the wraiths, on the other hand, love nothing more than Chitchatuk children," he said. "It is why Chitchatuk and the others are so puzzled by our young friend's presence this far north."

"Where are their children?" asked Aenea.

"Many hundreds of kilometers south," said the priest. "With the child-rearing bands. It is . . . tropical there. The ice is only thirty or forty meters thick and the atmosphere is almost breathable."

"Why don't the wraiths hunt the children there?" I asked.

"It is poor country for the wraiths . . . far too warm."

"Then why don't all the Chitchatuk play it safe and move south . . . ," I began, and stopped. The heavy g-load and cold must have been making me more stupid than I usually was.

"Exactly," said Father Glaucus, hearing comprehension in my silence. "The Chitchatuk totally depend upon the wraiths. The hunting bands—like our friend Cuchiat's—risk terrible odds to provide the child-rearing bands with meat, hides, and tools. The child-rearing bands run a chance of starving before the food is provided. The Chitchatuk have few children, but those few are precious to them. Or, as they would say—"Utchai tuk aichit chacutkuchit."

"More . . . sacred, I think the word is . . . than warmth," translated Aenea.

"Precisely," said the old priest. "But I am forgetting my manners. I shall show you all to your quarters—I keep several extra rooms furnished and heated, although you are my first non-Chitchatuk guests for . . . ah . . . five standard decades, I believe. While you settle in, I shall start warming our dinners."

43

I N THE MIDDLE OF HIS EXPLANATION of the real reason for de Soya's mission, Cardinal Lourdusamy leans back in his throne and waves his plump hand toward the distant ceiling. "What do you think of this room, Federico?"

Father Captain de Soya, poised to hear something vitally important, can only blink and lift his face. This great hall is as ornate as the others in the Borgia Apartment—more ornate, he realizes, for the colors are livelier, more vibrant—and then he sees the difference: these tapestries and frescoes are more current, depicting Pope Julius VI receiving the cruciform from an angel of the Lord, another showing God reaching down—in an echo of Michelangelo's ceiling of the Sistine Chapel—to confer the Sacrament of Resurrection on Julius. He sees the evil antipope, Teilhard I, being banished by an archangel with a flaming sword. Other ceiling images and wall tapestries proclaim the glory of the first great century of the Church's own resurrection and Pax expansion.

"The original ceiling in here collapsed in A.D. 1500," rumbles Cardinal Lourdusamy, "almost killing Pope Alexander. Most of the original decoration was destroyed. Leo the Tenth had it replaced after the death of Julius the Second, but the work was inferior to the original. His Holiness commissioned the new work one hundred thirty standard years ago. Notice the central fresco—it is by Halaman Ghena of Renaissance Vector. The Pax Ascending Tapestry—there—is by Shiroku. The architectural restoration was by the cream of Pacem's own artisans, including Peter Baines Cort-Bilgruth."

De Soya nods politely, having no clue as to how this relates to what they were discussing. Perhaps the Cardinal, as is true of many men and women of power, has become used to digressing at will because his underlings never protest the loss of focus.

As if reading the priest-captain's mind, Lourdusamy chuckles and sets his soft hand on the leather surface of the table. "I mention this for a reason, Federico. Would you agree that the Church and Pax have brought an era of unprecedented peace and prosperity to humanity?"

De Soya pauses. He has read history but is not sure if this era has been unprecedented. And as for "peace" . . . memories of burning orbital forests and ravaged worlds still haunt his dreams. "The Church and its Pax allies have certainly improved the situation for most of the former Web worlds I have visited, Your Excellency," he says. "And no one can deny the unprecedented gift of resurrection."

Lourdusamy's throat rumbles with amusement. "The saints save us . . . a diplomat!" The Cardinal rubs his thin upper lip. "Yes, yes, you are perfectly correct, Federico. Every age has its shortcomings, and ours includes a constant struggle against the Ousters and an even more urgent struggle to establish the Reign of Our Lord and Savior in the hearts of all men and women. But, as you see"—his hand gestures once again toward the frescoes and tapestries—"we are in the midst of a Renaissance every bit as real as that imbued with the spirit of the early Renaissance, which gave us the Chapel of Nicholas the Fifth and the other wonders you saw on the way in. And this Renaissance is truly one of the spirit, Federico. . . ."

De Soya waits.

"This . . . abomination . . . will   destroy   all   that," says Lourdusamy, his voice deadly serious now. "As I said to you one year ago, this is not a child we seek, it is a virus. And we know now whence that virus comes."

De Soya listens.

"His Holiness has had one of his visions," the Cardinal says in a voice so soft, it is just above a whisper. "You are aware, Federico, that the Holy Father is often visited by dreams granted by God?"

"I have heard rumors, Your Excellency." This magical aspect of the Church has always had the least appeal to de Soya. He waits.

Lourdusamy waves his hand as if brushing away the sillier rumors. "It is true that His Holiness has received vital revelations after much prayer, much fasting, and exhibiting the utmost humility. Such a revelation was the source of our knowledge on when and where the child would appear on Hyperion. His Holiness was correct to the moment, was he not?"

De Soya bows his head.

"And it was one of these sacred revelations which prompted the Holy Father to ask for you in this service, Federico. He saw that your fate and the salvation of our Church and society were inextricably entwined."

Father Captain de Soya can only stare without blinking.

"And now," rumbles Cardinal Lourdusamy, "the threat to the future of humankind has been revealed in much greater detail." The Cardinal rises to his feet, but when de Soya and Monsignor Oddi hurry to stand, the huge man waves them back to their chairs. De Soya sits and watches the giant mass of red and white move through the pools of light in the dark room, the flesh of the Cardinal's cheeks gleaming, his small eyes lost in shadows from the overhead spots.

"This is, indeed, the AI TechnoCore's great attempt at our destruction, Federico. The same mechanical evil which destroyed Old Earth, which preyed upon humanity's minds and souls through their parasitic farcasters, and which prompted the Ouster attack that presaged the Fall . . . the same Evil is at work here. The cybrid offspring, this . . . Aenea . . . is their instrument. That is why the farcasters have worked for her when they admit no one else. That is why the Shrike demon slayed thousands of our people and soon may slay millions—perhaps billions. Unless stopped, this . . . *succubus* . . . will succeed in returning us to the Rule of the Machine."

De Soya watches the great red form of the Cardinal move from light to dark. None of this is new.

Lourdusamy stops his pacing. "But His Holiness now knows that this cybrid spawn is not only the agent of the Core, Federico . . . she is the instrument of the Machine God."

De Soya understands. When the Inquisition had queried him about the *Cantos,* his insides had turned to jelly at the thought of punishment for having read the banned poem. But even this book on the Index admitted that the elements of the AI Core had been working for centuries to produce an Ultimate Intelligence—a cybernetic deity that would spread its power back through time to dominate the universe. Indeed, both the *Cantos* and official Church history acknowledged the battle across time between this false god and Our Lord. The Keats cybrid—cybrids, actually, since there had been a replacement after one sect of the Core destroyed the first one in the megasphere—had been falsely represented as a candidate for the messiah of the "human UI"—that blasphemous Teilhardian concept of an evolved human god—in the prohibited *Cantos*. That poem had talked about *empathy* being the key to human spiritual evolution. The Church had corrected that, pointing out that obeying God's Will was the source of revelation and salvation.

"Through revelation," Lourdusamy says, "His Holiness knows where the cybrid spawn and her dupes are at this very moment."

De Soya sits forward. "Where, Your Excellency?"

"On the abandoned ice world of Sol Draconi Septem," rumbles the Cardinal. "His Holiness is quite clear on that. And he is quite clear on the consequences if she is not stopped." Lourdusamy walks around the long desk and stands next to the priest-captain. De Soya looks up to see gleaming red, brilliant white, the tiny eyes boring into him. "She runs now to find allies," comes the Cardinal's sincere growl. "Allies to help in the destruction of the Pax and the desecration of the Church. To this moment she has been like a deadly virus in an empty region—a potential danger, but containable. Soon, if she escapes us now, she shall grow to maturity and full power . . . the full power of the Evil One."

Above the Cardinal's gleaming shoulder, de Soya can see the writhing figures of the ceiling fresco.

"Every one of the old farcaster portals will open simultaneously," rumbles the red form. "The Shrike demon . . . in a million iterations . . . will step through to slaughter Christians. The Ousters will be empowered by TechnoCore weapons and terrible AI technologies. Already they have used subcellular machinery to make themselves something more and less than human. Already they have traded their immortal souls for the machinery to adapt to space, to eat sunlight, to exist like . . . like plants in darkness. Their war-making abilities will be augmented a thousandfold by the Core's secret engines. That hideous strength will not be denied, even by the Church. Billions will die the true death, their cruciforms torn from them, their souls ripped out of their bodies like beating hearts from living chests. Tens of billions will die. The Ousters will burn their way across the Pax, laying waste like the Vandals and Visigoths, destroying Pacem, the Vatican, and everything we know. They will kill peace. They will deny life and desecrate our principle of the dignity of the individual."

De Soya sits and waits.

"This does not have to happen," says Secretariat Cardinal Lourdusamy. "His Holiness prays every day that it will *not* happen. But these are perilous times, Federico . . . for the Church, for the Pax, for the future of the race of man. He has seen what *may* be and has dedicated all our lives and sacred honors as Princes of the Church to preventing the birth of such a terrible reality."

De Soya looks up as the Cardinal leans closer.

"I must reveal something to you at this moment, Federico, which billions of the Faithful will not learn for months. . . . Today, this hour, at the Interstellar Synod of Bishops . . . His Holiness is announcing a Crusade."

"A Crusade?" repeats de Soya. Even the unflappable Monsignor Oddi makes a low noise in his throat.

"A Crusade against the Ouster menace," rumbles Cardinal Lourdusamy. "For centuries we have defended ourselves—the Great Wall is a defensive strategem, putting Christian bodies and ships and lives in the way of the Ouster aggression—but as of this day, by the grace of God, the Church and Pax will go on the offensive."

"How?" says de Soya. He knows that the battles already rage in the no-man's-land of gray space between the Pax and Ouster regions, filling thousands of parsecs with fleet lunge and parry, thrust and retreat. But with the time-debt—the maximum voyage from Pacem to the farthest reaches of the Great Wall is two years of shiptime, more than twenty years of time-debt—there can be little or no coordination of either offense or defense.

Lourdusamy smiles grimly and answers. "Even as we speak, every world in the Pax and Protectorate is being asked . . . commanded . . . to devote planetary resources to build one great ship . . . one ship for each world."

"We have thousands of ships . . . ," begins the priest-captain and stops.

"Yes," purrs the Cardinal. "These ships will use the new archangel technology. But they will not be like your *Raphael*—a lightly armed courier—but the deadliest battle cruisers this spiral arm has ever seen. Capable of translating anywhere in the galaxy in less time than it takes a dropship to rise to orbit. Each ship named after its homeworld, each staffed by devoted Pax officers such as yourself—men and women willing to suffer death and receive resurrection—and each capable of destroying entire Swarms."

De Soya nods. "Is this the Holy Father's answer to his revelation of the child's threat, Your Excellency?"

Lourdusamy moves back around the desk and settles into his high-backed throne as if exhausted. "In part, Federico. In part. These new craft will begin to be built within the next standard decade. The technology is difficult . . . *very* difficult. Meanwhile, the cybrid *succubus* continues to circulate disease like a spreading virus. That part depends upon you—you and your enhanced crew of virus seekers."

"Enhanced?" repeats de Soya. "May Sergeant Gregorius and Corporal Kee still travel with me?"

"Yes," rumbles the Cardinal. "They have already been assigned."

"Where does the enhancement come in?" asks de Soya, dreading the possibility that a Cardinal from the Holy Office will be assigned to his mission.

Cardinal Lourdusamy opens his fat fingers as if lifting the lid of a treasure box. "Just one addition to your crew, Federico."

"An officer of the Church?" asks the priest-captain, wondering if the papal diskey is to be passed to a different Commander.

Lourdusamy shakes his head. His great jowls flow with the movement. "A simple warrior, Father Captain de Soya. A new breed of warrior, bred for the renewed Army of Christ."

De Soya does not understand. It sounds as if the Church is answering Ouster nanotechnology with biomodifications of its own. That would defy all of the Church doctrine de Soya has been taught.

Once again, the Cardinal seems to read the priest-captain's thoughts. "Nothing like that, Federico. Some . . . augmentations . . . and much unique training from a new branch of the Pax military, but still totally human . . . and Christian."

"One trooper?" says de Soya, mystified.

"One warrior," says Lourdusamy. "Not within the Pax Fleet chain of command. The first member of the elite Legions which shall spearhead the Crusade that His Holiness will announce today."

De Soya rubs his chin. "And will he be under my direct command, as Gregorius and Kee have been?"

"Of course, of course," rumbles Lourdasamy, sitting back and folding his hands on his ample stomach. "There will be just one change, as was deemed necessary by His Holiness in council with the Holy Office. She will have her own papal diskey, for separate authority on military decisions and those actions deemed necessary for the preservation of the Church."

"She," repeats de Soya, trying hard to understand this. If both he and this mystery "warrior" have equal papal authority, how can they make decisions at all? Every aspect of their quest for the child so far has had military facets and implications. Every decision he has made has been dedicated to the preservation of the Church. It would be better if he were simply dismissed and replaced rather than this false sharing of power.

Before he can articulate this, Cardinal Lourdusamy leans forward and speaks as softly as the bass rumble will allow. "Federico, His Holiness still sees you involved in this . . . and primarily responsible. But Our Lord has revealed a terrible necessity which the Holy Father seeks to take from your hands, knowing you as the ultimate man of conscience you are."

"Terrible necessity?" says de Soya, knowing with an immediate and total sinking feeling exactly what it is.

Lourdusamy's features are all bright light and deep shadow as he leans across the desk. "The cybrid-spawned *succubus* must be terminated. Destroyed. The virus eradicated from the Body of Christ as the first step toward the corrective surgery which is to come."

De Soya counts to eight before speaking. "I find the child," he says. "This . . . warrior . . . kills her."

"Yes," says Lourdusamy. There is no discussion of whether Father Captain de Soya will accept this modified mission. Born-again Christians, priests, Jesuits in particular, and Pax Fleet officers do not quibble when the Holy Father and the Holy Mother Church assign them duties.

"When do I meet this warrior, Your Excellency?" asks de Soya.

"The *Raphael* will translate to Sol Draconi System this very afternoon," pipes up Monsignor Oddi from his place behind and to the left of de Soya. "Your new crew member is already aboard."

"May I ask her name and rank?" says de Soya, turning to look at the tall Monsignor.

Secretary Cardinal Simon Augustino Lourdusamy answers. "She has no formal rank as of yet, Father Captain de Soya. Eventually she will be an officer in the newly formed Legions of the Crusade. As of now, you and your troopers may refer to her by her name."

De Soya waits.

"Which is Nemes," rumbles the Cardinal. "Rhadamanth Nemes." His small eyes flick to Lucas Oddi. The Monsignor stands. De Soya hurries to his feet. The audience is obviously at an end.

Lourdusamy's pudgy hand rises in a three-fingered benediction. De Soya bows his head.

"May Our Lord and Savior, Jesus Christ, keep you and preserve you and give you success on this most important of voyages. In the name of Jesus we ask this."

"Amen," murmurs Monsignor Lucas Oddi.

"Amen," says de Soya.

44

I T WAS NOT JUST A SINGLE BUILDING frozen in the ice. An entire city was buried here in Sol Draconi Septem's resublimated atmosphere, a small bit of the old Hegemony's hubris frozen in place like an ancient insect locked in amber.

Father Glaucus was a gentle, humorous, generous man. We soon learned that he had been exiled to Sol Draconi Septem as a punishment for belonging to one of the last Teilhardian orders in the Church. While his order had rejected the basic tenets of Teilhard after Julius VI had published a bull proclaiming the antipope's philosophy as blasphemy, the order was dissolved and its members either excommunicated or sent to the ass-ends of the Pax's dominion. Father Glaucus did not refer to his fifty-seven standard years in this icy tomb as exile—he called it his mission.

While admitting that none of the Chitchatuk had shown the slightest interest in converting, Father Glaucus confessed that he had little interest in converting them. He admired their courage, respected their honesty, and was fascinated with their hard-earned culture. Before he had become blind—snowblindness, he called it, not simple cataracts . . . a combination of cold, vacuum, and hard radiation found on the surface—Father Glaucus had traveled with numerous Chitchatuk bands. "There were more then," said the old priest as we sat in his brightly lit study. "Attrition has taken its toll. Where there were tens of thousands of the Chitchatuk in this region fifty years ago, only a few hundred survive today."

In the first day or two, while Aenea, A. Bettik, and the blind priest spoke, I spent much of my time exploring the frozen city.

Father Glaucus illuminated four floors of one tall building with the fuel-pellet lanterns. "To keep away the wraiths," he said. "They hate the light." I found a stairway and descended into the darkness with a hand-lamp and my rifle ready. Twenty-some stories lower and a warren of ice tunnels led to the other buildings in the city. Decades earlier, Father Glaucus had marked the entrances to these buried structures with a light pen—WAREHOUSE, COURTHOUSE, COMMUNICATIONS CENTER, HEGEMONY DOME, HOTEL, and so forth. I explored some of these, seeing signs of the priest's more recent visits here. On my third exploration I found the deep vaults where the high-energy fuel pellets were stored. These were the source of both heat and light for the old priest, and they were also his principal bargaining chip to bring the Chitchatuk in to visit.

"The wraiths give them everything except combustible material," he had said. "The pellets give them light and a wee bit of heat. We enjoy the barter—they give me wraith-meat and hides, I give them light and heat and garrulous conversation. I think they first began talking to me because my band consisted of the most elegant prime number . . . one! In the early days I used to hide the location of the cache. Now I know that the Chitchatuk would never steal from me. Even if their lives depended on it. Even if the lives of their *children* depended on it."

There was little else to see in the buried city. The darkness was absolute down there, and my handlamp did little to dispel the gloom. If I had harbored hopes of finding some easy way to get us downriver to the second arch—a giant blowtorch perhaps, or a fusion borer—those hopes were soon dashed. The city was, with the exception of Father Glaucus's four floors of furniture, books, light, food, warmth, and conversation, as cold and dead as the ninth circle of hell.

ON OUR THIRD OR FOURTH DAY THERE, just prior to our mealtime, I joined them in the old priest's study as they chatted. I had already gone over the books on the shelf: volumes of philosophy and theology, mysteries, astronomy texts, ethnology studies, newanthro tomes, adventure novels, carpentry guides, medical texts, zoology books . . .

"The greatest sadness of my blindness thirty years ago," Father Glaucus had said, that first day he proudly showed us his library, "was that I could no longer read my dear books. I am Prospero denied. You can't imagine the time it took me to drag these three thousand volumes up from the library fifty stories down!"

In the afternoons, while I explored and A. Bettik went off to read by himself, Aenea would read aloud to the old priest. Once when I entered the room without knocking, I saw tears on the ancient missionary's cheeks.

This day when I joined them, Father Glaucus was explaining Teilhard—the original Jesuit, not the antipope whom Julius VI had supplanted.

"He was a stretcher bearer in World War One," Father Glaucus was saying. "He could have been a chaplain and stayed out of the line of fire, but he chose to be a stretcher bearer. They awarded him medals for his courage, including one called the Legion of Honor."

A. Bettik cleared his throat politely. "Excuse me, Father," he said softly. "Am I correct in assuming that the First World War was a pre-Hegira conflict limited to Old Earth?"

The bearded priest smiled. "Precisely, precisely, my dear friend. Early twentieth century. Terrible conflict. Terrible. And Teilhard was in the thick of it. His hatred of war lasted the rest of his life."

Father Glaucus had long ago built his own rocking chair, and now he rocked back and forth in front of the fuel-pellet fire set in a crudely fashioned fireplace. The golden embers threw long shadows and more warmth than we had enjoyed since coming through the farcaster portal. "Teilhard was a geologist and paleontologist. It was in China—a nation-state on Old Earth, my friends—in the 1930's that he devised his theories that evolution was an uncompleted process, yet one with a design. He saw the universe as God's design to bring together the Christ of Evolution, the Personal, and the Universal into a single conscious entity. Teilhard de Chardin saw every step of evolution as a hopeful sign—even mass extinctions as a cause for joy—with cosmogenesis, his word, occurring when humanity became central to the universe, noogenesis as the continued evolution of man's mind, and hominization and ultrahominization as the stages of *Homo sapiens* evolving to true humanity."

"Excuse me, Father," I heard myself saying, only slightly aware of the incongruity of this abstract discussion amid the frozen city, beneath the frozen atmosphere, surrounded by wraith-killers and cold, "but wasn't Teilhard's heresy that humankind could evolve into God?"

The blind priest shook his head, his expression still pleasant. "During his lifetime, my son, Teilhard was never sanctioned for heresy. In 1962 the Holy Office—it was quite a different Holy Office then, I assure you—issued a monitum—"

"A what?" said Aenea, who sat on the carpet near the fire.

"A monitum is a warning against uncritical acceptance of his ideas," said Father Glaucus. "And Teilhard did not say that human beings would *become* God . . . he said that the entire conscious universe was part of a process of evolving toward the day—he called it the Omega Point—where all of creation, humanity included, would become one with the Godhead."

"Would Teilhard have included the TechnoCore in that evolution?" Aenea asked softly. She was hugging her knees.

The blind priest stopped rocking and combed his fingers through his beard. "Teilhardian scholars have wrestled with that for centuries, my dear. I am no scholar, but I am certain that he would have included the Core in his optimism."

"But they are descended from machines," said A. Bettik. "And their concept of an Ultimate Intelligence is quite different from Christianity's—

a cold, dispassionate mind, a predictive power able to absorb all variables."

Father Glaucus was nodding. "But they think, my son. Their earliest self-conscious progenitors were designed from living DNA—"

"Designed from DNA to *compute*," I said, appalled at the thought of Core machines being given the benefit of the doubt when it came to souls.

"And what was *our* DNA designed to do for the first few hundred million years, my son? Eat? Kill? Procreate? Were we any less ignoble in our beginnings than the pre-Hegira silicon and DNA-based AIs? As Teilhard would have it, it is *consciousness* which God has created to accelerate the universe's self-awareness as a means to understanding His will."

"The TechnoCore wanted to use humanity as part of its UI project," I said, "and then to destroy us."

"But it did not," said Father Glaucus.

"No thanks to the Core," I said.

"Humanity has evolved—as far as it *has* evolved," continued the old priest, "with no thanks to its predecessors or itself. Evolution brings human beings. Human beings, through a long and painful process, bring humanity."

"Empathy," Aenea said softly.

Father Glaucus turned his blind eyes in her direction. "Precisely, my dear. But we are not the only avatars of humanity. Once our computing machines achieved self-consciousness, they became part of this design. They may resist it. They may try to undo it for their own complex purposes. But the universe continues to weave its own design."

"You make the universe and its processes sound like a machine," I said. "Programmed, unstoppable, inevitable."

The old man shook his head slowly. "No, no . . . never a machine. And never inevitable. If Christ's coming taught us anything, it is that nothing is inevitable. The outcome is always in doubt. Decisions for light or dark are always ours to make—ours and every conscious entity's."

"But Teilhard thought that consciousness and empathy would win?" said Aenea.

Father Glaucus waved a bony hand at the bookcase behind her. "There should be a book there . . . on the third shelf . . . it had a blue bookmark in it when last I looked, thirty-some years ago. Do you see it?"

"The Journals, Notebooks, and Correspondences of Teilhard de Chardin?" said Aenea.

"Yes, yes. Open it to where the blue bookmark is. Do you see the passage I have annotated? It is one of the last things these old eyes saw before the darkness closed. . . ."

"The entry marked twelve December, 1919?" said Aenea.

"Yes. Read it, please."

Aenea held the book closer to the light of the fire.

" 'Note this well,' " she read. " 'I attribute no definitive and absolute value to the various constructions of man. I believe that they will disappear, recast in a new whole that we cannot yet conceive. At the same time I admit that they have an essential provisional role—that they are necessary, inevitable phases which we (we or the race) must pass through in the course of our metamorphosis. What I love in them is not their particular form, but their function, which is to build up, in some mysterious way, first something divinizable—and then, through the grace of Christ alighting on our effort, something divine.' "

There was a moment of silence broken only by the soft hiss of the fuel-pellet fire and the creak and groan of the tens of millions of tons of ice above and around us. Finally Father Glaucus said, "That hope was Teilhard's heresy in the eyes of the current Pope. Belief in that hope was my great sin. This"—he gestured to the outer wall where ice and darkness pressed against the glass—"this is my punishment."

None of us spoke for another moment.

Father Glaucus laughed and set bony hands on his knees. "But my mother taught me there is no punishment or pain where there are friends and food and conversation. And we have all of these. M. Bettik! I say 'M. Bettik' because your honorific does you no honor, sir. It sets you apart from humanity by falsely inventing false categories. M. Bettik!"

"Sir?"

"Would you do this old man the favor of going into the kitchen to retrieve the coffee that should be ready? I will see to the stew and the bread that is heating. M. Endymion?"

"Yes, Father?"

"Would you like to descend to the wine cellars to select the finest vintage available?"

I smiled, knowing that the old priest could not see me. "And how many floors must I descend before finding the cellar, Father? Not fifty-nine, I hope?"

The old man's teeth showed through his beard. "I have wine with every meal, my son, so I would be in far better physical shape if that were the case. No, lazy old thing that I am, I keep the wine in the closet one flight below. Near the stairwell."

"I'll find it," I said.

"I'll set the table," said Aenea. "And tomorrow night I cook."

We all scattered to our duties.

45

HE *RAPHAEL* SPINS DOWN into Sol Draconi System. Contrary to the explanations received by Father Captain de Soya and others who travel by archangel craft, its drive mechanism is not a modification of the ancient Hawking drive that has defied the light-speed barrier since before the Hegira. *Raphael*'s drive is largely a hoax: when it reaches near-quantum velocities, it keys a signal on a medium once referred to as the Void Which Binds. An energy source from elsewhere triggers a distant device that ruptures a subplane of that medium, tearing through the fabric of space and time itself. That rupture is instantly fatal to the human crew, who die in agony—cells rupturing, bones being ground to powder, synapses misfiring, bowels releasing, organs liquefying. They are never to know the details: all memory of the final microseconds of horror and death are erased during cruciform reconstruction and resurrection.

Now *Raphael* begins its braking trajectory toward Sol Draconi Septem, its very-real fusion drive slowing the ship under two hundred gravities of strain. In their acceleration couches/resurrection creches, Father Captain de Soya, Sergeant Gregorius, and Corporal Kee lie dead, their shredded bodies being pulverized a second time because the ship automatically conserves energy by not initializing internal fields until resurrection is well under way. Besides the three dead humans on board, there is one other pair of eyes. Rhadamanth Nemes has opened the lid of her resurrection creche and now lies on the exposed couch, her compact body buffeted but not damaged by the terrible deceleration. As per standard programming, the life support in the general cabin is off: there is no oxygen, atmospheric pressure is too low to allow a human to survive without a spacesuit, and the temperature is minus-thirty degrees centigrade. Nemes is indifferent. In her crimson jumpsuit, she lies on the couch and watches the monitors, occasionally querying the ship and receiving a reply on a fiberthread datalink.

Six hours later, before the internal fields switch on and the bodies begin to be repaired in their complex sarcophagi, even while the cabin is still in virtual vacuum, Nemes stands, shoulders two hundred gravities with no expression, and walks to the conference cubby and the plotting table. She calls up a map of Sol Draconi Septem and quickly finds the former route of River Tethys. Ordering the ship to overlay its long-range visuals, she runs her fingers across the holoed image of ice rills, sestrugi dunes, and glacial crevasses. The top of one building rises from the atmospheric glacier. Nemes double-checks the plot: it is within thirty kilometers of the buried river.

After eleven hours of braking, *Raphael* swings into orbit around the gleaming white snowball of Sol Draconi Septem. The internal fields have long since switched on, the life-support systems are fully functional, but Rhadamanth Nemes takes no more note of this than she had of the weight and vacuum. Before leaving the ship, she checks the resurrection-creche monitors. She has more than two days before de Soya and his troopers will begin to stir in their creches.

Settling into the dropship, Nemes runs a fiber-optic link from her wrist to the console, commands separation, and guides the ship across the terminator into atmosphere without consulting instruments or controls. Eighteen minutes later the dropship sets down on the surface within two hundred meters of the stubby, ice-limned tower.

The sunlight is brilliant on the terraced glacier, but the sky is flat black. No stars are visible. Although the atmosphere here is negligible, the planet's massive thermal systems flowing from pole to pole drive incessant "winds" accelerating ice crystals to four hundred kilometers per hour. Ignoring the spacesuits and hazardous-atmosphere suits hanging in the air lock, Rhadamanth Nemes cycles the doors open. Not waiting for the ladder to deploy, she jumps the three meters to the surface, landing upright in the one-point-seven-g field. Ice needles strike her at flechette-gun velocities.

Nemes triggers an internal source that activates a biomorphic field within point-eight millimeters of her body. To an outside observer the compact woman with short black hair and flat black eyes suddenly becomes a reflective quicksilver sculpture in human form. The form jogs across the jagged ice at thirty klicks an hour, stops at the building, finds no entrance, and shatters a panel of plasteel with her fist. Stepping through the gash, she walks easily across glare ice to the top of an elevator shaft. She rips open the sagging doors. The elevators have long since dropped to the basement eighty-some stories below.

Rhadamanth Nemes steps into the open shaft and drops into it, plummeting 108.8 feet per second into the darkness. When she sees the light flashing past, she grabs a steel girder to stop herself. She has already reached her terminal velocity of more than five hundred klicks per hour and decelerates to zero in less than three hundredths of a second.

Nemes strides from the elevator into the room, taking note of the furniture, the lanterns, the bookcases. The old man is in the kitchen. His head comes up when he hears the rapid footsteps. "Raul?" he says. "Aenea?"

"Exactly," says Rhadamanth Nemes, inserting two fingers under the old priest's collar bone and lifting him off the ground. "Where is the girl Aenea?" she asks softly. "Where are all of them?"

Amazingly, the blind priest does not cry out in pain. His worn teeth are clenched and his blind eyes stare at the ceiling, but he says only, "I do not know."

Nemes nods and drops the priest to the floor. Straddling his chest, she sets her forefinger to his eye and fires a seeker microfilament into his brain, the seeker probe finding its way to a precise region of his cerebral cortex.

"Now, Father," she says, "let us try again. Where is the girl? Who is with her? Where are they?"

The answers begin flowing through the microfilament as coded bursts of dying neural energy.

46

O UR DAYS WITH FATHER GLAUCUS were memorable for their comfort, their slowed pace after so many weeks of hurrying to and fro, and their conversations. Mostly, I think, I remember the conversations.

It was shortly before the Chitchatuk returned that I learned one of the reasons for A. Bettik's having taken this voyage with me.

"Do you have siblings, M. Bettik?" Father Glaucus asked, still refusing to use the android honorific.

To my amazement A. Bettik said, "Yes." How could this be? Androids were designed and biofactured, assembled out of component genetic elements and grown in vats . . . like organs grown for transplants, I had always thought.

"During our biofacture," A. Bettik went on after the old priest prompted, "androids were traditionally cloned in growth colonies of five —usually four males and one female."

"Quintuplets," said Father Glaucus from his rocking chair. "You have three brothers and a sister."

"Yes," said the blue-skinned man.

"But surely you weren't . . . ," I began, and stopped. I rubbed my chin. I had shaved there at Father Glaucus's strange home—it had seemed the civilized thing to do—and the feel of smooth skin almost startled me. "But surely you didn't grow up together," I said. "I mean, weren't androids . . ."

"Biofactured as adults?" said A. Bettik with the same slight smile. "No. Our growth process was accelerated—we reached maturity at approximately eight standard years—but there was a period of infancy and childhood. This delay was one of the reasons that android biofacture was almost prohibitively expensive."

"What are your brothers' and sister's names?" asked Father Glaucus.

A. Bettik closed the book he had been leafing through. "The tradition was to name each member of the quint group in alphabetic order," he said. "My siblings included A. Anttibe, A. Corresson, A. Darria, and A. Evvik."

"Which was your sister?" asked Aenea. "Darria?"

"Yes."

"What was your childhood like?" said the girl.

"Primarily one of being educated, trained for duties, and having service parameters defined," said A. Bettik.

Aenea was lying on the carpet, cupping her chin in her hands. "Did you go to school? Did you play?"

"We were tutored at the factory, although the bulk of our knowledge came through RNA transfer." The bald man looked at Aenea. "And if by 'play' you mean to find time to relax with my siblings, the answer is yes."

"What happened to your siblings?" asked Aenea.

A. Bettik slowly shook his head. "We were initially transferred to service together, but we were separated shortly thereafter. I was purchased by the Kingdom of Monaco-in-Exile and shipped to Asquith. It was my understanding at the time that each of us would render service in different parts of the Web or Outback."

"And you never heard from any of them again?" I said.

"No," said A. Bettik. "Although there were a large number of android laborers imported for the construction of the Poet's City during the transfer of King William the Twenty-third's colony to that world, most had been in service on Asquith before my time, and none had encountered one of my siblings during their transshipment periods."

"During the Web days," I said, "it should have been easy to search the other worlds by farcaster and datasphere."

"Yes," said A. Bettik, "except for the fact that androids were forbidden by law and RNA inhibitors to travel by farcasters or access the datasphere directly. And, of course, it became illegal to biofacture or own androids within the Hegemony shortly after my own creation."

"So you were used in the Outback," I said. "On distant worlds like Hyperion."

"Precisely, M. Endymion."

I took a breath. "And is that why you wished to make this trip? To find one of your siblings . . . one of your brothers or your sister?"

A. Bettik smiled. "The odds against running across one of my clone siblings would be truly astronomical, M. Endymion. Not only would the coincidence be unlikely, but the chance that any of them would have survived the wholesale destruction of androids following the Fall would be very slight. But—" A. Bettik stopped and opened his hands as if explaining foolishness.

IT WAS THAT LAST EVENING before the band returned that I heard Aenea discuss her theory of love for the first time. It began with her questioning us about Martin Silenus's *Cantos*.

"All right," she said, "I understand that it was placed on the Index of Prohibited Books as soon as the Pax took over anywhere, but what about those worlds not yet swallowed by the Pax when it came out? Did he receive the critical acclaim he had been hungry for?"

"I remember arguing the *Cantos* in seminary," chuckled Father Glaucus. "We knew it was prohibited, but that just made the allure all the greater. We resisted reading Virgil, but waited our turn to read that dog-eared copy of doggerel that was the *Cantos*."

"Was it doggerel?" asked Aenea. "I always thought of Uncle Martin as a great poet, but that's only because he told me he was. My mother always told me that he was a pain in the ass."

"Poets can be both," said Father Glaucus. He chuckled again. "In fact, it seems they often are both. As I remember it, most of the critics dismissed the *Cantos* in what few literary circles existed before the Church absorbed them. Some took him seriously . . . as a poet, not as a chronicler of what actually happened on Hyperion just before the Fall. But most made fun of his apotheosis of love toward the end of his second volume. . . ."

"I remember that," I said. "The character of Sol—the old scholar whose daughter has been aging backward—he discovers that love was the answer to what he had called The Abraham Dilemma."

"I remember one nasty critic who reviewed the poem in our capital city," chuckled Father Glaucus, "who quoted some graffiti found on a wall of an excavated Old Earth city before the Hegira—'If love is the answer, what was the question?' "

Aenea looked at me for an explanation.

"In the *Cantos*," I said, "the scholar character seems to discover that the thing the AI Core had called the Void Which Binds is love. That love is a basic force of the universe, like gravity and electromagnetism, like strong and weak nuclear force. In the poem Sol sees that the Core Ultimate Intelligence will never be capable of understanding that empathy is inseparable from that source . . . from love. The old poet described love as 'the subquantum impossibility that carried information/ from photon to photon. . . .' "

"Teilhard would not have disagreed," said Father Glaucus, "although he would have phrased it differently."

"Anyway," I said, "the almost universal reaction to the poem—according to Grandam—was that it was weakened by this sentimentality."

Aenea was shaking her head. "Uncle Martin was right," she said. "Love *is* one of the basic forces of the universe. I know that Sol Weintraub really believed he had discovered that. He said as much to Mother before he and his daughter disappeared in the Sphinx, riding it to the child's future."

The blind priest quit rocking and leaned forward, his elbows propped on his bony knees. His padded cassock would have looked comical on a less dignified man. "Is this more complicated than saying that God is love?" he said.

"Yes!" said Aenea, standing in front of the fire now. She seemed older to me at that moment, as if she had grown and matured during our months together. "The Greeks saw gravity at work, but explained it as one of the four elements—earth—'rushing back to its family.' What Sol Weintraub glimpsed was a bit of the *physics* of love . . . where it resides, how it works, how one can understand and harness it. The difference between 'God is love' and what Sol Weintraub saw—and what Uncle Martin tried to explain—is the difference between the Greek explanation of gravity and Isaac Newton's equations. One is a clever phrase. The other sees the *thing itself*."

Father Glaucus shook his head. "You make it sound quantifiable and mechanical, my dear."

"No," said Aenea, and her voice was about as strong as I had ever heard it. "Just as you explained how Teilhard knew that the universe evolving toward greater consciousness could never be purely mechanical . . . that the forces were not dispassionate, as science had always assumed, but derived from the absolute passion of divinity . . . well, so an understanding of love's part of the Void Which Binds can never be mechanical. In a sense, it's the essence of humanity."

I stifled the urge to laugh. "So you're saying that there needs to be another Isaac Newton to explain the physics of love?" I said. "To give us its laws of thermodynamics, its rules of entropy? To show us the calculus of love?"

"Yes!" said the girl, her dark eyes very bright.

Father Glaucus was still leaning forward, his hands now gripping his knees very tightly. "Are you that person, young Aenea from Hyperion?"

Aenea turned away quickly, walking almost out of the light toward the darkness and ice beyond the smart glass before turning and slowly stepping back into the circle of warmth. Her face was downcast. Her lashes were wet with tears. When she spoke, her voice was soft, almost tremulous. "Yes," she said. "I am afraid I am. I do not want to be. But I am. Or could be . . . if I survive."

This sent chills down my back. I was sorry we had started this conversation.

"Will you tell us now?" said Father Glaucus. His voice held the simple entreaty of a child.

Aenea raised her face and then slowly shook her head. "I cannot. I am not ready. I'm sorry, Father."

The blind priest sat back in his chair and suddenly looked very old. "It is all right, my child. I have met you. That is something."

Aenea went over to the old man in his rocking chair and hugged him for a long minute.

CUCHIAT AND HIS BAND returned before we had awakened and got out of our beds and sleeping robes the next morning. During our days with the Chitchatuk, we had almost become accustomed to sleeping a few hours at a time and then resuming the march in the eternal ice gloom, but here with Father Glaucus we followed his system—dimming the lights a bit in the innermost rooms for a full eight hours of "night." It was my observation that one was always weary in a one-point-seven-g environment.

The Chitchatuk disliked coming very far into the building, so they stood in the open window, which was more ice tunnel than interior, and made a variation of their soft ululation until we hurriedly dressed and came running.

The band was back up to the healthy prime of twenty-three, although where they had found their new member—a woman—Father Glaucus did not ask and the rest of us were never to learn. When I came into the room, the image struck me then and it has stayed with me ever since—the powerful, wraith-robed Chitchatuk squatting in their most typical posture, Father Glaucus squatting and chatting with Cuchiat, the old priest's quilted and heavily patched cassock spreading out on the ice like a black flower, the glow of the fuel-pellet lanterns prisming light from the crystals at the entrance to the ice cave, and—beyond the smart glass—that terrible sense of ice and weight and darkness pressing . . . pressing.

We had long since asked Father Glaucus to be our interpreter in making—remaking, actually—our request of help to the indigenies, and now the old man broached the subject, asking the white-robed figures if they would indeed like to help us get our raft downriver. The Chitchatuk responded in turn, each waiting to address Father Glaucus and the rest of us individually, and each saying essentially the same thing—they were ready to make the voyage.

It was not to be a simple voyage. Cuchiat confirmed that there were tunnels descending all the way to the river at the second arch, almost two hundred meters lower than where we now sat, and that there was a stretch of open water where the river passed beneath this second farcaster, but . . .

There were no connecting tunnels between here and the second arch some twenty-eight kilometers to the north.

"I've been meaning to ask," said Aenea. "Where do these tunnels come from, anyway? They're too round and regular to be crevasses or fissures. Did the Chitchatuk make them at some time in the past?"

Father Glaucus looked at the child with an expression of bearded incredulity. "You mean you don't know?" he said. He turned his head and rattled syllables at the Chitchatuk. Their reaction was almost explosive—excited chatter, the near barking that we associated with laughter.

"I hope I didn't offend you, my dear," said the old priest. He was smiling, his blind eyes turned in Aenea's direction. "It is just such a given of our existence here, that it struck me—and the Indivisible People—as strangely humorous that someone could move through the ice and not know."

"The Indivisible People?" said A. Bettik.

"Chitchatuk," said Father Glaucus. "It means 'indivisible'—or perhaps closer to the actual shading of the word—'incapable of being made more perfect.' "

Aenea was smiling. "I'm not offended. I'd just like in on the joke. What *did* make the tunnels?"

"The wraiths," I guessed before the priest could speak.

His smile turned in my direction. "Precisely, my friend Raul. Precisely."

Aenea frowned. "Their claws are formidable, but even on the adults they couldn't carve tunnels that extensive through such solid ice . . . could they?"

I shook my head. "I don't think we've really seen the adult form."

"Precisely, precisely." The old man was nodding deeply as he tended to do. "Raul is correct, my dear. The Chitchatuk hunt the youngest cubs when possible. The older cubs hunt the Chitchatuk when possible. But the wraith cub-form you see is the larval stage of the creature. It feeds and moves about the surface during that stage, but within three of Sol Draconi Septem's orbits—"

"That would be twenty-nine years, standard," murmured A. Bettik.

"Precisely, precisely," nodded the priest. "Within three local years, twenty-nine standard, the immature wraith—the "cub," although that word is usually used with mammals—passes through metamorphosis and becomes the true wraith, which bores through the ice at approximately twenty kilometers per hour. It is approximately fifteen meters long and . . . well, you may well encounter one on your trip north."

I cleared my throat. "I believe Cuchiat and Chiaku were explaining that there were no tunnels connecting this area to the farcaster tunnels some twenty-eight klicks north. . . ."

"Ah, yes," said Father Glaucus, and resumed his conversation in the clattering Chitchatuk language. When Cuchiat had responded, the blind man said, "Approximately twenty-five kilometers across the surface, which is more than the Indivisible People like to do at one spell. And Aichacut kindly points out that this area is thick with wraiths—both cub and adult—that the Indivisible People who lived there for centuries have all been turned into skull necklaces for the wraiths. He points out that the summer storms are battering the surface this month. But for you, my friends, they are willing to make the voyage."

I shook my head. "I don't understand. The surface is essentially airless, isn't it? I mean . . ."

"They have all the materials you will need for the trip, Raul, my son," said Father Glaucus.

Aichacut snarled something. Cuchiat added something in a more tempered tone.

"They are ready to depart when you are, my friends. Cuchiat says that it will take two sleeps and three marches to return to your raft. And then they will head north until the burrows run out. . . ." The old priest paused and turned his face away for a moment.

"What is it?" asked Aenea, concern in her voice.

Father Glaucus turned back. His smile was forced. He ran bony fingers through his beard. "I will miss you. It has been a long time since . . . hah! I am getting senile. Come, we will help you pack, have a fast breakfast, and see if we can round out your provisions with a few things from the storeroom."

THE LEAVE-TAKING WAS PAINFUL. The thought of the old man alone there in the ice once again, fending off wraiths and the planetary glacier with nothing more than a few lighted lamps . . . it made my chest hurt to think of it. Aenea wept. When A. Bettik went to shake the old priest's hand, Father Glaucus fiercely hugged the startled android. "Your day is yet to come, my friend M. Bettik. I feel this. I feel this strongly."

A. Bettik did not respond, but later, as we followed the Chitchatuk into the deep glacier, I saw the blue man glancing back toward the tall silhouette against the light before we rounded another corner in the tunnel and lost sight of the building, the light, and the old priest.

It did take us three marches and two sleeps before we slid and scraped our way down the final steep incline of ice, twisted right through a narrow break in the ice, and came out where the raft was tied up. I saw no way that the logs could be transported around the bends and turns of these endless tunnels, but this time the Chitchatuk wasted not a minute admiring the ice-laden craft, but immediately went to work unlashing it and separating log from log.

The entire band had marveled most visibly at our ax during the first visit, and now I was able to show them how it worked as I chopped each log into shorter segments, each segment only a meter and a half in length. Using my fading flashlight laser, A. Bettik and Aenea were doing the same thing on our impromptu assembly line—the Chitchatuk scraping ice off the almost-sinking craft, cutting or untying knots, and handing the long segments up where we cut and stacked. When we were done, the stone hearth, extra lanterns, and ice were on the iceshelf and the wood was piled up the long tunnel like next year's firewood.

The thought amused me at first, but then I realized how welcome a store of combustible material such as this might have been to the Chitchatuk—heat, light to drive the wraiths away. I looked at our dismantled raft in a different way. Well, if we failed to get through the second portal . . .

Using Aenea as our translator now, we communicated to Cuchiat that we would like to leave the ax, the hearth, and the other odds and ends with them. It is fair to say that the faces behind the wraith-teeth visors looked stunned. The Chitchatuk milled around, hugging and patting us on the back with enough strength to knock the wind out of each of us. Even angry Aichacut patted and shoved us with something like rough affection.

Each member of the band lashed three or four of the log segments to his or her back; A. Bettik, Aenea, and I did the same—they were as heavy as concrete in this g-field—and we began the long trek uphill toward the surface, vacuum, storm, and wraiths.

47

I T TAKES LESS THAN A MINUTE for Rhadamanth Nemes's neural tap to finish its probe of Father Glaucus's brain. In a combination of visual images, language, and raw synaptic chemical data, Nemes has as full a picture of Aenea's visit to the frozen city as she will get without a complete neurological disassembly. She withdraws the microfilament and allows herself a few seconds to ponder the data.

Aenea, her human companion, Raul, and the android left three and a half standard days earlier, but at least one of those days will have been taken up with cutting their raft apart. The second farcaster is almost thirty klicks to the north, and the Chitchatuk will lead them over the surface, which is dangerous and slow traveling. Nemes knows that there is a good chance that Aenea has not survived the surface trek—Nemes has seen in the old priest's mind the crude means by which the Indivisible People try to cope with the surface conditions.

Rhadamanth Nemes smiles thinly. She will not leave such things to chance.

Father Glaucus moans feebly.

Nemes pauses with her knee on the old priest's chest. The neural probe has done little harm: a sophisticated medkit could heal the filament bore between the old man's eye and brain. And he was already blind when she arrived.

Nemes considers the situation. Encountering a Pax priest on this world had not been part of the equation. As Father Glaucus begins to stir, his bony hands lifting toward his face, Nemes weighs the balance: leaving the priest alive will pose very little risk—a forgotten missionary, in exile, destined to die in this place anyway. On the other hand, Nemes knows, not leaving him alive poses no risk whatsoever. It is a simple equation.

"Who . . . are you?" moans the priest as Nemes easily lifts him and carries him from the kitchen through the dining area, from the dining area through the book-lined library with its warm fuel-pellet fire, from the library to the hallway to the building's central core. Even here lanterns burn to discourage wraiths.

"Who *are* you?" says the blind priest again, struggling in her grip like a two-year-old in the arms of a strong adult. "Why are you doing this?" says the old man as Nemes reaches the elevator shaft, kicks the plasteel doors open, and holds the priest a final moment.

There is a blast of cold air rushing down from the surface to the glacial depths two hundred meters below. The noise sounds as if the frozen planet is screaming. At the last second Father Glaucus realizes precisely what is happening. "Ah, dear Jesus, Lord," he whispers, his chapped lips quivering. "Ah, St. Teilhard . . . dear Jesus . . ."

Nemes drops the old man into the shaft and turns away, only mildly surprised that no scream echoes behind her. She takes the frozen stairway to the surface, leaping four or five steps at a time in the weighted g-field. At the top, she must punch her way up the icy waterfall where the frozen atmosphere has dribbled down five or six flights of stairs. Standing on the roof of the building, the sky black with vacuum and the katabatik storm whipping ice crystals at her face, she activates the phase-shift field and jogs across the ice to the dropship.

There are three immature wraiths investigating the ship. In a second Nemes takes note of the creatures—nonmammalian, the white "fur" actually tubuled scales capable of holding gaseous atmosphere, which acts to hold in body heat, eyes working on the deep infrared, redundant lung capacity, which allows them to go twelve hours or more without oxygen, each animal more than five meters long, forearms immensely powerful, rear legs designed for digging and disemboweling, each beast very fast.

They turn toward her as she jogs closer. Seen against the black background, the wraiths look more like immense white weasels or iguanas than anything else. Their elongated bodies move with blinding speed.

Nemes considers bypassing them, but if they attack the ship, it could cause complications during takeoff. She shifts into fast time. The wraiths freeze in midmotion. The blowing ice crystals hang suspended against the black sky.

Working efficiently, using only her right hand and the diamond-hard blade of her phase-shifted forearm, she butchers the three animals. During the work two things mildly surprise her: each wraith has two huge five-chambered hearts, and the beasts seem capable of fighting on with only one intact; each wears a necklace of small human skulls. When she is finished and has shifted back to slow time, after the three wraiths have dropped like giant bags of organic offal onto the ice, Nemes takes a moment to inspect the necklaces. Human skulls. Probably from human children. Interesting.

Nemes activates the dropship and flies north—keeping it on reaction thrusters since the stubby wings can find no lift in this near vacuum. Deep radar probes the ice until the river becomes visible. Above the level of the river are many hundreds of kilometers of tunnels. The wraiths have been very busy in this area. On the deep-radar display, the metal arch of the farcaster portal stands out like a bright light in dark fog. The instrument is less successful in finding living, moving things under the ice. Various echoes show the clear track of adult wraiths tunneling their way through the atmosphere glacier, but these soundings are klicks to the north and east.

She lands the dropship directly above the farcaster portal and searches the sastrugi-patterned surface for a cave entrance. Finding one, she moves into the glacier at a jog, dropping her biomorphic shield when the pressure moves above three psi and the temperature rises within thirty degrees of freezing.

The tunnel maze is daunting, but she keeps her bearings relative to the great mass of portal metal a third of a kilometer beneath her, and within an hour she is nearing the level of the river. It is too near absolute darkness down there to see by light amplification or infrared, and she has not brought a flashlight, but she opens her mouth, and a brilliant beam of yellow light illuminates the tunnel and ice fog ahead of her.

She hears their approach long before the dim ember-lanterns come into view down the long, descending corridor. Killing the light, Rhadamanth Nemes stands in the tunnel and waits. When they first round the corner, it looks more like a herd of diminutive wraiths than a band of human beings, but she recognizes them from Father Glaucus's memory: Cuchiat's band of Chitchatuk. They stop in surprise at the sight of a lone female without robes or outer insulation standing in the glacier tunnel.

Cuchiat steps forward and speaks rapidly. "The Indivisible People greet the warrior/hunter/seeker who chooses to travel in the glow of the next-to-perfect indivisibility. If you need warmth, food, weapons, or friends, speak, for our band loves all those who walk on two feet and respect the path of the prime."

In the Chitchatuk language she has taken from the old priest, Rhadamanth Nemes says, "I seek my friends—Aenea, Raul, and the blue man. Have they passed through the metal arch yet?"

The twenty-three Chitchatuk talk among themselves of the strange woman's command of their language. They reason that she must be a friend or kin of the glaucus, for this person speaks with precisely the same dialect as the blind man in black who shares his warmth with visitors. Still, Cuchiat speaks with something like suspicion. "They have passed under the ice and out of sight through the arch. They wished us well and gave us gifts. We wish you well and offer you gifts. Is the next-to-perfect indivisibility wishing to travel the magical riverway with your friends?"

"In a moment," says Rhadamanth Nemes with her thin smile. This encounter offers the same equation as the quandary of what to do with the old priest. She takes a step forward. The twenty-three Chitchatuk exclaim with almost childish delight as she phase-shifts into featureless quicksilver. She knows that their ember light reflecting from a thousand ice facets must be mirrored now on her surface. Shifting into fast time, she kills the twenty-three men and women without wasting motion or effort.

Dropping out of fast time, she chooses the nearest corpse and fires a neural probe through the corner of the man's eye. The brain's neural network is collapsing from lack of blood and oxygen, creating the usual burst of hallucinations and wild creativity common to the death of such networks—human or AI—but in the middle of the life-to-death synaptic replay of birth images . . . emerging from long tunnels into bright light and warmth . . . she catches the fading images of the child, the tall man, and the android pushing off the crudely rebuilt raft, ducking their heads as they pass under the low ice beneath the frozen-in-place arch.

"Damn," breathes Nemes.

Leaving the bodies piled where they fell in the darkening tunnel, she jogs the last kilometer or so to the level of the river.

There is little open water here, and the farcaster portal is only a brief metal chord in the jagged ice above. Icy fog and mist roil around her as she stands on the low, broad shelf of ice where heat imprints show how the Chitchatuk had gathered to bid farewell to their friends.

Nemes wants to interrogate the farcaster, but to reach the arch, she has to either bore through many meters of ice or climb the overhanging ceiling to the exposed section twenty-some meters above. She phase-shifts just her hands and feet and climbs, digging steps and handholds deep into the ice.

Hanging upside down from the exposed curve of the arch, Nemes sets her hand on a panel and waits until the frosted metal folds back on itself like skin being pulled back from a wound. Extending both microfilaments and a fiber-optic probe, she contacts the interface module that puts her in touch with the actual farcaster. Whispers impinging directly upon her auditory nerve tell her that the Three Sectors of Consciousness are monitoring her and discussing events.

All during the centuries of the Hegemony of Man, everyone knew that there were hundreds of thousands, perhaps millions, of TechnoCore-created farcaster portals—from the smallest doorway to the larger River Tethys arches to the huge spaceborne portals. Everyone was wrong. There is only one farcaster portal. But it is everywhere.

Using the interface module, Rhadamanth Nemes queries the pulsing, living warmth of the true farcaster within its camouflage disguise of metal, electronics, and fusion shield. For centuries, humans jumping by farcaster within the Web—at its height, one human analyst suggested that there were more than one billion jumps a second taking place—had served the Ultimates, those elements of the TechnoCore who existed to create a more advanced AI . . . the Ultimate Intelligence whose consciousness would absorb the galaxy, perhaps the universe. Every time a human had accessed the fatline-connected dataspheres or farcast during those Webdays, that human being's synapses and DNA had added to the computing power of the Web-wide neural net the Core had built. The Core had cared nothing for humankind's visceral urge to move about, to travel without energy expenditure or time lapse, but the farcaster Web had been the perfect bait to weave the very fabric of those teeming hundreds of billions of primitive, organic brains into something useful.

Now, its hiding place in the interstices of space/time ferreted out by Meina Gladstone and her damned Hyperion pilgrims, its web-within-the-Web home attacked by the deathwand device the Core had helped human-ity to build, its fatline connections severed by powers from somewhere beyond the known circle of the megasphere, all facets of the single, omni-present farcaster portal are dead and useless.

Except this one. It has just been used. The interface module reports to Nemes what she and all the Sectors already know—the facet has been activated by Something Else. From Somewhere Else.

The portal still registers its connection points in real space/time in its bubble memory of modulated neutrinos. Nemes accesses this memory.

Aenea and the others have farcast to Qom-Riyadh. Nemes must ponder another puzzle. She can lift the dropship to the archangel *Raphael* and be in Qom-Riyadh System within a few minutes. But she will have to interrupt de Soya's and the others' resurrection cycle to do so, as well as come up with a plausible explanation as to the reason for the shift. In addition, Qom-Riyadh is a Pax-quarantined system: officially listed as having been overrun by the Ousters, it is one of the early Justice and Peace projects. As had been the case with Hebron, neither the Pax nor its advis-ers can allow de Soya and his men to see the truth the planet represents. Finally, Nemes knows that the River Tethys runs for only a few kilome-ters, crossing through red-rock desert of the southern hemisphere and passing the Grand Mosque in Mashhad. If she allows *Raphael*'s resurrec-tion cycle to run its course, de Soya and the others will not be active for three standard days, allowing Aenea and her raft of misfits time to pass the length of the section of Tethys. Once again the equation seems to demand that Nemes finish de Soya and the others and press on alone. But her instructions have been to avoid that possibility unless absolutely neces-sary. De Soya's involvement with the final capture of the One Who Teaches, the Aenea Threat, has been registered in too many full simula-tions, recorded in too many Full-Sector Looks Forward, to be ignored without hazard. The fabric of space/time is much like one of the elaborate Vatican tapestries, thinks Nemes, and she who begins pulling on loose threads does so at the peril of watching the whole tapestry ravel.

Nemes takes several seconds to consider this. Finally she extends a neural network filament deeper into the interface module's synapses. All of the farcaster's activation route is there—past and present. The memory pattern of Aenea and her accomplices is a fleeting bubble memory, but

Nemes can easily see the recent past and future openings. There are only two more downriver possibilities in the foreseeable future. After Qom-Riyadh the Something Else has structured the portals to open only onto God's Grove, and then . . .

Nemes gasps and withdraws the microfilament before the full import of the last activation can sear her. That last is obviously Aenea's goal—or more precisely, the goal of the Something Else who opens the way for her —and it is inaccessible to both the Church Pax and the Three Sectors.

But the timing will be about right. Nemes can keep de Soya and his men alive while still jumping ahead to the God's Grove System. She has already thought of a plausible explanation. Assuming two days to transit Qom-Riyadh and another full day on the River system on God's Grove, she will still be able to intercept the raft and do what she has to do before de Soya's resurrection. She will even have an hour or two to tidy up, so that when she drops to God's Grove with the priest-captain and Swiss Guard commandos, there will be nothing visible except signs that the child and her friends have passed that way and farcast on.

Nemes withdraws her probe, jogs to the surface, takes the dropship to *Raphael,* erases any record in the ship's computer that she has awakened or used the dropship, plants a false message in the ship's computer, and crawls into her resurrection creche to sleep. While in Pacem System, she had removed the creche from the resurrection system and rewired the telltales to simulate activity, and now she lies back in the humming coffin and closes her eyes. The jumps to fast time and the use of the phase-shift skin in such quantities tires her. She welcomes the rest before de Soya and the others arise from death.

Remembering that detail with a smile, Rhadamanth Nemes activates a phase-shift glove and touches her chest between her breasts, reddening and rearranging the skin there into the simulation of a cruciform. She carries no such parasite, of course, but the men in the ship may glimpse her naked, and she has no intention of revealing anything through a stupid lapse of attention to detail.

The *Raphael* continues to orbit the glaring ice world of Sol Draconi Septem while three of its crew lie in their creche coffins, the monitoring lights and telltales recording their slow climb up from death. Their other passenger sleeps. She does not dream.

48

A S WE FLOATED THROUGH the desert world, blinking in the harsh light of the G2 sun and drinking water from the air/water wraith-gut pouches we had brought with us, our final couple of days on Sol Draconi Septem seemed like a quickly fading dream to me.

Cuchiat and his band had paused fifty-some meters beneath the surface—we had noticed the air getting noticeably thinner in the tunnels—and there, in the jagged ice corridor, we had prepared for our expedition. To our amazement, the Chitchatuk stripped naked. Even while glancing away in embarrassment, we noticed how muscular and solid their bodies were—the women as well as the men—as if a bodybuilder on a one-g world had been flattened and compressed into a more compact specimen. Cuchiat and the female warrior Chatchia came over to supervise our own undressing and preparation for the surface, while Chiaku and the others pulled items from their hide packs.

We watched the Chitchatuk and followed their lead in dressing, with help from Cuchiat and Chatchia. For the few seconds that we were actually naked—standing on the wraith-robes we had been wearing so that our feet would not freeze—the cold burned at us. Then we pulled on a thin membrane material—an inner skin of the wraith, we later learned—that had been tailored for arms and legs and a head. But obviously for *smaller* arms and legs and heads. As it was, the membrane was tighter than skintight: the translucent skin hugged me so firmly that I must have looked like so many cannonballs stuffed into a sausage skin. A. Bettik looked no better. I realized after a moment that these must be the Chitchatuk equivalent of pressure suits—perhaps even of the sophisticated skinsuits the Hegemony military once used in space. The membranes passed sweat and provided much of their own heating and cooling while serving well to keep the lungs from exploding in vacuum, the skin bruising, or the blood boiling. The membranes pulled low over our foreheads and up to our chins like a cowl, leaving our eyes, noses, and mouths uncovered.

Cuchiat and Chatchia removed membrane masks from the pack. The other Chitchatuk had already donned theirs. These were obviously created-things—the mask itself was made of the same inner skin as the pressure suit, with wraith-hide padding sewn in here and there. The eyepieces were made from the outer lense of the wraith-eyes, offering the same limited access to the infrared as our outer-robe eyes. From the snout of the mask ran a length of coiled wraith-intestine, the end of which Cuchiat carefully sewed into one of their water bags.

Not just a water bag, I realized as the Chitchatuk began breathing through their masks: the fuel-pellet brazier melted the glacier ice into both water and atmosphere gas. They had somehow filtered this atmosphere mix until they had adequate quantities of breathable air. I tried breathing through the mask—my eyes watered from the other compounds there, definitely a hint of methane and perhaps even of ammonia, but breathable. I guessed that there must be only a couple of hours of air in the bag.

With our g-suit skins on, we donned the outer layer of wraith-robes. Cuchiat pulled the heads of the robes lower than we had ever worn them before, locking the teeth shut so we were peering through the lenses, the head acting as a crude helmet above our pressure suit. We then donned an outer pair of wraith-hide bootees, which laced up our calves almost to the knee. The outer robe was then quickly stitched shut with a few bold strokes from Chiaku's bone needle. The water bag and air bag hung from straps beneath our robes, near a flap that could be unstitched and opened quickly when the bags needed to be refilled. Chichticu, our fuel-pellet fire carrier, was constantly busy melting atmosphere into water and air, even as we hiked, and he handed the replacement skin bags out in precise order, from Cuchiat, first, to me, last. At least I now understood the band's pecking order. I also understood why—when danger threatened on the surface—the band moved into a protective circle with Chichticu, the fire carrier, in the center. It was not just that he held religious and symbolic importance. His constant vigilance and labors kept us alive.

There was one final addition to our wardrobe as we emerged from the cave onto the whirling wind and surface ice. From a cache near the entrance, Chiaku and the others retrieved a store of long black skate blades, sharp as razors on the bottom, flat and broad on top where our booteed feet fit quite nicely. Once again wraith-hide thongs were used to lash us to the blades. The things were an effective combination of skates and cross-country skis, and I awkwardly skated ten meters across the patterned ice of the glacier before I realized that we were skiing on wraith-claws.

I admit that I had a great fear of falling in 1.7-g since every tumble felt like the equivalent of seven tenths of another Raul Endymion falling on top of me, but we soon got the hang of movement on the things and we were well padded for falls. I ended up using one of the cut-up logs from the raft as a plump ski pole when the surface got too rough, poling myself along as if I were a one-man raft.

I'll confess here that I wish I had a holo-image or photograph of our party on that outing. With our wraith-hides, inner-skin g-suits, wraith-gut air bags, lower-intestine air hoses, bone spears, my plasma rifle, packs, and claw-skis, we must have looked like some Old Earth Paleolithic astronauts.

It all worked. We moved more quickly across the snow and ice-crystal sastrugi than we had in the ice tunnels. When the wind blew from the south, which it did during only a short part of our surface trek, we could spread our wraith-robed arms and be propelled across flat sections of the ice like sailing ships.

WALKING THE SURFACE of Sol Draconi Septem's frozen atmosphere had a harsh but memorable beauty to it. The sky was vacuum and moon-surface black when the sun was up, but an instant after sunset many thousands of stars seemed to explode into existence. Our robes and inner suits handled the near-space high and low temperatures well during the day, but it was obvious that even the Chitchatuk could not survive the cold at night. Luckily we moved quickly enough across the surface that we had only one six-hour darkness period to shelter from, and the Chitchatuk had planned our departure so that we got the benefit of a full day's sunlight before that nightfall.

There were no mountains or other surface features larger than ice ridges or rills, except for our first few hours on the ice when the rising sun struck an icy object far to the south of us. This, I realized, was the tip of Father Glaucus's skyscraper protruding from the ice many kilometers away. Other than that, the surface was so featureless that I wondered for a minute how the Chitchatuk were managing to navigate, but then I saw Cuchiat glancing at the sun and then at his own shadow. We continued skating north during the brief day.

The Chitchatuk moved in a tight defensive pattern as they skated/ skied, with the fire-carrier and medicine man, who tended the fire and air/ water bags in the center, warriors with ready spears on the wings, Cuchiat in the lead, and Chiaku—obviously second in command, we realized now —bringing up the rear and skating almost backward in his vigilance. Each Chitchatuk had a length of wraith-rope wrapped around his or her robe— they had wound some around the three of us when we were dressed—and I better understood the purpose of all that line after Cuchiat stopped abruptly and skated to the east to avoid several crevasses that had been invisible to my eye. I looked down in one of these—the rift seemed to drop into eternal darkness—and tried to imagine what that fall would be like. It was late the same afternoon that one of the outriders disappeared in a sudden, silent burst of ice crystals—only to reappear a moment later as Chiaku and Cuchiat were readying rescue ropes. The warrior had arrested his own fall and then pulled off his black claw-skates, and was now using them as climbing tools, hacking his way up the sheer wall of the crevasse like a technical climber on an icefall. I was learning not to underestimate the Chitchatuk.

We saw no wraiths that first day. As the sun set, we realized—through our exhaustion—that Cuchiat and the others had ceased skating north and were circling, peering down into the ice as if looking for something. All this while the thin winds lashed ice crystals against us. If we had been on the surface in spacesuits, I am convinced that the visor would have been scratched and marred. The wraith-robes and eye lenses showed no damage.

Finally Aichacut waved his arms from where he had skated far to our west—there was no verbal communication through masks and vacuum—and we all skated in that direction, finally stopping at a place that looked no different from all the rest of the pressure-rippled surface. Cuchiat waved us back, untied our gift of the ax from where he had lashed it onto his back, and began chopping at the ice. When the surface layer broke away, we could see that this was not another crevasse or rill, but the narrow entrance to an ice cave. Four of the warriors readied their spears, Chichticu joined them with his ember-lamp, and—with Cuchiat leading—the group crawled into the hole while the rest of us waited in a defensive circle.

A moment later Cuchiat's robed head emerged and he waved us in. He still held the ax, and I could imagine him grinning broadly behind his wraith-teeth visor and membrane mask. The ax had been an important gift.

We spent the night in the wraith-den. I helped Chiaku caulk the entrance with snow and ice, we packed another meter of the entrance tunnel with loose ice crystal and larger fragments, and then we went in to watch Chichticu heat blocks of snow-ice until the ice den was filled with enough atmosphere to breathe. We slept bundled together, the twenty-three Indivisible People and the three Indivisible Travelers, still wearing our robes and pressure membranes but masks removed, breathing the welcome scent of each other's sweat. Our huddled warmth kept us alive through the terrible night outside as the Coriolis and katabatik storms blasted ice crystals at nearly the speed of sound . . . had there been any sound in that near vacuum.

I remember one other detail about our last night with the Chitchatuk. The wraith-den was lined, completely lined, with human skulls and bones, each set into the circular ice wall of the den with what seemed to be an artist's care.

WE SAW NO WRAITHS—cubs or ice-boring adults—during our next day's travel, and shortly before sunset we doffed and cached our skates, then entered the ice tunnels above the second farcaster. When we were deep enough to be in captured atmosphere again, we removed the masks and pressure-suit membranes, handing them back to Chatchia with something like reluctance. It was as if we were surrendering our membership badges to the Indivisible People.

Cuchiat spoke briefly. I could not follow the quick syllables, but Aenea translated—"We were lucky . . . something and something about how unusual it is not to have to fight wraiths when crossing the surface . . . but, he says, luck on one day almost always leads to bad luck the next."

"Tell him that I hope he's wrong," I said.

The open river with its floating mist and ice ceiling was almost a shock to see. Even though everyone was exhausted, we set to work at once. Assembling the shortened raft was difficult with wraith-mittens on, but the Chitchatuk worked quickly to help, and within two hours we had a cut-down, awkward version of our earlier vessel—minus the foremast, tent, and hearthstone. But the steering oar was in place, and although the push-poles were shorter and clumsy-looking when lashed together, we thought they should work on this shallow stretch of the Tethys.

The leave-taking was sadder than I would have imagined. Everyone hugged everyone else at least twice. There was ice on Aenea's long lashes, and I had to admit a strain of powerful emotion in my own throat.

Then we were shoving off into the current—it felt strange to be traveling while standing still, I still had the push-and-glide motion of the claw-skates echoing in my muscles and mind—the farcaster portal and ice wall approached, we ducked under the ever-lower ledge of ice, and suddenly we were . . . elsewhere.

WE POLED INTO SUNRISE. The river was wide and unruffled here, the current slow but steady. The riverbanks were of red rock, striated like wide, gradual steps climbing up from the water; the desert was red rock with small yellow shrubs; the distant slabs of hill and arch were also of smooth red stone. All this redness was ignited by the huge red sun rising to our left. The temperature was already a hundred degrees above what it had been in the ice cave. We shielded our eyes and pulled off our wraith-robes, setting them like thick white rugs near the stern of the shortened raft. Layers of ice on the logs first glistened and then melted in the morning sun.

We decided that we were on Qom-Riyadh even before consulting the comlog or Tethys guidebook. It was the red-rock desert that cued us— bridges of the bright-red sandstone, fluted columns of red rock rising against the pink sky, delicate red arches dwarfing the receding farcaster portal. The river ran through canyons overarched by these red stone parabolas, then curved into a wider valley where the hot wind blew the yellow sage and raised a red grit that caught in the long, tubular 'hairs' of the wraith-robes and lodged in our mouths and eyes. By midday we were moving through a more fertile valley. Irrigation canals ran at right angles from our river, and short yellow palms and magenta bottlebrushes lined the waterways. Soon small buildings came into sight, and shortly after, an entire village of pink and ocher homes, but no people.

"It's like Hebron," whispered Aenea.

"We don't know that," I said. "Maybe they're just working out of sight somewhere."

But midday heated to midafternoon—Qom-Riyadh had a twenty-two-hour day, according to the guidebook—and although the canals proliferated, plants multiplied, and villages became more common, there was no hint of humans or their domestic animals. We poled the raft ashore twice—once to draw water from an artesian well and again to explore a small village from which sounds of hammering could be heard on the river. It was a broken awning banging in the desert wind.

Suddenly Aenea doubled over with a cry of pain. I dropped to one knee and swept the empty street with the plasma pistol as A. Bettik ran to her side. There was no one on the street. The windows were empty of movement.

"It's all right," the girl gasped as the android held her. "A sudden pain . . ."

I jogged to her, feeling foolish for having drawn the weapon. Setting it in my belt holster, I went to one knee and held her hand. "What's the matter, kiddo?" She was sobbing.

"I . . . don't . . . know," she managed between sobs. "Something . . . terrible has . . . I don't know."

We carried her back to the raft. "Please," whispered Aenea, her teeth chattering despite the heat, "let's go. Let's get out of here."

A. Bettik set up the microtent, even though it now took up most of our abbreviated raft. We pulled the wraith-robes into the shade, laid the girl on them, and gave her water from one of the water bags.

"Is it this village?" I said. "Did something about it—"

"No," said Aenea between dry sobs. I could see her fighting the waves of emotion that were crashing over her. "No . . . something awful . . . this world, but also . . . behind us."

"Behind us?" I looked out the door of the tent and upriver, but there was nothing but the valley, the wide canal of a river, and the receding village with its wind-tossed yellow palms.

"Behind us on the ice world?" A. Bettik asked softly.

"Yes," managed Aenea before doubling up with pain. "It . . . hurts."

I laid my palm on her forehead and bare stomach. Her skin was hotter than it should have been, even accounting for the heat of the valley and the day's sunburn on her face and arms. We pulled one of the medkits from my backpack and I set a diagnostic patch in place. It showed a high fever, pain in the 6.3 range of the dolorometer, muscle cramps, and an uneven EEG. It recommended water, ibuprofen, and contacting a doctor.

"There's a city," said the android as the river rounded a bluff.

I stepped out of the tent to see. The rose-red towers, domes, and minarets were still far away—perhaps fifteen kilometers across the widening valley floor—and the current on this river was in no hurry. "You stay with her," I said, and moved to starboard side to pole. Our shortened raft was considerably lighter than the old one, and we moved quickly with the current.

A. BETTIK AND I CONSULTED the water-warped guidebook and decided that the city was Mashhad, the capital of the southern continent and home of the Grand Mosque, whose minarets we could see clearly now as the river moved through thickening villages, suburbs, industrial areas, and into the city proper. Aenea was sleeping fitfully. Her temperature had risen, and the medkit diagnostic was blinking red lights to suggest a doctor's intervention.

Mashhad was as eerily empty as New Jerusalem had been.

"I seem to remember rumor that the Qom-Riyadh System had fallen to the Ousters about the same time they took the Coal Sack," I said. A. Bettik agreed, saying that they had monitored Pax radio traffic to that effect from the university city.

We tied the raft up at a low pier, and I carried the girl into the shade of the city streets. This was a replay of Hebron, only this time I was the healthy one and the girl unconscious. I made a mental note to avoid desert worlds from now on if I could help it.

The streets were less tidy than New Jerusalem had been: groundcars parked at odd angles and left abandoned on the sidewalks, detritus blowing in the streets, windows and doors open to the red sand, and strange little carpets lying on sidewalks, streets, and dying lawns. I paused at the first cluster of rugs we encountered, thinking that they might be hawking mats. They were only rugs. And they were all oriented in the same direction.

"Prayer mats," said A. Bettik as we moved back into the shade of the city street. Even the tallest buildings were not overly tall here—none as high as the minarets, which looked out from a park area with tropical trees. "The population of Qom-Riyadh was almost one hundred percent Islamic," he continued. "The Pax was said to have found no inroads here, even with the promise of resurrection. The people wanted nothing to do with the Protectorate."

I turned the corner, still hunting for a hospital or any sign that might lead us to one. Aenea's hot forehead was against my neck. Her breathing was rapid and shallow. "I think this place was in the *Cantos*," I said. The child seemed to weigh nothing.

A. Bettik nodded. "M. Silenus wrote of Colonel Kassad's victory over the so-called New Prophet here some three hundred years ago."

"The Shi'ites took power again once the Web fell, didn't they?" I said. We looked down another side street. I was looking for a red crescent rather than the universal red-cross sign of medical help.

"Yes," said A. Bettik, "and they have been violently opposed to the Pax. The supposition was that they had welcomed the Ousters when the Pax Fleet retreated from this sector."

I looked at the empty streets. "Well, it looks like the Ousters didn't appreciate the welcome. This is like Hebron. Where do you think they've all gone? Could they have taken an entire planetary population hostage and—"

"Look, a caduceus," interrupted A. Bettik.

The age-old symbol of a winged staff wrapped with two entwined serpents was on the window of a tall building. The interior was littered and tossed about, but it seemed more a standard office building than any sort of hospital I had been in. A. Bettik walked to a digital sign that was scrolling lines of text in Arabic. It was also muttering in a machine voice.

"Do you read Arabic?" I said.

"I do," said the android. "I also understand some of the spoken language, which is Farsi. There is a private clinic on the tenth floor. I would think that it would have a full diagnostic center and perhaps an autosurgeon."

I headed for the stairway with Aenea in my arms, but A. Bettik tried the elevator. The empty glass shaft hummed, and a levitation car floated to a stop at our level.

"Uncanny that the power's still on," I said.

We rode the lift to the tenth floor. Aenea was awakening and moaning as we walked down the tiled hallway, across an open terrace-garden where yellow and green palms rustled in the wind, and into an airy, glassed-in room with banks of autosurgeon beds and centralized diagnostic equipment. We chose the bed closest to the window, stripped the child to her underwear, and laid her between clean sheets. Replacing the medkit diagnostic patches with patch filaments, we waited for the diagnostic panels. The synthesized voice was in Arabic and Farsi, as was part of the display readout, but there was a Web English band and we switched to it.

The autosurgeon diagnosed exhaustion, dehydration, and an unusual EEG pattern, which might have resulted from a serious blow to the head. A. Bettik and I looked at each other. Aenea had received no blow to the head.

We authorized treatment for the exhaustion and dehydration and stepped back as flowfoam restrainers extruded from the bed panels, pseudo-fingers felt for Aenea's vein, and an IV was started with a sedative and saline solution.

Within minutes the child was sleeping easily. The diagnostic panel spoke in Arabic, and A. Bettik translated before I could walk over to read the monitor. "It says that the patient should have a good night's sleep and be better in the morning."

I shifted the plasma rifle from where I had been carrying it on my back. Our dusty packs sat on one of the visiting chairs. Moving to the window, I said, "I'll check out the city before it gets dark. Make sure we're alone."

A. Bettik folded his arms and watched the great red sun touch the tops of the buildings across the street. "I think that we are very much alone," he said. "It took a little longer here, is all."

"What took longer?"

"Whatever it was that stole the people. On Hebron there was no sign of panic or struggle. Here people had time to abandon their vehicles. But the prayer rugs are the surest sign." I noticed for the first time that there were fine wrinkles in the blue skin of the android's forehead and around his eyes and mouth.

"Surest sign of what?" I said.

"They knew that something was happening to them," said A. Bettik, "and they spent their last minutes in prayer."

I set the plasma rifle next to the visitor's chair and unclipped the flap over my holster. "I'm still going to take a look," I said. "You watch her in case she wakes, okay?" I pulled the two com units out of my pack, tossed one to the android, and clipped the other onto my collar with the bead mike in place. "Leave the common frequency open. I'll check in. Call me if there's a problem."

A. Bettik was standing by her bedside. His large hand gently touched the sleeping girl's forehead. "I will be here when she wakes, M. Endymion."

IT IS ODD THAT I remember that evening's walk through the abandoned city so clearly. A digital sign on a bank said that it was 40 degrees centigrade—104 Fahrenheit—but the dry wind from the red-rock desert quickly carried away any perspiration, and the pink-and-red sunset had a calming effect on me. Perhaps I remember that evening because it was the last night of our voyage before things changed forever.

Mashhad was a strange mixture of modern city and bazaar from *The Thousand and One Nights,* a wonderful series of stories Grandam used to tell me as we sat under Hyperion's starry sky. This place had a musky hint of romance about it. On the corner there would be a news kiosk and automatic banking machine, and as soon as one turned the corner, there would be stalls in the middle of the street with brightly striped awnings and heaps of fruit rotting in bins. I could imagine the din and movement here—camels or horses or some other pre-Hegira beasts milling and stamping, dogs barking, sellers shouting and buyers haggling, women in black chadors and lacy *burqas,* or veils, gliding by, and on either side the baroque and inefficient groundcars growling and spewing out filthy carbon monoxide or ketones or whatever dirty stuff the old internal-combustion engines used to pour into the atmosphere. . . .

I was shocked out of my reverie by a man's voice calling musically, the words echoing down the stone-and-steel canyons of the city. It seemed to be coming from the park only a block or two to my left, and I ran in that direction, holding my hand on the grip of my pistol in the unbuttoned holster as I went.

"You hear this?" I said into the bead mike as I ran.

"Yes," came A. Bettik's voice in my hearplug. "I have the door to the terrace open and the sound is quite clear here."

"It sounds Arabic. Can you translate?" I was panting only slightly as I finished the two-block sprint and came out into the open park area where the mosque dominated the entire block. A few minutes before, I had looked down one of the connecting streets and glimpsed the last of the red sunset painting the side of one of the minarets, but now the stone tower was a dull gray and only the highest wisps of cirrus caught the light.

"Yes," said A. Bettik. "It is a muezzin call to evening prayer."

I pulled the binoculars from my belt pouch and scanned the minarets. The man's voice was coming from loudspeakers on a balcony encircling each tower. There was no sign of movement there. Suddenly the rhythmic cry ended and birds chattered within the branches of the forested square.

"It is most probably a recording," said A. Bettik.

"I'll check it out." Setting away the binoculars, I followed a crushed-stone path through the extensive lawns and yellowish palm trees to the mosque's entrance. I passed through a courtyard and paused at the entrance to the mosque proper. I could see the interior—it was filled with hundreds of the prayer mats. Elaborate arches of striped stone were supported by elegant pillars, and on the far wall a beautiful arch opened on a semicircular niche. To the right of this niche there was a flight of steps guarded by a lovingly carved stone railing, and a stone-canopied platform at the top. Not yet entering the large space, I described it to A. Bettik.

"The niche is the mihrab," he responded. "It's reserved for the prayer leader, the imam. The balcony to the right of it is the minbar, the pulpit. Is there anyone in either place?"

"No." I could see the red dust on the prayer rugs and stone steps.

"Then there is no doubt that the call to prayer was a timed recording," said A. Bettik.

I had the urge to enter the great stone space, but the urge was canceled by my reluctance to profane anyone's sacred house. I had felt this as a child in the Catholic cathedral at Beak's End, and as an adult when a friend in the Home Guard wanted to take me to one of the last Zen Gnostic temples on Hyperion. I had realized when I was a boy that I would always be an outsider when it came to holy places . . . never having one of my own, never feeling comfortable in another's. I did not enter.

Walking back through the cooling and darkening streets, I found a palm-lined boulevard through an attractive section of town. Pushcarts held food and toys for sale. I paused by a cart selling fried dough and sniffed one of the bracelet-sized dough rings. It had gone bad days, not weeks or months, ago.

The boulevard came out by the river, and I turned to my left, taking the riverside esplanade back to the street that would lead me once again to the clinic. Occasionally I checked in with A. Bettik. Aenea was still sleeping soundly.

The stars were dimmed by dust in the atmosphere as night settled on the city. Only a few of the downtown buildings had lights on—whatever had stolen the populace must have happened in the daytime—but stately old streetlamps ran the length of the esplanade and they were glowing with gaslight. If it had not been for one of these lamps at the street end of the pier where we had tied the raft, I probably would have turned back toward the clinic without seeing it. As it was, the lamplight allowed me to spot it from more than a hundred meters away.

Someone was standing on our raft. The figure was motionless, very tall, and seemed to be wearing a silver suit. Lamplight gleamed from the figure's surface as if it were wearing a chrome spacesuit.

Whispering to A. Bettik to guard the girl, that there was an intruder on the raft, I pulled my pistol from my holster and the binoculars from my belt. The second I focused the glasses, the gleaming silver shaped turned its head in my direction.

49

FATHER CAPTAIN DE SOYA awakens in the familiar warmth of *Raphael*'s creche. After the first few moments of inevitable confusion and disorientation, he pulls himself from the enclosed couch and drifts, naked, to the command console.

Things are as they should be: in orbit around Sol Draconi Septem—the world a blinding white sphere just beyond the command console's windows, the braking burn optimum, the other three creches close to reawakening their valuable human cargo, the internal field set to zero-g until they all reacquire strength, internal temperature and atmosphere optimum for reawakening, the ship in proper geosynchronous orbit. The priest-captain gives his first command of this new life—he orders the ship to begin brewing coffee for all of them in the wardroom cubby. Usually his first thought upon resurrection is of his coffee bulb, tucked in the plotting table/wardroom table niche, filling with the hot black drink.

Then de Soya notices the ship's computer flashing a priority-message light. No message had arrived while he was conscious in Pacem System, and it seems unlikely that one has found them here in this remote ex-colony system. There is no Pax presence in Sol Draconi System—at most, transiting torchships use the three gas giants in the system for refueling their hydrogen tanks—and a brief query of the ship's computer confirms that no other ship was contacted during the three days of braking and orbit insertion. The same query brings forth the fact that there is no Church mission on the planet below them, the last missionary contact lost more than fifty standard years ago.

De Soya plays the message. Papal authority routed through Pax Fleet. According to the display codes, the message arrived mere hundredths of a second before *Raphael* had gone quantum in Pacem space. It is a text-only message and brief—HIS HOLINESS COUNTERMANDS MISSION TO SOL DRACONI SEPTEM. NEW AREA OF ACQUISITION: GOD'S GROVE. PROCEED THERE IMMEDIATELY. AUTHORIZATION LOURDUSAMY AND MARUSYN. MESSAGE ENDS.

De Soya sighs. This trip, these deaths and resurrections, have been for nothing. For a moment the priest-captain does not move but sits naked in the command couch, pondering the glaring white limb of the ice planet that fills the curved window above him. Then he sighs again and moves off to shower, stopping by the wardroom cubby to take his first sip of coffee. He reaches out automatically for the bulb while he taps commands into the shower-cubby console—needle spray, as hot as he can stand it. He makes a note to find some bathrobes somewhere. This is no longer an all-male locker room.

Suddenly de Soya freezes in irritation. His questing hand has not closed on the handle of his coffee bulb. Someone has shifted the bulb in its niche.

THEIR NEW RECRUIT, Corporal Rhadamanth Nemes, is the last to leave her creche. All three of the men avert their eyes as she leaves her creche and kicks off for the shower/wardrobe cubby, but there are enough reflective surfaces in *Raphael*'s crowded command bubble for each of them to catch a glimpse of the small woman's firm body, her pale skin, and the livid cruciform between her small breasts.

Corporal Nemes joins them in taking Communion and seems disoriented and vulnerable as they sip their coffee and allow the internal fields to build to one-sixth-g.

"Your first resurrection?" de Soya asks gently.

The corporal nods. Her hair is very black and cut short, the bangs hanging limply on the pale forehead.

"I'd like to say that you get used to it," says the priest-captain, "but the truth is, every awakening is like the first one . . . difficult and exhilarating."

Nemes sips her coffee bulb. She seems tentative in the microgravity. Her crimson-and-black uniform makes her skin seem all the more pale in contrast.

"Shouldn't we be leaving immediately for the God's Grove system?" she says tentatively.

"Soon enough," says Father Captain de Soya. "I've instructed *Raphael* to break orbit here in fifteen minutes. We'll accelerate out to the closest translation point at two-g's so we can recover for a few hours before we have to go back to the couches and the creches."

Corporal Nemes appears to shudder a bit at the thought of another resurrection. As if eager to change the subject, she glances at the blinding limb of the planet filling the windows and viewscreen. "How can anyone be traveling a river on all that ice?"

"Under it, I'd think," says Sergeant Gregorius. The giant trooper has been watching Nemes carefully. " 'Tis the atmosphere that's frozen there again since the Fall. The Tethys must flow beneath it."

Corporal Nemes raises a dark eyebrow in surprise. "And what is God's Grove like?"

"Ye don't know it?" asks Gregorius. "I thought everyone in the Pax'd heard of God's Grove."

Nemes shakes her head. "I grew up on Esperance. It's a farming and fishing world, mostly. People there don't pay too much interest in other places. Not other worlds of the Pax . . . not old stories of the Web. Most of us are too busy scraping a living from the land or sea."

"God's Grove is the old Templar world," says Father Captain de Soya, setting his coffee bulb in its niche in the plotting table. "It was burned pretty badly during the Ouster invasion preceding the Fall. In its time it was beautiful."

"Aye," nods Sergeant Gregorius, "the Templar Brotherhood of the Muir was a sort of nature-worship cult. They turned God's Grove into a world forest—trees taller and more beautiful than the redwoods and sequoias of Old Earth. The Templars lived there, all twenty-some million've 'em—in cities and platforms in those lovely trees. But they chose the wrong side in the war. . . ."

Corporal Nemes looks up from sipping her coffee. "You mean they were on the Ousters' side?" She sounds shocked at the idea.

"That they were, lass," says Gregorius. "Perhaps it was because they had spacegoing trees in those days. . . ."

Nemes laughs. It is a short, brittle sound.

"He's serious," says Corporal Kee. "The Templars used ergs— energy-binders from Aldebaren—to encapsulate the trees in a Class-nine containment field and provide a reaction drive in-system. They even had regular Hawking drives installed for interstellar flight."

"Flying trees," says Corporal Nemes, and laughs harshly again.

"Some o' them flew off in such trees when the Ousters paid back their allegiance with a Swarm attack on God's Grove," continues Gregorius, "but most of them burned . . . just as most of the planet burned. For a century, they say, most of the world was ash. The clouds o' smoke created a nuclear winter effect."

"Nuclear winter?" says Nemes.

De Soya is watching the young woman carefully, wondering why one so naive has been chosen to carry the papal diskey under certain circumstances. Was the ingenuousness part of her strength as a killer, should the need arise?

"Corporal," he says, speaking to the woman, "you say you grew up on Esperance. . . . Did you join the Home Guard there?"

She shakes her head. "I went directly into the Pax army, Father Captain. There was a potato famine . . . the recruiters offered offworld travel . . . and, well . . ."

"Where did ye serve?" asks Gregorius.

"Just training on Freeholm," says Nemes.

Gregorius leans on his elbows. The one-sixth g makes sitting easier. "Which brigade?"

"The Twenty-third," says the woman. "Sixth Regiment."

"The Screaming Eagles," says Corporal Kee. "I had a female buddy who transferred there. Was Commander Coleman your CO?"

Nemes shakes her head again. "Commander Deering was in charge while I was there. I just spent ten local months . . . ah . . . about eight and a half standard, I guess. I was trained as a general combat specialist. Then they asked for volunteers for the First Legion. . . ." She trails off as if this is classified material.

Gregorius scratches his chin. "It's odd I haven't heard of this outfit in the building. Nothing stays secret very long in the military. How long did ye say ye were training with this . . . legion?"

Nemes gives the big man a direct stare. "Two standard years, Sergeant. And it *has* been secret . . . until now. Most of our training was on Lee Three and the Lambert Ring Territories."

"Lambert," muses the big sergeant. "So ye've had your share of low-g and zero-g training."

"More than my share," agrees Corporal Rhadamanth Nemes with a thin smile. "While in the Lambert Ring, we trained in the Peregrine Trojan Cluster for five months."

Father Captain de Soya feels the conversation turning into an interrogation. He does not want their new crewmate to feel assaulted by their questions, but he is as curious as Kee and Gregorius. Besides that, he feels something . . . not right. "So the Legions' job will be pretty much like the Marines?" he says. "Ship-to-ship fighting?"

Nemes shakes her head. "Uh-uh . . . Captain. Not just zero-g combat tactics for ship to ship. The Legions are being formed to take the war to the enemy."

"What does that mean, Corporal?" asks the priest-captain softly. "In all my years in the Fleet, ninety percent of our battles were in Ouster territory."

"Yes," says Nemes, her small smile returning, "but you hit and run . . . Fleet actions. The Legions will *occupy*."

"But most of the Ouster holdings are in vacuum!" says Kee. "Asteroids, orbital forests, deep space itself . . ."

"Exactly," says Nemes, her smile remaining. "The Legions will fight them on their own ground . . . or vacuum, as the case may be."

Gregorius catches de Soya's glance saying, *No more questions,* but the sergeant shakes his head and says, "Well, I don't see what these vaunted legions are learning that the Swiss Guard hasn't done—and done well—for sixteen centuries."

De Soya floats to his feet. "Acceleration in two minutes. Let's get to our couches. We'll talk more about God's Grove and the mission there during our drive to the translation point."

IT HAD TAKEN *Raphael* almost eleven hours of braking deceleration at two hundred gravities to kill its near light-speed upon entry into the system, but the computer has located an adequate translation point to God's Grove only thirty-five million klicks out from Sol Draconi Septem. The ship could accelerate at a leisurely one-g and reach that point in around twenty-five hours, but de Soya has ordered it to lift out of the planet's gravity well at a constant two-g's for six hours before using more energy to bring on the internal fields during the last hour's dash at one-hundred-g's.

When the fields finally come up, the team goes through their final checklist for God's Grove—three days to resurrect, then immediate dropship deployment with Sergeant Gregorius in charge of the ground party, surveillance of the fifty-eight-klick Tethys River segment between portals, and then final preparation for the capture of Aenea and her party.

"After all this, why does His Holiness start directing us in the search?" asks Corporal Kee as they move to their creches.

"Revelation," says Father Captain de Soya. "Okay . . . everyone tuck in. I'll watch the boards."

For the last few minutes before translation, it has been their custom to close their creches. Only the captain stays on watch.

In the few minutes he has alone at the command board, de Soya quickly calls up the records of their abortive entry and escape from Hebron System. He had viewed these before their departure from Pacem System, but now he fast-forwards through the visual and data records again. It's all there and it all seems correct: the shots from orbit around Hebron while he and his two troopers were still in creche—the burning cities, cratered landscape, and shattered villages of Hebron lifting smoke into the desert atmosphere, New Jerusalem in radioactive ruins—and then the radar acquisition by three Swarm cruisers. *Raphael* had aborted the resurrection cycles and made a run for it, lifting out of the system at the two hundred and eighty gravities her enhanced fusion drive could provide with her cargo of dead men. The Ousters, on the other hand, had to divert energy to their internal fields or die—no resurrection for heathens—and could never muster more than eighty-g's during the stern chase.

The visuals were there, though—the long green tails of the Ouster fusion drives, their attempts to lance *Raphael* at a distance of almost a full AU, the ship's record of the defense fields easily handling the lance energy at that distance, the final translation to Mare Infinitus System since that was the closest jump point . . .

It all made sense. The visuals were compelling. De Soya did not believe a bit of it.

The father-captain was not sure why he was so skeptical. The visual records meant nothing, of course; for more than a thousand years, since the beginning of the Digital Age, even the most compelling visual images could be faked by a child at a home computer. But ship's records would require a gigantic effort—a technical conspiracy—to falsify. Why should he not trust *Raphael*'s memory now?

With only a few minutes before translation, de Soya calls up the records of their recent descent into Sol Draconi Septem's system. He glances over his shoulder from the command couch—all three creche couches are sealed and silent, their telltales green. Gregorius, Kee, and Nemes are still awake, waiting for translation and death. De Soya knows that the sergeant prays during these last minutes. Kee usually reads a book from his creche monitor. De Soya has no idea what the woman is doing within her comfortable coffin.

He knows he is being paranoid. *My coffee bulb was moved out of place. The handle was shifted sideways.* During his hours awake de Soya has tried to remember whether someone might have been in the wardrobe cubby and jarred the bulb in Pacem System. No—they had not used the wardrobe cubby during the climb out of Pacem's gravity well. The woman, Nemes, had been aboard before the others, but de Soya had used the coffee bulb and returned it to its place after she had gone to her couch/creche. He was sure of that. He had been the last to turn in, just as he always was. Acceleration or deceleration might smash bulbs not designed for terrible gravities, but the deceleration vector *Raphael* had been following was linear along the courier ship's line of travel and would not have moved things laterally. The coffee-bulb niche was designed to hold things in place.

Father Captain de Soya is part of a millennia-long line of sailors, sea and space, who become fanatic about a place for everything and everything in its place. He is a spacer. Almost two decades of serving in frigates, destroyers, and torchships have shown him that anything he leaves out of place will literally be in his face as soon as the ship goes to zero-g. More important, he has the age-old sailor's need to be able to reach out and find anything without looking, in darkness or storm. Granted, he thinks, the alignment of the handle of his coffee bulb is not a major issue . . . except it is. Each man has learned to use one of the chair niches at the five-person plotting table that doubles for the mess table in the crowded command pod. When they are using the table to plot courses or view planetary maps, each of the men—Rettig included when he was alive—had sat or stood or floated at their usual places at the table. It was human nature. It was second nature to spacers to keep their habits neat and predictable.

Someone had tapped his coffee bulb handle out of alignment—perhaps with a knee nestled there in zero-g to hold him . . . *her* . . . in place. Paranoid. Definitely.

In addition, there had been the troubling news whispered to him by Sergeant Gregorius in the minutes between that man's emergence from the resurrection creche and Corporal Nemes's awakening.

"A friend of mine in the Swiss Guard in the Vatican, Captain. Had a drink with him the night before we left. He knew us all—Kee and Rettig—and he swore he saw Lancer Rettig bein' carried unconscious on a litter to an ambulance outside the Vatican infirmary."

"Impossible," de Soya had said. "Lancer Rettig died of resurrection complications and was buried in space while in Mare Infinitus space."

"Aye," Gregorius had growled, "but my friend was sure . . . almost sure . . . that it was Rettig in the ambulance. Unconscious, life-support paks attached, oxygen mask an' all, but Rettig."

"That makes no sense," de Soya had said. He had always been suspicious of conspiracy theories, knowing from personal experience that secrets shared by more than two people rarely stayed secrets for long. "Why would Pax Fleet and the Church lie to us about Rettig? And where is he if he was alive on Pacem?"

Gregorius had shrugged. "Maybe it wasn't him, Captain. That's what I've been telling myself. But the ambulance—"

"What about it?" de Soya had snapped, more sharply than he had intended.

"It was headed for Castel Sant'Angelo, sir," said Gregorius. "Headquarters for the Holy Office."

Paranoia.

The records of the eleven hours of deceleration are normal—high-g braking, the usual three-day resurrection cycle ensuring the maximum chance for their safe recovery. De Soya glances at the orbital-insertion figures and runs the video of Sol Draconi Septem's slow rotation. He always wonders at those lost days—*Raphael* carrying out her simple tasks while the creches revive him and the others—he wonders at the eery silence that must fill the ship.

"Three minutes until translation," comes *Raphael's* crude synthesized voice. "All personnel should be in creche couches."

De Soya ignores the warning and calls up data files on the two and a half days the ship spent in orbit around Sol Draconi Septem before he and the others regained life. He is not sure what he was looking for . . . no record of dropship deployment . . . no sign of early life-support activation . . . all creche monitors reporting the regular cycle, the first quickenings of life in the last hours of the third day . . . all orbital ship records normal . . . *wait!*

"Two minutes until translation," says the flat ship's voice.

There on the first day, shortly after attaining standard geosynchronous orbit . . . and there again about four hours later. Everything normal except the dry details of four small reactor-thruster firings. To attain and hold a perfect geosynchronous orbit, a ship like *Raphael* will fire dozens of little thruster tweaks such as these. But most such fine-tunings, de Soya knows, involve the large reaction-thruster pods on the stern near the fusion drive, and on the command-pod boom at the bow of the awkwardly configured courier ship. These thruster burps were similar—first a double firing to stabilize the ship during a roll so the command pod was facing away from the planet—normal during rotisserie mode to spread the solar heating uniformly along the ship's surface without using field coolant—but only eight minutes here—and here! And after the roll, those paired reaction tweaks. Two and two. Then the final paired burps, which might accompany the larger thruster firings that would roll the ship back with the command-pod cameras aimed down at the planet. Then, four hours and eight minutes later, the entire sequence again. There are thirty-eight other station-keeping thruster sequences on the record, and none of the major thruster firings that would signify a roll of the entire ship stack, but these twin four-burp interludes stand out to de Soya's trained eye.

"One minute until translation," warns *Raphael*.

De Soya can hear the huge field generators beginning to whine in preparation for the shift to the modified Hawking system that will kill him in fifty-six seconds. He ignores it. His command chair will carry his dead body to the creche after translation if he does not move now. The ship is designed that way—messy, but necessary.

Father Captain Federico de Soya has been a torchship captain for many years. He has made more than a dozen archangel-courier jumps. He knows that double-burp, roll, double-burp signature on a reaction-thruster record. Even with the actual roll event deleted from the ship's records, the fingerprints for the maneuver is there in outline. The roll is to orient the dropship, which is tied down on the opposite side of the command-pod cluster, to the planet's atmosphere. The second double burp— the one still on record here—is to counteract the propellant squids separating the dropship from the center of *Raphael*'s mass. The final double firing is to stabilize the stack once the ship has returned to normal attitude, command-pod cameras trained on the planet below once again.

None of this is as obvious as it sounds, since the entire stack is slowly rotating in rotisserie mode during the entire time, occasional tweaks aligning the stack for better heating or cooling purposes. But to de Soya the signature is unmistakable. He taps directions to bring up the other records again. Negative sign of dropship deployment. Negative record of dropship deployment roll maneuver. Positive indicators of constant dropship attachment. Negative sign of life-support activation prior to everyone's resurrection a few hours before. Negative images of the dropship moving toward atmosphere on video records. Constant image-record of dropship attached and empty.

The only anomaly is two eight-minute thruster-tweak sequences four hours apart. Eight minutes of roll away from the planet would allow a dropship to disappear into atmosphere without main-camera visual record. Or to reappear and rendezvous. Boom cameras and radar would have recorded the event unless commanded to ignore it prior to dropship separation. That would have required less tampering with the record after the fact.

If someone had ordered the ship's computer to delete all records of dropship deployment, *Raphael*'s limited AI might have altered the record in just such a way, not realizing that the small-thruster firings during rotisserie mode would leave any footprint. And for anyone less experienced than a twelve-year torchship captain, it would not have. If de Soya had an hour or so to call up all the hydrogen fuel data, cross-check against dropship refueling needs and system-entry requirements, then double-check with the Bussard hydrogen collector input during deceleration, he would have a better idea if the main stack-roll maneuvers and dropship deployment had occurred. If he had an hour or so to himself.

"Thirty seconds until translation."

De Soya does not have time to reach his creche couch. He does have time to call up a special command sequence for ship operations, tap in his override code, confirm it, change monitor parameters, and do it twice more. He has just heard the confirmation acknowledgment on the third override when the quantum leap to archangel C-plus occurs.

The translation literally tears de Soya apart within the confines of his couch. He dies grinning fiercely.

50

"RAUL!"

It was at least an hour before Qom-Riyadh's sunrise. Both A. Bettik and I were sitting in chairs in the room where Aenea slept. I had been dozing. A. Bettik was awake—as he always seemed to be —but I reached the girl's bedside first. The light from the biomonitor readouts over the bed was the only illumination. Outside, the dust storm had been howling for hours.

"Raul . . ." The readouts said that her fever was down, pain was gone, that only the erratic EEGs remained.

"Right here, kiddo." I took her right hand in mine. Her fingers no longer felt feverish.

"You saw the Shrike?"

This caught me by surprise, but I realized in a moment that it did not have to be prescience or telepathy at work here. I had radioed A. Bettik about the sighting. He must have had the com unit's speakers on and Aenea had been awake enough to register it.

"Yeah," I said, "but it's okay. It's not here."

"But you saw it."

"Yes."

She gripped my hand with both of hers and sat up in bed. I could see her dark eyes gleaming in the faint light. "Where, Raul? Where did you see it?"

"On the raft." I used my free hand to push her back onto the pillows. The pillowcase and her undershirt were soaked with sweat. "It's all right, kiddo. It didn't do anything. It was there when I left."

"Did it turn its head, Raul? Did it look at you?"

"Well, yes, but . . ." I stopped. She was moaning softly, her head thrashing back and forth on the pillow. "Kiddo . . . Aenea . . . it's all right. . . ."

"No, it's not," said the girl. "Ah, God, Raul. I asked him to come with me. That last night. Did you know that I asked him to come along? He said no—"

"Who said no?" I asked. "The Shrike?" A. Bettik came up behind me. Outside, the red sand chafed at the windows and sliding door.

"No, no, no," said Aenea. Her cheeks were moist, although whether it was from tears or her fever breaking, I did not know. "Father Glaucus," she said, her voice almost lost under the wind noise. "That last night . . . I asked Father Glaucus to come with us. I shouldn't have asked him, Raul . . . it was not part of my . . . my dreams . . . but I did ask, and if I asked, I should have insisted. . . ."

"It's all right," I said, pushing a damp tendril of hair off her brow. "Father Glaucus is all right."

"No, he's not," said the girl, and moaned softly. "He's dead. The thing that's chasing us killed him. Him and all the Chitchatuk."

I looked at the monitor board again. It still showed improvement from the fever, despite her ravings. I looked at A. Bettik, but the android was staring intently at the child.

"You mean the Shrike killed them?" I said.

"No, not the Shrike," she said softly, and laid her wrist against her lips. "At least I don't think so. No, it wasn't the Shrike." Suddenly she gripped my hand in both of hers. "Raul, do you love me?"

I could only stare a moment. Then, not withdrawing my hand, I said, "Sure, kiddo. I mean . . ."

Aenea seemed to really look at me then for the first time since she had come awake and called my name. "No, stop," she said. She laughed softly. "I'm sorry. I came unglued in time for a minute. Of course you don't love me. I forgot when we were . . . who we were to each other now."

"No, it's all right," I said, not understanding. I patted her hand. "I do care for you, kiddo. So does A. Bettik, and we're going to—"

"Hush," said Aenea. She freed her hand and set one finger against my lips. "Hush. I was lost for a moment. I thought we were . . . us. The way we're going to . . ." She lay back deeper in the pillows and sighed. "My God, it's the night before God's Grove. Our last night traveling . . ."

I was not sure if she was making sense yet. I waited.

A. Bettik said, "M. Aenea, is God's Grove our next destination on the river?"

"I guess so," said the girl, sounding more like the child I knew. "Yes. I don't know. It all fades. . . ." She sat up again. "It's not the Shrike chasing us, you know. Nor the Pax."

"Of course it's the Pax," I said, trying to get her to make contact with reality. "They've been after us since . . ."

Aenea was shaking her head adamantly. Her hair hung in damp tendrils. "No," she said softly but very firmly. "The Pax is after us because the Core tells it we're dangerous to them."

"The Core?" I said. "But it's . . . ever since the Fall it's been . . ."

"Alive and dangerous," said Aenea. "After Gladstone and the others destroyed the farcaster system that provided the Core with its neural net, it retreated . . . but it never went far, Raul. Can't you see that?"

"No," I said. "I can't. Where has it been if it didn't go far?"

"The Pax," the girl said simply. "My father—his persona in Mother's Schrön Loop—explained it to me before I was born. The Core waited until the Church began being revitalized under Paul Duré . . . Pope Teilhard I. Duré was a good man, Raul. My mother and Uncle Martin knew him. He carried two cruciforms . . . his own and Father Lenar Hoyt's. But Hoyt was . . . weak."

I patted her wrist. "But what does this have to do with—"

"Listen!" said the girl, pulling her arm back. "Anything can happen tomorrow on God's Grove. I can die. We can all die. The future is never written . . . only penciled in. If I die but you survive, I want you to explain to Uncle Martin . . . to whoever will listen . . ."

"You're not going to die, Aenea—"

"Just listen!" pleaded the girl. There were tears in her eyes again.

I nodded and listened. Even the wind howl seemed to abate.

"Teilhard was murdered in his ninth year. My father predicted it. I don't know if it was by TechnoCore agents . . . they use cybrids . . . or just Vatican politics, but when Lenar Hoyt was resurrected from their shared cruciforms, the Core acted. It was the Core that provided the technology of allowing the cruciform to revive humans without the sexlessness or idiocy visited on the Bikura tribe on Hyperion. . . ."

"But how?" I said. "How could the TechnoCore AIs know how to tame the cruciform symbiote?" I saw the answer even before she spoke.

"They created the cruciforms," said Aenea. "Not the current Core, but the UI they create in the future. It sent the things back in time on Hyperion just as it did the Time Tombs. Tested the parasites on the lost tribe . . . the Bikura . . . saw the problems . . ."

"Little problems," I said, "like resurrection destroying reproductive organs and intelligence."

"Yes," said Aenea. She took my hand again. "The Core was able to correct those problems with their technology. Technology they gave the Church under its new Pope . . . Lenar Hoyt. Julius VI."

I began to understand. "A Faustian bargain . . . ," I said.

"The Faustian bargain," said the girl. "All the Church had to do to gain the universe was sell its soul."

"And thus the Pax Protectorate was born," A. Bettik said softly. "Political power through the barrel of a parasite . . ."

"It's the *Core* that's after us . . . after me," continued the child. "I'm a threat to them, not just to the Church."

I shook my head slowly. "How are you a threat to the Core? You're one child. . . ."

"One child who was in touch with a renegade cybrid persona before I was born," she whispered. "My father was loose, Raul. Not just in the datasphere or the megasphere . . . but in the metasphere. Loose in the wider psychocerbernet that even the Core was terrified of. . . ."

"Lions and tigers and bears," muttered A. Bettik.

"Exactly," said Aenea. "When my father's persona penetrated the Core megasphere, he asked the AI, Ummon, what the Core was afraid of. They said that they didn't range farther in the metasphere because it was full of lions and tigers and bears."

"I don't get it, kiddo," I said. "I'm lost."

She leaned forward and squeezed my hand. Her breath on my cheek was warm and sweet. "Raul, you know Uncle Martin's *Cantos*. What happened to the Earth?"

"Old Earth?" I said stupidly. "In the *Cantos* the AI Ummon said that the three elements of the TechnoCore were at war. . . . We talked about this."

"Tell me again."

"Ummon told the Keats persona . . . your father . . . that the Volatiles wanted to destroy humanity. The Stables . . . his group . . . wanted to save it. They faked the black-hole destruction of Old Earth and spirited it away to either the Magellanic Clouds or the Hercules Cluster. The Ultimates, the third group, didn't give a damn what happened to Old Earth or humanity as long as their Ultimate Intelligent project came to fruition."

Aenea waited.

"And the Church agrees with what everyone else believes," I continued somewhat lamely. "That Old Earth was swallowed by the black hole and died when it was supposed to have died."

"Which version do you believe, Raul?"

I took a breath. "I don't know," I said. "I'd like Old Earth to still exist, I guess, but somehow it doesn't seem that important."

"What if there was a third possibility?" said Aenea.

The glass doors suddenly rattled and shook. I put my hand on the plasma pistol, half expecting the Shrike to be scratching at the glass. Only the desert wind howled there. "A third possibility?" I said.

"Ummon lied," said Aenea. "The AI lied to my father. No element of the Core moved the Earth . . . not the Stables, not the Volatiles, not the Ultimates."

"So it *was* destroyed," I said.

"No," said Aenea. "My father did not understand then. He did later. Old Earth was moved to the Magellanic Clouds, all right, but not by any element of the Core. They didn't have the technology or the energy resources or that level of control of the Void Which Binds. The Core can't even *travel* to the Magellanic Cloud. It's too far . . . unimaginably distant."

"Who, then?" I said. "Who stole Old Earth?"

Aenea laid back on the pillows. "I don't know. I don't think the Core knows, either. But they don't want to know—and they're terrified that we'll find out."

A. Bettik stepped closer. "So it is not the Core that is activating the farcasters on our voyage?"

"No," said Aenea.

"Will we find out who is?" I said.

"If we live," said Aenea. "If we live." Her eyes looked tired now, not feverish. "They'll be waiting for us tomorrow, Raul. And I don't mean that priest-captain and his men. Someone . . . some*thing* from the Core will be waiting for us."

"The thing that you think killed Father Glaucus, Cuchiat, and the others," I said.

"Yes."

"Is this some sort of vision?" I said. "To know about Father Glaucus, I mean."

"Not a vision," said the girl in an empty voice. "Just a memory from the future. A certain memory."

I looked out at the diminishing storm. "We can stay here," I said. "We can get a skimmer or EMV that works, fly to the northern hemisphere, and hide in Ali or one of the bigger cities that the guidebook talks about. We don't have to play their game and go through that farcaster portal tomorrow."

"Yes," said Aenea, "we do."

I started to protest and then remained silent. After a while I said, "And where does the Shrike come in?"

"I don't know," said the girl. "It depends upon who sent it this time. Or it could be acting on its own. I don't know."

"On its own?" I said. "I thought it was just a machine."

"Oh, no," said Aenea. "Not just a machine."

I rubbed my cheek. "I don't understand. It could be a friend?"

"Never a friend," said the girl. She sat up and put her hand on my cheek where I had rubbed it a second before. "I'm sorry, Raul, I don't mean to talk in circles. It's just that I don't *know*. Nothing's written. Everything's fluid. And when I do get a glimpse of things shifting, it's like watching a beautiful sand painting in the second before the wind gets it. . . ."

The last of the desert storm rattled the windows as if to demonstrate her simile. She smiled at me. "I'm sorry I got unstuck in time a while ago. . . ."

"Unstuck?" I said.

"That bit about your loving me," she said with a rueful smile. "I forget where and when we are."

After a moment I said, "It doesn't matter, kiddo. I *do* love you. And I'll die before I let anyone hurt you tomorrow—not the Church, not the Core, not anyone."

"And I also will strive to prevent such an eventuality, M. Aenea," said A. Bettik.

The girl smiled and touched both our hands. "The Tin Woodsman and the Scarecrow," she said. "I don't deserve such friends."

It was my turn to smile. Grandam had told me that old story. "Where's the Cowardly Lion?" I said.

Aenea's smile went away. "That's me," she said very quietly. "I'm the cowardly one."

None of us slept any more that night. We loaded up and went down to the raft when the first hint of dawn touched the red hills beyond the city.

51

B ECAUSE OF *RAPHAEL*'S RELATIVELY low velocity at the translation point in Sol Draconi System, she has less speed to kill while spinning down into God's Grove space. The deceleration is mild—never more than twenty-five-g's—and lasts only three hours. Rhadamanth Nemes lies in her padded resurrection creche and waits.

When the ship slides into its orbit around the planet, Nemes opens her coffin door and kicks off to the wardrobe cubby to suit up. Before leaving the command pod for the dropship tube, she checks the creche monitors and makes a direct connection to ship's operations. The other three creches are functioning normally, programmed for the nominal three-day revival period. By the time de Soya and his men are awake, Nemes knows, this issue will have been settled. Using the microfilament connection to the ship's main computer, she sets the same programming directives and recording overrides she had used in Sol Draconi System. The ship acknowledges the coming dropship roll program and prepares to forget it.

Before kicking up the tube to the dropship air lock, Nemes taps the combination for her private locker. Besides a few changes of clothes and some false personal items—holos of "family" and some forged letters from her fictional brother—the only thing in the locker is an extra belt with the usual pouches. Someone examining those pouches would find only a playing-card computer of the kind available at any convenience store for eight or ten florins, a spool of thread, three vials of pills, and a packet of tampons. She slides the belt around her waist and heads for the drop-ship.

Even from orbit at thirty thousand kilometers, God's Grove—where it is visible at all through the heavy cloud layers—reveals itself as the damaged world it is. Rather than being divided into discrete continents and oceans, the planet has tectonically evolved as a single landmass with thousands of long salty-sea "lochs" raking across the landscape like claw marks on a green baize billiard table. Besides the sea-lochs and countless fingerlakes following the fault lines through the verdant landmasses, there are now thousands of brown slash marks where the Ouster invasion—what the humans still think of as the Ouster invasion—had lanced and relanced the peaceful land almost three hundred years ago.

As the dropship hurtles through atmosphere entry and ionization, ripping into solid atmosphere with a triple sonic boom, Nemes looks down at the landscape coming into sight from beneath the extensive cloud masses. Most of the two-hundred-meter-tall recombinant redwood and sequoia forests that had originally attracted the Brotherhood of the Muir to this world are gone, burned away in the planetwide forest fire that had brought on the nuclear winter. Large segments of the northern and southern hemispheres still glare white from the snowfall and glaciation, which only now is beginning to abate as the cloud cover recedes from a thousand-klick band on either side of the equator. It is precisely this recovering equatorial region that is Nemes's destination.

Taking over manual control of the lifting-body dropship, Nemes clips in her filament jack. She rifles through the planetary maps she has downloaded from *Raphael*'s main library: there it is . . . the River Tethys had once run some 160 klicks, primarily west to east, around the roots of God's Grove Worldtree and past the Muir Museum. Nemes sees that most of the Tethys Tour had been in a giant semicircular arc as the river winds around a small bite of the northern circumference of Worldtree. The Templars had fancied themselves the ecological conscience of the Hegemony—always inserting their unsolicited opinion into any terraforming effort in the Web or Outback—and the Worldtree had been the symbol of their arrogance. Indeed, the tree had been unique in the known universe: with a trunk diameter of more than eighty kilometers and a branch diameter of more than five hundred klicks, equal to the base of Mars's legendary Olympus Mons, the single living organism had thrust its upper branches into the fringes of space.

It is gone now, of course, shattered and burned by the "Ouster" fleet that slagged the entire planet just before the Fall. Instead of the glorious, living Tree, there is now only the Worldstump, a heap of ash and carbon looking like the eroded remains of an ancient shield volcano. With the Templars gone—killed or fled in their erg-powered treeships on the day of the attack—God's Grove has lain fallow for more than two and a half centuries. Nemes knows that the Pax would have recolonized the world long ago if the Core had not ordered them to desist: the AIs have their own long-term plan for God's Grove, and it does not involve missionaries and human colonies.

Nemes finds the upriver farcaster portal—looking tiny compared to the ashy slopes of the Worldstump to the south—and hovers above it.

Secondary growth has come up along the river and on the eroded ash slopes there, looking like mere weeds compared to the old forests but still boasting trees twenty meters and more in height, and Nemes can see the occasional tangle of thick undergrowth where the sunlight strikes the gullies. Not a good place for an ambush. Nemes lands the dropship on the north bank of the river and walks to the farcaster arch.

Discarding an access panel, she finds an interface module and peels off the human flesh on her right hand and wrist. Carefully storing the skin for her return to *Raphael,* she jacks directly into the module and reviews the data. This portal has not been activated since the Fall. Aenea's group has not yet passed this way.

Nemes returns to the dropship and flies downriver, trying to find the perfect spot. It should be a place where they cannot escape by land— enough forest growth to conceal her and her traps, but not so much as to give Aenea and her companions cover—and, finally, a place where Nemes can clean up the mess after it is all over. She would prefer a rocky surface: something easy to hose down before returning to *Raphael.*

She finds the perfect spot only fifteen klicks downriver. The Tethys enters a rocky gorge at this point, a series of rapids created by the Ouster slagging and subsequent avalanches. New trees have grown up along the ash slopes by the entrance to this stretch of rapids and along the narrow ravines feeding into it. The narrow canyon itself is bordered by tumbled boulders and by great slabs of black lava that had flowed downhill during the Ouster slagging and formed into terraces as they cooled. The rough terrain makes a portage impossible, and anyone piloting a raft toward these rapids will be intent upon guiding their craft into white water and will have little time to watch the rocks or riverbanks.

She lands the dropship a klick to the south, pulls a vacuum-locked specimen bag from the EVA locker, tucks it into her belt, conceals the dropship under branches, and jogs quickly back to the river.

Nemes removes the spool of thread from her kit, tosses away the thread, and extrudes several hundred meters of invisible monofilament. She runs this back and forth across the river above the rapids like an unseen spider's web, spreading clear, saplike polycarbon goo on the landward side of objects where she loops the wire, both to give her a visual reference and to prevent the monofilament from slicing through trees and boulders wherever it touches them. Even if someone were hiking the boulders and lava fields here, the goo would show up only as a faint line of sap or as lichen on the rocks. The monofilament web would slice through *Raphael* in a dozen places if someone tried to drive the spacecraft through here now.

When she has woven the monofilament trap, Nemes moves upriver along the only flat shelf of land, opens her pill case, and spreads several hundred miniclaymores on the ground and in the trees there. The chameleon-polymered microexplosives immediately blend in color and texture with the surface on which they have fallen. Each claymore will leap toward the walking or running target before it explodes, and its blast is shaped to burrow inward. The claymores are triggered by the proximity of pulse, carbon-dioxide exhalations, and body heat, as well as by the pressure of a footstep within ten meters.

Nemes assesses the terrain. This flat area is the only section of riverbank near the rapids where a person on foot can retreat, and with the claymores scattered there, nothing on foot will survive. Nemes jogs back to the boulder field and activates the claymores' sensors with a coded pulse.

To prevent someone from swimming back upriver, she breaks open the tampon casings and seeds the river bottom with ceramic-encased earwig eggs. These lie on the river bottom looking exactly like the water-worn pebbles around them. When one or more living beings pass above them, they activate themselves. If someone then tries to return upriver, the gnat-sized earwigs will burst through their ceramic eggs and scream through water or air to bore into their target's skull, exploding into a mass of wiry filaments only after making contact with brain tissue.

Waiting on a boulder ten meters above the rapids, Rhadamanth Nemes lies back to wait. The two items left in her belt are the playing-card computer and the specimen bag.

The "computer" is the most advanced item she has brought on this hunting trip. Called the "sphinx trap" by those entities that created it for her, named after the Sphinx Tomb on Hyperion, which had been designed by the same species of AIs, the card is capable of creating its own five-meter bubble of antientropic or hyperentropic tides. The energy needed to create this bubble could power a crowded planet such as Renaissance Vector for a decade, but Nemes needs only three minutes of temporal displacement. Fingering the flat card, Nemes thinks that it should be called the Shrike trap.

The short woman with the skinless hand looks upriver. Any time now. Even though the portal is fifteen klicks away, she will have some warning: Nemes is sensitive to the farcaster distortion. She expects the Shrike to be with them and anticipates that it will treat her as an adversary. Indeed, she would be disappointed if the Shrike were not there and adversarial.

Rhadamanth Nemes fingers the last item on her belt. The specimen bag is just what it appears to be—a vacuum-locked EVA specimen bag. In it she will transport the girl's head back to the *Raphael*, where she will store it in the secret locker behind the fusion-drive access panel. Her masters want proof.

Smiling slightly, Nemes lies back on the black lava, shifts her position so the afternoon sun warms her face, covers her eyes with her wrist, and allows herself to take a brief nap. Everything is ready.

52

I ADMIT THAT I EXPECTED the Shrike to be gone when we reached the riverfront street of Mashhad on Qom-Riyadh just before dawn of that last, fateful day. It was not gone.

We all stopped in our tracks at the sight of the three-meter-tall chrome-and-blade sculpture on our little raft. The thing was standing just as I had last seen it the night before. I had backed away warily then, rifle raised, and now I took another wary step closer, rifle raised.

"Easy," said Aenea, her hand on my forearm.

"What the hell does it want?" I said, slipping off the safety on the rifle. I levered the first plasma cartridge into the firing chamber.

"I don't know," said Aenea. "But your weapon won't hurt it."

I licked my lips and looked down at the child. I wanted to tell her that a plasma bolt would hurt *anything* not wrapped in twenty centimeters of Web-era impact armor. Aenea looked pale and drawn. There were dark circles under her eyes. I said nothing.

"Well," I said, lowering the rifle a bit, "we can't get on the raft while that thing's there."

Aenea squeezed my arm and released it. "We have to." She started walking toward the concrete pier.

I looked at A. Bettik, who seemed no happier at this idea than I was; then we both jogged to keep up with the girl.

Close up, the Shrike was even more terrifying than when seen from a distance. I used the word "sculpture" earlier, and there was something sculpted about the creature—if one can imagine a sculpture done in chromed spikes, razor wire, blades, thorns, and smooth metal carapace. It was *large*—more than a meter taller than I, and I am not short. The actual form of the thing was complicated—solid legs with joints sheathed in thorn-studded bands; a flat foot with curved blades where the toes should be and a long spoon-shaped blade at the heel, which might be a perfect utensil for disemboweling; a complicated upper carapace of smooth chromed shell interspersed with bands of razor wire; arms that were too long, too jointed, and too many—there was an extra pair tucked under the longer, upper set of arms; and four huge bladed hands hanging limply by the thing's side.

The skull was mostly smooth and strangely elongated, with a steam-shovel jaw set in with row upon row of metal teeth. There was a curved blade on the creature's forehead and another high up on the armored skull. The eyes were large, deep-set, and dull red.

"You want to get on the raft with that . . . *thing*?" I whispered to Aenea as we stood four meters away on the pier. The Shrike had not turned its head to watch us as we approached, and its eyes seemed as dead as glass reflectors, but the urge to back away from the thing and then turn and run was very strong.

"We have to get on the raft," the girl whispered back. "We have to get out of here today. Today is the last day."

Without really taking my eye off the monster, I glanced at the sky and buildings behind us. With the night's wild dust storm, one would have expected the sky to be pinker with more sand in the air, but the storm seemed to have cleared the air a bit. While reddish clouds still stirred on the last desert breeze, the sky above was bluer than it had been the day before. Sunlight was just touching the tops of the taller buildings now.

"Maybe we could find a working EMV and travel in style," I whispered, the rifle raised. "Something without this type of hood ornament." The joke sounded lame even to my ear, but it took most of the bravado I had that morning to attempt any joke at all.

"Come on," whispered Aenea, and went down the iron ladder off the pier and onto the battered raft. I hurried to keep up with her, one hand keeping the rifle trained on the chrome nightmare, the other grasping the old ladder. A. Bettik followed us without a word.

I had not paid attention to how battered and flimsy the raft seemed. The abbreviated logs were torn and splintered in places, water came over the forward third and lapped around the Shrike's huge feet, and the tent was filled with red sand from the night's storm. The steering-oar assembly looked as if it would give way any second, and the gear we had left aboard had an abandoned look to it. We dropped our packs into the tent and stood indecisively, watching the back of the Shrike and waiting for movement—three mice who had crawled onto the sleeping cat's carpet.

The Shrike did not turn. Its back was no more reassuring than its front, with the exception that its dull-red eyes no longer were watching us.

Aenea sighed and walked up to the thing. She raised one small hand but did not actually touch that spiked and razor-wired shoulder. Turning back to us, she said, "It's all right. Let's go."

"How can it be all right?" I whispered fiercely at her. I don't know why I was whispering . . . but for some reason it was next to impossible to speak normally around that thing.

"If it was going to kill us today, we would be dead already," the girl said flatly. She walked to the port side, her face still pale and shoulders drooping, and picked up one of the poles. "Cast off the lines, please," she said to A. Bettik. "We have to go."

The android did not flinch as he walked within monster-arm's length of the Shrike to untie the forward line and curl it into a loop. I untied our stern line with one hand while holding the rifle with the other.

The raft rode lower with the mass of the creature on the front end, and water lapped across the boards almost back to the tent. Several of the front and port-side logs were hanging loose.

"We need to work on the raft," I said, taking the steering oar in hand and laying the rifle at my feet.

"Not on this world," said Aenea, still straining against the pole to move us out into the center current. "After we go through the portal."

"Do you know where we're headed?" I said.

She shook her head. Her hair seemed dull this morning. "I just know that this is the last day."

She had said that a few minutes earlier, and I had felt the same stab of alarm then as I did now. "Are you sure, kiddo?"

"Yes."

"But you don't know where we're going?"

"No. Not exactly."

"What do you know? I mean . . ."

She smiled wanly. "I know what you mean, Raul. I know that if we survive the next few hours, we hunt for the building I've seen in my dreams."

"What does it look like?"

Aenea opened her mouth to speak but then just rested against the pole a moment. We were moving quickly now in the center of the river. The tall downtown buildings gave way to small parks and walkways on either bank. "I'll know the building when I see it." She laid the pole down and walked closer, pulling at my sleeve. I bent to hear her whisper. "Raul, if I don't . . . make it . . . and you do . . . please get home to tell Uncle Martin about what I said. About the lions and tigers and bears . . . and what the Core is up to."

I grabbed her by her thin shoulder. "Don't talk like that. We're all going to make it. *You* tell Martin when we see him."

Aenea nodded without conviction and went back to the pole. The Shrike continued to stare ahead, water lapping at its feet and the morning light beginning to glint on its thorns and razor surfaces.

I HAD EXPECTED US to move into open desert beyond the city of Mashhad, but once again my expectations were mistaken. The riverside parks and walkways grew more luxuriant with trees—everblues, deciduous Old Earth varieties, and a proliferation of yellow and green palms. Soon the city buildings were behind us and the wide, straight river was passing through a rich forest. It was still early morning, but the heat of the rising sun was very powerful.

The steering oar was not really needed in the central current. I lashed it in place, took off my shirt, folded it on top of my pack, and took the port push-pole from the obviously exhausted girl. She looked at me with dark eyes but did not complain.

A. Bettik had collapsed the microtent and shaken out most of the accumulated sand. Now he sat near me as the current moved us around a wide bend and into an even thicker tropical rain forest. He was wearing the loose shirt and ragged shorts of yellow linen I had seen him in on Hebron and Mare Infinitus. The broad-brimmed straw hat was at his feet. Surprisingly, Aenea moved to the front of the raft to sit near the motionless Shrike as we drifted deeper into the heavy jungle.

"This can't be native," I said, straightening the raft as the current tried to swing it sideways. "There can't be enough rainfall in this desert to support all this."

"I believe it was an extensive garden area planeted by the Shi'a religious pilgrims, M. Endymion," said A. Bettik. "Listen."

I listened. The rain forest was alive with the rustle of birds and wind. Beneath these sounds I could hear the hiss and rattle of sprinkler systems. "Incredible," I said. "That they'd use precious water to maintain this ecosystem. It must stretch for kilometers."

"Paradise," said Aenea.

"What, kiddo?" I poled us back into the center current.

"The Muslims were primarily desert people on Old Earth," she said softly. "Water and greenery was their idea of paradise. Mashhad was a religious center. Maybe this was to give the faithful a glimpse of what was to come if the teachings of Allah in the Qur'an were obeyed."

"Expensive sneak preview," I said, dragging the pole a bit as we turned again to the left as the river widened. "I wonder what happened to the people."

"The Pax," said Aenea.

"What?" I did not understand. "These worlds . . . Hebron, Qom-Riyadh . . . were under Ouster control when the population disappeared."

"According to the Pax," said Aenea.

I thought about this.

"What do the two worlds have in common, Raul?" she said.

It took no time to answer that. "They were both adamantly non-Christian," I said. "They refused to accept the cross. Jew and Muslim."

Aenea said nothing.

"That's a terrible thought," I said. My stomach hurt. "The Church may be misguided . . . the Pax can be arrogant with its power . . . but . . ." I wiped sweat out of my eyes. "My God . . . ," I said, struggling to say the one word. "Genocide?"

Aenea shifted to look at me. Just behind her the Shrike's bladed legs caught the light. "We don't know that," she said very quietly. "But there are elements of the Church and of the Pax that would do it, Raul. Remember, the Vatican depends almost totally on the Core to maintain its control of resurrection—and through that, its control of all the people on all the worlds."

I was shaking my head. "But . . . genocide? I can't believe it." That concept belonged with the legends of Horace Glennon-Height and Adolf Hitler, not with people and institutions I had seen in my lifetime.

"Something terrible is going on," said Aenea. "That has to be why we were routed this way . . . through Hebron and Qom-Riyadh."

"You said that before," I said, pushing hard on the pole. "Routed. But not by the Core. Then by whom?" I looked at the back of the Shrike. I was pouring sweat in the heat of the day. The looming creature was all cool blades and thorns.

"I don't know," said Aenea. She swiveled back around and rested her forearms on her knees. "There's the farcaster."

The portal rose, vine shrouded and rusted, from the overgrown jungle. If this was still Qom-Riyadh's paradise park, it had grown out of control. Above the green canopy, the blue sky carried a hint of red dust clouds on the wind.

Steering for the center of the river, I laid the pole along the port side and went back to pick up my rifle. My stomach was still tight with the thought of genocide. Now it tightened further with the image of ice caves, waterfalls, ocean worlds, and of the Shrike coming to life as we passed into whatever waited.

"Hang on," I said needlessly as we passed under the metal arch.

The view ahead of us faded and shifted as if a curtain of heat haze had begun to shimmer ahead of us and around us. Suddenly the light changed, the gravity changed, and our world changed.

53

FATHER CAPTAIN DE SOYA awakes to screaming. It is several minutes before he realizes it is his voice doing the screaming.

Thumbing open the coffin-lid catch, he pulls himself to a sitting position within the creche. Lights are blinking red and amber on the monitor panel, although all of the essential guidelines are green. Moaning in pain and confusion, de Soya starts to pull himself out. His body floats above the open creche, his flailing hands can get no grip. He notices that his hands and arms are glistening red and pink, as if all his skin has been burned off.

"Dear Mother of Mary . . . where am I?" He is weeping. The tears hang in front of his eyes in tumbling beads. "Zero-g . . . where am I? The *Balthasar*? What's . . . happened? Space battle? Burns?"

No. He is aboard the *Raphael*. Slowly the outraged dendrites in his brain begin to work. He is floating in instrument-lighted darkness. The *Raphael*. It should be in orbit around God's Grove. He had set the creche cycles for Gregorius, Kee, and him for a dangerous six hours rather than the usual three days. *Playing God with the troopers' lives,* he remembers thinking. The chances for unsuccessful resurrection are very high at this hurried pace. De Soya remembers the second courier who had brought orders to him on the *Balthasar*, Father Gawronski—it seems like decades ago to him—he had not achieved successful resurrection . . . the resurrection chaplain on *Balthasar* . . . what was that old bastard's name? Father Sapieha . . . had said that it would take weeks or months for Father Gawronski to be resurrected after that initial failure . . . a slow, painful process, the resurrection chaplain had said accusingly . . .

Father Captain de Soya's mind is clearing as he floats above the creche. Still in free fall as he had programmed. He remembers thinking that he might not be in shape to walk in one-g. He is not.

Kicking off to the wardrobe cubby, de Soya checks himself in the mirror there—his body glistens redly, he does look like a burn victim, and the cruciform is a livid welt in all that pink, raw flesh.

De Soya closes his eyes and pulls on his underclothes and cassock. The cotton hurts his raw skin, but he ignores the pain. The coffee has percolated as programmed. He lifts his bulb from the plotting table and kicks back into the common room.

Corporal Kee's creche glows green in the last seconds of revival. Gregorius's creche has flashing warning lights. De Soya curses softly and pulls himself down to the sergeant's creche panel. The resurrection cycle has been aborted. The hurried revival has failed.

"Goddammit," whispers de Soya, and then offers an Act of Contrition for taking the Lord's name in vain. He needed Gregorius.

Kee revives safely, however, although the corporal is confused and in pain. De Soya lifts him out, kicks off with him to the wardroom cubby to sponge-bathe the other man's burning skin and to offer him a drink of orange juice. Within minutes Kee can understand.

"Something was wrong," de Soya explains. "I had to take this risk to see what Corporal Nemes was up to."

Kee nods his understanding. Even though dressed with the cabin temperature set high, the corporal is shivering violently.

De Soya leads the way back to the command core. Sergeant Gregorius's creche is all amber lights now as the cycle surrenders the big man to death again. Corporal Rhadamanth Nemes's creche shows green lights for the normal three-day resurrection. Monitor displays show that she is inside, lifeless, and receiving the secret sacramental ministrations of resurrection. De Soya taps the release code.

Warning lights blink. "Creche release not allowed during resurrection cycle," comes *Raphael*'s emotionless voice. "Any attempt to open the creche now could result in true death."

De Soya ignores the lights and warning buzzers and tugs at the lid. It stays locked. "Give me that pry bar," he says to Kee.

The corporal tosses the iron bar across the weightless space. De Soya finds a niche for the head of the bar, says a silent prayer that he is not wrong and paranoid, and pries up the lid. Alarm bells fill the ship.

The creche is empty.

"Where is Corporal Nemes?" de Soya asks the ship.

"All instruments and sensors show her in her creche," says the ship's computer.

"Yeah," says de Soya, tossing the bar aside. It tumbles into a corner in zero-g slow motion. "Come on," he says to the corporal, and the two kick back to the wardroom cubby. The shower stall is empty. There is no place to hide in the common area. De Soya kicks forward to his command chair while Kee heads for the connecting tube.

Status lights show geosynchronous orbit at thirty thousand kilometers. De Soya looks out the window and sees a world of swirling cloud banks except for a wide band at the equator, where slash marks cut across green and brown terrain. Instruments show the dropship attached and powered down. Voice queries have the ship confirm that the dropship is where it should be, its air lock undisturbed since translation. "Corporal Kee?" de Soya says on the intercom. He must concentrate to keep his teeth from chattering. The pain is very real; it is as if his skin is on fire. He has a tremendous urge to close his eyes and sleep. "Report," commands de Soya.

"The dropship's gone, Captain," says Kee from the access tunnel. "All the connector lights are green, but if I cycled the air lock, I'd be breathing vacuum. I can see out the port here that the dropship's gone."

"*Merde*," whispers de Soya. "All right, come on back here." He studies the other instruments while he waits. The telltale double burps are there on the thruster record . . . about three hours ago. Calling up the map of the equatorial region of God's Grove, de Soya keys in a telescope and deep-radar search of the stretch of river around the stump of the Worldtree. "Find the first farcaster portal and show me every stretch of the river in between. Report on location of dropship transponder."

"Instruments show dropship attached to the command-core boom," says the ship. "Transponder confirms this."

"Okay," says de Soya, imagining himself punching out silicon chips like teeth, "ignore the dropship beacon. Just begin telescope and deep-radar searches of this region. Report any life-forms or artifacts. All data on main screens."

"Affirmative," says the computer. De Soya sees the screen lurch forward as telescopic magnification begins. He is looking down on a farcaster portal now from only a few hundred meters above it. "Pan downriver," he says.

"Affirmative."

Corporal Kee slides into the copilot's seat and straps himself in. "With the dropship gone," he says, "there's no way we can get down there."

"Combat suits," says de Soya through the ripples of pain that shake him. "They have an ablative shield . . . hundreds of microlayers of colored ablative in case of a coherent light firefight, right?"

"Correct," says Corporal Kee, "but—"

"My plan was for you and Sergeant Gregorius to use the ablative for reentry," continues de Soya. "I could get *Raphael* in as low an orbit as possible. You use an auxiliary reaction pak for retro thrust. The suits should survive reentry, shouldn't they?"

"Possibly," says Kee, "but—"

"Then you go to EM repulsors and find this . . . woman," says de Soya. "Find her and stop her. Afterward, you use the dropship to get back."

Corporal Kee rubs his eyes. "Yes, sir. But I checked the suits. All of them have integrity breaches. . . ."

"Integrity . . . ," repeats de Soya stupidly.

"Someone slashed the ablative armor," says Kee. "Not noticeable to the eye, but I ran a class-three integrity diagnostic. We'd be dead before ionization blackout."

"All the suits?" says de Soya weakly.

"All of them, sir."

The priest-captain overcomes the urge to curse again. "I'm going to bring the ship lower anyway, Corporal."

"Why, sir?" says Kee. "Anything that happens down there is still going to be several hundred klicks away, and we can't do a damn thing about it."

De Soya nods but taps in the parameters he wants to the guidance core. His befuddled brain makes several mistakes—at least one of which would burn them up in the atmosphere of God's Grove—but the ship catches them. De Soya resets the parameters.

"I advise against such a low orbit," says the sexless ship's voice. "God's Grove has a volatile upper atmosphere, and three hundred kilometers does not satisfy safety-margin requirements as listed in the—"

"Shut up and do it," says Father Captain de Soya.

He closes his eyes as the main thrusters fire. The return of weight makes the pain in his flesh and body all the more fierce. De Soya hears Kee groan in the copilot's couch.

"Internal containment-field activation will alleviate the discomfort of four-g deceleration," says the ship.

"No," says de Soya. He is going to save power.

The noise, vibration, and pain continue. The limb of God's Grove grows in the windscreen until it fills the view.

What if that . . . traitor . . . has programmed the ship to drive us into atmosphere if we awake and try any maneuver? de Soya suddenly thinks. He grins despite the punishing g-pull. *Then she doesn't go home either.*

The punishment continues.

54

T HE Shrike was gone when we came through the other side of the portal.

After a moment I lowered my rifle and looked around. The river was broad and shallow here. The sky was a deep blue, darker than Hyperion's lapis lazuli, and towering stratocumulus were visible far to the north. The cloud columns seemed to be catching evening light, and a glance behind us showed a large sun low in the sky. My feeling was that it was near sunset rather than just after sunrise.

The riverbanks showed rocks, weeds, and ashy soil. The very air smelled of ash, as if we were moving through an area destroyed by forest fire. The low growth supported that impression. To our right, many kilometers away, from the look of it, rose a blackened shield volcano.

"God's Grove, I think," said A. Bettik. "That is the remnant of the Worldtree."

I looked again at the black volcanic cone. No tree could ever have grown that large.

"Where's the Shrike?" I said.

Aenea stood and walked to the place where the creature had stood a moment before. She passed her hand through the air as if the monster had become invisible.

"Hang on!" I said again. The raft was coming up on a modest set of rapids. I returned to the steering oar and unlashed it while the android and girl took up poles on either side. We bounced, splashed, and tried to turn end to end, but were soon past the white ripples.

"That was fun!" said Aenea. It was the most animated I had heard her in some time.

"Yeah," I said, "fun. But the raft's coming apart." This was a slight exaggeration, but not total hyperbole. The loose logs at the front were coming untethered. Our gear was rattling around loose on the collapsed microtent fabric.

"There is a flat space to put in," said A. Bettik, pointing to a grassy area along the right riverbank. "The hills look more formidable ahead."

I pulled the binoculars out and studied those black ridges. "You're right," I said. "There may be real rapids ahead, and few places to put in. Let's tie up loose ends here."

The girl and android poled us to the right bank. I jumped out and pulled the raft higher onto the muddy shore. Damage was not serious to the front and starboard sides, just loose wraith-hide thongs and a few splintered boards. I glanced upriver. The sun was lower, although it looked as if we had another hour or so of light.

"Do we camp tonight?" I said, thinking that this might be the last good place. "Or keep on moving?"

"Keep moving," Aenea said adamantly.

I understood the impulse. It was still morning, Qom-Riyadh time. "I don't want to be caught on white water after dark," I said.

Aenea squinted at the low sun. "And I don't want to be sitting here after dark," she said. "Let's get as far as we can." She borrowed the binoculars and studied the black ridges to our right, the dark hills to the left of the river. "They wouldn't have put the Tethys section on a river with dangerous rapids, would they?"

A. Bettik cleared his throat. "It would be my guess," he said, "that much of that lava flow was created during the Ouster attack on this world. Very severe rapids may have resulted from the seismic disruption such a lancing would cause."

"It wasn't the Ousters," Aenea said softly.

"What was that, kiddo?"

"It wasn't the Ousters," she said more firmly. "It was the TechnoCore that built ships to attack the Web . . . they were simulating an Ouster invasion."

"Okay," I said. I had forgotten that Martin Silenus had said as much toward the end of his *Cantos*. That part had not made much sense to me when I was learning the poem. It was all irrelevant now. "But the slagged hills are still there, and some nasty white water may be as well. White water or actual waterfalls. It could be that we can't get the raft through it."

Aenea nodded and set the binoculars back in my pack. "If we can't, we can't. We'll walk it and swim through the next portal. But let's fix the raft quickly and get as far as we can. If we see bad rapids, we'll pole for the closest bank."

"It may be more cliff than riverbank," I said. "That lava looks mean."

Aenea shrugged. "Then we'll climb and keep hiking."

I admit that I admired that child that evening. I knew that she was tired, sick, overwhelmed by some emotion I could not understand, and scared half to death. But I had never seen her ready to quit.

"Well," I said, "at least the Shrike's gone. That's a good sign."

Aenea only looked at me. But she tried to smile.

THE REPAIRS TOOK ONLY TWENTY MINUTES. We relashed the bindings, shifted some of the center supports to the front, and laid the microtent fabric down as a sort of liner to keep our feet dry.

"If we're going to travel in the dark," said Aenea, "we should rig our lantern mast again."

"Yeah," I said. I had kept a tall pole free for just that purpose and now set it in its socket and lashed its base in place. I used my knife to cut a niche for the lantern handle. "Shall I light it?" I said.

"Not yet," said Aenea, glancing at the setting sun behind us.

"Okay," I said, "if we're going to be bouncing through any white water, we should keep gear in our packs and load the most important things in the waterproof shoulder bags." We set to work doing just that. In my shoulder bag I put an extra shirt, an extra coil of rope, the folded plasma rifle, a handlamp, and the flashlight laser. I started to toss the useless comlog into my regular backpack, thought, *It's useless, but it doesn't weigh much,* and clipped it around my wrist instead. We had fully charged the comlog, laser, and handlamp batteries at the Qom-Riyadh clinic.

"All set?" I asked, ready to pole us out into the current again. Our raft *looked* better with its new floor and mast, packs loaded and tied down for white water, lantern ready to be lit at the bow.

"Ready," said Aenea.

A. Bettik nodded and leaned on his pole. We moved out onto the river.

THE CURRENT WAS FAST—at least twenty or twenty-five klicks per hour—and the sun was still above the horizon when we moved into the black lava country. Riverbanks changed to bluffs on either side, and we bounced through a few ripples of white water, coming out high and dry each time, and I began to search the banks for places to set in if we heard the roar of a waterfall or wild rapids ahead. There were places—gullies and flat areas—but the land was visibly rougher ahead. I noticed that there was more growth here in the ravines—everblues and stunted redwoods—and the low sun painted the higher branches in rich light. I was beginning to think about getting our lunch . . . dinner . . . whatever, out of the packs and fixing something hot when A. Bettik called, "Rapids ahead."

I leaned on the steering oar and looked. Rocks in the river, white water, some spray. My years as a bargeman on the Kans helped assess this stretch of rapids. "It'll be all right," I said. "Keep your legs braced, move a bit toward the center if it gets too wild. Push hard when I say push. The trick will be to keep the front headed where we want it, but we can do it. If you go over, swim for the raft. I've got a line ready." I had one booted foot on the coiled rope.

I did not like the black lava cliffs and boulders on the right side of the river ahead, but the river looked wider and milder beyond this stretch of rough water. If this was all we faced, we could probably continue on into the night, using the lantern and widebeam laser to light our way.

All three of us were concentrating on lining the raft up properly to enter the rapids, trying to miss several boulders rising from the frothing water, when it all began. If it had not been for an eddy there that spun us around twice, it would have been over before I'd known what was happening. As it was, it almost happened that way.

Aenea was shouting in glee. I was grinning. Even A. Bettik had a smile. Mild white water does that, I knew from experience. Class V rapids usually just freeze a rictus of terror on people's faces, but harmless bumps like this were fun. We shouted directions at one another—Push! Hard right! Avoid that rock!—Aenea was a few steps to my right, A. Bettik a few steps farther to my left, and we had just been grabbed by the swirling eddy downstream from the large rock we had avoided, when I looked up to see the mast at the front and the hanging lantern suddenly sliced into pieces.

"What the hell?" I had time to say, and then the old memories hit, and with them, the reflexes I would have guessed had atrophied years before.

We were spinning to my left. I screamed "Down!" at the top of my lungs, abandoned the steering oar, and tackled Aenea headfirst. Both of us rolled off the raft into white water.

A. Bettik had reacted almost instantly, throwing himself down and toward the stern of the raft, and the monofilaments that had sliced the mast and lantern like soft butter must have missed him by millimeters. I came up out of the water with my boots scraping against rocks and my forearm around Aenea's chest in time to see the underwater monofilament slice the raft in two sections, then reslice it as the eddy swirled the logs around. The filaments were invisible, of course, but that kind of cutting power meant only one thing. I had seen this trick used on buddies of mine in the brigade on Ursus; the rebels had strung monofilament across the road, sliced through a bus hauling thirty guys back from the cinema in town, and decapitated all of them.

I tried to shout at A. Bettik, but the water was roaring and it filled my mouth. I grabbed at a boulder, missed it, scrabbled my feet against the bottom, and caught the next rock. My scrotum tightened as I thought of those goddamn wires underwater, in front of my face. . . .

The android saw the raft being sliced a third time and dived into the shallow water. The current flipped him over, his left arm rising instinctively as his head was forced under. There was a brief mist of blood as the arm was sliced off just below his elbow. His head came above the water, but he did not cry out as he grabbed a sharp rock with his right hand and hung on. His left arm and still-spasming hand were swept out of sight downriver.

"Oh, Jesus!" I yelled. "Damn . . . damn!"

Aenea pulled her face out of the water and looked at me with wild eyes. But there was no panic there.

"Are you all right?" I shouted over the rapids. A monofilament slices so cleanly that you could be missing a leg and not know it for half a minute.

She nodded.

"Hang on to my neck!" I yelled. I had to get my left arm free. She clung to me, her skin already cold from the freezing water.

"Damn, damn, damn," I said as a mantra while I fumbled in my shoulder bag with my left hand. My pistol was in its holster, pinned under my right hip against the river bottom. It was shallow here . . . less than a meter in places . . . barely enough water to dive for cover when the sniper started shooting. But that was irrelevant—any attempt to dive would sweep us downriver, into the monofilaments.

I could see A. Bettik hanging on for his life eight meters or so downriver. He lifted his left arm from the water. Blood spurted from the stump. I could see him grimace and almost lose his grip on the rock as the pain began to pour through shock. *Do androids die like humans?* I shook the thought away. His blood was very red.

I scanned the lava flows and boulder fields for a glint of dying sunlight on metal. Next would come the sniper's bullet or bolt. We would not hear it. It was a beautiful ambush—straight out of the book. And I had literally steered us into it.

I found the flashlight laser in the bag, resealed the bag, and clamped the laser cylinder in my teeth. Fumbling underwater with my left hand, I undid my belt and tugged it out of the water. I nodded wildly for Aenea to grab the pistol with her free hand.

Still clinging to my neck with her left arm, she unsnapped the cover and pulled the pistol out. I knew that she would never use it, but that did not matter right now. I needed the belt. I fumbled, setting the laser under my chin and holding it in place while my left hand straightened the belt.

"Bettik!" I screamed.

The android looked up at us. His eyes held agony. "Catch!" I screamed, pulling my arm back over my head and throwing the leather belt at him. I almost lost the flashlight laser with the maneuver, but grabbed it as it hit the water and gripped it in my left hand.

The android could not release his right hand from the rock. His left hand was gone. But he used the bleeding stump of his arm and his chest to

stop the hurtling belt. The throw had been perfect . . . but, then, I had
had only one chance.

"Medkit!" I shouted, leaning my head toward the bag rising and
falling next to me. "Tourniquet now!"

I don't think that he heard me, but he did not have to. Pulling himself
up against the rock, trying to lodge himself on the upstream side of it, he
pulled the leather belt around his left arm below the elbow and pulled
tight on the strap with his teeth. There was no notch that low on the belt,
but he pulled it tight with a jerk of his head, wrapped it again, and pulled
it tight again.

By this time I had triggered on the flashlight laser, set the beam to
widest dispersal, and played it above the river.

The wire was monofilament but not superconducting monofilament.
That would not have glowed. This did. There was a web of heated wire,
glowing red like crisscrossed laser beams, streaking back and forth above
and into the river. A. Bettik had floated down beneath some of the glowing
wires. Others disappeared into the water to the left and right of him. The
first filaments began about a meter in front of Aenea's feet.

I moved the widebeam, playing it above us and to our left and right.
Nothing glowed there. The wires above A. Bettik glowed for a few seconds
as they dissipated heat, and then disappeared as if they had never existed. I
fanned the widebeam across them again, bringing them back into existence, then dialed a tighter beam. The filament I had targeted glowed
white but did not melt. It wasn't a superconductor, but it wasn't going to
go away with the low energies I could pour into it with a flashlight laser.

Where is the sniper? Maybe it was just a passive trap. Years old.
Nobody waiting in ambush.

I did not believe it for a second. I could see A. Bettik's grip on the
rock slip as the current threatened to pull him under.

"Shit," I said. Setting the laser into the waistband of my pants, I
grabbed Aenea with my left arm. "Hang on."

With my right arm I pulled myself higher onto the slippery boulder.
It was triangular in shape and very slick. Wedging my body on the upstream side, I pulled Aenea there. The current was like someone battering
me with body blows. "Can you hold on?" I shouted.

"Yeah!" Her face was white. Her hair was plastered to her skull. I
could see scratches on her cheek and temple and a rising bruise near her
chin, but no other sign of injury.

I patted her on the shoulder, made sure her arms were secure on the
rock, and let go. Downstream, I could see the raft—now sliced into half a
dozen segments—tumbling into the curve of white water by the lava cliffs.

Bouncing and scraping along the bottom, trying to stand but being
swept and battered by the current, I managed to hit A. Bettik's small rock
without knocking him off or myself out. I grabbed him and hung on,
noticing that his shirt had been almost ripped off him by the sharp rocks

and current. Blood oozed from a dozen scratches in his blue skin, but it was his left arm I wanted to see. He moaned when I lifted the arm from the water.

The tourniquet was helping to staunch the bleeding, but not enough. Red swirled in the sunlit waters. I thought of the rainbow sharks on Mare Infinitus and shivered.

"Come on," I said, half lifting him, prying his cold hand from the rock. "We're leaving."

The water was only to my waist when I stood, but it had the force of several fire hoses. Somehow, despite shock and serious loss of blood, A. Bettik helped. Our boots scrabbled at the sharp rocks on the river bottom. *Where is the sniper's bolt?* My shoulder blades ached from the tension.

The closest riverbank was to our right—a flat, grassy shelf that was the last easy spot to reach as far as I could see downriver. It was inviting. Far too inviting.

Besides, Aenea was still clinging to the rock eight meters upstream.

With A. Bettik's good arm over my shoulder, we staggered, lurched, half swam, and half crawled our way upstream, the water battering us and splashing in our faces. I was half-blind by the time we reached Aenea's rock. Her fingers were white with cold and strain.

"The bank!" she shouted as I helped her to her feet. Our first step took us into a hole, and the current battered against her chest and neck, covering her face with white spray.

I shook my head. "Upriver!" I shouted, and the three of us began leaning into the current, water pounding and spraying to both sides. Only my maniacal strength at that moment kept us upright and moving. Every time the current threatened to throw us down, to pull us under, I imagined myself as solid as the Worldtree that had once stood to the south, roots running deep into the bedrock. I had my eye on a fallen log perhaps twenty meters up on the right bank. If we could shelter behind that . . . I knew that I had to get the medkit tourniquet on A. Bettik's arm within minutes, or he would be dead. If we tried to stop here in the river to do it, the medkit, shoulder bag, and everything else ran the risk of being whirled downriver. But I did not want to lie exposed on that inviting shelf of grassy riverbank. . . .

Monofilaments. I tugged the flashlight laser from my waistband and played its wideband in the air over the river upstream. No wires. *But they could be* under *the water, waiting to slice us off at the ankles.*

Trying to shut down my imagination, I pulled the three of us upstream against the force of the river. The flashlight laser was slippery in my hand. A. Bettik's grip was growing weaker around my shoulder. Aenea clung to my left arm as if it was her only lifeline. It *was* her only lifeline.

We had struggled less than ten meters upstream when the water ahead of us exploded. I almost tumbled backward. Aenea's head went under and I pulled her up, gripping her soaked shirt with frenzied fingers. A. Bettik seemed to slump against me.

The Shrike exploded out of the river directly upstream from us, red eyes blazing, arms lifting.

"Holy shit!" I don't know which one of us shouted. Perhaps all three.

We turned, all of us looking over our shoulders, as the bladed fingers sliced through the air centimeters behind us.

A. Bettik went down. I grabbed him under the arm and pulled him out. The temptation to surrender to that current and ride it downriver was very powerful. Aenea tripped, pulled herself up, and pointed to the right riverbank. I nodded and we struggled in that direction.

Behind us, the Shrike stood in the middle of the river, each of its metallic arms raised and bobbing like a metal scorpion's tail. When I looked back again, it was gone.

We each fell half a dozen times before my feet felt mud rather than rocks under foot. I shoved Aenea up on the bank, then turned and rolled A. Bettik onto the grass. The river still roared to my waist. I did not bother crawling out myself, but tossed the shoulderbag onto the grass, away from the water. "Medkit," I gasped, trying to pull myself out. My arms were almost useless. My lower torso was numb from the freezing water.

Aenea's fingers were also cold—they fumbled at the medpak stick-strips and the tourniquet sleeve—but she managed. A. Bettik was unconscious as she attached the diagnostic patches, pulled off my leather belt, and tightened the sleeve around his amputated lower arm. The sleeve hissed and tightened, then hissed again as it injected painkiller or stimulant. Monitor lights blinked urgently.

I tried again, succeeded in getting my upper body on the bank, and pulled myself out of the river. My teeth were chattering as I said to Aenea, "Where's . . . the . . . pistol?"

She shook her head. Her teeth were also chattering. "I lost it . . . when we . . . the . . . Shrike . . . came . . . up. . . ."

I had just enough energy to nod. The river was empty. "Maybe he went away," I said, jaws clenching between words. Where was the thermal blanket? Swept away downriver in the pack. Everything not in my shoulderbag was gone.

Lifting my head, I looked downriver. The last sunlight of the day lighted the treetops, but the canyon was already in gloom. A woman was walking down the lava rocks toward us.

I lifted the flashlight laser and thumbed the select to tightbeam.

"You wouldn't use that on me, would you?" asked the woman in amused tones.

Aenea looked up from the medkit diagnostics and stared at the figure. The woman was wearing a crimson-and-black uniform that I was not familiar with. She was not a large person. Her hair was short and dark; her face was pale in the fading light. Her right hand to above the wrist seemed to have been flayed and embedded with carbon-fiber bones.

Aenea began shaking, not in fear but out of some deeper emotion. Her eyes narrowed, and I would have described the girl's expression at that moment as something between feral and fearless. Her cold hand made a fist.

The woman laughed. "Somehow I expected something more interesting," she said, and stepped down off the rock and onto the grass.

55

IT HAD BEEN A LONG, BORING AFTERNOON FOR NEMES. She had napped away a few hours, awakening when she felt the displacement disruption as the farcaster portal was activated some fifteen klicks upriver. She had moved up the rock a few meters, hiding herself behind deadfall, and waited for the next act.

The next act, she thought, had been a farce. She had watched the flailing around in the river, the awkward rescue of the artificial man—artificial man minus one artificial arm, she amended—and then, with some interest, the odd appearance of the Shrike. She had known the Shrike was around, of course, since the displacement tremors of its movement through the continuum were not that different from the portal's opening. She had even shifted to fast time to watch it wade into the river and play bogeyman for the humans. It bemused her: what was the obsolete creature doing? Keeping the humans out of her earwig trap or just herding them back toward her, like a good little sheepdog? Nemes knew that the answer depended upon which powers had sent the bladed monstrosity on this mission in the first place.

It was largely irrelevant. It was thought in the Core that the Shrike had been created and sent back in time by an early iteration of the UI. It was known that the Shrike had failed and that it would be defeated again in the far-future struggles between the fledgling human UI and the maturing Machine God. Whichever the case, the Shrike was a failure and a footnote to this journey. Nemes's only interest in the thing was her fading hope that it might provide a moment's excitement as an adversary.

Now, watching the exhausted humans and comatose android sprawl on the grass, she grows bored of being passive. Tucking the specimen bag more firmly in her belt and slipping the Sphinx-trap card into the sticktight band at her wrist, she walks down the rock and onto the grassy shelf.

THE YOUNG MAN, Raul, is on one knee adjusting a low-power laser. Nemes cannot help but smile. "You wouldn't use that on me, would you?" she says.

The man does not answer. He lifts the laser. Nemes thinks that if he uses it on her, in an attempt to blind her, no doubt, she will phase-shift and ram it all the way up past his colon into his lower intestine—without turning the beam off.

Aenea looks at her for the first time. Nemes can see why the Core is nervous about the young human's potential—access elements of the Void Which Binds shimmer around the girl like static electricity—but Nemes also sees that the girl is years away from using any potential she has in that area. All this *Sturm und Drang* and galloping urgency has been for nothing. The human girl is not just immature in her powers, she is innocent of their true meaning.

Nemes realizes that she has harbored some small anxiety that the child herself would pose a problem in the final seconds, somehow tapping into a Void interface and creating difficulties. Nemes realizes that she was mistaken to have worried. Oddly enough, it is a disappointment. "Somehow I expected something more interesting," she says aloud, and takes another step closer.

"What do you want?" demands young Raul, struggling to his feet. Nemes sees that the man has become exhausted just pulling his friends from the river.

"I want nothing from you," she says easily. "Nor from your dying blue friend. From Aenea, I need just a few seconds of conversation." Nemes nods toward the nearby trees where the claymores are seeded. "Why don't you take your golem into the trees and wait for the girl to join you? We'll just have a word in private, and then she's yours." She takes another step closer.

"Stay back," says Raul, and lifts the little flashlight laser.

Nemes holds up her hands as if frightened. "Hey, don't shoot, pardner," she says. If the laser carried ten thousand times the amperage it did, Nemes would not be worried.

"Just back away," says Raul. His thumb is on the trigger button. The toy laser is aimed at Nemes's eyes.

"All right, all right," says Nemes. She takes a step back. And phase-shifts into a gleaming chrome figure only sketchily human.

"Raul!" cries Aenea.

Nemes is bored. She shifts into fast time. The tableau in front of her is frozen. Aenea's mouth is open, still speaking, but the vibrations in the air do not move. The rushing river is frozen, as if in a photograph with an impossibly high shutter speed. Droplets of spray hang in the air. Another droplet of water hangs suspended a millimeter beneath Raul's dripping chin.

Nemes strides over and takes the flashlight laser from Raul's hand. She is tempted to act on her earlier impulse right now and then drop to slow time to watch everyone's reaction, but she sees Aenea out of the corner of her eye—the girl's little hand is still molded into a fist—and Nemes realizes that she has work to do before having fun.

She drops her phase-shifted morphic layer long enough to retrieve the specimen bag from her belt and then shifts again. She walks over to the crouching girl, holds the open bag like a waiting basket beneath the child's chin with her left hand, and rigidifies the edge of her phase-shifted right hand and all of her forearm into a cutting blade not much duller than the monofilament wire still hanging over the river.

Nemes smiles behind her chrome mask. "So long . . . kiddo," she says. She had eavesdropped on their conversation when the trio had been kilometers upriver.

She brings her blade-sharp forearm down in a killing arc.

"WHAT THE HELL'S GOING ON?" shouts Corporal Kee. "I can't see."

"Quiet," orders de Soya. Both men are in their command chairs, leaning over the telescope monitors.

"Nemes turned . . . I don't know . . . metallic," says Kee, playing the video again in an insert box while watching the milling tableau below, "and then she disappeared."

"Radar doesn't show her," says de Soya, keying through different sensor modes. "No IR . . . although the ambient temperature's risen almost ten degrees centigrade in the immediate region. Heavy ionization."

"Local storm cell?" says Kee, bewildered. Before de Soya can answer, Kee points to the monitor. "Now what? The girl's down. Something's happening with the guy. . . ."

"Raul Endymion," says de Soya, trying to improve the image quality on the monitor. The rising heat and atmospheric turbulence makes the image ripple and blur in spite of the computer's best efforts to stabilize it. *Raphael* is holding its place only 280 klicks above hypothetical sea level on God's Grove, far too low for an easy geosynchronous orbit and low enough that the ship is paranoid about expansion of the atmosphere adding to the already molecular heating the ship is encountering.

Father Captain de Soya has seen enough to make a decision. "Divert all power from ship functions and drop life support to minimal levels," his voice orders. "Bring the fusion core to one hundred fifteen percent and kill forward deflection shields. Shift power for tactical use."

"That would not be advisable—" begins the ship's voice.

"Override all voice response and safety protocols," snaps de Soya. "Priority code delta-nine-nine-two-zero. Papal diskey override . . . now. Readout confirmation."

The monitors fill with data columns superimposed over the shifting image on the ground. Kee is watching wide-eyed. "Dear sweet Jesus," whispers the corporal. "My God."

"Yes," whispers de Soya, watching the power to all systems except visual monitoring and tactical fall beneath red lines.

The explosions on the surface begin then.

AT THIS POINT I had precisely enough time to have a retinal echo of the woman becoming silver blur, I blinked, and the flashlight laser was gone from my fingers. The air was becoming superheated. On either side of Aenea the air suddenly misted and seemed filled with a struggling chrome figure—six arms, four legs, flailing blades—and then I was leaping at the girl, knowing that nothing I could do would be in time, but—amazingly—reaching her in time to pull her down and roll aside from the blast of hot air and blurred motion.

The medkit warning alarm went off like fingers on slate—a sound impossible to ignore. We were losing A. Bettik. I covered Aenea with my body and pulled her toward A. Bettik's body. Then the explosions began in the woods behind us.

NEMES SWINGS HER ARM, expecting to feel nothing as the edge slices through muscle and vertebrae, and is shocked by the violent contact.

She looks down. The sharpened edge of her phase-shifted hand is in the grip of two sets of fingerblades. Her forearm is gripped by two other scalpel-sharp hands. The bulk of the Shrike presses close, the blades on the lower body almost in the frozen girl's face. The creature's eyes are bright red.

Nemes is momentarily startled and seriously irritated, but not alarmed. She rips her hand away and jumps back.

The tableau is exactly as it had been a second before—river in freeze time, Raul Endymion's empty hand outstretched as if pressing the firing stud on the little laser, the android dying on the ground with medpak lights frozen in midblink—only the girl is now overshadowed by the huge bulk of the Shrike.

Nemes smiles beneath her chrome mask. She had been concentrating on the girl's neck and not noticed the clumsy thing coming up on her in fast time. That is a mistake she will not make again.

"You want her?" says Nemes. "Have you also been sent to kill her? Be my guest . . . as long as I get the head."

The Shrike pulls its arms back and steps around the child, its thorns and knee blades missing her eyes by less than a centimeter. Legs apart, the Shrike stands between Nemes and Aenea.

"Oh," says Nemes, "you don't want her? Then I'll have to take her back." Nemes moves faster than fast time, feinting left, circling right, and swinging down. If the space around her had not been warped by displacement, sonic booms would have shattered everything within kilometers.

The Shrike blocks the blow. Sparks leap from chrome, and lightning discharges into the ground. The creature slashes the air where Nemes had been a nanosecond before. She comes around from the rear, kicking at the child's back with a blow that will drive the girl's spine and heart out through her chest.

The Shrike deflects the kick and sends Nemes flying. The chromed woman shape is hurled thirty meters into the trees, smashing branches and trunks, which hang in midair after she has passed. The Shrike hurtles through fast time after her.

Nemes strikes a boulder and is embedded five centimeters in solid rock. She senses the Shrike shifting down to slow time as it flies toward her, and she follows the displacement back into noise and motion. The trees snap, break, and burst into flame. The miniclaymores sense no heartbeat or respiration, but they feel the pressure and leap toward it, hundreds exploding in a chain reaction of shaped charges that drive Aenea and the Shrike together like halves of an old imploding uranium bomb.

The Shrike has a long curved blade on its chest. Nemes has heard all the stories about the victims the creature has impaled and dragged off to stick on the longer thorns of its Tree of Pain. She is not impressed. As the two are driven together by the shaped charges exploding all around them, Nemes's displacement field bends the Shrike's chest thorn back on itself. The creature opens steam-shovel jaws and roars in the ultrasonic. Nemes swings a bladed forearm into its neck and sends it fifteen meters into the river.

She ignores the Shrike and turns toward Aenea and the others. Raul has thrown himself across the girl. *How touching,* thinks Nemes, and shifts up into fast time, freezing even the billowing clouds of orange flame that spread from where she stands in the heart of the explosion's flowering.

She jogs out through the semisolid wall of the shock wave and breaks into a run toward the girl and her friend. She will sever both their heads, keeping the man's as a memento after delivering the girl's.

Nemes is within a meter of the brat when the Shrike emerges from the cloud of steam that had been the river and blindsides her from the left. Her swinging arm misses the two human heads by centimeters as she and the Shrike roll away from the river, slicing up turf to bedrock and snapping off trees until they slam into another rock wall. The Shrike's carapace throws sparks as the huge jaws open, teeth closing on Nemes's throat.

"You've . . . got . . . to be . . . fucking . . . kidding," she gasps behind the displacement mask. Being chewed to death by an obsolete time-shifter is not on her itinerary for today. Nemes makes a blade of her hand and drives it deep into the Shrike's thorax as the rows of teeth throw sparks and lightning from her shielded throat. Nemes grins as she feels the four fingers of her hand penetrate armor and carapace. She grabs a fistful of innards and jerks them out, hoping to remove whatever foul organs keep the beast alive but coming away with only a handful of razor-wire tendons and shards of carapace. But the Shrike staggers backward, four arms swinging like scythes. Its massive jaws are still working as if the creature cannot believe it is not chewing bits of its victim.

"Come on!" says Nemes, stepping toward the thing. "Come on!" She wants to destroy it—her blood is up, as the humans used to say—but she is still calm enough to know that this is not her purpose. She has only to distract it or disable it to the point that she can decapitate the human child. Then the Shrike will be irrelevant forever. Perhaps Nemes and her kind will keep it in a zoo to hunt it when they are bored. "Come on," she taunts, taking another step forward.

The creature is hurt enough to drop out of fast time without dropping the displacement fields around it. Nemes could have destroyed it at her leisure except for the displacement field; if she walks around it now, it can shift up to fast time behind her. She follows it down to slow time, pleased to conserve energy.

"JESUS!" I CRIED, looking up from where I had thrown myself across Aenea. She was watching from the protective circle of my arm.

It was all happening at once. A. Bettik's medkit alarm was screeching, the air was as hot as a breath from a blast furnace, the forest behind us exploded in flame and noise, splinters from trees exploded by superheated steam filled the air above us, the river erupted in a geyser of steam, and suddenly the Shrike and a chromed human shape were feinting and slashing not three meters from us.

Aenea ignored the carnage and crawled out from the shelter of my body, scrabbling across the muddy ground to get to A. Bettik. I slid along behind her, watching the chrome blurs surging and smashing into each other. Static electricity whipped from the two forms and leaped to the rocks and savaged ground.

"CPR!" cried the girl, and began administering to A. Bettik. I jumped to the other side and read the medkit telltales. He was not breathing. His heart had stopped half a minute before. Too much blood loss.

Something silver and sharp hurtled toward Aenea's back. I moved to pull her down, but before I could reach her, another metallic shape intercepted the first one and the air exploded with the sound of metal striking metal. "Let me!" I shouted, pulling her around the android's body, trying to keep her behind me while picking up the rhythm of resuscitation. The medkit lights showed that blood was being pumped to A. Bettik's brain by our efforts. His lungs were receiving and expelling air, although not without our help. I continued the motion, watching over my shoulder as two figures crashed, rolled, and collided with near-supersonic speed. The air stank of ozone. Embers from the burning forest drifted around us and steam clouds billowed and hissed.

"Next . . . year . . . ," shouted Aenea above the din, her teeth chattering despite the sweat-dripping heat, "we . . . take . . . our vacation . . . somewhere else."

I lifted my head to stare, thinking that she had gone insane. Her eyes were bright but not totally crazy. That was my diagnosis. The medkit chirped alarm, and I continued my ministrations.

Behind us there was a sudden implosion, quite audible over the crackling of flames, hissing of steam, and clashing of metal surfaces. I turned to look over my shoulder, never ceasing the CPR motions on A. Bettik.

The air shimmered, and a single chrome figure stood where the two forms had been warring. Then the metallic surface rippled and disappeared. The woman from the rock was standing there. Her hair was not mussed and she showed no signs of exertion.

"Now," said the woman, "where were we?" She came forward at an easy walk.

IN THOSE LAST SECONDS OF THE BATTLE, it was not easy getting the Sphinx trap in place. Nemes is using all her energy fighting off the Shrike's whirring blades. It is like fighting several spinning propellers at once, she thinks. She has been on worlds with propeller-driven aircraft. Two centuries earlier she had killed the Hegemony Consul on such a world.

Now she bats away whirling arms, never removing her gaze from the glaring red eyes. *Your time has passed,* she thinks at the Shrike as their displacement-shrouded arms and legs slash and counterslash like invisible scythes. Reaching through the thing's less-focused field, she seizes a joint on its upper arm and rips thorns and blades away. That arm falls away, but five scalpels on the lower hand dig at her abdomen, trying to disembowel her through the field.

"Uh-uh," she says, kicking the thing's right leg out from under it for a split second. "Not so fast."

The Shrike staggers, and in that instant of vulnerability she slips the Sphinx card from her wristband, slides it through a five-nanosecond gap in her displacement field squarely into the palm of her hand, and slaps it onto a spike rising from the Shrike's banded neck.

"That's all," cries Nemes as she jumps back, shifts to fast time to bat away the Shrike's attempt to remove the card, and activates it by thinking of a red circle.

She leaps back farther as the hyperentropic field hums into existence, propelling the flailing monster five minutes into the future. It has no way back while the field exists.

Rhadamanth Nemes shifts down from fast time and drops the field. The breeze—superheated and ember laden as it is—feels delightfully cool to her. "Now," she says, enjoying the look in the two pairs of human eyes, "where were we?"

"DO IT!" SHOUTS CORPORAL KEE.

"I can't," says de Soya at the controls. His finger is in the tactical omnigrip. "Groundwater. Steam explosion. It would kill them all." *Raphael*'s boards show every erg of energy diverted, but it does no good.

Kee flips down his microphone bead, throws the switch to all channels, and begins broadcasting on tightbeam, making sure that the reticule is on the man and girl, not on the advancing woman.

"That won't do any good," says de Soya. He has never been so frustrated in his life.

"Rocks," Kee is shouting into his bead mike. "Rocks!"

I WAS STANDING, pushing Aenea behind and wishing that I had the pistol, the flashlight laser, anything, as the woman approached. The plasma rifle was still in the watertight shoulder bag near the riverbank just two meters away. All I had to do was jump, unseal the bag, lever off the safety, snap open the folding stock, aim, and fire. I did not think that the smiling woman would give me the time. Nor did I believe that Aenea would be alive when I turned to fire.

At that moment the idiot comlog bracelet on my wrist started vibrating its inner lining against my skin like one of those antique soundless alarm watches. I ignored it. The comlog began pricking tiny needles into my wrist. I raised the stupid thing to my ear. It whispered at me, "Get to the rocks. Take the girl and get to the lava rocks."

Nothing made sense. I looked down at A. Bettik, the telltales shifting from green through amber as I watched, and began backing away from the smiling woman, keeping my body between her and Aenea as we stumbled backward.

"Now, now," said the woman. "That's not very nice. Aenea, if you come here, your boyfriend can live. Your phony blue man can live also, if your boyfriend can keep him alive."

I glanced down to see Aenea's face, afraid that she would accept the offer. She clung to my arm. Her eyes showed a terrible intensity, but still no fear. "It'll be all right, kiddo," I whispered, still moving to our left. Behind us was the river. Five meters to our left and the lava rocks began.

The woman moved right, blocking our movement. "This is taking too long," she said softly. "I only have another four minutes. Oodles and oodles of time. An eternity of time."

"Come on." I grabbed Aenea's wrist and ran for the rocks. I had no plan. I had only the nonsensical words whispered in a voice that was not the comlog's.

We never reached the lava rocks. There was a blast of heated air and the chrome shape of the woman was ahead of us, standing three meters above us on the black rock face. "Bye, bye, Raul Endymion," the chrome mask said. The shimmering metal arm rose.

The blast of heat burned off my eyebrows, set fire to my shirt, and threw the girl and me backward through the air. We hit hard and rolled away from the unspeakable heat. Aenea's hair was smoldering, and I batted my forearms against her, trying to keep her hair from bursting into flame. A. Bettik's medkit was screeching again, but the avalanche roar of superheated air behind us drowned the noise. I saw that my shirtsleeve was smoking, and I ripped it away before it ignited. Aenea and I turned our backs to the heat and crawled and scrabbled away as quickly as we could. It was like being on the lip of a volcano.

We grabbed A. Bettik's body and pulled him to the riverbank, not hesitating a second before sliding into the steaming current. I struggled to keep the unconscious android's head above water while Aenea fought to keep both of us from sliding away on the current. Just above the surface of the water, where our faces were pressed against the wet mud of the riverbank, the air was almost cool enough to breathe.

Feeling the blisters forming on my forehead, not yet knowing that my eyebrows and swaths of hair were missing, I raised my head to the edge of the riverbank and peered over.

The chromed figure stood in the center of a three-meter circle of orange light that stretched up to the heavens and disappeared only when it narrowed to an infinite point hundreds of kilometers above. The air rippled and roiled where the beam of almost solid energy ripped through the atmosphere.

The metallic woman-shape tried to move toward us, but the high-energy lance seemed to exert too much pressure. Still, she stood, the chrome field around her turning red, then green, then a blinding white. But still she stood, her fist raised and shaking at the sky. Beneath her feet the lava rock boiled, turned red, and ran downhill in great molten rivers. Some ran into the river not ten meters downstream from us, and the steam clouds billowed up with a loud hissing. At that moment I admit that I considered becoming religious for the first time in my life.

The chrome shape seemed to see the danger seconds before it was too late. It disappeared, reappeared as a blur—fist shaking toward the sky —disappeared again, reappeared a final time, and then sank into the lava under its feet where solid rock had been an instant earlier.

The beam stayed on for another full minute. I could not look directly at it any longer, and the heat was burning away the skin of my cheeks. I pressed my face against the cool mud again and held A. Bettik and the girl against the bank even as the current tried to pull us downstream into the steam and lava and microfilament wires.

I looked up one final time, saw the chromed fist sinking beneath the surface of the lava, and then the field seemed to shift down in colors for a moment before it winked off. The lava began to cool at once. By the time I had pulled Aenea and A. Bettik out of the water and we had begun CPR again, the rock was solidifying with only rivulets and pseudo-pods of lava still flowing. Bits of cooling rock flaked off and rose in the heated air, joining the embers from the forest fire still raging behind us. There was no sign of the chrome woman.

Amazingly, the medkit was still functioning. Lights went from red to amber as we kept blood moving to A. Bettik's brain and limbs and breathed life back into him. The tourniquet sleeve was tight. When he seemed to be holding his own, I looked up at the girl crouched across from me. "What next?" I said.

There was a soft implosion of air behind us, and I turned in time to see the Shrike flash into existence.

"Jesus wept," I said softly.

Aenea was shaking her head. I could see the heat blisters on her lips and forehead. Strands of her hair had burned away, and her shirt was a sooty mess. Other than that, she seemed all right. "No," she said. "It's all right."

I had stood and was fumbling in the shoulder bag for the plasma rifle. No use. It had been too close to the beam of energy. The trigger guard was half-melted and plastic elements in the folded stock had fused with the metal barrel. It was a miracle that the plasma cartridges had not gone off and blasted us to vapor. I dropped the bag and faced the Shrike with my fists balled. Let it come through me, goddamn it.

"It's all right," Aenea said again, pulling me back. "It won't do anything. It's all right."

We crouched next to A. Bettik. The android's eyelashes were fluttering. "Did I miss anything?" he whispered hoarsely.

We did not laugh. Aenea touched the blue man's cheek and looked at me. The Shrike stayed where it had first appeared, burning embers drifting by its red eyes and soot settling on its carapace.

A. Bettik closed his eyes and the telltales began to blink again. "We need to get him serious help," I whispered to Aenea, "or we're going to lose him."

She nodded. I thought she had whispered something back, but it was not her voice speaking.

I lifted my left arm, ignoring the tattered shirt and rising red welts there. All the hair had been burned off my forearm.

We both listened. The comlog was speaking in a familiar man's voice.

56

ATHER DE SOYA IS SURPRISED when they finally respond on the common band. He had not thought their archaic comlog capable of transmitting on the tightbeam the ship was holding on them. There is even a visual display—the fuzzy holographic image of two burned and sooty faces float above the main monitor.

Corporal Kee looks at de Soya. "Well I'll be damned, Father."

"Me too," says de Soya. To the waiting faces he says, "I am Father Captain de Soya on the Pax ship *Raphael*. . . ."

"I remember you," says the girl. De Soya realizes that the ship is transmitting holo images and that they can see him—no doubt a miniature ghostly face above a Roman collar, all floating above the comlog on the man's wrist.

"I remember you, too," is all de Soya can think to say. It has been a long search. He looks at the dark eyes and pale skin beneath the soot and superficial burns. So close . . .

The image of Raul Endymion speaks. "Who was that? *What* was that?"

Father Captain de Soya shakes his head. "I don't know. Her name was Rhadamanth Nemes. She was assigned to us just a few days ago. She said that she was part of a new Legion they are training—" He stops. All of this is classified. He is speaking to the enemy. De Soya looks at Corporal Kee. In the other man's slight smile, he sees their situation. They are condemned men anyway. "She said she was part of a new Legion of Pax warriors," he continues, "but I don't think that was the truth. I don't think she was human."

"Amen," says the image of Raul Endymion. The face looks away from the comlog for a minute and then returns. "Our friend is dying, Father Captain de Soya. Can you do anything to help?"

The priest-captain shakes his head. "We can't get to you. The Nemes creature took our dropship and overrode the remote autopilot. We can't even get the beacon to respond. But if you can get to it, it has an autosurgeon."

"Where is it?" says the girl.

Corporal Kee leans into the imaging field. "Our radar shows it to be about a klick and a half southeast of you," he says. "In the hills. It has some camouflage crap on it, but you'll be able to find it. We'll lead you there."

Raul Endymion says, "It was *your* voice on the comlog. Telling us to get to the rocks."

"Well, yeah," says Kee. "We had everything diverted into the ship's tactical fire-control system—that was about eighty gigawatts that we could deliver through atmosphere—but the groundwater would have turned to steam and killed all of you. The rocks seemed the best bet."

"She beat us there," says Raul with a crooked smile.

"That was the idea," responds Corporal Kee.

"Thank you," says Aenea.

Kee nods, embarrassed, and ducks out of the imaging field. "As the good corporal said," continues Father Captain de Soya, "we will help guide you to the dropship."

"Why?" says the blurred image of Raul. "And why did you kill your own creature?"

De Soya shakes his head. "She was not my creature."

"The Church's, then," insists Raul. "Why?"

"I hope she was not the Church's creature," de Soya says quietly. "If she was, then my Church has become the monster."

There is a silence broken only by the hiss of the tightbeam. "You'd better get moving," de Soya says at last. "It is getting dark."

Both faces in the holo look around them almost comically, as if they have forgotten their surroundings. "Yeah," says Raul, "and your lance or CPB or whatever it was melted my handlamp to slag."

"I could light your way," says de Soya without smiling, "but it would mean activating the main weapons system again."

"Never mind," says Raul. "We'll manage. I'm shutting down the imager, but I'll keep the audio channel open until we get to the dropship."

57

I T TOOK US MORE THAN TWO HOURS to go the kilometer and a half. The lava hills were *very* rough. It would have been easy to break an ankle on those rills and fissures without the added weight of A. Bettik on my back. It was very dark—clouds had moved in to occlude the stars—and I don't think we would have made it at all that night if Aenea hadn't found the flashlight laser lying in the grass when we were packing up to move out.

"How the hell did that get there?" I said. The last I remembered of the little laser, I had been ready to trigger it at the hell-woman's eyes. Then it had been gone. *Well,* I thought, *to hell with it.* It had been a day for mysteries. We left with one last mystery behind us—the silent form of the Shrike, still frozen where it had reappeared. It did not attempt to follow us.

With Aenea leading the way with the flashlight set at widebeam, we struggled and scrabbled our way across the black rock and shifting ash back into the hills. We would have made it in half the time if A. Bettik had not required constant treatment.

The medkit had used up its modest share of antibiotics, stimulants, painkillers, plasma, and IV drip. A. Bettik was alive because of the kit's work, but it was still a close thing. He had simply lost too much blood in the river; the tourniquet had made a difference, but the belt had not been tight enough to staunch all the bleeding. We administered CPR when we had to, just to keep the blood flowing to his brain if nothing else, and stopped when the medkit alarms started squawking. The comlog kept us on track in the Pax corporal's voice, and I decided that even if this was all a trick to capture Aenea, we owed those two men up there a hell of a debt of gratitude. And all the time we were scrambling through the darkness, Aenea's flashlight beam playing over black lava and the skeletons of dead trees, I expected that hell-woman's chromed hand to slash up through the rock and grab me by the ankle.

We found the dropship right where they said it would be. Aenea started up the metal ladder, but I grabbed her tattered pant leg and made her come down.

"I don't want you in the ship, kiddo," I said. "We only have their word that they can't fly it by remote. If you get in and they can fly it from up there, they've got you."

She sagged against the ladder. I had never seen her look so exhausted. "I trust them," she said. "They said—"

"Yeah, but they can't grab you if you're not in there. You stay here while I carry A. Bettik up and see if there's an autosurgeon."

As I went up the ladder, I had a stomach-twisting thought. What if the metal door above me was locked and the keys were in the hell-woman's jumper pocket?

There was a lighted diskey pad. "Six-nine-nine-two," said Corporal Kee's voice from the comlog.

I tapped it in and the outer air-lock door slid open. The autosurgeon was in there and it came alive with a touch. I gently lowered my blue friend into the cushioned enclosure—taking great pains not to hit the raw stump of his arm—made sure that the diagnostic patches and pressure cuffs were placing themselves properly, and then closed the lid. It felt too much like closing a coffin.

The readouts were not promising, but the surgeon went to work. I watched the monitor for a moment until I realized that my eyes were blurring and that I was dozing on my feet. Rubbing my cheeks, I went back to the open air lock.

"You can stand on the ladder, kiddo. If the ship starts to take off, jump."

Aenea stepped up onto the ladder and winked off the flashlight laser. Our light came from the glowing autosurgeon and from some of the console lights. "Then what?" said Aenea. "I jump off and the ship takes off with you and A. Bettik. Then what do I do?"

"Head for the next farcaster portal," I said.

The comlog said, "We don't blame you for being suspicious." It spoke in Father Captain de Soya's voice.

Sitting in the open hatch, listening to the breeze rustle the broken branches tossed atop the aircraft-sized lifting body, I said, "Why this change of heart and program, Father Captain? You came to get Aenea. Why the turnabout?" I remembered the chase through Parvati System, his order to fire on us at Renaissance Vector.

Instead of answering, the priest-captain's voice said, "I have your hawking mat, Raul Endymion."

"Yeah?" I said tiredly. I tried to remember where I had seen it last. Flying toward the platform station on Mare Infinitus. "Small universe," I said as if it did not matter. Inwardly, I would have given anything to have that little flying carpet right now. Aenea clung to the ladder and listened. From time to time, we both glanced over to make sure the autosurgeon had not given up.

"Yes," said the voice of Father Captain de Soya, "and I have begun to understand a little of how you think, my friends. Perhaps someday you will understand how I think."

"Perhaps," I said. I did not know it then, but that would be literally true someday.

His voice became businesslike, almost brusque. "We believe that Corporal Nemes defeated the remote autopilot with some program override, but we won't try to convince you of that. Feel free to use the dropship to continue your voyage without fear of our trying to capture Aenea."

"How do we do that?" I said. The burns were beginning to hurt. In a minute I would find the energy to go through the bins above the autosurgeon and find out if the ship had its own medkit. I was sure it would.

"We will leave the system," said Father Captain de Soya.

I perked up. "How can we be sure of that?"

The comlog chuckled. "A ship climbing out of a planet's gravity well on fusion power is rather obvious," he said. "Our telescope shows that you have only scattered clouds above you at the moment. You will see us."

"See you leaving near orbit," I said. "How can we know you've translated out of system?"

Aenea pulled my wrist down and spoke into the comlog. "Father? Where are you going?"

There was a hiss of silence. "Back to Pacem," de Soya said eventually. "We have one of the three fastest ships in the universe, and my corporal friend and I have each silently considered heading . . . elsewhere . . . but when it comes down to it, we are both soldiers. In the Pax Fleet and in the Army of Christ. We will return to Pacem and answer questions . . . face whatever we must face."

Even on Hyperion the Holy Office of the Inquisition had cast its cold shadow. I shivered, and it was not just the cold wind from the ash heap of the Worldtree that made me cold.

"Besides," continued de Soya, "we have a third comrade here who did not come through resurrection successfully. We must return to Pacem for medical care."

I looked at the humming autosurgeon and—for the first time that endless day—believed that the priest above us was not an enemy.

"Father de Soya," said Aenea, still holding my hand so that the comlog was near her, "what will they do to you? To all of you?"

Again came the sound of a chuckle above the static. "If we're lucky, they will execute us and then excommunicate us. If unlucky, they will reverse the order of those two events."

I could see that Aenea was not amused. "Father Captain de Soya . . . Corporal Kee . . . come down and join us. Send the ship back with your friend, and join us to go through the next portal."

This time the silence stretched long enough that I feared the tightbeam connection had broken. Then came de Soya's soft voice. "I am tempted, my young friend. Both of us are tempted. I would love to travel by farcaster someday, and even more, I would love to get to know you. But we are faithful servants of the Church, my dear, and our duties are clear. It is my hope that this . . . aberration . . . that was Corporal Nemes was a mistake. We must return if we are ever to know."

Suddenly there was a burst of light. I leaned out of the air lock, and we both watched the blue-white fusion tail cross between the scattered clouds.

"Besides that," came de Soya's voice, strained now as if under a g-load, "we really do not have any way down to you without the drop-ship. The Nemes thing slashed the troopers' combat suits, so even that desperate attempt is not an option."

Aenea and I were both sitting on the edge of the open air lock now, watching the fusion tail grow longer and brighter. It seemed a lifetime since we had flown in our own ship. A thought struck me like a blow to the stomach, and I lifted the comlog. "Father Captain, is this . . . Nemes . . . dead? I mean, we saw her buried in molten lava . . . but could she be burrowing out even as we speak?"

"We have no idea," said Father Captain de Soya over the tightbeam hiss. "My recommendation would be to get out of there as soon as possible. The dropship is our parting gift to you. Use it in good health."

I looked out at the black lava landscape for a minute. Every time the wind rustled dead branches or scraped ash on ash, I was sure it was the hell-woman gliding toward us.

"Aenea," came the priest-captain's voice.

"Yes, Father Captain?"

"We're going to shut off the tightbeam in a second . . . we'll be passing out of line-of-sight anyway . . . but I have to tell you one thing."

"What's that, Father?"

"My child, if they order me back to find you . . . not to hurt you, but to find you . . . well, I am an obedient servant of the Church and a Pax Fleet officer. . . ."

"I understand, Father," said Aenea. Her eyes were still on the sky where the fusion tail was fading near the eastern horizon. "Good-bye, Father. Good-bye, Corporal Kee. Thank you."

"Good-bye, my daughter," said Father Captain de Soya. "God bless you." We could both hear the sound of a benediction. Then the tightbeam snapped off and there was only silence.

"Come on in," I said to Aenea. "We're leaving. Now."

Closing the inner and outer air-lock doors was a simple enough task.

We checked on the autosurgeon a final time—all of the lights were amber but steady—and then strapped ourselves into the heavy acceleration couches. There were shields to cover the windscreen, but they were raised, and we could see across the dark lava fields. A few stars were visible in the east.

"Okay," I said, looking at the myriad switches, diskeys, touchplates, holopads, monitors, flatscreens, buttons, and gewgaws. There was a low console between us and two omnicontrollers there, each with finger insets and more diskey patterns. I could see half a dozen places where one could jack in directly. "Okay," I said again, looking at the pale girl dwarfed by her padded chair, "any ideas?"

"Get out and walk?" she said.

I sighed. "That might be the best plan except for—" I jerked my thumb back toward the humming autosurgeon.

"I know," said Aenea. She sagged in the heavy straps. "I was joking."

I touched her hand on the console. As always, there was a jolt of electricity there—a sort of physical déjà vu. Pulling my hand away, I said, "Goddammit, the more advanced a technology's supposed to be, the simpler it's supposed to be. This looks like something out of an eighteenth-century Old Earth fighter-plane cockpit."

"It's built for professionals to fly," said Aenea. "We just need a professional pilot."

"You have one," chirped the comlog. It was speaking in its own voice.

"You know how to fly a ship?" I said suspiciously.

"In essence, I *am* a ship," the comlog said primly. The clasp panel clicked open. "Please connect the red filament jack to any red interface port."

I connected it to the console. Immediately the panel came alive, monitors glowed, instruments checked in, the dropship's ventilators hummed, and the omnicontroller twitched. A flatscreen monitor in the center of the dash glowed yellow, and the comlog's voice said, "Where do you wish to go, M. Edymion? M. Aenea?"

The girl spoke first. "The next farcaster," she said softly. "The last farcaster."

58

I T WAS DAYLIGHT ON THE OTHER SIDE. We hovered above the stream and moved forward slowly. The comlog had shown us how to use the controllers while it ran all the rest of the ship's systems and kept us from making stupid mistakes. Aenea and I glanced at each other and inched the dropship over the treetops. Unless the hell-woman could transit a farcaster portal, we were safe.

It felt strange making our last farcaster shift without the raft, but the raft would not have worked here anyway. The River Tethys had become little more than a trickling stream between deep banks—the creek could not have been more than eight or ten centimeters deep and only three or four meters wide. It meandered through heavily wooded countryside. The trees were strange, but familiar at the same time . . . mostly deciduous like champa or weirwood, but broadleafed and expansive like halfoak. The leaves were bright yellow and brilliant red, and carpets of them lined the banks of the streambed.

The sky was a pleasant blue—not as deep blue as Hyperion's, but deeper than most earthlike worlds we had seen on this trip. The sun was large and bright but not overpowering. Sunlight came through the windscreen and fell across our laps.

"I wonder what it's like out there," I said.

The comlog . . . ship . . . whatever it was now, must have thought I was talking to it. The central monitor pulsed and data began to flow down it.

Atmosphere: 0.77 N_2
             0.21 O_2
             0.009 Ar
             0.0003 CO_2
             variable H_2O (−0.01)
Surface pressure: 0.986 bar
Magnetic field: 0.318 gauss
Mass: 5.976×10^{24} kg
Escape velocity: 11.2 km/s
Surface gravity: 980 km/s
Tilt angle of magnetic axis: 11.5°
Dipole moment: 7.9×10^{25} gauss/cm^3

"That's strange," said the ship. "An improbable coincidence."

"What?" I said, already knowing.

"These planetary data match almost perfectly with my database for Old Earth," said the ship. "It is very unusual for any world to match so closely with—"

"Stop!" screamed Aenea, pointing out the windscreen. "Land! Please, now."

I would have smashed into trees on the way down, but the ship took over, found us a flat, rocky spot within twenty meters of the tree-lined streambed, and set us down without a bump. Aenea was punching the air-lock combination while I was still staring out the windscreen at the flat roof of the house beyond the trees.

She was down the ladder before I could talk to her. I paused to check the autosurgeon, was pleased to see several of the lights switched to green, and said to the ship, "Watch over him. Keep everything ready for a quick getaway."

"I shall, M. Endymion."

WE CAME AT THE HOUSE from downstream and across the stream from it. The building is hard to describe, but I will try.

The house itself was built out over a modest waterfall that spilled only three or four meters to a small natural pool beneath. Yellow leaves floated in the pool before being whisked away downstream on the quickening current. The most noticeable features of the house were the thin roofs and rectangular terraces that seemed to hang out over the stream and waterfall as if defying gravity. The house appeared to be built of stone and glass, concrete and some steel. To the left of the slabs of terrace, a stone wall rose three floors with a glass-cornered window rising in it almost the entire height. The metal framework around those windows was painted a gentle orange.

"Cantilevered," said Aenea.

"What?"

"That's what the architect calls those overhanging terraces," she said. "Cantilevered. They echo the limestone ledges that have been here for millions of years."

I paused in our walk to look at her. The dropship was out of sight beyond the trees behind us. "This is your house," I said. "The one you dreamed of before you were born."

"Yes." Her lips were trembling slightly. "I even know its name now, Raul. Fallingwater."

I nodded and sniffed the air. The scent was rich with decaying leaves, living plants, rich soil, water, and a certain tang to the air. It was very different from Hyperion's air, but it somehow smelled like home. "Old Earth," I whispered. "Can it be?"

"Just . . . Earth," said Aenea. She touched my hand. "Let's go in."

We crossed the stream on a small bridge upstream from the house, crunched our way up a gravel drive, and entered through a loggia and narrow entranceway. It was like coming into a comfortable cave.

Pausing in the large living room, we called, but no one answered. Aenea walked across the open space as if in a trance, running her fingers over wood and stone surfaces, exclaiming at small discoveries.

The floor was carpeted in places, bare stone in others. Books filled low shelves in at least one alcove, but I did not take time to check the titles. Metal shelves ran under the low ceiling, but these were empty—perhaps just a design element. The far wall was taken up by a huge fireplace. The hearth was of rough stone—perhaps the top of the boulder upon which the house seemed to balance—and ran out two meters or so from the fireplace.

A large fire was crackling in the fireplace, despite the warmth of the sunny autumn day. I called again, but the silence was heavy. "They were expecting us," I said, making a weak joke. The only weapon I had now was the flashlight laser in my pocket.

"Yes, they were," said Aenea. She went over to the left of the fire-place and placed her small hands on a metal sphere that was set into its own hemispherical niche in the stone wall. The sphere was a meter and a half or so in diameter and was painted a rich, rusty red.

"The architect meant this as a kettle to heat wine in," Aenea said softly. "It was only used once . . . and the wine was heated in the kitchen and brought here. It's too big. And the paint is probably toxic."

"This is the architect you're looking for?" I said. "The one you plan to study with?"

"Yes."

"I thought he was a genius. Why would he make a wine kettle too big and too toxic to use?"

Aenea turned and smiled. No—she *grinned*. "Geniuses screw up, Raul. Look at our trip if you need proof. Come on, let's look around."

The terraces were lovely, the view from above the little waterfall pleasant. Inside, the ceilings and overhangs were low, but that just gave one more of a sense of peering out of a cave into the green world of the forest through all that glass. In the living room again, a glass-and-metal hatchway folded back to steps—supported by bars from the floor above—which led down only to a larger cement platform over a pool in the stream above the waterfall.

"The plunge," said Aenea, as if coming home to something very familiar.

"What's it for?" I said, peering around.

"Nothing practical," said Aenea. "But the architect considered it—and I quote—'absolutely necessary from every standpoint.' "

I touched her shoulder. She turned and smiled at me, not mechanically or dreamily, but with an almost radiant vitality.

"Where are we, Aenea?"

"Fallingwater," she said. "Bear Run. In western Pennsylvania."

"Is that a nation?" I said.

"Province," said Aenea. "State, I mean. In the former United States of America. North American continent. Planet Earth."

"Earth," I repeated. I looked around. "Where is everybody? Where's your architect?"

The girl shook her head. "I don't know. We should know soon."

"How long are we going to stay here, kiddo?" I had thoughts of laying in food, weapons, and other equipment while A. Bettik recovered and before we headed off again.

"A few years," said Aenea. "No more than six or seven, I think."

"Years?" I had stopped on the upper terrace where we had stepped out at the head of the flight of stairs. "Years?"

"I have to study under this man, Raul. I have to learn something."

"About architecture?"

"Yes, and about myself."

"And what will I be doing while you're . . . learning about yourself?"

Instead of making a joke, Aenea nodded seriously. "I know. It doesn't seem fair. But there will be a few things for you to do while I'm . . . growing up."

I waited.

"The Earth needs to be explored," she said. "My mother and father visited here. It was Mother's idea that the . . . lions and tigers and bears —the forces that stole the Earth away before the TechnoCore could destroy it . . . it was Mother's idea that they were running experiments here."

"Experiments?" I said. "What kind of experiments?"

"Experiments in genius, mostly," said Aenea. "Although perhaps experiments in humanity would be a better phrase."

"Explain."

Aenea gestured toward the house around us. "This place was completed in 1937."

"A.D.?" I said.

"Yes. I'm sure it was destroyed in the twenty-first-century North American class riots, if not before. Whoever brought the Earth here rebuilt it somehow. Just as they rebuilt nineteenth-century Rome for my father."

"Rome?" I felt that I was standing around with my thumb in my ear repeating everything the child said. It was one of those days.

"The Rome where John Keats spent his last days," said Aenea. "But that's another story."

"Yeah," I said, "I read it in your Uncle Martin's *Cantos*. And I didn't understand it then, either."

Aenea made the gesture with her hands that I was growing used to. "I don't understand it, Raul. But whoever brought the Earth here brings back people as well as old cities and buildings. They create . . . *dynamics*."

"Through resurrection?" My voice was doubtful.

"No . . . more like . . . well, my father was a cybrid. His persona resided in an AI matrix, his body was human."

"But you're not a cybrid."

Aenea shook her head. "You know I'm not." She led me farther out on the terrace. Below us, the stream rushed over the little waterfall. "There will be other things for you to do while I'm . . . in school."

"Such as?"

"Besides exploring all of the Earth and figuring out just what these . . . entities . . . are up to here, you'll need to leave before I do and go back to fetch our ship."

"Our ship?" I resolved to pull my metaphorical thumb out of my ear. "You mean travel by farcaster to get the Consul's ship."

"Yep."

"And bring it here?"

She shook her head. "That would take a few centuries. We'll agree to meet somewhere in the former Web."

I rubbed my cheek, feeling the whiskers scratch. "Anything else? Any other little ten-year odysseys to keep me occupied?"

"Just the trip to the Outback to see the Ousters," she said. "But I'll be going with you on that trip."

"Good," I said. "I hope that's all the adventures that we'll have waiting for us. I'm not as young as I used to be, you know."

I was trying to be light about all this, but Aenea's eyes were deep and serious. She put her fingers in my palm. "No, Raul," she said. "That's just the beginning."

The comlog beeped and tapped. "What?" I said with a spasm of concern about A. Bettik.

"I've just received coordinates on the common band," came the comlog/ship's voice. It sounded puzzled.

"Any voice or visual transmissions?" I said.

"No, just travel coordinates and optimum cruise altitudes. It's a flight plan."

"To where?" I said.

"A point on this continent some three thousand kilometers to the southwest of our current position," said the ship.

I looked at Aenea. She shook her head.

"No idea?" I said.

"An idea," she said. "Not a certainty. Let's go be surprised."

Her small hand was still in mine. I did not release it as we walked back through the yellow leaves and morning sunlight to the waiting drop-ship.

59

I ONCE SAID TO YOU that you were reading this for the wrong reason. What I should have said was that I was writing this for the wrong reason.

I have filled these seamless days and nights and smooth pages of microvellum with memories of Aenea, of Aenea as a child, with not one word of her life as the messiah whom you must know and perhaps whom you mistakenly worship. But I have not written these pages for you, I discover, nor have I written them for myself. I have brought Aenea the child alive in my writing because I want Aenea the woman to be alive—despite logic, despite fact, despite all loss of hope.

Each morning—each self-programmed brightening of the lights, I should say—I awaken in this three-by-six-meter Schrödinger cat box and find myself amazed to be alive. There has been no scent of bitter almonds in the night.

Each morning I fight despair and terror by writing these memories on my text slate, stacking the microvellum pages as they accumulate. But the recycler in this little world is limited; it can produce only a dozen or so pages at a time. So as I finish each dozen or so pages of memory, I feed the oldest pages into the recycler to have them come out fresh and empty so as to have new pages upon which to write. It is the snake swallowing its own tail. It is insanity. Or the absolute essence of sanity.

It is possible that the chip in the text slate has the full memory of what I have written here . . . what I shall write in the coming days if fate grants me those days . . . but the truth is, I do not really care. Only the dozen pages of microvellum are of interest to me each day—pristine, empty pages in the morning, crowded, ink-splashed pages filled with my small and spidery script each evening.

Aenea comes alive for me then.

BUT LAST NIGHT—when the lights in my Schrödinger cat box were off and nothing separated me from the universe but the static-dynamic shell of frozen energy around me with its little vial of cyanide, its ticking timer, and its foolproof radiation detector—last night I heard Aenea calling my name. I sat up in the absolute blackness, too startled and hopeful even to command the lights on, certain that I was still dreaming, when I felt her fingers touch my cheek. They were her fingers. I knew them when she was a child. I kissed them when she was a woman. I touched them with my lips when they took her away for the final time.

Her fingers touched my cheek. Her breath was warm and sweet against my face. Her lips were warm against the corner of my mouth.

"We're leaving here, Raul, my darling," she whispered in the darkness last night. "Not soon, but as soon as you finish our tale. As soon as you remember it all and understand it all."

I reached for her then, but her warmth was receding. When the lights came on, my egg-shaped world was empty.

I admit that I paced back and forth until the normal waking time arrived. My greatest fear these days or months has not been death—Aenea had taught me how to put death in perspective—but insanity. Madness would rob me of clarity, of memory . . . of Aenea.

Then I saw something that stopped me. The text slate was activated. The stylus was lying not in its usual place, but tucked behind the slate cover, much as Aenea had kept her pen folded away in her journal during our voyages after leaving Earth. My fingers shaking, I recycled yesterday's writings and activated the printer port.

Only one page emerged, crowded with handwritten lines. It was Aenea's writing; I know it well.

This is a turning point for me. Either I am truly insane and none of this matters, or I am saved and everything matters very much.

I read this, as you do, with hope for my sanity and hope for salvation, not of my soul, but salvation of self in the renewed certainty of reunion—real reunion, physical reunion—with the one whom I remember and love above all others.

And this is the best reason to read.

60

R AUL, CONSIDER THIS A POSTSCRIPT to the memories you wrote about today, and which I read tonight. Years ago, years ago . . . those last three hours of our first journey together, when you, my darling Raul, and dear sleeping A. Bettik and I flew the dropship southwest toward Taliesin West and my long apprenticeship there, I longed to tell you everything that day—the dreams that showed us being lovers of whom the poets would sing, visions of the great dangers that lay ahead, dreams of the discovery of friends, dreams of the deaths of friends, certainty of unspeakable sorrow to be borne, certainty of unimaginable triumphs still unborn.

I said nothing.

Do you remember? We dozed during our flight. How strange life is that way . . . our last few hours alone together, this ending to one of the most intimate periods of our life together, the end of my childhood and the beginning of our time as equals, and we spent most of our last minutes sleeping. In separate couches. Life is brutal that way . . . the loss of irrecoverable moments amid trivia and distraction.

But we were tired. It had been a rough few days.

As the dropship was beginning to descend over the southwestern desert toward Taliesin West and my new life, I took a page from my soiled journal—it had survived the water and flames when most of my clothing had not—and wrote a hasty note to you. You were sleeping. Your face was against the vinyl of the acceleration chair and you were drooling slightly. Your eyelashes were burned away, as was a patch of hair at the crown of your head, and the effect was to make you look comical—a clown surprised in the act of sleeping. (We later talked of clowns, remember, Raul? During our Ouster odyssey. You had seen clowns at a circus in Port

Romance as a teenager; I had seen clowns in Jacktown during the annual First Settlers Fair.)

The burns and burn ointment we had liberally applied to your cheeks and temples, eyes and upper lip, looked for all the world like clown makeup—red and white. You were beautiful. I loved you then. I loved you backward and forward in time. I loved you beyond boundaries of time and space.

I wrote my note hurriedly, tucked it in what was left of the pocket on your ruined shirt, and kissed you ever so softly on the corner of your mouth, in the one spot that was not burned or salved. You stirred but did not wake. You did not mention the note the next day—nor ever again— and I always wondered if you found it, or if it fell out of the pocket, or was tossed away unread when you threw away the shirt at Taliesin.

The words were my father's. He wrote them centuries ago. Then he died, was reborn—after a fashion—as a cybrid persona, and died again as a man. But still he lived in essence, his persona roving through metaspace, and eventually leaving Hyperion with the Consul, in the DNA coils of the ship's AI. His final spoken words to my mother will never be known, despite Uncle Martin's creative license in the *Cantos*. But these words were discovered in my mother's text stylus when she awoke that morning after he left forever, and she kept the original printout for the rest of her life. I know . . . I used to sneak into her room in Jacktown on Hyperion and read the hurried handwriting on that yellowed slip of vellum, at least once a week from the time I was two.

These were the words that I gave to you with a sleeping kiss that last hour of our last day of our first voyage, my darling Raul. These are the words I leave tonight with a waking kiss. These are the words I will claim from you when I return next, when the tale is complete and our final voyage begins.

A thing of beauty is a joy forever:
Its loveliness increases; it will never
Pass into nothingness; but still will keep
A bower quiet for us, and a sleep
Full of sweet dreams, and health, and quiet breathing.

And so, Raul Endymion, until we meet again on your pages, in wild ecstasy, I bid you *adieu*—

Thou foster-child of silence and slow time,
Sylvan historian, who canst thus express
A flowery tale more sweetly than our rhyme:
What leaf-fringed legend haunts about thy shape
Of deities or mortals, or of both,

In Tempe or the tales of Arcady?
What men or gods are these? What maidens loth?
What mad pursuit? What struggle to escape?
What pipes and timbrels? What wild ecstasy?

For now, my love, I wish you sweet dreams, and health, and quiet breathing.

About the Author

Dan Simmons's first novel, *Song of Kali,* won the World Fantasy Award, his science fiction novel *Hyperion* received the Hugo, and the Horror Writers of America awarded him its highest honor for his novel *Carrion Comfort.*

Simmons is also the author of *Phases of Gravity,* Hugo and Nebula Awards finalist *The Fall of Hyperion, The Hollow Man,* his "Elm Haven triptych"—*Summer of Night, Children of the Night,* and *Fires of Eden*—and two collections of short fiction, *Prayers to Broken Stones* and *Lovedeath.* He lives in Colorado along the Front Range of the Rockies.